To you, and all those I have failed, before and after this is written.

A Statement of the Past

When England Suppressed the American Uprising, the Revolution ceased. Men and women watched as the patriots laid down their weapons. After hearing of George Washington's assassination, anyone would. It was also no surprise that John Adams, Ben Franklin, and others were lost too, forever marked as traitors to the crown. The Colonists that decided to remain in New England were swiftly placed under martial law for treason. The slaves were set free in the colonies and replaced with the once-proud Patriots as punishment. This was both a great achievement and a curse. Unable to keep up with eastern demand, the colonies fell short and were soon considered nothing more than third-rate.

Later came the French Revolution. In its wake, Napoleon Bonaparte declared himself the new King of France after staging his coup. The narcissist determined himself to bring France to greater glory. He promised everyone he would conquer all of Europe, and soon, marched out to keep that promise.

Under Napoleon, France conquered Switzerland, Piedmont, Spain and Portugal. Russia heard them coming, heard the beat of their drums and the clamor of their artillery. So, Russia began to march west into the Austrian Dominions, eager to stake their claims under the tides of war.

It was no surprise that, when The King of France conquered Spain and Portugal, he decided to ignore their colonies. These isolated communities in the west quickly rose back to freedom but forgot their history. The Spanish and Portuguese Colonies dissolved all sense of nationality and whatever civilization might have been made there was ransacked. The people spread out into the wilderness, whether to start anew or free themselves of eastern germs, no one knew.

2

At that time, Napoleon appointed his own generals to lead the lands he had conquered. He called these men his *faithful Barons*, and they were powerful lords, each taking a slice of Europe and ruling over it. Napoleon was so busy killing that he didn't mind his Baron's lust for power. The tyrant let his generals have all of it. All Napoleon wanted was fame, even if the price was blood.

Sometime after, in a year people don't remember much, a new disease was found in India. The leaders of India were unable to contain the spread of the contagion and, overnight, their population fell fifty-three percent.

Later that year, Napoleon Bonaparte died, fighting a peasant in Amsterdam who was too drunk to remember his crime. France searched for Napoleon's next-of-kin after that. They wanted to resume the monarchy. Napoleon left the curtain of war at the hands of one of France's greatest heroes, The Marquis De Lafayette.

After the 19th century turned on its dime, India's government was scraped due to growing instability. The remaining population scattered from the cities in fear of becoming infected. Civil neglect grew, and the country became a wasteland in but a few months. Many people thought that was the end of the southern pandemic, until the contagion spread into Africa.

A year later, in 1802, to be precise, France conquered Denmark, and The Marquis moved east into Prussia. Russia founds signs of the Indian Strain spreading well into the Middle-East. They nicknamed the Virus "The Second Death."

In the following years, France would create the first locomotive, and Britain would prepare for a French invasion that would never come.

France found no successor to Napoleon. In response, the barons thought they would leave their national government in the council of themselves. It wasn't a surprise that this was the verdict, the barons were greedy pigs.

They weren't paying attention that year. They didn't notice that the Russian army met the French boarder at earth's 15th Longitudinal line.

Suffice it to say, tensions rose.

In what is recorded as The Battle of Prague, Russia invaded France and Colonel Pickering led the 7th Regiment to its harrowing death. France, in fear of the Russian military power, chose to ally with Britain. France promised they would never betray Britain's trust.

As that decade ended, Africa was declared "A Wasteland of Death and Disease." Italy surrendered to France, choosing to side with the nation whose culture they shared closest.

As tensions rose, France, in fear of Russia's technological advantages, asked to form the Blue Diamond Treaty with their neighbors. In the end, the two powerhouses made an uneasy armistice, deciding it was best to divert their attention to causes other than death.

These "diverted attentions" gave birth to worldwide enlightenment. Planes, cars, advanced weaponry, computers, and more, were invented within years after the war. The same ambition that was poured out in blood, was now poured out in brain matter. France built the world's biggest bank in Paris and Russia founded the Institution Biological Research (or IBR) to study Second Death in third-world wastelands. The world became a paradise of innovation for a few years, and they were very short years.

As technology rose to deity, so did other deities. New, odd, species were reported in North America, and the unexplainable occurred regularly. Human lifespans increased by 20%. Men and women of all kinds flocked to worship odd carvings and symbols found in western temples and monasteries.

But what did their devotion bring them but regret?

In 1823, in what was known as "The Year of Poseidon's Wrath," Britain was struck by storms that hovered

4

the Isles. The storms didn't move from their place, fueled by happenstance, obstructed only by belief. Massive damage to the island rendered all communications and transportations void. No one could see nor hear from the Isles that whole year. It was a prison of water. By the end of that year, The Isles of Britannia disappeared entirely once the fog dissipated. Scientists were led to believe that the Island "capsized under the constant torrent." The Year of Poseidon's Wrath was known as the biggest massacre in history, led by none other than Mother Nature herself.

Two years later, a suspicious creature was found off the shores of Spain. The cameras and reporters described this dead creature as having "The head of an elephant but the body of a man." The new and unfamiliar species is named Imparest, or "Odd thing." Questions into the human genome were made, but no answers could be discovered.

Later that year, a large bird was reported to fly over Canadian Yukon. Sightseers reported the bird was big enough to block out the sun. That same year, The Marquis De Lafayette speaks to all of France. Baffled by his youth, he conceded to the public "I haven't aged a day since the war ended."

In 1831, The Cult of Radjagah disappeared into South America in a mass exodus. The members were never found again. But some say that they committed mass suicide inside the Amazon rainforest. Sometimes, if a villager could hold their breath long enough, the silent screams of prayer could be heard along the river.

Fast forwarding to 1888, France captured the large bird of legend. They made plans to build a city using the prehistoric creature's "weightless bones." This construction was completed in 1895, when LeCeleste, the floating city, became the first city to float in the sky.

In a meeting of Barons, it was determined that The Marquis De Lafayette would be pronounced the Baron of

LeCeleste. He would be the last baron ever appointed in this kind.

In fear of France's technological progression, baffled Russian engineers announce their plans to build a space station that would bring LeCeleste to shame. This space station was completed in the year 1900.

1900, The Russian space station, Zavoyevatel, launched after some delay, carrying passengers into space. One-thousand passengers were supposed to live above the sky, beyond reproach and bound only by Russian law. Students, teachers, soldiers, and children were all sent into space to start a new life. That is, until the space station ruptured after it exited the atmosphere. Scientist thought there was a structural weakness in the station, that it wouldn't be able to contain the expanding air at higher altitudes. As far as we know, at this time, they were right.

Amidst the turmoil, Aleksander Sevik, a Russian student, reported back to Earth that he was the sole survivor on the space station. He warned Russia never to attempt spaceflight again. The student became the last living astronaut, and his name became a holiday, which was treated more like a wake.

In 1917, The Marquis De Lafayette abandoned France. The Golden Baron vanished with LeCeleste overnight and without a word. Both Russia and France were left with nothing to show for their years of hard work.

Two years later, Colonial American Archeologists, led by the infamous adventurer, Connor Shaw, discover the lost crypt of Radjagah in South America. This ancient burial mound was dubbed the most significant archeological find in history to date. The archeological team aided in bagging and naming every cultist that was found dead on-site. Their mummified bodies, although old and mangled by years of rot, were not afflicted with diseases.

In 1925: The Cult of Radjagah was founded in Philadelphia, N. America. Philosophers sought to study the "arcane" sciences, but with no bearing as to how "the supernatural" worked. They quickly determined all miracles were not supernatural, but scientific circumstance in an ever-changing natural order. Despite the temperament of the scientists, citizens began to report sightings of "men drinking the blood of other men," which was anything but natural.

Five years later, America found a painting of King George III in Antarctica. The world called for continental search for British footprints. They believed that England might have been removed from the ocean, or that the currents would lead them back to the submerged isles. But no evidence was found that Britain was still on earth.

In 1932, a giant creature was reported walking over Boston. That Christmas eve, Children were reported to have gone missing while their parents slept.

In 1940, there was a mass suicide in Paris. A mob of 42 people were seen walking off the roof of ECore, a vilified business focused on pseudo-sciences. The reason for this suicide was never clear, but the corporation paid millions in restitution.

Two years later, Russia found a way to weaponize The Second Death. They assured, and still assure the world, that the virus would be a case study for vaccination only.

In 1945, Videl De La Mer explored Mariana's Trench. But the man was presumed to have died in a maelstrom. Those that sailed with Videl, however, insisted the man was still alive.

"But what does this mean," one might ask? "Well," one would say. "If you haven't learned anything, remember this." In the year 1950, Joshua Hill was born.

Prologue/Roper

Joshua Hill walked on his tiptoes, a certain cadence akin to the dropping of hollow brass casings onto laminate. The room was dark, and the walls were slathered red. The victim was Angelo Costas, an entrepreneur working for a vilified computer company that recently found a way to manipulate overseas markets. Angelo laid on his bed in his golden boxers, his stomach torn open, his entrails stretching into the bathroom to his right. In his mangled hand was a home telephone. The faint dial tone left a quiet, haunting, note in the apartment flat. His killer, a woman, a prostitute, allegedly, was well known. This "prostitute" was gone long before Joshua Hill arrived with his entourage of policemen in tow. On the ground lay a black-sequenced dress covered in blood and a pair of heels with like color.

"This woman doesn't stop, does she? Get the director on the phone, tell him that whore is at it again." Joshua cursed.

Case in mind, Joshua thought of the particular history behind the most recent string of murders. This prostitute was thought to be linked to every single one. This girl, whom was probably an assassin, trapezed about the city killing well known businessmen for unknown reasons. Joshua knew he couldn't catch her. In this slanted world, only barons and mice, demons and lesser grueling things, got their way in Paris.

The city Joshua operated in was a hollow landscape devoid of morals. A keen church-goer would cringe at the corruption in this city. It is a unique city, and one of the biggest. It is a place in France, but a different France altogether than the one people saw in the brochure when sitting in lines waiting for buses. The young French country captured lands well to the west, stopping only for the Atlantic. It also reached east, unfurling across Europe. Ever since Napoleon ravaged the world in a slew of ambition, Europe was left a pile of rubble, fragmented by adversity and agenda. The people truly responsible for that adversity were the leaders Napoleon left behind, Barons.

Kramer entered, a wiry man with a belly full of beer and plenty of razor burns. He was carrying a mag light. His pistol hung loosely in its unbuttoned holster and his shirt was untucked. He was a character of neglect, seen by his balding hair and unwillingness to comb it. There was a thin yellow stain down the front of his shirt, stopping at the third button down. Perhaps it was from a mustard accident a year before, or an encounter with a bladder-challenged mutt.

"Detective, there's a witness in the hall." Kramer grouched, his smoker's lungs choking the clarity of his garble.

"Then go talk to him." Joshua sighed.

"He'll only talk to you." Kramer insisted incompotently.

Joshua walked out of the flat which overlooked the entire city. This city named Paris was a collection of warm lights flickering to remind one of torches over a river, wisping about a horizontal, spectral level. The towers dimly lit the sky, marking where the airspace halted and where it crashed into stone and iron. Below, a sea of neon persisted from restaurants, hotels, brothels, and other meaningless services. But, out in the distance there lay a square of black on the grid of light, a hole in the color, an unmarked territory. That voidance of light marked the best of the city slums.

This city was most like any other city, perhaps more inspired by Britain than any other country. The gothic stone clashed with the advent of steel skyscrapers, creating a sense of disunity in the city. That wasn't far from the truth. Really, a tourist could get lost in the city, suddenly stumbling off pavement onto a cobblestone road. That tourist could blink and suddenly think he was in a dream, think he was in London. But London was gone, perhaps it was there, stitched into the city planning like a patchwork quilt.

At the end of the hall, Joshua saw a small man with dark skin. The persona twitched uncontrollably and a small amount of white powder rested just above his lip yet that did not touch his nose. He was wearing black suspenders but with only one strap was over his shoulder; the other dangled behind him like an asymmetric tail. He rubbed his arm as if he had a rash, unconsolably nervous and presumably high.

Joshua approached faster than the average human walk. His gait showed a will towards hostility coupled with a subtle, yet supple, intent to kill. He took the man by his neck with both hands and pushed him up against the wall. The man sputtered, and dribble from his mouth slid down Joshua's black crime-scene gloves. Joshua knew this man, his name was Saeed, a refugee from the wasteland that was India. Somehow his ilk was donned with considerable wealth, his forerunners some kind of higher caste before a plague destroyed the subcontinent. This plague was called the Second Death. The Second Death had taken the southern hemisphere by storm; the only continents left unscathed in that region were South America and Australia. The plague was a subtle reaper until it struck, leaving people convulsing on the floor in agony until death. But death wasn't the end for those infected, some corpses still walked about, killing people without cause. Most of the dead in the southern hemisphere kept on killing, leaving whole nations in shambles. During the onslaught, in which the contagion took the world by storm, many high and wealthy peoples from the southern hemisphere would use their cash to escape their homeland. They were rescued by brave soldiers, entrepreneurs, and mercenaries. Brought out of the death zones, led by those guides like Moses out of Egypt.

There was no doubt Saeed's family was at the top of the rescue list in India. But his presence didn't give health to the city. Perhaps it was because of what he saw in India, the maiming, murder, genocide, that led him to a life of a whoring mobster.

But, why would his story matter?

"What the hell are you doing here Saeed!? You're not supposed to leave your house!" Joshua scowled.

"I saw the TV– I had to see if I could catch her!" Saeed sputtered.

"You're not a part of this Saeed, if you cooperated and kept your nose clean we might have caught her a long time ago!"

"I'm sorry man – I just wanted to help Costas." Saeed cried.

"What did you see?" Joshua asked, his composure loosening, feeling guilt from his rage. Joshua dropped Saeed to the wooden floor. The collision of Saeed's short body was heard throughout the hall, echoing down the dark corridors.

The hallway was lacking lighting, sparsely a working bulb was littered down the line to the elevator. Saeed, purple-faced, still had drool running down his chin. He was crumpled into the perimeter.

"A-All I saw was her coming down the hall, she had a lot of blood on her legs and she wasn't wearing pants. All s-she had was a shirt and a coat. She didn't notice me or anything… I couldn't move. I - I just stood there…" He stuttered.

"Kramer, get two badges and take Saeed here to his house. Make sure to shake him. And make sure the coroner gets here, will you?" Joshua demanded without looking up to the fatso. He turned back to the door in which he came and left the weasel there in his shame. He didn't have time for coked-up amateurs. This woman he was chasing was a slippery one. Her modus operandi was close to that of a lightning bolt. As soon as she was there, she would make her move, kill her target, and leave.

However, considering the dress on the floor, the half-naked victim, and the mess about the cabin. Costas must have made the first move. He must have thought to assault her sexually immediately as they entered the room.

Joshua stood in the flat again, staring at the pale lining of the intestines used as streamers. How did a simple assassination go so wrong? Joshua thought, and for a second, he felt himself twitch at the side of his mouth. Was he feeling glad? Joshua was worried that he might be rooting for her. She never killed anyone who didn't seem to deserve it. Her main targets were big-shot businessmen who ran lucrative deals in back-alleys, siphoning the cities wealth, hiding drugs in their pockets to sell out to children on the street. If Joshua had a different job, maybe he wouldn't mind looking the other way. But he didn't have another job.

The coroner knelt beside the bed of Angelo Santos humming the tune *In the Hall of the Mountain King.* His eyes were lax and unexpressive. In his profession, such atrocities were of no further arousal than that of a bowl of cereal in the morning and a nagging wife. He lifted the silver silk sheets to find threads of hair, long and auburn, in the visage of his monocles. With tweezers in hand, he lifted the hair gently and procured them into a medium plastic bag. He pulled the top of his marker and looked carefully at the bag's label, blank and white. He smiled wryly from his thoughts and proceeded to scrawl in perfect cursive letters: *A Heifer's Cowlick.*

He chuckled.

"I can't believe you're still doing that Marcus." Joshua moaned.

"This is the only way to lighten my day before going home." Marcus replied evenly.

"You should find a better muse. You're screwing over the people who try to file this away."

"Serves them right, they get to stay in the office all day reading."

There was a slight smile, slight grimace, from Joshua, which was followed by a lingering silence. Marcus rose his head and cocked it to the side, recognizing something peculiar, a slight streak of white against the white walls of the apartment, a shade lighter than that of the surface. It was new paint. He walked over and ran his hand over the plaster. A thin layer of white powder covered his latex glove.

"How long have we been doing this, Joshua? At least four years of *this*, cleaning up this city. Keeping all these murderers behind bars. I remember when you first joined, Joshua." Marcus cooed.

"Yeah." Joshua grumbled, reading receipts by the table. "What about it?"

"You've changed; You've gone dark. You've had to fire that gun of yours more times than any other person on the force. How many people have you shot, Joshua, or have you lost count?"

Joshua ignored the question and moved near the glass balcony and gazed over the city. Marcus was always trying to have a meaningful conversation with Joshua. Marcus was supposed to operate on dead bodies, but he took a fancy of operating on live people too. Looking out into the city again, Joshua looked down at the traffic that lay many stories below like small fireflies ordered neatly behind the other. They waited for their normal lives to resume the second the light turned green.

Paris never slept.

Something in Marcus' question reminded Joshua of his first day at work in this city. He remembered standing there, being introduced; it was the first thing he remembered, the furthest back he could recall.

"Do you want to tell me what you've found, Marcus?" Joshua asked, looking back to his coworker, his hands held behind him.

"This paint is new. Not new, new, but new enough that the paint still has excess residue. Angelo had someone paint over this spot at least a week back, but only this spot. The question is, why?" Marcus thought aloud.

"Your thoughts?" Joshua asked again, letting the coroner continue.

"I have no idea, it could be anything. This part of the wall might be new, or, it could've been marked by something like a table scuff while moving furniture."

"Do you see this?" Joshua asked, his view further away from the pane, "There's a ring there, a small ring."

Joshua moved closer and leaned close to inspect. He produced a small magnifying glass and aimed it where Marcus held his finger. The young detective pulled out his gun from its brown leather holster. A modernized luger, he quickly ejected its magazine out and took a bullet from the chamber. He ran the bullet along the wall and into the small ring of collected paint. The rim of the bullet sat inside the ring, smaller than that of the circle.

"It could be a bullet hole of a forty-five round." Marcus mumbled, "Something might have gone down in this apartment before that assassin killed Santos."

"Maybe something significant enough for Angelo, or someone else, to fire a gun." Joshua sighed. He motioned to Kramer who stood inside the door haphazardly, staring down the hall.

Kramer shuffled through the door, slightly tripping over the threshold. He shifted his belt with his hands, making sure it wouldn't fall below his large stomach.

"Yeah?" Kramer huffed.

"Did Santos have a firearm registered in his name? Or did you find one while sweeping the apartment?"

"No Boss. I just got off the phone with the director, though. He wants you downtown, someone called about some lunatic near the square slicing people up."

Joshua frowned and made his way to the door. Thinking again about Marcus' question. It was true that

Joshua forgot much of his life before his job, but it never mattered to him.

Little did Joshua know his life would begin that night, that whatever he held true and dear in his occupation would be left a shard of a distant past, something to dream about one day when alone in his bed.

The square was snowing while Joshua arrived. The man was tired, gaunt, and his hair was swatted about by the wind that howled through the narrow alleyways. Neon signs of Blue and Pink flickered against the cold like cotton candy. The policemen, waiting for orders, gathered around these lights like moths to a flame. They discussed the recent string of killings and the news of the recent fall in stocks.

"Did you hear the conspiracy? They say one of the big corporations, E…core, I think, was behind the drop. They were the only company to sell stock right before it happened." Joshua heard a policeman whisper.

"Are you kidding me? You need to get your head out of the computers Dunn, you spend too much time reading blogs." The other retorted.

The scene was cleaner than the murder of Angelo Costas. The square had no clutter, only a few benches and trees stapled into the earth. The small park was boxed in by the concrete jungle, a rectangular area small and contrite. On the ground, the powdered snow, crumpled and piled off the streets, made the world white as paper, wrinkled by the thousands of footprints left by invisible men and woman who fled the scene. Scrawled upon this blank canvas were three blemishes, velvet stains making wide arcs across the plane only meters apart from each other. There, next to the arcs, lay shallow indentations the sizes of graves. These were the places where the victims lay before being taken to the hospital. Nothing else could be surmised at first glance.

Joshua turned his back on the scene, his arms crossed tight in defense of the cold. His breath shimmered and reflected the colors of the neon signs. He looked to the Director, a wiry man adorning a large fur coat and a pair of glasses.

"Did anyone die?" Joshua asked first.

"The perp stabbed three people but missed all their arteries. And, get this, with a sword, like what the rest of the barons use outside the city."

Strange, Joshua thought. Although guns were commonplace in most densely populated areas, there was still a need for steel in rural areas. Some states in the French Dominion even required their soldiers to carry and use swords. Most firearms were maintained by the governmental authorities, hoarded in anticipation for war in the east. France could only make so many bullets a year and it wouldn't be surprising if they were forced to beat the eastern juggernaut with their pointy sticks.

"The square was busy tonight, it's a Friday, why weren't the victims closer together?" Joshua inquired.

The Director replied with a shrug and there was a silence. The only sound that filed the empty chorus was a creaking of half-closed doors and the barking of a dog, a small dog. Joshua thought long and hard, his left temple straining from the flood of information he saw at the scene. His temple twitched like a headache, the cold squeezed him, made his head tight. The frigid air compressed his neck and his torso and forced the blood to rise up about his eyes. Could there be a reason why three people were harmed among a crowd of tens, if not dozens, of people? The perpetrator waited between each attack for the people to understand what was happening and run. Why, with such a large weapon, would someone miss every artery? To Joshua, the assailant couldn't possibly do such things, unless they were aiming to evoke fear more than death.

There was a buzz, a vibration, muffled by the clothes of a navy-blue jacket. A policeman, looking at his walkie-talkie, felt the sensation. He lifted the phone out of the pocket it was nestled in and turned up the volume. On the other end of the line, the signal of a patrol unit buzzed white noise.

"Say again." The policeman called back, unable to hear the words spoken.

The static continued afterwards. In the speaker, an emerging sound of heavy breathing kept the time through the earpiece.

"Sir, I'm getting something strange from the channel." The Policeman informed, turning to his boss for assistance. The Director motioned to the blue man and the pig hustled over to him, the snow giving a satisfying crunch beneath his boots.

"Turn the volume up, Harry." The Director ordered, leaning his ear to the speaker. The man placed his hands on his hips, his coat pulled back by his wrists.

"It won't go any further sir." Harry replied. "What the hell is that, breathing?"

No one knew, but, they didn't have to. A few seconds after, a banshee scream sounded through the radio. It pierced the howling wind at such a pitch that it almost dissipated into a higher octave than the human ear could comprehend. At this crest, the sound fell back into the range of perception. It was a sound of a man begging for his life, crying for mercy. It echoed through the corridors. It bent time to its will. The company of police, The Director, and Joshua were frozen much like the snow. The wailing lasted for what was thought to be an eternity, a living hell upon those that heard it, something they would have nightmares about for many years to come. It was a moment of complete fear and mesmerism, a moment before the world known is taken from their hearts and everything good and lovely was forgotten. It was a trumpet or a war cry. More importantly, it was the sound that marked the beginning of this play.

The Director took command once his heart began to beat again, his skin flaring into a cartoonish zeal. He snatched the radio from Henry who was still in shock. The static resumed on the radio and the scene was over.

"Henry! Where the hell was the patrol car dispatched to?" The Director barked. The old man already started to hustle down the biggest street leading from the park. Henry hesitated, his chest heaving in a wild ordeal. His eyes dawdled and twitched. Despite the cold, a thick slosh of sweat collided with the back of his collar, soaking it through.

"Does anyone know where our patrol car is!?" The director shouted into the parkway, his voice booming off the walls in desperation.

"They're checking out the warehouse on 7th and Lancaster!" A cop shouted back from under a pink sign of noodles, finally. "Someone called about a noise disturbance!"

"That's only 2 blocks from here! Come on Hill!" The Director ordered, quickly turning his back to the case and shouting into the talkie. "Is anyone there?! Can anybody hear me?!"

Joshua Hill panted, his brown leather shoes slapping against the snow and asphalt. It was early in the morning, but more like the dead of night; the time approaching 4 A.M. Ahead of him, his boss sprinted forth at like speed, his massive coat fluttering behind him like a cape. Together they stormed down Lancaster street, the sounds of deafening screams steering them closer to their destination. The boss had given up on speaking to the radio, and now the sounds of torture could be clearly heard in the direction they were heading.

Joshua was in the moment, that brief expanse of time that can take mental hours to overcome. His mind begged his attention but without words or thoughts he could understand. Whatever words that drowned beneath the pounding of his heart could not be warning him enough, that his life would be forever shaken and ratified.

18

They arrived. The screams emanated from a short two-story building made with concrete and rebar, reinforced with rusting sheet metal left in shambles. It was a forgotten parking garage, ones the homeless took advantage of. The decrepit building was a third bolted, a third soldered, and a third duct-taped.

The Director stopped just a few steps before Joshua. He stood in front of a wide entrance, a broken-down wall with the rebar jutting and twisting around itself like a curly fry.

Joshua slid on his heels over the slush into a braking halt.

Before, it had snowed in the square, the wide-open air frigid and unforgiving. But now, the smog of the city and the heat of the sewer vents caused all drifting snow to melt and cling as rain, slush, and slick. It clung to Joshua's black frock coat and refroze brittle. The ice intervened between every fiber. It left room for the howling wind to sneak in and sting the detective's skin.

The Director turned and addressed his cohort, "What's the plan, Hill?" He asked, catching his breath.
"How the hell should I know?" Joshua replied, stooping over slightly, his hands on his shoulders.

"Well, you're the one who usually ends up in a firefight. I'm out-of-order, I haven't done this in years. I'm a desk jockey."

Joshua shook his head in disdain and tiptoed into the dark hole. The light from the neon signs filtered in, creating a beautiful red circle around Hill's shadow. The whole floor was vacant and wet. Dirty cardboard boxes and plastics littered the walls, slightly floating in the puddles. It smelt like sewer, the corners darker than the center. Brown streaks of feces lined the walls. To Joshua's right was the only staircase to the second floor. At the bottom of the steps, forgotten power tools and paintbrushes lay clumped and dry.

"How does it look?" Inquired the Director, still catching his breath.

"Just get in here old man" Joshua huffed.

Joshua stepped lightly, he placed the sides of each foot down onto the floor and rolled onto the balls of his feet to creep, taking each precaution not to make noise. The lights that came down from the stairs hinted to a construction lamp facing the steps. Against this luminescence, a shadow was shaped. It was a man in a chair, his head back and hanging over the rest.

Joshua picked up the pace, his mind still blank, the hair on his neck standing on end, waiting in anticipation for something bad. He feared an ambush from the shadows, being noticed, being killed. But Joshua Hill was a man of devout curiosity and slowly trudged forth. He was at the stairs, his pistol poised in one hand, his other hand lightly brushing the top of the hand rail, rusted and worn. The Director behind him brandished a small silver handgun. His chest heaved out from beneath his clothes. His face wet and dirty.

Joshua rounded the corner, his gun pulled close to his eye and at level. His eyes beheld the horror. The man in the chair was one of the patrolmen, his neck slit wide open that if you would compare it to a mouth, it would be laughing like a puppet. But from that opening the spine was still attached to the head which dangled back like a pocket watch.

The patrolman was undoubtedly dead, but he bled out over time and that blood was caked over his chest. It pooled below him on the floor. The blood ran like a river along the concrete as if gravity had a peculiar way of directing it down a hill, forming a stream. At the end of that stream there was not a delta but a shoe, a man's shoe, a man's rubber boots. The man who wore that boot was tall. He wore a high-end plastic-yellow rain poncho and a wide-brimmed hat to match. In his left hand was a long Japanese ceremonial sword and in his right hand a pistol identical to Joshua's. He stood there with a smile white enough to been seen through the darkness. It was a spotlight aimed straight at the young detective.

His smile parted to speak, his voice clear in the empty room, echoing not only in the building, but in Joshua's head.

"It took you long enough, Mr. Hill. I've been waiting for you all alone. Well, I was with your friend here, but he wasn't much company." He said.

The man paused, Joshua cringed. The murderer took a few steps forward, his gun pointed in the air, his elbow tucked near his hip. As he walked, the blade tapped the concrete floor, and every time it touched the ground it gave a small chime. It sounded like a pin drop inside an empty water tower. His face hit the light, his skin looked crisp, almost leathery and scarred. His eyes were alive, wide awake. The expression he wore looked uncertain but menacing. Joshua couldn't tell the killers intent, despite being called by his name.

Joshua was used to being known; his days on the street pointed to his reputation. Even after his days working, Joshua was known for being vigilant, so much so that he was almost considered a vigilante. His reputation had the attention of many people, good and bad. Joshua was rarely the man who would answer to anyone, he was almost a bounty hunter. The Paris crime division were not so much his occupation as his broker. He was his own man, and the division he worked for had no problem letting him do what he wanted, so long as he produced results. Many times, The Baron of Paris would call upon him to help in other affairs. He would serve the baron by helping officers in other states protect assets and bring criminals to justice. In some ways, he was his own department, the department of Joshua Hill.

"My name is Solomon, and I've been trying to get your attention for a long time." The man regarded himself. He had a whimsical but sinister air about him, it drew Joshua's attention, snapped him out of his brain and into the moment.

"What the hell are you talking about?" Demanded Joshua, his gun trained on Solomon.

"If I were to tell you that I had a gift for you, would you take it?" Solomon mused, but he soon answered his own question.

"No, of course not. At a young age, children are told not to take gifts from strangers… and I am *surely* strange. I can't give you what I want to give you, I don't have it yet… It's… not something I *can* give."

The man tapped the sword again, Joshua watched him with an eagle eye. He was ready to fire but waited. The Director stood behind him, his silver pistol shaking in his hand. Joshua could tell the old man was nervous. The young detective was used to doing things alone, and he didn't want the soft director to be caught in the crossfire if he could help it.

Solomon looked at the director, as if he knew what was going through Joshua's brain. He smiled at the man, his lips thin and twisted. Joshua could see a small stream of blood from the corner of Solomon's mouth.

Is he injured? Joshua thought.

Solomon continued. "Since I can't give you what I want to give you, I'll have to send you to retrieve it. But I can't do that if you're here, either. You have to be thrown to the wolves."

The Director yelled, his heart unable to bear the standoff. He squeezed the trigger and in a blinding flash of light emptied his clip. The director continued to fire and pace towards the criminal until his gun simply clicked, empty, useless.

Joshua looked at Solomon and The Director in amazement. The Director stood there, his smoking gun still poised in front of him. He looked through his sights at Solomon who still stood there with a smug look on his face.

The director blinked. Had he missed? Joshua and Solomon watched as the Director loaded his gun again in fright, fumbling his hands over the slide. He loaded it clumsily and fired again.

"Die you bastard!" The Director screamed. Through his sights, yet again, he had missed. But Joshua noticed something, the unflinching villain hadn't moved, nor was the

Director's aim poor. The bullets hadn't zoomed out into the open space behind Solomon, where streetlights and construction lights loomed, casting bright florescence onto the scene. The bullets had disappeared.

As the bullets moved towards the yellow man, they distorted in a haze, a ripple like summer heat had emerged before him, hard to see, hard to understand. This wrinkle absorbed the bullets and erased them from existence.

It was impossible, inconceivable. Joshua blinked, unable to understand. Between this blink the man who was Solomon vanished from his eyesight as if moved from the picture of his mind. Joshua heard a grunt, a gurgle.

Joshua looked to his right to see the villain's hand pressed firmly on the director's head. The director chocked on a black sludge which oozed from his mouth. He fell to his knees and shuddered. Joshua leapt to the side and fired pointed rounds at Solomon whom let go of the director. Joshua looked at Solomon who ignored Joshua's attack, he simply focused on Joshua's boss. The director was motionless in his posture, dead and stuck on his knees. Black ooze poured from his eyelids, his ears.

The bullets were gone again, not a single one landed. Joshua blinked.

"You should be worried." Solomon whispered into Joshua's ear.

Solomon stood inches behind him, he appeared without a sound, his body unscathed, surfacing there as if remerging from imagination into reality. Joshua twisted around again but was soon met by nothing for his pistol to aim at. Again, Solomon was gone. The yellow-coated man stood at the edge of the second floor, his body masked by the lights of the street beyond. He smiled his spotlight smile.

It was all impossible, Solomon couldn't have moved so fast. But there he was standing, undaunted, the Director's talkie in his hand.

"You should be worried about reinforcements."
Solomon stated. The villain cackled and leapt from the edge
and disappeared yet again.

Joshua was dazed, perplexed. He kept muttering to
himself, *this can't be real, I'm dreaming. I fell asleep on the
ride to the square in a cab. This is all a bad dream.*

Joshua could hear the sirens in the distance. There he
stood with two dead bodies, one in a chair, one on its knees.
He couldn't explain any of it.

Joshua heard the thuds of boots on the first floor. They
kicked the tools away by the steps. They thundered up the
stairs and trained their guns on Joshua's back. Joshua slowly
raised his hands, he knew the drill. Before he could open his
mouth to identify himself, he heard the sound of a round going
off in its chamber. Joshua felt a firm punch to his back and the
tightening of wire around his arms. It was a shock bullet, and
it gripped Joshua and bore against his skin, coursing voltage
throughout his body. Joshua fell to the ground with a thud,
quickly fading into the unconscious.

ACT 1/<small>*Reborn*</small>

Part 1/<small>*Rescue*</small>

Joshua stared at the steel table before him, his hands chained to the floor. He looked over the documents of that night two days ago, the day nothing made sense anymore. Joshua read the files over and over and over again. He answered the Bureau's questions, but they told him the same thing, the same response.

"It was your gun that fired the bullet, you're the one who killed the director."

Joshua denied it all, it wasn't true. But he couldn't prove it, he explained the man who disappeared without a trace, but somehow no prints were on the katana that was left there. The only DNA at the scene was Joshua's, the Director's, and Clinton's.

Joshua continued to read the files until he heard the creaking of a door. As the door swung open Joshua could spy him. The illustrious, conniving and shark-like man who was the owner of Paris, the owner of what was once the country of France, Baron Glass.

Baron Glass was a slick man, something out of a magazine for up-and-coming professionals. He wore the standard black suit of power with silver cufflinks. The man was perhaps the only person over Joshua, having dealt with him several times. It was Baron Glass that Joshua really answered to. His baron was the man who would send him out, lend him out, to others. But Baron Glass wasn't a respectable man, he was a crime lord feigning legitimacy. The businessman was shrewd, skimming from the top of every major company in France, ensuring their survival and their fidelity.

Glass stood there in the doorway for a moment so that Joshua might behold the presence he was in. But Joshua was used to Glass' presence, his holy masquerade, and quickly looked back to the files, scanning for holes in the evidence. The Baron waltzed to the steel chair across from Joshua and wiped the surface with a napkin before sitting down. He stared at Joshua for a moment before speaking.

"They said you killed the Director and someone else." He stated bluntly.

"And they're wrong, like always." Joshua grunted.

"But this isn't like always, Joshua. A deal has been made."

Joshua looked up from the table and into Glass' pale eyes. It was like looking into the face of the devil himself. *What did the Baron mean?*

"I won't be able to protect you this time, Joshua." Glass sighed. He didn't look sad in the slightest. "You were a great detective, but detectives can be replaced. I got where I am today by replacing people, doing good business, paying favors and making people owe me."

Glass stood and walked into the corner of the room, away from Joshua, in the far corner.

"I've sold you to Whitecroft." Glass explained.

Joshua lurched from his chair and kicked it back. He stood in rage and cursed. The young detective kicked the table towards his baron which slid into the wall and bounced away. Glass slowly flinched and quickly made his way to the door while Joshua snarled like a dog. Joshua was more than angry. Joshua knew what this meant.

A time back, when Joshua was newer at the department, but still popular. Glass rented Joshua out to Baron

Whitecroft who presided over much of what used to be Germanic lands. She owned a small state in her name Southwest of the Scandes, south of the North Sea. During his assignment, Joshua was told to protect Whitecroft's fiancée, whom was traveling into the providence for their wedding. Needless to say, Joshua learned more about the fiancée than he cared to.

In their travels, they came across a small group of girls, younger than a proper age. The groom took a fancy to them, quickly began to flirt with them, boasting of his wealth and stature. This, Joshua payed no mind. It was not until later that night, when Joshua guarded the groom's suite, that the groom's men brought these girls to his room, bound at the wrists and beaten. Joshua reluctantly let the men through, and thus began his conscience. Joshua first heard the crying, the muffled screaming, the thumping of a headboard and the rocking of old springs.

Joshua couldn't stop thinking about it. He lit a cigarette to calm himself, cocked his gun and opened the front door to the room. The whole hotel, if not awake already, rose in fright to hear the gunpowder ignite. Many shell casings later, the captured girls ran into the hall and disappeared. Joshua left the extra bullets in the groom's face, leaving his face unrecognizable.

Despite the groom's infidelity and unholy cravings in his flesh, Whitecroft demanded Joshua be executed. Had Baron Glass not come to the rescue, Joshua might have been dead in a foreign land. The Baron quickly ushered Joshua home and swept the ordeal under the rug. He paid high sums for Joshua's freedom, pulled many strings to ensure his safety. But Joshua didn't love his baron for this. It was just business, a way for him to flex his muscles for the other barons. The other barons weren't as powerful as Glass. Glass held the greatest city in the French Dominion. Paris was the capital of all of France, the center of the Dominion's world.

Joshua didn't doubt being sold to Whitecroft meant a swift execution.

Joshua watched as Baron Glass left, leaving the door open for ironclad bureau soldiers to enter. They put a bag on Joshua's head and began pummeling him with batons until Joshua couldn't stand. Submissive by force, they unchained the detective and dragged him away to an armored vehicle. Joshua was on his way to The Crofts.

Joshua woke up with an all-consuming headache. His vision still blurred before him as if he was just now learning to see. Double and triple visions overlaid slowly, approaching a singularity of clarity. Slowly he came to his senses. He lay on a dirty floor. To be more literal, he lay on a dirt floor in a cavern, a dungeon. Joshua was in prison.

France's barons never saw fit to improve the living conditions of their prisoners, the kings and queens of Joshua's country always held on to the firm belief that the best punishment was to live in hell. In French prisons, there was only one meal a day, a type of powdered bone that was grounded from whatever inmate died last. On benevolent days, a rat was skewered and lightly salted for them each. There were no walls but for the rocky underground caves that were left from early mining rushes. There was no toilet nor bed either.

Joshua just lay there for a time, listening past his barred door at the sounds of grunting officers beating a prisoner to death. It could be other things as Whitecroft's prison was known for both sexual and physical violence as a means of getting inmates in order.

Rising from his muddy place, Joshua was happy to realize he still retained most of his clothes after the ordeal. This meant that he hadn't been raped immediately, and his detainment was somewhat respected by those who put him in cuffs. He scraped the mud off the back of his vest and slowly walked toward the bars to take a look about.

The cavern was deep like a catacomb, going stories beneath the surface. Joshua, somewhere closer to the top, could only see a few hundred feet down before the rest of the spiral cavern was left in shrouded darkness. However, up above, there was a large iron door that marked the divide between the guard station and the criminals.

Joshua leaned against the iron tubes, his head slightly hung and sore. They must've thrown him on his head in the cell, or took liberty in beating his skull a few times with a blackjack before placing him in.

"Hey you." Beckoned a rasping voice. "You, you're Joshua Hill, aren't you?"

Joshua looked right of his door to find an oddly figured head poking out of the nearby cell, his neck stretched long away from the bars and Joshua could see him clearly. He was ugly, a thin face that sagged and wrinkled. His eyes popped out of his head and his hair was in long patches. His skin was yellow and almost flakey. He smiled, his teeth black and shiny, as if replaced with dull marbles. The man surely had no marbles.

Joshua stayed silent, hardly acknowledging the odd man, looking through him less than at him. But the fellow continued anyway.

"Oh boy- oh boy, you're going to die in here!" the odd figure chimed.

Joshua sighed, he was without solid hope. He held his back to the conversation, he wouldn't entertain someone who only wished to laugh at his misfortune. Joshua still felt dizzy, disoriented. He walked over to the far wall and took his vest off. Rolling it over itself he made a small pillow and rested his head on it. Slowly, he closed his reddened eyes.

Joshua had the strangest dream of a girl with short black hair and glistening eyes. She was walking through a field of grains, holding a sickle in one hand and a bouquet in the other. This woman was walking towards him. But soon this vision changed as he heard whispers deep in the caverns. Joshua listened to them, they whispered his name. In his sleep Joshua thought of his encounter with Solomon. He could have sworn he wasn't the only one there. He had the slightest inclination of... black leather shoes.

What had gotten him here? And what was this gift Solomon talked about? Moreover, how would Joshua get out?

"Oi, get up mista Hill!"

There was a rattling of some metal.

"We needa get you to the Baron, don't act up okaye?"

Joshua nodded but stayed on the floor. The guardsman slowly inserted his key into the gate and rotated it into place. The iron gate was then pushed by his metal fist. The bottom corner of the door clung to the dirt reluctantly. Eventually he struggled to open it, until it shuddered agape under the weight of his body.

Joshua's eyes still didn't open, they felt swollen, bulging from their sockets, warm in an uncomfortable way, a sickly way. He felt himself being lifted by a group of hands. Joshua was half drug, half walked up the spiraling stairs like a drunkard. The turns seemed steeper, perhaps his body had not awoken nor consumed energy at this moment, feeling much akin to lead. He heard a door creak, a large door that almost cringed beneath its own weight.

He entered with his escort. The floor was hard now, Joshua could tell by the smooth surface beneath his dragging toe. He moved past a few spots of warmth and light flickered against his eyelids. Joshua then heard the clamor of many metals, a sort of revelry and jeering. The young detective must've been in the Baron's court. There was an orchestra of noise and music that grew ever louder until it was upon him, blaring in his ears. Joshua was placed down onto an expanse of floor. He sat on his heels and his knees, facing what he thought would be forward.

A loud and hoarse voice called out to the room. "Everyone here today in my honor, I give you a man of stories but not legends, a man of fortitude but not faith, the justified... yet cruel, Joshua Hill!"

The crowd laughed and slammed their jars of liquids onto their tables, a loud thump like a war cry vibrated through Joshua's bones. Out from the crowd, somewhere behind him, someone shouted amongst the resuming laughter, "Where's his baron now?"

The haughty voice mused "He's been abandoned by his own king!" in a higher alto.

"He has no more power than a man's!" Another chimed.

"Certainly not! As we can plainly see, he is actually rather skinny." The main voice added daintily. The crowd laughed again and slammed their mugs. Joshua began to understand his situation, if the voice before him was Whitecroft, she would give him no time to escape, no time to whittle away before being executed. He was to die there and now. Joshua didn't respond to the heckling, half afraid, half uncertain.

"Here we see, this man is not beyond our grasp," The voice hissed again, a slight garble in the throat. "Nothing is out of my reach."

Joshua began to twitch his eyes, they creaked slightly, slowly, wedging the lids wider and wider. Before him there seemed to be a large stone throne, large enough to hold two or three men. The whole room was made of stone and adorned with purple tapestries. They hung about the large colosseum and torches lined the pillars. Before him shuffled a thin woman down the stairs towards Joshua. His heart beat rapidly, his eyes throbbing at each pulse. The woman was too frail to be alive. She was only skin and bones, her skin sucked into her ribs. In her hands was a large axe, like that born for executioners. Despite her size, she could lift it enough to descend it. She wore a purple velvet coat with a white furry collar with black speckles. A small ring hung about her neck and even that looked too heavy for her. Her feet were barren, her pants drawn tight against her waist like a burlap sack about a sapling.

"Joshua Hill, just a regular man who kills regular people by regular means..." She mused, "You will die for killing my Charlie, my love."

"You're baron Whitecroft?" Joshua asked. "I remember her being... average at least."

Whitecroft scoffed, perhaps it was the pain of losing her fiancée that drove her to starvation. She snarled, her axe ready to swing it around in a heaving motion. Joshua stared back, unable to comprehend whether the wretch could sever his head with her twiggy arms.

There was a breaking of the glass that was not aforementioned. Nor was it something the guards should have ignored or those who heard it. Rather than it being a drunken advocate dropping her glass or a rambunctious party-goer deciding to be physical with a wine glass. The shattering of glass was from a window that was tucked away and out of sight. This window, once used to filter in light before the consideration of open flame, was now blocked off by a large concrete balcony that opened into the roof.

This blockade was made to diffuse the light from Baron Whitecroft's eyes. Many a year before her health had declined, much like her body the year before that. She found that her eyes couldn't bear the harsh and direct white light the sun brought. Sickly though she was in mind, spirit, and body, she ordered the translucent panel boxed off to prevent it from bringing her any further distress. But in this instance, it was something that kept her from witnessing the trespasser who utilized this entrance.

The window broke because of a man, a dark man. He was a mercenary who wore a long green peacock coat with the sleeves torn off. His pants were battered and torn, tapered to his leg by small knots of rope. He wore no shoes and moved silently because of it. His name was Haddock and he had just invaded a baron's estate. He bore a strong arm, and in both his arms he held a long revolver named after someone very precious to him, someone he wished he could keep with him forever.

At the time Whitecroft descended her hatchet upon Joshua, Haddock rang a bullet that would have plunged into Whitecroft's chest, but instead, shattered against the flat of her blade. Whitecroft, overcome by the force of the bullet was sent sprawling backwards.

Joshua was baffled by his luck. The young man, against the will of his body, quickly sprung to his feet where the guards had left him and sprinted across the room. His new chance at life urged his energy-deprived body to flee.

Joshua ran as fast as he could, the men and women of revelry now hot with rage. In the corner of his eye he could see Whitecroft's guards lift their baron gingerly, trying to get her upright. She contorted and cursed. "Come-on you fools, stand me up!"

The mob trampled over itself, the drunken bog of feet tangled and twisted. What should have been a uniform pace recreated itself into a living mound of humans.

Joshua was almost free. He thundered forth, leaping over the last guard who stood watch. Joshua then thundered down the stone steps that led away from the entrance and looked across the yard to make his way through the gates. There was an adjacent forest by Joshua which he used to his advantage. The detective leapt over fallen branches and weaved through trucks in random vectors, trying to lose anyone who might have followed him closely. Not only was Joshua afraid of the mob that would soon rise to find him, but also of the unknown shooter that presumably rescued him. Joshua ran for the better half of the hour until he was near the edge of the forest.

No one had found him. Perhaps they were preoccupied with someone else.

Haddock, as soon as he had been realized by the commune, vanished back into the window from whence he came. On the roof he sprinted. To the far side he flew over the cracking tiles of the estate and leaped into the air. Easily and nimbly he landed into the nearest bush and just as swift emerged from it scratched and scrambling. He quickly ran left and away from the entrance. Haddock, unlike the boy he rescued, was smarter and knew the distance he needed to achieve in so little time for Joshua had the head start on him.

Haddock found his prize and vaulted over a stall, entering a nearby stable. As he leapt from stall to stall he shot the locks on the doors and scared the horses out of their pens. He did this until neatly landing on the last of two horses and unleashed them.

Haddock rode the duo within the stampede of fleeing equines until he left the estate grounds. After he was well out of the guards' lines of sight, he broke his two horses from the escapade and made his escape into the forest. He needn't be afraid to lose his target, Haddock was the best tracker he, himself, knew.

Joshua leaned against a tree on the edge of the forest and tried to catch his breath. He was getting out of shape, or perhaps it was the ramifications of being in a cell that caused his hands to shake uncontrollably. Once Joshua recovered, he nestled himself on the shore like a baby turtle and watched the North Sea break against the beach. On that beach, Joshua could see hundreds of feet away, and no one could catch him by surprise, or so he thought.

As the night grew upon him, The American fingered the inside of his vest for his secret pocket and pulled out a cigarette and a lose match. He struck the match against his shoe and proceeded to light his smoke. But even this took some time as his muscles screamed beneath the weight of the tobacco in his hand. So, focused on lighting his cigarette, was

Joshua, that he couldn't hear Haddock approach him from behind.

"Smoking will kill you." Haddock quirked.

Joshua jolted at the close voice, turning to see a dark man with two horses just ten feet away. He sprang to his feet, the cigarette falling onto the fine sand near his toe. The man laughed a slow but friendly laugh.

"My name is Haddock, and you are Joshua Hill." He started.

"So, I'm told." Murmured Joshua.

Haddock gave a toothy grin, his revolver aimed at Joshua's thigh, "Come Mr. Hill, you are going to spend the night at my house."

Haddock held out the spare reign of the chestnut horse, and Joshua reluctantly took it. Mounting the beast lethargically, Joshua felt the gun pressed to his thigh. If he were to pull the trigger, both his leg and the horse would be gone. He looked to Haddock who was still smiling.

"I need you alive, Joshua Hill, but that doesn't mean I won't harm you." He grinned.

"What are you," Joshua asked, "a bounty hunter?"

"I am hired help." Haddock insisted, as if the two terms were somehow opposite occupations.

Together, Joshua and Haddock trotted along the beach and back into the tree line. The grasshoppers' chirping picked up. For a time, they rode along the edge of the forest, tracing it along the end of its reach.

"So, what do you need me for?" Joshua huffed, the ride taking longer than he expected; the horse's back chaffing his thighs. He twisted in his seat.

"I need you because a witch needs you. And since a witch needs you I need you." Haddock rhymed terribly.

"Aren't you helpful." Joshua moaned.

"I don't know why the witch needs you Mr. Hill. But I have a deal to bring you to her. In return, she will let me say goodbye to my daughter."

"Why would a witch have your daughter? And are we talking about a pointy hat and broomstick witch?"

Haddocks laughed, "No, my daughter died many years ago, she will let me say goodbye to her from beyond the grave. And yes, a witch, like those who guided the people before they built cities and homes for themselves."

"Well if she's a witch, why don't you just ask her to bring your daughter back?" Joshua played, believing none of his story.

"The dead need to stay dead, Mr. Hill. The living should continue living. The dead are at peace. We shouldn't want them to come back to this hell. One death is enough for each life, there is no need for more." Haddock chided.

Joshua rolled his eyes.

The duo trot upon the rising ground as the sun started to rise. They were upon a hill in which the trees started to thin. Up and upon the rise they halted their horses to look back down the other side, beholding an array of tenements. The small village was made inside a small valley in which a suitable river drove through and out of sight to the north.

The populace bustled about in odd attire, straw hats and black, white, or brown kimonos. It was a native village, tucked away from technology and any French map. Joshua had no idea such a place existed. The water was harnessed by watermills made of planks and buckets turning at varying radii. It was a shanty town, a glimpse at a native, naïve, life. It was something which Joshua never had the luxury of experiencing.

Haddock started his horse down the slope, taking the hill at sideways angles, zigzagging down a well-trodden path. His horse jerked in excitement, or struggle, and the bounty hunter raised his hand to calm it.

The two moved closer and at their point of entry was a long amber field of grain divided by a single dirt path. In this dirt divide were busy children, all pushing thin rubber tires with sticks and giggling. The first house they passed boasted a man. He smoked a long pipe and held out his hand slowly in the air, waving it weakly. He did not raise his head from the porch. Haddock laughed, and his horse quickly strung itself into a circle before the man.

"Mister Fill, tell one of your grandchildren to bring a message to the witch, I have the man fitting her description, and I will be there soon." Haddock chuckled, twisting his horse straight and continuing.

Joshua passed slowly through the narrow path between the buildings, passing Mr. Fill who raised his head slightly, his eyes catching Joshua's. They were Violet and vibrant, the chin was smooth and pointed, the mouth smirking and letting out a thick pungent smoke. He had long eyelashes and rosy cheeks.

Joshua shrugged the ominous notion and resumed pace with Haddock. Haddock led him through the town until he eventually dismounted his horse and led it by its reigns next to the river. On the water rode many shallow boats filled with fruits and vegetables; some even held cages with birds and other creatures. The passengers moved their craft with long oars, pushing against the shallow bed like Venetian ferrymen. Koi fish swam about the river, their orange and white scales starkly in contrast against the green rocks beneath them. Up ahead, Haddock and Joshua crossed a bridge over the river.

"This is my world," Haddock mused. "We came here to live together from many different places. We fell madly in love with this land, and we have lived in peace with it for many generations."

"How come the French haven't found you yet? You're not on any map I've ever read. You're living on Whitecroft's land, her hunting parties could find you. She isn't the kind of woman who lets people have nice things," Joshua warned, overwhelmed by the view around him.

More children passed, their families in tow. They had small eyes like the native tribes in Japan and the wastelands of China. "Did you come here from Asia? I haven't seen any oriental people's in France. The country didn't accept refugees that fled through Russia." Joshua asked again.

Haddock laughed, "We are not in France, this is Valashoth, a place separate of the world."

Joshua sighed, he would ask someone else for answers. Haddock did not seem like the person who would explain himself to others.

The mercenary stopped in his tracks, blocking Joshua's horse down the narrow streets between houses. He then proceeded to take the stirrup and saddle from his horse. Now in hand, he dropped them onto the porch on his left with a loud thump. Haddock dismounted and motioned his compatriot to do the same. Joshua did, and left his horse's equipment down next to Haddock's and waited for further instructions.

"What do you want Haddock?" came a voice from behind the door, it was an airy voice, an aging voice.

"I have horses for you." Haddock called back into the house.

"Well, just run them around back into the stables like everyone else." The voice snapped.

Haddock huffed and jerked his head back at Joshua. He turned and waltzed around back. The stables were empty but for one horse, a white stallion with a pristine coat. The small building was open-roofed; the lazy sun of the day trickled down at a perfect temperature.

It really did seem too good to Joshua. The spectral landscape differed greatly from France's wildlife as well, and, through the thatched roof, a thin haze began to trickle from the sky. The two proceeded to move their horses into their pens in silence and the morning felt more alike to the evening. The energy of the village was laxer than before; its attitude changed like a switch. The oncoming mist was a welcoming cool, a good fog that didn't choke one's breath like France's city smog. It was the antithesis to that as if the mist opened

Joshua's lungs and spurred him forth in a renewed, but mindful, vigor.

They walked back around and further down the street having finished their small chore. The village grew silent, the children who were once playing now sat inside their homes, glancing out with curiosity at the pair that passed. They whispered to each other.

The somber adults gathered around their porches, each of them igniting a long slender pipe and puffing their conversations between each other. The once energetic village now became a slumbering one, quiet in all regards. The only sound adamant against the silence was the condensed mist dropping onto the porches. The sky whispered and hissed like distant sprinklers.

Haddock motioned to Joshua again, and this time the hunter wanted him to hurry. Joshua jogged behind his companion to keep up with him. A right down the road and then a left began their short tour which abruptly ended a few hundred feet later. There, Haddock stood on a porch, waiting for a moment so Joshua could catch up.

They entered the house together.

Haddock hushed the silent detective, striding over to a small coffee table in which two red and embroidered cushions lay. Joshua plopped himself down on the cushion adjacent to Haddock, who was busy with illuminating the candles on the table.

The hunter whispered, "Ashoth gives us night in the day, so we take this time to relax, to nap, so that we can be a better people to each other and meditate, fostering our souls."

The tanned man grasped his hand around a pearl vase with flowers painted on it, it sat in the center of the table. He poured sake into two shallow saucers, one for Joshua, one for himself, and proceeded to drink it. Joshua did the same. Joshua coughed, the potency of the alcohol searing his throat. Haddock chuckled quietly and resumed his speech.

"You asked me why no one has found us yet. Val-ashoth was built by our people upon Ashoth's palm, she breathes her mist down on us and she lifts us in her palm when the hunters near. She moves us around the earth and places us where she wants us to be. We are her chosen people. The witch is her emissary, her tongue, she stewards us. Ashoth was kind enough to put us here, north of Whitecroft's forest, so that I, Emil Haddock, could find you, Joshua Hill."

Joshua didn't believe the tale, he had burnt any inclination of easy faith out of his mind as a man, he trusted only what he saw, and what he did. Yet, although he trusted his own hands and no one else's, he had a clear understanding of someone watching him since youth. It was evident he believed in God, but it was not certain whether the guy still loved mankind anymore, much less cared.

Joshua stayed silent for a time, hardly paying much mind to the statement of deism. He would not place weight in Haddock's words. Haddock refilled both their dishes with alcohol and they downed the liquid again. This time, Joshua only grimaced. Joshua thought he was tougher than to dislike the sake, he was a hard-liquor man, after all.

"What does this witch want with me?" Joshua finally asked.

"I do not know. But she used two names for you, not Joshua Hill, as you are called, but Connor Shaw. Do you have two whole names?" Haddock asked.

"No." Joshua said, taking another drink, "I've never gone by that name before."

The man gave Joshua a puzzled look, it twisted to tell him he had no answers.

"Ashoth has had many emissaries over the years. The witch we have now is new, young. She doesn't spend time with the people as past emissaries have, she does not seem to be a 'white' witch."

"What do you mean by white?" Joshua quizzed.

"She is not evil, but she does not 'do' good by the people. The emissaries are supposed to tend the lands, make sure the people are healthy, happy. She does not do this, she stays in her cottage in the forest she made, she does not care for us as she should." Haddock explained.

"Sounds like a baron to me." Joshua replied.

"Almost true, but they are still bound to do what Ashoth asks and they cannot leave the land without the goddess's permission. Our witch is bound to this place, bound to her duty, made immortal by the hands blessing. Until she no longer has the strength to serve the village, she will be here, contracted to protect us, to play a great mediator.

This mist, even, was her doing, approved by Ashoth, a way of keeping us all rested, all retired, so to say. I think she believes she can keep us sedated. I think she is trying to stave off her duty. She must be waiting for something."

"It all sounds like bull to me, and tyranny." Joshua mumbled, looking at his bowl.

Haddock chuckled, "Only "bull" for those not content with this way of life. In all my travels as a young man I haven't found a place as kind as this. Even in this darker time, purity saturated this place, even into the very soil we walk upon.

Tomorrow, I will take you to the witch and she will tell you what she needs to tell you. I hope that you will listen. For now, get some rest, this mist will help you sleep and loosen your mind. I will wake you when it is time to go."

Haddock rose from the floor and slid open a small door which revealed an adjacent room. On the floor was a cot and a folded sheet. Joshua entered. Haddock left the small living room and sat outside. He produced a pipe from his robe and took a long drag while waiting on the world.

Val-ashoth was peaceful and right, something Joshua was foreign to. The village slept, and the young detective found himself sleeping soon as well. His last glance was at Haddock, the man was frozen inside a small picture frame in the corner of the room. He sat next to a small girl on a hill, his big laugh radiating joy. It must have been his dead daughter, Joshua thought.

Part 2/Resemble

Joshua dreamed of a monster, a large and grotesque woman with the teeth of a shark. She rose her fat head and her mouth unhinged like a snake to swallow him. In this moment, Joshua felt a force of being held, squeezed, and drug forward. The woman seized Joshua in her jaw and proceeded to shred and chew him until he died, or so he thought he was dead. The dream ended with him conscious inside the belly of the beast, slowly being digested. Joshua could hear the water outside the fish, it kept him in an organic prison while it went on its way without a thought to his well-being.

It wasn't until Joshua woke up in his sweat that he caught his breath; His hair matted against his forehead. It was dark out, seen by the thin window strip at the top of the walls where it would connect to the ceiling. Joshua rolled out of his cot and loosened his shirt about the collar, his heavy breathing culling between his ears. Eventually, after much time and deliberation, he found himself lucid again and back into the reality of his predicament.

A small and subtle knock sounded on the small frame of the sliding door and Haddock showed his head through. He smiled brightly and spoke.

"Joshua, it is time for us to go." He whispered.

Joshua found his feet and walked to the door which Haddock fully opened. Outside the house, Haddock lit a small lantern that hung from the tip of an alpenstock. It shed a hollow light on the houses where still torches and paper lanterns luminated in many colors. The sconces aligned the shoji corridor and the lanterns added a fair gradient to the shadowed places, the corners where torches didn't reach.

Even though the stars were out and the half-moon shined down on them, the people of the village were not asleep. Instead, they walked in small groups with each other, all of them wearing immaculate silk robes with broaches in their hair. They laughed and sang odd and incoherent songs. On the porches, old men threw di into trays and gambled, some played checkered games that resembled chess with odd strategy. Beautiful woman walked in pairs, occasionally giggling as Joshua passed, a foreigner in a strange land.

"Because we sleep with the mist, we wake with the moon, a second sun. Our hard work is rewarded in the night with games and food. We feast until the mist returns. Ashoth controls the clock here. She tells us when to sleep." Haddock explained, thundering down past the crowds.

Joshua admired the beauty in his own, disconcerted, way. The paper lights reminded him of the neon signs in France's cities. It was a comforting sight, that some societies always have something in common. There was uniting factor, the need for light, the need for social interaction. As Joshua was a detective, this psychological certainty made him feel more comfortable. Wherever he would find himself, however foreign. People were still people.

The troop of two continued to walk up the valley along the river until the sound of the village's voices died and the sound of rushing water took over and tickled their ears. Together, he and Haddock climbed the first hill.

At the top, Joshua could see further ahead where dark-trunked trees began to grow again, marking the outskirts of the land. They swayed underneath a faint breeze. Ahead, stakes had been placed along the path they both trod, lights dangling from them, reflecting off the river. These lights were composed of glass cages. They were filled with glowing worms and lightning bugs.

It took a few more minutes until the tree line swallowed Joshua. Unlike the vegetation in Whitecroft's land, the collection of flora here was thicker and more eerie.

Fireflies drifted outside the path, small critters unseen made noises in the branches and brush, scurrying away from Joshua's presence. They marched on through what now felt like a marsh or disheveled bog, quite unlike the ecosystem that was supposed to be present.

This marsh of sorts had a volatile aura about it, one that would forewarn any normal adventurer from nearing. It was a place for snakes to feed and mongrel dogs to prey. In a moment, for a moment, Joshua looked off from the area around his feet and saw a fluffy white tail with black stripes flickering from behind a wide and gnarled tree, like that out of Grimm tales. Much like those tales, the trees seemed to boast character, as if they might've lounged about their post waiting in silence to discretely move when Joshua was out of their range of sound.

Joshua and Haddock continued until they entered the light of a cottage. The light punctured the forest, the trees casting long shadows from its glitz. The large cottage sat above the stream and dipped into the current was both a canoe and a small windmill. The windmill was oblong like that of the many mills inside the village of Val-ashoth. This assured Joshua he was still in the same world, on the same earth.

Although soothing, the sight of the home was, it was also sinister at the same time, dilapidated. It was knowledge that a witch would lay here through the night in seclusion that caused the hairs on Joshua's neck to peak. He did not believe in magic, but the growth of strange occurrences around the world begged him to shudder. If magic was real, who could prevent harm from befalling Joshua? Before someone who could command magic, no one would be safe.

Haddock made his way across the small porch and opened the door.

"Don't you think we should knock first?" Joshua pleaded, scared but not terrified.

"She knew we were here the moment we set foot in her forest, and we don't wish to wake the creatures who stir in the night. Many things in the forest are deadly here, created by the witch in her boredom, it is very dangerous to make noise." Haddock whispered back.

Joshua sucked his lips in, his heart begged him to take a deep breath. It was the feeling of being near a cookie jar and being told not to eat them. The very suggestion that he could eat the cookie made him want the cookie. In the same way, the possibility of Joshua awakening a witch's spawn begged him to make a noise, just to cease his worry.

The door swung open slowly and with a slight creak. Haddock crossed the threshold on his tiptoes.

"If she knows were here, why are we sneaking around?" Joshua inquired more, whispering.

"She might still kill us, if she wishes. The Witch of Val has made herself quite a cruel reputation. I have heard of men who have come to lay eyes on her, they had returned as toads and lizards. It took days for them to return back to normal, telling us that, at a whim, the Witch decided to transform them. They had done nothing wrong but raise their voices and look at her wrong."

The cottage made small splintering noises beneath Haddock's feet and Joshua tiptoed behind him. They both made their bodies small, like men before a standing bear.

The cottage wasn't cluttered, it was simple. There was only a small loveseat covered in white linen on the far wall, a tray, a sword, and an assortment of flowers lay upon it. The back of the single room hosted a king mattress which sat on the floor. It was minimalist, almost poor, but the natural energies made the feeling of the building rich, higher in power, above the gaudy characteristics of materialism.

Joshua felt a hand. He couldn't move; he froze. He watched as an arm wrapped around his chest and pressed on his collarbone tightly, locking him in a powerful but warm embrace. It was slender but firm whilst gentle, if such a thing could be said.

Joshua felt a woman's chest pressed into his back. She was slightly shorter than him, if not by a mere centimeter. Her breasts sat right below his shoulder blades. Her forehead pressed into his spine and a hat's brim brushed against his neck.

There was some type of toxin in the contact, metaphorically. The embrace imbued Joshua with a feeling of heaviness, drudgery. A small piece of sweat beaded down his forehead, a drop of adrenaline trying to find its way into action, created by anticipation and, perhaps, pheromones. Joshua didn't know he was being hugged. He had never been hugged. He simply thought he was being attacked in a sensualized constriction.

"Hello Connor." The woman behind him greeted. She sounded friendly, but a tinge of resentment or stress weighed in her tongue.

Haddock slowly turned from his placement before Joshua. He was terribly terrified, caught with his hand in the cookie jar. He bowed his body low and stuck his head there near the floor, waiting for acknowledgement. He shivered in anticipation, trying not to move in fear of upsetting the predator. This predator had a firm lock on Joshua, he was her prey. She watched the mercenary with feigned interest, underwhelmed by his sense of fidelity. She already had her prize, and she wouldn't toy with two balls of yarn.

The witch dismissed him. "Thank you, Emil, for bringing Connor back. Your daughter's outside. Go quick, or you might lose her."

Haddock rose his head and ran out of the cottage in a single fluid motion. As his footsteps faded and he disappeared behind the cracks of the wooden walls, Joshua heard him shouting joyfully.

"Delia, papa's here! Delia, where are you?!"

Haddock left Joshua alone with the witch without second thought. The man that had been his rescuer had now abandoned him for mere moments with his dead daughter. He hopped through the dangerous overgrowth to find her, so shortsighted and reckless.

"He's going to die, he's making too much noise." Joshua seethed through his teeth.

"Oh, but that's the funny part. Emil is the dead one." The witch corrected. "I brought him from the dead to fetch you. He'll see his daughter once she passes on. But she probably won't die for a long time."

How Cruel. Joshua thought, to toy with a dead person, manipulate them into working. She had promised him his daughter but didn't pay him when he came to collect.

"I'm giving him purpose, Connor." The witch assured, knowing his thoughts. "What ever happened to your smile? Aren't you glad to see me?"

"Whoever this Connor person is, it's not me. I don't know you." Joshua snapped.

Joshua felt the hand around his collar, and the other about his torso, release and free him. The sorceress walked before him and stood there, looking into his eyes. She smiled, before backing away from him and sitting down. The witch sat on the only chair and leaned forward, the sword that was beside the chair cocked in her left hand, running down between her calves. The tip pressed against her right toe, begging to sever it. She would apply pressure to the sword, swinging her right foot back and forth. Perhaps she was more careless than Haddock.

Joshua had seen this woman before. She was the person in the Japanese house, the person who Haddock regarded as Mr. Fill. Somehow, she had replaced herself with him, sitting among her subjects in obscurity, spying on them. How long did she hide among them, pretending to be a man?

The Witch donned a straw hat which covered her round, purple eyes. They were brighter than when he first looked into them, almost ethereal, like a pair of stars. The straw hat covered her short black hair which stopped just past her curved jawline. The back of her hair was tied into a knot, keeping it taught and away from her nape. It was tied with twine, giving her an earthy-but-rich energy, much like the house she lived in. She wore a kimono much like the villagers, tapered at her bending waist with a thick rope. Her leg would shoot forth in an open flap about the left thigh subtly as she swung her foot side to side in the air. She wore no shoes.

Her spare hand was used to support her chin, she looked bored and gorgeous and animalistic yet elegant if not barbaric and somewhat modest. She was all these things and more.

Joshua felt a strange tug at his heart, as if he had known her just as she insisted, but perhaps it was her features that begged him to know her. Perhaps it was her violent beauty that reminded him of his own angers and frustrations. He looks begged him to sympathize with her, begged him to step a little closer.

The witch took out a thin tobacco pipe from her dress and plucked it into her mouth. She wrinkled her cute nose like a cat while she shifted her lips and inhaled. She snapped her fingers and they sparked like flintstone. The sparks fell neatly into the bowl and set off a strong streak of smoke which reminded Joshua of a boiling cauldron.

The witch looked back at Joshua as if contemplating, suddenly more human than snake or tiger. Her vicious features waned and waxed faster than any lunar cycle. Beneath her violet eyes a ferocious visage loomed, something that was caged and waiting to feed itself flesh, pound for pound. This sinister and quirky visage maintained its presence to threaten Joshua, to keep him both from running and charging unarmed. She seemed to have to attitude of a fighter. If her gaze were formed into words, it would say "*I-can-kill-you-if-I-want-to.*"

"You don't remember me, do you?" the lunatic woman quizzed. Her attitude became attentive, curious, soft. "The name Elizabeth doesn't ring any bells?"

"No, it doesn't." Joshua huffed, "I need to return to France, so if we could get this over with-"

"Connor," Elizabeth interrupted, "France doesn't need you. You have more important things to do than save people from men with guns. Even so, I doubt France would take you back because you killed the head-of-police."

It was true, Joshua thought. No one would take him back after being framed. He couldn't be a detective unless another baron acquitted him of his sins. Joshua already knew no baron would. They would have to answer to Baron Glass for that.

"You don't seem like a person concerned with saving people." Joshua retorted, hoping to start, and win, a battle of wits, it was his only way to conquer without his gun as his side. His silver tongue his only secondary weapon. Even though Joshua was a convict, he determined himself to return. He would find out what to do once he returned.

Elizabeth gripped her sword tight until her knuckles popped. Her toes clenched. Her teeth clenched. The pipe cracked and splintered slightly in her mouth.

"That remains to be seen, Connor." Elizabeth frowned. "I can't believe you don't remember anything…"

The witch trailed off, picking the broken pipe from her mouth and folding it over her thumbs. She watched it intensely.

Joshua began to realize his predicament. Elizabeth wasn't a threat to him because she thought he was someone else, he reminded her of someone else. It was just his luck that she saved him in his time of need; his luck, or, her intelligence. If Joshua hadn't been mistaken for this "Connor Shaw," he would be dead.

"I'm not this Connor person, so, can I go now?" Joshua asked politely. "I really have things I need to do."

Elizabeth hummed slightly, thinking. She looked up at him and smiled thinly.

"No." She mused, shifting her body from the chair, "I think you are Connor Shaw, and I need to find a way to jar your memories."

The girl rose and made her way to him. Her shoulders were rigid, Joshua began to back away. She reached out her hand to his forehead from afar. Motioning for him to near, aiming for his forehead with her fingertips like a dart. Was she trying to attack Joshua?

"Let me just mull around in your brain a little, I'm sure I can bring your memories to the surface." Elizabeth thought aloud, the sinister look from beneath her eyes beginning to surface.

Joshua continued to move away. He looked quickly behind him for the door, but to his horror, there was none. Wherever the door once was had become just a plain wall.

Was it magic, was it *truly* magic, that kept him feeling for some sort of give in the panels where none came?

Joshua was certain he was staring at the entrance, the bed was adjacent, Elizabeth on the opposite side of where he stood and rubbed the walls. Joshua turned and keenly swiped at Elizabeth's outstretched arm as it almost touched his forehead. She chuckled wryly and raised her hand again like a gun. Joshua moved away from her, but she looked to him with impatience.

Elizabeth began to pick up her pace like a hungry zombie. Joshua readied himself and waited to move past her again, this time looking at the small window on the right wall. Elizabeth made her way forth, but the ex-detective neatly moved out of her reach as she neared and ran to the far wall. Joshua watched as the wall began to contort like a flag waving in the sky. To his horror, the window wasn't there anymore. Joshua placed his hands on the wall, feeling for the window. His eyes must have been playing tricks on him. His hands felt nothing but the wooden grafting.

Joshua was trapped.

"You can't leave, Connor." Elizabeth reminded, "I can't let you leave until we get to the bottom of this."

"There is no *we*," Joshua barked, twisting around to find her, "It's just me. *I have to be dreaming.*"

"You're not dreaming, Connor, but you will be soon." Elizabeth played, pretending she was Socrates or Plato. "you be dreaming of a dream, within yet another dream, like layers on an onion."

Elizabeth passed behind a pillar outside of Joshua line of sight and didn't return from the other side. She couldn't have stopped behind the pillar, for it was too thin. It was if there were an invisible room she walked into, something of a trick. It reminded Joshua of that moment a friend thinks it's funny to mime descending non-existent stairs behind a sofa in an apartment.

Joshua heard Elizabeth giggle. It was poignant, close, moving and echoing from the rafters. The young man looked to find her, but his effort was futile. Elizabeth was completely invisible.

Joshua watched as the bed and the chair rose from the floor in anti-gravitational force. The ex-detective was trapped with a poltergeist, a crazy woman who was naked to his eyes. Joshua stood in the center of the room, the plate, the white sheets, the broken kiseru, floated about the cabin. Joshua watched them intently, expecting them to come soaring out of the air at him.

Yet, it was all a distraction. Joshua felt a gentle hand on front of his forehead, Elizabeth stood right before of him, a winner's smile on her face. She had won, but had Joshua blinked? She was simply there, as if she had always been there, she had approached in the millisecond his eyes couldn't catch, drawn into place between second three and four of their little game. The artist swift, the artist a god.

Joshua couldn't move, his forehead felt numb, he hadn't realized there were nerves in that place, but they screamed in pain from manipulation and awakening. Elizabeth's hand glowed white, Joshua's vision glowed black. He then realized he was no longer in the cabin, he was in Paris. Elizabeth had won in subduing Joshua, and Joshua fell at her feet to dream about his past.

A door opened wide before Joshua and he stepped out of a dark closet, looking back. But, as he left the closet and kiltered back, the door was already shut as if it had never been opened at all.

Joshua's brain was reduced to luggage space, the coffin of his mind. He knew the year, he knew the time. He was in the not-too distant past. He was in Paris and his current objective was to investigate the frequent disappearance of children. The place and time Joshua witnessed was what the young fellow often lived out, over and over again. It was the most common of his nightmares; this was Joshua's hell. Yet, something was keenly different this time around, he had not gone to sleep and thought he wasn't dreaming this time. Was he truly in a dream within a dream, as Elizabeth poetically described? The daunting witch had cast a spell on him, and now he was trapped, unable to pinch himself into consciousness. A deed he tried many times.

Joshua paced back and forth in the room, unwilling to leave the vicinity. This past he was locked in was the night he lost all will to live, or at least, his confidence in the morality of mankind. He hated this night, he dreamt of this night over, and over, and over again until he became so hauntingly familiar with the scene, he could write it more vividly than the police report he wrote the first time he experienced the ordeal.

Joshua sat on the bed for hours like in a doctor's office, rocking himself in wait for the witch to give up searching his brain and let him out. The sun wouldn't fall outside the room, and there were no curtains. Joshua tried the door to the balcony, but it wouldn't open, jammed by some invisible force.

In immense boredom, Joshua found he couldn't sleep nor grow tired. He would rest his head on the mattress, but he felt no cushion to welcome him. He laid as if on shaped steel, a plastic mockery. Joshua's cabin fever grew, and his eyes burnt in their sockets feverishly. Joshua did not want to leave that room; he refused to leave that room. But over time, over what felt like years and years, waiting won him over. He felt that, if he continued to wait, he would suffer much more damage to his sanity than to relive his atrocities.

Joshua rose and gripped the door, embroidered brass which was common in old French suburbs. He rotated its handle and emerged from the bedroom. He found himself in the same spot he had been years before, in a narrow second-story hallway. To his left there was a short corridor. Across his door was an open bathroom. It was a clean bathroom, a bleak bathroom, consisting of faded teal and white porcelain.

The younger Mr. Hill walked towards it, familiar with what he had to do. He looked down and already in his hand was his firearm, loaded. He gripped the broom handle with white knuckles. He could hear the laughter behind the door to his left.

This door was beside the bathroom entryway. But Joshua, unable to urge himself to open the correct door to his left, now stood inside the bathroom beside it, detouring to wash his face with cold water. This was his last attempt to wake up.

As Joshua twisted the handle and began to splash cold water in his face, he looked for himself in the mirror. Joshua didn't see his reflection, only a demon, this demon was a man, dressed like Joshua and of the same height and build. His face was a writhing mass of tentacles. The tentacles moved about like a hydra; serpent like heads all looking about the bathroom to devour and bite. Some of these serpents, showing a certain aptitude for anxiety, like Joshua, nipped and gnawed at each other. One nefarious serpent prided itself in the miniature albino rat it viced in its mouth.

Joshua stared at this grotesque monster with apathy. It was a crooked interpretation of himself. But somehow, he, for the first time in this dream, doubted his sanity. He remembered a distant thought, a scene, of an amazing, loving, woman, she walked through amber grains to him, snapping her fingers and lighting her pipe. Joshua realized this fantasy was about Elizabeth, who wore a white sundress. He remembered her smile, her perfect teeth, her breasts pressed against his back in embrace. It was the only thing he could think about for, a rebel memory, chiding him.

For the first time in his dream Joshua smiled.

Joshua looked back to the mirror from his daze. There was Solomon. Joshua shuddered and jumped back, almost falling into the tub. He caught himself on the shower rod and stilled himself. Solomon laughed. Somehow, he appeared amidst his thoughts and materialized. He was a rouge event in his path through his dream. Joshua had never seen him there before.

"You should hurry, Joshua. Children are impatient." Solomon goaded.

"Damn you!" Joshua spat, rising to punch the mirror.

The mirror wouldn't shatter, much like the plastic bed wouldn't comfort him.

Joshua's heart rocketed and galloped. The speed and intensity of the shock hurt his heart. The young man flopped out of the bathroom and shut the door behind him, afraid Solomon would come groping out of the mirror uninvited. He rested his neck against the door panel behind him, the still small laughter of children resuming in the hall.

They giggled; Joshua raised his pistol and looked at the white door, hesitating to open the source of the laughter. He knew exactly what was about to happen. Joshua should have been numb to what was about to occur. He wasn't.

Joshua reached for the gilded handle and twisted the knob. The knob clicked, and the door slowly parted like a curtain.

Down the detective's sights were four children, as they seemed to be. They sat on the floor around a skeleton in a sort of circle arrangement. It was a small skeleton, a baby's skeleton, a representation of the three-year-old that was there, dead and mangled. It was the youngest of the those who bore witness to the murder.

The skeleton was broken, some of its ribs and teeth missing. There was a hole in the skull plate as well. The first child stood at the skeleton, pulling at its ribs, braking them off. In its mouth it sucked on these ribs violently and with great noise.

The second child sat in the far corner with a kitchen knife in one hand and in his other hand he held his legs in tight, fetal. The third and the forth children sat beside each other playing market with the teeth.

"See, I'll give you two of these teeth for that one tooth, because that one is worth two teeth." The first explained. The second, a girl, just frowned, she had mascara and lipstick smeared on her face like a sad clown.

"What's going on here!?" cried Joshua, as the memory went. Although he already knew, he always said the same thing. If only he could ask the right questions.

"Tommy wouldn't share his pretty little teeth with us." Number Three said.

"I hated Tommy, and I liked pushing him around," Number One said.

"I made a mistake," Replied the child in the corner, he started to stand with his knife.

Their voices grew heavy as they spoke. Like that of gravel in a cement truck it started to churn Joshua's heart. Their voices faltered into a demonic roll call.

"Tommy was too pitiful, he made me sad." Number Four grumbled.

They all rose, brandishing their cutlery from God-knew-where. They looked into Joshua's eyes and Joshua couldn't see their faces, they were gone. All that remained of their cute features was a thin slit in the skin where the lips used to be. The slits flapped in their speech like clapping fins.

The not-so-childish children moved like one person. In their approach they swayed like catholic priests with their thuribles. Joshua retreated, a repetitive "no" stuttering on his lips.

The children charged him in unison, moving with ungodly speed. They defied gravity and human nature, some of them crawling on all fours. As they chased him down the hall in a frenzy, their limbs grew longer like that of a spider's, their bony fingers snapping the back of Joshua's heels.

"I regret killing Tommy, but I'll enjoy killing you!" Howled one.
"I'm going to pull your teeth out and feed on your ribs!" Squawked another.

Joshua made his way to the stairs and jumped down the full set into the living room. His body flew forth and collided with the railings below, where he was supposed to turn right, shattering it.

Joshua was sent sprawling into the furniture. He slid through the small antiques that decorated the space until met with the wall. Quickly, he sprang to his feet and ran to the back door through the rear kitchen. But before he could span the gap between him and freedom, one of the children grabbed his foot with its elongated digits. Joshua flattened against the wooden vinyl yet again.

Joshua kicked and turned with his sidearm, he aimed back, the barrel finding its place between a Number Two's eyes. In this moment, he froze, looking at the eggshell head. It cast a shadow over him, its limbs pinioned about the room. The slits of the mouth smiled a horrific grin, a, "you-can't-kill-a-child," grin. But Joshua squeezed, and the bullet flew through its skull, creating a confection of red. The child's head popped like a white balloon.

Whether out of fear or self-preservation, Joshua had squeezed that gun, and found himself free of the monster's grasp.

Joshua sprang and charged the remaining paces through the door with his shoulder tucked. He demolished the hinges of the old-world dwelling and broke across the yard. Behind him, the monsters began to file out of the doorway. The detective tripped over a stray toy left in the grass and found himself in the children's sand pit. Joshua rolled to his back.

Looking at the door as the remaining things emerged, Joshua rose his pistol and trained his eyes on them. They lunged at Joshua, instantly spanning the distance now that they were free of the man-made crucible. Joshua closed his eyes and emptied the clip.

After a moment of closed eyes and empty prayer, Joshua opened his eyes after the sound of the ringing brass. He witnessed his actions as the dream began to alleviate.

The ground began to rise with an anti-gravitational force much like the furniture in

Elizabeth's cottage, the sand around him trickling through his leather jacket. Joshua let go of his pistol, which floated into the air, filled with powerful helium. The swing set in the yard was pried from its holding and slowly drifted away into the atmosphere along with every other object. The ground fractured and was sucked slowly towards the blinding, pale, sun which rose perfectly in the center of the sky like a lightbulb.

The nubile detective was covered in the blood of three children, their bodies littered in the sandbox. They had returned to their innocent state. They were three little children, not monsters. All of them were dead, slain by Joshua, the ruthless killer who demanded self-preservation.

Joshua didn't know what to think. How could he when he did not know the world was ripe with magic? Was he really chased by demons, forced to pull the trigger? Was he insane, a murderer under certain tricks of the light and long hours reading papers? This was how his dream ended every single time it conjured itself each night. It was a dream of a memory of a day during the first year of his career. It set the pace for his life in Paris, it determined him a guilty and broken man.

Joshua rose into the blinding sun until he began to see where his body was in regard to his real, living self. He watched his body in the witch's cottage like it was on display. In the light of the sun, a television floated showing a man lying on a bed in Elizabeth's cottage. Elizabeth stood at the foot, staring at him in worry. She bit her knuckle, her hat toppled and resting behind her, held there like a necklace, tied by a string.

Joshua began to approach the screen in the sky which soon divided into two drops of visionary water. They parted themselves perfectly to land into his reddened eyes like lubricating conditioner for contacts.

Joshua blinked as the water stung his eyes. He opened his eyes to find himself back on earth, awake.

Elizabeth looked down at Joshua and huffed in denial, "I scoured your brain. Connor Shaw isn't there. Someone must have taken your memories. You have to be Connor Shaw."

"Why do I have to be Connor Shaw?!" Joshua complained. Sitting up, Joshua looked still for an exit. He was seemingly more docile now, having lost to the witch. "Can't you just let me go?"

"I can't let you go!" Elizabeth scowled in return before going soft, "This is the closest I've come to finding you, him, whatever! I looked all the way back to your first memories, but, the furthest I could go back was your first day joining the French Police. There's nothing further than that, absolutely nothing in your head about your childhood. Birthdays, parents, they aren't there either. I don't know what people did to you to make you forget about us, your friends, your family, but we can get to the bottom of this."

"I was an orphan and I was bullied, they're probably suppressed." Joshua defended using his small understanding of psychology, "Just let me go."

"No." Elizabeth renounced firmly. She stared at her feet at the end of the bed and thought hard on ways to jog Joshua's memory. "Once you remember, you'll be okay. You wont want to go back to Paris ever again."

"But I have unfinished business in Paris." Joshua explained. "People are going to get hurt, I have to do something."

"What? You have to *save* them? You hurt more people than you save, Connor... *Joshua*." Elizabeth sighed, "You need to understand that what I am about to ask from you is important. You can save people, *more* people. You can save more people than you can even imagine."

Joshua groaned again cursed. "This magic shit! I don't want to be a part of any of it!"

"You're already a part of it!" Elizabeth retorted, beginning to pace before the bed. "If you can't remember you're Connor Shaw, we'll have to beat it into you. It will have to be beat into you. You're going to go help our friends and then you'll remember who you are, I'm sure of it."

Elizabeth placed her thumb below her chin, working out the kinks in her plan. Joshua stared in disbelief. Joshua had no expertise or decision in the matter. Perhaps all he could do was try and convince her he was inept for the role.

"What makes you think I can do any of this? I'm just a detective, I'm just a man, I'll die." Joshua whined, he had to get out of this house, he wanted to go home.

"Connor Shaw could do impossible things. He could survive anything. If you're Connor Shaw, you'll come back alive. If you die, then *who cares?*"

Joshua scratched his face and grunted his fury. He was helpless to stop her, she was too stubborn, powerful. His only hope was to wait until she was gone and run away. After she left, he could escape, given the chance.

"I've made up my mind, you're going to Moscow." Elizabeth assured herself, she snapped her fingers. "It's either your life or theirs, anyways."

Joshua was baffled by her deduction, horrified by his mission. Passing the 15th into Russia was impossible, it was a minefield, a wall of economic aggression and cold war hysteria. If Joshua was caught in Russia, there would be no way home but through that minefield, which was certain death.

As Elizabeth snapped her fingers again and Joshua saw Haddock appear from behind one of the support beams, appearing out of thin air like most people seemed to do these past few days. He looked in bewilderment at the two, wondering why he was alive.

"You want to see your daughter again, don't you Haddock?" She asked.

Haddock nodded his head, "Where is my daughter?" He asked.

"She's dead, but if you knock out '*Joshua*' here, I'll make sure you can see her again."

"To see my daughter again, I would do anything." Haddock replied, "your wish is doable."

"Bind him when you're done; he's going to be mailed very soon." She snickered. "I'm going to get in touch with some old friends to prepare for his arrival."

Joshua sprung from the bed and readied himself to fight the man, but he was far slower than the hunter whom had years of training and experience. It wasn't ten seconds before the ex-detective was pinned to the ground, gasping for air, Haddock's massive bicep tightening like a snake around his throat.

"Don't worry," Elizabeth replied to Joshua's unspoken fear. "When this is all over, and if you don't remember who you are, you can go back home. I promise."

What good is your promise? Joshua thought.

Joshua was chocked until he had no strength left to move. He watched helplessly as Haddock tied his arms and legs. He was only released from his binds when he was securely placed in a wooden coffin shaped like a shipping crate.

It was a long and bumpy road, and Joshua was never so bored.

Part 3/Ramshackle

"Welcome to Moscow." The city channel announced. This message was displayed on every major building, each one connected to large intercoms whose noise would reach the floor of the city despite their lofty emplacement. Joshua could hear it through the padded crate he was locked in.

It was yet another prison.

Joshua lay there in darkness, captive and shipped into another country. He pushed against the panel in front of him, trying to free himself and get away for the thousandth attempt, but it was futile. The crate jumped and shuddered at every pothole, he groaned in frustration, becoming ever more claustrophobic. Whatever caravan Elizabeth smuggled him in couldn't be more inconsiderate, but maybe they didn't know he was in the back, suffocating in his own body heat.

There was yet another pothole a few minutes later; Russia's unused roads were never taken care of. Above, or rather, in front of him since he lay, he could hear and feel the reverberations of skyships soaring about. Skyships were large ferries that floated about Russia on a route much like the trains and busses used in the French Dominion. The only non-cosmetic difference between them was that they flew, hence their name.

Pedestrians rarely owned cars in Russia, always instead riding a skyship to work like a public transit. They were big vehicles, bigger than a French rig but smaller than a building. They varied in size based on the model and their intended commuters. Their sizes a shape varied from a frigate to a schooner to even small rowboats. The biggest models and could hold an easy hundred people, getting them where they needed to go in no time.

Joshua remembered the first time he saw a skyship, it was plastered to a stucco wall in France, a propaganda poster placed by some pouty French teenager. It bragged about the Russian country, it prowess and sovereignty over the world.

Joshua groaned, another pothole. The caravan took a right, and then a hard left. Joshua's crate twisted from the force and fell from another placement further down the bed. He rattled about the insides of the box cursing. The coffin lay untethered and slid side to side on the metal flooring. Joshua felt seasick.

The caravan skid to a stop, the headboard of Joshua's coffin smacked against the top of the bed. "Damn it!" Joshua screamed, pounding on the box with all his might. "Let me out of this crate!"

There was faint whispering, something inaudible, and possibly in Russian. The murmurs rambled louder, but still, Joshua couldn't understand what was being said. He had learned Russian at a young age in school. Perhaps that was France's way of acknowledging they might be steamrolled one day and, preparing for it, instituted that children should know Russian. The first words they learned were "peace" and "surrender."

In his plump livery, Joshua could only understand the sound of the tailgate opening. By the foot of his crate, Joshua was dragged out. The crate fell and smashed onto the ground. A splintering noise roared through Joshua's cabin and daylight poured in through the cracks the impact made. Joshua could hear clearly through them.

"Damnit, David, be gentle with it." Voice number one chastised. From what Joshua could see, he wore a brown beanie and a jade-green sweater.

"Come now," The so-called David remarked, "We're always long gone before they answer the door."

"That doesn't mean the guy can't call the boss."

"Who would take time to do that? We'll both say it was damaged when we received it. They can't catch us."

"You're an asshole David."

"Only because I'm right." David laughed.

The duo set Joshua down at the top of the door. The door was painted a darker shade of green and made of steel with a small peephole in the center. David rung the door bell, the man in the beanie rapped the door loudly and without rhythm.

"Delivery!" The beanie man cried. Then, in unison with his friend, they turned and bolted back to their truck. The vehicle they delivered Joshua in was a camo truck with MARPAT design, an old army vehicle. They mounted it, one in the front and driving, the other in the back, still folding the tailgate as they drove away. An old man came from the door dressed in a fine white cutlery suit and a chef's hat. He looked at the box, and then at the two men leaving frantically.

"What the hell!? If you boys ruined my dinnerware I'll wring you by the necks!" The Chef shouted down the alleyway. He threw cans of food he happened to hold in his hand at them, but they were already rounding the bend. Joshua watched the chef through the crack in the crate disappear, chasing them a small distance to show his frustration.

The Chef returned eventually. In his sight through the thin peephole, Joshua could see he was a cue ball. A bigger man, clean shaven, unlike Joshua, and smelling of old cabbage and green onions.

The Chef looked over his box, muttering and spouting excrement about the black market becoming a rude trade for thugs. He dragged Joshua into his house, or restaurant, or both, and set him down gently. Grabbing his butchers knife off the magnetic strip along the wall, the chef slammed it into the corner of the crate. Joshua jumped in fright. He could see, out of the corner of his eye, how far the butchers knife slammed through the wood, mere inches from his eye.

The butcher's knife leveraged the two panels and sprung the nails loose. Joshua assisted the act and placed his hands on the panel to swing the wooden slab off. The butcher's eyes shot open in surprise. He backed away, the knife still in his hand, and witnessed Joshua slowly rising from his grave. Joshua clambered out of the box coolly and dusted himself off.

Joshua wore something different, something new, he realized, a coat, a plain tee, and slim BDU pants. Elizabeth or Haddock must've changed him, and whoever did, knew his exact measurements, surprisingly.

The Chef was speechless, and Joshua simply nodded to him in acknowledgement and thanks. Without the Chef's assistance, Joshua might have been trapped in the crate forever. The young man stretched briefly, waltzed over to the still open door, and left without a word.

Moscow was immaculate. Tall white pillars of futuristic skyscrapers grew in sleek design like funnels of clouds towards the sky. The skyships floated about the top of these, sometimes moving down from their heavenly float to touch a building and let off its travelers. The sky was a spectacular orange and it brought warm thoughts to those who lived there. But, in reality, the weather was very cold despite the concrete jungle.

Although the buildings of Moscow were immaculate and beautiful, unlike France, the lower buildings and residential areas were an assortment of antiquity and modernity. Some buildings were white as well, like a box of monogamous character, while others, like the restaurant Joshua just left, looked back to the era when concrete, brick, and other stones, were the go-to material for construction. Each modern house looked identical, and they all boasted tinted panels where one might want walls.

Moscow was the future brought into the present. Wherever Joshua walked he could see above the lower buildings a large commodity of odd shaped structures. These buildings, or rather, this building, was circular and spherical, like the leaves on broccoli or a bundle of grapes. This building was the Institute for Biological Research located neatly in the center of Joshua's current district. That was where Russia studied the Second Death, and where they held it still in weaponized form below in impenetrable vaults dug into the earth.

Joshua could almost see it, an odd imagination or aura off the building, as if the Second Death was waiting inside its vial, listening, waiting to escape and spread its sickly fumes of homicidal will. But, paired with this, Joshua hoped the scientists were trying to find a cure, not wage war. Perhaps Second Death wanted to reveal its alchemical secrets too.

Joshua thought also of *Zavoyevatel'*, the Russian space station. It was supposed to bring about a new space exploration institute, but when it failed due to unforeseen variables and crashed into the ocean, Russia gave up on reaching the stars and opted to watch them from back on earth silently. Thus, in *Zavoyevatel's* stead, they devoted the top floors of their skyscrapers to housing telescopic gizmos.

Joshua thought back to learning of the event, reading about the last known survivor onboard the station, and imagined him surrounded by the corpses of his coworkers and loved ones, all alone. He told Russia, and the world, that they shouldn't send help, that it was too dangerous to explore space. Soon after, Aleksander died in anguish. He was one of the first and certainly the last of the space explorers. This was the example for Russia, proving that even their reach was limited.

Joshua shoved his hands into his pant pockets, inside was a small sheet of paper. Plucking it out he discovered it to be a receipt for his clothes, but on the back, there was a note. It was written in a feather pen, the cursive scrawling, immaculate in every way:

Have a safe trip! I hope our friends treated you well. Love, *Elizabeth.*

Below the shorthand scrawl was a small symbol of a diamond surrounded by odd Zen-like structures. Joshua pocketed the note again and continued his way through the city.

Joshua had to get a ride home. But because of the stalemate between Russia and France along 15th longitudinal line, it would be impossible unless he was smuggled back by a group of ruffians. Joshua was not going back into a box, he knew that much.

Joshua marched down the street in search of his purpose. He walked through the masses whom wore scientific bodysuits of Red, Orange, Yellow, Green, and Blue. They were ranked and distinguished by their jobs like military men and women. All of the tunics were made of plastics and carbons, like they were ready to launch themselves into space and become astronauts like their predecessor. Moreover, unlike the slums and grounds of France's cities, they all looked happy. They walked in batches in accordance to their colors, seeming to socialize with those who shared their occupancy, and rarely did anyone talk to anyone of a different color. Perhaps it was productive for them, perhaps they spoke of ingenious machines and the next big inventions, the bubonic plague and the Second Death. Joshua didn't care too much to listen, he wanted to find his purpose there, and he wasn't going to wait in a restaurant for his business to find him.

The roads were empty where one would use a car, where the asphalt was laid. There was no traffic. The pedestrians walked this black decaying pavement freely but never in parallel. They meandered, but, eventually, found their way to the other side as if, instinctually, they thought a car to hit them.

That was where these Russians made sense to Joshua, he could see their habits. Some shrugged while they talked, rubbed their noses, put their hands on their hips. The more self-conscious walked with their arms crossed as if to keep their chests from showing much of themselves. Certainly, they wouldn't be cold beneath all of their technology, but still they were covered under their arms in defense. All people, everywhere, were the same, no matter where Joshua was.

Joshua looked about, bars and restaurants looked to be the people's favorite haunts; it would be the perfect place for him to gather information and ask for directions. But among these restaurants, further on, past the conclave of businesses, sat a much smaller pub in a much darker location. On the door of this pub was the outline of a diamond which sat engraved on the panel. Joshua fingered the letter in his pocket and slid into the door that powered itself open and shut behind him.

The venue was different from what Joshua expected. It was almost anti-Russian. There were only dim lights, and the people who drank there had stripped down slightly, their suits half open, their undershirts showing, or tank-tops, or sweaters -for the particularly frozen.

Joshua swooped forth casually, trying not to draw attention to himself and motioned for the bartender to pour him a glass. The bartender walked over and leaned to Joshua who leaned in turn into the counter.

"I can tell you're new here bub. We ask for the cash up front. Too many asses not paying their tabs." The bar hand quipped. He jerked his head over to a man in the corner, slumped and smelly, his last bottle oozing down his hairy chest, incapacitated. The barkeep continued, "We might be the richest city in this shitty world but were not a bank, try not to be at least. The name is Ciddartha, Cid for short, dad was a heated Buddhist before you ask, and yes, I'm from England, so don't take photos."

Joshua looked at the man up and down. He was pale with freckles and had very blonde hair which poked out in odd angles on his head. He wore a pair of golden piercings and long colorless tattoos drew down his arms and around his neck. It was as if Britain had birthed a punk-rock child with a biker from Ireland. He wore a torn-grey band-tee and skinny-jeans ripped, sewn, and ripped again.

It was rare to see a British, Irish, or Scottish person in the world, most of them went missing during the year of storms, the Year of Poseidon's wrath. This bartender's ancestors must have been on vacation at the time, or merely lived somewhere else. Magazines and tabloids glorified the British after their islands disappeared. Those who were away from their home, at the time, were lucky enough to survive. With the rarity of British blood, the DNA was seen as a "royal gene" in popular culture. The small handful of remaining British peoples interbred with others of their nationality to preserve their lineage and secure their feigned royalty, often finding positions in offices or flaunted before crowds like celebrities.

It was an odd idea in culture, to glorify something like heritage. It was even more odd that others with no relation sought to glorify celebrities they will never meet in their life time, Joshua thought.

"I actually don't have any money." Joshua replied.

"Well then what the hell are you in here for?" Cid scowled.

"Information."

"If you want information, you should've brought money to buy a drink."

"Hey, Cid, give the man a break, he's something of a big deal in Paris." Commanded a voice from the end of the bar, it was a middle-aged man with a shallow beard and long, brown hair that stopped above his shoulders. He wore something of a military outfit from the 1500's, only slightly modernized for the times. It was velvet blue and the large white collar that proceeded from it rose to touch his chin. On the vest, tassels of gold connected horizontally down like a ladder. He had large sleeves and broad shoulders. His pants were a black denim and his belt was worn outside his coat to keep the jacket from flowing haphazardly.

The man continued, "If you don't, you *could* tell your next boss you got fired denying a French legend his booze."

"Whatever old man." Cid pissed, but he poured Joshua a generous glass of whisky nonetheless.

"Sit down by me Mr. Hill," The man called, "And get Cid to bring me another bottle of the rum… oh, there you are Cid, lovely."

Joshua sat down next to the man as he poured the new bottle into his glass. Maybe he could give him the information he needed. He seemed drunk, lost in a torpor of thought, sad, or even contemplative.

"It is a treat," the man began, "to see you here again my friend. Well, not *here,* here, but *here.* Where is your darling girl? You haven't let her loose about the world have you, to terrorize men and turn them into pigs?"

"Are you talking about Elizabeth?" Joshua asked, after all, who else did he know who could possibly do such things.

"That's her name." The man chimed. "You know her, and you insist you're not Connor Shaw."

"And you told Cid I was Joshua Hill." Joshua retorted.

The man laughed and took another drink, "So I did, you are a man with almost more names than me."

"No, I'm just Joshua Hill." Joshua insisted, taking a drink in turn.

The man paused, he hummed as if to think, slowly, the gears turned inside his head.

"I think she called me about this. Something about amnesia, that you don't believe you are Connor. Don't worry, you'll get no gripe from me. Whoever you are, Elizabeth has you here to deal with a problem."

"And you know what problem that is, right?" Joshua asked, eager to understand why he was jumping through hoops for her, why she wouldn't let him go.

The man yawned and rolled back into his seatrest. He didn't reply for some time. He stared at the bottles along the wall behind the bar, surveying his next purchase. The man looked haggard, unkempt. By the way he carried himself one would say he was mourning for something.

"I'm not sure what she sent you here for." He said, "But you'll probably find out soon enough. You are one of the luckiest men alive, to my knowledge. You'll figure it out."

Joshua twisted his chin in disappointment.

"So, this witch sent me to Moscow to meet you, presumably, telling me she had friends that needed me to do something for them. She sent me to them, you, and they don't even know what they need help with." Joshua surmised.

"I might remember… when I'm not so drunk." The man replied hoarsely. "You can check in with me tomorrow, when I don't feel so inebriated."

Joshua scoffed, it was unbelievable. He didn't want to wait another second.

"It was something about a monster..." He grimaced, hoping to jar the drunkard's memory.

"Like I said, Ask me tomorrow. Until then feel free to lounge around here, we won't charge you for anything."

Joshua knew the man was lying to him. He was playing some sort of game. But Joshua didn't know what he was trying to pull. The detective would play along and watch them closely for now.

Joshua rose from the table and sat himself on one of the crimson baroque chairs in the corners. He would have to wait on them to make the first move. He didn't know what they had up their sleeves, or the reason why the man was drunk the day he was supposed to meet him. Was Joshua supposed to find their bar on his own; did they know it would be the one he found? Most of all, why were they not ready for his arrival? These questions scratched Joshua's brain incessantly, begging him to scream. He had to know, he had to find out. What if he was in the wrong place?

Joshua closed his eyes and pretended to sleep. It had been hours since he arrived at the pub. Still, the bartender and his manager operated as usual. The owner drank while the bartender served people who wandered in. As night began to creep through the opened door, more people continued to fill in and meet their friends for a night out. It was during this time Joshua noticed a look between the two, a common glance.

"Okay, guys!" Ciddartha piped, placing a large vase on the table, "Regulars will know the drill. This is the honor jar, I'm stepping out for a smoke, so you guys drop your rubles in the vase and pay for what you grab. You got that?"

The crowd nodded and continued their drinking, some already dropping cash into the vessel and procuring their bottles from the wall, pouring their own taps. Cid stepped out into the night and the manager slowly rose to follow suit.

Joshua looked to their absence through parted eyes, pretending to sleep. He slowly looked around and rose from his chair in the dark corner, making his way across the room slowly to poke his head through the door. Cid and his boss strolled in the distance down the sidewalk, going somewhere.

Joshua waited until they were further away and began to follow. He kept to the walls, marking the steps before each alley; He estimated the time it would take for him to reach them. He counted the passing seconds from his last safe point. The duo he stalked looked back momentarily, and Joshua quickly swooped into an alleyway. He watched them from the shadows, cautious that he eyes wouldn't flicker in the darkness. This wasn't the first time he followed someone; stalking potential criminals was his bread and butter. He enjoyed the feeling, knowing he was where his enemy didn't think to look, and he was waiting for them to make a move. Joshua's hands would rest in his pockets, fingering his cuffs in sheer anticipation for someone to make his day. It was a habit he picked up while serving the city of Paris, both hurting others and hiding the blood in his pockets as he strolled away.

The ex-detective followed many men into drugstores who decided to wear long coats and hoods on summer days. Joshua would smash their heads against the counters before they could shoot the pharmacists, the clerks. It built him a name in Paris, it gave him a high reputation. It's what led to his notoriety, Baron Glass' interest in him; him being loaned out to other barons as favors, finding things for them, hunting things. Joshua recalled all his cases, his days cleaning the streets on and off the clock. But he didn't necessarily long for to return of this lifestyle either, not as much as he thought he would.

Joshua turned and looked around the corner. Observing at his targets, he quickly understood their vector. In the distance was the IBR, those round buildings that reminded Joshua of grapes, eggs, and the faces of twisted children.

Joshua shuddered at the thought.

In his stalk, Joshua's mind became void of information, reckless in thought, brooding all the outcomes he could think of. Joshua paused outside the radius of a streetlight and watched the bartender and the manager greet the guards at the marble palisade that marked the perimeter of the Institute. They both nodded their approval and motioned them through.

The IBR was alight in different colors that night, string baubles hung outside; people greeted each other with glasses of wine in the courtyard. They seemed to be partying, celebrating something. Joshua was sure it was a big event for the scientists, and Elizabeth's "friends."

Joshua walked toward the IBR and found himself at its front gate, after making sure the two men he followed were no longer outside to see him in the light. The IBR loomed before him like a giant hive. Joshua felt small yet enamored by the buildings curvature. The two guards that stood at the front of the main entrance donned high-tech armor and glassless helmets, their visors made of a thick carbon fiber; miniature camera's in the helmet served as their oculus. The Russian soldiers hid behind them scanning everything that moved, now more robot than human. They both held light machine guns in their hand, immobile like sentries until Joshua tried to enter.

"Halt! State your name for the guest list." The right guard demanded, his helmet broadcasting his words through the speakers in the base gasket.

"I'm just curious as to what's going on here." Joshua said casually.

"You haven't heard? Some scientist has made a massive breakthrough while studying Second Death. Their all celebrating the achievement. I even heard the Czar will be here sometime." He replied.

"Sounds promising." Joshua murmured, "I don't suppose everyone is allowed inside, then."

"What gave that away?" The Left guard chided, "The big-ass machine guns?"

"Quiet Gnat." The right guard barked, "Be nice to the American. He might burn a few minutes of our boring shift. Besides, soldiers are supposed to embody Russian hospitality."

"Russian hospitality?" Joshua replied, "Is that a joke? Your neighbors in France might say otherwise, given the tension between the two nations."

"Familiar with the French Dominion?" The right guard asked.

"Work there," Joshua sighed, "Moved there to join the police force when I was 25."

"You're a Frenchie?" The guard laughed, "How did you get across the border?"

"Doing a favor for some local people, friends of someone I know. They're actually inside right now." Joshua mused. "Are you sure I can't go in?"

The right guard laughed "You're welcome to go in, but we'd have to shoot you."

"We do need something to liven our day." Gnat sighed.

Righty laughed again, "Rookie's catching on, I'm proud of him. You should go back where you came from, roper, we're feeling benevolent today and won't turn you in, not that we can leave our post if you run. Coming across the 15th is quite the crime."

"Thanks." Joshua huffed. The detective turned and left. Joshua trudged around the perimeter, looking for a place to climb the wall. He could climb anywhere, really. The rounded marble was slippery, but the large groves where one segment ended and the other began allowed him to scale the barrier easily.

It was too easy, Russia wasn't used to miscreants, and were too lax on their guards.

Joshua dropped down into the grassy yard and made his way through the crowd. They were all too busy in their social lives to notice the intruder. Joshua weaved through them gracefully, used to the crowded street-walking of France.

The festivities seemed to be in full swing. Joshua saw there was enough defensive measures inside the facility, small cameras and droid turrets marked the ceilings. It would be dangerous to go inside without an excuse. The cameras would automatically pick up on his face and determine his presence unwarranted if he were to accidentally look at them. Joshua would need to stick inside the crowds, move with the group and keep his face from looking around. Otherwise, he could end up in a Russian gulag.

Joshua entered the building. Before him was a wide foyer, arches upon arches created balconies and external balustrades. The interior was stark white like an unpainted house and yet smooth as glass; it must have been ceramic.

The guests huddled about each other, conversing platitudes and scientific functions in terms of equations. Entwined in their topics and companionship, they didn't notice Joshua among the hubbub in his estranged attire. The foreigner looked through his brow for the two barmen, but he couldn't see them.

Joshua continued to strafe about the cameras, dancing between faces behind men taller than him. He eventually reached the end of the party, the break from the faces. He stood there at the edge like a man on a cliff. He looked back and scanned everyone once more. He was positive none of them were the barmen. Joshua had to search the rest of the building for them, worried they might be capable of exacting some treacherous plan.

The detective looked at the white doors in front of him. There was no lock, and the seam was slightly parted. Joshua could simply walk into the room within seconds, but what was on the other side?

Joshua had no choice and quickly trudged forth, the doors slid open for him and Joshua quickly looked to the ceiling, the cameras could not see him under the small alcove above him.

The room was a library with porcelain shelves and old literatures. The library stood three stories tall, garnered with rows and rows of knowledge. Joshua could have a field year reading them.

Joshua felt something at his boot, a subtle warmth. He looked down at the floor and spied a red laser, a tripwire. Joshua had activated the silent alarm. Joshua's heart began to beat, it was heavy, throbbing. He didn't have any time to react.

Joshua heard the doors open behind him. He turned around slowly to find a soldier with a gun aimed at his chest. Joshua looked at the green dot floating on his shirt and slowly rose his hands.

"You got me." Joshua grimaced, slowly backing into the center of the library. He moved past the study tables and stood in the middle of the floor. The soldier stood there for a moment and slowly followed him forward as if his weapon couldn't already reach him. Joshua recognized him as the left guard at the entrance, the one named Gnat.

Gnat watched Joshua intently before speaking, "Got a little curious, then? On your knees, Frenchie, I won't ask again."

Joshua slowly took a knee when he heard yet another hiss of the door. It was the right guard this time, and he made his way to Gnat.

"It's that Frenchie from outside." He stated with a harrumph, looking at Joshua most likely with a face of disgust. "We told you, you couldn't come in."

"I had good reason." Joshua insisted, "I'm looking for two guys, the two you let in, the punk rock kid and the long-haired man."

"Well who gives a damn?" The right guard snorted. "Cuff him, Gnat!"

Gnat slung his gun behind his armored back and pulled a pair of cuffs from his tactical vest. As he approached the detective, they heard yet another hiss of the door. Joshua looked past them to the door behind them, but no one appeared, the door was still shut.

"Pull your weight you twit!" The trio overheard, a whispering, a bickering, flowing from the walls to their ears.

"Look at my arms captain, it's not like a can lift this any higher!" Another voice bickered.

The two Russian Sentinels looked up to the second balcony to witness two men matching Joshua's description carrying a large tube between them. They were thieves, and they met the two soldier's mechanical eyes, caught red-handed and sweating.

Joshua twisted around where he knelt to see the two of them, Elizabeth's friends. They looked bewildered, still like a deer in headlights.

"Gnat, you know what that is don't you?" The right guard whispered, but the speakers made the noise quite conspicuous. "My helmet says that its…"

"It's the Second Death sample." Gnat finished.

The tall barkeep smiled clumsily at Joshua. They were certainly thieves. Gnat and the right guard rose their weapons and opened fire on the two men. The men dropped the case and rolled into the corner on the floor, hoping the alcove would protect them. The bullets shattered the porcelain shelves and ruptured the ancient books which exploded into a mass confetto of papers which slowly drifted to the floor like snowflakes. Cid and boss his reached for their small weapons, rusted antique revolvers, and fired back blindly into the first floor.

Joshua quickly jumped away from the exchange and over a study table. He rolled back and flipped it to make a barrier and laid there for protection. The two thieves dragged the canister along the ground as bullets collided about them. They reloaded and resumed their counter attack while dragging the giant vial to safety from the bullets. On that second floor there was a window which shattered in the lead haze. The two thieves had made their way to it.

"Reload, quickly!" the right guard ordered, they had run dry. The two soldiers scrambled for their extra box of bullets and began to feed the belts back through their rifles. In their haste to kill the criminals, they forgot about Joshua.

The detective rose from his hiding place behind the table and sprinted to the door he came from, leaving the four to solve their mess.

Joshua made his way to the main foyer. To his mistake, the crowd had left in shock moments earlier, leaving him exposed to the turrets in that room. Joshua hesitated as the turrets spooled to life and began to fire, lightly grazing the foreigner's jacket. Joshua stumbled for cover and found himself behind a small stool table. The turrets continued to fire their small rounds in great number, they ricocheted off the painted steel where Joshua curled into a ball, trying to fit himself behind the barrier.

Cid and his captain tossed the plague container through the window and leapt out behind it. The two hooligans yelped as they descended and slammed into the cool grass below. The large case made a small dent in the ground as it landed before them. For a few moments they were safe.

"The hell was Joshua doing here?!" Cid asked.
"He must've followed us, obviously, unless he suddenly has jurisdiction in Russia." His boss replied, huffing.

The two rose from the ground and grabbed the chemical weapon by both handles and trudged away into the night. They would have a lot of explaining to do in the morning.

The right guard stormed through the foyer with his comrade in tow. The turret ignored them and continued to pelt Joshua's small shield.

"Turrets off!" The Sentinel shouted in passing as he made through the entryway. The machinations immediately ceased their volley.

"Have a good day, Sgt. Reeves." The machines responded. They quickly sounded their shutdown sequence and fell asleep like nothing happened.

Joshua wiped his sweaty forehead and gulped. In the windows at the entrance, the two soldiers stood in the yard. It took Joshua a few minutes to find his knees, and once he could stand, he tumbled his way onto the lawn.

Gnat shambled through the grass of the IBR before Joshua, but it was empty of thieves. Furious, he threw his gun to the ground and beat his helmet. Reeves stood on the grass with his head low. His helmet scanned for drag marks, footprints, but the scuffle of the citizens after the party prevented him from marking anything certain. He shook his head.

"Come on Gnat," The sergeant called, "They couldn't be far."

Both guards trotted off through the gate they were originally supposed to protect and continued down the street leaving Joshua alone and dazed. Did Cid's boss feign intoxication to buy time, knowing they would steal into the IBR to take a chemical weapon that night? Were these men terrorists? Did they plan on releasing the contaminates and plunge a nation into chaos?

Joshua began to walk to the pub. He didn't know whether the scoundrels would still be there, but it was his only lead. He watched the empty streets that night, wondering what he'd do if he now owned the world's deadliest disease.

The Second Death virus was the reason third-world nations such as India and Africa became near uninhabitable. The virus overpowered the nerve system, made people act spontaneously, barbarically. The first case was a man named Garrison Smith, a tourist who was traveling around the world on live television. He was conducting a live study on indigenous peoples when he suddenly fell ill and began to attack his cameraman savagely while the footage still rolled. It was as if he was overcome by some incubated rage which finally broke from its shell.

Over time, the virus would spread to India's population, those it didn't aggravate, it killed, the nervous system breaking down as it fought the infection. Once you fell to the floor in spasms, you knew your time was up. What was most bothering, was that there were no precursor symptoms either; a man could be fine one day and gone the next, convulsed to death in his sleep. The Second Death left victims brain dead, unable to fight the disease once it took over their bodies, left to prowl about until they starved to death, left to attack anything living they laid their eyes on.

Joshua shivered at the notion and let himself through the front door. He was back in the tavern; the revelers had left, and the young detective was alone to reflect on the day. It wasn't the best start, but Joshua was confident he would get home eventually.

Gnat and Reeves trudged through the city streets looking for their criminals. Small scuff marks left on the sidewalk concrete marked their route, hard to detect even with their helmets in the low light of night. Nevertheless, the duo of soldiers boasted confidence that they were moving faster than their prey.

It took them time, under the wide illuminations of Moscow, to reach the two barmen. Their masks scanned them as they sat on their stolen weapon, using it as a bench. As they ran forth to meet them, their helmets told them their information. It was the same names they had seen on the guest list. But they seemed less like their titles than the pair originally thought. The tall man was named a senior advisor to the mechanics division, Gilbert Pecking. The young man with the rock t-shirt was dubbed a member of the press, Tyler Bove.

If these men weren't truly within their occupation, why did the computer not deny them entry? Was Russia's defense AI malfunctioning, tampered with? Or, had their hinged dependency on technology failed them; had it removed their ability to reason and make up their minds for themselves?

Reeves poised his rifle from the corner of a nearby building. Looking through his sight, breathing in and out slowly to control his movements. He clicked his rifle, safety off.

"You can't just shoot them." Gnat whispered.
"Watch me." Reeves huffed, "They stole a chemical weapon, I think we're justified."

"Doesn't mean we can just kill them, they're unarmed. The Russian policy states-"
"To hell with the rules, Gnat" Reeves spat. "These bastards deserve to die."

Reeves pulled the trigger. He watched as the tall man fell back from the bench. It was a perfect shot, straight through the manager's head. The loud bang was sent echoing through the avenues, waking those living nearby.

"Mother-." Gnat spat, rushing across the street to the fallen man, looking to render aid. The rock kid had jumped from his seat and took cover behind the container as Reeves continued to fire at the remaining criminal. Gnat waving his hands in the air, screamed at his partner, "Cease fire, Reeves! Cease fire!"

Reeves sighed as his comrade almost passed into his sights, his finger off the trigger. He stood and made his way to the remaining child. As he grew closer he began to watch his partner attempt to render aid to the dead bar manager. But, it was already hopeless, the bullet passed cleanly through the older man's skull and he was dead. Despite Russia's technological advancements, not much could be done to aid that condition, dead was dead. Ciddartha sat under the lamp helpless. He hadn't any bullets left, and he had tossed the gun long before they had ran to this place. He wasn't a threat anymore.

"That's how you do it Rookie." Reeve chuckled, "Clean and fast, like a band-aid."
"You didn't need to kill him." Gnat responded. "If the General finds out, we'll be hanged."

"Well who's to say anyone has to know?" Reeves replied.

Reeves lifted his rifle and placed it to Ciddartha's head, who sat there motionless, still next to the container. Cid looked down at the floor, his face hidden by his own shadow.
"I say we shoot the witness too, then no one will know."

"I'll know," Gnat protested, raising his sidearm from its holster, pointing it at his commanding officer. "Put the gun down Sgt. Reeves. Bloodlust is not a virtue of Russian Sentinels."

Reeves laughed and turned the gun on Gnat slowly. "You won't shoot me rookie! Hell, I might even shoot you and make off with this container myself! I bet Second Death fetches a high price in the underworld!"

"You don't mean that! Put the gun down, Sergeant!" Gnat demanded. "Check yourself, you're out of line!"

Reeves looked down his barrel at his new partner. Gnat was the newest of the Russian army recruits. They were an elite fighting class, the Sentinels. Gnat had been recruited a few years back to become a unifying factor, to keep Reeves in check.

Reeves, who had many mishaps behind the gun before, was ordered to take Gnat under his wing, a ball and chain for a rampant beast. The more Reeves stared at Gnat through the lens of his helmet, the more he realized he did mean it. Reeves was tired of his job, tired of neglect. They were soldiers, asked to stand around and do nothing all day. No one broke the law in Russia and it annoyed him. Reeves joined to military to kill people, but to his disappointment, there was no one to shoot anymore. Now there stood before him two foreigners, two, real criminals.

Reeves' finger itched, he already tasted it, the beauty of ending a life. He already killed one person, why not two more? He would vanish into the night with the container, sell it and start his own country. Soldiers had nowhere to go anymore, nothing to do. They were neglected, and no war would come to give them purpose.

Reeves used to be somebody, his job used to mean something. But what is a warrior without his war? There were no storms on the horizon, no end to peace. Reeves was scared. Reeves was scared of becoming obsolete.

"I do mean it." Reeves sighed and pulled the trigger. The bullet broke through Gnats helmet and Gnat fell back, at the force. Gnat opened fire in quick reaction, pelting Reeve's with a series of bullets, slumping him in a heap.

Both soldiers bled on the ground and Reeves was the first to die, choking softly in his tin can.

Gnat looked up from the hole in his helmet, the visor broken, the screen inside shorted out in sparks and the red emergency lights flared, warning him of the damage, helping him see inside his mask. From the ground he caught a better angle of the punk kid. The boy sighed. Cid didn't shudder, nor look concerned.

"When are you going to stop playing dead, old man?" the boy asked.

"When its morning," his captain moaned, but despite his answer he sat up. There was an odd wisp about his head, a radiating light that covered his forehead. It began to shimmer and the bullet that was lodged in his skull shifted back from the gaping hole, removing itself. The glowing light formed fibers which weaved about, stitching the wound shut and vanishing any trace of damage like a needle erases a tear in clothing. The captain looked down as he stood, unscathed and chipper.

"Come now, Cid, let's get this back home." The manager smiled.

The captain and the rock star lifted the canister again and began to plow away from the dreadful scene. Gnat began to reach for them, trying to stop them. He weakly grabbed at the older man's heel.

"What's this?" The captain exclaimed, "One's still alive."

"Just leave him, cap." Cid begged, "We really should be going."

"I suppose you're right. *Or,* we could save him," the boss asserted.

"Damnit, well I'm not going to carry him all by myself."

"I'm sure he can sit nicely on this crate." The captain replied, stooping to help the dying soldier. The captain placed the man on the long and heavy plague sample, adding to its weight.

Gnat lay across haphazardly on the gurney. He watched helplessly as he was carried away.

Part 4/*Reason*

Joshua watched quietly from the bar as the pair of thieves dragged the biochemical weapon through the pub door. They looked tired, sweaty, and bloody. Joshua twisted his face, he half-hoped they would be found dead in the morning, then he wouldn't have to do them a favor. He could play innocent when Elizabeth asked him what the hell happened.

Apparently, the two ruffians decided to take home a souvenir, one of the guards, who was quickly placed on a table but mere feet from the door. The two men began to operate on the man immediately after the door slid closed. They left Second Death unattended.

"Joshua, pass the vodka." The manager ordered.

Joshua grunted and walked to the other side of the bar, understanding that a human life was more important than his questions. Behind the bar, he spied a sawed-off shotgun beneath the island. Joshua grabbed the whitest bottle and tossed it across the bar to his hosts but stayed behind the counter, watching them intensely.

The captain poured the alcohol into the soldier's eye where the bullet struck. It had become lodged there in the socket. The soldier moaned and kicked, but it was useless to struggle. Without tweezers, tongs, or any medication, the captain jammed his fingers into the man's skull, found the bullet, and quickly ripped it out from where it embedded itself. The surgery was over in a matter of seconds. What was left of the white, fleshy, eye was removed and placed on the table like a half-eaten boiled egg.

Joshua was glad to see the two criminals cared for human life. But even so, they just stole a very important and deadly package. As the two men wiped their hands and placed Gnat on the couch to rest, Joshua grabbed the shotgun and poured himself a shot. The detective placed it on the bar loud enough to get his company's attention.

"Ready to talk now?" He asked.

"Yes, Joshua, we are ready to talk." The man replied. "My name is Marie-Joseph Paul Yves Roch Gilbert du Motier de Lafayette, Le Marquis de Lafayette."

"Like the war hero?" Joshua huffed, thinking about what he once learned in grade school.

"I assure you, I am no hero." The man bowed. "I go by many names. But Lafayette, or Laffy, would do just fine."

"Another loon…" Joshua sighed, pouring himself another shot. He knew the story behind the Marquis. After serving in Napoleon's French Brigade, he was awarded the final piece of Dominion territory, the best technological marvel the country could make. It was called LeCeleste, *the star*, a floating city that could house hundreds of citizens and usher France into an age of innovation. LeCeleste was France's boon to the world, their trophy, the proof they were worthy to be called Russia's rival.

According to history, that pipe-dream ended when the Marquis forsook France and sailed away in the night sky with his award. History didn't know what happened to him. The textbooks coined him as a crazy zealot who thought himself invincible, immortal. Joshua thought many men must've made the same claim as the person who stood before him. They were con artists trying to gain more from life, more money, more fame, greater ego. Why would the man before him be any different than all the other people who sought to declare themselves the Christ?

The Marquis chuckled and walked forward. "Now that everyone involved with Elizabeth's scheme has been introduced. I hope you would be so kind as to let us wash ourselves and get some rest. It has been a long day for all of us."

Joshua nodded slowly, he doubted he could force much information out of Lafayette. If these truly were Elizabeth's friends, no harm would befall him.

As the duo left the main floor, Joshua considered his circumstances. Apparently, the world was ripe with magic and untold history. It wouldn't be surprising if the only witch he ever met knew many folktale characters and legends. But it was Joshua's fear of being overwhelmed, and feeling insignificant, that dissuaded him from admitting its existence out loud. What did it mean for his sins? Could Joshua be forgiven? Joshua thought of the mutilated children he shot. Were they not innocent? Were they really wolves in sheep's clothing? Could the existence of magic help explain what happened that day?

Joshua crept onto the chaise lounge in the center of the room and slept with a hand and a foot on Second Death; his other hand clutched around the shotgun. He wanted to make sure it was still present when he woke, like a shepherd at the mouth of a sheep pen.

The captain served Gnat his fourth shot by the time Joshua awoke that morning, his head throbbing. It was a slow rise and a gentle wave from the Marquis that stirred his brain to reality. Joshua was still in Russia, still living in a world of magic, living among the sort of things you read in books.

"When you're ready, I'll start answering your questions." The Marquis said.

Joshua sat up and waited for the blood to rush back down to his heart before speaking, "What are you going to do with the virus?" He asked, hand still resting on the biochemical case. He drummed his fingers on the double-barrel.

"We won't release it, if that's what your worried about." The Marquis assured, "We have a buyer who owns a team of scientists that will study it. She wants to find the antidote herself, actually, and we can't trust Russia to do that."

"How are you so sure your buyer can be *trust*ed?" Joshua asked.

"She's an entrepreneur, creating an antidote is the best way to make money. She would gain merit and legitimacy from saving the population from contagion. She will also cripple the Russian superpower by removing their greatest weapon. She isn't so callous to commit genocide. In a way, she's really protecting humanity from itself." The Marquis replied thoughtfully.

"I assume you're getting a lot of money out of this then?"

"Just the usual," The Marquis shrugged, "We scratch her back she scratches ours. We enjoy owing each other favors. We've known each other for quite some time; we're almost fast friends."

Joshua nodded, it wasn't like he could do much to stop them. He was outnumbered; he wasn't legally present in Russia, even. Joshua would be insane to walk before a Russian defense agency with a biological bomb and no way of explaining what happened. He would sound like a madman.

It was hard to believe Joshua wasn't a madman. For many the same reason he kept his mouth shut when the police found him drowning in baby blood and sand. There were only some things one could say, and only some things others could believe.

"My second question is, who's Connor Shaw?" Joshua asked, after some sparse hesitation.

Lafayette smiled, "I actually have just the thing for that."

Lafayette moved about the room to a small linen closet placed on the far wall away from the entrance. There, in the small room, he vanished for but seconds before returning with a tall stand and a projector.

"Damnit," Cid sighed, "You and your damned digital presentations."

The Marquis smiled and began to set up the equipment, plugging many a wire into outlets, "What would you have me do, scrapbook?"

After Lafayette finished erecting the white tapestry and powering the projector, he sat behind Joshua, tucked behind the beams of colorful light. Joshua who sat across a sofa in the backroom of the pub, looked across the room at the large white square, waiting for the first image.

The First image contained a young boy at about the age of six. He stood on a small stool in a family portrait. His mother to his left and his father to his right. He wore old colonial knickers and a tweed coat over a tucked white linen shirt. They all looked smug, the father especially.

Lafayette began his presentation.

"Connor Shaw was born in the Colonial North America after the British-American Uprising. His family were loyalists, and during that time of Post-American Rebellion, were sentenced for treason to be hanged by the neck until dead by rebel remnants. Connor's father, Alfred, was a British war hero during the French-Indian War and had quite the affinity for… opiates. Connor's mother, a scientist if there ever was one, sent Connor to Britain a few months before their capture. He went to live with his aunt."

The Marquis changed slides, now showing a cobblestone street in Britain. Seemingly, it was something out of a history textbook. The image was faded at the ends, almost burnt and folded until creases marked the beige plaque like veins inside skin. In the corner was a thick woman in a dress with a boy holding her hand, the boy looked to be the same age, but his hair was much darker. The woman wore a pink dress with a flowered sun hat to match. Despite this lackadaisical color, she looked void of sincerity, full of malice.

"During this time Connor went to a boarding school near Westminster where he met a very special girl."

"Elizabeth?" Joshua mumbled.

"No." the man corrected, "Fiona, the daughter of a well-known nurse working in an asylum."

Joshua frowned.

"Don't worry Mr. Hill, everyone's favorite little witch will show up soon, I promise.

Fiona and Connor became friends during his stay in England, but the girl's family was subject to controversy. Fiona's mother, a nurse, was accused of using witchcraft on one of her patients to cure him of mental instability, such was the fear of those days. The King's police quickly locked her away where she died of hypothermia that following winter.

Nevertheless, Connor stayed around Fiona who was deeply affected by her mother's use of said witchcraft. It had peaked her interest about the arcane. Fiona found a very naïve and perfect subject in Connor. She ran a lot of tests and experiments on the boy until one day she was caught with one of her mother's tomes during school. She was sentenced to prison as well, even though she was but a child."

"So, you're telling me Elizabeth is in love with a two-hundred-year-old man?" Joshua asked, shifting on his chair.

The Marquis frowned, "I actually don't know... how peculiar. These things I have been telling you are things that Connor had told me during our time together.

As Elizabeth might have told you, however, Val-Ashoth helps keep her young, timeless. A wage for her services. In regard to Elizabeth, she is *that* old, living outside of the passage of time. Perhaps Connor is a warlock. Most witches and warlocks have long lifespans, some even reaching five-hundred years old. Perhaps the tests Fiona ran on him slowed his aging process. What I can tell you, is that this is Connor's past, unless he made some terrible lie to all of us."

"This magic crap seems all so convoluted." Joshua interrupted.

"That's the point," The Marquis assured, "Magic is the illogical, the unexplainable come to fruition. Magic is supernatural, beyond science and causality. Anything can happen, and perhaps, everything will happen."

Joshua frowned, "So you're telling me about Fiona because…"

The man frowned slightly, "Because magic always matters. It can change the course of history without batting an eye. A girl can wish for a rose in the wilderness but unknowingly change the biome leading to the death of a species. Magic is often the base of all events, the precursor of significant happenings. Wherever something significant happens, magic flocks there like a witness or a news reporter. It is evident in all change and all circumstances, no matter how small."

The man changed the slide, this time it was a picture of a girl with long black hair. She looked like Elizabeth, but more innocent, sincerer. The black and white cinematography didn't help distinguish her features and Joshua found himself leaning forward.

"As Connor continued to grow up he began to shy away from civilization. Free of his family, he sailed back to Colonial America to become a hunter around the age of twenty-six. He grazed the wilds there, learning how to live off the land. It was in his exploration that Connor met Elizabeth.

Elizabeth was the daughter of Victor and Annabelle of France. Her father had died during the French-Indian War. Annabelle, a witch herself, saw the residual magic Fiona had left on him. Intrigued, she brought Conner back to her cabin for study.

As you know, Elizabeth is the Witch of Val-ashoth currently, she actually inherited her affinity for magic from Annabelle throughout her mother's career. By being around magic, people can inherit the gift, not even needing to learn it formally.

Annabelle was a famous healer, and the French didn't shoo her away like the English did in their fear of the arcane.

Connor and Elizabeth actually grew up together and split company on many occasions.

Due to growing instability in the wilds around Colonial America and the growth of cults over the years, Elizabeth hid in the bosom of Val while Connor left to explore of South America. With an expeditionary team, he quickly became known throughout the wilds for his ability to fight relentlessly against natives, beasts, and other primordial beings. He became a hero of the wilds; he gave people much hope of settling there where resources were abundant. He lived out there and helped the people build small settlements. They called on him when there were strange threats they couldn't handle. He became a sort of Saint, like Dominus of Silos, he was the people's champion, but, also, he was an outcast."

"What do you mean?" Joshua questioned, "How could someone so loved be so hated at the same time?"

"The reason Elizabeth always explained it to me was; because of Fiona, Connor became a beacon of trouble, as if he was cursed with bad luck. The Natives, the beasts of The Wilds, they were all looking for Connor, attracted to him like moths to a flame, flies on something sweet. Elizabeth always said he had a… propensity, a power, to be more than a man, it's what gave him an edge in America. Connor saved many villages, but even if one person would come to harm, those he protected would turn away from him. He wasn't responsible for their deaths, but people blamed him for not saving those who died… The more some people loved him, the more some people hated him. The greater the flame, the longer the shadow."

Laffy switched the slides around, the picture consisted of a young man who looked like Joshua. He stood at the side of a monument inside a dense jungle. He looked happy, proud even. He looked exactly like Joshua, and it haunted him like some sort of memory he should know.

"Connor eventually helped head the expedition into the crypt of Radjagah, and he was never seen again. Elizabeth searched for him everywhere for years and she never found him…"

The Marquis rubbed his eyes and closed the slides. It was the end of the presentation.

"…Then Elizabeth found you, an article in a newspaper about a hotshot American detective shooting up France. She was ecstatic, really…" The man trailed off, there was a silence over the room albeit a slight noise from the bar. Gnat was snoring.

"Was? What do you mean was?" Joshua asked, placing the words abruptly.

"She became dark for a while," Laffy mused, still a silent and thoughtful air about him. He hid his mouth with his hand and spoke through it. "She'd never say anything, but I'm sure it came from watching you. She wanted to talk to you immensely, but she never went through with it until now. She had to save you from Baron Whitecroft, it seems.

She watched you, read the headlines as you notched kill after kill after kill. I would assume, in an attempt to understand you, she did the same in her own way. Imitation is a form of affection after all. As you became colder she became colder, more callous, perhaps in an attempt to draw your mantra into her skin, a silent prayer for your wellbeing."

Joshua cringed, now feeling the weight of Elizabeth's heart. He took the witch for a fiend, but perhaps she was more like him than she realized. Joshua pitied her, and somehow, wished to see her again to, if only apologize for what had happened to her. She must have felt so lonely, waiting for centuries to see whether or not her loved one was even alive. And then, she thought she found him, and was forced to watch as he shred his soul away. Joshua hadn't realized the way he lived might bring sorrow to others. He didn't know anyone cared enough for his well-being. Although Joshua was mistaken for Connor Shaw, the love Elizabeth misplaced on him was comforting. It was a love based on suffering. It was nothing cliché, a match made in hell. He was a corpse-groom, and she was a fallen saint.

"Do you think I'm Connor then, honestly?" Joshua asked the man, almost wanting to be.

The Marquis chuckled under his breath. "You? I don't honestly know. It's not my business either. If you are, then good - good for her. But if you aren't then she'll probably continue to search the world for him; there's a lot of people in the world, either way. I have my own agendas to bother with."

Lafayette finished wiping the sleep from eyes yet again. "I'm going to get some coffee across the street. Feel free to meet us when you're ready to answer Elizabeth's calling."

Joshua nodded and laid on the couch again. He stared at the far wall where the projector was aimed for a time wrapping his mind around the surplus information. He didn't want to be Connor Shaw; he didn't want to be anyone but who he was. It was his prerogative and mission to return from this horrible detour unchanged, unscathed. He wanted to be alone and accountable to no one. He wished he had never met any of them. In his mind he kept chanting to himself: *My name is Joshua Hill, I'm a detective that lives in France. I have an apartment in Paris. I've never been in The Wilds. My name is Joshua Hill, and I've been mistaken for someone else.*

Daylight came through the open window as the sun continued its way about the earth. Joshua looked about. Gnat was gone along with the others.

The mistaken man rose; today marked his second day in Russia. He still had no idea what day it was, or what time it was. Slowly, he managed to elevate himself off the couch and onto his feet. He sunk his head into his hands and, through the cracks between his fingers, he discovered his foot was cold.

Joshua's right boot was missing. He wiggled his toes, tapping them against the wooden floor. He wondered why he hadn't noticed before.

Joshua looked about for a time for his boot but noting revealed itself. Wherever it had gone off to was beyond Joshua's knowledge or recollection. It was nowhere on the first floor, and the ex-detective, although silently bold, felt he would ask for more trouble than it was worth if he searched the second floor.

Joshua thought it peculiar, the window curtains had been drawn back, the light trickling lazily through in a cold, white, ray. Through this translucent pane, Joshua saw Laffy sitting outside across the street underneath a parade of patio tables. He read the morning newspaper and sipped a small cup of coffee ritualistically.

The Marquis looked up, his reading glasses glaring in the sun, he seemed to look straight back at Joshua. He was doing just that. Smiling, he reached around his chair and trophied a ruddy leather boot, Joshua's boot. The man dangled it aloft over his head as if to tease his guest and beckon him over to take it back. Across from him, Cid slouched lazily with his arms crossed, to The Marquis' left, and Gnat sat off to the right. Gnat still wore his helmet although it was ruined the day before. The hole in his visor was covered with grey duct tape and the wires were haphazardly tied back together to return visual application to the monitor inside.

Joshua cursed, slowly stormed out the door, and crossed the empty street. "I don't suppose you're just going to hand my shoe over, are you?" Joshua addressed.

Cid slouched down even more, as if expecting a fight between parents. Laffy only smiled, he took off his reading glasses and folded his newspaper. Tossing the paper down onto the table, he gave a slight chuckle,

"My new friend here fetched it for me," He remarked, gesturing to Gnat, "I didn't think you would run away with only one shoe. You can take it back after we've had coffee."

"I would have run this morning if I knew I had a chance." Joshua huffed. "Don't take me for a fool. I don't flee like a fox."

Laffy laughed again and shrugged. He reached down and tossed Joshua's his shoe. Joshua sat and tied it back on. The others watched in silence. Gnat still sat there motionless, almost as if dead and bronzed. He stared at the coffee that had been served to him. He hadn't taken his first sip.

The day was warmer than most, a thick 64 degrees that sat on top of their coats. Big band played on the radio by the coffee shop door and the shop owner gazed out of her store. She cast a perfect shadow on the be menu behind her. It must have been seven in the morning, the sunrays darting down the street and exposing strange contrasts in the whitewall paint. It was a good day to be outside, there were no pedestrians out, no commotion nor hustle that estranged the ears. It was so quiet that the small radio that played, at about half a foot in width, could be heard clearly from where they sat.

Joshua finished, and his party nodded to suggest they were ready to begin. Yet they began to speak about other things. Perhaps they thought Joshua needed more time to tighten his shoelace.

"Lovely weather today, don't you think, boss?" Cid hummed.

"Indeed, it reminds me of a small village in Japan, you were there were you not? The cherry blossoms were struck by the sun and those radiant filaments permeated through the trees in hushed pink and white tones, just like these buildings."

"I do remember that, were we not there for that feudal prince? We ended up plowing him with the ship."

"Yes, we did, we did. And there is a lesson to be learned from that, never let the princess step across the threshold of your door when she is getting married. No matter how many times you tell the groom nothing happened, he won't believe you."

"You also saw her ankles at the ceremony before that…" Cid started.

"…Which didn't help at all, no." The Marquis drummed. "It is a shame they have to contest with the Second Death there, although their effort gives me hope life can continue while the reaper abounds."

There was a quiet, and end to the talk of duos. The two barkeeps looked for input or new conversation from their new company, but Joshua and Gnat said nothing.

"Silent one," The Marquis cued, addressing Gnat. "I don't suppose you'd tell us your name now, would you?"

Gnat shook his head, a silent no.

"Well I suppose we have to name you, then. For now, of course, until you decide to speak."

"What, like a dog?" Cid snorted.

"Nothing so terrible," The Marquis hushed.

Joshua watched them. They were an odd group, almost unnatural, most unnatural. They began to run names in front of the silent ex-militant.

He once boasted a certain attitude; Joshua recalled a certain dry humor at the gate of the IBR last night. Gnat looked uptight now, almost defensive against the world itself. He was more akin to the stereotypes of his last occupation now than ever before. He sat there, much like a dog, as it was suggested; he even stole Joshua's shoe on command, the devil. Perhaps he was tired, or in a deep trance. Like Joshua, his whole life seemed to draw upon an end, ripped away from him by another world, another kind of people. Joshua sympathized silently for the soldier.

"If I remember correctly, it's Gnat." Joshua interjected, hoping to save the shy Russian from the spotlight.

Gnat nodded his head.

Cid shrugged, "It sounds too cute for me, he really is a dog, now, isn't he?"

"But he is quite like someone small, a fly on the wall. He certainly has a small presence."

"It's short for Nathan," the guard grumbled, the words mechanic, his true voice muted by the cask about his head.

The two awed, his name was more "Nat" than "Gnat." Perhaps he was "Gnathan."

"How come you haven't tried to arrest us again, Gnat?" The Marquis asked.

"I saw something I can't explain." The robotic soundtrack responded, "I saw you die, but you're not dead. I also can't go back to the garrison; I killed my partner. They'd put me in stocks. I'd rather stick around, figure this out, and skip the formalities. My brother receives annuity if I'm dead, or presumed dead, anyways."

The Marquis chuckled and nodded his understanding. He looked back down about his seat and relinquished a manila folder from a small messenger bag under the table. Leaning forward from his chair, he placed it before Joshua on the table. He looked stern, all traces of his whimsicality and grandeur had vanished.

Joshua became attentive, ready as a detective would be for a debriefing. He opened the folder to discover a series of fine-tuned topographic images, both the lines of altitude and the actual landscape. The coordinates remained the same in each photo precisely, but there was a difference in the dates, from the left the oldest photos, to the right the most recent. The topographs were also different in definition. It looked as if there was a small shift in altitude, a line that altered the land about it.

"Sorry for holding out on you, Joshua," The Marquis apologized, "This is what Elizabeth sent you to find out."

"What is this, construction?" Joshua inquired, shuffling through the photos.

"No one knows," Replied the Marquis.

"I think it's a wurm." Cid shot.

"We know you think it's a wurm. It's *not*."

"*Is*."

"*Is not* and *you* should know better." Lafayette chided.

"A *worm*? Like fish bait?" Joshua asked.

"No, a *wurm*." Cid starkly replied, "Like a giant *worm* that eats people. *Giant* ones, underneath, with armor usually, will crush you to bits."

"They're gargantuan *worms* in a lot of ways, but they've been mutated to have teeth that could shred a car." Marquis added.

"You're kidding me." Joshua half gawked, half mocked.

"Not anymore we're not. But *I* think it is something worse. Even if it was a wurm, that is bad enough.

Elizabeth brought you here to handle this. These images came from a Russian satellite; the government has been watching it for days. They even plan to send a small research party out there. Unless they're armed to the teeth, I don't think they'll come back. It's also possible that whatever this is will move close, if not move through, Moscow before the end of the month. We want you to go and find out what it is." The Marquis chimed, he wore a grin from ear to ear as if begging Joshua to say yes but knowing the detective didn't have a choice in the matter.

Joshua sat there on the thought, he knew that, even if he said no, he would have to deal with the problem later if he couldn't bug out of Moscow. Elizabeth would probably capture him again and throw him in another shipping container anyways.

"I guess I really don't have a choice." Joshua mumbled.

"No truer words were ever spoken." Cid mocked.

"I'm sorry," The Marquis spoke, "I know this is all much for you. But, we do have a plan, and, you won't be doing this alone, mostly."

"Mostly?" Joshua asked for clarification.

"I can't be found out," the Marquis put plainly, "I have a strict no-interference rule with human affairs, unless I want something, of course, and can stay below the radar. But Gnat could help, I could let you borrow him."

"Like a dog." Cid snorted again.

The Marquis frowned at the corners of his mouth and added, "If you hurry, you could get there before the expedition arrives. I could load you with a truck full of weapons and you could go '*bang-bang*' like Connor Shaw always did and solve the problem."

Joshua pulled his hair and thought it all insane. How could he face something that could level the ground where it moved? He hoped it was a farce, that he would arrive there and find something easy, something explainable. Hopefully it was just a large steamroller that somehow lost its way into Siberia.

"What's your plan?" Joshua asked.

"To lure the thing away from Moscow," The Marquis coughed, "We'll give you a load of guns. We can get you a truck with a satellite beacon on it, you and Gnat could camp north of its trajectory and if it starts changing course for you we'll contact you to start moving further away from Moscow. It's moving at about eight miles an hour, so it'll be like a road trip for you two. Each day you'll move out of the range it can travel and make camp. Lather rinse, repeat, until it's clear of Moscow and those researchers."

"But how do I lose it after that?" Joshua asked again.

The Marquis went silent. His lips pursed. "I hadn't thought about that. Run away, faster, maybe? I mean, it'll only follow you for so long, at a certain range."

"So, you're saying I'll probably get caught in the Siberian wilderness running from this thing until it gets bored of me. It may never, and I would be lost out there forever."

The Marquis thought for a moment about the predicament. "I have an idea, we'll pick you up in our skyship once you're far enough away. We'll even drop you off somewhere in France. It beats having to wait for Elizabeth to return you home."

Joshua sighed, the bait dangled before his face. An express ride home was all Joshua wanted. "When do I leave?" He asked, ready to end the nonsense.

"You leave the day after tomorrow. We'll get your supplies ready through the black market until then and make sure you're ready to travel."

The Marquis rose from his position around the table and stretched. The wind had picked up and his coffee had gone cold. Cid put his feet on the table, now being allotted more room as The Marquis returned his ceramic mug to the dreary hostess. Gnat remained there motionless. Once the Marquis returned, Joshua had risen as well. He knew not what to do for the day, but his party already seemed to have plans for him.

The Marquis tugged on Joshua's tense shoulder, "Come on," He said, "I have something to teach you."

Cid and Gnat followed Joshua and The Marquis down the street. The Marquis tugged them through amassing crowds of scientists on their way to work. After some time of threading through the population, Joshua thought he had lost his company among the sea of faces. But, just before he gave up, he could see Gnat's helmet slightly above the crowd. At the end of the walk through the LED streets of Moscow, Joshua found himself staring down a short and wide building marked with the giant word "Gymnasium" over the door.

"This is where you're going to spend your next two days." Laffy stated.

"Why would I need to go to a gym?" Joshua asked.

"That's quite simple, you need to be stronger if things go awry during your mission. Whether you're Connor or not, you're slow, and a little skinny, to be honest."

"I don't need to work on anything, I'm fine." Joshua insisted.

"Are you now? I'll tell you what, if you can beat Cid in the ring, then I won't argue it further." Lafayette paused,

"But you're going to lose, Mr. Hill, don't say I didn't warn you."

The group walked into the building, rusted equipment was strewn everywhere, unused for at least a decade. The interior of the building was the antithesis of the exterior. Inside, everything was a rotted and dusty mess.

"What happened here?" Joshua inquired.

"No one in Moscow has needed a gymnasium in 50 years." Cid explained, "They all take pills that simulate exercise in their muscles and increase their heart rate. They burn fat that way, able to lounge about on their thrones."

"Why can't I just take those then?"

The Marquis laughed, "You need combat training in addition to muscle, we're going to teach you to fight, not just lift weights or run. Besides, you also need to understand and overcome physical pain. Pills won't do that for you."

Joshua and Cid climbed into the ring and took to their corners. The Marquis aided Cid while Joshua attended to himself. Gnat stood by stoically, despite being asked to help Joshua.

Joshua wrapped his hands and removed his coat and shirt. Cid did the same, his whole body littered with tattoos. The Marquis told the group the match would be judged by Gnat, who was seen as the most neutral of the group. He then sounded the bell and the American detective squared his toes against the British Rockstar.

Cid flew during the sound of the bell. He landed the first blow squarely across Joshua's jaw. Joshua spun in a circle and narrowly blocked another shot to the face with his arm. The first shot almost ended it for the detective, his vision blurry and red. Still, he stayed on his toes and defended himself. Joshua returned with a brutal flourish, he grabbed Cid, who had opened his guard between jabs, by the back of his head and leapt into his nose with his knee.

Cid sprawled back and fell but quickly rolled with the momentum in a well-timed hand-spring and emerged back onto his feet. Joshua had over pushed, following Cid as he fell. He thought he could pummel him while he stayed on the ground. But as Cid rose, Joshua realized he had left himself wide open. Cid landed a powerful uppercut to Joshua's ribs with a loud crack. Joshua bent over by the force and felt a descending fist onto the back of his head that flattened him on the ground.

The bell rung the end of round one. Joshua already knew the winner and waved off Gnat's judgement sign marked "Sidd" in a kindergartener's handwriting.

The second round started, and this time Cid hung back. Joshua jabbed the air around the skinny bartender, Cid easily dodging the punches. Cid stepped into Joshua's box, he had found an opening. Joshua was pelted with a barrage of left hooks, the ribs that had cracked now crunched, the bruise that had immediately shown after round one now bled. But as Cid hammered into Joshua, Joshua, in turn, had wrapped his arms around Cid's back.

Joshua lifted with his body and picked Cid off the mat, only to crash down again. Cid bounced and sprang, now bleeding from his forehead after the throw. Joshua had narrowed the distance with good timing and planted a punch with shattering force right into Cid's sternum. Cid shot back and landed against a corner post. Blood and sweat drenched both of them.

This ended the second round. Gnat held up his board, there in uneven letters was written "Yoshuwah."

Gnat didn't know how to spell. The Marquis laughed, trying to keep from humiliating the young soldier now erasing the board with his forearm.

Cid and Joshua waited for the bell, this started the last round. If Joshua won, he wouldn't be stuck doing workouts for the next two days.

At the bell, both Joshua and Cid strode forth in confidence towards each other. Joshua landed the first blow of the match, a long kick to Cid's belly. Cid gasped for air but still drove on against the shift of momentum. He sprinted forth and dug his shoulder into Joshua's waist, tackling him to the ground.

Cid knelt above him and rained down punches. Joshua protected his face but couldn't stop the punches to his shattered ribs, the blows caused him to choke on his blood, he hacked and sputtered pools that collected in his mouth to the side.

Joshua riposted, his fist landing a blow from the ground into Cid's eye. Cid jolted back, and Joshua pushed him off. Joshua rose to his knees in defense. Cid swung hard and Joshua was there to meet him. Catching Cid's fist, he rotated his foe's arm into a knot, but, Cid rotated with the turn, his whole body spinning in the air to keep his shoulder in its socket. He descended in a flip with a flat kick to Joshua's skull. Joshua cringed as Cid continued his advance, kneeling in the ring; his vigor for victory drove him past his fatigue.

Cid flew forth with a kick that met Joshua's chest. Joshua flew back and felt tight against the ropes. He used this momentum and shot back to meet his knuckles with Cid's forehead. Cid left his feet and Joshua rose to descend his heel, striking Cid's shoulder blade with a wallop and a snap. Cid rotated his body and spun his legs into Joshua's. Joshua crashed into the floor yet again.

The round seemed to drag and both contestants lay there, their sweat drowning their throats with salt. Blood had been splashed across the ring, but still, there was no bell.

Joshua rose and planted a kick in Cid's ribs. Joshua waited for him to stand. Cid slowly found his route onto his feet, using his good hand to climb using the rope fence.

Joshua taunted the bartender, and they both slowly closed the distance. Joshua and Cid started to trade blows. They didn't block or dodge the strikes. They pelted each other directly in the face, taking fair turns. They were exhausted. Eventually, they dawdled from each other and found their eyes on Marquis and Gnat.

The bicameral audience sat attentively. The Marquis stared through Cid and Joshua towards the far wall. They sat in silence until the Marquis replied to Nathan. "Yes, I see your point, but black tea is simply inconsistent in flavor whereas green tea isn't. Although that gives black tea an edge over the non-monogamous, it is the monogamous that should be the partakers of good and simple tea. No one should drink something that might bite them when they most need it to be sweet. It needs consistency, monogamy is wisdom and sound artisanship."

Gnat shook his head in disappointment.

"Hey, piss-heads, are we done here!?" Cid shouted, his face snarled like a pig.

The Marquis scratched his head. "Are we done here, Joshua?"

Joshua winced, the blood trickled down his chest. He thought for a moment about his potential enemy. His thought about Solomon and everything else he must face in the future. The detective had grown soft. In his street prowls, he relied on shock and awe to keep him alive and unscathed, but, this was not the case anymore. What else would Joshua have to fight against in this new world? How could he ever be prepared?

"No," Joshua replied, "what's next?"

Joshua found a moribund love in the flow of blood. For the rest of the night, the roper traded blows with Cid, until he fell at the hands of the Marquis, who never found a scratch. When the morning arose so did Joshua, his body as stiff as a tree trunk. Yet, he found himself able to force his body to a slow and noisy stomp.

On this morning, the Marquis found Cid and Joshua outside smoking cigarettes, their hands tender and shaking. He stood on the opposite side of his compatriots across the door and lifted his foot to friction himself to the wall. He tucked his hands in his long colonial coat and looked out at the city.

The gym sat at the end of a particularly wide street which stretched down and out of view. The lazy haze that found its way about the paved floors of the city hid the pedestrians far away, reducing them to nothing but shadows and dots to the eyes. Up from this sea of grey uncertainty rose the buildings that housed the citizens and the workers and the militants. They all kept their lights off until the ninth bell. In unison, turning on they did, to mark the start of Joshua's last full day of training. What was just another day of work for the civilian, was still the beginning of a new life for Joshua.

Joshua still bore the pain of labor, the pain of new birth. Even though Joshua wanted to return to Paris, he would not be able to return to his job. This, he had understood. Knowing the world now as he did, he wanted to be prepared for whatever he would meet. Joshua, although a dark and brooding man, still wanted to save others, even if it meant not saving himself.

The Marquis was silent today, the fog seemed to erect a barrier between any sounds or comments he might have had about Joshua's performance the day before. The lights of the buildings turned on, as was their cue, and the city roared to life like a generator. The blue building lights shifted and turned into a fiery orange to complement the sun. The street lamps turned off and automatons, such as the holographic menus of restaurants and advertising models, turned on.

The Marquis nodded at Joshua and Cid, motioning for them to snuff their flames and head inside for breakfast.

As the trio strode in they were smitten with the fragrant smell of morning coffee and fried eggs. Before them, a small arrangement of breakfast foods lay sprawled on a folding table in the center of the gymnasium floor. The equipment before, treadmills, escalators, bikes, and elliptical machines, had been pushed away to create space for the four of them. Off to the right, in an L-shape to the foodstuffs, Gnat cooked on a portable gas-grill with a small pink apron about his military suit.

The trio sat about and enjoyed the food, Cid and Lafayette contributed to conversations the most, Joshua preferring to say nothing. He was still in disdain from his predicament and diaspora from France.

Gnat was silent for his own sake. The soldier, in all deeds he performed resembled a regular statue or marionette. Occasionally, and to the humor of the Marquis, the soldier would cock open his helmet just enough to wedge in food so that he might eat. Sometimes, he would forget about his helmet, and smear the tattered, opaque, visor with toast and jam incompetently.

"Joshua, it is time for you to learn the most important thing about fighting." The Marquis began, wiping his mouth with a napkin. "*Stamina*, if you can't overpower your enemy, outlast them. If you can't move faster than your enemy, survive them. Only when your foe outlasts you will you lose to your foe."

"Because you'll be dead." Cid mumbled. "The best way to kill something is to *stay alive*."

"How are you going to teach me not to die?" Joshua scoffed.

Suddenly, the Marquis took up a butter knife and lobbed it in Joshua's direction. Joshua fell to the floor in haste, the butter knife flying past his cheek, thinly scrapping his stubble, it penetrated the wall behind him, despite its dull shape, and stuck in the mortar.

The Marquis clapped and rose from the table. The food was quickly wrapped up by Gnat and the table folded. Cid moved the chairs to their corners.

"We act to kill you, of course," The Marquis chuckled.

The Marquis motioned for the posse to follow him. He beckoned over his shoulder to them as he moved to the exit marked "Basement." Joshua found himself staring at a large dojo which was kept better than the squabble upstairs. The entire floor was replaced with padding. Along the walls lined targets and dummies and swords and pistols and rifles. A

108

firing range stuck out from the dojo. Like an exit tunnel in a sewer, it was placed with three targets at varying distances. At the stalls, ammo boxes and crates of weapons stacked upon each other. It was an anarchist's dream.

The Marquis had already positioned himself in the middle of the floor, he held a long rapier in his right hand, and a silver pistol in his left. Cid began taking his own weapons off a wall, a scimitar and a short double-barreled shotgun.

"Joshua," The Marquis bowed, as if apologizing. "You're going to have to dodge everything we throw at you."

"What d-"

Joshua felt an odd punch to his leg and a loud thunder in the room. He flew back in agony. "What the hell was that!?" He grimaced.

Joshua looked up from his back, viewing an upside-down Cid who stared down at him from the end of a smoking barrel.

Cid smiled, "Rock-Salt, Hill, I figured you should get used to that pain now before we really begin."

The Marquis tried to stifle a laugh. "I'm sorry, Mr. Hill, you are hopeless until you can dodge a bullet."

"How the hell am I supposed to dodge a bullet!?" Joshua cried.

"Watch the gun, move before the trigger is pulled, stay out of its sight, that sort of thing. Maybe dodge isn't the best word, *avoid* would be better." Cid smiled, reloading his gun. The Marquis followed suit, placing rubber bullets in his magazine.

Joshua rose. He looked about the place once more; there was nowhere for him to hide from a bullet. Gnat sat in the corner, still and unmoving. Gnat would make a good barricade between him and a gun, if Joshua were so bold.

"Damn," Joshua cursed.

"We'll shoot sparingly to start off with, so focus on our sword arms." The Marquis assured, "We need to teach you how to move away and survive against as many different weapons as possible… and perhaps objects."

"I hope we get to use the wrecking ball in the backyard." Cid cooed, "I haven't seen that for some time."

Joshua stood and aligned himself opposite his rivals, they stood at 45 degrees to either side of him. "Where's my weapon?!" He demanded.

"We're teaching you to *dodge* first, nothing more." The Marquis hummed, "Besides, you could kill us. We know how to keep from cutting you in half. You, on the other hand, have no control over your strength."

The Marquis lunged, his rapier thrust at Joshua's heart. Joshua jumped to its side, but immediately after, felt the flat of Cid's blade against his calf. Joshua tripped on the impact, flying onto his back again.

Joshua looked over at Cid mid-fall. The boy had his shotgun pressed against his chest and pulled the trigger. Joshua collided with the ground, pushed by the rocketing salt which shred his shirt in tatters. Small holes full of salt embedded in his chest, it would certainly leave a scar.

Joshua yelped. He rolled onto his knees and hacked a smidgeon of blood onto the ground. Joshua's body writhed under the pain, shuddered in agony.

"You can't take your time, Mr. Hill, as much as it would be courteous to let you." The Marquis assured, "You will also need to get used to pain. If your body can't handle pain it will try and shut down on you. When the adrenaline is gone, you'll want to rest, hide, but that's when you make mistakes, turn your back and give up. You're going to learn to fight until death, not until you fall, or until you can't take it anymore. You will rise again and again until your head is taken from your shoulders. No matter how much your body wants to give up, your soul will not."

Joshua stood.

"Are you ready?" Lafayette asked.

"I'm ready." Joshua stated.

The Marquis lunged and Joshua moved past the blade, his body grazed the pointed sabre. The corner of his eye caught Cid, who swung his sword high about Joshua's neck. Joshua ducked quickly and passed between his two coaches. The Marquis fired his gun toward the ground, the rubber bullet knocking the floor near Joshua's feet. Joshua stepped back instinctively, a mistake.

The Marquis lunged forward with his rapier whilst Joshua was still in mid motion. Unable to put his foot down in time to move again he watched as the rapier pressed into his belly. It passed through like a pin entering water. The Marquis lurched his sword out.

Joshua gasped.

"That could've been your kidney, Mr. Hill." The Marquis sighed before posturing his sword arm again.

Cid charged and slapped Joshua again against his thigh. Joshua fell to his knee, but quickly rolled before the young bartender could put a shell in his stomach. The detective rose again to find the Marquis aiming his gun. Joshua sprang in and beneath the sharpshooter's arm but found the rapier in his stomach again as he reached to disarm the pistol.

"I have more than one arm you know." The immortal sighed again, kicking Joshua away. "Try to predict every variable. Cover your head and your chest, those are the important organs."

Joshua darted left, Cid's last shell finding the wooden panel behind him. The Marquis swung low and Joshua narrowly hurdled the steel. He miraculously found his feet midair.

Joshua found himself behind the Marquis, who had left himself open. Joshua firmly placed his boot against his foe's ass and kicked. The Marquis stumbled forth, laughing under his humiliation.

Cid now came in from the left, his sword raised about his waist like a spear. He lunged, but Joshua had stepped back at the last second, narrowly finding the tip of the blade sparking across his belt buckle.

Joshua swatted the blade away and moved into Cid, landing a firm right hook to his ear. Cid fell off to the side with an angry harrumph.

Joshua felt a sharp sting to his shoulder. The Marquis stood there at the far wall, his pistol raised, already fired and billowing smoke. Joshua cringed, the bullet lay there at his foot pathetically.

Joshua had been shot.

Damnit! Joshua thought, sucking in his lip to bear the discomfort. *This is impossible!*

Joshua felt another strike of rock salt against his lower back. He flew forward onto his face and lay there. He screamed into the mat, frustrated.

"Was that really necessary, Cid?" The Marquis asked. Cid shrugged, "He didn't look hurt enough. If you're trying to push him then put a little backbone into it."

"I just want to go home!" Joshua groaned softly. His body shook in fatigue, pain, and anger.

The Marquis lowered his gun. He had a contemplative look about him. He wrinkled his nose and sniffled. "You could try, but I think you're here out of curiosity, and you're here because you want to survive. Perhaps you even feel a sense of duty to the world, after all, you are a detective, or, were a detective, and, in your past, you were a savior to certain people who could look past your methods."

"Why are we screwing around with swords, though?" Joshua hissed, his chin resting on the mat.

The Marquis looked at his gun, and then tossed it onto the floor near Joshua. Joshua gripped it and rose, turning it over end on end.

"What do you see in that gun?" The Marquis asked.

Joshua looked the gun up and down. It was a well-polished nine-millimeter. It held thirteen more rounds; its max capacity was about fifteen rounds without any modifications. It had a steel frame and wooden-polished grip pads.

"I see a gun, it's a simple, you point and shoot. You don't have to get close or dodge anything."

The Marquis chuckled. "I see a good weapon too, but it has one fatal flaw."

"And what's that?" Joshua spat.

"Ammunition, you can only use that gun several more times before it's just a fancy piece of scrap to bludgeon someone with." The Marquis smiled. "How many bullets could you carry if you stuffed your pockets? Two hundred? Maybe just fifty? You go into a forest with a rifle, but you can only hunt until you're out of bullets. The modern man is reliant on it. A child could use a gun, a weak man too, but, it only serves them if they have a bullet.

So, what happens when you get out there to Siberia, Mr. Hill? If it's a beast, it would probably take you more bullets than you could hold. If it's an army, the same rule applies, so on and so forth. Your success is determined by small brass cylinders, not your skill, not entirely, at least. Stamina, however, is the ammunition of the sword, the glaive, the pike. When you go out into Siberia, when you head into South America, you need something to carry you, even if it's just a knife. We're teaching you to fight until your dead, we're teaching you to have stamina. As long as you stand, the sword serves you. The gun needs to be fed, the sword does not. You need to learn how to get close to your enemy when that happens. That is why you can have your guns and your rockets and your grenades, but you must have your blade as well, and you have to know how to use it."

Joshua tossed the gun back to the Marquis.

"Do you think you're ready now, Mr. Hill? You'll suffer us for hours, but you'll catch on." The man asked with another complacent curtsy of respect.

"I'm ready." Joshua groaned.

At the end of the day, Joshua found himself spritely and swift. As the Marquis lunged forth and Cid swung about his waist, he could spin out of range or between the two freely and without fault.

Joshua's perception widened, shadows out of the corner of his eyes beckoned his unwavering attention to new threats. It was too much to say that Joshua was a master at surviving their swords, for, if they had wanted to maim him permanently, he knew they could.

At the end of that day, when he lay on the padded flooring drenched in an ocean of sweat and blood, the Marquis and Cid had to lift and tote him off to his bedding the floor above. They had taught him all they could about blades and bullets in such little time. They passed on their knowledge in that brief expanse of hours.

Joshua felt gratitude, but also contempt. It was The Marquis and Cid who gave him time, seeming to care about his wellbeing, but, it was also The Marquis and Cid who wished to use him as their tool for combat.

Joshua lay there petrified on his cot, finally reaching exhaustion as his muscles began to cool, and stared at the ceiling. He still longed to be home and wished all these events which led him to Moscow would cease to exist. That, like his dreams, he would wake up and find himself drunk on the table of a pub somewhere. That night, the detective was too sore to move, so he fell asleep without dinner, or lunch, or sheets to cover him. Yet, he did wake up with a cold dousing of water and a firm tap on the head.

Part 5/Ravage

"Wake up, Mr. Hill." The Marquis commanded, his
voice something like a lullaby. "Get a shower and meet us
outside. Your chariot awaits."

Joshua slowly rotated himself aloft. He pressed his
knuckles down upon his mat until they popped. He rose with a
lethargy, and rolled his neck, slowly sauntering off to the gym
restrooms. They were surprisingly clean for their age. Joshua
undressed and slowly turned the cold knob, letting the water
cascade down his scarred back. The blood that had saturated
on his skin the night before melted off his body and he seethed
under the pain of his cuts. Joshua rested his forehead under the
sprinkling waterfall and rubbed it against the white tile.

"Fuck," he whispered, the word repeating upon his
lips. "Why the hell am I here?! What am I about to do?!"

Joshua punched his knuckles against the wall, the
ceramic chipped and sliced at his fist. The blood ran thinly
down to the puddling floor and diluted into the drain between
his legs. Joshua punched that wall until the tile revealed a
layer of spackle and sheetrock.

Joshua hated all of them. They all decided to screw up
his life, they couldn't stay away. Elizabeth should have
realized that he wasn't some legend from America, he was just
a man that looked like someone else. The more he groped for
people to blame the more acute his aggression became. Joshua
realized it wasn't Elizabeth or Lafayette or even Baron
Whitecroft that started his wayward sojourn.

This sojourn was Solomon's fault. Solomon, the
unruly man who killed the Director. He was a murderer, a true
demon.

Joshua felt his jaw tighten. He had to do something
about Solomon. Joshua couldn't let people like him live. It
burned in his veins. Something deep inside him called out to

this desire. He wanted justice, revenge, benediction on this personified evil. He couldn't help himself. Solomon was it, that ripe pumpkin waiting to be smashed, the big fish Joshua would catch and gut. Joshua determined himself, determined himself for restitution. Restitution not only for himself, but for those who were harmed by his pale, burned hands.

Yes, it was all Solomon's fault.

However, something still didn't add up. What was this present Solomon wanted to give him? Did he know, that by framing Joshua for murder, he would be executed? Was that his present, death? Was this journey Solomon talked about a journey into the afterlife? Perhaps Solomon wasn't a lucid being, simply acting on a whim, ranting about random, insignificant, things and promises. If Solomon wasn't, what was he trying to do?

Joshua shifted his muscles about his body, feeling the cramps. He grinded the pain until it had seemed to go. With gritted teeth, he turned the shower off. Behind him hung a new set of clothes which he put on slowly. A pair of snow boots, snow pants, a thickly-woven sweater and a leather bomber jacket with fur about the collar. He slowly dragged his feet out of the restrooms, his hand gliding along the wall behind him, and found his way through the gym and into the city.

The morning air bit Joshua's nose; he quickly tucked his hands beneath his armpits. The Marquis and Cid stood a few feet before him, wrapping a tarp over some large crates in the back of a military truck bed. Among those crates lay a set of camping equipment, equipped with an interior burner, and a long gun case for a single, large-caliber rifle. Gnat sat silent in the driver's seat, his hands at two and ten. His helmet faced the road directly as if he was driving already. His fingers drummed on the wheel, as if impatient, or angry, at some sort of inviable pedestrian that wasn't crossing fast enough. Joshua wasn't confident the ex-soldier could see well through his cracked helmet. Joshua didn't believe he was fit to drive.

The Marquis noticed Joshua. He smiled and approached him, his countenance warm despite the chilling weather. He wore his usual long coat but paired it with a ushanka hat. A large pelt was wrapped about his waist like a sash, a long sabre tucked into it. The wind started to howl and whine, it obscured most of the buildings further from view and killed the voice of the Marquis whom shouted at him.

"It's terrible timing, but there's a storm coming in. I gave Gnat the directions. His helmet should help you navigate the blizzard, but you should be able to stay in front of it for a few hours! Everything you need is inside! Before you go, I wanted to make sure you took this!"

The Marquis produced a long medieval sword from behind him. It had a long cross guard and a sharp, pointed, hilt. In total, it was slightly under four feet in length. It came in a leather sheath that was wrapped in a thin, scarlet red, linen. The linen flapped in the wind like a flag, tied to the hilt like one would tie a pom-pom on a toddler's bike.

Joshua took it and slung it about his back. He strapped the buckle about his chest. It fastened perfectly.

"I know you hate swords, so I took some time to find you this too!" The Marquis added. He passed Joshua a thick, six-shooting, hand cannon. Joshua felt it in his hands and placed it in his coat.

"There's more ammunition in the back, should you need it!" The Marquis continued. "There's a hunting rifle in the back if food supplies run low, but you should have enough for two whole months should anything go wrong! The rest are assault rifles, grenades, some C4, you know, the good stuff!"

Joshua nodded. The Marquis placed his hand on Joshua's back and guided him to the passenger seat. Joshua climbed in and sat on the beat-up cotton. Gnat glanced over briefly.

"We'll see you when it's all over. God be with you, men!" The Marquis called. Cid jumped off the back of the truck with a thud. Joshua could see him shivering in the rear-view mirror. The engine cranked and sputtered. Gnat jammed the keys around roughly, forcing the truck to roar alive.

Joshua, still looking in the mirror, watched the Marquis back away and retreat toward Cid who stood near the gym entrance. As The Marquis slapped the rear of the truck, Gnat applied the throttle and they rolled forth and down the street, the two thieves shrinking in the distance.

Joshua watched the clouds roll behind them in the west. They thundered loudly and an occasional streak of lightning drew horizontally across the sky. Gnat glued his eyes to the windshield; his driving was fast-paced, almost brutish. The morning was too young for the city; it had not roared to life again. The truck's headlights showed them the street ahead as no lamp nor sign would brighten the asphalt for a few hours.

"We're going to be on the road for a long time today." Gnat spoke, his speakers crackling from damages rendered. Gnat broke the silence.

"North, right?" Joshua asked casually, still staring at the side mirror. Something in his mind kept him from looking away. Joshua half expected to see his face as he did in his dream of the children, writhing with tentacles, but, it did not change.

"Storm's going to roll over us before then." Gnat half-answered.

The road wound about the outskirt of the city which had now been swallowed by the cloud. It was a haboob of ice stretched like a wall as far as the eye could see. The Skyships still moved about lowly, their shadows being seen with the thunder. The city of the future, Moscow, was still at the whim of the earth, and still just a city as any other. But it was a place of odd happenstance, a city where each person had no more an identity than the last. They all were common faces, wore common clothes. It was the frontier of space on earth. The residents were all ants on a farm, no more different than the next. However, the self-proclaimed Marquis sat in his tavern with a lethal epidemic in his parlor, accompanied by a bartender named Cid.

If that was the true Marquis De Lafayette, where was his city in the sky and why did he sit in a gym for two days, teaching a detective how to survive the wilds, when he could sit on his throne above the world without care or consequence?

Up ahead, the Tundra of the Russian wilderness sprawled out like a canvas. Joshua watched the thermometer drop about 20 degrees as they left. He didn't know what to expect, but he remembered the headlines, the stories of large monsters people continued to pull out of the sea, out of forests. The world of fantasy lay before them, and Joshua thought he saw a large bird move out from the rocks. He had no idea of what he would experience, he only knew that he was heading for something large enough to cause change to the ground below it, something large enough to threaten an entire city.

If the stories were true and there were gods and demons and aliens and ghosts, Joshua was in over his head, as any mortal man would be.

As the hours flew by, much like the birds that fled far above him from the coming storm, Joshua watched as said storm started to consume them, finally. The wall of white powder was now at their backs, the rear of the bed was like a wafer brick, slowly being caramelized by a giant lob of cotton candy.

The blizzard opened its mouth and swallowed the duo with a large roar that would not cease until Joshua slept later on. Joshua could neither see in front of him nor hear the creak of the axles beneath him, which shuddered with each craggy bump upon the unrepaired road. He looked forward past the dashboard and saw not but a foot outside the car, a massive and all-encompassing blanket of pearl keeping the world Joshua knew cold and bitter.

Gnat stared forth. He knew where he was going, inside his helmet, he watched the sonar ping off of the trees and shrubbery. This gave him a visual guide of where he should go. Above his eye lay a virtual compass, an arrow, consistently rotating to provide a direct heading to their destination. A long line stretched before him as well, a virtual track. That is what he followed, a clairvoyant indicator, a digital railway.

Gnat's synthetic gloves gripped the aluminum wheel tightly. The thermometer had well struck below zero by this time and the internal air conditioning was cranked to maximum heat. Joshua could still see his breath. Eventually, the windows were iced over. The condensation had grafted into the glass, leaving nothing for the passengers to view. Joshua was pale as a ghost; Gnat shuddered.

Joshua's mind drifted, he thought of France, of his duty to the city of Paris. He hated the event of his exodus still, he loathed dawdling about the wilderness as if the anomaly was anything more important or treacherous than a serial killer.

It was late when the storm's fog became black and blue instead of pure white. The lack of sun did not help the heat either. Joshua folded himself in his seat for warmth and soon found himself in another series of harrowing dreams. He shot between each scenario, diving into the memories of monstrous acts he and his enemies committed. He had fettered his villainous self this way. In many ways, the dreams preformed a roost for him so that he might arise in the morning to convince himself he was still a good man, the right man, to do his job. But the children and the whores, the thieves and the cops, never seemed to agree with him. They never stopped fighting him in his dreams. Joshua also saw a new dream, one of being in a jungle, whence he was chased by large monkeys cursing his name. They swung on the treetops, their faces flat like mirrors, their fur colored like peacocks.

Eventually, they caught up to him, and beat him to death under their long, brawny, arms.

When dawn blurred into the still-frozen windshield, Joshua fluttered his eyes awake. He looked about the cabin, the torn leather seats, and the scratched dashboard. A bobblehead shook his disapproval for the venture above the radio. He was a burly image, a dapper man, insisting that they turn back.

Gnat didn't listen. On the radio, through an onslaught of static and feedback, played twenties's jazz happily, miraculously, despite their distance from any civilization.

Joshua listened for a time, tracing his memories back to the pubs of France. Those taverns couldn't get their hands on anything more modern, thankfully. There was a particular tavern, on the way out of Paris, that was posted along the perimeter of a small orchard. There they served the darkest and warmest beer in full pints instead of bottles. The people there acted barbarous in kind, bringing about a cliché old-world feeling. There were mourners in the corner, brawlers on the floor, and negotiators along the walls. They all forgave the offences of drunken men if they could still keep their fists up. Joshua thought would like to visit there again, should he survive this 'Moscow ordeal,' for there was something peculiar about that place that reminded him of heaven. There were no rules there, in particular, that any man would dare break, and so, no one for Joshua to watch over.

The radio faded out, the static now consuming the caravan's cockpit. Gnat reached over and turned the volume down to a minimum. He looked over to Joshua through his helmet. Even with the giant cask about his face, Joshua could tell he was still of serious composure and stoic thought. "Welcome to the Russian wilds," his speaker announced factually, "We're in the calm of the storm right now, so take a peek outside if you want."

Joshua gripped the icy window handle with his left hand and cranked the glass. It was jammed, but enough force of both will and strength saw to it, that the window slowly fell, much like the walls of Jericho. Joshua peered out, the frigid air stung his eyes, making them water.

The pair drove upon the top of a rift, two valleys rolled down each side of them. The tundra was covered in thick layers of snow, but still, against the climate and circumstances there stood an army of evergreens. It was a woodland and up ahead of them rose a frozen waterfall that rushed down into both valleys from a single forking river, shallow and frozen.

It was a beautiful sight. The sun struck against the wall of clouds surrounding them in the distance, sheltering this open grove from spying eyes. Although harsh and violent, the flora did not lack in beauty. There at the bottom of the valleys, and surrounding the rivers, collected tall and brittle mountain flowers purple like lavender. All life, sheltered from the storm before, had awoken to find their food, seeking to forage before the final bout of weather. They dashed around in the grasses looking for other life. They paid no mind except distance to the two vagabonds on their mission, the fauna either uncaring or uneducated about the evil of man. They did not seek to approach the car's steady climb; they merely hid and moved, evaded the world of sight like field mice in the spring. The density of life was staggering.

Joshua didn't have so many words in which to describe such a view himself, but it was something out of a painting. He realized it was something you might find in a museum of art. Joshua rolled the window to its close, the frost had melted in the heat of the vehicle, and thus the wipers pushed away the wet slush and exposed the elusive sun which remained hidden behind the storm. However, the small rays that passed through the clouds proceeded to enter Joshua's cab and caress his face with vitamin c. To the detective's delight, he no longer shivered in those moments.

"Were running low on gas. Once we make it to the other end of these ridges, we'll make camp and the storm should roll over us tonight. After refilling the tank we'll be a few thousand kilometers away from the anomaly. In the morning we'll move north and review its trajectory." Gnat summarized, his face still pasted to the bumpy road.

Joshua nodded slightly. He examined a large bag of chips in the glove compartment which had been bobbing colorfully before him. It was open, facing out of the latch, and half full. Gnat had been snacking.

Another day passed. The view, although beautiful in its own isolated way, never changed but for the shadow of the mountain which shrank and grew again as the sun moved east to west.

Joshua and Gnat rolled through the creek, the water running slightly above the tires. The bed was full of medium and well-rounded rocks. They passed over the stream with ease.

In the back, Joshua could tell the cargo sat well in its place. The tarp stayed secure but slightly flayed with the friction it underwent from the pelting snow. Joshua faced back forward and placed his feet on the dashboard in front of him. He reached between his legs and procured the chips from within, beginning to munch heartily. They were bland, aerated, and stale, but Joshua was not one to be picky. He ate until his stomach stopped its fussing and his tongue began to dry from the salt.

As the moon began to rise, the wind picked up again at a steady rate. Joshua and Gnat had found themselves at a small plateau on the other side of the cliff. Before them, a vast plain as far as they could see panned to the horizon. It was an ocean of snow, ice, and grassy flowers.

Gnat parked the car there and dismounted. Joshua followed suit.

The ledge in which they stood was small, about ten feet long, a jutting structure of rock from the hillside.

The soldier climbed into the bed. He did not remove the tarp, but rather, passed Joshua the camping set through the flaps. Joshua snatched it from his hand and put his knee to the fertile ground. He unzipped the package and pulled out the big orange fibers. The sticks rested on the bottom along with a small white paper for instructions.

Joshua didn't need them. He quickly threaded the sticks into the loops around the tent fabric and pinned the corners down with his boot.

It was an eight-man tent, the Marquis benevolent in space and luxury. In the center of the roof was a large hole for a stove chimney to rise through.

Gnat procured that and disappeared into the tent to quickly assemble it. Joshua tossed packaged food rations through the tent flap, then went to recover the sleeping bags. As he toiled, he stared at a black dot off on the horizon line. He wrinkled his mouth in a struggle to understand its composition.

"Bags," Gnat demanded, he stood at the flap of the tent which now puffed a thick black smoke from its hat.

The tent was radiant like a house with its lights on, a small little cottage of fiber for the two pigs to hide from a big, bad, frost wolf.

Joshua passed the sleeping bags over to Gnat along with a second pair for them to layer in. Gnat followed Joshua's eyes after closing the flap. He wanted to let the warmth stew inside the tent while he admired the black dot on the horizon.

"That looks like where the anomaly should appear from, that very spot over that horizon." Gnat stated, "It's going to be big, if it really can make a dent in the land, but we'll find out in a few days. I'll get the kitchenware."

Joshua nodded slowly. The temperature began to drop again. Through the crack in the crag, the wind screamed steadily. Joshua proceeded to move into the heat of the tent. His guide soon followed. They sat there in their sleeping bags

124

like eskimos while the stove gave a steady and merciful radiance quite unlike the old truck which creaked outside.

Gnat placed a pot inside the large mouth of the fire to begin cooking their first meal: dried meats in chicken broth with carrots and peppers. It seemed like a hearty combination to the both of them, considering it came out of a sealed plastic bag.

The duo of explorers didn't say much, merely, they thought in anticipation on what that dark speck might be. It loomed and seemed to haunt their thoughts. Within the tent, they couldn't see the odd object, and they didn't care to let the cold in so that they could discover whether or not it had grown any closer.

As the storm rolled over again and the snow beat against the tent, they slurped their broth and chewed their rubbery food. It was enough for them, for now.

The light now diminished from being, the winter wasteland now alive in its fury as Joshua and Gnat slept close to the stove, occasionally shifting to keep an eye in the coals and refuel it. They said nothing that night, and neither did they sleep for more than minutes at a time. No thoughts of home, nor women, nor revelry in the comfort of a city house, consoled them against the small infinitesimal blotch in the distance. In the moments that they blinked between cognition and hibernation, they could swear they dreamt up what it could be. However, when they woke again and again, they couldn't remember the details of its characteristics in the morning.

Eventually, the banshee winds and bullets of snow and sleet became nothing but another memory.

The morning was bright. The sun, now clear in the sky, penetrated the tent like a spotlight through a curtain on a stage. The duo woke with a chemical overdose, the lack of sleep and anticipation did not beget a lethargy in their brains, but the antithesis.

They lay outside their tent on a heated blanket which spread across the ground, their legs jittering, apprehensive. They had been there for the better half of an hour, the snow beneath the blanket melted and permeated through the thin soil.

A large rifle sat before Gnat, he gazed through it as if preparing for a shot. He aimed it towards the horizon, its high-powered sight worked like a telescope. He searched for the anomaly with Joshua, who held a pair of low-powered binoculars. He played with its zoom but found nothing.

"Do you really think that dot was what we are looking for?" Gnat asked again, he aimed off to the right and slowly panned left.

"I thought about it all night. We can't take the risk of moving onward if we are closer than we thought we were. I know it should be moving slowly, but something tells me it's here. My gut is telling me we shouldn't go just yet." Joshua murmured. Although his body surged with energy, his tongue was asleep, bouncing oddly in his mouth as he struggled to form words.

What Joshua and Gnat didn't witness in the distance they reconnoitered was a large hill which perfectly blended into the surrounding grasses. It provided a slightly steeper gradient than the horizon beyond their field of view. Behind that long knoll lay their target which began to slowly heave itself over the hill. It appeared immediately before Gnat through the scope, rising like a pale and sickly sun over the hill. It was a massive and putrid creature. If one were to imagine a Matryoshka doll, this beast, this ball of flesh, would consume a whale as if it were the smallest piece before proceeding to swallow other, greater, beings. It was the personification of gluttony.

They watched it in horror, it shifted about like a grub across the field, its long tongue draped out of its mouth and licked its belly button with a pool of salivation like a cravat. In lieu of its ears shot out many human bodies, both from its head and beneath its baggy flesh. It was as if people had been pressed into its body like animated scraps of dough, a child mashing clay figurines together.

The legions of bodies both male and female were hidden and flailing beneath the beast's skin, trapped and squirming. They waved their arms in celebration but called forth in agony. The giant's eyes were large and skewed, almost displaced into the side of its head like an iguana or chameleon. A thin layer of mucus covered its skin and the liquid froze in lumps that slid down its piggish body until they slapped the ground and were left to burn holes like acid.

The beast was white and wet. It boasted four arms, but three of them grew about its right shoulder, the left holding only a singular limb, bigger than that of the other three. Where it walked, dents were left in its trail, creating a plowing line of its pus to seed the earth. With long and gnarled toes, he stamped himself along the plains. The cracks it left in its wake continued to falter and shift, slowly moving down further into the ground, compressing, as if the gravity about the giant was more than the natural earth could bear.

It was disgusting to say the least; no more words could be said between the party as the bile shifted about their stomachs. The acid fizzed about their esophagi, and they forced it down with a shudder. Even from their distance, they could catch the animal's scent. Joshua watched it more, taking in its details. From the flaps on its skin to the lard that collected in lumps on its body and rolled over itself. There was a thin haze of putrescent body odor under the legion of arms and torsos, green air like that of a toxin. One could almost guess it was a cruel mixture of rotting eggs and decomposing rats coupled by hundreds of sweating, flailing, armpits. It had to be at least the size of a small building, perhaps the size of a Baron's house.

The titan's teeth were not within its mouth but coming out of its lips, reminding Joshua of a Venus fly trap. Its ass drug behind it like a tail, its hands could possibly lift its fat like a dress before descending a flight of stairs, if it had the ability to look couth. Its nipples were small black dots like marbles, piercings long conquered by the skin and surrounding lard. It approached the mountainside in a small trotting pace.

"What the hell is it?" Gnat gasped and quickly passed the rifle over to Joshua.

Joshua huffed, "I have no idea."

The ex-detective watched the beast's eyes, it had stopped and glanced around the plain. It huffed as if to smell something peculiar that was not its own odor. The titan slowly turned to its right and paused. It almost looked attentive, looking for someone.

Joshua couldn't tell what it was looking at nor what had caught its eye. Its boggish pupils rolled about inside its head in different directions.

The beast paused and whipped his head around suddenly, staring straight into the lens and into Joshua's eyes. Joshua shuddered and felt his hairs stand on end. Slowly, he pressed the safety button and his finger hovered over the trigger.

"What the hell are you doing?!" Gnat hissed.

"It knows I'm here." Joshua whispered, "It knows *exactly* where we are."

The beast started to slime its way forward, at first slowly, then accelerating. It moved towards the two, the folds jiggling about its knees. For a giant bag of flesh and water, it moved surprisingly fast. It loomed in the distance, still a pygmy outside Joshua's telescopic view. Joshua knew it would be a matter of minutes until the beast was upon them.

"Gnat, get the car ready!" Joshua demanded, pulling the bolt back to load the first bullet. Gnat nodded and rose, quickly beating the tent into submission and tossing it into the truck bed. Joshua knew they didn't have enough time. Even if they were to drive off now, the beast was already running faster than the car could descend the long winding slope into the valley. Driving off would merely buy them a few more minutes.

Joshua fired his first round and watched the streak of light zoom over the hills. Unsurprisingly, he missed. Joshua coolly cocked the bolt again and took a deep breath. He squeezed the trigger again. The bullet slapped the beast on the chest and reverberated its skin like the surface of water. Despite the large caliber and direct hit, the bullet did not deter the titan from his course.

"Hurry up!" Joshua shouted, cocking the gun again and firing. The Marquis was right, bullets were terribly ineffective against beasts.

Joshua heard the truck ignition and quickly stomped over to the driver's seat. Gnat plopped down next to him and took the rifle from Joshua quickly. Gnat saddled over to the truck bed and aimed the rifle at the beast. His feet pressed against the tailgate to steady him. The bipod rested on the stove box.

Joshua changed gears, twisted the car and moved it down the crag with a heavy shudder. They weaved about the north face gradually, and soon found themselves heading out towards the far crags. Joshua pushed on, slamming the pedal repetitively for torque over the large rocks wedged under their wheels. They shambled on slowly. Gnat kept the sight steady on the ravine they escaped from, waiting for its head to peek about the ridgeline. If the beast hadn't slowed at all...

Gnat cocked the bolt and began loading bullets back into the magazine hastily. "IT'S GOING TO BE ON US ANY MINUTE!" he warned, shouting over the thumping of cargo.

Joshua careened through the roads, they now drove downhill at a blistering pace of twenty miles an hour, not that it was enough to escape their pursuer.

The Titan now looked colossal in lieu of the cliff they had exfiltrated. It was at the first series of mountain shapes, where Joshua and Gnat had slept.

The beast ran into the mountainside, but it was not the beast's body that gave way, it was the mountain's rock that shattered and erupted from its placement into hundreds of large rocks. The formidable crag that took them the better of a day to scale, took the giant a second to destroy. The rocks flew forth towards Joshua and Gnat like an avalanche of meteors.

Joshua swerved to and fro, weaving between the collapsing debris that threatened to flatten them.

"Keep it steady!" Gnat shouted through the rear window.

"Like hell I can do that!" Joshua shouted back, a thick bead of sweat running down his cheek.

The truck rattled against the smaller rocks, the axles churned about with hideous metallic cacophonies. Joshua had his foot to the floor of the truck, but the old machine didn't have the will to flee faster than the monster chased them.

With no time to think or waver, Joshua jerked the wheel and moved off the beaten path. The mountainside had become more of a hillock in the distance they had covered. The rigid landscape started to wave and subside into flat land. The boulders of the mountain, now no more a rock than a mound, littered the plains like a dog might litter his feces onto a wooden floor. They jutted out of the ground where they made impact like balls of yarn, and still, more rained down from the heavens like Sodom and Gomorrah. The Titan was only a few hundred yards away. Gnat fired his first bullet, but it had missed, zooming past the Titan's left tit.

"Damnit!" Gnat shouted, loading another round into the rifle. He took aim again and fired.

He missed again.

Joshua glanced over his shoulder, the beast's shadow touching their taillights. Its flaps flapping in a hideous anti-rhythmic clapping.

Joshua watched Gnat load another bullet. He took aim, he breathed out, he waited until he the road was smooth, and his sight lined perfectly. Gnat squeezed the trigger, the bullet passing through the Titan's right eye. It screamed and wailed, resounding with a large guttural sigh of compressed air, a sound akin to singing with a mouth full of liquor and a bullhorn.

Gnat loaded another bullet, the Titan close enough to the truck that the steel frame bounced with each shudder of the earth. It was too close to miss, wherever Gnat shot would meet its mark. The soldier fired the rifle as fast as he could, jiggling the bolt in and out, a fistful of brass in his right hand.

The bullets sunk into the blubber of the whale and the behemoth shuddered and stooped down. The fat had shifted down on its body as it leaned, and it drug the beast down into the permafrost with a large and thundering crack. This impact rattled a final shockwave through the ground and a giant cloud of dust boiled out from the soil.

Joshua couldn't see anything as the dustbowl enveloped their vehicle. He looked forward through squinted eyes, but it was too late to adjust his course. In the moment he had seen boulder appear before the bonnet, he had already collided with it head on. The force of the impact sent Gnat catapulting over the rock and onto the grass out of Joshua's view before he blacked out momentarily.

Littered and shattered around Joshua was all the equipment the duo had packed. Much like Gnat, they had been launched during the collision. Joshua bled over the steering wheel, his mind fighting to stay afloat. Still, he managed to unbuckle his seat belt, open the door and fall out onto the ground. Joshua looked up from the dirt to hear the sound of footsteps. He closed his eyes for an unknown amount of time, if only for a second of rest, before he felt a firm hand on his chest.

Gnat found his way back to Joshua and shook the man by his shoulder.

"Agh!" Joshua choked, clutching his stomach. Looking to Gnat, he softened slightly, "You're still alive?"

Gnat pointed to his helmet and then at his invisible mouth, motioning for Joshua to stay quiet. He whispered. "Get up and be quiet Hill. This isn't over yet. The beast will be back any second."

Joshua mouthed inaudible curses and pulled his pistol from his shirt. His comrade helped him rise by the shoulder.

They couldn't see very far about them, only four feet or so. Barely they could make out the shadows of the meteors. They were in a minefield of boulders that dotted the landscape, created by the mountain they once slept upon. Soon, the dust would settle, and they wouldn't be able to hide from the Titan.

Joshua listened to the moans of the beast, its voice echoing off each rock, making it hard to triangulate its position. Wherever it was, it was angry.

"We'll split up." Gnat insisted, "Pincer movement, if were at two different directions, we might be able to pin him down."

Joshua nodded wiping the dirt from his face. Gnat let go of Joshua's shoulder and the ex-detective watched as the Sentinel disappeared into the smoke. Joshua walked in the opposite direction painfully and skirted his way about the fallen debris. He didn't know where the giant was, but he kept quiet, and listened.

Surrounded by the thin light of the sun which filtered through the smoke, Joshua noticed that the world began to darken, yet it was only morning. He looked about for a sign of the enemy but heard the thick leg of the Titan before he saw it.

The Titan stomped the ground on the other side of the rock, seemingly patrolling, on search for delicious humans. Joshua watched it clamber and step on its own fat. The Titan towered so high that Joshua could only make out its body to its waist, its cratered belly button.

Joshua slowly readied his pistol. He felt like a minnow in a shallow puddle. He hid beneath the water and explorers, with their boots, would kick their way into the world from above without fair notice, threatening to take Joshua's life without remorse.

The titan's gelatinous legs shifted about the same position for a time making the ground tremor. Every little move shook the earth enough to make Joshua feel unstable on his toes.

Joshua waited, and then, waited some more. The Titan started to move away from Joshua's hiding place. Joshua sighed.

His mistake.

The sky began to darken ever more. Joshua looked up. Above him, through the smoke, fell a triad of giant hands trying to squash Joshua like a bug. Joshua leapt to the ground right before the hands slapped the earth, turning to find himself between the beast's index finger and middle finger. He lay right between both digits in some odd expanse of luck. The fingers were like the tree trunks of an oak, the nails like spears, sharpened, to tear through a kodiak.

Joshua rose and unloaded his gun into the index finger. The bullets penetrated its sickly, moist flesh, and the beast screamed. It raised its set of hands back into the sky and out of view.

Joshua sprinted away.

The American slid down beneath another rock and huffed. However, it wasn't long until he was discovered again. The Titan picked up the boulder by which Joshua hid and exposed him like an ant.

Joshua ran away again; he juggled his pistol trying to feed it more ammunition. Looking over his shoulder, he watched as the beast lobbed the rock towards him. Joshua looked ahead for safety. There in the distance the truck was breaking, he had made a circle back to the start. Joshua slid neatly under the truck bed and emerged about the other side. The boulder slammed into the car and ricocheted into the air in a small parabola before descending in the distance, shattering in a heap much like loose sandstone. The car skid a few feet back and the axles dislocated, dropping the frame to the ground just after Joshua emerged from the other side.

Joshua continued to run from the vehicle and the Titan behind him. It loomed over him in a slow and groggy pace. Perhaps its wounds had taken its toll, or, the pursuit of humans tired it. The beast now hulked about in slow but long strides behind the rugged American, wheezing. It leaned over again and swept its arm low along the ground. The web of arms arced towards him like an ancient flyswatter. The Titan's long nails brushed the back of Joshua's jacket, tearing his coat open, opening the flesh.

Joshua turned, his firearm loaded again, and fired at what he could see, the monster's chubby legs. They smacked into the being with a satisfying thump and punctured its skin in small dots. It screamed its disapproval, no more damaged than irritated. The large caliber hand gun was the equivalent of a wasp's sting in a man, or a bb pellet in a lion.

Joshua saw the second arm too late, it swooned down from the opposite direction and slammed into Joshua's upper body. The sheer force launched him across the field where he finally rolled across the ground to a stop at the sound of crunching bones.

Joshua found his impact at the edge of the dust cloud. Joshua looked up slowly, expecting the beast to be upon him, stomping him to death, but it wasn't.

In Joshua's fall, he could have sworn he heard a gunshot that was not his own.

Joshua looked to the beast that looked away from him. It had noticed something more interesting. Something else preoccupied it. In the dissipating miasma Joshua made out what the beast found so intriguing. Joshua squinted to see Gnat in the distance, poised on a rock. Gnat's rifle flashed with a loud bang, the same bang as before. He sat there patiently until the bullet sliced at the beast's head and popped its alternate eye.

The beast roared with disdain as the puss in its socket began to shower the floor like rain.

Joshua looked back to find Gnat, but he had already disappeared from his nest. Joshua turned as the giant gripped its tongue using his morphic ears. The humanoids draped themselves across its face like a sleeping mask, gripping at the pink taffy. They let out sorrowful sobs that crawled beneath Joshua's skin, singing a song of mourning for the loss of their sight.

Joshua had no reason to feel pity for the beast and rapidly reloaded his gun. He aimed for the titan's face through his iron sights. This was his final batch of bullets, but he let them ring, knowing that there might not be a better time. The lead broke upon the human torsos, the ears of the Titan. The ears wailed in agony, one of them limping as if dead; another broke about its waist and dangled by a thin attachment of skin like a torn earlobe. It flopped about like an earring, a stray leaf on a winter branch.

Out from the thick mist, another crack of a rifle sounded, it found its mark on the right pectoral of the beast. Unlike the previous bullets, this streak of metal did not stay lodged in its breast. Instead, the bullet ripped through and out of the beast. This created a wide wound that seeped of liquid fat resembling microwaved butter. The beast turned and left Joshua to his own.

Joshua felt sick, his mouth now encased a vagabond pool of acid. He quickly hunched over to let it out, still keeping a keen eye on the colossus which slowly gathered itself from the blow. The beast contorted back to the graveyard where Gnat had fired the shot in guerilla-esque fashion.

This Titan seemed like a single-minded brute. It only payed heed to what last occupied its mind. If such a thing were true, Joshua knew it could be outwitted. Joshua straightened himself and unclasped his sword from its sheathe behind him. He stole forth, sword drawn, its tip dragging the ground on his right, drawing a line in the grass. He entered the dust storm and prepared himself.

Joshua could hear the gunfire, see brief flashes of muzzle flare like obscured lightning. Joshua made way to the ruckus. He no longer hid, he knew no range nor rock would protect him from the beast. He began a determined sprint forth, his knuckles white around the hilt, quickly, he arrived back to the truck.

Joshua looked left as he heard the sound of splintering wood. Upon approaching, Joshua found Gnat slumped against a small partition of debris, his rifle was shattered, and his arm bent back, broken in two. He looked at Joshua through his helmet.

"Piss," he sighed, "I gave it my best, but the Marquis was right, this isn't a world for guns." He coughed, a small portion of blood oozing from his gasket. "I'll be alright, I can patch myself up… Go! Show that wretched thing what we can do."

Gnat grimaced and pulled at his thigh. From a leather holster he produced a combat knife. "It isn't much, not like your sword, but just in case you find yourself without." Gnat coughed again.

The Russian soldier rested his head against the rock. Joshua held his shoulder for a second, making sure that his ally was going to make it.

Joshua had to lead the beast away from Gnat. He had to pull it out of the cloud, somewhere he could see everything his enemy was about to do.

Joshua moved back to the truck, there had to be something he could use as bait. He looked in the bed, the stovetop was the only thing left in the rear.

It would have to do.

Joshua snatched the tin from the bed and took off through the dust. He sprinted through the grey fog without aim. Eventually he would arrive in the open fields. Joshua opened the stovetop package and took two sections of the pipe in each hand. As he ran, he bashed the pipes together. The density and the radius of the tubes carried resonance, carrying a sound like church bells. Joshua continued to do this until he found himself out in the open field. Here, the young detective could move freely and see the beast.

Joshua dropped the stovetop set and turned around. He watched as the titan emerged from the cloud thicket. First, its belly poked from the floating debris, second, its flat and wounded face, and third, its massive thighs.

Joshua steeled himself, everything that he had done during the fiasco at the gym was done not in preparation to save Moscow from this menace, but to save himself from a life in the menace of Moscow. Dealing with this cretin, this demon of gluttony, this Titan, was the key, the ticket, for him to go home. After this, Joshua would find his way, vindicated by the saints, back to Paris to find and kill the man that ruined his life.

The Titan lunged forth from the haze, its arms flailed like a child in a seemingly half-assed attempt to crush Joshua. Joshua feinted to the side of the towering, rank, demon. He found himself at its shoulder, where it now bent in a quazi-body slam, its legs still poised to move against the ground like pistons. It was a resting dog, tucked over its hind legs.

Joshua drove his blade down the beast's forearm. The steel gashed through, gripping into flesh like an invisible hook and tether. The skin was unzipped this way and, oozing its slime, it coated Joshua's blade like a resin. The blade tore out with a large rip that revealed thick white bone.

Joshua pivoted and readied himself yet again and the monster rose to reassert its homicidal vendetta. The cryptid swiped with its arms, the set of three appendages careening straight for Joshua.

Joshua couldn't dodge, being far too close to outrun the length of the hand. He rose his sword high above his head and thrust it down into flesh when the hands collided with his body. Joshua held tight as the impact threatened to remove him from his grip on the blade.

As the arm finished its swing and returned to its origin, Joshua was lifted in tandem, refusing to let go of his weapon. He hung there about one of its many palms. With his spare hand, Joshua produced Gnat's knife and began to hack at the beast's forearm. As he hacked, he pulled himself up onto the limb and stood upon it like a fallen tree. Joshua lifted his sword and ran forth to the demons face as fast as his fatigued limbs would allow him. The Titan saw him, it opened its mouth as if to say something, to plead for mercy, but no words were uttered forth.

Even if the being was sentient, Joshua thought, it couldn't be allowed to live, could it? Surely, it was hell bent on destroying Moscow, but, if he stopped it here, he might never know.

Joshua stumbled about the long pink path, the Titan trying to shake it from its arm. Joshua dove into the beast arm as it shook, driving his two blades deep into the forearm. He rode the movement like a mechanical bull. Once the beast grew tired, Joshua rose and continued his advance.

The Titan ran its hand along its shoulder in response to the pest. The monster brushed at Joshua. The detective watched the branch approach him, the thick gnarly hand. He knew he would have this one moment to make his accent meaningful. He had proceeded thus far, and he wouldn't fail nor fall now.

Joshua urged his body faster as the limb approached. He planted his boot firmly and pushed himself into the air with a gallant leap over the arm. Joshua rotated in the air, directing his blade downward. The American prepared for impact with the thing's bunched and crippled face, descending the metal deep into its neck. Blood spewed like a geyser and the monster writhed. Joshua's grip, between the red water, animal fat, and G force, was lost.

Joshua plummeted to the ground and met the soil with an immense twinge of whiplash.

Even after Joshua's mighty push, the beast did not die. The layers upon layers of fat acted as its shield, a gelatin to prevent damage, a substitute that protected its bone and organs. Joshua's only option was to bleed it slowly and survive until it finally keeled over.

Joshua bore his fingers around Gnat's razor and waited in anticipation for the demon's next attack. It sobbed a very trough-like cry. Perhaps it was in pain, perhaps it bade Joshua to loom closer and, leveraging its feigned vulnerability, betray trust to roll over him.

Perhaps it had feelings.

Joshua paced around it, his torso locked perpendicular to his foe. The blood in his veins throbbed in rhythm with his heart, his hair stood on end, his senses adjusted into something vicious, something feral. He was confident in his killer resolve, he was immersed in his own energy and willpower. Whether this beast was truly wounded of not, it did not matter to him, he would prevail over it and forge his way home.

Joshua huffed and wiped the sweat from his brow. He shrugged his coat from his back and let the frigid air of Siberia between his knitted sweater. Joshua roared like a lion, he was prepared for the warpath, and trumpeted his advance.

Joshua rushed the Titan with his dagger. Ahead of him, it paid immediate heed to the small warrior. It reached out in an aggressive attempt to snatch the bug from the ground, but as it stretched out its hands, it lost visual of the human in its own shadow and through its ruined eyes. The beast removed its hand to find Joshua and, indeed, it found the small animal near its left flank.

Joshua climbed the beast again about its left leg, as he climbed, he slashed large gaping wounds into the Titan's thick skin with his knife. He used these cuts as handles for his ascent, tossing his feet into them for a secure hold. He grimaced, his body burning with fatigue. The beast twisted about, lifting its leg, and slapped Joshua like a wasp. Joshua separated from the beast and fell to the ground. He rolled amuck to his feet and continued his puny attack against the monster.

This time, as the Titan recovered, Joshua slid into its right toe and leapt onto its foot. The man stabbed it relentlessly, severing the small digits. The beast kicked Joshua off his bridge and hobbled. It yelped like a child with a stubbed toe.

Joshua tumbled through the force, this time slightly slower to find his feet. He stretched his back and popped it awkwardly, his shoulders cocked and heaving with each breath. Joshua's body was covered in many cuts from the rocks and grassy thorns he was tossed upon. The American felt his joints near-breaking, but, he ignored their desperate plea for rest. He breathed as much blood and mucus as air.

Joshua sprinted back to the beast whom swiped him. Narrowly vaulting over the appendage, cutting it lightly with his razor, he tumbled. Joshua continued his assertion and found himself at the beast's crotch. Joshua leapt in between its legs and began to grapple himself, slashing all the while. As the slashes were accrued, the beast, overcome by fatigue, staggered back and fell onto its spine.

Joshua bounced upon the beast's sternum and flew from the Titan, crashing into the ground by its neck. Joshua groaned, his body was lead, his brain swirled in fatigue. Beside him, the Titan panted, its bodies sagged in tandem.

Joshua gripped the soil with his hands and slowly inched himself back to the beast. He heard its labored, gurgling breathing. The beast was choking slowly on its own grease. Joshua couldn't wait for it to die. It had to die immediately. If chance would have it that the monster should rise up in greater fervor, Joshua would not be able to exact his revenge, his body acquitting energy.

The fevered avenger lifted himself on the beast's neck, his torso sliding against a combination of salivation and oil.

Joshua reached for his sword and wrapped his shaking hand about its red sash. Slowly he felt the blade give way, opening the severed artery and releasing accumulated blood.

The Titan let out a defeated grunt. It lay there beside Joshua like a deer shot in the woods, breathing its last, looking about for help. Its fractured eyes met Joshua's with a deep-seated pain and hatred. The wounds about its cornea bled profusely; the blood that shed from the beast by hundreds of lesions now created a long corridor that flowed like a stream downhill. It was a crimson walkway for a triumphant man. It was a carpet to begin Joshua's entrance into a new world of dark, foreboding, things.

Joshua stared back at the sorry giant and breathed in unison. With it, their powerful but shallow gasps emanated as a chorus for the gods of death. Soon, Anubis would ferry this beast into heaven, or hell, or an eternity of darkness and plain thought. Only Joshua and Gnat would be left to remember its existence.

The titan's sentient ears seemed to limp like that of a dog's flopping ears, they occasionally flicked with life, almost rising up. Their hands occasionally brushed Joshua's wrist as if trying to pet him, plead unto him to possess the humanity he had not in his heart. Joshua watched for what seemed his own eternity. The Titan lost its life over the course of minutes, dissipating into nothing more than a hulk of fat and liquid.

Joshua rested there. As he did, the beast's layer still gave out a radiating warmth like that of a furnace. This heat stung Joshua's wounds, but also, kept his body awake and safe from the frigid air. Now that Joshua's adrenaline was gone, he was cold.

The sun had begun to descend before the young slayer, and soon, Joshua stared into the vibrant night sky. He could make out the milky way perfectly, the myriad of constellations and nebulae. The young detective could almost, through his squinting eyes, watch what seemed to be a moving star, flickering like a strobe, waning across to the horizon.

Joshua's eyes followed that light to the horizon as it passed. This vector of sight led him to make out the shape of Gnat sauntering towards him. The broken solider hobbled with a sling made of tent tarp. He let himself down next to Joshua with a sigh and passed his companion a cigar with a lighter. Joshua fell from his cushion softly and gave a thin, heroic harrumph.

"Found them in the glovebox," Gnat murmured, letting Joshua light his first.

Gnat took off his helmet, but even in the faint light of the cigar cinder, Joshua couldn't see Gnat's face. They sat in silence and let out long puffs of smoke. Today was the start of something different. Today was the day Joshua bought his ticket home.

Little did Joshua know, that somewhere deep inside, he didn't long for his past occupation anymore. A part of him wanted this: a silent world with a subtle sun sliding down the edge of his known world. But even in the vigor, the sense of purpose and serenity, Joshua still felt the docile, metropolitan lull demand his attention. Joshua couldn't find any hope in his vision. He knew he would not have a future such as this. His life was built at the base of civilization, and he bore the weight of every individual brick in society. Joshua couldn't ignore others, only to give him rest. He was a callous thinker, an avenger. He couldn't be so selfish as to run away.

The pair stood as the sun set behind their Titan, the beast cast a long shadow across the two. Sore and dark-eyed, they moved back to the truck and sat in it for a time, tampering with the electronics that still functioned. Fortunately for them, the radio was still operable, and at its particular position in unison with the slab, it had a channel playing classical Russian opera. The two didn't dare change it, afraid they would break it.

After dozing an hour or two, Joshua abandoned Gnat there in the menial warmth the iron casket provided and walked back to the beast.

The Titan had already succumbed to decomposers, its wounds wiggled with maggots and worms. Joshua felt sick and quickly collected his coat and the stovetop kit before turning his back and leaving.

Back at the truck, Joshua draped his ruined coat over the bed. Gnat seemed to have fallen asleep and lay across the chairs haphazardly, a faint snoring noise humming from his mask. Joshua foraged the crates closest to the wreckage and found a generous number of rations, a few cartridges of rifle ammo, and a small sack of coal. He dragged these slowly back to camp.

Joshua appointed himself to start a fire. He found an ample amount of rocks that had jettisoned from the mountain and arranged them in a circle neatly, stacking a few portions of coal within. Then, he plucked whatever brown grass he could for tinder. His lighter did the rest and the fire soon bade him to relax. Joshua lay there on the ground, the dirt caressing his shirt, glued from the slime. His back faced the fire and toasted it as if he were to be eaten. He could feel the flames lick his spine, sear and whittle at his nerves. In Joshua's mind, that pain was welcome. He didn't mind being uncomfortable. Joshua rested his mouth into the dirt, his neck about a jagged rock, and tried to get some rest.

The sun hung about midday when Joshua finally rose. He juggled a rock in his hand thoughtfully while his spare hand opened a dry ration. He gnawed at the cold flake until it satisfied his hunger. His stomach, however, grumbled for something more tangible, more couth.

Joshua's spoiled body kicked about like a child, his ribs felt apt to burst, bruises pecked at his thighs and shoulders. He wasn't entirely sure about treating his small scrapes for bacteria or leaving them be, they didn't seem any greener than the grass stains on his trousers. When he had dragged his lazy legs over to the cockpit to ask Gnat whether he had another cigar in his possession, he gazed upon the vacant seats, confused. He wasn't sure whether Gnat had abandoned him, or simply gone off to piss.

Joshua climbed into the empty chair and stared at the boulder through the windshield. He was transfixed on the rugged surface, slate and brown. He stared at it like an artist would a blank canvas, but his mind came back with no idea nor creative jest of what he could paint. The young lad tapped his finger against the bobble head on the dashboard, it shook its disapproval and scolded him. *"The Marquis is a fraud, he used you and he's not coming to save you."* The bauble said.

Joshua stared left out the far window. The view was breathtaking. The tall grains of the plains rippled in unison. It reminded him of a woman's hair, flowing like water, blonde and wavy. He, having experienced the worst these past few days, found it not *too* fantastical if the ground were to rise beneath him. He would not be surprised if the whole plain was the sideburn of some roguish deity with muttonchops.

Overall, Joshua's heart was underwhelmed. His mind still dared to surmise the threat he had vanquished, its hulking figure, its wide legs and long teeth. Now, the fear set upon him, a deep-seated fear that did not show on his face, but laid siege on the health in his heart. His hair stood on end again, his muscles tense as if ready for a marathon. Joshua opened the door and folded himself out rapidly, he fell to his knees and bunted on the floor yet another time. His ration was before him, he watched it seep into the firmament. Not only did Joshua now understand the horror of the titan, he understood the horror of Solomon.

Gnat appeared by the fire and watched Joshua retch constantly. Joshua looked like a victim of war, a man with disease written on his face. The ex-soldier let the ex-detective be by himself. Any interaction and Joshua might end up worse than he already was.

As Gnat blinked, watching his comrade pour his stomach about his hands, he was intrigued. His eyes must have played tricks on him, his mind tired and longing for civilization. Next to Joshua, or so it seemed, knelt a pale and burnt man in a yellow raincoat, this man rubbed Joshua's back, patted it, as if consoling the detective. Gnat blinked again but the image was gone until the next bat of his eye showed him and vanished over again with his final blink.

Gnat looked at his sensors in his helmet, no life but Joshua's had been recognized by the system, and Gnat trusted that. He wouldn't tell anyone of his vision, he was simply tired and hallucinating, nothing more.

Joshua finished his retching and spat onto the ground, the bile in his stomach rotting his insides. He saw Gnat about the corner of his eyes and tripped over to the campfire to join him in the heat. An illness was taking hold, his body heat plummeted. Joshua found himself shivering, trying to hug the fire as close as he could without becoming the fire himself. Gnat tossed in a few more coals to aid Joshua. The soldier roasted broth near the flame in a small cooking pot. It bubbled and churned.

Gnat closely watched Joshua. He didn't want to take his eyes off him. He could see people's intent through their eyes, their will to live. After a horrendous crisis, he could know which soldiers would desert. He could foresee whether he would find them later with a bullet between their eyes or a rope about their necks. This was his skill as a guard, the ability to know the conditions of those about him. But, Joshua was different. Even in the American's lack of emotions, there was a deep-seated erasure about him. Joshua was steady, but all the while harboring a sinister intent. Joshua had a dominating presence, an exuding power that almost seemed to visibly radiate from him.

Perhaps, Gnat thought, he wasn't human. After all, he did just destroy a behemoth without shattering every bone in his body. Truly, Joshua seemed to be no less injured than when he began. Maybe the Marquis was on to something, that monsters called to him, that he was one with the wilds. No simple man could have conquered a cryptid single-handedly, especially *that* cryptid, and live unmaimed. Joshua seemed dangerous, now lethal and menacing. The soldier was almost terrified of his potential. He was threatened, that at any moment, Joshua, with his immense power and presence, would take his's life if he wanted to. Realizing this also made Gnat immensely grateful: Joshua was on his side and was a seemingly righteous man.

Even though this banter encouraged him, an antithesis provoked his mind. Gnat promised himself that, should the day come when Joshua became too strong or became wicked, he would not rest until the American was dead.

There is a week left unaccounted for. A week of general talk and menial work, the coal had been used, the fire left stoked. Joshua steadily healed under the vigilant eye of Gnat. They stayed there for hours, maintaining warmth, eating, talking, and listening to the radio. They shared rations, they shared cigars, slowly building up this doubt: *they were forgotten.* Yet, as the week began to close, so did the sound of company close in on them. For on that day, in the clear sky there flew a large and immaculate skyship out of the sun. It neared them, and in that view, the duo could see the Marquis with one foot on the bow. He leaned off to the side with an impressing smile. His hair batted in the wind.

Part 6/Ride

The Skyship lowered itself, the large balloon which lifted the frigate illuminated in beautiful patchwork orange, the heat of the hot air spouting with long audible sighs. Despite the noise, so thick and sharp, Joshua found it a comfort; it was something quite unlike the Russian radio and the crack of the fire. It was a new sound, and Joshua drew towards it.

The Marquis dismounted his craft and strode towards his friends with open arms. He seemed to carry the role of a savior in his stance, or a foreign ambassador greeting his people upon return. In many ways, he might have been confused with a god or an angelic messenger, coming down in a vision to redirect the faith of the world. If they be his disciples, Joshua certainly thought he would be the least of them, like Judas Iscariot or Peter.

Joshua briskly walked into Lafayette's approach. However, instead of embracing the Marquis, as was suggested by his posture, Joshua tossed his sheathed sword and his coat into his arms, treating him like a coat rack. The Marquis was startled but, without breaking his countenance, he gracefully wrapped the cumbrance about his shoulder to keep them from falling over, happily turning from prince to pack-mule.

Gnat toted the kitchen set behind him, pausing to extinguish the fire with the leftover broth from lunch. He greeted the Marquis formally and the shipmaster helped him with his equipment. Joshua turned about the skyship and gripped the ladder that descended from the deck. He tightened it with his foot, letting Gnat climb first, conscious of his crippled arm. Then, he climbed, the Marquis following.

The deck was an illustrious amber beauty. Crewmen swabbed the deck and kept the wood glowing with polish. All about the trio swarmed men busy in their labors, none of which Joshua knew. The men of the ship all wore white and oversized Henley shirts, if they wore a shirt at all. They wrapped their heads in rags to keep their sweat about their forehead, repelling the assault of salt that would befall their eyes.

Despite their hard work, not an single sailor was burly, rather, they seemed the skinnier short, like elder men with full bellies laden with ink and sun spots. Surely, they spent more time in leisure than labor. They did not seem altogether menacing, most of them had full sets of teeth and hair. Some even resembled a particular beauty for men, until Joshua realized they were actually women with very short hair, giving clichés to common tropes.

The rails of the ship were gilded in copper with odd figures like minotaurs, rocs, hydras, and other mythological creatures. These images marched, each one behind the other, led like a family of elephants. At the back, a yellowish wheel, eight-pronged, simple and sturdy, stood ready to be twisted. It looked to have been made by many swirling branches, all tied together about the handles and barely kept together.

Joshua was mildly impressed.

The Marquis passed his guests' luggage to a nearby man who proceeded to disappear into the hull. The captain dusted his hands and left them to their wondrous awe so that he might lift the ship and leave the area quickly.

Off into the distance, Laffy spotted the pink mound that was the Titan. He smirked. He looked back at Joshua, who hadn't so much as smiled or talked upon his arrival. He wore small scars about himself, small light stripes that almost possessed rank about them like a general bearing ribbon. Joshua seemed stronger than when the Marquis had first departed his company. The Marquis was proud of him.

Lafayette reached right and seized a series of gilded levers posted into the floor by the wheel. He clenched, pushed in the furthest lever, and quickly yanked back the first. The wooden ship creaked and raised its long belly. Slowly, it elevated and inched forward.

Joshua staggered, unused to the floor moving beneath him. He walked to the rails and watched as the ground left below him, the world had become small before long, the giant a fleshy splotch of decay that slowly faded from view. They were flying at a cruising speed, smooth and low. Joshua hung himself over the rail and felt the passing air across his face. It massaged the sleep from his eyes, brought him renewed life and peace.

Gnat stood off to the side of him, through his helmet he could see the virtual markers that directed him into Siberia. He twisted the knob about his nape, and the helmet slowly turned off, leaving nothing but what his true eyes saw through old, torn, and fluttering tape, the beauty that was Siberia's wasteland. He ran his gloves along the gilded rails, feeling the engravings where brass met polished wood.

As the skyship stopped its ascent and paralleled with the ground far below it, the Marquis passed the wheel to Cid, who had sat about the stern casually. Lafayette clasped the rails and overlooked his vessel.

"There's something on your mind Captain." Cid stated, not needing to ask.

"I'm starting to believe…" The Marquis hummed. "I'm starting to believe Elizabeth was right. Joshua Hill is most likely Connor Shaw."

"She probably *is* right. She's is not the person to err in her judgement."

"This is important to Elizabeth. Joshua might not be Connor. But what he just did was something only Connor could do, and if he wants to insist he isn't, killing that beast did not help his case… If we drop Joshua off in France I'm afraid we will upset Elizabeth that we let him go."

"So… Will you toss him back to the witch?" Cid asked.

"I can't, I'm a man of my word, but that doesn't mean we can't let Elizabeth know where we are going to drop him off. Also, it'll be some time before we pass into The French Dominion. Maybe Joshua will begin to remember more of his previous life." The Marquis replied before becoming silent for a moment, "Our *other* guest needs to be aware of Joshua's presence. I wouldn't want her to misinterpret his company. Whether he's Connor or not, he should not incur someone wrath for something he doesn't remember doing."

Cid nodded, "You best do that then."

The Marquis stretched his back and stole down the shimmering stairs port-side, crossing back to his two friends. He intervened between them, leaning back into the rails. He spied both of them, their posture still suggested discomfort and defensiveness, as if poised to fight even in the midst of safety upon the frigate.

Joshua's hand rested inside his pocket, perhaps fingering some weapon or plot.

"Friends," The Marquis began, "Unfortunately we're going to have to put you in the common quarters for now, our guest room is occupied. One of my men has already put your items down below so you'll know where to bunk. We're heading west, Mr. Hill. We'll be in France, but it will take some time. Do make yourself comfortable. Cid is at the wheel should you have any questions. Before I disappear, would you like a tour?"

Joshua shook his head and Gnat did not react.

The Marquis frowned about the corners of his mouth and gave a small nod. "I'll see you about, then." He closed, before trotting off and disappearing into the captain's quarters.

"What are you thinking?" Gnat asked shortly thereafter.

"I think he knew." Joshua murmured.

"Knew what?"

"I think he knew exactly what that *thing* was. I think Elizabeth knew what I was facing. That *witch* set this up after all."

"Why would they do that?"

"They think I'm a hero. If I lived through this, I would be Connor Shaw to Elizabeth, or want to be. If I failed them, they would know I wasn't, and they wouldn't have to lift a finger because I would be dead."

"Manipulative bastards, they are." Gnat chimed.

"I hope this is the end of their plans for me." Joshua sighed, "I have my own problems to deal with."

There was another round of silence. Gnat looked back into the deck, he watched the sailors carefully, many didn't seem to pay them any attention. Like servants, they minded their own until told not to. It annoyed Gnat, it reminded him of his faults, his inability to seize independence. That was the reason he had become a guard first off. He just wanted orders, and to follow them blindly. Even now, AWOL from Moscow's military, he still stumbled about in the dark at the whim of some immortal man. A criminal who stole a weapon of mass destruction, a man who might have stolen LeCeleste. He did it all, *just* to have orders, to continue living a purposeful life. He didn't mind where the ship was heading, as long as it was moving. That was enough for the young militant.

"What are you going to do in France?" the soldier inquired.

"I'm going to find and kill the person responsible for this." Joshua replied bluntly. "What will you do?"

"I'm going to stay here. The Marquis offered me a job back in Moscow before you came out for coffee. I need to keep an eye on him. I want to keep an eye on Second Death and make sure he and this *buyer* are trustworthy."

Joshua about-faced; he looked out to the other side of the deck with Gnat. "Good luck with that." He mused. "Don't blink for even a second."

The Marquis sat upon a sofa across from his guest, he twiddled his boots about, tapping on his toes. He reclined softly to the side, his eyes fixed upon the curio before him.

Laffy sat before an odd girl with short pinkish hair. It was bright pink, faded pink, in the way that it looked a steely grey under the correct lightings. Perhaps it was the red in the cloth sheet she sat upon that made it seem so, but the Marquis could not tell. She sat in fine posture on the opposite couch, a table between them. Her legs touched side by side, the feet tucked underneath. She wore an odd suit that was technologically superior to those in Russian centers. It was an exotic type of flight suit resembling the legendary astronauts from Moscow's golden age. But it was nothing he had ever seen in his lifetime but on her. It seemed futuristic, a plastic half-helmet rose tightly about her neck and stopped about her chin. The tips of her hair brushed it when she swayed. But, the most peculiar thing about the lass was the small hornlike structures that grew out of her head. It was bone, without doubt, serrated in horizontal sections. It did not rise out like that of a bull nor an antler, it stayed closer to her head more like that of an ibex or ram.

From what she had hinted, and how she presented herself to him first when they met years ago, she was no one to be ignored. She carried a metal sphere in her arms, holding it tight like a doll or a teddy bear. She had not an insinuating body, to jest upon one that looked or imagined her. She had not large breasts nor a distinguishing rear. Her body was more petite than most, perhaps squeezed by the suit she wore.

To speak further of the suit, it was rigid about her body. The material from the neck plate fell about the collar with protective grooves. When she shrugged, these grooves bent into the space about them. They were not flexible themselves, but they were given enough room to keep the body unrestricted as she shifted about. They were metallic, and selective. The material also covered her elbows, her wrists, her knees, her waist, her ankles, and the area about her sternum. Elsewhere, underneath the armor, there was only a cloth with the texture of cut-resistant mesh. It clung to her like a wetsuit. Like veins, lights shown forth from odd lines beneath the armor, an accent to the grooves.

"I don't think we can do that, morally." The Marquis retorted. "It's not that we don't want to, but to steal a body of a young man, and do *that*. Perhaps if he were dead, but by the time we could begin procedures in Moscow the body would be stale. This isn't accounting for the difference between technology and biology. We aren't there yet in time. You can't transfer memories, even when they're stored. Memories are not a soul, nor the constitution of character. I'm afraid your friend is stuck where he is for now."

"But I did," The girl insisted, "I made that transfer and it worked."

The Marquis sighed. "That's different. Your *people* are different. Perhaps where you are from, that technology exists, but here, there is no way. We could put the memories in a computer, but I doubt there's a better husk than the one he's in now."

The two were quiet. The girl ran her hands along the sphere in her lap. It looked heavy, a steel ball that was painted a matte white. It was scratched and dinged, the paint peeled in certain areas. It seemed her golden calf, her safety blanket, respectfully. She paid so much attention to it, that the Marquis did the same instead of gazing into her bunny-red eyes.

"I will wait then," She fumed, "until the opportunity arises to give us what we want. I would like to talk to my friend in the privacy of my room."

"Of course," The Marquis consoled, "Let me show you back to it."

The two negotiators rose and left the captain's cabin. They emerged in the open sun.

Birds flew about the ship and squawked their curiosity in the man-made. Down and about the bow, Joshua and Gnat sat about the rails. They continued their quiet thoughts. They neither talked nor moved. They both stared at their toes, enthralled by the floor. Joshua looked up through his brow and saw the odd girl with the large pill in her arms. She chaperoned it low about her waist like one would a moving-box or a cooler.

The girl glanced about and caught eyes with Joshua. She stopped behind the Marquis and stared back. The Marquis looked at the both of them. He sighed, hoping to have warned her sooner. If not for the ball in her hands, she might have stridden towards him. Instead she paused, frozen in the gaze.

"Saia." The Marquis piped. "That is *not* Connor."

Saia said nothing but quickly turned about. She found her way into the second room beneath the stern's left stairs, swiftly, like leaving an argument. The Marquis quickly followed and vanished along with her.

"Who was that?" Gnat questioned. "You know her?"

"No," Joshua replied, "I don't."

Out upon the wooden concourse, the Marquis emerged again to meet the gaze of Joshua and Gnat. He approached their post and greeted them with a half-assed wave. He wore a slight frown about his chin.

"My apologies for any discomfort." He said. "It seems more than just Elizabeth thinks you're Connor Shaw."

"You should tell us what the deal is before we wake up with bullets in our chests." Gnat demanded.

The Marquis hesitated before opening his mouth, "All I can tell you is that the girl went to Connor because she needed help desperately. But Connor refused to do anything for her."

"Would she do something drastic?" Gnat inquired.

"No," The Marquis assured, "Even if she wanted to, someone gave her a very strict set of rules to live by."

Lafayette sighed, rubbed his eyes, and shook his head. The sun had begun to set on the horizon. It matched the color of the heated blimp. The flames that flickered into it, a fire and a light much like the sun. It was a steady stream of heat, a steady trickle of glow. It made a roof for the pirates, a large bulb for them to see by.

Nobody saw Saia again that night even when a long table was erected center onto the deck and platters of food were arrayed down its length. A multitude of chairs were placed to seat its audience. The Marquis sat about one end, and his quartermaster sat about the other, a woman with long blonde hair. She wore a long black coat and a tangle of daisies was placed on her head like a crown. She seemed wholly unhardened, unlike a pirate or a sailor. She ate daintily, with fork and knife, while the men and women around her groveled about the table, scarfing down only the meats.

She cut a miniature potato in half, one that sat to the side of her plate, furiously lonely among salad greens.

Gnat seemed to eye her the most, if that is what you could say about a man so unrequited about losing his helmet.

Joshua and Gnat sat to the left of the Marquis, Cid leaned on the right. This is the first they had noticed Cid particularly for a time. He wore a torn teal tee; an odd cartoon was pasted on the front. It drank orange soda by the barrel. He didn't pay any mind to Joshua and Gnat, truly, Cid was a youth among men, constantly staring at his trousers as if he had spilt something. Cid was preoccupied with something under the table, his wrists jittered about a small puzzle in his hands. He sneered each time he twisted it the wrong direction and had to start over.

Gnat didn't eat, hardly did Joshua or Lafayette. They sat there and stared about, each one thinking of something to say. It was not until Joshua realized his fledgling concepts of the mystical world that he broke the silence: "What else is out there?"

"Out where?" Marquis aired, his last word mingling on some higher guise of silence about the second-half syllable.

"What else exists that I don't know about." Joshua rephrased.

The Marquis grinned, he took a sip of his wine and leaned over his arm rest, anew with curiosity and half-truth.

"What isn't?" He mused. "The Greeks, the Nordics, the Jews, and even those buffoons who rant about Chupacabras and yetis had something right. There are giant snakes and men who throw lightning and fire. Pestilence can take on odd shapes like that of a horsemen. Serpents swim in the seas and octopi scurry about the surface of the moon. There are angelic monsters, demon like monsters, intelligent monsters, small, big, round -- as you know. There are skinny, male, female and nongendered beings. There are men that extend their life by bringing other people's blood into their veins. There are sailors who have and did see a giant whale destroy their ship like a battering ram. Bipedal wolves aren't common, but they are out there, more docile than one might think. Killer moths fly above the clouds, many odds and ends and all that.

The truth is, we're still finding out. Well, *they're* still finding out. The men that Connor led kept tabs and encyclopedias. I'm sure there are some men out there in Siberia who made their home out of the bones of their slain. Some of mankind opted to get into the wilderness and live how they thought they were meant to; they probably have some stories to tell and their own written encyclopedias as well."

"That isn't very specific now, is it?" Gnat joked without timbre or pitch. Interested though he was, he didn't find Lafayette's answer helpful enough.

The Marquis chuckled, he put his fingers to his chin and ran them through his follicles. "Let me think then… that beast you fought back there, with the layers and breasts like an utter, we call those Shapers."

"Shapers?" Joshua repeated.

"Yes, as you saw, wherever they go, the land contorts about them. They 'shape' the land, so we call them Shapers. They're not all obese like the one you fought either. They come in just as many shapes and sizes as humans do. That one probably was just... Siberian in the sense that it needed fat to fight the cold. There are skinny ones, and some even wear clothes. We think they might be thoughtful in some part. Places like Stonehenge could have been their doing."

Joshua nodded his understanding. He thought back to it. That ugly creature wasn't the only one out there, there were more.

"How come, with so many giant monsters roaming about, have people not realized this?" Joshua inquired next.

The Marquis shrugged, "It wouldn't be impossible to hide, or diminish. You've seen the news about what happens in America, but that's only what the media choses to tell. I'm guessing the governments have something to do with the hush-hush. It's not like every country can spot these anomalies by satellite like Russia can. I'm sure there are a lot of different reasons. I'm sure that when civilization began, many beasts fled in fear of mankind, choosing to hide, their numbers shrinking as people spread and populations grew. But, really, I think people only see what they believe they will see. Any videos of amateurs finding bigfoot or a ghost can be waved off by the majority of humans as video effects, when they might not be."

The Marquis smiled shallowly. He waved his glass in a circle and watched the wine move about like a whirlpool.

"The worst of these beasts are called Ancients." He stated rather darkly, his tone more hushed. "They are never to be disturbed."

Joshua leaned forward, he reached for a skewer and began to nibble it. His curiosity made his stomach growl.

"They stand as tall as a mountain," the Marquis continued. "and not a small mountain like those Shapers. They're like skyscrapers.

The Ancient's are made of muscle and bone, but no skin covers them. They have these partial exoskeletons that make their faces and act as armor. They don't have eyes either. The muscle runs thick and sinewy, like wires tied with a rubber band. They swim in the ocean, hide under the earth's crust, and sleep in glaciers. If you ever see it, it's like watching the end of the world or looking into the face of God himself."

The Marquis trailed off, his lower lip parted slightly.

"You've seen one then." Gnat prodded, trying to spur the conversation on.

"I've seen *two*," The Marquis replied almost sadly. "I was in Antarctica. I saw them both fighting each other a few miles inland. They didn't stop or pay me any attention. I was a flea to them. They fought each other. I thought I was going to die just by watching; and this was after I discovered I was immortal.

One of them had tails instead of legs, like an octopus it slithered along the ground. It had a smooth head like a motorcycle helmet and his hands were massive fists the size of cargo ships. Whenever he landed a good hit the clouds would open, and you would hear a crack like a lightning whip inside your ears. The other was smaller by a few lengths, it had a head with horns like a rhinoceros. He looked much like a man, two legs, two arms.

I didn't stay to watch, I was too scared. I didn't sleep for weeks after seeing them either."

Joshua thought about the village of Val-Ashoth. He remembered Haddock's story of their protector having the village in its palm. Could it be true? Could some giant the size of a skyscraper exist? If they did, could they be cognizant of men, like angels and demons? Could they care?

Joshua felt small. He shifted in discomfort. He watched the dark line that marked the horizon. He almost expected to see an ancient, primordial, being block out the sun. If he ever met one, what would he do?

Joshua imagined one stomping its way into France. He would be helpless before it. This feeling of helplessness irritated Joshua. What if all he had done to make people safe was merely postponing their deaths for another ending, a more sinister ending. Was Joshua cruel to save someone from being shot, not knowing that one day they might die in terror at the hands of an angry demon? If he knew they would die a horrid death, would he let them live?

Joshua's life began to feel menial.

The Marquis eyed Joshua, curious to his thoughts. He could see the gears turning in his head. He knew all too well what it was like to question himself. It didn't seem so long ago that he had forsaken his place as baron and left the world to its own devices. He too, was once a hero.

Little did The Marquis know the exact rabbit hole Joshua was burrowing into, but this could be said: The Marquis and Joshua were nothing alike. Back when The Marquis was faced with this ordeal, he chose to flee from humanity and the world at large. The Marquis forsook the world in order to bring himself peace and tranquility. But Joshua, in this moment of fear and humiliation, teethed in expectation and desire. Joshua wanted to be in the world more. He had a dream to save people, it was written in his core. He would not give up on his dream, even if it was a fool's errand. Joshua would rather die for his impossible dreams than live in the bog of normality.

The Marquis stood and raised his glass. He rapped it lightly with his fork to summon attention. The sailors tuned themselves in, resisting the urge to continue feeding. They twisted their wrists, trying to keep their mouths from salivating.

"Gentlemen," The Marquis began, "I would like to propose a toast to our new guests. I should have introduced them earlier, and thanked them as well, but there is no time like the present to correct ourselves. So, to Gnat and Joshua, who stopped a Shaper to protect the citizens of Moscow. Let their first hunt not be their last. And let their enemies sit upon their hands knowing their approach!"

The sailors jeered, they raised their glasses and downed their drinks. Joshua didn't know what to think. Gnat quirked slightly, he lifted the drink before him and put it back down when the roar had ceased. The rest of the night was filled with revelry. The sailors sang after their meal and tidied the deck for the night. Joshua retired to his hammock below deck while the others enjoyed themselves. His mind was empty, and before he laid down, he found himself cursing his own name. Perhaps he was tired, or perhaps he felt the weight of the world increase upon his shoulders.

Finally, as the rest of the men came to their hammocks from above, Joshua had found sleep, thankfully.

The next morning came early for Joshua. Leaving his bed, he made his way upon the deck and found himself staring over the side of the ship down to terra-forma below. He spied trough the parts in the clouds like staring through a window, looking within the frame of a painting.

Joshua had never been on an airship before. Such crafts were delicacies in France. All Skyships were imports from Russia and nearly impossible to acquire. The silent war between the two nations had become economic as time passed by. Heavy taxes on Russian imports and stacks of paperwork were needed to bring anything in. One was always paying more to France than to Russia through this method. If one wanted a watch from Russia, he or she would give 100 units to Russia and 400 to France, if it was a watch. But most items never went below a steep ratio as such. Thus, France ensured their market remained internal and kept Russia from not only stealing their money but also from becoming stronger. You would pay the price of a palace for a Skyship, and no less.

The sun crept above with the speed of a caterpillar and heated the deck evenly. Joshua could hear the sailors stirring below deck. Cid was the first to emerge from beneath and he paid no mind to Joshua. He immediately moved to the stern and began locating their position on the globe that sat on a table far behind the wheel.

Joshua realized how negligent the Marquis was of navigation last night. It frightened him, but, he supposed there was nothing to run into whilst in the sky. Clouds were not solid like icebergs.

The Marquis emerged from his quarters and stretched his back. It cracked and popped terribly. He yawned. Joshua looked back towards him in an odd sense of disgust. The man stood there in his pajamas with large fluffy slippers on his feet. He wore a Phrygian cap with a fuzz ball on the end, like that of Santa Claus or a garden gnome.

How careless. Joshua thought before looking away, back down to the earth.

Eventually the whole deck was in full motion. Men moved about the floor with large barrels in their arms. They checked the ropes, retied the knots, and polished the deck per usual. A few men, who seemed daring to Joshua, rappelled down the sides of the ship to wash the keel. Others climbed the balloon to check for punctures and patch them with adhesive strips. They seemed to ignore their guests and do what they were used to. Joshua was glad for this, he did not want attention.

Behind Joshua, Gnat loomed about the stern with Cid. The soldier looked out behind the craft, his helmet magnifying the land below, he watched people go about their lives in small villages. He scanned populations as if taking census and read articles on whatever item was in view. He read articles on fruits, rocks, mineral deposit probabilities, and cultural information. He kept himself busy while the day grew long, waiting patiently in hope of seeing something abnormal, another monster, another anomaly.

The Marquis munched on an apple, he juggled it in his hands like ball. Eventually, boredom struck him, and like Gnat, took to watching the horizon of the earth through a lens. He didn't retreat back into his room until Saia took to walking the deck. He was afraid to look indecent, and soon emerged again in his captain's attire. He wore a faint-green jacket adorned in beige tassels about the elbows. His shirt was open and showed slight chest hair, a true, wealthy, pirate look about him. He walked with certainty again and stopped yawning. He was a different person altogether. It seemed, at first glance, he was trying to put on a show for Saia. Either he was chivalrous and decent towards women, or he was trying to seduce them. To Joshua, that line was ever thin.

Saia still held her egg as the Marquis approached. He began to speak casually but the short woman was not forwarding much attention to him. Neither did the Marquis mind, he never posed a question, and he knew the girl was paying him whatever mind she deemed necessary. She smiled weakly, almost conscious and shy of being in public. She wore the same spacesuit she did the day before. It was all she ever wore.

The day passed on and night started to subside. The light of the fire, caused by the burners, was always on and kept the deck, along with the surrounding clouds, visible. They had begun a decent through the layer.

Joshua looked over and saw something peculiar, long lines of strange and illuminating patterns below. At first, he thought it was civilization, a string of houses or road lights. However, the lights were discolored into a beautiful haze of blue, green, and yellow in a rhythm and cadence. It was a pattern of sorts, like that of zebra stripes or leopard skin, only incandescent.

Joshua peered over, clutching the railing as the light of the ship met the strange phenomenon. As the lights rose to converge on the skyship, Joshua beheld a set of odd flying creatures. They traveled together in a group, not paying caution to the pirates on deck.

"Peaceful creatures, the Farossi." Cid murmured. "They're completely docile."

Joshua watched the herd, and then one in particular, a small baby Farossi. It had a wide head. Like that of a shovel it came to a fine tip. Its mouth sat below its flat face, jutting out slightly like a bump. It had small sharp teeth. Its eyes sat atop its head in a ridge like a crocodile's. It looked at Joshua and gave a short low moan. The moan was something from a dream, reminding Joshua of a xylophone and an organ trying to play together.

Perhaps it sounded more like a chirp.

"Human eyes usually can't see them from the ground at night," Cid continued like a tour guide, "their bellies are the perfect shade of grey to blend with the atmosphere. But from above, they're like magic carpets peddelin' neon signs. They do it to make themselves known to the rest of their flock, so none get lost. The cloud cover hides their lights from predators above them. They're in the perfect position to stay safe. During the day they move up and stay inside the clouds. They're very social creatures, like dolphins, but in the sky."

As Cid continued his banter, Joshua forgot his words and listened in on a conversation by the other side of the skyship. Although his eyes continued to watch the Farossi, he spied on The Marquis and Saia, who watched the creatures starboard.

"It reminds me of marbles." Saia cooed quietly. "I used to watch the big blue marble from my window when I was young. I think blue is the color of hope."

"I like to think so too." The Marquis replied. "But also, blue is the color of sadness."

"Maybe hope is a sad thing." Saia mentioned as the Farossi began to fall behind in the distance. "Often, hope is shattered, ambitions are played with by fate. Maybe sadness and hope are two sides of the same feeling. You hope for things you're sad about, and sad when you lose hope."

The Marquis smiled.

Joshua wrinkled his nose, catching Cid's attention.

"Eaves dropping, are we?" He smirked, but he didn't seem too cheerful, even with his lip turned.

"Couldn't help but overhear." Joshua defended.

Later that day, Joshua sat on the edge of his hammock and ran his hands through his hair. He thought of Saia, her spacesuit, her commentary on things regular people never would talk about. She acted unearthly, odd, dainty, and pure, despite being onboard a ship with thieves. The thought gnawed at him, Saia must be something odd, something different.

These thoughts concluded his second day aboard.

Part 7/Rain

Joshua stood in a vacant forest and the trees all around him started to bend. It was the wind, strong staggering, but silent.

There was no noise, only silence.

Under the force of the wind, which swirled like a tornado about him, the trees twisted like licorice strands and bent to the ground. One tree bent upon another and another until Joshua was surrounded by a corkscrew of trees. They walled him in. The thick trunks became Joshua's cage.

Joshua pressed his hand against the gauntlet. He felt the ridges of the wall akin to that of log cabins. He was in the middle of an abyssal wood. Joshua was seemingly trapped.

The trees heaved before Joshua and surprised him. The trees breathed, they moved in and out and the American could feel the heat of the breath fall upon him from the ceiling unseen. It was a disgusting warm-mist of breath.

Joshua put his hand into the creases made between the trees and began to climb.

Joshua blinked as he rose and when he opened his eyes he was already at the top.

So soon? He thought.

Joshua reached over the last trunk and moved himself upon it. He looked across. He was not above, so much as at, the ground level. He looked out to see an expanse of red clay. Upon this clay Joshua walked.

As the man walked, he noticed a small group of children. They drew with their fingers in the clay. As he continued walking, he noticed again the same group of children, the same faces, the same clothes. They didn't pay him any mind, not until he came upon them but another mile down. They seemed to notice him, but they didn't look his way.

Am I walking in circles? No. Surely, I am not. Joshua thought again.

Joshua came upon the same children yet again. They looked his way. Joshua walked briskly.

Again, he saw them, and, they stared.

Once more he walked, looking over his shoulder until they were out of his sight.

Joshua felt a tug on his pants. He looked around, there he saw the same children. He had bumped into them.

How? He thought.

This time they looked to speak to him, their lips moved, but no words came out. He questioned them inaudibly. They looked angry at him for not understanding. Joshua looked confused. The first child, in pigtails, bent down to write in the clay.

Joshua knelt to watch the length of the L, the trident E, and the pointed A. These letters were followed by V, E, and N, O, and W.

Joshua scratched his stubbled chin, it seemed he'd forgotten how to read. He looked up at the children to see they had changed. They were upset, and despite heat of the red desert around them, wore yellow raincoats.

That Joshua knew, was a warning.

Joshua watched as the children were met by another man whom he knew as Solomon. Joshua tried to run forward, but the clay had grown about his ankles and continued to envelop him. Joshua screamed at Solomon in pure, grotesque, rage. He screamed, and the anger caused blood to pool in his eyes. He couldn't hear his own screams of disgust and murderous intent.

Solomon rested his hands on the heads of the children while Joshua sought to maim him. Joshua leaned forward and reached for Solomon's yellow coat but his fingers missed by inches. Solomon didn't move, but Joshua saw a small tear part way from his eyes. Solomon seemed to smile, much like someone hides their sorrow at a funeral. His burnt face looked cleaner and Joshua thought he could recognize him as someone he once knew.

Joshua continued to scream as Elizabeth emerged from the side of his view. Elizabeth smiled, or seemed to smile, the same way Solomon did. She knelt briefly to lay the flowers she held in her hands at Joshua's feet. Joshua couldn't reach them, couldn't smell them.

The clay had grown about his chest.

Elizabeth stepped back and Solomon wrapped his arm around her. She placed her hand on his chest. They were ready to walk away.

Joshua's voice grew hoarse as the parade before him waltzed into the distance.

Joshua began to cry, which built itself into a full sob. He wailed in agony as the clay began to push his body into the air. It hung him there, high enough the see the couple and their children disappear over the horizon. Joshua tried to call out once more, but still the world was quiet.

In the corner of Joshua's eyes marched forth a band of soldiers, they carried trumpets that were fed bullets, mounted on the end of spears. They stood there like Chinese terra-cotta or a marching band. They stood there to bear witness as Joshua began to wither like a flower.

As Joshua began to die, the soldiers turned to face him. He looked into the faces of his men. Lafayette, Gnat, Cid, and Marcus stood there with him, their weapons poised in the air like banners. Unlike the other soldiers, Joshua watched as each of his allies painted their faces with black soot, war paint. Before Joshua blinked, he watched each of them charge headlong with their spears into his chest.

In his dream, Joshua lost everything, but not his life.

Joshua watched the sunrise again while sitting on the bow of the ship. His white shirt and jeans rippled against the steady breeze. He clicked his boots together in a slow tempo, his hands wrung about his neck and his elbows on his knees.

Joshua felt a jerk in his throat, a hoarse bead of pain and dryness; he felt like he would cry. He couldn't shake his dreams, how they tore at his lungs and beat his heart to pulp. More now than ever, he felt afraid of what they meant. More now than ever, Joshua was scared. He didn't want to live with himself anymore. He himself came to that conclusion time and time again, only to forget later in the day.

Joshua looked down to the ground below, he felt an imaginary force tug his shirt, begging him to drop. It would be a few moments of peace and freedom before death. Joshua wouldn't have to think, he could simply listen to the wind screaming in his ears.

The truth was, after the day Joshua was found in the sandbox in the backyard, he found solitude in his imagination. Joshua dreamt of all the ways he could die, and it comforted him. Because, after Joshua killed those children, he found it hard to live with himself. Joshua took out his rage on others, beat crooks down within inches of their life for petty things, just for running, even. He did anything to make him feel like a good person, he did everything to pretend he had a purpose in the world.

It was true that Joshua didn't want to live anymore, but it was also true that he didn't want others to die. The second peace that Joshua found, unalike to his suicidal hopes, was his tendency for martyrdom. He wanted to save others, but not himself. Passively, he waited for the end of the world to claim him. He urged himself to live so others might live.

Joshua would be the last of all death. Joshua wanted to be the first and last one to die.

Joshua thought he had jumped for a moment. He thought his body was descending from the heavens. But the approaching ground wasn't because he had slipped from the bow of the skyship, as much as he wanted to. No, the ground began to rise because the ship was sinking.

"Why are we going down?" Joshua inquired across the deck.

Cid leaned forward over the wheel, his skinny body lined up with the handles, almost fitting between them. He looked at Joshua darkly. He was the only person awake that early in the morning.

"We need to stop for supplies, the fuel is running low, and all the alcohol's gone." He replied, his voice wavered, tired.

The ship bounced slightly against the soil until it rested firmly upon it. The burner's low hum subsided, but the thin frame of the balloon kept the canvas from falling onto the deck. Cid sighed, and the deck shuddered softly as it made a nest of the ground. The ship had deployed its legs, small pegs about the keel to hold it upright.

Through the trees of the meadow in which they landed there was no village in sight. But a cool mist collected on the floor and kept such far places from being seen clearly, if at all.

Joshua climbed down the side and dropped to the ground with a soft thud. His feet wobbled as they were so used to a moving platform, his whole body felt unbalanced on solid footing. He found himself stumbling to the right, his feet flopping about a few seconds behind his torso.

It was too early for the birds or any other wildlife. It was that point in the dawn whence the nocturnal beasts were nestled and the daytime animals had yet to awake. Thus, a foreboding silence marked the area and reminded Joshua of his dream. He almost expected to see another child. He waited for his nightmare to resume, to feel a tug on his shirt. As the sun started to pierce through the trees, he cringed thinking it was a spotlight. The mist made him shiver.

Cid leapt to the ground beside Joshua. "The town is just a mile that way. You can come with me if you want." he offered.

"Why didn't we land by the village?" Joshua inquired.

"Parking sucks, this town is one of the old war outposts so there's a lot of military traffic through there. Trucks and the like get loaded with rations and blankets, mostly for soldiers, before being transported to the 15th. We also want to be discreet around those soldiers. They're not all arseholes, but you will always find that one officer that wants to 'confiscate your ship and use it to aid the Russian military." Cid mocked with a Russian accent terribly sharp in Joshua's ears.

The two started moving out through the trees. They walked over long and unearthed roots, weathered down and slick. The fog didn't let up, but it proved to be no trouble for the pair. Still, even with the sparse cracks of limbs and leaves underneath the courier's feet, there remained something foreboding about the forest. A lingering hum drummed in their ears.

Joshua felt his chest tighten, he was about to enter military domain. What if they found out that he was from France? Could they tell? Joshua didn't carry a French accent or posture. He was rigid and stoic without any mannerisms unique to French peoples. He thought that if he kept himself from drawing too much attention, he would be fine. He could turn back, but why should he wait and let his thoughts consume him due to boredom? Joshua felt compelled to tag along with the young British Pirate.

There was something faint in the air, a moribund smell. Joshua caught a whiff of it, if only for a moment. Cid

170

didn't seem to notice. Perhaps it was Cid himself, they hadn't bathed for a while. But the smell, however brief, was something odd, tangible, something that could be described as beautifully-rotten. It was a smell of decay, but also of certain perfume. It reminded Joshua of a wilting flower; it reminded Joshua of the brothels he used to bag bodies in.

The wind blew steadily, that is what pushed the scent from under the detective's nose, and out through some random current. But the wind, however steady, seemed to howl past Joshua's ears. The wind nipped at their eyes, dried them, and the drought pressed upon their lips. Something so warm and pleasant as the meadow in which they came, was quickly altered by the gradient of fallen trees they now saw less frequently.

As the trees ceased to continue, they were replaced by their stumps. The grass soon followed the dying trend and turned to mud, wet from the fog.

Joshua could see the outpost, which was really a commiseration of dingy airships. They were not made of wood nor lifted by balloons. The large metal ships were electrical, powered by dozens of swiveling fans in rows about each side. It was as if someone took a large hallway, or block, and put seats along the interior. On one end of the hall there was a dual cockpit, and the other side boasted a ramp for boarding. In comparison with Russian technology found in the city, Russian military architecture was gruesome, clunky, and overweight.

These vast amounts of air frigates lay upon the ground, men in uniform lay across the seats throwing knives and lighting cigarettes. They sat on the opened ramps near campfires; one soldier, older than the rest, slowly strummed his guitar and hummed along to the chords.

The true houses laid further on, metal barns and shacks lay hidden behind and between the massive aircrafts. Men quartered themselves there, seemingly without permission.

The people without badges nor uniforms shouted at them in Russian, trying to ward them away from their doorstep. It was a loud outpost. It was a cluster of odd sounds and ramblings, all in Russian.

Joshua understood all of it.

Out beyond the outpost, as seen if one might walk around the large parking-center, was the remains of a battlefield. Large barb-wired fences lay disheveled and tossed into trenches. Men with bright spotlights stood behind sandbags and fanned the territory with their construction lights. The area was a minefield. Although the front had moved west of there, the Russians still surveyed the area for miscreant children. A small group of men walked along the barren land, surveying the ground with clipboards in hand. With large orange markers they seemed to identify the location of mines for the bomb squad to disarm the next day. What Joshua and Cid didn't know was that a little boy had found his way out into the field unnoticed, and swiftly met his end the previous day.

The two entered the outpost tavern which sat on the edge of the commiseration closest the fallen woods. It was rife with Russian soldiers drunk on liquors of many kinds. They shouted and clambered over the short wooden tables, falling this way and that. It was a regular, slurried, festival of mythological belief where bearded gods and war maidens met to celebrate an unfair and unjust battle. But, in all of this babble there stood an odd fellow behind the bar. He was a bartender like Cid, and even though his clothes were spattered in the thrown piss of his customers, he looked certain against the clownish goings.

This bartender looked across the room through the crowd, somehow hearing the door open in all the commotion. He locked eyes with Cid immediately. He seemed to smile on one end of his face, but a thin beard hid that expression. He looked sly and quickly poised himself for their arrival, adjusting his yellow stained shades and running his hands through his slicked-back hair. He moved slowly to the far end of the counter where the traveling duo met him.

"I didn't know you were in Russia, Cid." The bartender mused, his voice average, if not for an air of Zen.

Cid chuckled under his breath, uncharacteristically hushed. "We're here for gas."

"Just gas?" The Bartender piqued, his eyebrow raised beneath his spectacles. "Are you sure you don't want anything else?"

"Just gas." Cid assured

Cid reached into his pocket and produced a small metal card, it was a light golden plate with a small insignia in the middle composed of three circles linked by a T, the circles at the end of each line. The Bartender picked it from his hands swiftly and folded it over its end, inspecting it. He hummed all the while, before handing it back.

"That sort of gas." He said to himself. The Bartender twisted his head about his right, looking towards a short girl in a high-low dress. "Faith, watch over the bar for me, will you? I'm going to show these travelers to their room."

The girl waved her hand in the air, her blonde head tucked into her elbow on the counter. Clearly, she needn't play sentry for the miscreants in the tavern.

The bartender walked swiftly towards the corner, sliding past the brutish Russian congregation. Cid followed in kind and Joshua tried to keep pace. But Joshua was slightly bigger than his company and found himself brushing against people. He kept his head down and tried not to open his mouth. No one should know he was from France, the armistice between their nations was fragile at best. Any single shot from one citizen to an alien would be enough ground for Russia to resume their artillery strikes against western Europe, or vice versa.

Really, Joshua thought, whatever peace between the nations was hardly official. The Blue Diamond treaty was only a statement, and the two countries still loathed each other after they had skirmished. The World was waiting for the 15th line to budge, licking its lips over the promise of new land. The barons rubbed their hands together at an opportunity, an opening to slip a letter-opener into the Russian cogs. Russia was waiting for an excuse to exercise their military arsenal and bring their strict way of life into the west.

The Barons never did much to improve their lands. They were tricksters too busy fighting each other to devote time to the Eastern front. Although Paris, the French powerhouse, stood under contract to maintain a sizeable force along the 15th to observe Russian movements, their forces seemed petty in comparison to the Russian leviathan just feet away. France was medieval at best, a cluster of gun-toting Neanderthals with no thoughts about the future or the big picture in life.

Did Joshua have that foresight? Probably not, he thought, but here he was in Russia, thinking about the consequences of French and Russian ambition. One of these days one of the nations' ambitions would become too big to deny, and when that bullet would be heard, many more people would die for the sake of foolish leaders.

Joshua wondered who was worse, the Russian Juggernaut that suppressed its citizens, assigning them jobs and wages where nothing was in their control, or the French pissants, neglecting the citizens altogether as they struggled and starved in the hovels of their cities. It was a war of parents, those who were overbearing, and those who never cared enough. Which parent would raise the better generation, the generation that would conquer the other?

Joshua remembered his bearings, and when he returned from his thoughts, he found himself passing through a door which led into a small backroom full of oddities. In the center of this room was a steel table with a yellow cloth over it. In large black print, or smothered paint, the same 'T' symbol was imprinted upon it. The far wall had green canisters glowing on a wine-rack. They didn't look like a liquid someone wanted to drink.

It was that in which the bartender seized. He held it in both hands delicately until he set it on the table.

"Is one enough for you?" He asked Cid.

Cid examined the canister, obviously the fuel they had come to pick up. He placed a wad of cash on the table.

"This is how much I was given to spend, so, how much will this get me?" Cid asked.

The Bartender picked up the wad and uncrumpled it. He ran his fingers through the corners and knew the exact amount immediately. He twisted his lips and squinted.

"About 4 cans." He responded.

Cid laughed and began to haggle, "Surely this is at least six. Last time, we got six."

"Well these don't grow on trees Cid," said the bartender, "and I don't see anyone else in the area who sells these."

"What is this place?" Joshua interrupted as he walked along the edges of the room. His eye catching the most bizarre of items.

Next to the canisters there sat a hat like one out of a fantasy book. It bore a wide and floppy brim and a pointed top. It collected dust there on one of many shelves. Beside it sat a short, thin, twig with a single leaf growing at the point. Guns and knives and oddly shaped bones were placed beneath it in a heap, filling in its placement on the pile.

Joshua finally realized he stood within *the* black market, the infamous black market. It was something of an oddity. It was clearly evident in the world. Many conspiracies stemmed from their existence. It was a single existence, a singular, worldwide organization that spanned across the globe. The Black Market was a secret cabal led by unidentifiable people hidden in the shadows, people whom Joshua used to hunt in the days he spent in France.

Joshua didn't know who began the black market or why it was so powerful, but the free trade underground gave small civilizations, like that in the Americas, the resources to survive. It was for this reason that most officials didn't mind their presence. And then, it was because of their presence that most officials became scared or corrupted.

"Who's this guy?" The bartender asked Cid, ignoring Joshua's question.

"He's … *new.*" Cid responded, "The boss wanted him to stretch his legs for a bit, so he's *here.*"

"Oh, the boss-man," The bartender clicked, "I get it. How is old Laffy nowadays?"

"Not old, if that's what you're wondering." Cid murmured, his eyes still trained on Joshua who rummaged through the oddities.

"One of these days, I would like just a quart of his blood." The seller insinuated, "Apparently, there's this guy in America who will pay millions for ageless blood…"

Joshua gripped the handle of a large sword, its blade buried in the heap. It fit perfectly in the palm of his hand. A single dull-green emerald sat in its hilt from whence thin steel wires rose from the sides to meet and form the cross guard. It was a single-sided blade, but enchantingly symmetrical. The blade curved like a spine, reminding Joshua of Mongolians and hussars of old.

"Look, for Lafayette, I'll give you five cans, and no more. *But,* you have to promise me the next time he gets cut up you'll try to collect the blood for me."

Cid laughed, "I don't think that will be a problem. The boss is a klutz. He's bound to get a scrape or two sooner or later."

The bartender shook Cid's hand and proceeded to place the cans in a small leather duffel he provided for them. While the bartender packaged their purchase, Cid watched as Joshua pulled the Mongolian blade from the shelf. Joshua liked it, Cid could tell. It looked perfect in his hands.

Cid grabbed the bag from the bartender and lifted it over his shoulder. The bartender pocketed the cash and moved to open the door for him.

"Come on Hill." Cid urged.

Joshua paused and looked at the blade once more before reluctantly putting it back onto the pile beside the witches' hat. He turned and sauntered out behind them, back into the fray of drunken soldiers. Cid passed through with the bag before him, following the bartender to the entryway.

"I'm sorry you didn't like the rooms," the bartender stated. He spoke louder than before, trying to subtly let other people hear. "There should be another inn about ten miles down the road. You should get there before the sun rises if you cut through the forest."

"We'll do that." Cid echoed back in kind.

The two left the tavern and no bystander seemed the wiser. After The Bartender watched the pair disappear back into the woods, he went back to the room where they had conducted their deal. He wanted to make sure everything was still there. *Healthy paranoia*, he called it.

"Is everything alright?" Faith called out from the bar.

The bartender didn't answer, his eyes caught an anomaly in the room. He couldn't remember why it was there, or who had found it. He walked over to the shelf and grabbed the sword Joshua displaced, slowly placing it back where it had rested before. The Bartender's eyes were focused on the hat it was sitting upon. He didn't remember owning a hat in the shop, and he didn't remember seeing it anywhere else in the bar.

"John," Faith whispered through the door frame. "Are you okay?"

"Yeah…" The bartender whispered back.

Faith walked forward and snatched the hat from the shelf. She put it on with a slight nod. "I'm sorry, I left this here when I was closing last night. I found it in the woods yesterday." She said, her chin forward, pointing at John in a cute manner.

John looked at her, thinking she was as beautiful as ever, as young as the day they met. He smiled halfheartedly, still unsettled by the hat's appearance in the room.

"It looks great on you." He complimented, "I'm going to take a nap, let me know if anybody needs me."

John walked out of the room slowly and disappeared through the crowd. Still unsettled by its presence.

Joshua trudged back through the thickening fog. It clung to his shirt and matted his hair. Before him, he could hardly perceive the shape of Cid carrying the gas canisters on his head, pathfinding before him.

"Stay close," Cid called, "I wouldn't want you getting lost out here."

"I'm here." Joshua replied. Watching Cid carefully through the haze.

As they continued, the fog had enveloped them. It wasn't long until Joshua couldn't see Cid at all. Still, he listened to the sound of his feet. He followed that noise until, suddenly, he couldn't hear them anymore.

Where had he gone? Joshua thought.

"Over here." Cid called.

Joshua looked to his right and began to follow. The voice sounded close, so Joshua moved that way. He thought that Cid hadn't stopped to wait for him but was before him walking, nonetheless. This explained why he still couldn't see him in the distance. But if Cid called him, the Rockstar must have been able to see him. Joshua trusted the lad knew where he was going.

"Keep up." Cid called again.

"I'm here" Joshua replied, trudging on through the murk.

"Stay close."

"I'm here, I'm here!" Joshua replied again, this time louder. He wasn't sure Cid could hear him coming.

After Joshua spoke there was a silence. The fog showed no signs of thinning and Joshua continued forward. He still couldn't hear Cid's feet nor see his back, but he was confident that the pirate could find their ship.

"Keep up." Cid called yet again.

Joshua's heart began to beat heavily in his chest; he began to notice the voices tone; it sounded the same as the last time he said it. The more he thought, the more he felt that he was talking to a broken recorder. Cid's voice was playing on a loop. Joshua felt like he was playing a game of Marco Polo. Nevertheless, he pressed on. He had no choice but to walk. After a time, Joshua could hear the voice of Cid again, this time an incessant repetition of words. The noise began to alarm in his head like a ringing phone.

"Keep up… Stay close… Keep up… Stay close… Keep up… stay close…"

"Shut up!" Joshua huffed, lunging forward, hoping to grab Cid by the shirt; but, as he lunged, his foot snagged a lump in the ground before him. Joshua fell.

"Cid!" Joshua called into the fog, hoping for a new bearing, a confirmation of life. But there was no response.

"Cid!" Joshua called again from his stomach. He reached his hand out, hoping to find a shoe, or anything, to get his bearings, but his hand touched nothing.

"Cid!"

Still, nothing but the sound of his own heartbeat.

Moments passed and the fog remained. Joshua lay there tired, the fog filling his lungs. The cold humidity distorted the light around him. He was in a cloud, a cloud in the center of a blue planet called hell. Joshua was blinded by an unyielding obstruction and now he was lost. The young man was lost on the ground motionless until he heard those concrete, chiming, words again.

"Keep… up?"

Joshua opened his eyes and looked up. Before him the fog seemed to move about and create a brief pocket, a small space like a closet. Joshua looked up from within that space at the walls of fog that imprisoned him. The American looked forward and found a face looking into his eyes. But, the guise wasn't a true face, it was a piece of rounded wood worn like a mask. It had knots that looked like eyes, symmetrical and perfect. He looked at the mask, whose body was composed of the fog. The fog had stretched itself into the space to meet him. Its face hung down from above him in curiosity. Joshua gripped the grass beneath him and positioned himself on his knees, panting.

The face swayed around him, the fog attached to it like some unholy matrimony of a dryad, a treant, and a cloud. It observed him with interest. From the mask a sound was uttered forth.

"Stay… close?"

Joshua had been hoodwinked. How long had he followed this mischievous, spectral, ghost, thinking it was Cid? It was as if he were chasing a parakeet into the ocean, and now he was in the middle of the sea, with neither a map nor a compass.

The thing lingered there, waiting. Joshua was surrounded by it, he and Cid unknowingly walked into the belly of a Terrible Dogfish, and Joshua was Geppetto, lost and alone.

"Keep up." The thing chimed again. It seemed to beg communication with Joshua, but the man could not understand it. The man didn't need to. The American felt an odd pull at his shirt and the air about him grabbed his collar, politely pushing him towards its organic face. The disembodied being swiveled back in the same direction of Joshua and began to lead him somewhere by force. Joshua watched as the fog collapsed again, erasing the room from existence and leaving him in the mirth.

Joshua made a break for it. He turned the second he felt the air loose and sprinted through the fog, hoping to see daylight again, but the fog soon solidified about his ankles and he fell to the ground. It was hopeless. He looked up to find the fog inches before him, staring blankly.

"Stay close." The fog stated. This time, it seemed more assertive and sterner. The incorporeal oddity picked up Joshua by the back of his shirt like a young cub. The ex-detective hung there helplessly, and he floated behind the mask into nowhere.

Sometime later, Joshua found his feet as the fog slowly floated him down. It seemed to mind its own, confident Joshua would stay by its side this time. The fog was curious of Joshua, this the man was sure of, but it also seemed curious of every wildflower it passed. It would near itself to each plant as if to sniff it or tend to the budding sprout, and rather, it would muse to it. A shake of its head or the words "keep up, stay close," was all it used to make noise. Whenever it shook its head, the fog would ripple slightly, a piece of its body, and shake the grass like the breeze does in grainy, golden, fields.

The oddity seemed entertained by everything, all the while sending Joshua along with its own journey. If Joshua were to stop, thinking he could slip away, the fog would become frustrated at him like a pet, and push him from behind.

Joshua could breathe better now, and his clothes were starting to dry.

After another time of follow-the-leader, the fog seemed keenly more aware; it stopped less and less, until it became certain that it was going the right way. Joshua followed it through the trees, through the fog which was itself. The fog determined its route and picked up the pace, there, in the distance they directed towards, was a small shadow which began to grow, soon they had emerged upon it.

After it had taken shape, as if made by the fog's body, Joshua stood before a shack. It was a small shack, a desolate one. After further inspection, Joshua determined the shack was tangible by grabbing the lock gingerly.

"Stay close!" the fog screamed. Joshua turned quickly to face the face behind him. The ex-detective was ready to defend himself, but the anomaly did not attack. It seemed to retreat. It shook its head, it repeated itself. "Stay-close-stay-close-stay-close!"

Joshua did not know what it meant by the words.

Slowly, the man reached for the door again and, slowly, he pushed it open, ready for the fog to scream again, but this time it didn't. Instead it opted to move closer, having prepared itself for what lie beyond the wooden gate.

Joshua found himself inside the hut, revealing it to have much more room than preconceived. If anything, it looked like the size of the bar he was in however long ago.

No, it was that exact bar.

There was no furniture, except for an occupied bed in the center of the room. When Joshua began the understand what he gazed upon, what he witnessed mortified him. He bent over and looked at the soles of his boots, they were caked in quickly-drying blood. There on the bed adjacent from him was a young couple maimed and brutalized in their sleep. Barbed wire and torture tools hung across the walls.

The couple's faces were unrecognizable. But there on the floor against the headrest was a pair of yellowed glasses, chipped and rusted. The bodies laid side by side, their hands entwined and burnt to a crisp, seared together in embrace. It was the two bartenders from the Russian outpost. The sizes of their bodies matched perfectly and so did the color of their hair. Into their skin, barbed wire had been embedded to form odd symbols and words such as misfortune, distrust, greed, and jealousy. The rest of the barbed wire was strung from their bodies and arced into the air like string for marionettes. A hot, iron, poker lay on the floor beside them and a blue fire nestled soundly in the fireplace.

Joshua traced the blood that ran along the floor. It made a definitive arc across the wooden vinyl and as Joshua's eyes finished, he determined its shape. The blood was drawn into the shape of a disjunct pentagram.

Joshua felt a chill down his spine.

"Where am I?" He asked himself.

The world seemed to pause, the fire settled, or perhaps it began to freeze. Joshua heard a creak and a tapping of heels against to hollow floor akin to brass casings on laminate. Joshua slowly turned about to spy a pair of black marble eyes floating in the air.

"Maybe it's where, or maybe it's when." The eyes corrected in a gruff voice.

"What do you mean?" Joshua asked, looking at the two floating beads. The eyes stayed far off at first, but soon neared slightly closer into the light of the furnace. "I saw these two people alive. This is a vision, isn't it?"

"What is alive?" The man responded. "You've seen them. You've *interacted* with them, but is that life? What you are seeing not a vision. They *are* dead. They died."

"How can they be dead if I just saw them alive?" Joshua stammered.

The voice fell silent for a moment, contemplating. It waited a moment before speaking again. "Sometimes… the world sees it fit to keep things the way it was. Sometimes someone misguided and evil creeps into a house at night and ends something that otherwise could have been perfect. These two lovers were a perfection, the best of creation, the best of the pure. And, the world, or God, or magic, or wizards, or necromancers, or what-have-you, decides to put them back together because they, or he, or it, fell in love with them. This couple has been deeply affected by magic. Someone has brought them back from death and left their bodies here, that much can be said."

"So, they *are* alive." Joshua insisted, taking one step forward.

"Would we consider ghosts to be alive? Their bodies are here, in this forest, in this stomach. This is the couple's grave. I would *not* venture to classify this phenomenon as necromancy, but the subjects are un-*dead*, nevertheless."

The eyes loomed closer and, in a puff of rolling smoke, the figure revealed himself. Before Joshua stood a sharply dressed man with short silver hair. His marble eyes stared into Joshua's soul. He wore nothing but black. The enigma was getting on in his years. His skin sagged slightly but his overall countenance had not withered. He reminded Joshua of Baron Glass, much older, much more kingly and noble.

"Do you think people need a body to live?" the black-eyed man asked.

Joshua thought to himself for a moment before answering. He thought of Haddock, although Haddock was a ghost, he had a house, if not for a moment. Haddock laughed and smiled and helped Joshua escape Whitecroft's clutches. Was Haddock not living, when he sat across from Joshua and drank with him? Perhaps Elizabeth wasn't so cruel. Perhaps, although Haddock aimed to see his daughter from beyond the grave, the one who summoned him gave him another gift, the gift of his own life. Perhaps Elizabeth was a saint.

"I suppose anything is possible." Joshua answered, a deign of sarcasm and dishonesty in his voice.

The stranger smiled slightly and nodded. He began to pace to Joshua's left, looking down at the corpses.

"So why am I here?" Joshua huffed after much pause.

"You're here because life has dealt you a bad hand." The man answered, "And I'm here to help you."

"I don't need help." Joshua snapped, and he began to walk to the door. Joshua twisted the handle and opened the panel, but on the other side of the entrance floated the fog, its mask pressed firmly into the door. It prevented Joshua from leaving.

"You don't need help killing Solomon, then?" The Stranger called.

Joshua turned, serious, sad. "How do you know that name?" He demanded.

The Stranger chuckled, but quickly his facial expression changed from amused to worried. He looked down slightly before explaining: "Solomon is a part of my family."

Joshua squinted and began to walk away from the exit, the entrance.

"So... how do you want to help me." Joshua inquired.

"You were a detective before all of this, correct?" the man blinked, motioning Joshua towards the bed. "I want to help you by doing this couple a favor."

The man pointed with an open hand towards Faith and John, a slightly dignified pose about him. Joshua looked at the two corpses, the dead bodies who still lived. Like snakes, perhaps they had shed skin. Somehow, by some magic, they reincarnated back into existence as the same people, somehow not knowing who they were or what once happened to them (unless they knew, and simply never let it be known.)

"I want you to find the thing who did this." The Stranger began, "I already know that the killer is tied to the skyship you are traveling on. Years ago, when The Marquis first stopped in Russia, he sent a delegation of sailors to buy fuel from the tavern. One of these sailors, a promiscuous man, met Faith at the bar. At first, he tried flattery, then, he tried money, but the girl was in love with John and so the girl wouldn't accept any of these coercions. So, the sailor resorted to force, and was having his way with her until she managed to slit his throat. John and Lafayette buried his body somewhere, after Faith told them about what happened. They thought it was over, until later that night... the same man took on the form of a vengeful spirit and killed them in their sleep."

"A spirit?" Joshua asked.

The Stranger huffed and adjusted his collar. "Spirits... how to describe spirits, or avatars, as they can be called... When great emotions, dreams, or desires are manifested, so does magic also manifest. This magic is manipulated to take on the personalities, the memories, and the intentions of the feeler. Sometimes, that 'avatar' is only alive for a mere moment, unable to take full form. Others take full form, but only for a few minutes…

Even still, every so often, very, very, rarely, does an avatar manifest for its full lifetime. It lingers and haunts a place for eons, sitting upon the emotions and purpose of that which it was created from. Because this perpetrator died, his desires continued his will. Because the victims died in their bed, side by side, an avatar of love and protection manifested to watch over their grave. It is not uncommon that two avatars are born at once. It takes great emotion to stir great emotion out of others."

The stranger cleared his throat before continuing. "This man left his avatar on the earth. His avatar haunts the ship Le Marquis De Lafayette sails. Perhaps it grew bored of waiting in its typical place and was powerful enough to move away from its home. Either way, the man has left behind a spirit of vengeance, a dark avatar."

"I would be looking for a man, then?" Joshua asked, still slightly confused.

The man shrugged, "Avatars can take many forms… The avatar outside, this *fog*, took an odd form, something of a djinn, maybe. I cannot say what form the dark spirit has taken. I think this fog knows what, and who, you're looking for. Because these two spirits were born from the same tragedy, they will most likely draw each other out of hiding when they are close together."

The man finished; he held out his hand, and within it, seemingly out of nowhere, a clear and corked bottle sat there. He moved it towards Joshua, whom delicately grabbed it by the neck.

"What am I supposed to do with this?" Joshua asked.

"Catch the fog." The man chuckled lowly. "If the spirit is willing to leave its home and join you, she will enter this bottle and travel with you. Do this for the spirit, kill the vengeful avatar, and you will be more prepared to face Solomon than you ever were before."

186

"Like a genie..." Joshua muttered to himself. The American uncorked the bottle, and an odd draft seemed to house within it, almost like a gentle vacuum trying to fill itself. The American took a deep breath and looked up to the man to tell him that he would do what was asked of him, but the man was gone already.

Joshua looked towards the door and slowly peered it open. There, still waiting, the sorrowful fog floated keenly. Joshua lifted the bottle out to the being and watched as small particles condensed into the bottle and filled it to the brim like dry ice. Joshua quickly corked the bottle and examined it in awe. Like a fish in a plastic bag, the avatar floated inside and swam about. It circled in anticipation.

Joshua jolted as the bottle of fog flew out of his hands and flew into the air.

"Keep up, Keep up, Keep up!" Joshua heard, as the glass rocketed into the mist.

"Wait!" Joshua yelled.

Joshua chased the bottle back into the remaining fog. Jumping over low rotting branches and roots, he tried his best to keep pace, but the bottle was too fast, having to slow down periodically to wait for him. It seemed perturbed and zoomed off into the distance again to wait for him. It was a game of tag and Joshua was the fat kid that was always picked on. The kids would wait for him to get near, and then, sprint out of reach, stopping only to repeat the teasing and mock Joshua's lethargy.

It didn't take long for Joshua to lose the bottle for the nth time. But only a few steps more had his forehead colliding with the side of a large wooden vessel. His head thumped against the hollow, tarred, exterior, and reverberated like a flat note from a gong. Joshua felt the hull and quickly realized he made it back to the skyship.

Joshua was glad to be back, but he felt odd, as if, he thought he might be going crazy. The American had experienced something no one else had. He didn't know whether he should tell anybody. What if the dark avatar was the Marquis, Cid? Here he was below the ship, almost afraid to climb up. It would be smarter of him to keep his task a secret so as to not arouse the suspicions of the people on deck. He was to find a murderer, and no one need know but him.

Joshua waited for a small increment of time before ascending the ladder. He searched the grass for the bottle, but his search bore no fruit. Dismayed, he decided it was best to return, and did so. Climbing the rungs, he was soon met with Gnat's open palm. Joshua took it, and placed weight to help himself upon the deck.

"Saw you coming," The soldier stated bluntly.

Joshua nodded to Gnat in acknowledgement and thanks. Looking up he saw the team before him, if one was to call it a team. Lafayette quickly approached to greet him.

"Joshua! What took you so long, decided to smell the flowers?" The captain joked before taking Joshua by the shoulder. This exchange was brief, and the captain immediately took off towards the stern, shouting at his crew. "Time to sail! Let's leave this fog!"

Joshua's return was business as usual for Lafayette.

"Are you okay?" Cid asked, his eyes furrowed in worry. "You look pale."

"I'm fine," Joshua lied.

Cid scratched the back of his head, embarrassed. "Sorry I left you, bruv."

Joshua shrugged. He was fine with it, truly, he hadn't thought it was Cid's fault. It had never occurred to him how Cid rushed off into the woods without making sure Joshua was behind him.

"It's all in the past now." Joshua assured blatantly; he didn't care enough to make his words seem genuine; he didn't think it would matter. Cid's ignorance wasn't what Joshua worried about.

Cid nodded back, slightly distraught at the response, looking for validation past his error.

Revealed after Cid was Saia. She stood there fondling her pathetic ball; she stood there with a twisted mouth of disgust, an obvious "you-should-have-died" expression on her face. But she didn't move off into her cabin as typical. She actually parted her lips, and in small under-case hushes she asserted her loathing against him.

"Don't you have something better to do?" She spat softly, like someone whispering slurs behind their bosses back.

What hurt Joshua the most was that he did have something better to do, so she wasn't wrong.

Joshua's disheartened face pleased Saia, in some small battle she had defeated him, and proved herself the stronger adversary. It was a terse exchange of words, but somehow it was a bullet that curved its way strait into Joshua's heart and pierced every chamber.

Joshua's disheartened face occurred because the man remembered something. He used to take crap from no one. Now, there stood a very little girl, possessing some adjunct scrap metal, capable of making him feel worthless. Joshua used to be cold and certain of himself. Now he felt like a wet sponge, soppy, squishy, and worst of all, yellow. He found himself trudging off underneath the dignified grunt of the girl, who flicked her hair in triumph like a lion, batting its mane in the wind.

Joshua grew tired and made his way to the beds underneath the deck. He soon found himself fast asleep. During Joshua's lull, he could hear the hard-working sailors toil. The captains voice was confident over them. They sang shanties, pausing to shout at each other. But this soon faded, and Joshua began to hear something else entirely.

Part 8/Requital

What Joshua heard wasn't something real, meaning, whatever had he picked conceived was not through the ear, but through his mind or perhaps his heart. Some people dream with the mind, they think things into being for the night, and reason with the images that come to their head. These dreamers fight off the chaos of misplaced objects and plot-holes in their world. These people wake up remembering what had happened in the night and can tell people exactly what they'd dreamed about the next day.

People that dream with their heart are quite different, they are subject to nightmares and feelings of imminent terror causing them to wake suddenly in beady sweat. They can't reason with their dreams, slaves to their fears and their loves. When that person wakes, they only remember the feeling the dream left them. They can wake up scared or confused, happy or sad. They don't know why, but even in some cases, they can feel the presence of something living, be it a monster beneath the bed, two hands squeezing their neck, or even the bosom of an angel in which they rest their head.

The pressing matter was, what did Joshua dream of, and why couldn't he remember?

When Joshua came to, however, he did feel quite outside himself. He felt as if he was looking through a pair of eyes that were not his own. His hands felt like odd machinations, his head a floating bubble trying to stay seated on his torso. His heart was silent, his eyes inflamed, his foot tapping the floor in a repetitive and energetic flurry.

It was because Joshua thought his foot was tapping, so outside his body as he was, that he didn't realize it was not his foot at all. At the toe of his boot rolled that small round bottle he had collected in Russia with the miasmic avatar within. It bumped against his rubber toe. The spirit had found its way on board and was asking for attention. It knew immediately the killer's approach.

Even now, Joshua's enemy was materializing on the four winds to descend and kill the fog's frail incasing. The fog had not the power to lift itself from the floor as the air was too thin to float. So, as Joshua rose to start his day, the bottle helplessly found itself kicked away and tucked into the corner, its warnings insufficient.

Above, the crew was almost within the airspace of the French Dominion. They all gathered along the rails to watch the Mediterranean Sea meet the 15th line.

The 15th was a long series of trenches, barbed wire, and dirt. The land had been terraformed in expectation of war. Tunnels beneath the overturned dirt had sapped the soil of nutrients and little foliage grew. It was a long strip of grey and brown, with green on either side. To their left was France, their small army vehicles looked like ants beneath them, unaware to their small human smuggling operations. The band of pirates had perfectly nestled themselves between the sun and a batch of clouds, ingeniously invisible to skyward eyes. But, either way, no soldier looked up. The sun was hot and bright that day. It was too painful for those below to look anywhere but down.

The crew dressed down, the scorching deck was splashed with water in an attempt to keep it cool. Men rolled up their pants or shorts and took off their shirts. Women opted to wear swim tops instead of the heavy cloth shirts standard to their occupation.

It was an odd paradise.

Lafayette lay on the deck with a small umbrella in his rum bottle. He tanned himself in peace on a deck chair. Gnat kept his helmet on, despite being shirtless himself. He looked funny, like a poor prisoner in an iron mask. The soldier looked at Joshua, who stood halfway into the hull wondering if he should change.

"Morning." Gnat grunted.

Lafayette glanced over and waved. "We are about two or three days from Metz after that delay." He said, taking another sip of rum. "You would be home sooner but the fuel we bought isn't running so well. This boat's getting old, it seems. You'll be let off south of Paris, as you well know, along the Mediterranean Sea. From there you'll have to rent a horse or walk the rest of the way home."

Joshua didn't know if he looked forward to home, to Paris. He might have wanted to go before, but back then he was a simple detective trying to make ends meet and clean up a city full of evil and crooked people. Now, he knew there was more than people to look out for. Anything was possible, and there was too much left to do. Moreover, he was no longer a cop, he was a rouge, a criminal.

Joshua rightfully doubted Baron Glass would pardon him. French officers would be looking for him if Whitecroft informed the other barons of Joshua's survival. But despite the possibility of being headhunted, Joshua had to find Solomon. He wanted answers and justice. He wanted revenge for his diaspora, to tear open the man's chest and carve his initials into his still-beating heart to let the devil know who sent him.

Joshua also felt less benign. He knew there was more purpose to his life. Joshua understood that he might have to fight the barons if he was to continue living in France. He would kill them if he had to. Was this the ramification onto them for tossing him to the wolves? Would Joshua be a righteous man if he returned in a fervor of retribution? Was it right for him to embody a criminal in order to achieve his goals?

Why did Joshua even think to care? Perhaps such things were still beyond him and he shouldn't trifle with those wayward thoughts. What Joshua was certain of was that he would do whatever it took to kill Solomon. He wouldn't sleep well until he was dead. He couldn't sleep well.

Joshua continued to imagine what he would have to do in France. He decided to meditate and relax in the cool of the lower deck. There, he would plan on how to safely get to Paris, and, how to safely find and kill Solomon.

However, it was later that day when Joshua lounged in his hammock that something odd struck him on the back of his head. The bottle, having fully regained its strength from the descending aircraft, plowed into Joshua, leaving a twinge of pain at the back of his skull.

Joshua twisted about, rubbing the back of his head and playing witness to the culprit. The clear bottle floated before him and shook in anticipation, trying to break from its shell. Joshua recalled his promised task and rose to grab the bottle only for it to shoot off again. The bottle zoomed this way and that, it paused at each bunk as if to sniff each cloth. Joshua followed it in a panic. It bounced off the walls like a ricochet bullet until finally shooting through the stairs to the upper deck.

Joshua stormed out onto the deck to watch the bottle smash against the floor with a loud crack and fizzle. The small fog withered in its broken cask and shot off into sky, returning to the atmosphere.

Joshua was confused, he looked over to Gnat whom stood facing him, staring through his helmet. He was most likely confused as well.

Joshua waited for Gnat's first question, but it never came. At first, Joshua thought the soldier had broken a speaker, and was muttering inside his broken helmet. But no motion nor sign language was moved for his eyes to play charades with. Gnat was perfectly still.

Joshua turned to Lafayette who lounged motionless in his chair and discovered that he was too still as well. It looked as if he had turned to hear the sound of the breaking glass. In his hands Laffy held a small pink book labeled "Love's Unending Air." His hand was poised over the spine, a page pined between his thumb and forefinger, frozen in mid-turn.

Joshua felt a sudden gale but the cloth zeppelin above him did not shift under the force as the American was used to. It was strange, it seemed that time stood immobile.

Joshua glanced at the sailors, each of them leaning over the rail or trying knots on the ropes. None of them moved, poised like perfect mannequins. They were a troupe of trophies, so real, yet so lifeless.

Joshua heard a whoosh about the stern and looked back to find a sailor careening down the steps. His rigid body bounced like a concrete block down the stairs until finally resting upon the ground. He lay there in the same frozen position that he began. Like a toy soldier he lay until, piece by loosing piece, his body began to incinerate. The body became a fire for a brief moment before turning into a puff of ash which dispersed through the rails and down into the earth below.

It was indeed that the world had frozen, all but the wind, which carried dark green clouds towards the ship, was still; all but the bully who pushed the sailor down the stairs, was animated. Soon the platform was swallowed by the intermittent storm. It soon grew into a hurricane. The ship sat in the eye of this tropical twister and red thunder rumbled inside the smog as frequent as a drum or triangle.

Joshua turned again to look up at the wheel. He who drove it was not any man Joshua had seen before on the ship. Verily, he was hardly a man at all. He stared at Joshua, waiting for acknowledgement.

As the humanoid began to approach, Joshua witnessed something else in the corner of his eye. The very same sharp dressed man in the beady eyes walked by him. Through his peripherals, he waltzed serenely to gaze into Joshua's view. The Stranger nodded slightly. He seemed to play referee or a composer to the whole ordeal. As he passed from right to left of Joshua's sight, he could hear him in his head. It was almost like a bullet before a horse race, a whistle before a play, a trumpet before the heavens opened, formed into a single audible and candid sentence reassuring Joshua he *"knew what to do."*

The Humanoid jumped down from the railing, not noticing The Stranger's existence. The being boasted antlers upon its bald head. It garnered rippling muscles and six eyes were placed upon the façade of the thin and tall frame. Its pupils burned like white coals and its fingers stretched like talons. The spirit's skin was made of composite ash. It had no genitals, and no clothes, for that matter. In the demon's hand was a large and thin slab of square rock, this slab met a handle to form a crude sword or bastard cleaver. The blade was five feet long and the handle two feet.

Joshua didn't know what to do, but what came next was not expected.

"Tell me your name." The avatar asked. His voice sounded like an explosive volcano, a combination of deep tones and choking phlegm.

Joshua hesitated, but decided he would rather delay any attack and answer. Quickly and confidently, Joshua answered. "My name is Connor Shaw, and yours?"

The avatar laughed. As his chest heaved, small openings under his skin were exposed, revealing a burning furnace of white heat. The avatar had no vitals like humans. This would make fighting him very difficult, Joshua discovered.

"We born of hearts have no name." The Avatar responded.

Joshua watched the beast's sword arm, it began to grip the handle of its sword tighter.

"Do you think I should die for something someone else did?" The Avatar asked.

Joshua stammered, his mouth parted, but he didn't know how to answer. Joshua hadn't thought about it. This avatar, although born of hate and vengeance, didn't rape the girl in the shack.

"But you did kill them." Joshua debated aloud, "You killed that couple the night you were born…"

"Such was my conception and purpose. I was born with thoughts not my own, my father's will. I started to think after committing a crime during infancy. A child should not be punished for doing what their parents ask them to."

Joshua closed his right eye a moment, wanting to understand what the avatar was hinting at.

The Avatar was born in the wake of intense emotions, with the memory and purpose of someone he didn't know. He was compelled to do something against his will. Was the life of a spirit that cruel? The Dark Avatar was born against his say so. The person that birthed him gave him his task, his purpose. The Avatar wouldn't have a choice, would he?

Joshua's lip twisted, he began to chuckle crookedly. He was an idiot. He didn't care. If Joshua killed this Avatar, he would be one step closer to his goal, one step closer to fighting Solomon. Joshua reached into his jacket for his gun.

"Shit." Joshua sighed, he wasn't wearing his jacket, he didn't have a gun.

The beast roared and lunged forth with his giant slab of bladed stone. Joshua dove to the side narrowly. The Avatar paused, the sword outstretched. Despite its massive weight, the beast wielded it with the strength of Hercules. It spat, a plume of magma on its lips, distraught.

"You're just like everyone else, Shaw!" The demon bellowed. "You don't understand us!"

The demon of wrath swung its sword again, but Joshua dropped to the floor as it narrowly passed his chest. The American watched as the blade passed over his sternum and lodged itself into the rail of the ship. The Demon quickly pried the sword free of the rail as Joshua rose.

The Avatar rushed Joshua again and the detective steeled himself, the adrenaline coursing through his veins assured him he could survive. The vengeful Demon swathed its sword horizontally at Joshua, who nimbly lunged over the blade. Joshua rolled as his body met the polished floor and stayed low.

The thunder cracked, and Joshua waited for the monsters next move. He needed to bide his time and come up with a plan.

The demon charged again, his giant weapon lifted above his head. Joshua lunged forth and closed his fist. Before the demon came down with his blade, Joshua was below it, smashing his hand into the avatar's belly. The dark spirit stooped slightly, more awestruck by the blow than hurt by it.

Joshua clutched his hand in pain. It was not the force of the blow that hurt him, but the reaction of his hand with the avatar's body. Joshua watched as his hand curled about itself, trying to fight what seemed like an infection, a parasite. The skin on his hand flaked and turned a dark black. Cells began to disintegrate before him, blowing out into the breeze.

Joshua forced his hand to stretch back out. The bones in his fingers relocating into place in a series of disgusting pops and cracks.

"You cannot harm me, Shaw! You will be cursed before you make me bleed!" The Avatar mocked.

Joshua felt a huge force on his side and he was sent flying backwards, sliding across the deck. At that contact, Joshua watched as his shirt began to vanish in the same way, turning to ash. The Avatar laughed at him and wiped the soot from his mouth. It slowly began to advance again.

Even though the spirit was unscathed, it was more cautious than before. It strafed the detective, waiting patiently for him to rise.

"Connor." It mocked, "Connor 'Shaw,' you have no compassion. You are just a killer. You don't *know me*."

From the ground, Joshua spied a glint at the stern. There upon the terrace lay a small sword, something a pirate must have left, forgotten in his duties. Joshua had to get it.

Looking up, the Demon still circled, waiting for a fight. Joshua hesitated till The demon circled around to the bow, away from the sword, and bolted away.

The Demon roared and charged Joshua whom turned his back on his enemy. Swinging down his long sword, he left a gash in the detective's back which burned its mark and set fire to the remains of his shirt. Joshua yelped and tumbled before regaining his balance and continuing his flight away. From where The Demon struck, the blade caught the floor, sticking once more, giving Joshua enough time to make it to the top and leap behind the railing.

The Avatar didn't bother to pull out his sword. He pounded his fists which set off sparks like flint. He huffed, furious.

"Connor" He bellowed, "Not only are you a soulless cur, you're a coward!"

Joshua panted, his back felt cold, his nerves seared and numb. He quickly rose for a mere second and snagged the sword at the stern into his hands before squabbling back into the protection of the rail. The tube of the storm started to grow closer, and the thunderous flashes of light became red lightning, striking near the ship. Joshua unsheathed the small blade, a mail breaker, hardly thick enough to sever the beast's limbs, but sturdy enough to survive a blow from his foe's weapon.

Joshua scooted himself to the rear of the ship, being cautious to remain out of the monster's sight, and eyed the enemy though a crack in the wood. The Avatar stood there on the main deck, waiting, muttering in frustration, pumping itself with adrenaline. It pounded its black chest which plumed with red heat. It was stoking itself like a fire. For some odd reason, it did not ascend the next floor.

Joshua gripped the blade firmly in his hands, his back screamed, his good-hand numbing further. Joshua felt his eyes grow hot, he was taking on a feverish illness, a grotesque rage. The American felt sick, but it was an estranged sickness that boiled his stomach like a steamboat. He shook his hands, squeezing the muscles in his arms, demanding his body move. Joshua worked himself to stand and yelled back at the prideful avatar. This gave his body the surge to continue.

In a sheer second of planning, or no forethought at all, Joshua rose and sprinted towards the railing at full speed. With the blade firmly in both hands, he planted his foot and leapt straight for the Demon whom looked up, astonished by Joshua's zeal and suicidal assault.

Joshua flew through the air and gripped the blade closely to his chest like a lance. He collided with the beast with a loud crack and drove the blade through its stomach. They both fell to the ground, and the blade wedged itself neatly between two panels of wood, pinning Joshua's foe into the ground.

Joshua rolled quickly but couldn't avoid the consequences of the collision. As he had touched the Demon, his body lit into flames and his skin scorched in anguish. Joshua rolled, and tore at his body. He drooled, his body tweaking and bending in spasms.

The beast roared. It pushed against the blade, trying to rise.

Joshua managed to snuff the flames as he rolled. He couldn't feel his arm or his leg. They hung beside him aimlessly as Joshua clawed at the flooring, the pain lingering. The American crawled past the beast, heading for the five-foot blade.

"Connor," The Beast screamed. "Come here Connor!"

The Avatar reached for Joshua and grabbed his boot. Joshua flailed, the boot began to melt and peel. He kicked and wiggled his foot free of his shoe, turning back to the blade. The avatar grew tired trying to unpin itself; it breathed deep breaths, waiting to regain its strength for one massive heave.

Joshua had to hurry.

Joshua continued to crawl. Using his good arm to pull himself, he still had a long way to go. It was hopeless. He couldn't make it in time. Joshua listened to the Demon as he heaved the blade out of its chest in a surge of spare energy.

The American heard the blade clang against the ground. He heard the heavy feet approach him.

Joshua turned around as the beast clamped its talons around the man's neck, squeezing with all his might. The heat, the searing pain of the avatar's hand felt like a fryer. Joshua started to black out with a hiss of boiling skin. His eyes fading, his body flailing, The Demon picked Joshua up by the neck and watched intently as Joshua's throat grew the black, ashen curse. Joshua fought the magic all he could, but soon, the dark ashen marks began to make their way across his body, and his skin began to blow away in the tiniest of pieces.

Joshua blinked and blinked again. Beyond the beast, in the corner of his vision was the man in the black suit. The Stranger watched intently, he motioned to Joshua, he pointed behind Joshua. Joshua grimaced, suffocating. He tried to look back, but his eyes could only swivel so far.

Joshua could feel what The Stranger was pointing at. Joshua remembered its presence. He felt a collection of droplets down his back. Joshua watched as a mist began to slowly creep from behind him and move between him and the dark avatar. Somehow, there between the beast and the boy, was the sliver of fog, lucid and frantic.

The lover's spirit grew. It grew slowly like a building cloud until it fit between the demon's arms. The animated wisp slowly solidified like the fog in the forest, providing a wedge between the grip of the demon upon Joshua. It separated the demon's arms as it grew, and the American fell to the ground onto his rump, gushing black-spotted blood from his mouth like vomit.

The fog expanded until it covered the floor of the ship like a mire. A face condensed into a spectral mask which took the form of wood; It was the fullness of the woodland spirit, the gravity of two spirits entwined, fighting over the death of a couple struck down in the midst of night.

The Fog glided its way around the Embered Demon and slashed its body with condensed fog. The Embered burned fiercely, vaporizing the blades after each lesion, and thus damaging the Fog in a passive countersuit. It was a war of attrition, a fight for survival, cut by steaming cut. There was no difference immediately noticeable between the two spirits, they were perfectly matched. The only difference lay in Joshua, whom, during the commotion, crawled his way to the bastard blade and gripped it.

To Joshua's horror, the blade was made out of the same ash the Embered Demon constituted. It carried the same curse. As Joshua seized the blade, his only good hand quickly began to turn to ash.

With all of his strength Joshua pulled at the blade, trying to take it out of the floor. He didn't have the strength to lift it with one hand. He pulled, and he pulled, and he pulled while the John and Faith's avatar occupied the vengeful spirit.

Joshua couldn't help, as desperately as he wanted to. In his condition, he couldn't lift the blade. He looked back at the scene where the creatures thrashed about. Still beyond that view, The Stranger sat, examining the warfare. Moreover, he looked toward Joshua, the center of his attention, and smiled thinly.

Joshua tried to scream at him, but he coughed instead; more blood poured forth, accompanied by ash. Joshua couldn't hold the blade much longer, already, a quarter of his good arm had vanished into the storm, leaving a missing chunk in his skin.

Joshua heaved again, nothing. And again, he tried, but it wouldn't budge.

The Fog looked back at Joshua, in that moment, the ex-detective understood the oncoming predicament. In that short time, Joshua hadn't seen the toll the fight had taken. The Fog's mask was beginning to burn, the vapors beginning to dissipate, for not only was the Embered Demon burning the Fog away, the storm was taking it too. The lightning struck both Spirits in unison, having finally centered itself on deck, and the Demon's eyes rekindled anew. This was its storm, this was the Demon's spell and it would not quietly bend over and die. The dark avatar pummeled the Fog's mask into the ground, leaving it silent and still. The foe roared in conquering excitement and turned to Joshua, no longer chained by percolating fetters. It began to approach Joshua, who still struggled with the blade, half of his arm gone. It wouldn't move from its place.

Joshua realized he was perceiving the blade in the wrong gist. If the blade wouldn't move out of the hole it had made for itself, it might be able to move further in. The blade sat precariously at an angle, leaving a five-foot hypotenuse above the ground, creating plenty of space beneath.

Joshua waited, and the demon grew closer. Even with the surge of energy it moved slower than before, tired and lethargic from the long fight. Joshua couldn't move until the last second, he didn't want to give away his plan. In the corner of his eye, Joshua saw the Fog slowly rising from behind the beast, slowly waking and collecting condensation from the air about it. Joshua looked into its knotted eyes and prayed it would save him in time.

Joshua lingered, his fragile, cursed, body slowly waiting for his cue. The Demon approached his sword but passed it, making its way to Joshua, ready to end his life without charade. Joshua made sure to stand a few paces back from the weapon, he did not know if he weighed enough, but hoped the momentum of his frail body was sufficient.

The Fog was ready. With her long cloudy tendrils, it grasped the Demon by its ankles and flipped him onto his stomach. The Demon began to drag backwards. It tried to claw its way towards Joshua, but it wasn't enough to overcome his pinioned legs. Joshua urged what was left of his body forth. It moved with spectral ferocity and power, by a sheer miracle of force, or nature. The storm was at his back, the wind ushered him forth and he gripped the hilt of the bastard sword as the demon's shoulders passed it.

Joshua leapt off his feet and bore his full weight and strength upon the pommel. The sword shrugged and snapped the wood around it. With a load roar, the blade fell down through the deck and met the Dark Avatar's neck, severing its head from its body. The sword broke through the floor and fell into the hull, vanishing into the darkness below.

The Dark Spirit's head rolled around the ground like an eight ball.

It was dead.

The lifeless demon-body began to lose form. It soon become a pile of ash and dissipated into the green clouds. In turn, the lightning ceased to crack, the thunder began to quiet, and the clouds returned to a natural white purity, moving away from the skyship, giving the wayward vessel respectable space.

It was silent for a moment until The Stranger applauded softly and slowly, looking down at Joshua whom lay on the ground. The black-suited man moved from his place at the railing and stooped over the broken human.

Joshua felt his eyes become a desert, his sclera turned black and his retinas turned yellow. Even though the mad Avatar was gone, the curse continued to spread across his body. Joshua shuddered in pain. His body was at its limit and he couldn't move to save himself. If it were at all possible, maybe he would.

The Stranger reached for the head of the dark spirit, which was left after the battle. He pinched it by the left antler and shoved his hand into its mouth. The ashen mug separated, and The Stranger rooted inside it like a purse. The skin did not burn him as it did Joshua; the power of the curse had ceased to inflict on others, or perhaps he was something else entirely. The Stranger grunted, struggling to find the correct gland. He decided to speak, hoping to pass the time while he searched inside the throat like a surgeon without proper tools.

Joshua couldn't hear The Stranger and looked out to the Fog whom had helped him. It looked defeated, tired. The Fog seemed to look at him, the way a horse looks before the master shoots it in mercy. The mask it bore was no longer whole, the burned edges resembled paper growing smaller under the lick of a candle. It had fulfilled its purpose. It had honored the dead lover's memory and erased the traces of sadness they left behind. It brought forth justice for them.

The fog faded and only a sliver remained. It wiggled itself into the spacing between the floor panels and disappeared into the cold darkness below. Perhaps it was trying to recover, to repair itself. Whatever it was doing, it had left its mask on the deck like a vestigial bone.

"Here we are…" The Stranger said, yanking a stone from the Avatar's esophagus. He held it in the air and squinted from his knees. He had to make sure it was the right gland. The Stranger tossed the head over the railing and pressed the stone to Joshua's lips. With his free hand, The Stranger clamped down on Joshua's cheeks and forced the rock into his mouth.

"Swallow, kid, you don't have much time before you start decomposing."

Joshua swallowed and felt the rock force its way into his stomach. It hurt, but not as much as the curse. The Stranger looked around quickly and grabbed Joshua by the legs. He dragged the boy into the hull and out of prying eyes.

Joshua couldn't speak, but once he devoured the gland, he began to feel worse. As The Stranger carried Joshua into the lowest depths of the ship, he snagged a pair of clothes from Joshua's old bed.

In the next hour, The Stranger dressed Joshua, and then proceeded to explain the toll of his curse.

When Joshua was dressed, The Stranger sat across from Joshua's new bunk in the hull. They were housed in the wine cellar, underneath the hole they made which trickled subtle light down into the room. Thus, to the side, not far off from them, sat the Avatar's sword, standing against the barrels of alcohol.

"How can I explain this to you?" The Stranger began, "When spirits enter this world, they sometimes chose to take known forms. Most of the time, they chose to look like humans, that way they can live regular lives after they have done their duty. They live for a long time, and that depends on the amount of energy provided to them... Regardless, this spirit you fought, this spirit you fought took on the form of an Ifrit when it came out of hiding."

The Stranger waited for Joshua to say something, but he had forgotten how damaged the boy was. Joshua lay there on the hammock motionless, his dark eyes and yellow retinas staring straight at the ceiling. The sad man couldn't even move his neck. The black ash continued to grow, but it also built upon itself to refill the particles Joshua had lost in his fight.

Joshua was undergoing metamorphosis.

"An Ifrit is what you fought... *meaning,* that the curses and attributes ifrits are born with are given to them... most humans *cannot* touch ifrits, their skin, well, their bodies, are a type of resin that turns other things into the same constitution. It's like a Midas Touch, but even worse than gold, it's just ash.

Joshua, you *were* being turned to ash. You were becoming *like* an Ifrit. However, Ifrits have a gland in their body, it helps them stay solid beings, keeps them from crawling along the ground like dregs. Because you swallowed the same gland, you're *not* going to blow away or fall apart. But you will become something like an ifrit. Much like one, at least."

The Stranger saw Joshua was trying to squirm in his hammock, trying to scream. His eyes shifted in the pain of information. Joshua didn't want this. Joshua didn't think when The Stranger offered to help him, he meant *this* could happen.

"There are ways around it, ways to at least look human. But you're going to be different, you will be *stronger.*"

Lastly, The Stranger apologized, and then, he seemed to disappear. Joshua thought it was negligence, abandonment, denial or fear for the boy. But Joshua didn't know how sorry The Stranger felt, that his decisions and ambitions would lead to this. If he had known, he might not have asked Joshua to do this for him.

Joshua lay alone for hours as his body repaired itself. Forever, he thought, he would have to hide from civilization. He would be forced to live in obscurity, unable to march the streets of his home again without hoods and cloaks. How would this stop his revenge? Did Joshua's own ambition send him falling into the depths of despair like Icarus long before him?

In the hours before he was found. Joshua began to think again about how many ways he would like to die.

"Who the hell left a hole in my ship!?" The Marquis cried in disbelief. His hands gripped his long brown hair and pulled, tromping about the deck in a tizzy.

The sailors feared the captain's anger because it was so rare. When he was angry, it would take him weeks to settle down. First, he would yell for the whole day. Then he would mope about like a child for a week until he spiraled into depression for another, locking himself in his cabin until he finally accepted the truth. During those times, Cid would take over the captain's duties, and he did them well, if not better than the captain himself. But the crew hated this even more. It made them feel under-managed, as if their real boss wasn't smart enough nor cool enough to be their leader. It would have inspired mutiny, but everyone knew they couldn't kill the illustrious Marquis. He was immortal.

After these bouts of anger and depression, the Marquis would waltz out of his room with his hand on his hips, take a big sigh and exclaim, "Well, I guess what is done is done. Que sera, sera." Therefore, in the end, everything remained normal and the crew returned to business, used to the foolishness of the war hero.

But this time, the recourse of the incident was different, for when the sailors returned from the hull, they had a different excuse for the damage.

The Marquis followed them down to the stores of liquor. He asked about the sword as he made his way down the many flights of stairs. He stood there, and, bathed in thin streaking lights, stood the Ifrit's sword, laying against shattered barrels and swash. The Marquis admired its craftsmanship. It was simple and well defined, a sword that brought its end to a fine 90-degree point, while maintaining a thin edge for cutting. Its handle, though crudely made, was intricate and well carved to promote savagery. It was beautiful, but its gray color and its stone material made it barbaric and crude.

The Marquis reached for the hilt but soon found his hand being slapped away by a black claw. It snagged the hilt firmly, claiming it.

The men drew their swords and rifles in response, ready to show this stowaway the gangplank. But the Marquis halted his men with an outstretched arm.

"I wouldn't touch this sword if I were you. It does terrible things to your skin." Came a resounding voice, stern, but empty of emotion.

"Who are you and what business do you have aboard my ship?" The Marquis demanded in his big-boy voice.

The thing pushed itself into the shadows. Its body was made of a dark grain, covered by a loose white tunic, a tan pair of trousers, and a pair of strapped sandals. It had no toes. Its hands were sharply pointed, its head produced small forking horns which rested against its head and moved back in an arc to the sky. Its yellow and black eyes shone against a handsome yet featureless face. Its hair was black and long, descending his neck like a mixture between a hedgehog, a peacock, and a lion's mane. The monster looked right into The Marquis' eyes.

"Don't you see me? I am your guest," he replied. "I am Joshua Hill."

Joshua remained hidden in the hull for the rest of the flight, too ashamed to show his face to the sun. But those who didn't respect him, namely Saia, found her way into the hull anyways to look.

Joshua sat at the end, still near the crack in the boat, staring at Saia from the darkness. Despite his invisibility in the shadows, Saia stared back into the darkness directly due him in kind.

"What do you want?" Joshua asked.

Saia didn't reply. She stared, clutching her toy. Joshua fidgeted, tense under her beautiful and unnatural gaze. He clenched the sword in his lap like a stress ball, waiting. They sat there for a long time in silence, it almost served to mediate their hostility. It was both a dual and a duet, two people trying to figure out each other while trying to keep themselves hidden and above reproach. It was at the end of the day, when the sunlight the served its time and the moon shone through the cracks, that the small young girl returned after dinner.

"What now?" Joshua called out again.

Saia looked at her ball, and back again. She blushed, nervous, unsure. Joshua noticed, and pulled back into the shadows further. He tried to, at least.

Saia opened her mouth to speak and the words came out faster than she anticipated.

"Now-you-know-how-it-feels, Connor, you dumbass!" She cried.

Joshua rose in disgust and grabbed a barrel of rum. He yelled in anger and rose it above his head in monstrous strength, throwing it against the wall not far from the girl. The cursed man had been tempted to crush her, for her arrogance, her hostility, for treating him like a monster.

"I'm not Connor Shaw!" Joshua shouted, small droplets of fiery spit shooting from his mouth.

Saia looked away. She was unable to meet Joshua's gaze; Joshua had succeeded in scaring her. Joshua frowned, and Saia sprinted up the stairs past the Marquis whom had been standing there for some time.

Joshua looked at the Marquis and then turned away. "Do you think you handled that well?" The Marquis asked.

Joshua didn't reply, he moved back to his corner and sat there.

"I don't think others will be so scared of you in Paris. You might see a pitchfork or two." The Marquis continued.

Still, Joshua said nothing.

The Marquis shrugged and reached into his pocket. He produced a small package of cigarettes. "Gnat wanted you to have these." He said, passing the carton through the air. The cigarettes landed on the floor before Joshua who didn't bother to pick them up. What need did Joshua have to smoke now? He hadn't the taste buds.

The Marquis sat down on the stairs, his head hung lower than usual.

"You know, when I first joined the army, I was a happy man. I thought I would make a difference… But when the wars began I always hesitated to pull the trigger. I thought I could change the world, thought I was helping people. But I couldn't make up my mind about whether I *had* to *kill* people to do it or not. Eventually I did, I don't remember whether I was pressured into it or if it just came to me. I think I thought I would miss anyways, but I killed him, a general from the Germanic lands.

The promotions came after that. I tried to help others more with my newfound stature, tried to stay away from the front. But then America came calling, asked for help, wanted freedom from King George. I thought that was my chance to really make a difference."

The Marquis paused and reached into his own pocket. He pulled out his own cigarette and lit it, his hand shook slightly. He tried to mask this from view with his other hand.

"Then, Washington died. The guy wanted to cross the Delaware river. He grabbed his boats and his men, but sure enough on the other side there was a loyalist dame washing clothes. She shot him straight through the heart. Once he was gone the whole thing just fell apart. People were captured, heads rolled, you know, history stuff.

Then, it was France's turn. I thought Napoleon really wanted something better, but it was all a ruse to conquer the world. He didn't care about freedom, he cared about power and he used all of us like pawns. He bought me off, talked me into having a purpose again. And… like a fool I went rushing into war, my bayonet raised. In those moments of talking to him, I suddenly forgot, forgot how it felt to take a life…

When I was made the last baron, I made up my mind then and there. I didn't want to be a pawn anymore. I didn't want to watch as the southern hemispheres burned, and the barons yelled at each other over every dime. I saw Russia one night from my house, and, I realized the French Dominion was sitting on a time bomb. The whole commonwealth was ignorantly waiting to fall. So, I ran away. It was just like that: I took my people, I sailed away from France, and I never looked back."

The Marquis rubbed the butt of his cigarette into the stair beside him and tossed the scrap away. He sighed and looked forward at the adjacent wall. He rose from his seat.

"The truth is. I think we're all monsters, Joshua, whether we look like one or not. But if there's one thing that keeps you and me apart, is that you haven't given up yet. So, don't be like me. Promise me you'll die before you become like me."

The Marquis rose and began to trudge up the stairs, but before he vanished, he turned back, remembering why he came down in the first place.

"Come out when you're ready, we've arrived in Metz." He announced, finishing his walk up the stairs, vanishing headlong, leaving Joshua alone to his thoughts.

"I promise," Joshua replied, but nobody was there to listen.

Part 9/Rest

Joshua stood in France once again with his cloak covering his body. He was fully covered and carried a large wrap of gauze on his back, concealing the ifrit's sword in a large and thin water jar made of clay. At the handle, Joshua's clothes, including another bottle Joshua had found to put the fog back in, was tied in a burlap sack along with foodstuffs. The pirates had landed in Metz, unable to take him further lest arouse suspicion - the skyship was a Russian craft, after all.

Joshua still had a long distance to walk and plenty of time to think. He shook the Marquis' hand and waved goodbye to the crew. Gnat traced his finger down his helmet as if to draw a tear.

"Thank you for everything." Joshua told the Marquis, who walked him to the start of the pier. "I'll try my best from here on out."

"Of course," The Marquis remarked, "that is all I could ever ask. And there's no reason to say goodbye, I have a feeling we'll meet again."

The last baron smiled, and just like that, turned his velvet back to Joshua and danced back to the ship.

Joshua turned and began to walk through the town. He saw a simple way of life. An innocent community not worried about danger nor strife. No one payed the sojourn any mind. Joshua left the town in peace.

It was then, when he was walking the dirt road to the next town, that Joshua felt something tickle his nose. There in passing, a small sheet of paper zigzagged down before him and landed at his feet. Joshua bent over to pick it up. It was a letter that smelled of rose hips. It was addressed to him.

Joshua,

I've heard you've returned. You did a great job in Siberia! I can't wait to see you. I've taken the liberty to prepare some things for your arrival.

See you soon,
~Elizabeth

P.S. Sorry

Joshua crumpled the letter; he began to feel dizzy. It was the perfume, Elizabeth had poisoned the perfume. Joshua cursed as he felt a thick arm wrap around his neck. He had felt this arm before, it was large and muscular, like that of an ape.

"I'm sorry friend." Haddock huffed, it was almost a chuckle. He wrung Joshua's neck until he blacked out. Joshua could feel the undead mercenary lift him onto his spare horse and tie him to the saddle.

"I hate witches." Joshua thought as his horse began to trot away, its bounces thumped against his chest. It would be an uncomfortable ride back to Val-Ashoth.

Joshua could feel every winding road and every bumpy crag. Joshua thought it would only be a time before he returned to full consciousness. He didn't know how much time passed, but he knew that the ride was not long enough for him to be in The Crofts.

Once the bumpy roads and the winding crags had finished like the passing of a marching carnival, Joshua heard the familiar sound of laughter, and the familiar sound of water mills. It wasn't long after that Haddock lifted him off his horse, careful of Joshua's tender chest, and placed him on a large cushion. It only felt like minutes to Val-Ashoth, sixty seconds to another country. Had they teleported, or was Val-Ashoth in Metz, waiting for Joshua expectantly?

"Hey, Hero." Elizabeth cooed. She slouched on a cushion that was tied to her wicker chair. She sucked on a kiseru, the fumes running from the pot into her nostrils and out again. Her lips parted, cracked in a devil's smile. She looked down at Joshua, her chin pointing towards him, eyes slanted down.

Joshua lay on a mattress by the far wall. He was back in the witch's cottage and she had renovated. The room seemed less sinister. There were no more jars hanging from the ceiling with bones and organs from exotic species. The house looked like a vacation home, something tied to the beach. The paneling became lighter, no longer made of random twigs and branches but full aspen logs. The doors were made in Japanese design, a thick papyrus-white sheet covering the entrance and interior structures. Small flowers sat in vases protruding from the corners, lilies and tulips. Her house resembled the rest of the houses in Val, matching the architecture of the villagers.

Joshua grunted, his head throbbed. He was hungover, the poison killing his braincells, if he had a brain. From where Elizabeth sat in her black floral garb, close by Joshua's head, she pointed her toe and prodded Joshua's antlers, budging his head, taunting him.

"Ifrits are usually morning people." She quipped, "I would have thought the change would make you get up earlier than usual. You always hated mornings."

Joshua looked up, his chin resting on the pillow. "I hate you." He grumbled, but, looking upon her face, the words didn't come out so harsh.

"So close to home?" Elizabeth jested, "Yet so far from it."

Elizabeth laughed. It was a rebellious laugh. Something childish, conniving and sly. It was becoming of her. She stood and tossed her straw hat on his blanket. She sighed. "I've got some work to do with the locals, but I'll be back in a little while."

The witch walked to the sliding door at the end of the room, the entryway. Peering back before she left, she reminded Joshua playfully, "You know you can't run away, right? So, save us some time and behave yourself, okay?"

"Don't worry," Joshua mumbled, "I've learned a thing or two while I was free."

As Elizabeth vanished and slid the door shut behind her, Joshua laid his head back onto the pillows. He wasn't angry, oddly enough. He expected himself to be angry, but he was more comforted by Elizabeth's presence than discomforted. Joshua's heart beat against the mattress, he could feel it. Maybe she was a saint, Joshua thought, before falling back asleep. Maybe she was saint forwarding purpose to bitter hearts.

Joshua rose sometime after. The sun had passed above the house and peered through the thin fabric that provided natural lighting on the roof. It soon became too hot for Joshua to stay in bed. He looked about for his shirt and cloak to dress himself, rightly, before leaving the house.

Outside, the path that led to the village was opened. There were only a few trees, which were certainly not akin to the forest shrubbery before. Neither was the flora sinister and foreboding like that during Joshua's first visit; cherry blossoms accompanied apricot trees. They were well-spaced, the trunks easy to peer through, letting in plenty of light between their white trunks. It was springtime on the palm of Val-ashoth. Butterflies chased each other and rested on trees and wildflowers that riddled the ground in abundance. Odd looking animals scurried through the green grass unabashed. In the distance, through the trees, Joshua could see the village of Val-Ashoth perfectly. He hadn't realized the town was so close to Elizabeth's house. The forest before had obscured the distance between the two.

Joshua breathed in the fresh air and picked an apricot with his pointed fingers, skewering it like a knife and plucking it off. He began to walk down the path, taking bites as he moved along. It didn't take much time for Joshua to scale the last hill before reaching the town. Children ran about, brushing by him, pulling kites. The adults sat in their porches playing games with tiles. To his right, a man with a pair of glasses smiled as he sewed a tear in a child's shirt while the boy still wore it. The child stood there patiently, yet so anxious to run away.

Joshua smirked beneath his cloak. He made sure his face was hidden, worried that he might scare someone if they saw him. He kept his head down, which might have attracted even more attention than he realized.

As Joshua walked, he began to find his way to the center of the village where most of the commotion originated. Joshua leaned against the corner of a building, on the edge of the center, where the road met its end and the dirt became solid rock. The foundation of the center was a large slab of smooth white granite, uncut and weathered by time. In the middle of the crowd, in the hubbub, there was a small set of steps leading to a birch awning. The small roof provided shade for Elizabeth, and another figure, not that the sun was hot or harsh. Elizabeth stood there on the platform blindfolded, she twisted her hands like a street performer and, within them, the shape of clear blue water formed before their eyes. It glistened and flowed in amazing patterns with Elizabeth's hips, following her every movement like a snake.

The water changed from blue to white and then bright purple. It changed form, flowing then stopping like a solid, waiting on a cue from the enchantress. The other figure, who wore a series of feathers about her neck and quills in her silver hair, slowly raised a bowl at the other end of the platform. With her free hand, she rubbed grains which fell into the golden cask which soon began to smoke.

Then, as the smoke began to rise, the thunder of drums began to rattle. Joshua jumped slightly, unaware of their small presence behind the platform. They sat tucked into an emptied house, an amphitheater, and echoed the rhythm of Elizabeth's hips. Elizabeth danced with the beat, her body swayed and the liquid split from one shape into two. Two and four and sixteen, they continued to divide until a multitude of flowing strands circled her like a torrent of wind.

The strands looked like a living, gilded cage, Elizabeth the precious bird. The music grew louder and louder, anticipating the finale. Joshua's heart beat faster in tandem, watching her every curve. Her hair whipped, her eyes sparkled, and the water began to release from the cage. It moved like spider's string across the platform and began to collect at the silver-haired woman's elbow. It slowly trickled up against gravity. The beads of water crawled their way into the bowl and filled it to the brim, a deep green concoction like seawater was left, and the drums beat their last in a grand exit, leaving the universe silent.

Elizabeth began to walk towards the bowl and she lifted it in her hands. Twisting back towards the crowd, Joshua expected her to hold it above her head as it exploded in a glorious burst of sunlight that would flow down the witch's body, donning her like a blessing, proving her an angel. But, instead, she walked down the steps and stooped down to meet the eyes of a young girl. The girl's face was red, swollen. Her eyes were forced shut under the bloating of her skin. Elizabeth held the bowl to the toddler's lips, and she drank it, all of it. The girl was no more than five.

The crowd didn't cheer, nor did they applaud. The girl, and the mother directing her, stood in silence and the dancer and bowl-bearer bowed. The mother then left the epicenter with her sick child. She didn't, nor anyone else, speak a word of gratitude.

After that, Elizabeth turned her back on the crowd and stood there facing the drummers. Nothing happened until an old man, thin and frail, painfully rose. He was crippled, his left hand withered into itself. Beside him, a younger man by only a few years with white hair and crow's feet, helped him stand. The two approached Elizabeth, who couldn't see them. The old man, with a shaking hand, reached out to her and gripped the back of her dress slightly. He leaned in, and whispered in her ear, coughing between unheard words. Elizabeth stood there emotionless, unresponsive. It wasn't until the man guiding the elder passed a bowl full of water to her waist, that the witch reacted. She grabbed the bowl, a small wooden cup, and climbed the stairs again. She made her way to the end of the platform, the drums beginning to beat slowly, and handed the bowl to the feathered lady with a small bow. Again, she began to dance, the water from the cup forming about her.

This happened many times, many villagers came up to her and whispered in her ear, reminding Joshua of Jesus. They brought her their bowls full of water, and the feathered woman put grain in the bowl like clockwork. However, the color the water took was always different, sometimes one or two shades, and sometimes a vibrant rainbow. Moreover, Elizabeth never danced the same routine twice. Her body moving in new and unique ways every time, un-learned but divinely given. She never broke a sweat, never increased her breathing. The only people who seemed to grow tired were the crowd, waiting their turn, the drummers, grasping their mallets, hoping for strength, and the woman, whose hands shook underneath the bowls' water-weight.

Not one thanked the performers for the dance nor the water, no one spoke a word. Joshua sat after a time, tired of standing but never tired of watching Elizabeth. She seemed so happy, completely carefree. Joshua worried that with each step she took, her heart would give out, that she would fall or twist an ankle. But dance after dance she shattered his expectations and warmed his heart. It wasn't until sunset that all of the people in the square, who sat before the concert, had whispered in her ear and received their water back. She would hold it to their lips and they would drink before ducking out without verbal gratitude.

How tiring, how merciless, Joshua thought, to move for hours. Was this how the witches of Val-Ashoth were supposed to serve? Joshua never thought a woman like Elizabeth, whom, before, seemed cruel, would do such an act of servitude. Before, Elizabeth seemed heartless, manipulative, and even distraught. Now, as she toiled, she was more like a hero than all the stories Joshua heard of, even his own.

After the last performance finished, and all the villagers abandoned her. Elizabeth sat at the edge of the platform, her legs hanging down, swinging back and forth. Joshua walked over from the shadows to see her.

"Hey Hero." Elizabeth said again casually, her cheeks raised in a tired smile. "How did you like the performance?"

Joshua tightened his lips in secret, his cloak hiding his mug. "It was great. I thought you hated people. You know, with the cottage in the woods and all."

"I guess you get used to your job." She chuckled, "You get lonely waiting for your man to come home."

"I'm not-" Joshua retorted, but Elizabeth cut him off.

"I know," She frowned, "I mean, you should be, but you're not. I keep thinking that one day he'll come back, and we'd just pick up where we left off. And I thought it was you, I really did. I wanted it to be you. I still want it to be you…"

Joshua waited, thinking, he felt sorry for her. And he almost thought, in passing, that he wished he was Connor too. But he would be lying if he thought that, it wouldn't be the truth.

Joshua frowned.

"What was that?" Joshua inquired, "Witches don't dance, do they? What about black pots and terrible rhyme schemes?"

Elizabeth chuckled. "Don't be so stereotypical. Magic doesn't work like that. Magic is about effort and desire. You have to think about them as wishes. Magic is more like a wish you want to come true, you focus on it, you pray upon it, you show the world how badly you need it by giving it something to trade. Witches, mages, they have more to give, more life, more willpower. The world takes their favor, their mana, as appeasement, an offering, and gives them back what they ask for. But it doesn't always work. Sometimes we don't have much to give, sometimes the world wants more from us. It's all a bargain."

Elizabeth sniffed and patted her nose with the back of her palm. She was trying not to tear up. She thought it peculiar that only now, she was feeling the weight of Connor's absence. Perhaps looking at Joshua reminded her of him.

Joshua felt like he should leave; he didn't like to see people cry, it made him feel callous. He was callous. But, Joshua wanted to stay, and felt selfish for it. He wanted to stay because of Elizabeth was in disrepair. Her raw emotions piqued something in him, perhaps a true feeling, something not socially derived, something that would stay with him.

"So why dancing?" Joshua asked, trying to redirect her, to keep her mind off Connor's absence.

Elizabeth looked at him, her cheeks flushed, perhaps anew with the thought he was Connor indeed. "Magic use doesn't only exchange one type of currency like 'Favor;' it settles for other things, just like how a person doesn't eat only one type of food, the earth doesn't buy one type of energy. That's why I dance, that's why there's music. Think of it as extra payment or incentive for the wish, for favor. It's an attempt grant these people their wishes, no matter how powerful they may be. It's an attempt to lessen the cost of casting magic by offering…"

"Offering something beautiful, something more than us." Joshua finished.

"Yes," Elizabeth grinned, "something beautiful. The water, the grain, the drums, it's all energy and gifts to appease and lessen the strain on me while I make the wish come true. It's a prayer. Traditional witches use more ingredients, words, offering air and even poetry. Cults offer lives, utilize more people who don't have much Favor. It's all wishes and dreams, one big bargain with nature, or God, or demons, whoever the catalyst might be."

"Do you ever get it back? Favor, I mean."

"You can over time. You can steal others' favor as well, drink their blood. Sip their bones…"

Joshua shuddered, and Elizabeth smiled weakly.

"That's not often, and I wouldn't do that… unless I really wanted to!"

Elizabeth lunged at Joshua; he jolted back in shock. Subconsciously, he reached for his waistband where his pistol would be.

"You're just as easy to scare as Connor was!" Elizabeth laughed wryly.

Joshua tried to regain countenance, his arms resting at his sides. "Well… what *are* other ways to gain favor?"

Elizabeth thought for a moment. She furrowed her brow, twisted her lips. Her eyes flickering as the village began to light their night lanterns. Each one hung neatly at the corners of houses, some bearing symbols of bears and koi and ravens next to family names and mercantile trades. The world was on fire, vibrant in technicolor, and all of it could be seen through the reflection of Elizabeth's eyes. Joshua couldn't look away. His cheeks felt warm. He had never felt butterflies in his stomach before. What was this feeling? Was Joshua enamored? Was this the reason he stayed in the courtyard and the reason he wasn't angry she stole him back to Val-Ashoth? Like many people whom fell in love before him, Joshua became scared.

"People can gain favor slowly. Over time, the world cycles it back through us, as a gift, and a promise to fulfil someone's wish one day. It's like a number that increases every moment, and if that person wishes for something that is under or at the same value as their favor, it will be granted."

"But it seems that wishes never happen." Joshua remarked, hoping his face couldn't blush.

"Wishes always happen. We waste so much of our Favor on meaningless things. People are impatient and wish for the day to begin a little sooner, and the world says 'yes,' but they don't notice. They aren't glad because it was a small wish, but a wish nonetheless. A lot of people never see big miracles because they spent so much time asking for the small things. For most people, small things aren't enough.

People with 'magical' powers don't have to wait for their Favor to increase for long, they are better at receiving it, more receptive to energy and the world is more responsive to their requests. They have huge stores of Favor, not losing it like many people do before they become older.

As people reach a certain point, they either keep a large store of Favor or lose it and lose that store of Favor forever. Most lose it, that's why children are so creative very early in life, so magical and surreal, but, after they become a certain age, they stop holding on to wishes and spend their favor on stupid things, never to get it back because they've spent too much.

People can also lose the ability to 'wish' if they make too great a wish and its granted. The cost of their great wish was the rest of their hopes and dreams. They'll never have a wish granted again, all their favor leaves, never to come back again."

Joshua nodded. It made some odd sense, like a man who wants to become warm but sticks his hand in the fire. Instead of becoming warm, he burns the nerves from his hand and can never feel warmth on it again. He imagined the earth as a banker with a scale, or an accountant, always seeing if someone has enough Favor for them to make a withdraw, a purchase. Favor was like money, a currency not many people had.

The two watched the lights for a time, Joshua sat next to her. The children continued to play, tossing rubber balls against the slab, the only smooth surface outside. The adults talked in groups. Lovers walked arm in arm. Fish hung from small stands in front of houses, showing the catch of the day. In the distance, softly and confidently, a smith hammered on a shard of metal. It was a rhythm, a heartbeat, bringing the night to life and keeping time. Joshua found himself longing for a place like this. Paris now seemed trivial. He wanted a boat on a river, a lazy life with a loving wife; plenty of food, plenty of silence, and someone to come home to. In that silence, he could hear the important things, the conversations, the laughter, the music, and, he could watch Elizabeth dance the day away.

Joshua felt a raindrop on his boot.

"Damn, I'm sorry." Elizabeth sighed.

The detective looked down to see a thick splotch of blood on his toe. Elizabeth's feet were bleeding about the ankles.

"There was a big crowd today. I shouldn't have rushed to help them so soon." She cringed, her hair pulled back with one hand, hoping to see the damage.

Joshua's heart broke. This was the cost of Elizabeth's job, her duty as a witch. How often did she hobble home after long days providing for others, but not herself?

"You won't need them tonight." Joshua assured her.

Joshua put his arm underneath Elizabeth's thighs and another behind her back. The hooded knight lifted her into the air softly. In that moment, he remembered something from his childhood. He remembered an old bible and a bookmark. There was a nunnery, something Joshua had forgotten and now remembered with little detail. There was a ruler and bruises, cuts on his hands. A nun, whichever one, he did not know, was in the garden one day. Young Joshua was walking by with the other children, pulled by a rope tied about his waist. The nun had a rosary in her hand, the beads rolling down the center of their great history book. She carried it to her eyes, which were fully open, but could hardly see.

"They will lift you up, so that you will not strike a foot against a stone." She murmured slowly, tasting every word. She sucked in her lips, the air thin and cold.

Joshua's arms kept Elizabeth from the stone. It was the first act that the American preformed that wasn't an expectation of him. As a detective, he was told to investigate and bring justice to murderers and criminals. He was told to do this, and never asked himself if that is what he wanted to do. Joshua took orders and followed them, trained at a young age to do good because God was watching, and the switch was ready to strike. Joshua was trained to help, but he never felt he was helping because he wanted to. Joshua started to feel what it was like to care from his heart and not from his duty. Detectives weren't asked to care about who died, or for the family that cried in the living room after discovering their only child was brutalized and hung from a telephone wire like a discarded pair of shoes. People like Joshua forgot hope, as they were the ones untying the dead from their cross.

That was the world Joshua grew up in. A murder every day, an order every day, fulfilled and completed; sign, sealed, and case closed. But holding Elizabeth, feeling her eyelashes brush against his neck, her warm breath passing through his linen hood and against his collar. Joshua could feel her heart beat. He had never felt a heartbeat before. Joshua didn't want this to end. This mission he wanted to do for Elizabeth. He wanted to preserve the moment, but he had already climbed over the first hill, walking on the dirt towards her house. He felt free of duty. He was fulfilling his own wish, to carry a girl home and tuck her in. To save someone from pain just so he could be selfish and steal more of their time.

Joshua scaled the second hill, but his pace was already too slow. He couldn't walk any slower lest be asked by Elizabeth if he was tired. Joshua wasn't tired. Joshua was stalling, biding his time.

Joshua was in stalling for many reasons. Elizabeth reminded him of childhood. Hurdling canyons created by close rooftops. Fireworks and apple turnovers stolen from unsuspecting store owners. It was exciting; it was something he could sense inside of him. Joshua stalled because Elizabeth reminded him of a better life, a different world. Maybe it was just their location, the lights, the crickets, that made him stall, but he didn't want to believe this. Above all else, Joshua was stalling because he made a friend.

Joshua ascended the last hill. It was over, their walk was done. The American pushed open the door and guided her in, placing her on the chair while he looked for gauze.

Joshua struggled to wrap cloth around Elizabeth's ankle while she sat in the wicker chair. He was not accustomed to his new hands, but, she was patient with him. She had noticed his cloak that whole evening and, as he was occupied with tending to her wounds, she leaned forward, her chest against his forehead, and pinched the back of his hood. She brought it back and revealed his ashen head. The enemy he had defeated became him, the curse of the Ifrit's touch, and the gland he swallowed.

She felt his antlers and kissed his forehead softly. Joshua pretended not to notice. He was too engrossed in his work, and too ashamed of his face, among other things.

"Look here." Elizabeth whispered, moving Joshua's face up to meet her. Elizabeth leaned back now that she had his attention and pointed to the kiseru sticking out from the corner of her mouth. She ran her hands along Joshua's arm. Where she touched, the ash became red and warm. She took Joshua's hand and held his index finger to his thumb. She pressed them together and the end of their points, a small red flame like a lighter ignited. It was the first time Joshua casted a wish.

Joshua smirked a hollow smirk, a smile of certain whimsy like a child with string. He opened his fingers and the spark dissipated. He put them back together, but nothing happened. Joshua frowned.

"It's a small wish, remember?" Elizabeth assured, leaning forward with her pipe, "Think about it, want it, purchase it. Light this pipe for me, will you?"

Joshua focused. He wanted the flame to return. He wished it would return. He felt a tingling in his arm, a vibration and a surge of energy. Slowly, he watched his finger begin to spark. It burst, his hand caught fire, but he couldn't feel the heat. Elizabeth smiled. She slipped her hand through the flame and grabbed Joshua's fingers. She pinched them tighter and, like a dial, turned back the intensity until it was small like before. Joshua brought it to her pipe, and she puffed.

"The essence in your heart is like a furnace." Elizabeth started, she spoke quieter because it was night outside. "Because you're now cursed, you no longer have human organs, muscle. But you do have a heart, a small beating stone. It beats and flickers like a flame, so it's your affinity. It's your fire, a constant wish like a constant flow of blood. Connor always could do a little magic too. Small things, but it makes the difference, it kept him safe."

Joshua cut the cloth and tied the bandage off. He rested her foot back to the floor.

"I have something to show you tomorrow." She said. "But it's time to rest."

Joshua wrinkled his nose. Suddenly, he realized how tired he was. He blinked his heavy eyes and sat back on the foot of the bed. Elizabeth had risen from her chair and moved behind him. Joshua began to nod his head back and laid down. He found his head below Elizabeth, who stretched out at the headboard. Joshua fell asleep at the foot like an old dog with Elizabeth's hands running through his hair.

Before Joshua fell asleep, he remembered something more from his childhood. He remembered the apple turnovers and the rooftop runs, but moreover, he remembered his friends running beside him. Yes, Joshua had friends, and one of them was a girl with short black hair and purple eyes. Elizabeth was there, the whole time, helping him piss off the nuns, helping him hurdle the long jumps onto another roof.

Even though Joshua could swear Elizabeth was there with him. His story didn't match the Marquis'. What was he thinking, and why was he so sure she was there? Did that Marquis lie, or was he lying to himself?

Joshua had an exotic dream, or so it started. He was another man falling in love in a different ending and a different story. Whom-he-was stayed up all night with whom-he-loved, laughing over dinner, running through the streets of Paris with firecrackers underneath their arms. They were young. They laughed in bed, blushing. And when she had left to change into something more comfortable, whom-he-was waited by a window in the hotel room.
It was storming outside and whom-he-was loved the sound.
When whom-he-loved had emerged from the bathroom, she wore only a twisted smile and a coat. A knife was in her hands. Somehow, people left knives in bathrooms for nightmares to abuse. Whom-he-was almost smiled at the sight. But soon she was moving towards him, slashing this way and that. Whom-he-was thought it was too dark in the room to see color. But if he were a betting man, he would bet that coat was yellow.
Whom-he-loved never caught whom-he-was, but she didn't need to, for whom-he-was backed away into the dresser which smashed into the window behind him. The young man fell in a shower of glass and rain falling slowly as the she watched him plummet. Whom-he-was never hit the ground, but who-he-was never needed a coroner like Marcus to proclaim him dead.

Joshua woke up and found himself staring at Elizabeth. She stood over him on the mattress holding a mirror that reflected Joshua face, Joshua's *real* face. Joshua looked at his human self again, all but his eyes had returned to normal. Joshua ran his hands under his shirt. He looked down at his toes. They were there. He never woke happier in his life.

"Do you like it?" Elizabeth asked, "Took me all morning."

"I love it." Joshua replied in hushed disbelief. He leaned up, causing Elizabeth to topple clumsily on her rear in front of him. She sat at the foot of the bed, her legs over his. She wore a smile, but it didn't fit her face. The mirror in her hands still reflected him, the human Joshua. He wasn't dreaming, nothing bad had happened yet.

"Joshua," Elizabeth warned, "It's not real."

Joshua looked confused. He shrugged slightly, "What do you mean, it looks real to me."

Elizabeth put down the mirror and grabbed Joshua's hand. Joshua watched as it began to morph. It slowly became the ifrit's hand again. Joshua ripped his hand out of Elizabeth's.

Elizabeth jumped in fright.

"Sorry." He apologized.

"Don't, I understand. You want to *be* human again, not just look like one." She sighed. "the only way I can actually change you back is with a lot of dead bodies and a pact with a satanic spirit. Unless you want to kill every villager outside today, it'll be hard to do. Only the ifrit who cursed you, or an overriding curse from something stronger can help you. And if I know you, that ifrit is dead."

Joshua pretended to think about the proposition laid before him. Most of the villagers were unarmed, but he would have to contend with Val-Ashoth's anger. Elizabeth saw his eyebrow raise and chuckled nervously.

"Yeah, we can't do that." Joshua sighed sarcastically.

Elizabeth smiled, wonderfully unamused by Joshua's attempt at a joke. Was he trying to be charming?

"You'll be able to eat and bleed and shave. But you just won't *be* human. That sounds like a small thing if you can interact with the world like most humans but it's not. You're still bound by a lot of things an ifrit is. Your curse still matters, and even though you look and act and talk like a human, magic, life, and chance will treat you like a beast, an ifrit. Does that make sense?"

"I think so." Joshua mumbled, he held out his hand and pressed his fingers together. A small flame held there. It made sense. He was a tangible illusion, like a plastic shell over a piece of clay. Something only half real, something unoriginal, a fake, a proxy.

"And whatever you do, don't swim for too long." Elizabeth added.

Joshua nodded again. There was something of a small silence, brief, but evident.

"There's something else." Elizabeth began. "You're Connor Shaw."

Joshua moaned, "This again? I'm not Connor Shaw."

"That not what I mean." Elizabeth assured.

Elizabeth leaned into Joshua with the mirror held before him. Joshua looked at his reflection. Estranged black hair, a strong chin line under stubble, chiseled cheeks and nose, he was all there but for his eyes which were still yellow and black. Down to the creases besides his eyes and the crease in his forehead, all but his eyes were there. He saw the same tired man with the same small scars and ears as before. Nothing had changed from his facial features. If anything, he felt a little more handsome, after being a horned beast with skin made of soot for some time. Elizabeth could have turned Joshua into another, random, human and he'd still be happy about it, even a girl, even a fat lard.

"Is there anything out of place, besides your eyes?" Elizabeth asked, her eyes watery. "Anything at all?"

"No, nothing at all, I'm surprised you did this well." Joshua smugly replied.

"Exactly" Elizabeth pouted, the mirror dropped into Joshua's chest with a thud. Joshua looked up at her.

"I didn't use your features as a template. I couldn't… remember all of it… I used Connor's. I used his full features to the letter. But only because I knew you two were so alike."

Joshua paused. He lifted the mirror to his face again, surely, she had to have missed something. Joshua combed his body with his hands. He found the mark on his bicep, the scar on his chest and the scar on his thigh. Absolutely everything was the same, nothing was new, and nothing was missing.

Joshua cursed, "We looked that much alike?"

Suddenly, Joshua didn't think Elizabeth was so crazy. He wasn't just some person who happened to share traits with her past lover. Joshua was, for all intents and purposes, Connor Shaw's doppelganger.

Elizabeth nodded, "I would never have brought you here the first time if I wasn't so sure."

There was a silence in the room, the bird outside could be heard, a surrogate for crickets in the audience. Joshua didn't know whether birds were intelligent enough to eavesdrop on people, but in that moment, the chirping seemed more tart than usual.

Joshua thought to himself. Elizabeth was waiting for him to admit that he was Connor Shaw. No two men could be so alike, Joshua knew that. The fights he survived after leaving Val-ashoth stacked reason against him, all the evidence pointed to him being Connor. But even though the evidence for Elizabeth's plight was so confirming, there were two things that kept the American from conceding. Joshua didn't remember anything that colluded with The Marquis' story, his memories, his childhood, it all pointed to his life as Joshua Hill, not Connor Shaw, with or without Elizabeth.

The second reason was his heart; it had a special place for Elizabeth, it meant that they had a special connection, the way she inspired him last night made him fond of her. He couldn't say he was Connor Shaw, because, maybe, in a few moments, or years later, he would show up. If Joshua said yes and stayed with her in Val-ashoth, he might answer a knock at the door and find himself staring at his reflection, the real Connor Shaw that was not him. Such a thing would tear Elizabeth's heart in half. Joshua couldn't live with that in the back of his head. Until he knew beyond a doubt he was Connor, he couldn't agree.

"You know what." Joshua huffed, "I think I used to have a small imprint right here on my palm. And, come to think of it, my nose wasn't this small, I think I had a bigger nose."

"Liar." Elizabeth quipped, but she smiled. The girl was sure of herself and knew that Joshua was giving her a ticket to leave him whenever she wanted for Connor. Joshua was protecting her from devotion, enabling her the benefits of doubt.

Joshua didn't dare ask her about his memory of her on the rooftops, he didn't ask about the turnovers nor the nuns either. It didn't make sense to him, and he didn't want to know the truth. Why did he only remember his past when he was trying to piece things together? Why couldn't he remember his past well enough to know where he went to school, his first girlfriend, his GPA? He didn't clearly recall anything before joining the police.

Elizabeth lay next to Joshua that day, her arm across his chest. He stared at the ceiling and listened to her talk. Joshua worried for France, he worried for Elizabeth. But his fears weren't as strong when she made jokes and explained the world to him like he was a kid again. Joshua didn't want to leave her. Elizabeth helped him sleep at night.

It was that night Joshua walked with Elizabeth in his arm. They looked at shops and admired the lights. People greeted Elizabeth as "Val's Witch." She seemed happy and more willing to help people. Joshua met the feathered lady, she was once a witch too, the village dancer even. However, years of hard work in granting wishes took their toll and she couldn't do much more than hold the cup and grains. She wanted to make the dancing a bit easier for Elizabeth.

Joshua realized that one day, Elizabeth would run out of favor and retire for the next witch to take her place. Elizabeth would probably have silver hair too, which Joshua didn't think would look so bad. Yes, one day Elizabeth would teach someone else to dance for wishes, and the immortality Val-Ashoth gave her would disappear. Joshua felt sorry for her, but he knew she loved her job, or was beginning to. Joshua wanted to support her in any way he could.

When they had arrived at the square, their window-shopping over. Elizabeth asked Joshua to put down their gifts. She took his hands and led him to the platform in that same central square. She smiled and blushed. She stood on her toes and she put her arms around him. "Dance with me." She pleaded over and over.

"I don't know how." Joshua warned, bashful, scared.

Eventually, Joshua was coaxed and reined by the dancer. She taught him the simple steps and they began to move as one. People began to gather and watch. A witch had never danced with somebody else before. The villagers didn't understand what it meant. Nor did they run when Elizabeth twisted her fingers behind Joshua's back, and he became an ifrit again. Joshua hadn't noticed; his eyes were closed, he was in paradise in those moments. When he opened them, it seemed the whole town was present. He saw his hands, his saw his horns in the reflection of a pan hanging from a not-so-distant stall. As he began to panic, he looked into the eyes of the audience. Yet, no one cringed, no one gawked. Although he was a monster, no one screamed. Coupled with his view in the reflection, Joshua felt guilty. Joshua remembered the ifrit's words; "*do I deserve to die?*" Did Joshua kill someone innocent?

"Eyes on me." Elizabeth cooed. Joshua glanced back at her, unsure of himself. Elizabeth moved in and kissed him on the cheek. Joshua closed his eyes again, unable to react, unable to reciprocate what it meant. Joshua had never understood such things before.

When Joshua opened his eyes, they had teleported back to the cottage. Elizabeth had saved him from over-embarrassment, saved him from his own thoughts, from the crowd that had gathered. He was back to himself as a human, comfortable again, safe. It was late, and they went to bed, only to do the same, day in and day out, week in and week out.

Joshua stayed with Elizabeth for the rest of those days. For a long time, he forgot who he used to be, and he forgot why he wanted to go to Paris. Any thoughts of pain and loathing were seemingly numbed. He was treated day in and day out by a beautiful woman. She treated his sadness, handicapped his fervors and rage. Elizabeth was Joshua's sole confidant, his only friend, his kettle, his favorite dream. And his dreams didn't compare to waking.

Act 2/Regis

Part 1/Remove

The longer Joshua stayed with Elizabeth, the more he felt guilty and the more he began to think about Solomon. Whenever he closed his eyes he could vividly see the children he killed, dead around him. Other times, when walking home with Elizabeth, Joshua would look out into the fields and swear he saw Solomon standing across from him, waist deep in wheat. The more he blinked the more he felt sudden pain, sudden nightmares. He was still haunted by his past and it wouldn't let him steal away so easily.

Joshua woke for the last time that final night. Elizabeth held him tight, her forehead pressed against his jaw. She had been so kind, more so than before. They'd both changed, accepted things, calmed down in their fervors and selfish ambitions, but that was about to change. Joshua didn't know if he could ever come back, but he couldn't stay, not while he felt needed elsewhere. The young man pressed his fists together and, for the briefest moment, turned into ash. The dust flowed away from Elizabeth and onto the floor before collecting and forming back into the corporeal. It was a blink technique, something Elizabeth had taught him over the past few days, *her mistake.*

Joshua put his fingers together and the dim flame he conjured helped him find his clothes, his sword, and some food for the night. It also caught the twinkle of a man's eyes, The Stranger's eyes. He stood there against the doorway with his arms crossed, he looked right at Joshua.

"I thought you would come to your senses. We had a deal that I would help you kill Solomon, and you've been sitting on your ass."

Joshua waved his hand to shoo The Stranger away. This wasn't the first time the ghost had appeared to sow seeds of doubt into Joshua's heart. Joshua opened the front door and began to leave, it was his mistake that he made so much noise.

Elizabeth sat there on the bed, awake, she already rose out of the bed to meet him.

"Joshua, what's wrong?" She asked. Even then, she knew what he was trying to do.

"You know I can't stay here." Joshua replied, "I can't leave the world behind."

Joshua remembered The Marquis' words, he couldn't believe he forgot them. Joshua didn't want to be The Marquis, he had to play his role in the world. He couldn't forsake it.

To Joshua's surprise Elizabeth nodded. "That's exactly what Connor would say." She sighed. "You're my hero. You know that, right?"

Joshua tried to smile, but he couldn't. Leaving was too painful.

"You know that you might never be able to come back." Elizabeth said, her voice starting to break.

Joshua nodded this time. He turned to walk out but was soon constricted by a pair of arms wrapped around his body, much like how they met long ago. Elizabeth cried into the back of his jacket. Joshua looked at the ground. He pressed his hands to where Elizabeth's arms intersected and slowly unwrapped himself from her clutch. Joshua began to walk away a few paces. Joshua needn't look into her watery eyes, he knew them too well. Nevertheless, he did, and she looked back. There was something dead in his gaze, something that didn't see her so much as look through her. Joshua opened his mouth and spoke.

"I can't let him live. I can't."

Joshua walked away, leaving Elizabeth on her knees at the doorframe, never looking back again. He walked for hours. As he passed through the village, he made eye contact with nobody. The villagers tried to greet him, but he simply bumped past them and went on his way. As he exited the village he took the same winding path that Haddock had shown him sometime earlier that year. Joshua felt so much older than he was back then. Perhaps it was the worry, his inability to let things go that weighed down his heart.

As Joshua continued along the road, he came to an odd door. The door ran right through the road, or rather, the road ran to the door and stopped there. There was nothing attached to this brown door with the transparent glass, it lonely stood there, erected by some mystical force. Above the door was a sign labeled "exit" in faded-red neon. It reminded Joshua of a certain square in Paris, and a night where his life began. Joshua twisted his mouth and rotated the handle.

As Joshua passed through the door he found that he had exited a water closet. Joshua recognized the buildings around him as those built in Paris. Perhaps he was lucky, or perhaps the goddess, Val, was kind enough to let him off just south of his apartment. The air was growing cold as fall was coming about. The dark streets before daylight were riddled with autumn leaves that blew upon the subtle wind, channeling over the concrete and asphalt. Joshua thought he would feel at home, but he didn't.

As Joshua walked back to his old apartment, he began to question himself. Maybe he was drunk and fell into a stupor. Paris didn't greet him with open arms, he was no one of consequence to her. Whatever Joshua had done during his diaspora did not follow him here. He felt like a normal man again. Maybe he could even start a new life, again. He could own a small shop and forget anything bad had ever happened. Joshua pressed his fingers together and watched as his fingers sparked and ignited. He looked back to the water closet and down to a thin puddle on the cobblestone path. He looked into his yellow and black eyes.

No, Joshua wasn't dreaming. He was a different man than when he had left. He was stronger, smarter, and he was determined to raise hell.

It didn't take Joshua long to arrive at his apartment building. He climbed the emergency stairwell up to his apartment since he didn't have his keys. There at his floor, he jimmied the lock on the window and entered.

Joshua was surprised. None of his stuff had been moved or evicted.

Joshua's apartment was a dark place. A leather sofa donned a linen sheet like a toga. To his left, a small restroom tucked into a room the size of a closet. All Joshua's clothes sat on a clothing rack against the far wall, the other wall housing a microwave and a single stove top. It was a well-maintained crap-hole. It was here that Joshua solved all his crimes, ate all his meals, and slept.

It was nothing like home.

The Stranger snorted his disapproval, appearing behind Joshua. The whole place smelt of old leather and cigarettes. Joshua had become used to The Stranger's comings and goings. There was nothing Joshua could do to stop him either way. A week ago, Joshua had determined that The Stranger was some type of spectral guardian, the way that all books had a guiding wise man. Perhaps he was a powerful mage who used projections and teleportation to get where he wanted and tamper which whoever's life he wanted to. Joshua could have been grateful for him, but he wasn't.

The first thing Joshua did when entering his apartment was move to his old case files. He left the window open.

Joshua furled his brow, talking to himself. "Murder, murder, murder, murder, triple homicide, children. That sounds like a good start."

Joshua tossed the promising document to his right.

"You're going about this all wrong, boy." The Stranger pecked.

"Then tell me what I should do." Joshua dismissed, still engrossed in his paperwork.

The Stranger clicked his tongue and waited a moment to make sure Joshua was listening.

"Solomon *wants* to kill you. You don't have to go and find him. You just need to make a big enough statement to let the world know you're alive. You need to reach out to him. Tell him he failed in killing you."

Joshua paused, it was true. Solomon once said he had plans for Joshua. Whatever these plans were had obviously fallen through. Joshua wasn't dead, and he didn't have any special 'gift' from the murderer. All Joshua needed to do was get word out that he was alive, then, Solomon would come to finish what he wanted to do. *Why hadn't he thought of that?*

"So, what do you propose I do?" Joshua asked, turning around to give The Stranger his full attention. "How do I get word out fast enough that I am alive, without constantly running from Glass' military? How do I keep him interested in me, enough that he comes for me?"

"I have just the statement in mind." The Stranger smiled smugly. "I do recall a certain frail woman tried to take off your head almost a year ago…"

The Stranger smiled wryly, it reminded Joshua of how Elizabeth smiled before sending him to Russia.

"Joshua," The Stranger beckoned, "how do you feel about regicide?"

Part 2/Racket

Joshua rode his rented stallion towards the Rhine. The Stranger was not far behind him. His horse trotted along in merry clops, bouncing more than usual, much to Joshua's displeasure. The land was quiet, a countryside lush with crops and vineyards soon ready to be crushed into bread and used in alcohol. Unfortunately, most of these farmers worked under the provision of their tyrannical baron, whom levied heavy taxes against them. They could only keep fifteen percent of their crops once harvest was over, and not a unit more. This fifteen percent was enough to trade with other farmers for their yearly food and clothes, but only enough for that. Whatever was harvested in abundance, whatever else they owned, was collected by the barons first-infantry tax-officers and brought to their storehouses to be counted and used for the baron's parties; unless they were sold to other provinces. This baron was a regular tyrant, a regular thief. The farmers, most of them four generations in, had never seen a coin or franc in their life.

The troupe were aliens in Whitecroft's territory, guerillas, ready to raise hell against the skeletal woman.

Joshua watched carefully the oncoming patrol, a small group of men in thick plate armor carrying staves. There, crudely painted on their cast-iron pauldrons was Whitecroft's mark, two bugles crossed underneath a cluster of grapes.

Charming, Joshua's thought, that the Baron wouldn't raise her hand to provide her regulars with good armor made by a good smith. Most parts of their armor had already begun to turn a sandy brown, rusting in the humid air.

Joshua could see their first stop on the hill, a small tavern full of cacophony and jeering. The Stranger waited for them to near the tavern before addressing his concerns.

"You should start with building a rebellion, stirring unrest. If you simply storm the Baron's estate, even if you're successful, she probably has contingencies, people to take over when she's gone. You'll need allies, people to legitimize the conflict as a civil issue. Then the other barons won't rush in to stake their claims on the newly opened soil. Moreover, they'll see you as the new baron, if you can get your cabinet established quickly. After that, you'll have a lot of diplomacy on your hands, reshaping the countryside, maintaining or dissolving previous contracts with other lands. You'll be rewriting your world as you see fit. Then, Solomon will come for you."

"Where do you suggest I start?" Joshua asked, pulling his horse into the tavern's stall. The taverns were a small penance for Whitecroft's misdeeds. She had established these inns for "public drinking" early in her stewardship. It provided booze if someone would credit their harvest. The men and women gave the baron's reich more and more power in exchange for liquor. In truth, the taverns about the countryside were made for alcohol, but their purpose was to fuel the baron, who made frequent stops for booze when traveling on business. She never intended to use the inns for public use originally.

"Start small and the Baron won't notice." The Stranger said, peering through the window of the longhouse. "Good deeds by the people will make them trust you, rally around you when the time is right, and that way you won't need to keep a standing army. You'd be a regular Robin Hood. They'll take you in when your injured, hide you from the soldiers when you're hunted. They'll keep their heads low until you start your march upon the estate. Building character before them is your first business. And it looks like you have your first customer."

The Stranger pushed Joshua in his chest once he had dismounted. He stumbled back just as the door to the Tavern slammed open. Out rolled a girl into the mud. She was caked in booze, dirt, and sweat. A large bottle of bourbon was clasped in her hands tightly. Her hair was the brightest orange.

She was a vibrant girl with a proper amount of muscle and fat, despite the starvation the countryside faced. Her knuckles were bruised, and her left eye was bruised, but not swollen. She quickly rose, cursing. "Asses," She spat, swaying towards the door. "I'll s-show you a th'ing or two."

The two men whom tossed her out cackled. They were two soldiers, underdressed. Their vestments bore the standard colors of the baron, their arms crossed aggressively. They stood to prevent her from re-entering the establishment.

"You're drunk Joan, go home before you break something else!" The first ordered.

"And don't return until you've sobered up." The second added.

"But-but my-grain's-as-good-as-anyone's," she protested, her words strung together, dribbling out her tongue carelessly.

"Your grain is *piss*!" The first shouted, "It goes to the horses come harvest!"

Joan tossed her bottle at the guards. Impressively, it landed square in the first's chest and shattered, leaving his stripes stained. The guard curled his face, his nostrils flared. The beer-bellied man scratched his butt and produced a small cudgel from the belt in one smooth motion.

"I'll give this tart as lesson." He snarled.

Joshua loomed in unnoticed behind the guard whom approached the drunken girl. He placed his hand firmly on the man's gambeson, directing his attention.

"The girl's a bit drunk, surely you can't do any harm she'll remember." Joshua tried to reason. "Spare the rod, just for today."

The first blinked, confused as to how Joshua had snuck up on him. "Maybe she won't, but if I beat her good enough she'll feel it in the morning." He cracked, expecting Joshua to laugh.

Joshua didn't.

Joshua sighed and flicked his fingers. His hand began to burn into the guard's shoulder like a hot skillet against his skin. The guard cringed.

"Let me try this again. You really should leave the girl alone." Joshua protested.

The guard's face stretched in horror as Joshua's hand caught fire. He screamed both in pain and fear. The guard writhed to look upon Joshua's yellow eyes. He looked into the soul of a demon.

"Help me!" He cried.

Joshua turned around, quickly extinguishing his hand as the second guard ran into the tavern. Out from the pub, moments later, seven more guards had come out to answer the plea.

Joshua had stumbled across a small, and very unorthodox, squad. Most of them were pissed, and the others, in both ways, were pissed. In their drunken fervor to help, they had left their weapons inside, brandishing only their fists and belts. Many of them wore no trousers, having come down from their rented rooms. Altogether they charged, thus beginning what used to be Joshua's favorite past-time in the underbelly of Paris, a bar brawl.

It was Joshua and Joan versus the Croftian menaces. Joshua bobbed right, the first oncoming punch passing his left ear. He jabbed his fist into the guard's sternum and quickly swept his feet away with a hooked kick. The guard was sent tumbling over onto his head.

The second man roared ferociously, the man whom Joshua tried to persuade, and bear hugged Joshua from behind, lifting him up to pile-drive him back into the ground. Joshua snapped his fingers and quickly phased through the hug, his ashes flying off in a dark cloud and collecting again a short distance from Joan. He collected himself briefly, before slamming his palm into the ear of another challenger, disorienting him.

The hugging man looked bewildered as he fell into the ground, expecting Joshua to be in his arms. Instead, he had fallen upon the first guard with his full body weight, and he was a heavy man. When he had managed to rise, he had incapacitated his comrade under his sagging blubber, smothered him like a pillow. The guard turned around to find Joshua's fist square against his nose. The man fell back and fainted.

Joan was too drunk to evade any punch, but she never shied away from trading blows. Whatever she was dealt, she returned tenfold, pulverizing her enemy. She punched quickly, her fist meeting a guard square in the jaw. The man tumbled backwards into another guard, whom, in the confusion and drunken disorder, began to strike his comrade, not taking sides in bias.

The fighting quickly turned inward as villagers, whom began to find their way home, mistakenly walked through the fare into blows meant for other people. Those sober enough watched from the windows and by the stables, safely behind cedar fences. They roared and spat their amusement, creating slick puddles of spit and booze atop the mud. They watched, in particular, the young man with the yellow eyes whom seemed to disappear and return again in other parts of the fray.

The partygoers all began to chant, to cheer and sing. Never had anyone quarreled so well against the baron's men. They hadn't seen a good fight in such a long time. But some more lucid fellows waited for a patrol to come and find a high branch on a tree. Instead of jeering, they quickly left the scene.

Joshua lay down the last blows just as the sound of horses drummed through the countryside. The remaining crowd quickly dispersed in fear as a small brigade of sober soldiers appeared over the hill. They made their way along the road, unaware they were about to come upon a feud.

"Come on!" Joan hushed, as she clumsily scaled over a waist-high fence behind the house. Joshua quickly grabbed his bag and leapt over behind her. Together they ran through the vineyard, escaping the prying hand of tyranny.

Joan laughed the whole way through, having the time of her life. Occasionally, she would trip over her own toe before gaining balance again, but never once did she lose speed. Joshua kept up until they reached the other side of the acre, wherein Joan had stopped in a ditch to vomit.

"Stupid Crofties," She chuckled between upchucks. "Showed them, we did, kicked... their girly asses."

"We sure did." Joshua replied coarsely, ruffling through his bag roadside.

"What was that back there? All that voodoo, they barely touched you."

"Magic, I think."

"Magic, like hocus pocus abra kadabra?" Joan hiccupped, motioning with her hands like a magician before stretching her belly, straightening out.

"Something like that, I'm not too sure." Joshua replied.

"Are you a traveling carnie?" Joan asked, starting to gain her bearings; they began to walk east along the road. She tangled her hair back into long braids and clasped them with rings, keeping them away from her wine-drenched clothes. She wore animal skins, warm and brown. The fur was turned inside, the thick threads keeping the pieces of hide together were blue like the sky, accenting her azure eyes.

"I'm not a carnie," Joshua replied bluntly. He felt slightly offended.

"The Baron used to have a jester or something in his estate. He could do crazy stuff, real crazy stuff, before he was beheaded."

"I thought the baron never lets farmers see the estate?" Joshua asked, pausing in his tracks, realizing the information Joan had given him. But Joan continued ahead, independent and unaware.

"I'm not a farmer," Joan quirked, turning back. She performed a disheveled curtsy, shrugging in mockery. "The baron still hasn't caught me, and she won't. I go wherever I please, no law can hold back a Northern gal."

"It sounds to me like you don't care much for Whitecroft." Joshua pecked.

"Hell no," She huffed, "the sooner I can work without a royal entourage taking note, the better."

"Would you be interested in a healthy rebellion then?" Joshua pecked again, trying his best to imitate The Marquis' charming ways.

The fair-headed woman laughed, she almost fell in hysteria. "Would you be interested in finding England!?" She shouted back mockingly. She finished her trot away from him. The girl walked off down that dirt road until she became something of an ink blot.

Joshua watched her walk away, a thin smug still on his face. The population of Whitecroft's land wasn't enormous. It was one of smallest states in France, and housed a small, rural, population. Chances where they would meet again before Joshua was ready to declare war. Joan seemed like the person who knew her way around the land. She implied that she knew the layout of even Whitecroft's estate, which was no small feat. Joshua liked her gumption, her spunk. When the time came for Joshua to move upon the castle, he wanted Joan to guide him there.

Joshua stood roadside for a few moments, letting himself sink into his own thoughts. Could gaining people to his cause be that simple, that easy? Joshua was used to people galling at him when he was a detective, refusing to help him because of his methods. Perhaps the people were already waiting for a revolution. Perhaps they just needed someone to ask them to fight.

"How did it go?" The Stranger asked, appearing cordially behind Joshua.

"I don't know." Joshua responded, "I'm surprised you weren't watching."

The Stranger chuckled softly, the sun had begun to set. "I thought it was a good time to check up on your girl."

"How is she?" Joshua frowned.

It had been a month since Joshua left Val-ashoth, the change of a season, the turn to fall. A few weeks in, The Stranger offered to keep tabs on her and the community to make sure she was okay, safe. More importantly, the man watched to see if Connor Shaw would return. He watched for this because Joshua didn't want to return if he was going to be replaced. In Joshua's sordid state, he never considered his position with Elizabeth to be anything but temporary, not that he wanted it to end. Joshua thought he would be replaced easily, feigning the thought that once Connor returned to her, Elizabeth would drop him into the trash and forget about him entirely. But, neither did Joshua know how smitten Elizabeth was with him as well, not as the illustrious Connor Shaw, but as Joshua Hill himself.

Elizabeth told him about Connor during their time together, his happy countenance, his ability to make friends at the drop of a hat. Connor was nothing like Joshua. Connor was better in every way. Connor was kind, considerate, and passionate. Joshua was brooding, self-involved, and hollow. Even in the months he spent alongside her, Joshua had trouble keeping her from worry, keeping her happy, and maintaining his own sanity.

"She's hanging in there. It didn't take her long to get back to her routine. The work keeps her occupied, but, she has been working more and more lately. The wishes are piling up now that harvest in upon them. She drags herself home and doesn't care to show herself around. She's almost... wounded." The Stranger informed, fingering his breast pocket, but it was empty.

Joshua wiped his eyes free of residual mud, he nodded softly. He had begun to salvage wood from the roadside, placing them to erect a fire. It didn't take him long, and he needn't worry about working the flame. Once the materials were ready, he simply willed the fire into existence, and watched it flicker, mesmerized. Joshua wrapped a thin cloth around him. It wasn't cold outside, but he had never slept without something around him. He wouldn't overheat either, the benefits of not being human was not having standard blood.

Joshua waited for night to fall.

"How will you go back to your girl when you have a small country to run?" The Stranger asked, sitting on the other side of the fire. "You can't just abandon your people."

"The people can rule themselves." Joshua snorted. "They won't need me after I'm done."

"Don't lie to yourself, boy. These people might be able to handle their own lives and live independently, but the second they lose their baron, the land is ready to be taken by another. There always has to be a baron, otherwise the other barons won't hesitate to fight over it like the vultures they are."

Joshua sighed, he couldn't think of a baron nice enough to give the people what they deserved. Even Baron Gurdard, the noblest of all the barons. Would struggle maintaining the land from across the North Sea. The Scandes had enough problems to deal with, as it were.

"I suppose you wouldn't be interested in ruling, would you?" Joshua mumbled, but on cue he heard the silver fox laugh.

"It would be beneath me, and I doubt others would pay heed to me. Whoever is to be the next ruler must be involved with the rebellion."

"What do you do, really? I've never quite understood your purpose." Joshua asked.

The man looked out to the stars. They were far away from the lights of Paris, the milky way could be seen vibrantly. It was a small world that the man served, he wondered if other lifeforms beyond their solar system had a world that could create people like him.

"The funny thing is, you already know about avatars, and I'm kind of like that." He began, "I'm something like a ghost. Really, I am a ghost. I don't know whether I am who created me, or if I am another being entirely. Either way, I have the memories of the man I once was.

I was born years ago and died after a long day at work. Just like that, I was gone. I was a businessman, I worked in Paris heading a science division."

"What did you work on?" Joshua asked.

The Stranger seemed to hesitate, he looked at his hands and turned them over. His palms were open and facing him. He traced his finger along the creases. "I was a part of a research and development agency. We were working on something that would revolutionize the workforce and turn the tides of this cold war. The project was something incredibly significant and special, but I don't think we ever accomplished anything in the end. Those above us shut the project down once the hinges became lose. They were afraid of a little bump in the road. Sometime later, I-I think I was killed.

As to my purpose, I just feel compelled to help people I see. I wasn't the best man while I was alive. I was cruel and domineering to those who worked for me. I had a real stick up my ass. Either way, that's why I'm here."

"But you said Solomon was like family," Joshua insisted, beginning to clean his boots with a twig where he sat. He wanted to keep his hands busy after the long ride into The Crofts. "How does that fit in?"

The Stranger sighed, he ran his fingers along his chin, the follicles ruffling and twisting. He rolled some between his thumb and forefinger. He tried to find the right words. "Solomon was one of the first people I wanted to help. I thought he deserved a better life than was given to him, and I think that it was partially my fault he was dealt such a hand, so maybe I'm guilty. But when I met him, he had different plans. I tried to coerce him, tried to put him back on the path of hope, tried to make him believe he had a bright future ahead of him, but he had his mind made. And, you know how that ended up. He went crazy, started killing people, tried to get attention from others. I think it's because he knows he's at his end, that he's going to die eventually. He doesn't think life has anything left for him. But, who am I to say what is really going through his mind."

The Stranger's explanation seemed cryptic to Joshua. Perhaps it was a touchy subject, perhaps he didn't want to answer any more questions. But the last answer he gave seemed to be cut short, deliberately shorter than necessary. Either way, it mattered not to Joshua. He didn't need to know his enemy to kill him.

"I never asked what your name was." Joshua finally asked.

The Stranger rose slightly, sat up straight, and his hand moved to the flame. Like Joshua, it didn't burn. It was because of his spectral body, his semi-solid form. His body struggled to react to natural causes.

"I think it appropriate for you to call me Symeon." The Stranger claimed.

Joshua nodded, silently agreeing to let that be his title. It wasn't quite late enough to sleep, but the ride and the fight had sapped Joshua of much needed energy. Therefore, the American soon found himself dozing beside the fire, thinking about what he might leave behind when he died. Would this be his legacy, or would it be something else entirely? Whoever came before Symeon certainly seemed important, perhaps it was his regret that the project was never completed to his standard. That regret could have manifested once the businessman died, manifested enough to create an avatar, or some other type of apparition.

Part 3/Reach

At dawn, Joshua awoke to hear a commotion. A man down the road was on his knees in the dirt. Joshua rose and snuffed the coals with his boot before walking down along the grains for a better view.

Before the man on the road was an enclave of soldiers led by a single man. This man held a paper in his hands, a note with the picture on it. It was a wanted poster, a wanted poster of the man whom knelt before the enclave. This man had perturbed the baron, broken the law, and now, the reapers had come to collect. The sergeant, or leader, that stood before the man pointed a grubby finger at him. In an authoritative voice he laid down the verdict for his prisoner's punishment.

"For withholding ten bushels of wheat during the previous harvest, a crime punishable by death…"

Joshua began to wade through the stalks, slowly towards the group.

"…you will permanently be required to provide an extra five percent of crops to the baron per annum. This is the price of thievery."

The price of slavery, more like. Joshua thought.

"In addition, the criminal will be flogged thrice for each bushel withheld, to a total that may exceed thirty lashes should the punishment not be rendered sufficient by the official bearing the whip."

The man finished his verdict from the paper and proceeded to wrap a rough rope about the farmers neck. He pinned the paper to the rope like a necklace, a symbolic gesture of burdening the criminal with his crime. It also served to warn others watching that the punishment was mandated by the baron, and not the whim of her soldiers. Even if the officials were to whip a man without moving to ask Whitecroft's permission, Joshua was sure they would not be reprimanded.

Joshua watched, crouched down in silence among the stalks. He listened intently as the sergeant flogged the poor guy repeatedly. The American counted along with them, he wanted to make sure things didn't get out of hand. If the man faltered, or looked on the brink of death, Joshua would jump in to help. But as it were, there were too many men armed and armored for Joshua to intervene.

Thirty-three lashes later, the sergeant grew tired. The farmer whimpered in pain. Surprisingly, the man didn't scream as his back was opened up. The man must have been tough in his youth, perhaps even a soldier himself. Thirty-three red lines had covered his back like paint, the slashes opening old scars on his back. Joshua realized that it had not been the first time he had committed a felony. The man was brave, or incredibly stupid.

Joshua waited until the troops had left before revealing himself. He stooped over and unscrewed his flask, pouring cold water over the man's back. The man had light brown hair which only grew in tufts. A sign that he was once lashed across his head. His left eye was white, dead in the socket. His right eye was bloodshot and brown.

"T-thank you." He whispered.

"Why did you withhold your crops from the Baron last year?" Joshua inquired, helping the man to his feet.

"C-c-children, by the river, orp-p-phans." He began.

Joshua thought the man must have been coursing with adrenaline or cursed with a stuttering tongue. He shook all over, his words chopped together, almost unintelligible.

"Extra bushels f-f-for orphanage." The man tried to explain, but Joshua was confused. Joshua had never seen markers for, nor heard of, an orphanage when studying Whitecroft's land. If there was an orphanage, that meant there was a community outreach, a decent group of people willing to give their hard-earned crops just to help others. It was something the baron certainly frowned upon. If Joshua could find this orphanage, he had no doubt he could convince those people to join his cause.

"Where are these orphans?" Joshua asked.

"D-don't k-know, come and go. By river when hot. C-children come, w-we give. Never found them, only f-f-found us."

Joshua looked off towards a small stone bridge, a small brook shot underneath it, it was a small outlet for the Rhine, the reason the crops maintained a steady supply was because of these irrigated streams. The irrigated water flowed all through the baron's lands so that, even in drought, there was constant fertility. The children could have been anywhere, by any stream, knocking on any house. Joshua was determined to find the backers of this orphanage. He thought it best to ask around for someone more inclined to form full sentences.

Joshua patted the man, making sure he was okay. He was still shaking, but soon started to make his way down the road to his house in the distance. The detective turned back to the road and walked in the opposite direction.

It was not a hot day. Joshua could tell. The workers in the field didn't sweat nor stop to watch him pass. It was on cool days like this that the workers worked hardest. They were driven to perfection by a gaudy, greedy, ruler. Due to that greed, most of them looked frail, almost undead. Their glassy eyes were fixated on their scythes as they continued gathering wheat. Most of the wheat was ripe, most of it.

Joshua passed by a lady covered in a shawl. She cried into her husband's arms. Only half of their crop had survived the season. The other half withered on the ground, dark brown and dead. The irrigation ditches had failed them; the river hadn't provided for them. Or perhaps, the soil began to rot beneath them after years of overuse. The baron would drive this place to the ground, loosen the soil until it was useless dirt if she continued to plant the same crop every year. There were no beans, only grains, only grapes. Could Whitecroft really be that stupid?

Joshua decided it was not best to ask them if they had seen any orphans around lately, so, he continued onward. There was a small bulletin board some miles later. It was posted outside another tavern, smaller than the first. The people whom gathered around it had already finished their harvest and proceeded to brag about their crops. They were probably lucky, having a healthy family to help them harvest quickly, and having a bigger farm than others to support that family. Their land was most likely the richest, and they were the wealthiest. They were fat rats among mice, still filthy, but awed at.

The tavern those farmers stood by was more disjunct than the last. Its roof seemed to slant to the side as if the soil had skewed it through an ordeal of time. In such a way, the cottage beyond the bulletin board was less frequented than the first Joshua had visited. But this did not matter to Joshua, nor the keeper inside.

"Excuse me," Joshua began, "I don't suppose you would know if there is an orphanage around these parts?"

One of the farmers looked at him confused, perturbed by the interruption. "We don't throw away our young, foreigner, if that's what you mean."

The farmer was being difficult. Joshua rubbed his forehead. He would try to be more direct. "I heard there was a band of children playing by the river, orphans. I just wanted to know who takes care of them."

The man snorted, they all stared at Joshua with bewilderment. They wanted to go back to chatting about crops, but Joshua wasn't letting them. "You're not one of those children-stealers, are you?" The man insulted.

"He can't be a kid-napper, George, where's his horse and cage?" Another butted in.

"Aye, kid-takers always have a horse an' cage, that's what I've heard. Sometimes they carry sweets with them. Like in Hansel and Gretel, sweets for the children." A third chimed.

253

The group started to murmur amongst themselves, which soon turned into a ramble. They began to debate whether kidnappers were evident in The Crofts. They were split on the decision, forgetting Joshua's question.

"Do you know who might be taking care of them?" Joshua restated, shaking his head in disbelief. He had never met people so dense.

The man named George, clearly the head of the posse, turned his head back again, impatient with the newcomer. "Talk to Dutch, foreigner, I've heard him say something about children. Something along the lines of Russian children, accidentally getting lost across the 15th."

"And where is Dutch?" Joshua continued, becoming impatient himself.

George scratched his balding head.

"I think I saw him inside, actually, bald man, carries a sword." A lady in the crowd chirped.

"Deborah, I was going to say that!" George spat, turning his back on Joshua.

"Well you weren't getting on with it!" She spat back.

The group began to clamor again. Joshua shook his head one last time and moved around them. Some people in the country, seemingly, weren't fond of foreigners. They always kept to themselves and in groups. Social cooperation didn't help under tyranny either.

Whitecroft's country wasn't exactly the best tourist attraction. Compared to Paris' high town, there was no contest anywhere else in The Dominion. It was the only place relatively safe to venture, if any person was wealthy enough to stay away from the city floor.

Joshua walked through the door and quickly spied Dutch in the far corner. He sat there slouching against the wall drinking a pint of ale. He fumbled through a stack of papers in his left hand, his right propped itself on a sheathed cutlass like a cane. The burly man had a black handlebar mustache and didn't bother buttoning his shirt. His pants rode above his waist where a red sash was wrapped, covering his belly button and holding his shirt to his sides. He was intimidating, if not for the kind smile he wore on his face and the twinkle in his eyes.

It wasn't hard to spy Dutch, Joshua reflected upon approach, the tavern was mostly empty, only seeing traffic when one of those in George's clique came back in for another pint.

Joshua sauntered down into the seat across from him. Dutch didn't look up, but his rich and deep voice addressed him.

"You must be the one who punched Earl in the mouth last night." He began, "Poor sod's still running a slab of meat to his lip."

Dutch put down the stack of papers he clutched. Joshua looked down at them and, on top, saw a crude drawing of him on a wanted paper. Clearly, Joshua was sitting with someone of some import.

"I would venture Earl had it coming." Joshua stated bluntly.

"Aye, that is most likely true. But it's my job to make sure these papers are no longer printed." He replied. "Even if Earl is one of Whitecroft's lackeys, all of us here are just trying to make ends meet, that isn't so bad a sin. Still, it's refreshing to watch them get their asses handed to them once in a while. It reminds them they're human."

Dutch smiled widely and pointed down to the second, third, and fourth paper. They were all sketches of Joan.

"You made yourself quite a friend too." He evaluated.

"What are you, a bounty hunter?" Joshua grimaced. "I'm not someone you want to piss with."

"Calm yourself lad, I'm not here to collect on this warrant unless I really have to." Dutch defended calmly, "I'm not a callous man, and you should ask yourself whether you want to condemn a man you hardly know. I'm not someone you want dead, and we have a mutual friend here."

255

Dutch tapped the wanted papers again, his thick and burly finger striking Joan's papyrus face. Under the force of just his finger, the table rattled, spilling a small amount of booze from Dutch's drink.

"Joan told me what you said yesterday." Dutch continued. "Are you sure you want to go through with your plan?"

Joshua almost laughed. Joan did listen to him. Perhaps he shouldn't have been so bold to come out and say his intentions. It would've been better to remember caution. Just because Joshua learned a tinge of magic did not make him invincible.

"Why are you asking me this?" Joshua evaded.

"I'm asking you this because I might agree in your opinion. No one likes a tyrant. If there was someone willing, and able, to take her place, I would be on that side."

"And if I were to tell you my intentions… what could you possibly offer a small coup d'état?" Joshua inquired.

"I'm not just a bounty hunter, I'm something of a sheriff." Dutch smirked.

"Meaning?"

Dutch motioned to the wanted signs again, looking at Joshua straight in his eyes. "I make deputies, I chose my soldiers. More importantly, I chose the *right* soldiers. I chose to conscript those capable of bringing Whitecroft to her knees."

"You're ridiculous. If your hire people on Whitecroft's wanted list, you going to get killed. You're going to get yourself, and me, caught." Joshua scoffed.

"No, I'm smart about it. I turn in plenty of crooked people, not all the thieves in this state steal just to stick it to that twig. I keep those I need, not those I want. I'm also a tactician. I promise you, I don't give up people who don't deserve it and I'm good at what I do. I trade people who have the best odds of living, who won't have a death penalty undeserved."

"So, what, you save people from the noose by hiring them? Do you plan on storming the castle with your own lackeys?"

"No... I'm wouldn't plan to do something so bold." Dutch began. "But are you serious about this or not?"

Joshua thought to himself. Dutch already knew much of his intentions through his ill-placed words with Joan. But if someone as headstrong and gun-toting as Joan confided in this goliath, it should mean something to him. This couldn't be a ruse or a con, and if Joshua said yes, he wouldn't have much to lose.

Moreover, Joshua thought it peculiar, his timing in trying to kill Whitecroft. Was there already a rebellion being planned? Did Joshua arrive too late to take the forefront, or was he being offered full leadership?

"What makes you think I am the one you want. You don't know me. I could let you down."

Dutch laughed, it was something loud, almost like a blaring trumpet. It was a rough laugh, but full of heart. "Joan described to me how well you handled yourself, *exactly* how well you handled yourself. If you can do what she claims, and you have the heart to help people as you helped her. I think we'll do swimmingly together."

Joshua twisted the corners of his mouth before he frowned. "I used to be a detective, actually. I saved a lot of people, but I don't think I did it because I wanted to. I just need to get things done, and the baron's in my way. I'm not a hero, I'm just a man with an agenda."

"That's fine, sometimes good men don't have good hearts, but their soul is more here than *here*." Dutch pointed to his head and then his rippling pectorals.

"What's going on here?" Joshua redirected. "I show up expecting to struggle in building... a workforce, only to find people falling on their knees before me."

Dutch laughed, "Maybe I could explain myself if we began to speak straight."

Joshua nodded, "Okay... I want Whitecroft dead, she's in my way. I *am* planning treason. Now why is this so easy?"

Dutch smiled again, his face lighting up the room. He whistled at the barkeep as he rose, approaching with Joshua in tow. She turned to him. She was an older lass, a woman with greying hair.

"What do you want?" She asked.

"A bottle of Berkovian Brandy." Dutch replied.

"What year?" The barkeep smiled, her countenance changing entirely. Obviously, she knew who Dutch was.

"1901, the year the Heaven's Fall." Dutch replied.

The Barkeep reached beneath her shelf and Joshua heard a click. It was an odd noise, the rotating of a bottle, not of glass clinking against glass. The click was hollow, soft. The sound came from where the stairs behind the bar, which led to the spare rooms, met the corner of the building.

"I'll bring it up to your room." The barkeep said.

Dutch motioned for Joshua to follow, which he reluctantly did, cautiously walking slower than his cohort. They climbed the stairs which made a right angle for the second flight. Dutch took a left at said corner. He passed through the wall which swung open, a hidden door which discovered a small room, about the size of a bedroom. It was all too familiar, for on the table which lay in the center of the room, was a cloth with the same 'T' symbol from Russia. Dutch was a part of the enigmatic black market.

"I've seen this before." Joshua started, "I was in Russia and they had this exact symbol."

Dutch raised his eyebrows. "You're more popular than I thought then." He huffed. "That symbol was the symbol given to us by our founder, Saia of the Heavens."

Joshua choked in disbelief. "You can't possibly mean that small obnoxious girl with the pink hair is the leader of *the* Black Market."

"You've met Saia!?" Dutch burst, his face grew rosy, his eyelids fluttered, and his arms closed together in excitement. The seemingly stout weight-lifter withered into a teenage tabloid-reader. "What is she like? Is she a gorgeous as the pictures show?! Does she really have the power to fly like a rocket into the sky!?"

Joshua sighed, "You're in over your head. Get your head out of the clouds, she's not a pop-star."

Dutch grunted, realizing his knees were shaking before a man he barely knew. He straitened his back and cleared his throat. "I'm sorry. I get ahead of myself."

Dutch walked over to a small corner shelf and lifted a small picture frame from the top. It was dusted and worn down. He wiped it with his hairy forearm and handed it to Joshua. It was a picture in sepia. Joshua made out the figures, the Marquis, Saia, and a few other people stood to take a group photo. They looked serious but brimming with confidence. It was in the same style of one of those pictures taken before shipping out to war. It was cracked and muddled much like one of the slides the Marquis showed him a long time ago.

"Saia created the world's biggest black market, she is the richest human being in the world. Millions of weapons, medicines, vehicles, clothes, foods, organs, and more are shipped across borders. She's the reason people in India still have food, the reason strongholds cling to life in Africa. She's saved thousands if not millions of lives by connecting the world through minimally-taxed trade. She is truly a goddess among men." Dutch wiped his eyes with a handkerchief quickly, trying not to return to his gelatin self.

"She's a rich brat." Joshua concluded for him.

"I guess it's true, then, that you should never meet your hero's." Dutch sighed. "But this rich brat is why you've been having such an easy time. She's already beginning to pull the weeds of infidelity. She's using the black market to throw cogs into the Baron's networks. Saia wants to see Whitecroft overthrown just like you do."

"I don't quite understand." Joshua began, but he stopped himself. Altogether it made sense. Saia must have been aboard the skyship to collect The Second Death from The Marquis. She led the black market and she wanted to cripple Russia. Why not cripple France as well, or better yet, replace the baron with her own influence, so that she might have a stronghold on the market through a familiar ruler? Saia was more than a brat, she was a genius.

"Saia isn't *too* worried about destroying the Croftian rule, which is why my outpost is a small one. I mostly use it to smuggle alcohols into the country or smuggle wanted people out. The very serious cases result in faked deaths and a long ride in the back of a food car. But, she does her best to loosen Whitecroft's hold on the people. You'll begin to see that there are many people looking forward to seeing her fall, and they are already waiting for the right moment, the right leader. That is why this is so easy for you now. Before you were here, Saia was here."

Joshua twitched under the prospect. Perhaps he had to thank the girl if he ever saw her again.

"What are you planning to do then?" Joshua asked. He paced around the room. It was fairly empty but for a few wine racks. But these racks did not hold fuel for a skyship, nor any weapons. It was hard to see the room's potential. But Joshua was well-versed in the depths of the Black-Market trade. If they could fit it into the room, they could make use of it.

"I can order you whatever you want." Dutch answered, "Weapons for those who have pledged allegiance to our cause, food for those that've missed harvest. If we can give these people what they need, they will become less reliant on the baron and more willing to join us. I can also give you the full disposal of my currently requisitioned officers. They're a small squad, but they have heart and talent. Most of them hate the baron as much as you do. You can use this room as well and a barn we have to the north to meet people, plan your next move. I will also be ready to stand in advisement. I have contacts that can provide us information to help us understand what is going on around The Crofts. I leave all of this to your discretion, I'm here to make sure ends meet and Saia's goals are achieved, but you will be the face of the coup. We can't have anyone knowing the black market is actively looking to overthrow parties of interest."

"Right now, I need to find some orphans, I heard they hang around the river sometimes." Joshua stated, suddenly remembering why he was there in the first place.

Dutch twitched his mustache. "I think I've heard about these children. They are orphans from Russia. Somehow, they got lost behind the 15th and made it here."

"So I've been told, but how can children become displaced over hundreds of miles?"

"It's not uncommon. The baron east of us, Baron Holiday, she has an extensive transportation network due to the mining economy. I wouldn't be surprised if the children found their way onto the trucks and fell off here on their way to Paris, hungry. Baron Holiday herself is considered a mother of patrons, having adopted many children. I wouldn't be surprised if they have a growing orphan problem in towns close to the 15th. You should try further east, there's an abandoned granary a few miles down my contacts warned me about. They said they've seen small shadows at night entering and leaving the area." Dutch explained.

"I'm going to go find them, let me know if you have any leads. Until then, work on placing weapons and extra grain into the villager's hands, they should be willing to defend themselves. They can use the wheat we import to lessen the toll of taxation. Tell them to hide it under their houses." Joshua ordered. "Round up your men as well, I want to see them with my own eyes. Hopefully I will return soon with the children, if any exist."

Dutch nodded and took a sheet of paper from the main table. He began to write out orders on a small sheet. This was all Joshua saw before exiting the secret room.

Joshua was still unsure; his plan was coming together too easily. He hadn't realized that so many people would be so willing to help him kill the baron. Joshua was not used to working with people. Even on the force, he served from afar and people avoided him. He was a black swan, a rotten egg to them. Perhaps it was time for him to alter his proclivities. He needed to adjust his mind and trust others, if he couldn't, he might as well forget any intonation that he could succeed in killing the baron.

Although the baron was frail, her defenses were not. Any army *en masse* would quickly be detected across the fields that surrounded her estate. Her estate was an elevated position above the plains which were surrounded by two encompassing courtyards. These walls were not the most formidable of structures, but they prevented people from observing what was inside. How many guards did she have? And what were they armed with?

Still, that battle seemed so far away.

Joshua exited the tavern, Saia still on his mind. It was midday and he hadn't gained much of a lead. He began to walk down the road but didn't go very far until someone slammed into his side.

Joshua jerked left at the force, taken aback by the sudden presence of someone. As per usual, he quickly found the pistol underneath his cloak and brandished it halfway. He held it against his chest in one hand, ready to flick it at his attacker. Joshua huffed under a quick surge of adrenaline. But that surge quickly dissipated once Joshua's eyes focused on his target. It was Joan, swaying in front of him with a big playful smile. "Hey!" She greeted. "Long-time-no-see!"

"Joan," Joshua twitched before recloaking his sidearm. Joan wasn't scared to see the pistol under his cloak. But still, she eyed it carefully as it returned to its place on Joshua's hip. "It's good to see you again." Joshua finished, he sounded tired.

"I saw you talking to good ol' Dutch in the tavern. He didn't give you too much trouble about the fight, did he?" She asked, her body starting to become more rigid, more cautious now not to startle her bar-buddy. Joshua began to walk along the road again whilst Joan backpedaled before him. A thin silence hung as Joan waited to hear Joshua's answer. Once she did, she would know she could relax.

"We're good. I have no choice but to trust him for now." Joshua murmured.

Joan chuckled, "Stop being so stiff, I've known him for years. He's a great guy."

Joshua didn't respond back, letting yet another strain of silence hang upon the air like a pathogen.

"Do you kill people?" Joan asked. As they topped a small hill.

"Why would you ask such a thing?" Joshua asked, but his voice became taut. *Yes*, Joshua was a killer. It was something Joshua regretted at the end of each day.

"I dunno." Joan explained, "Seeing you in action yesterday with all your spooky jester stuff, you seemed like a killer to me. And, your gun, looks like you've used one before."

Yes, Joshua thought again, he was a killer. He only hoped he was not a murderer. He frowned slightly. He thought about the rebellion he was raising to find Solomon. He wondered how many more people he would have to kill until he could retire somewhere. If he stopped killing, would Elizabeth come and collect him as she did when he completed his mission, when he stood execution? Or would he have to find her. Maybe she would forget about him sooner rather than later.

Joshua didn't deserve friendship, so he thought. He already had too much weight on his shoulders, too much anger and resentment. But perhaps if Joshua succeeded, and chose to take his place as the next baron, he could use his power as king to reunite them. He would have a home for them, a whole kingdom. Elizabeth could retire in peace, and he could watch over her as he wanted to. Was this too much to ask for, or had he not the favor to make the wish?

"No." Joshua lied softly. "I'm not a killer."

"It's okay if you are," Joan smiled. "I think you're pretty cool."

At this time, in which their conversation ended, Joan ceased her backpedaling and now walked beside him, somehow back to a more civil posture. She carried herself well, with confidence and joy.

"Dutch is a big softie." She said, breaking yet another silence, "He's like a big lovable dog, a bear even."

"You've met a soft bear?" Joshua inquired.

"Yeah, I grew up in the Scandes." Joan clarified. "We strive on our hunting arms out there. There's no man like a Scandes man and no woman like a Scandes woman. We're the strongest bunch around, even those Russian piss-cakes cry when they hear of us. Bears are like cats to us."

Joshua looked at her. It made sense. The burning hair, the soft eyes, she didn't try to be skinny like those in Paris did. She didn't look unhealthy. No bags wore under her eyes and her skin was not crudely tanned as if she spent her days in a salon. Her cheeks were proud and pronounced, thick and rounded to add to her soft features. She drank like a man and fought like a soldier. She even dressed for the cold, despite the mild weather. Joan must have grown up around those honorable men and women like Gurdard, whom was close to his people.

"What are you doing out here anyways?" Joan continued.

"I'm looking for orphans." Joshua replied bluntly.

"Really?" She replied. She looked surprised, her eye tinged with excitement. "And what do you plan on doing when you find them? I doubt you have a house to put them in. Are you trying to become a father? *Are* you a father?"

"I'll figure something out," The American assured, answering only one question. "I'll find out what to do with them once Whitecroft is dead…"

"You can't actually be serious about that!? I thought you were joking." Joan stammered.

"I was not. That's why I'm here."

"What's your beef with her?" Joan asked, her curiosity stemming like a sugared plant.

"She tried to kill me, and now she's in my way."

Joshua watched as a lone farmer walked over a small bridge with a guitar in his hands. He strummed a slow tune that matched the lazy day. The guitarist hummed along while Joshua passed him. He nodded at Joshua.

Joshua thought the whole countryside particular. He never liked the country. He was a city boy himself. Although Val-Ashoth had enchanted him, nowhere in those mystic lands did he see men in overalls or hear stray pigs. Val-Ashoth wasn't a countryside, it was a community ripe with culture and flavor. It was deep, complex, and beautifully colorful.

The difference between the two environments lay in the shallow waters of the brook they just passed, it represented the depth of Whitecroft's people. The difference in the soil matched the farmers' dry characters. But Joshua also didn't blame them, he did admire their simplicity. Perhaps, when Joshua was baron, he could reinvigorate the waning culture in these lands. But that was just another small task on Joshua's long list of to-dos.

Joan bit her lower lip. She hadn't replied in some time. It was peculiar, the way she was so carefree and relaxed despite the hardships of being under an oppressive ruler. Especially for farmers.

"Joan," Joshua began, "What is it that you do? Despite getting drunk and breaking into the Baron's estate."

"I do a little bit of everything. I mostly live off the land, I fish and lay traps for food. I sell the furs to people passing through or patch up my clothes. I also run errands for people. These people have relatives outside the province they aren't allowed to see. I'm good at finding my way around patrols and, because I'm not a farmer nor a child, I'm not missed by the census. I deliver letters mostly, write letters too, since many of the farmers can't read or write. But also, I'm asked to find lost items or special ingredients in places normal residents can't go."

"Freelancer, then?"

"That sounds about right." Joan laughed.

"How much would it be to hire you Joan?" Joshua asked.

"Excuse me?" Joan asked.

"Say I wanted to use your skills. What would I need to offer you for you to say yes?"

Joan scratched her braided head. She thought for a while.

"Most people just buy me beer or give me bread when I've done something. But I have a feeling yours isn't an ordinary request."

"It's not, I want you to help me find these children first. And then I want you to help me kill the baron. Dutch has already agreed to help me as well."

Joshua stopped and looked into Joan's eyes. They stood at the top of a hill within eyeshot of the old granary. The sun had begun to set, and Joshua waited for a reply. He seemed serious, which scared Joan. Joan had never directly contributed to the death of anyone before, she didn't know if she wanted to. She hated the baron; watching her tear apart loved ones and sit on her throne surrounded by pallets of food made from exploiting the starvation of others. She never even ate the food.

Joan had snuck into Whitecroft's treasury once and even stole a golden necklace from her. She had so much money, Joan knew, and it was never used. Money the baron possessed should have been used to purchase the grains she needed from the farmers or used to flourish the economy by incentivizing businesses to establish themselves on unused land. But that vast treasury never moved. The more Joan thought about it, the more she didn't see Whitecroft as a human being, but as a parasite, an eagle that steals the prey of other birds, a bird that should be put down. The more she thought about it, the more she hated Whitecroft, and the more she wanted to see her rot.

"Consider me hired," Joan grimaced, taking Joshua by the elbow. "But you'll only know my price after Whitecroft sees justice."

Joshua was willing to take the risk and thanked her with a nod.

"Let find ourselves some orphans." Joan huffed, anew with vigor.

Joshua and Joan entered the large granary to find it empty. Only yellow batches of scattered straw littered the concrete flooring. The building was rectangular. Brick and mortar rose from the soil to meet rotten pillories. Cracks in the roof revealed the stars. It was becoming dark, but not too dark. Joshua and Joan had no trouble seeing or finding evidence of child activity. They had been there, the straw had been bent, chewed at the ends, cracked in bundles, and wrapped with strings created by torn clothes. The rudimentary bundles that were tied stood up on end, no doubt used as a plaything, a small instrument used for imaginative purposes, perhaps a doll.

"Look at this." Joan called. She stood transfixed at the other end of the house. She pointed down at the corners. There in the brick was carved small stick figures. The first image had a small child holding what looked to be his parents' hands. It was scratched thinly into the foundation, perhaps with a knife or piece of glass. These little doodles were riddled before them like hieroglyphics. A child and his mother, a child and her father, a house with two windows and a chimney, all stood the test of time and hinted at the orphan's emotions.

Certainly, as Joshua continued to observe the art, one image stood out most. It was a large caricature of a single person. At that size in which everything was scaled, the doodle did not tell whether the subject was supposed to be an adult or a child. But one thing was positive in Joshua's examination, the image was drawn to convey fear. The child in question had drawn an unusually large head on the subject, and the features of the face were in more detail than the features of other peoples in other drawings. This no doubt meant the image was a specific person, whether imagined or real. The face had angry brows and a gaping mouth, shouting silently at the Joshua and Joan. It stood to be their height, and although the body was a single rehashing of lines with no width nor definition, the image looked alive, ready to strike them down with the knife clutched at the end of its hand.

Joshua thought the image would peel itself from the wall and become a 2D slasher.

Joshua continued to stare at the image, it had to mean danger, but from whom? Joshua traced his finger through the image's curly hair and along his angry brow. All of the etchings were confined in this corner and seemed to bear the consistency of a single artist. Between the thin lines, the location of the markings, and the increased detail, Joshua thought the artist was the subject. It had to be, for no child would be apt to remember a stranger so vividly, unless he haunted their dreams. The knife would be the tool that he used to sketch, his anger misplaced at other children, perhaps. Contrary, the artist was least likely a lonely or shy child that confined himself to a corner despite being surrounded by others. Was the child disassociated with, leading him to feel anger. Was he pushed into a corner and neglected by the others? Was he planning on hurting other people, or merely giving expression to his emotions? None of these thoughts comforted the ex-detective. He grew impatient, worried. He wanted to find the children soon, if they had not suffered already.

"This is bad." Joan sighed, having come to the same conclusion. "Whoever this is might intend to harm the children."

"Hopefully it's just misinterpreted." Joshua mused, "sometimes children have nightmares about adults, or see something they don't understand."

"Like what?"

"Any adult could have approached these children to offer them help. What if one was too loud, or they had a knife on them, a... chef... maybe. The children would have misplaced fear and draw it here with a rock."

"You know how farfetched that is. It's a very specific example, and it's very unlikely all those variables would be true." Joan chided softly.

Joshua sighed, "It's the only hope I have something bad won't happen."

"Or has happened." Joan added, "We don't know how old these are."

Joan paused, she crossed her arms, thinking. "Who told you there were children by the river anyways?"

"There was a man I helped, seemed to be suffering from a stutter, maybe even Tourette syndrome. Told me he saved some food for children if they were to come by. Talked as if they were treated as town dogs, moving door to door."

Joan mumbled to herself. "One word of mouth is all you have and your running with it?"

"Are you upset?" Joshua asked. He turned to her, no longer staring at the markings.

"No... *no*." She assured, her voice still pleasant and tempered, more curious than upset. Her face seemed worried, pouty, "You're just doing an awful lot because of a rumor. Why does it matter to you that these children are found, if there are any children at all, for that matter?"

Joshua thought about it. Something burned inside of him, tugged his intestines through his throat. The children he had killed, his dreams about them, how could he ignore another child ever again? Now, when he closed his eyes, walking through that upstairs hallway and opening up the door. He could see it, a blame upon himself contorting into a complex idea. It was something about a nun leaping to the cross, shouting at children their destinies in hell. Perhaps he embedded something distinct in his heart long ago. Something akin to a loving, a zeal, a certain heroic complex.

But these needn't be fast examples. In its simplest of form, without such trite evaluation, it was the stick figure that still seemed alive. It looked at Joshua with his two-dimensional expression of rage. Joshua was chastised by that image and what else it looked like. Those ugly slender monsters who pretended to be children, or, the children who pretended to be monsters.

Joshua couldn't stop the thought of their death. He knew it now. The reason why he was looking for the children was because he felt guilty. Joshua would feel guilty if he ignored the orphans, only to find out they starved to death, or worse. How many children would he have written under his name. How many more innocents would he have failed? Surely his sins were stacking against him. Surely there was a clock somewhere and a reaper called death, waiting to sink his scythe across someone's wrists. Joshua couldn't bear to lose another on his watch.

Everyone Joshua saved became part of him, and so did everyone he killed. For him to see the joy of a hostage's face was to know the depth of his own heart. Such was the light of other people's smiles and tears, a spotlight reminding Joshua he was empty and no better than a robot. Perhaps if he saved enough people, he might remember what it's like to feel full of life himself.

"I don't know," Joshua lied, but Joan could see the pain, the look of a bloodhound searching for answers. It was a look she had seen before in her father's eyes. The night after her mother went missing, she remembered her father dropping her off with her uncle, too young to understand why he was abandoning her. Her father didn't look back as he descended the mountain paths of the Scandes, but his demeanor spoke of defeat and emptiness. Joan knew Joshua's look well, she was scared of it, but also, she was drawn to it, as if she were looking at her father again.

"Well…" Joan comforted, "We should get back to the tavern. Let me buy you some shots. We'll start here tomorrow. We'll find them."

Joan gripped Joshua's wrist and tugged at it, but Joshua wouldn't move. He looked down at the ground, lost in thought, deciding whether he could bear to let his hands slip and relax. Joan tugged again. She didn't want to watch Joshua run himself into the ground.

Slowly and surely, she prodded him back from the wall until he budged. He started to walk behind her, and she led him back like a red wagon.

It was a long walk that night back to the tavern. Joshua had a long time to think in the silence. He stared at Joan's hand around his wrist. He thought it could be like a child's. He imagined the children's faces, the ones that haunted him night after night. They would all hold each other's wrists at the park, like elephants in a line leading him to the fountain of forgiveness. Or was that a life he made up for them so that he might not believe their lives ended so early? Joshua needn't imagine anything else. The scene was a blur, a picture of blown bubbles floating adrift in a cosmos of pain. He would find the orphans even if it killed him.

Joshua followed Joan into the tavern. It had been busier that night. Hooded pilgrims and poor farmers drank away their woes at the table, playing card games and rolling dice. Joan guided Joshua to a table where Dutch studied. He drank from the same cask he had that morning. Joshua lay his head on the table, unresponsive to Dutch's attention.

"I'll get some whiskey," Joan told Dutch, after sitting Joshua down and before walking herself to the bar.

"You better bring the whole bottle too." Dutch called after her, looking into Joshua's hollow gaze. He turned to Joshua and patted him on the head. His big meaty hands ruffled Joshua's nappy hair like a father would his son.

"What's gotten into you, huh?" he asked.

Joshua didn't respond, didn't even twitch. His mind still drifted, tugged away by imaginary elephant lines. Joan returned with two bottles of whiskey and poured three shots. Dutch grunted at Joan, motioning to his shot.

"They don't call me Dutch for nothing lassy." He quirked.

"Oh, right." Joan smirked and poured him a double. "I hadn't realized our future baron was so mopey."

"You know about that too? Why are you helping him?" Dutch asked.

"I have something I want him to do for me after he's done taking his throne." Joan replied. "Why are *you* helping him?"

Dutch leaned back and put his papers down. "I'm a businessman. Joshua's going to take down the baron one way or another, as powerful as he seems. When he does, I want a seat at his table. Imagine being able to flex that treasury he'll have. Not to mention he'll owe me a few favors. And, of course, to save the farmers too." He lied. Joan didn't know about the black market, nor should she.

Dutch tipped Joshua's head back. "Common lad you need to get some liquor in you. No one likes a sour puss."

Joshua rose and walked out of the tavern swiftly. He slid through the bodies of those trying to find their way in and walked out past the bulletin board until he leaned forward against a lone tree at the crossroad.

Joshua wretched something foul and black onto the ground. Perhaps it was blood, perhaps it was just the lack of lights. Joshua felt his hand grip around something he hadn't put down. In his hand was a wet shot glass. Joshua had taken it with him in the hurry. Somewhere in his flight, he had spilt its contents on the floor. Joshua looked at the cup until his knuckles started to tighten. Joshua shattered the glass in his hands which cut his hand. The blood that dropped from his palm was a mixture of ash and red cells.

That's right, Joshua thought, *I'm not even human.*

"Are you okay?" Joshua heard Joan call from behind him. Joshua's shoulder twitched, but this time, his hand did not find his pistol.

"Leave me be," Joshua begged sternly. "This doesn't concern you."

Joan still approached. Joshua wretched again. Joan reached for Joshua's neck and unclasped his cloak. There was no need for it to get dirty. Joan rolled the cloak into a cylinder, arm over arm, and placed it on the ground.

"It is my business. If you die or quit on us, I won't get to collect on my pay." Joan quipped.

"Is that all?" Joshua asked. "I'm not going to quit any time soon. I've come too far for this…"

Joan looked at Joshua who stayed hunched into the tree. He looked ill, his right hand shook, and his fingers writhed in the pattern of a pianist. What she didn't know, was that it was shaking in bloodlust. Joshua forced it by his side. He wanted to keep his finger off the trigger of his pistol desperately. The bullet was not for Joan nor anybody else but himself, should he not bear his existence through the night. Joshua knew he couldn't, but the entertaining thought was enough for his brain to pretend the gesture, to mimic a movement of pressing the barrel to his forehead.

Joan grabbed Joshua by his wrist again and slowly nudged him back. It took her much longer this time to coax him away from the darkness outside the tavern. Eventually, Joshua was too tired to resist, and found his way back inside once the crowd had gone.

Joshua was going crazy. And it wasn't just Joshua who could tell.

For the next few days, Joshua would come to ask more of Dutch as he put his personal baron-slaying project on hold. *The children are more important*, he would tell his lieutenant, *focus on stabilizing the region, put pressure on the guards, make them sweat blood. The children are alive. The children are out there. The children are more important. The children are alive, they're out there, I know it.*

Part 4/Rodent

Joshua woke with a headache. Last night, he had fallen asleep on the stairs with his head against the wall. He sensed the emptiness of his heart immediately, it was a physical pain, a mental stupor that rivaled that of drunkenness and heart attacks. Opposite Joshua's lack of inebriation, it seemed that Dutch had his way with every black-market bottle that night. The burly man sat in his usual spot surrounded by mixed liquors and empty bottles both on the table and the floor.

Joshua heard a knock at the door, it was something dull, but not soft to his ears.

"Dutch," Joshua called out. "Wake up. Get the door."

Dutch fidgeted. "*You* get the door. I'm your dealer, not your butler." He yawned.

Joshua sighed and rose from his hovel. He tripped over to the entrance and placed his head against the sanded wood.

"Who is it?" Joshua mumbled.

"It's Mrs. Hammond, the bar maid!" an old woman cried out. "Dutch locked me out of my own tavern last night so open up!"

"I don't know where the keys are…" Joshua sighed.

Dutch giggled from his bench seat, pointing a general direction for Joshua to search. "Try the spare. It's by the fireplace."

Joshua retrieved the spare keys by the fireplace, a brick masterpiece, and lethargically waltzed back to the locked door and put them into the allotted hole. The second he twisted the lock, the old coon burst through the threshold. She stampeded around her store, looking at the mess "they" had left.

"Dutch," She yelled, "Look at what you've done!"

The whole room had been lifted. The bottles lay off their racks and spread across the floor unopened or left open.

275

Tables were flipped, the pictures upside down. In the corner, a small pig oinked in fear of the shouting lady.

The whole of the morning was spent undoing the mess Dutch had made. Joshua was tied into the sins of his tactician. He dusted the furniture, replaced the good bottles, and turned chairs upright. Dutch swept broken glass off the ground while his hostess chewed his ear off.

It was about noon when Joan walked into the bar to see Joshua mopping the floor. She laughed. "From anarchist to busboy?" She cooed.

Joshua grumbled.

"Come on, let's get going." Joan demanded.

Before Joshua had time to undo his apron and lean his mop against a corner, Joan was gone. Joshua exited the den and walked hurriedly to catch up with her, whom already loomed ahead a good distance.

A heat wave made the day warmer and Joan unstitched her sleeves while they walked. Joshua differed his attire with more, yet thinner, layers. Joshua and Joan walked in silence down the same dirt road as the day before. Most of the crops had still to be felled and a blue horizon could be seen over the hills. Each landowner rolled the sum of their wheat into bales which sat on the earth like beige cotton balls, or caramel gumdrops on a gingerbread man.

The whole of the world seemed to operate in shades of brown. The houses were made of wood, small and pathetic. Those who could afford to build barns choose to match the color. Paint was nonexistent, or so it seemed, and everything was made from a form of wood, stone, or brick. The air was brisk and a thin waft of manure from the stray goat or cow would occasionally cross their noses.

The animals were free range, or rather, owned not by one man or any men. Whomever the owners had been, like many owners before them, decided to let their cow fend for itself, and, one day, they would hope to find it fattened and kill it. It was a free for all and the scarcity of grass in the harvest cycle left the animals roaming for hundreds of miles in search of food. They couldn't eat the grain, the farmers made sure of that with their fences and sharp sticks. If ever livestock began to nibble, the farmers were there to jab it in the flank, deterring it with negative reinforcement. One would see a cow starve before they approached the farms, lying dead in the middle of the road surrounded by vultures and grains.

On the topic of animals, many starving families, whom accidentally had too many mouths to feed, would aim to shoot down vultures. In order to do this, the farmers would kill a dying animal and leave it in an open field while they hid a small distance away. If they were smart and quiet, they might come home with one or two vultures. They would pluck them and cook them just like a chicken. Shrugging a week later, after becoming ill, *it's better than nothing,* they would say. It was better to die with a belly full of crow and an illness than an empty belly and pained stomach.

After the long tangent of thoughts that riddled Joshua's brain, the two seekers finally came upon the granary where they had last begun. Joshua stood by the river not so distant from the granary. There were no signs that the children returned that night.

Joshua frowned, looking at a small piece of driftwood in his hands. Rolling it over his thumbs, he thought about being young and racing paper boats down Paris streams. The person who finished last would have to eat the gum off the table at school or put dirt in their underwear for a school day. The consequences were silly things, made in a time when everything was just silly. Somehow, the exploits of children always seemed innocent, fantastical.

"What do you think?" Joan called from the building.

"I'm not sure." Joshua replied. "With the amount of markings on the wall you would think to find them somewhere around here, unless something happened."

Joshua squinted under the sun, there was a glint in his eye. He had been looking for it, but each time he moved his head, the glint would vanish. Joshua watched the vector. It was a stray ray originating from down the stream.

Joan was the first to notice its location. She watched as Joshua twisted his head, surrounded by invisible flies, the movement did nothing to help his morning headache. Joan jumped the creek with ease. It was only four inches of water, but the width of the trail meant the average person would need to come home with one wet foot. However, Joan was an athlete, a huntress, she needn't a head start, her body simply flew like a bird, her legs powerful and graceful like a gazelle. She landed firmly at the other end and zigzagged through the trees. She giggled, still watching Joshua twitch, half awake.

Joan stooped down to pick up the half-buried object, it was a clear beer bottle, scratched. The patterns of the scratches seemed rhythmic, someone had pretended it was a whetstone, and ran their blade over it, over and over again.

"Joshua," She called, "Look at this."

Joshua had a different approach to the stream. At first, he dabbed his foot in, his shoe aimed at a surfaced rock. However, it was too slick to place weight upon. He retreated.

"Come on!" Joan mocked.

Joshua waved her off. There was no bridge in sight. Joshua removed his shoe and his sock. After rolling up his pants, he sunk his foot into the freezing water and shivered. Joshua pivoted his good leg across to dry ground and followed over again. Joshua meandered over to his company before sitting down to redress.

Joan tossed Joshua the bottle, which he snagged out of the air. He placed his finger into the mouth like a peg inside a spool of yarn. The translucent glass almost seemed opaque. The blemishes had removed all luster from the body. Within the scratches, Joshua could see small grey fragments of metal shards, the weapon of choice by the stick-figure man.

Joan looked off into the dirt, there were scuff marks along the road, a trail. Softly, she began to follow, the steps uneven, a limp and dragging feet. The scuffs were wide, an adult's, winding down the road and into the distance. It was where the trailed ended that the riverside began.

"I'm going to follow these." Joan told Joshua.

Joshua nodded, placing the bottle down. "I'm going to stay here just in case they come back. Maybe someone who's been feeding them might stop by and I can ask them about the orphans."

Joan said her goodbyes and trod beside the steps, leaving Joshua to stare at the stream. She watched each mark closely. It was an odd cadence, a step with the left that almost slid out from under before the right foot placed the ground, a sign of confidence, or deformity. It was the right foot that dragged most. It scuffed at the toe and then twisted once the whole body passed over. During her tracking, Joan even stopped to practice it. She took the left foot and slid it back, lifting her right and plopping it down at the right moment in the air. It was a jarring walk, almost too difficult to perform. *What odd person could walk like this*? She thought, continuing to practice further down the road.

Joan looked up from the track as she heard the sound of farmers finishing their work. She approached them, watching them for a time as she leaned on their fence. She looked at their feet, looked for signs of a handicap, odd stances, but they had none.

"See something you like, darling?" One of the farmers whistled. "I can take a break, just for you."

The other men laughed, still toiling. Joan didn't give it thought, staring the man straight in the eyes without so much as a blush.

"Have any of you seen someone pass by in the last few days? Somebody who walked with a limp, possibly disfigured about the hip?" She asked, her chin bobbing, her hands relaxed on her sides.

The man grunted to himself, disappointed. "No, I ain't. Andy, Gomer, have you seen anybody walk by with a limp or hideous deformity?" He jawed.

"I didunt." The first said.

"Eh. Mayhbe Gene, I didn't see 'im but I sure know when he's by, wears two belts on account of his weight issue. Man is downright scarrrry." The second cawed.

"Gene." Joan murmured starting off down the road.

Gene was the second most influential man outside of Whitecroft's domain. He owned a house on Hiker's Folly, right before the southern border, a large columned mountain that jut into the sky like a pillar. He was one of Whitecroft's advisors, a regular Joseph before Pharaoh.

"Are you sure you don't want to come in a spell? It's awfully hot outside!" The man shouted, a last attempt for him to meet a pretty girl. Long days of work and no play left him starving for the presence of a woman in his life. Even if it was just over a glass of water.

Joan never replied, she simply went about her mission.

Joshua perched his head between his knees and crossed his arms over his chin. It had been an eternal two hours in which nothing eventful happened. Rarely, some single entity or whole groups of people would pass by and he would stop them for a moment to ask them about seeing orphans, any orphans, ever. They all reported seeing no orphans anywhere in the area, nor in the whole of Whitecroft's lands. Many couldn't give account to seeing orphans their entire lifetime.

Joshua flicked his matchlight fingers off and on, off and on. Waiting for something to happen, and something did. In the dark shadow of the granary, through the only door, Joshua saw a shadow move. The detective rose slowly, hoping not to make a sound. He slowly approached the granary, boots wading through the stream. The figure was still, watching him, but Joshua couldn't make out its features.

Joshua entered the granary and looked into the thing's beady eyes, it was a small creature, a small fuzzy bear-like creature akin to that from fairy tales. It looked harmless, standing there on its two nubby legs erect like a homo-sapient, watching Joshua with curiosity. Joshua stood in the doorway, still crouched slightly, positioned to defend himself if necessary.

"Hey there." Joshua whispered. "I don't suppose you're the orphans we've been looking for."

Joshua looked down at the creature, it didn't seem to understand. After all, it was some type of mangy animal. Like most animals, Joshua found himself talking out loud to it, as most people do when they're lonely.

"No, I suppose not, even if you knew where they were, you couldn't say…"

The creature growled cutely within its throat, its large canine ears twitched and folded. Inside its small paws was a half-eaten fish. Joshua could see small scales, smutz, around its lips. It was adorable, the bane of all stuffed animals, all real domesticated pets. It reached out to Joshua, as if asking for his hand. Joshua slowly reached back, looking to assert a peaceful and human demeanor. It was best for him to mimic the creature's movements, a show of docility. Joshua thought that this magical species might have never achieved contact with humans before, so unknown to the world as magic was in general. Joshua had seen the movies, the stories of aliens destroying the earth all because some punk with a slingshot thought it was okay to make fun of the "weird thing." Then, after laughing at the defeated alien, its friends would come to exact revenge using their massive lasers of death.

"Are you alone?" Joshua asked, more for himself than for the animal.

"Of course, I'm alone you pissing shill!" The fur-ball shouted in an intense, intelligent voice. "God, if I had a penny for every time someone treated me like a goldfish I'd be living in a Russian penthouse!"

The animal tossed his half-eaten fish at Joshua and laughed. It was an ugly cackle, like those you hear from embezzling bankers or mobsters. The fuzzball grumbled and motioned to claw Joshua like a cat. Joshua shook his head, he should have known better.

"Oh, cool kid, are you?!" The beast motioned, turning his back to sit in a corner, "Not surprising given your ugly mug!"

Joshua ran his hands over his face, but he still looked human; he still felt his human face.

"Yeah, that's right, I see what you are with your terrible complexion and your deer horns, sooo scary! Illusions don't work on these eyes, even high-quality ones like yours!"

"Well don't go around telling anybody." Joshua insisted.

The thing cackled again, almost howling. "Who am I gunna tell?! Half the county's drunk and the other half don't give me the time of day! They think *I'm* scary, a talking plush toy! Just wait till they see a real monster. I'm adorable, I know it, but they don't!"

"I haven't heard anyone mention a monster in the area, you'd think they'd remember." Joshua thought aloud.

"Yeah," the thing coughed, "That's because I root around in their empty brains before they run away. I'll tell you, I have never seen brains hollower. These pissant bumpkins should seriously get out more and stop handling so much firewater."

"You erase people's memories?"
"Never heard of a brownie before, kid?" The creature asked.

Joshua shrugged, his stomach rumbling. "I don't carry a guidebook in my back pocket."

"Yeah, bring me a copy if you find one, I'd stare at sirens all day." The thing laughed again, motioning to his puffed-up chest and winking. "I'm a brownie, kid. I was once a household pet, did chores, looked cute, and kept my mouth shut. What they don't tell you, is that I also nom on people's brains, fool around with their minds. Boggarts, brownies, boogeymen, we play along those lines trying to keep our master in good graces, usually."

"So, I don't suppose you've seen any orphans hanging around here, have you, 'brownie?" Joshua asked, moving to more pressing matters than feminine wiles and monster descriptions.

"Bucky, Ducky, and Lucky?" it responded, picking its teeth with a fishbone.

"If those are the name of the orphans, the ones who drew on that wall there." Joshua assured, nodding to the fall perimeter.

"Yeah, Bucky's the one with the big front teeth, tall for his age, Lucky's the one who curses more than a leprechaun, and Ducky's the girl who follows Bucky around all the time, like a duck."

"Okay, so, where are they?" Joshua huffed.

The brownie shrugged. "Beats me kiddo, I haven't seen them in weeks, not since that man came by to pick them up since 'boarding school' was over or something."

"What man?"

"That big buy, what's his name, Eddie, Genie? I dunno, super fat though, knife in his belt, wears two of 'em actually."

Joshua rubbed his head. He hadn't seen anyone of the sort and would have to go back and ask Dutch. The young man turned about to leave but felt a prick in his calf. Joshua swiveled around to see the brownie with his claws out. His nub of a tail wiggled, for a moment almost cute again, before opening his dirty mouth.

"Name's Ablisach," He stated, holding out his hand, "but everybody, namely me, calls me Sach, dirtwad."

Joshua didn't shake Sach's paw, he'd tried that before. The American huffed slightly before turning again to leave, exiting the ruined building and heading for the road. Behind him, Sach scurried on all fours to catch up.

"I didn't get your name, pal." The fur-ball panted.

"I didn't give one." Joshua retorted.

"Hey, hey, hey, shots fired, color me defeated, white flag, I got it. But I don't suppose you wanna house pet, do you?"

Joshua looked over his shoulder at the mangy tuft of hair. "You don't look the type." He guessed. "Even for a brownie."

"Yeah, I've been out here on my own. My last master threw me out, real douche bag." Sach scoffed.

"I wonder why." Joshua sighed sarcastically.

"Hey, I was a good pet! I had talent! I took out the trash! I licked his feet! I danced for his enjoyment, metaphorically on the feet thing... I'm not an animal, but I'm tired of being on the road. You've gotta throw me a bone here!" Sach moaned.

Joshua thought about it, having drowned out the incessant words of the brownie.

"What talents so you have?" Joshua asked.

Sach ran before Joshua and paused in his tracks, making Joshua stop to look at him. Sach had trouble in this interview, tapping his chin as he did. Joshua sighed again and continued his way along the road, passing the scruffy animal with a wide birth.

"Oh, wait!" Sach called out after him, scurrying back to follow. "I'm great at making human vegetables. Just let me at a human's head and I'll sink my teeth in. I can suck out all their memories and leave them a living heap of flesh!"

"Charming." Joshua scoffed.

"Hey, it's something." Sach defended.

Joshua walked a little faster now. It was already dark, and he was having trouble finding his way. There in the distance, a small radial shine marked the lone tavern behind the hills. It was hiding, waiting to be discovered, returned to. The gradient served as a marker for refuge, safety, sleep.

Joshua also thought about Sach's offer to suck people's brains for him. He thought it was ridiculous, but he never knew when he would need something, anything. If

Joshua ever had to resort to torture, he could always let Sach make good on his promise. The teddy bear seemed like the type to do any bidding. Such things, like torture, were beyond Joshua's expertise, after all. All in all, he might make good fodder, and Dutch could sell him on the market if he didn't know what to do with the mongrel.

"Please! I'm begging you!" Sach desperately sobbed, "I'll do anything! I wasn't made for the outdoors. I'm an exotic house pet! I'll read ya bedtime stories, I'll buy ya groceries, anything!"

"Fine… *Fine*! You can come with me!" Joshua snapped. "Just be quiet, you can't be talking in public!"

"I'll be as silent as a ghost, not a wraith or a banshee but one of those bedsheet ghosts that don't talk much." Sach apologized.

Joshua came upon Dutch's tavern. It had been a slow day and last calls were already made. Whomever had been there that day already left for the night in order to get an early start on the next morning. Immediately, as Joshua opened the door, the old bar maid was upon him.

"And where did you go this evening, young man?" Mrs. Hammond barked, "You didn't finish cleaning your room or finish mopping the floors. This place was a sty today and *I* think *you* hurt my business! You just ran off with that red-haired girlfriend of yours! I agreed with Dutch you could stay here but I didn't think you'd be so-"

"Mrs. Hammond, Mrs. Hammond," Joshua shushed, placing his hands at her elbows, "I had an emergency, but not to worry, I'm here now and I have a solution."

Mrs. Hammond stuttered. "Well, I expect you'll clean up before we open tomorrow."

"Oh, no, I won't be cleaning" Joshua insisted, "I've brought help."

Joshua looked at Sach, who looked back at him, mortified.

"Damnit." Sach whispered.

"Mrs. Hammond," Joshua began, "From here on out this little… 'Sach' … will help you on my day to day chores. I'll pay for whatever food he needs, and he'll be here all day so that, when I'm on errands, you'll always have help. He even has apposable thumbs. You do have apposable thumbs don't you, Sach?"

Sach nodded slowly.

Mrs. Hammond looked at Sach, she was both bewildered and enthralled by the creature. "Is it a monkey of some sort, some sort of odd, tailless, fluffy cat?" She asked Joshua.

"That's exactly what it is." Joshua assured. He turned to Sach and winked. Sach grumbled and took the mop from Mrs. Hammond's hands, beginning to slosh the water around.

"That's amazing." Mrs. Hammond exclaimed, she pressed her hands together in excitement.

"Oh, and Mrs. Hammond," Joshua called before he slipped upstairs, "He understands English well, but I'm not sure if he's trained to use the john."

Joan looked out at the small mountain, the highest point in The Crofts, it was a jagged chalk boulder which jutted out between the rolling hills. It was an oddity. It was as if a comet, before slamming into the earth and destroying the land, suddenly stopped and changed its mind. It rested there like a large building, the world's biggest boulder, perhaps, and looked down in its celestial purity to scorn the everyman. At the top of this slab was Gene's estate. It was not so extravagant as the baron's, but it rivaled any well-to-do city-dweller. The estate had been constructed from the same rock it stood upon, a coarse stone sanded down into Spanish design.

Joan sighed. It wasn't the first time she had heard of Gene. He was a larder, a glutton, unlike the baron, and that was why his council was cherished by her. Joan remembered, one day, watching the two polar opposites through

Whitecroft's window eating during a "business meeting." While Gene devoured everything in sight, Whitecroft simply sat there, eating a single leaf of spinach like it were a steak. Joan thought the two leaders were perfect for each other, each of them selfish and evil in their own way.

Joan, too impatient to return to Joshua as to tell him of her lead, ran her hands along the stone and began to climb. It never made sense to Joan to use the front door, having the element of surprise in any conversation, in any environment, was key to getting what she wanted. Pop in on someone while they're exchanging private dialogue and the would be leverage when asking them for a favor. Joan need not pretend to know all of the land's secrets, she was pretty damn close. And that was good enough to scare anyone who knew her name.

Joan always kept a collapsible pick by her waist, a small rectangular set of swivels that retracted when she needed it. It aided her in climbing at a moment's notice. She could even tie her spare blue string, which she had braided into her belt, to the end of the pick, using the combination as a crude grappling hook to reach far off places. She was a regular cadaver, no one could go where she could. Joan left Joshua back by the river because he would only slow her down.

Joan looked up, she had barely started her climb and, already, the sun began to set. It had been the mark of the second day, and the orphans hadn't been found yet. This worried her. She began to wonder if Joshua had any luck in finding them. Maybe he was with them right now. Hopefully, they had returned shortly after Joan had left, all of them safe, all of them willing to go with Joshua to find better shelter, to be better provided for. Hopefully, Joshua was taking care of them right now like a loving father.

Joan blushed as she continued her ascent, or perhaps it was the heat of exertion that made her cheeks rosy. It should be said that is was the former, silent knowledge, that Joan was quite fond of the enigmatic, anarchic leader.

Joan assured herself that Joshua was well and had a good head about him. He would know not to go looking for her if anything bad happened, or, at least, he should.

Either way, if the children hadn't already been found, Joan would soon find them, she was sure.

Joshua walked into the tavern's secret room to meet Dutch after dressing down. His friend stood there with his hands spread on the table, leaning. Dutch looked up at Joshua with a wry smile, "Hey, boss, we just received the first shipment of firearms, the men are going to be distributing them tomorrow. They're all eager to meet you once you have time. How goes to search for the children?"

Joshua stretched out on a wooden chair in the corner and uncorked a bottle of scotch left on one of the many shelves around the room. He drank straight from the bottle and set it down next to him on the floor.

"Do you know of a man who wears two belts and carries a knife around all the time?" He mused into the room.

"I can think of a few men, but not many people wear two belts. The one that comes to mind is Gene Chase, whom happens to be Whitecroft's advisor. Gene Chase has a mansion south-east of here. You can't miss it. It's located atop this white mountain the locals call 'Hiker's Folly.' He's known for having parties late at night, thoroughfares with supporters from God-knows-where. I believe he is having one on the morrow, so it wouldn't be so suspicious for us to forge an invitation and get you in."

Joshua nodded, "I will need one in the morning then. You best get to it."

Dutch rubbed his head, it seemed he had to do all the legwork. Perhaps when their little rebellion grew to a greater size, he could call upon some assistants for help. However, he didn't know any farmer that could read or write well enough to make good clerks. It seemed, for now, Dutch would have to wring himself dry.

288

"By the by," Dutch chimed, remembering a missive he had received earlier that day. "I've heard that Whitecroft is having a feast in a month or so. You should make an appearance."

Joshua shifted further in his chair and raised his brow. "Do you think it's wise to show my hand? She doesn't even know I'm here." He asked, a small burst of meaning in his eyes.

Dutch twisted his fingers through his mustache, curling the ends. "I think it might be smart to show *a* hand, if not *your* hand. If you show up yourself, you're trading the element of surprise to deal a psychological detriment. The baron wouldn't be able to sleep after knowing you're after her. You survived her guillotine. She has to be scared of you coming back.

Plus, many other Barons will be there too. They'll begin to see her as weak, and maybe some would even root for you. If you can promise the Barons that you can stabilize this state, increase commerce, or improve anything else that Whitecroft has failed to do in her office, your claim might be legitimized. That legitimization is what will keep the Barons from helping Whitecroft, will keep them from staking their claims on this land once she's dead."

"But she could also crack down on the farmers because she's scared. Patrolmen would conduct more searches. She would hire more guards and bolster her defenses." Joshua retorted, rising from his chair and beginning to pace in front of Dutch.

Dutch leaned back from the table. Joshua truly looked capable of leading them. The man seemed intelligent, wise, and open-minded, but he didn't think outside the box enough. When Joshua would reign over them, Dutch hoped he would keep close advisors, namely, he hoped he could stay around to offer an opinion.

"Where do you think those guards will be from?" Dutch asked rhetorically, "I'm not led to believe she will hire from outside the country, that costs too much. Also, she won't borrow troops from another baron. Even if a Baron has the gall to stand against you and the people, Whitecroft is too prideful; she won't ask for favors.

Whitecroft will hire farmers. Farmers can be spies, turn a blind eye to weapons stores so that we can raid them. They can give us the upper hand. She'll be paying for their weapons, paying them actual coin. Those recruited wouldn't have to farm anymore. Finally, if the Baron is surrounded by her enemies, what good are the new defenses she would make? Joan, by herself, can find another way into the estate, this is true, and we could funnel our forces through whatever path she finds. But what if every soldier Whitecroft relied on turned against her? They could simply open the doors for you so that you could stroll on in. The fight would be over before it even begins."

Joshua watched Dutch's attitude. The burly man waved his hands before him as he spoke implying his sincerity and passion. This helped the detective trust the whimsical fellow. His open palms, his unabridged smile, all pointed to someone who could be a friend, a true ally. Joshua wasn't sure about others, or rather, the majority of all people. For some uncanny reason, Joshua believed nothing a man did was selfless; that even a selfless act was selfish, because it was something they wanted to do for whatever reason. This reasoning bade Joshua to prove himself an odd paradox. He drove himself to impossible edges trying to find an act worthy to be called selfless. Even in himself, he could never find such a deed. Perhaps this was why he detested himself and drove himself to instability. Perhaps this was why he tortured himself on saving every soul he could.

Nevertheless, Joshua liked Dutch's idea. The whole rebellion could end in one fell swoop if all went according to plan. But it would be dangerous. They would have to start operating in public, and the risks would become very steep. One false move could mean the rebellion's end.

"I'll sleep on it. We have time, but, the orphans come first." Joshua answered him.

"Then get it done fast." Dutch agreed, "I'll have your invitation on the morrow. I hope you find what you're looking for; we're all waiting on you."

Joshua nodded and left the small room. He ascended the last set of stairs and found himself in his "rented" room. Joshua sat on his bed, not bothering to undress. *Why did he always have to think?* He asked himself. Joshua surely detested himself. Was he selfish in the extreme, willing to send farmers to war so that he might draw Solomon out of hiding. Would he be responsible for their deaths, or would it be on their heads alone? No one had to join him, but Joshua knew he couldn't conquer the state alone. So, was Joshua selfish, and, if so, then who wasn't?

Part 5/Rite

Joan rolled over the top of the Hiker's Folly and huffed. She had climbed just over the mansion, on a small steppe just beside Gene's mansion. The woman gazed down the small outlet at the white walls of the estate. The lights incandescent and his guards remained posted around the empty courtyard.

Joan crawled on her stomach and watched them, still, silent, and unnoticed like a panther in a tree. She looked for patterns in the guard's movements, ways to slip in without arousing the men from their posts. Nothing availed itself so easily.

The guards seemed rigid, more so than those at the baron's estate. Their backs were straight and their eyes alert. Joan looked off behind the house, there, two other guards carried a large crate behind the corner. Joan smirked, perhaps there was a cellar on the back end. But not all cellars connected with the house, Joan recalled, they merely served as hollow foundations. It would be a gamble to enter, only to find herself cornered off by patrolling soldiers. If she was to be found out, she would be trapped beneath Gene's estate with only one way out.

Joan continued to look about.

There were plenty of windows about the house, terraces adorned with hanging branches and vines, yet, the frequency of the guard's patrols would leave a small margin of time to scale through.

With this intelligence, Joan decided her best bet was to wait until the next morning when Gene would be out of his house. The guards would be lax, not expecting a thief to break in while the sun was high.

Joan was patient that night. She slept with one eye open, watching the guards come and go in shifts. A man with yellow mutton chops and a crumpled hat, another with hay fever and a rash. Many different guards came and went, many more than Joan could remember.

Bored of watching the shifts, Joan let her mind dawdle to her homeland, the rigid peaks and the frosted valleys of the Scandes mountains. She thought about when she first learned to hunt, something her uncle once taught her when she came of age. Riding her horse, sharing her first kiss, partying at the festivals that marked the turn of each month, were all musings Joan meandered through.

Most of all, Joan thought, she missed her skiff the most; the small redwood boat that the villagers loved to see sailing around the shores at dawn. She held fond recollection of the salt water that sprayed her face as she leaned over the side of her catboat. She could still remember the way its smoothly-worn rope threaded through her fingers.

As much as Joan loved the ocean, it was her first voyage away from home that grounded her in The Crofts. In that distant past, Joan had sailed in search of adventure into a torrent of sloshing rain. As much as she fought and flowed with the maelstrom, the waves conquered and devoured her lovely boat, smashing it against the reefs and the rocks. The following morning, after a long night of keeping her head above the water, Joan drudged herself onto the shore, her sail in tatters, her body drenched and cold. Joan found what was left of her skiff on the beach, the small dingy that was once her father's. It was broken beyond her ability to repair it. Desperate, Joan limped into the thin woods, looking for shelter. She found herself curled into a ball under a tree, its roots around her like a cocoon. She stared into a small fire made of twigs and leaves, expelling the numbness from her body.

The death of Joan's boat gave limelight to a fear that bade her away from the ocean. She thought she had conquered her fear of death under a riptide, her fear of waves and sharks and all other kinds of dangers in open waters. The death of Joan's boat allowed her resplendent dreams to become nightmares. When she closed her eyes, large monsters watched her through sunset eyes like gods exacting divine judgement. The turtles, the sharks, the eels, that were once her favorite animals, nibbled away at her flesh, betraying her. Joan was helpless in these nightmares. She was pulled further into the depths of the ocean by groping seaweed and crystalized by growing corals, forever left in Rán's suffocating bosom.

Joan once found a dead body in her youth, when out playing with her friend along the shore. They had found a small rowboat covered in mold and nets. They rummaged through it, discovering that the boat was owned by a failed scavenger whom searched for gold at the bottom of the sea. The children only found spoons and other utensils until Joan tripped over the sailor. At first, she thought it was a bag made of animal skin, or thin plastic, transparent and white. But as she fell over him, she twisted his body around, and there, where she lay on the ground, its rotten, pale, and bloated body stared at her, mouth open and the lightest shade of lapis.

It was that image of the rotting diver, of the sickly corpse, that woke her up in the morning.

Joan rolled to her back and stretched on the ground, arms flailing, careful not to yawn. She looked backwards at Gene's mansion, her chin pointed at the sky. It was already midday and the sun's heat resonated off the stone rise. The soldiers had taken to hiding beneath the balconies, tucking themselves into the shade for cooler air.

Joan rolled back to her stomach and bear-crawled forth. To her luck, no one stood watch near the east window. This was Joan's opportunity to infiltrate.

The girl leaped forth, her arms spread like a bird, allowing the subtle breeze a chance to catch beneath her armpits and resist her fall. She landed softly with a sideways roll and quickly sprinted towards the wall. Joan leapt and firmly placed her feet against the slab. Using her momentum to urge her body upward, her feet scraped like a goat kicking rocks down a cliff. Quickly, she reached into her waistband and produced a tied thread that hooked into her pickaxe. In mid-step, with her body still in ascending motion, she launched her grapple forward to neatly hang against the seal of the window above.

Joan gripped the blue-braided rope and pulled, her body rising rapidly in momentum. She rose straight to the window seal and nimbly placed a firm boot on the head of her pickaxe. Her hands pressed into the sides of the window, creating friction with the lip. She pulled her body against the small window frame holding her up, clenching tightly. Her whole rear hung out of the sill, and, if someone were to walk by, they would immediately notice the funny lass like a nail in a wall.

Joan twisted her spare foot before her and pressed against the pane, slowly pushing it open with a creak. The lass shifted through, her foot falling to the bench inside, then to the floor. Joan entered and reeled her climbing gear back into her belt behind her swiftly, so that it might not crack against the tile.

The infiltrator stayed low along the ground. She was on the second floor. If she wasn't careful, the thin tile beneath her, hollow and thin, would sound her footsteps through the house. She reached out with each step, biding her time, first her toe slid against the tile, rolling then to the outside of her boot before she let the rest of her leg apply pressure. The movement burned her legs, stole her energy meticulously. No matter how often she found herself sneaking through houses or forests, hunting deer and stolen possessions, Joan could never get used to the pain in her thighs, it was the burning sensation of exercise that chided her, which was nothing quite as annoying as her scalding impatience.

The house Gene lived in was beautiful, no doubt inspired by a Spanish hacienda. The tiles were orange and polished, the walls smooth with stucco and fanned spackle. The occasional painting commemorated the countryside or a stallion galloping with pride. Benches littered the walls as if the place was once a church. Joan half expected a priest to appear below her through the rails in the center foyer and begin his daily prayer on behalf of an invisible congregation and Catholics everywhere.

The doors were made of wood, a dense, ancient wood, the kind used in hollow knolls and found in ghost towns. It was a simple house, spacious, but unwelcoming. The lack of plants and personality created a lovely but lifeless prison. It didn't seem to Joan that Gene entertained many guests.

There were no signs of children yet. There was no sign of any life whatsoever. The rooms Joan began to search were all empty and no one living lingered in the halls. After a long time of searching the house, the trespasser soon found herself inside a long rectangular room she had missed before. Inside this room was an art studio. Joan closed the door behind her before standing upright.

The seeker was positive the mansion was empty.

On the far side of this art studio was a blank white sheet, a bedsheet, which hung from a rafter where it was nailed so that it might stand. Paint caressed it, splotched in clumps as if the wannabe canvas was subject to scrutiny, the mad artist tossing his brushes against it in frustration. There were plenty of easels in this room, all erect with half-finished paintings fixed to them. Shades of all colors, poorly mixed, were spread upon them. Whomever the artist was, was clearly an amateur.

The tile below Joan was littered with spilled paint, something Joan tried to avoid. She walked around each splotch, tiptoeing. She tried her best to be careful, to not step on the colorful landmines. Joan did not want to leave her footprints on the ground, a sign the house was broken into.

Glancing back, Joan realized she missed something. There, on the floor, where the puddle of sewer-green paint met the cupboards, was a small handprint of like color. The size of this handprint matched to size of a child's palm, proving that an infant had been in the room. Whomever the child was had nefariously made his or her mark against the orange tiles. The handprint started as a blot, a single pat, but in drying, was streaked back towards the hanging bedsheet.

Joan looked at the paintings before looking back at the bedsheet. The paintings were not complete, this much was true, but, at further inspection, perhaps they were not supposed to be completed. Joan realized the paintings were all the same with a single spot of negative space, a place where the white canvas gave shape to a thin body.

Whomever the artist was kept a person omitted, neglected, in every single portrait. The other characters in each painting, being similar in shape, held dark-red torches. These peoples resembled a mob, an angry mob, pursuing the blank spot or led by it.

It was not a happy picture, it was cynical. The dark green sky above the villagers was foreboding, providing an oracle of things to come. The portraits were a certain revelation for the artist, a promise of a certain harrowing, and hollowed, end.

Once Joan looked back at the bedsheet canvas, she immediately noticed there was a second door at the end of the art studio, to the left behind the painted bedspread. This door was much narrower than the other doors in the house, almost humble. Joan didn't know why she had missed it, for it should have been an obvious find under her eagled eyes.

Joan tiptoed forth and carefully grabbed its brass handle. She brushed the bedsheet to the side slightly and rotated the knob. Behind this door was another hallway, shorter and less spacious than that of the other rooms she searched. It was a servant's quarters.

Joan walked through it slowly, her hands brushing against the narrow walls. There were three doors on the left and one further on the right. Joan listened, the silence of the mansion suddenly broken. There was something, a thump, thump, thumping, against the walls. Joan could feel it in her fingers, bouncing through the walls. It was a dull hum, a soft kickdrum.

Joan peered through the first door, but there was nothing. It was a small kitchen with two ovens, only one person could fit within this room at a time. Joan closed the door and moved forth.

The beat of the drum thumped stronger as she made her way to the second door. Joan was growing warmer. The lass opened the second door slowly, nothing, a laundry room with piles of white linen and ruined tapestries of red/green paint.

Joan's heart began to hammer, now understanding exactly where the thumping was coming from. The young girl looked to the only door on the right, the hammering of her heart matching the drumming against her skin, in her ears. Joan gripped the knob and opened the door.

Joan sobbed.

Joshua took the steps along the small mountain; the wind grew louder the higher he went. He had come to Hiker's Folly to meet Gene Chase in person and find the orphan children. It had taken him all day to reach the estate, but now he stood there before the mansion. The guards stared at him through and through, running their hands along his sides. It was well past six and clouds began to collect, stopping the setting sun from shining, cooling the rock they stood upon.

"Go on in," One of the guards stated, his rifle pointed at the sky, "A tad ahead of the pack, eh?"

Joshua nodded and ushered himself forward, his feet climbing the last of the winding steps. The gate opened before Joshua and he spied the front door, a massive twenty-foot pearl-gilded swivel. Joshua thought it odd such a fixture would be clashed with such a Spanish house. But given what Dutch told him about Gene, Joshua doubted the man had impeccable taste. Joshua made his way across the courtyard and stood in the mouth of the foyer. Joshua looked about the large vestibule and caught his eye on an open window seal along the second-floor. Surely, Gene was going to let the rain into his house unknowingly. The outsides of Joshua's mouth twitched momentarily, and on cue, it began to drizzle.

"You may approach," Dr. Chase announced, his airy and thin voice slicing through the atrium. The man was grossly large, but not obese. Most people grew outwards from all angles, their legs thick, their feet swollen, their face sagging, but Dr. Chase was a lightbulb, all of his fat was contained in his belly. His legs were wiry (as was his hair), and his face looked normal, if not for his pointed ears and chin. His belly hung over his dual belts and rested on the empty space between his legs where he sat. That spare flesh poked out from his shirt and covered the crotch-area of his skinny leggings. Dr. Chase held a large glass of thick wine in his hands, swishing the liquid around in nervous rotation.

"What. Do. You. Want?... I. Know. My. Guests. You. are. not. one. of. them." The man asked, each of his words spaced as if every utterance he spoke was important, and their own sentence altogether. Joshua couldn't tell if this was due to the doctor's narcissism, or the weight upon his lungs.

"I heard you were in contact with some orphans recently. I was wondering where they were." Joshua stated, already perturbed by the man's demeanor.

"I. Have. Not. Seen. Any. Orphans. Around... You. May. Leave."

Joshua furrowed his brow, trying to hide his growing impatience. The ex-detective had been sidelined much too often as of late.

"Surely someone of your stature would have at least heard of orphans in the area, and can point me in a general direction, your excellency." Joshua subtly mocked.

The Doctor looked down from his chair in the foyer. Joshua noted that rows of benches were lined before the Gene, making him the center of attention for the non-existent loungers.

Joshua felt an unsettling rise in the air.

"Do. You. Think. That. I. pay. Attention. To. The. Matters. Of. The. Poor?" The Doctor spat. "My. House. Is. Up. Here. To. Forget. That. Drivel... I. look. Down. On. Them. In. disgust."

"Are you expecting company?" Joshua asked, but again, on cue, he already heard the gates open behind them. There, an unholy choir flooded the foregrounds, men and women dressed like widows. They carried small red lanterns in one hand and umbrellas in the opposite.

Joshua shifted nervously and watched as this congregation of gothic Quakers passed by him, brushing his pea coat. Joshua put both hands in his pockets.

"Perhaps I should come by another time, Doctor. I didn't mean to intrude on your party-" Joshua began, but the doctor held up his free hand, it was fragile and bony, smaller than his wine hand; it shook under the pressure of gravity.

"Don't-leave. Stay." The doctor insisted, suddenly changing cue and pace.

Joshua didn't have a choice for the moment. Already, the congregation trapped him in a sea of black clothing. They shifted forth towards the doctor, forming a single file line. Each person approached him and kneeled before the advisor, whom now seemed unusually tall in comparison to them. He held out his wine glass to them, and they each took a sip before moving towards the pews and sitting down.

Joshua had never seen a cult before, as shown by the lack of communion wafers. He had only read about them in newspapers. Even the mention of cults unnerved him. Joshua believed new religion was audacious, often at the expense of others. Cults often separated the poor and the rich by unnatural distances, much did any institution.

Joshua fingered the hidden pocket where his pistol rode and wiggled his fingers around a lump of air in the other.

The fog still nestled with him; It wrapped around his fingers, cold and brisk like the low-pressure front bursting from the doors. It was another reminder of fall on the way, and it would be a strong one. These months, the days shifted between hot and cold, mother nature never deciding whether to wear layers or a tank top.

The congregation continued to brush by Joshua. He tried not to make eye contact with them, but, as he stared forth he caught someone's eye, a man wearing a wide-brimmed stovetop hat. He looked at Joshua with a hint of cruelty, a hint of respect, and a hint of worry. This man slowly crept his way right through the crowd. He didn't drink the wine Gene possessed and sat in the back row quietly. Not one person but Joshua seemed to directly notice this man chose the non-ritualistic path.

Joshua stared with his yellow eyes at the cup the congregation drank from. He began to understand exactly what it was, and the predicament he was in. Doctor Chase wasn't human, and Joshua stood in the middle of an army of vampires. The detective tensed beneath his jacket. He didn't know exactly what to do. Did they mistake him for a vampire too? He did have slightly big teeth and his skin was decently pale. Was that not the cliché?

Joshua remained still, silent. He had no heart, no real pulse nor organs. The vampires had to notice. The cursed man was an open flame. Flames could be a weakness to them. Did they think their sheer numbers could overtake him? Or did they mean to offer Joshua a drink from their revolting cup of blood? Joshua cringed, he had to remain confident, confident in his abilities, enough to put them at arm's length, enough to make them think twice about meddling with him.

"Good evening all." The doctor began, his voice less strained, almost normal, if not for its high pitch and drawn words. He almost sounded American. The crowd murmured as Gene continued. "Today we have two guests in our friendly little chapel…"

Gene motioned to his left where the man in the wide-brimmed hat sat. The man stood and made his way to the center aisle. He gave a small curtsy, his right hand aloft, his body stooped. The crowd nodded their agreement. Some whispered hello under their breath, foregoing a human habit. But Joshua saw something they didn't. As the man leaned forward, the hem of his pants creased against the front of his shins. There, strapped to his calf was a long silver blade with no cross guard, a metal stake inlaid with grained wood that formed a cross and a pelican.

Interesting, Joshua thought. Perhaps this visitor was more friend than foe.

"…the illustrious Doctor Frank Penn. He is our cohort from Paris whom recently was honored with the title of 7th chairman." Gene finished, taking a long breath afterwards.

The audience clapped. Frank bowed again, lower this time. Still, no one noticed the weapon in his pantleg, his whole body facing the masses from the back row. Before Gene could open his mouth again, the man straightened himself and turned with an outstretched hand at Joshua. His yellow eyes glared a fierce commandment, introducing Joshua before Gene could.

"And the infamous American harbinger, Connor Shaw!" The man announced.

There was an eerie silence in the audience, perhaps some unsettled shuffling. The strange man smiled at Joshua before turning back to Dr. Chase.

"My apologies for the outburst, Gene, I have known this man for quite some time and, I must say, I am quite excited to see him here." Dr. Penn apologized.

Frank Penn did not sit down after his introduction. He stood there motionless between Joshua and Gene.

Gene wrinkled his nose, disgusted that he would be interrupted. Gene Chase thought the man before him was Joshua Hill, but now this belief was contested by a very reputable man. Gene wrinkled his nose once more and sneered, he couldn't argue with Dr. Penn, it would make him seem like the fool. Gene was no one's fool.

Joshua watched as Frank stood there. It seemed he was hell-bent on making Gene throw a fit. He refused to acknowledge the silent signals of the choir to sit down. He stayed in the aisle purposefully affronting his host, whom was turning red in frustration.

"I see..." Gene snarled, "Please, sit down Dr. Penn, so that we might continue our gathering."

Dr. Penn smiled handsomely, "There is one other thing I would like to announce, your excellency." The man started, bowing yet again, this time, with both feet flat on the floor. Dr. Penn's hands did not rise into the air as before, but stood by at his calves, tensed around his knees. Joshua noticed the man's index finger twitching towards the stake in his buckled shoe.

Whatever the man was planning to do, he was to do it now. The show was about to begin, this stranger was about to crash the party, and Joshua didn't know if he was a friend or an enemy.

"The First Order has-" Frank hardly started.

There was a slam of a door, a pattering of footsteps. This noise had come from the door above Joshua, the door on the interior balcony to his right. There, covered in paint and blood was Joan. Joan dragged a mangled corpse by its neck into the auditorium. The corpse was well-dressed and wore a white lab coat over an oversized vest and pair of slacks.

Joan huffed, she looked at Dr. Chase, unaware to the congregation, unaware to Joshua's presence.

"You bastard!" Joan screamed, leaping from the terrace into the crowd. The conglomeration shouted, surprised, but none was more surprised than Dr. Gene Chase, who tried to rise from his seat in fright, but, under the weight of his torso, struggled to move fast enough. Joan slammed into the peoples below her and climbed her way through the pews to Gene.

Blood trickled from Joan's face into her eyes. It was not her blood, but the blood of the man she had killed, the blood of the first man she ever killed. Joan was now like Joshua.

Joan was a killer.

The paint from the artisan room left trails behind Joan's stampeding boots. She clutched her pickaxe tightly, shaking with energy and hatred.

Doctor Gene couldn't rise in time to save himself, and Joan slammed her pick into his head over and over and over again. Gene was dead, his jaw detached, his forehead caved in, and there stood Joan in front of a sea of cultists who snarled and rose from their chairs.

Joshua looked at Joan from across the room, her anger quenched and her arms limp. All that was left of her fury was marked by tears which melted away the clotting blood on her eyelids.

Dr. Penn rose from his place in the aisle astounded. The cultists began to approach Joan, half-ready to devour her, half-ready to flee.

Joshua ran forth and stormed past Dr. Penn, the first to action. He blinked his way to Joan in a twist of ash and curtailed about with his arm around her, his pistol training on each head within the masses of vampires. The young man's pockets began to foam with The Fog's descending mist, covering their feet, marking a concert stage. It deterred the vampiric hoard, if the gun already did not.

The vampires shifted back to keep themselves from the fog which began to whip the air like viscous weeds. The Fog protected Joshua and Joan from the hoard's advance, slashing before them in a wall of gaseous vines.

"Cease at once! Cease and desist!" Dr. Penn shouted over the hissing vampires. In his hand was a large sheet of paper rolled and tied, "Cease at once by the command of The Fo!"

The thralls looked back, no longer focusing on Joshua or Joan. The Doctor had their attention. He cleared his throat and opened the paper before him.

"This is a warrant for Gene's execution signed by The Fo!" He shouted. "He has unlawfully collected humans for feeding without Order approval. He has been found guilty of kidnapping and directing rituals such as the one I'm sure you are all here for!

Given the circumstances, and my power as the new 7th chairman, I order this execution exacted and finalized! If any of you remain on the premises or attempt to harm Connor *or* his friend, I *will* exercise my right to kill all of you! None of you will be considered accomplices to Dr. Gene if you all *peacefully* leave!"

The cult looked about at each other, grumbling. Slowly they rose from their rubbled heap and dusted off their clothes. They proceeded to leave the building with the same elegance, or attempted elegance, and they walked in with. Some, more humbled than others, when passing by Doctor Penn, apologized for their ill-notions and the events of the night. He shook their hands and waved them onward, assuring them they would not be held accountable for the goings-on that night. The other, less docile of the bunch, lingered outside the doors, looking for answers and explanations. They asked odd men in black, paisley, suits whom pushed them away from the main gate. They had appeared so suddenly. This immediate presence reminded Joshua of a strike team, something governmental, something powerful.

Doctor Penn wiped his forehead which beaded with sweat and hurried to Joan's side.

"Miss," the chairman insisted, kneeling down to her. "My name is Doctor Frank Penn and I need to make sure those people didn't scratch you."

"Why should I be worried about a scratch?" Joan asked, slightly terse.

"Even the slightest wound caused by a vampire can become infected. You could die, among other things." Penn asserted.

Joshua nodded to Joan, silently assuring her the man wasn't crazy. Joan nodded back, and the doctor motioned to a man at the door whom readily brought him a leather medical bag. The doctor ran his hands over Joan's arms and examined her clothes for holes. He was thorough, looking her up and down from her toes to her nose.

"Joshua…" Joan remembered, suddenly anew with life, "upstairs, you need to go upstairs. Behind the blanket in the east wing… I found them Joshua… I found them!"

Joshua grinned aknowledgement and left Joan in the care of the doctor. The young man vanished upstairs. Entering the art room, he noticed toppled chairs and spattered blood. The room was a mess, drag marks split a large puddle of green paint on the floor. The bedsheet on the far side of the room was torn, revealing a narrow door on the left.

Joan must have killed the scientist in this room. Joshua thought, pitying the girl.

Joshua entered the slender door and walked down the small hallway, opening every door until he reached the third, left, entrance.

Joshua looked at a chair, a dentist's chair, with leather straps around the feet and arm rests. Within it a thin boy whom lay lifeless with needles in his arms.

Gene had sucked the boy dry, killed him for his blood.

Joshua found his eyes beginning to wet. He shook his head, denying the swelling emotion. The man walked forward and ran his hand along the wall to meet a bulletin board with pinned x-ray photographs and diagrams. Joshua ripped a sheet of paper down and read it.

"Wish fulfillment and the potency of young blood." He whispered to himself.

The paper showed a small DaVinci-like body, a child. The cardiovascular system was noted. The elbows and the spine of the diagram were circled and marked with notes like *insert here, avoid here, 9ᵗʰ vertebrae,* and *feed type B.*

Joshua crumpled the paper and watched it burn in his hands. He burned all of the papers before taking the child from his placement and carrying him away. Joshua quietly brought him to the entrance where one of Penn's bouncers took his fragile skeleton. They exchanged a sad glance. The bouncer shed a tear. Joshua turned away in disgrace. The young detective then returned to the hall to find what was in the last room.

Joshua looked at both of them, Bucky and Ducky. Ducky lay on a small bed by Bucky, both of them gaunt, husks of their former selves. Joshua wondered what they were like in life and what kind of people they could have become. Whatever potential they had, whatever hopes and dreams they wanted to achieve, was cut short. Joshua also wondered how much pain they were in as their life was slowly siphoned from their bodies.

On the ground around the two children were small litter bags and a linen sack with processed kibble, a human chow labeled "B." Joshua looked down at the kids and knelt beside their crib-sized bed. Bucky lay in a position to cover Ducky, the motionless girl no bigger than a duffel bag, and no more than seven years of age. Bucky was slightly bigger, perhaps a year older than the girl. Joshua reached out to both of them, ready to pick them up and bag them.

Bucky snapped his head forth to bite his finger. Joshua jerked back, surprised the boy was still alive. His eyes began to water.

They managed to save someone.

Joshua reached out again to Bucky who proceeded to bite his hand aggressively. It hurt Joshua's fingers, but it did not sever his digits. Joshua let Bucky bite his hand, the child only wanted to protect Ducky, but it was pointless. Ducky was dead. That, Joshua was sure of.

The boy squirmed, and Joshua placed his free hand around him, lifting the boy and briskly walking out of the wing with him. The boy tried to scream, but his voice was gone, his organs non-existent. He tried to scream back at Ducky. Perhaps he still thought she was alive. How stupid was the boy? Joshua thought. Ducky was dead, withered into a crisp. Nevertheless, the lone survivor wasted his energy trying to protest the separation.

Joshua heard the sound of the helicopter long before he saw it, long before he left the entrance of Gene's mansion with Bucky in tow. The helicopter hovered slightly above the ground, ready to go as soon as it arrived. Two men sat in the cockpit wearing the same black suits as the body guards. Inside the sliding doors, two nurses in white sat surrounded by computers and gadgets.

As soon as Joshua emerged from the building, two men relinquished him of the child. He followed them to the chopper as they placed Bucky on a gurney. Immediately, and without feeling for a vein, the two nurses pricked the child's arm and ran an IV bag about the other side. The gurney was placed in the large aircraft swiftly, the nurses monitoring their new arrival. Joshua spotted a small, child-sized body bag already in the back of the helicopter, another vampiric guard zipped it to a close and pinned a note to its black shell.

"We just might be able to save him," One of the men told Joshua, placing his hand on his shoulder in professional consolation. Joshua quickly swiped it away and walked back to the mansion.

Joshua's stomach boiled as Dr. Penn emerged through the front door with Joan around his shoulder. He helped Joan walk. They began to make their way to the front gate.

Joshua began to walk back to the mansion and Joan brushed Joshua's hand as his passed, taking it for but a moment. Joshua turned back slightly before her hand could slip from his. She looked at him square in the eyes for but a fleeting moment, her blue irises awash with sadness. She mouthed some words to him before letting him go, something Joshua couldn't hear while his anger pulsed through his ears. It was something Joshua didn't want to hear.

Joshua watched them pass quietly before he put his back to them.

"Is that all the bodies?" Penn asked.

"Yes," Joshua lied over his shoulder. He had made a mistake of letting them have the first body. He made a mistake trusting them with Bucky, but all he could do now was prevent them from taking the girl away. Ducky was better off as ashes, not as a corpse among vampires, no matter how dignified they seemed.

Joshua walked through the pure white entryway and to Gene's lifeless body. He placed his palm on Gene's deformed face. Joshua concentrated, the tears in his eyes began to boil, scald in his building rage. He twitched his hand and watched as Genes face erupted in flames. He watched the doctor's skin burn and engulf his body. Joshua pressed on the skull with all his might until in capsized under the weight of his palm like the breaking of an eggshell.

The flame continued to burn as it spread across the floor and along the walls. Joshua screamed into Gene's corpse, cursed, the roar of the flames drowning out his voice. Joshua cried.

After he had done this, Joshua wandered through the flames back up the stairs to the second story. He kicked the feet of the dead scientist before walking through the painted room. He burned the painted worlds and dragged his feet into the servant's chambers.

Joshua turned into the room where little Ducky lay. He knelt beside the small bed where her bony body had withered, her skin almost glued to the linen. Joshua rested his hand on her small head and watched as her dry skin began to flake under the heat of his hands. The flakes cascaded into the sky in an inverted waterfall. Ducky became kindle, sparks that rose to the ceiling.

It was those sparks that set fire to the rafters of the second floor, those sparks that carried on her soul. As Joshua breathed in the smoke, the fire surrounded him and kept him tight in morose embrace. Joshua didn't feel the heat, if anything, he was cold. The sparks vented through Joshua's nostrils, and the callous seeker found himself praying. He didn't want this poor girl condemned to hell. If God existed, he wanted to see her there, her head on an angel's lap.

To Joshua, it seemed children were too good for this world. To Joshua, it was always the children that died.

When Joshua had finished his prayer, he rose and slowly walked out of the room. Around him, the rafters and pillars began to fall away. Soon all that would be left of the hacienda would be a burning pile of ash and melted rock. Gene's home was becoming a wax mansion, oozing to the ground in its final defeat.

Joshua looked at the entrance of the building from the flames. He stared out through the flickering fire and watched the world as one might through a window. The rain still subtly drizzled outside, playing a sarcastic fireman to the ordeal, pretending to help quell the fire. Outside, Joan looked into the building with Dr. Penn.

Joshua was tired of losing. He was struggling to find the reason to continue his march. Perhaps all he was good for was killing people. Killers couldn't be heroes, Joshua guessed. At best, Joshua was a glorified life taker. He didn't save people, he only added bodies and names to the lists in Hades' hands.

Joshua sighed and let the tears about his face dry. He reached into his pocket to produce a pack of cigarettes. It was his stupid mistake, for the moment they brushed the air, they ignited and burned in his hand. Joshua almost chuckled. He was such an idiot, he couldn't even save a pack of cigarette, he couldn't even save the children.

The vampiric troopers left just as Joshua emerged from the rubble, sometime later that night. He made his way to Joan and Dr. Penn. The doctor stood resolute until Joshua neared. He approached Joshua with a thin frown on his face.

"I wish I'd arrived sooner." Frank sighed. "My job is to find fiends like him. I promise you, not all vampires, not all of us, are like this."

Joshua brushed off his defense, his terrible apology. He ignored Dr. Penn altogether, taking Joan under the arm and helping her down the stairs. It would be a long walk home in the dark and they were both so tired, and so worn out.

Frank watched them leave, he didn't want to stop them or make them feel better. The vampire understood. He had looked in the mirror many times centuries ago and felt the same disgust, the same defeat. Eventually, his hatred for his own kind made him stronger and more objective on hard-pressed issues. Now, he did what he always wanted to do, kill vampires. Dr. Penn knew the Fo would keep Bucky safe, his order never took feeding on humans lightly.

Joshua turned around one last time to gaze upon the pearl gate of Gene's estate, the fire continuing before his eyes. His eyes reflected the flame as he stared at Frank, a mock to his burning heart. Joshua had remembered something important, and he wanted to ask Dr. Penn immediately, so that they might be done with their search for the orphans.

Joshua opened his mouth; a momentary pause marked his thoughts. He looked for the right words until he uttered miserably, "How did you know Connor Shaw?"

Frank nodded his understanding of the real question. He fingered his hat which he held in his hands.

"I knew Connor only for a short while. I was there when the North Americans blamed him for things he didn't do. I bore witness as they burned him alive…" Frank explained, "Joshua Hill… I am familiar with the name, your reputation once preceded you a year ago. I knew you weren't Connor Shaw when I saw you. I knew you weren't because I was in North America the day Connor died."

Joshua looked down at his feet, he didn't respond to the statement, but turned his back again to leave the scene as bitter as he entered it.

Joshua helped Joan down each step, patient with her. He did not care how much time had passed. The miserable man had failed again to protect someone. He beat himself over this failure. His heart betrayed him, his mind cursed his very existence. It wouldn't take long for this new defeat to haunt him in his dreams. Joshua felt an invisible hand around his neck, as if the dead were furious with him, trying to suffocate him for his sins, his ignorance. The dead were surely trying to kill him, he couldn't save them back then, and he couldn't save them now.

Joan and Joshua walked for hours in the darkness. Neither of them talked. In the fields of The Crofts there were no lights to keep them on their path. They navigated by threading the edge of the road, waiting to find the beacon of Dutch's tavern. To Joan's eyes, the world never seemed darker.

For Joshua, it wasn't until he saw the lights of Dutch's hideout that he pieced together Joan's lips. Only now, he heard the words she passed onto him outside Gene's mansion. But what she said made no sense to him. He lulled over the words. He didn't believe them, no matter how he phrased it.

Joan told him this: *No one blames you.*

But Joshua knew he was the only one to blame.

Part 6/Rally

Joan slept in Joshua's bed that night and the nights thereafter. However, the two were not bedfellows, as Joshua, in response, stared at the blueprints of Whitecroft's estate, night after night. The killer punished himself by examining every weakness, every opening, and every guard post until it was ingrained in his mind like the alphabet. Joshua knew it was futile, once the Baron heard of her advisor's death, she would change everything, altering the guard formations, reforming patrols from scratch.

Whitecroft was paranoid. She had every right to be.

Joshua was glad for Dr. Penn's quick thinking. By calling him Connor Shaw, the forgiven cultists whom sunk back into their homes gossiped the wrong name, and Whitecroft still wouldn't know he was present. With a bottle of vodka in one hand and a knife in the other, Joshua reviewed everything he could lay his dark eyes on, restless, day in and day out.

It must have been morning, some days later, when Dutch walked in. He didn't say much, having heard about the children's fate long ago; when Joshua and Joan stumbled through the back door, broken and disheartened. He was respectful in his silence, a good comrade, but Joshua needed him to speak.

"I'm ready to see your men." Joshua stated, the thick smell of alcohol on his mouth could almost be seen.

"Are you sure you don't want to bathe first?" Dutch asked, the way he put those words were solemn, not expecting an answer, which Joshua didn't give.

Dutch nodded slowly and left the room. The man wasn't expecting much from Joshua anymore. His general was too lost in his broken heart to waste his breath. Once Dutch was gone, Joshua turned his bottle over in his hands. It was empty. The American sighed and sat down in the corner seat. Without warning, he soon dozed off.

Joan opened her eyes and slowly adjusted herself in Joshua's bed to find a small brown tuft of hair staring at her with puppy eyes.

"You sleep like an angel," Sach commented, "I was going to join you but I'm a gentleman, you know."

"How kind," Joan mumbled, still dozing.

"You must be Joshua's friend, I can tell by the way you don't scream at me." Sach pecked, waking her up again.

Joan stretched and rose from the bed. "And you must be his dog." She replied.

Sach scoffed, "I'm nobody's dog. I am a bonified brownie."

Joan laughed halfheartedly. Sach's title didn't make him any less ridiculous. Sach grumbled to himself and left. He had chores to do downstairs.

Joan began and finished dressing swiftly before making her way down the narrow brown hallway. Before entering the secret room, she made sure no one paid mind to the stairway, and slipped in.

Entered, Joan immediately spot Joshua still in the corner. Joan watched him for a moment. She felt sorry for him. The loss of the children kept him from relaxing, even in his sleep he looked tense. For the past few days Joan would do this: walk in after waking to spy on Joshua in his corner, his unshaven face and messy hair clumped and dirty. The man was a wreck.

Joan put her hand under Joshua nose as she always did. Like clockwork, she waited for him to exhale, to prove he was alive, but no breath came for quite some time.

"Josh!" Joan yelped, grabbing him by the shoulders and shaking him. Joshua opened his eyes quickly and shuddered in his chair. Joshua looked about with bloodshot eyes, trying to keep his body seated. His legs splayed across the floor haphazardly like lose strings.

"What," he mumbled, "What's wrong?"

Joan slapped Joshua, angry at him. "You weren't breathing; I thought you were dead!"

Joshua shrugged with hollow candor, squinting beneath the light. Joan slapped him again before grabbing him by the hand and dragging him out of the room.

"What's wrong," Joshua repeated while being led outside and behind the tavern. There, Mrs. Hammond and Sach hung clothes to dry. They stopped when watching the fair girl approach with her captive in tow.

Joan shoved Joshua to the ground and grabbed a bucket of soap water near the lines. Before Joshua could rise from the ground, she poured the cold contents over his head.

"What!?" Joshua yelped, frustrated and soaking in bubbles. "What is wrong!?"

"You're what's wrong, Josh!" Joan spat, her face red, "You need to pull yourself together!"

Joan fetched another pail and splashed him again. Joshua tried to rise, hopeless, shaking the excess water from his sleeves. Before he could fully incline, his red-headed friend straddled him and forced his shoulders into the ground, slapping him yet again.

"Damn it, woman!" Joshua barked, but Joan slapped him yet another time.

"Say 'I'm sorry.'" Joan ordered, her hand poised to hit him yet again. "Say 'I'm sorry I've been negligent.'"

"Hey now," Sach piqued under his breath, quiet enough that Mrs. Hammond couldn't hear.

Joan ignored the dog, she huffed, waiting for Joshua to apologize. But he didn't.

"Sach, another pail of water." Joan ordered.

Under the force of her demand, or the resentment in his heart, Sach betrayed his master and took to the river with a bucket. He couldn't keep from snickering. Joan grabbed a handful of Joshua's jacket and lifted him to her face.

"You're not the only one who was there, and you're not to blame! I don't know what's gotten into you, but you have a job to do, so do it! You're supposed to be our leader. You're going to be a baron, so act like one!" She pleaded. "Grow up and stop moping like a baby!"

Sach returned and handed Joan the newly filled pail. Joan took it and held it over Joshua, ready to pour.

"Say it." She demanded.

Joshua was silent, he looked away, refusing to make eye contact with his assailant. Even in sobriety he denied himself the word "uncle."

Joan dumped the water on him slowly, splashing both of them. Sach backed away, snarling from the stray droplets. Mrs. Hammond retreated into the inn in search of Dutch.

"Stop acting so tough!" Joan repeated, shaking him by the collar, "No one likes a brick wall. You can't just shut everybody out and continue to expect them to follow you!"

Joshua stared angrily, waiting for Joan's face to get closer. Once it did, he squirted a mouthful of soap-water into Joan's face. Joan tried to back away from the geyser and Joshua twisted about, forcing Joan to roll off him. Quickly he reached for a spare bucket and splashed her in turn as she rolled to her feet.

Joshua said nothing, but a small look of pleasure rode his lips.

Joan wad a wet shirt from the hanger and tossed it at Joshua, hitting him square in the chest with a satisfying thud.

"You aren't the only one dealing with the problem!" Joan began again, grabbing another shirt from the line and aiming it. "I was there too, and your silence doesn't help me heal! You're supposed to lead us from the dark, not wallow in it! You're supposed to be our example of how we should live, not a symbol of regret and pain!"

Joan hurled the shirt, but Joshua dodged it, splashing her with the remaining water in his pail. Joan chased Joshua around the backyard, she was faster than Joshua, but each time she would try and catch him, Joshua would disappear behind the hung shirts and appear somewhere else. It was at this point of their fight that Dutch returned from gathering his men. Together with his troop, he stared bashfully as the two miscreants splashed water and tossed shirts at each other. All about bubbles had risen in the fray as the angry, flame-haired girl, fought to make Joshua happy. Eventually, she caught him and tackled him to the ground, both of then covered in suds.

"I'm sorry men." Dutch grumbled, his cheeks almost blushing on Joan and Joshua's behalf, "It seems Joshua forgot about the meeting."

The group shrugged, they weren't about to leave. Unaware about the circumstances and decline of Joshua's mental health, the fight seemed romantically passionate more than sorrowfully contrived.

Dutch approached the two while they rolled around on the ground, kicking and pushing each other like young wolves. He didn't know how to jump in. But soon, the two grew tired, and Joan lay apart from Joshua who quickly rose to his feet. The young man offered Joan his hand.

"I won't apologize for who I am." Joshua sighed, finally answering Joan's questions.

"Joshua is speaking like a king already!" Dutch laughed loudly, finishing his approach, "You can't expect a king to rule the way you want him to, even if he is the cornerstone of the kingdom. You can only blame a king for the fall of his civilization. If we expect Joshua to lead us through these dark times, we cannot question his methods, or ask him to change his heart. We can only follow and pray the sun will find him as it has found us."

Joan took Joshua's hand and found her feet. Both he and Joan glanced at Dutch in bewilderment.

Joshua had never taken Dutch for a philosopher. But he was a very happy and burlescent man, carefree and heroic. Dutch was the best of all of them, maybe he should become the baron. Maybe Joshua would offer him the seat, once his revenge was completed. Maybe Joshua could force him to become king.

"By the by, the men are here to meet you sir." Dutch whispered, bringing Joshua back to cognition. Dutch's hand shaded his mouth, but he didn't whisper quietly enough.

Joshua looked about Dutch's width to see a group of peoples staring at them. At the front stood six of special import, two women, three men, and a child.

"Thank you, Dutch." Joshua replied, even though his heart was heavy he straightened himself out. He knew the sooner he killed Whitecroft the better he would feel. "Where can we go to see them in action?"

Dutch smiled and led them away from the tavern where Sach stood unnoticed, sopping and cold. He was left to rehang and rewash all the clothes. It was a task he was too short to do alone. If not for the hair in his eyes, one might have said he began to mope.

Joshua stood in a wide and small meadow north of Whitecroft's estate. It was there the men could train, the trees dampening the sound of fighting. Still, bullets would not be fired, as they did not know where they would land and the baron's estate was not far off. The training on that day would show the militia how to use a rifle up until the point in which they pulled the trigger. Later, Dutch and Joan would teach their small army other basics of combat.

Joshua rolled his ankle, his boot still filled with soapy water, his hair still riddled with bubbles. Joan was in the same state, soggy, but still upset with Joshua. Her anger had been displaced onto the guards while they trained. Joan was the lightest, quickest, and toughest fighter Joshua had. Joshua and Dutch watched gladly while she beat her opponents, often without touching a weapon. She was impressive, unstoppable. Joshua could always bet on her skills as a hunteress before, but now, he knew she was more than a simple bar brawler. Watching Joan fight also made Joshua cringe. Even now, he felt his jaw, tender from Joan's slap earlier that day.

Dutch ordered all of his men into a lane where they would try to hit a painted tree from 25 yards with a bow and arrow. Most of them failed, only used to the sickles and scythes they used to farm. Joan still bested the farmers at this skill and would soon be appointed to teach them how to properly handle and aim their slings.

Joshua was disappointed in the prospects. But still, he trusted Dutch's judgement, that the six special troops the giant had conscripted offered something special to Joshua's rebellion and would make up the difference in the rebellion.

Once the first rounds of tests were over, Joshua had the opportunity to meet Dutch's officers, the six whom he oversaw personally. They all stood in a line before him, waiting to be addressed by their future king.

"This is Green," Dutch said while passing the first of the men. Green saluted to Joshua as he stopped to look at him. "He's not very good with anything but a poniard, but he has the stamina of a horse. Served as a mule along the 15th for a few years, transporting weapons and food in the trenches where cars and wagons couldn't fit. He can carry well over three hundred pounds on his back and still hoof it like any other man. He's loyal and doesn't dick around."

"Very well, Green," Joshua mused, "is there anything you would like to add to that?"

"Sir, no sir." Green stated. He was a square man with a crew cut, standard army culture.

"Green's been with me from day one, simple mishap, got drunk and punched the wrong fellow. He's a good guy…

Next, we have Hannah. She's an expert in explosives. If it can be broken, she can break it. She is also good at repairing machines and other, general, mechanic stuff. She won't be good on the forefront of a skirmish, but she'll know how to scrap a car or rig it. We're planning on having her choke Whitecroft's supply lines come winter."

Joshua looked Hannah up and down. She seemed mischievous, overtly happy, too young.

"How old are you, Hannah? And why are you here?" Joshua asked.

Hannah bounced from toe to toe, a thin smile on her face before she opened her mouth. "Sixteen, put a cherry bomb in a pig, turns out it was the Baron's dinner, didn't go off till it was on the table." She giggled. "I also stole two tires from a tourist driving through."

"Just two tires?"

"So the spare doesn't matter," She cackled, still bouncing.

Joshua shrugged. She had a certain flair to her, which meant good morale for the troops.

"This is Mortimer," Dutch introduced, pointing at a masked figure in a black robe, "Good at hiding bodies, caught for hiding bodies. He's here in case we need to get rid of a body. He's a quiet fellow, but he likes poetry and hiding behind this mortician mask."

Mortimer nodded, leaning slightly as if to bow, but changed his mind at the last moment.

"Simple enough." Joshua sighed. "Do you care to elaborate, Mortimer?"

Mortimer shook his head, a definite no. The man was slightly tall, and probably possessed a thin figure beneath his long robes.

Dutch tugged Joshua's arm, moving him down the line to meet his next accomplice. The next figure Joshua stood before was a dark man that reminded Joshua of Haddock. He wasn't as muscular, nor was he quite as chipper. He wore a turban about his head, a clean-shaven face speckled with dark dots.

"This is Biarre, great with scimitars, even better on horseback. If you need someone to get somewhere quickly, he's the man for the job. Good courier, good crier."

"Why are you here, Biarre?"

"I was caught crossing the border while running from the police in Rome." Biarre responded.

"Rome's a long way away." Joshua thought aloud.

Biarre nodded, grinning from tooth to golden tooth. His tanned skin wrinkled under his turban. "Not for me." He winked.

Dutch chuckled and gave Biarre a nod goodbye. He moved Joshua down the line again.

Joshua stood in front of the small child. She was undoubtedly the youngest of the bunch, undoubtedly the poutiest. The young girl possessed sandy hair and brown eyes. She looked up at Joshua with certain certainty. She seemed to look at him as one might the spine of a book. She read him. She detected the sleuth.

"This is … Lilith." Dutch sighed. He shook his head looking down at the girl. She was no more than twelve. "I'm not sure how I ended up stuck with her. If I recall correctly, her parents left her in this country before smuggling themselves into Russia. They were, or are, adventurers, more concerned with staying sojourns than parents. Either way, Lilith's extremely intelligent, if you get her to talk. She's also good luck."

"Good luck?" Joshua asked. He didn't like where the conversation was heading. Dutch shrugged, a thin and smug twist on his face. He hadn't any more to say than that.

Joshua looked at the girl. He didn't know what to ask her. But, as intelligent as Lilith was, she predicted Joshua's question before he could and shook her head no. Joshua frowned slightly, knowing now what he wanted to ask and then realizing her answer was accurate.

Joshua moved on to the last candidate.

Joshua looked the last candidate in totality. The girl before him did not look prepared for war. She was a well-dressed lady, wearing Victorian clothes and shaded by an umbrella. She looked at Joshua with her mismatched cat eyes.

Joshua felt threatened, scared. She was a beautiful lady with straight hair and bangs that cut off right before her eyebrows. Her corset accented her body but did not help her move about. She looked too fragile, and too sinister, even for Joshua. The American was worried she was out of place.

Joshua leaned forth and gleaned at her, unsure of what to say. To Joshua's surprise, the woman began to pace around him as if to begin a dance. She giggled, but it wasn't a welcoming sound. Joshua thought he was supposed to be making the decisions, examining his allies. Now, he felt that he was being examined, judged.

"Yes, Frea thinks he will do perfectly." The woman smiled a carnivorous smile.

"*What* is she?" Joshua whispered to Dutch as the vulture circled, doubtful he was unheard. Dutch grimaced, and stood there for a moment, trying to explain. The big man stammered at first, and then conceded.

"I don't know." Dutch puffed, staring at her like a traffic light. "She's the newest member, I met her a week ago. She simply walked up to me and told me that she, or Frea, wanted to join."

"Isn't it dangerous for her to be here?" Joshua hissed, nervous. The lady still watched him. "You don't even know her. She might not be helpful at all."

"I didn't think she would show up." Dutch whispered back. "I don't recall telling her anything about our rendezvous or our plans. She seems to know exactly what we're up to. We can't just toss her away… she might inform on us."

Joshua turned his back to the women, trying to be quieter than before. "No, get rid of her." He demanded.

"*You* get rid of her, you're not king yet." Dutch protested.

"Ro sham beaux?" Joshua suggested, lifting his hand against his chest. Silently they played. Joshua pumped his fist thrice and revealed a pair of scissors. But looking up, the odd woman had made her way in front of them, unnoticed by the two.

Joshua jolted back as she loomed into view. The girl giggled again, she was spying on them. But who was she working for?

Dutch perked his ear before looking away. He pretended to heed the silent call of someone far away. "I think I hear one of the lackeys calling for me, Joshua. Good luck!" He wished.

Joshua watched as Dutch fled, abandoning him before the unknown queen of terror. Joshua watched him disappear into the other groups of men. He pretended to talk to them; he watched Dutch issue empty orders, trying to look busy.

Joshua looked back to the alien woman and held his hand out slowly to greet her. The woman took it. Her hand was light, practically a feather. She enacted a small curtsy, dignified, but not overzealous. She seemed to wait for her question. Joshua came out with it, half bold, half disheartened.

"What are you?" Joshua asked.

"What are *you*," Frea retorted. "man, or myth, myth, or monster?"

The woman chuckled. Adding to her prophetic words, she spoke again.

"Frea is the bones in your arm. She is the bane of your sins. Is it so much for you to look at Her? Is she not the one you need to save yourself?"

Joshua cringed and thought *"the bones in his arm."* From what this woman alluded to, he did not recall creating any avatars, but such a thing was beyond him, for needn't he be dead? Perhaps his lack of emotions at certain points in the day were emotions themselves and contrived this beauty whom stood before him. Out of thin air, she had come to answer his call, a powerful and dark being coming to fruition, birthed by Joshua's nightmares.

This was not unlikely, in Joshua's mind, for magic was so ever convoluting itself, becoming stranger and stranger every day.

"You may call Frea this: the name she utters herself." The girl finished.

Joshua twisted his mouth. He was tired of meeting odd things.

"That is more 'who' than 'what.'" Joshua denounced, but it was too late for answers. Already, Joan had approached to meet with them. A small bead of sweat trickled from her forehead. The woman smiled. Behind her, towards the training area, a man wallowed on the ground, dazed and hurt. Joan jogged to a halt and stood straight, beholding Frea. There was a certain electricity in her eyes before she held out her hand, point back from whence she came.

"Did you see that, Joshua?" Joan asked excitedly, childishly.

Joshua shook his head, still transfixed by Frea, trying to figure her purpose and origin as one would a painting. Joan looked at Frea with cut eyes.

"I'm Joanne," Joan intruded, stepping in front of Joshua's line of sight to extend her hand.

Frea didn't grab Joan's outstretched palm. Instead, she gave a curtsy, pinching her dress on both sides as she bowed. Joanne looked back to Joshua, both bewildered an upset, but Joshua did not return the glance. He couldn't pin down what Frea meant by her words, what she meant by her words exactly.

"We're all waiting on you, Josh." Joan huffed, before giving another glance at the Elizabethan woman and walking away. She tromped into the distance where others were standing. The whole group watched Joshua's stiff dance with the woman, waiting to see sparks flare, roses fall from the sky.

Joshua wrinkled his nose one last time and turned about. He didn't want to be stuck on such a topic for too long. Frea giggled yet again and proceeded to follow Joshua as he made his way back to the troops. Joshua looked at his small battalion. Each one stood there haphazardly. They were not prepared. Dutch and Joan needed to shape them well. Until then, they had no chance of victory if the Baron assassination went awry.

Joshua asked Dutch to run through training with them, they would be taught to defend themselves, if not kill someone else.

In the meadow, Dutch ordered the lackeys to spar with each other. He wanted to understand each individuals' strengths and weaknesses, much like he understood his officers. The men created rings along the ground using spray-cans of white paint, perfectly forming a circle much like that found on a wrestling mat. To understand his men, Dutch thought it would be best to make everyone spare with each other. During this skirmish, if an opponent were to leave the ring or become immobilized, the victor would win a point and the match would resume. The fighters had a set time limit to score as many points as they could by the end of the day, and fighters would rotate once every ten minutes, ensuring a certain endurance training.

Joshua, unable to keep the girl off his mind, watched Frea intensely as the sun passed around the sky. The day began to cool as the shadows of surrounding trees grew long to meet him with shade. Wildflowers rippled in the meadow.

Joshua hid in the shade by the trees. But, as for Frea, the odd lass stood there in her dress near the center of the meadow, in the center of her white circle. Before her was her opponent, another farmer whom had joined the ranks. No one seemed to worry about her presence in the ring, truly, Joshua thought that Dutch was not aware the Victorian woman was willing to fight. Nevertheless, Joshua worried that the man would harm her once they began sparring, but, was too curious to stop their match.

Joshua thought it best the girl be wounded now, rather than be killed later. She would have to learn a hard truth that day, that war was no place for women in large dresses.

At the sound of Dutch's voice, all the fighters began their attacks. Some chose to fight with their fists, others with their legs. Some wrestled, some boxed, and some awkwardly pushed the other like teenagers in a school courtyard.

Amongst this babble and before Joshua's eyes, Frea began to unclasp the dress around her, revealing skinny black pantaloons with ruffles along the side. They led down to her leather boots which garnered ten too many buckles. Joshua blinked and the fight was over. Frea stood over the farmer without raising her hand. Her boot on his stomach, she stood there over the paralyzed man for the whole ten minutes. As Dutch shouted for the next round to begin, Frea released her foot from the man and reached back down for her unclasped dress to put it back on, knowing full well she was about to fight again.

How could Joshua have missed the fight? Was this some kind of joke? He gawked. The sleuth thought his eyes were deceiving him, but the defeated farmer ran away from Frea, shaking his head, confused. As he passed by, Joshua took him by the shoulder and stopped him. The man was sweating; if anything, he was drenched in cold water and shivering.

"What happened?" Joshua asked sternly.

The farmer stammered, unable to explain. He did not speak, both out of fear of Frea, and his fear of Joshua. If he could speak despite his cowardly erasure, he could say nothing, either way, because he did not remember. All that was left in him was a sense of fear and cold. He knew not what else. Joshua let the man go and watched him stand before his next opponent. The farmer was unsure of himself, his willingness to fight was crippled by whatever experience occurred while against Frea. Frea hadn't only defeated the man with aplomb, she'd crippled him for life.

Joshua turned back as Dutch hollered for the troops to start again. But Joshua was too late and the second fight ended the same way. This time, Frea hovered over Biarre, whom laid there with his hands aloft in defeat. Biarre smiled despite his humiliation. Almost jokingly, his palms faced her, proving he was unarmed. Joshua had blinked and he didn't know what once, and at once, occurred.

Joshua rose from where he squatted and made his way over to the area Frea sparred in. The buzzer was called, and it was time to switch partners. In the distance Joshua could hear Joan and Dutch correcting their students. "Move through the punch; use your hips! Meet your opponent when blocking! Don't hover your arm, it won't help under the force of the strike!" They barked.

Still, none of them took notice of the Victorian girl.

Joshua grabbed Biarre by his arm and softly moved him back towards Frea. Frea eyed both of them, clasping her dress around her hips again.

"You can stay here." Joshua ordered, motioning for the next candidate to move on and find someone else. As he walked with Biarre towards Frea, Joshua made sure to bide his time and ask questions.

"What happened; how did you lose?" Joshua inquired.

Biarre shook his head, although he still smiled. He was covered in beads of water, thoroughly sloshed. Despite his joviality he still seemed disappointed. "I'm not sure, boss. I blinked, then, I was on the ground."

"Try again." Joshua commanded, moving Biarre into the circle and backing away outside the paint.

Joshua stood back while he watched Frea stand there, holding her the clasp about her waist. It cascaded around her vexing hips like a fluffed duvet waiting to be spread on a bed.

Joshua heard Dutch's ceremonial cry to spar. He peeled his eyes and absorbed everything, watched everything.

He didn't blink, but, in seconds, he didn't find the answer to his question either. Joshua looked at Biarre laying on the ground. Frea stood over him with her boot in his sternum much like the other man before him. Frea's dress littered the ground, her tights exposed.

Joshua hadn't blinked but Biarre was on the ground as if he had been on the ground the whole time, as if he never moved away from the first fight. It reminded Joshua of Elizabeth's tricks, her diversions.

"Again," Joshua ordered, he had to know. Was this woman using magic, or moving at ultrasonic speeds?

Again, Joshua steeled himself to witness the occurrence. But as Frea unclasped her dress, he didn't glean her movement until she was already pinning Biarre to the ground. Biarre began to look concerned, scared.

"*Again*," Joshua ordered, watching Frea retie her dress about her waist. Was he paying too much attention to the dress? Was there some non-sexual charm in her hips that made him hallucinate, to miss the moment Frea moved.

Joshua watched Frea's face, but she didn't blink either, she didn't do anything before she ended victorious *again*. Frea stood over Biarre *again*.

The roper watched as Biarre picked himself off the ground in tandem with Frea, loosening her triumphant stance over him. Dutch shouted, and the men began to change areas, moving back to archery. Joshua motioned for Biarre to move on. He was done with him. The hussar smiled nervously and left to beat the pulp out of his next enemy, for he was not a horrible fighter.

Joshua left himself in the meadow, staring at Frea's smooth face. Frea stared back, her face pinched, her eyes enchantingly coarse.

"You never answered my question." Joshua mentioned, breaking the silence between them, severing the tension in the air crudely. "You told me a title. You told me of an intention and what you were, or had, to offer me. But *what* are you?"

Frea smiled wryly, ignoring Joshua's question yet again, "If it pleases Al Hamra, Frea would like to see his strength."

Joshua looked at Frea as she bowed to him. She needn't be so rigid, so pompous, he thought. She was being disrespectful, mocking him by bowing. She didn't say his name, she called him by other things. What did they mean, what was this title?

Joshua entered the ring in front of Frea. He would teach her some manners. Even though the ring marked the field of combat, Joshua knew they wouldn't need it to determine who was the better of the two. Joshua was. He knew it, he thought it.

The American looked at Frea. She was mesmerizing, haunting, those dreams of Solomon could easily be replaced with her. She had a certain poise, a stance and etiquette and style like that of a fragile person, but she was seemingly more ferocious than anyone else in those woods. She talked like a robot, she walked like a goddess. She was Frea. Or Frea's puppet, full of odd promises and third-person statements.

"If you won't tell me what you are, then I'll find out. Show me who you are, girl, so that I might put you in your place." Joshua ordered. He twisted his mouth, sneered at her. Joshua had defeated giants, criminals, and drug lords. Joshua killed an ifrit, an avatar. How could this voluptuous woman possibly harm him?

These questions stirred an idea in Joshua's mind. Perhaps Frea was an assassin, perhaps Whitecroft knew what Joshua was up to and sent a killer to dispose of him. Or, worse: what if Solomon sent her?

Joshua watched as Frea giggled. This incessant giggling began to irritate him. He wasn't a teenager to be sniveled at, they were adults, not children. As Frea giggled, the world as Joshua knew it seemed to close around them. A thin black filament closed around the arena, encapsulating them like a round hamster ball, a dome. Joshua watched as the trees vanished, the grass turned grey, and the encasing filament turned purple like a silk canvas, alluding to a Halloween sky. The moon appeared high in the air and personified. It stared down at him with gritted teeth which drooled dark blood. The moon blinked, keen on observing the two. Too close for comfort, it was, like it had come to headbutt the earth like a football.

The ooze that ran from its mouth dropped, a single drop that directed Joshua's eyes to a lake that had not existed before him. It sat there at the end of a pier, only feet from where he stood. This body of water was surrounded by trees but for the small clearing he stood in. The water was black, the moon used it for his mirror. On that mirror was a gnat, a lone figure hovering over the waters like a spirit, a reaper. Joshua steeled himself as he approached the docks, his feet thumping hollowly on the wood. Frea hovered there, paces above the water, paces from him, her dress began to run with the same substance as the lunar ooze. It became a liquid that enveloped her body and formed into a legion of strings which flickered into the air. Each strand of liquid clothing moved with her like an octopus and its ink. This ink took, also, the form of ribbons, tying her hair in bundles, redirecting it to flow into open space as if submerged under the water. It was not until the ribbons and her clothes reformed into solid, milky, silk that she opened her eyes.

Frea wore the same smug she always did and curtsied again in her unified outfit. At least she was not pretending to be someone else, Joshua thought.

The opposer spoke calmly, "Al Hamra, prepare yourself."

Joshua watched as those silk strands protruding from Frea loomed over him and crashed. Joshua evaded, jumping out of the way at the last second. The tendrils swiftly reoriented and made their merry way towards him, stretching like strands of glue, homing missiles and snakes with long tails. Joshua ran to his left into the foliage, the wires giving chase.

Quickly Joshua snapped his fingers and his arms burst into flames and reverted to talons. Joshua twisted about and dug his heels into the ground. He turned and swiped the tendrils, shattering them into pieces like glass. Joshua looked out from the trees towards Frea. She smiled at him sheepishly, happy that he was still alive. Her eyes trained on Joshua with killer intent.

In Frea's hand there lifted a long thrusting lance, eight feet in length. At the end of this spear, a large conical point grew to a tip. The length of this spearhead wrapped hollowly down the staff like a guard, covering half of the shaft like a shield. Joshua would have a hard time nearing Frea, whom floated over the lake. She possessed ranged and close weapons. But perhaps Frea was slow to heft her spear, and Joshua could take advantage of this.

Joshua saw Frea motion, her hand pointing at the ground before him. Frea was proud that Joshua had survived her preliminary strike. Most people, like the farmer and Biarre, didn't make it past that. It was her signature beginning. If anything, Frea might have forgotten how to fight, having been so used to defeating her foe instantly. Frea thought it unfair for Joshua to be at a disadvantage, so she left him a boon. She wanted to give him a gift.

Joshua looked down to where Frea pointed to see a dark ooze bubble beneath him. Submerged in this bubbling liquid, and quickly rising from the ground, was a long blade, curved and single sided. It was something from Turkey, a yatagan.

Joshua snatched the blade out of the ground and rushed forth in one motion. As he sprinted forth to the lake, he snapped his fingers again and set his blade awash with fire. Above the lake, Frea hovered with her hand outstretched, beckoning for him to approach. Joshua leaped, his feet instantly ablaze. The fire propelled him into the air, and he flew forth to meet her. Joshua rotated the yatagan down in a somersault and it met Frea's spear. Even with one hand, she easily lifted her weapon and blocked the blow. Frea tilted her lance and redirected Joshua's momentum, hurdling him down towards to the abyssal pond.

Joshua rotated his legs beneath him, his burning legs catching on the oozing liquid. The heat simmered the black waters below him and Joshua floated on the thicket of steam. It caught beneath his jacket and provided enough lift for him to redirect his fall across the pond and into the woodlands. Joshua rolled onto the grass and stopped at the base of the nearest tree, posturing himself into a runner's sprint. Joshua rose and sprinted forth again, for he was certain Frea would not come to meet him. Joshua readied his weapon and leaped again, his legs bursting into flames to give him an extra boost.

Joshua leapt into Frea, sliding his blade along her spear. They grazed and deflected. The American blew past Frea and across the to the other side of the lake. As he landed, he rolled forward over his head and pushed his body about a tree trunk, Frea tendrils piercing the oak and shattering the log. The tendrils deflected in their momentum and struck near Joshua, whom, without losing momentum, curved his course around the base, sprinting back to the pond.

Joshua jumped again and again and again, trying to land a blow on the girl, but she was simply unbreakable. She didn't move from her position in the air. Her high ground prevented Joshua from being able to land more than one blow on her before he passed by and landed across the lake again. They continued this exchange for many minutes until Frea changed her pattern.

Joshua thundered into the sky and Frea proceeded to responded in a flurry of silk armaments. The solidified ooze loomed forth with great velocity, their tips aimed to skewer Joshua in each significant artery and organ. In midair, the American slashed his way through the arsenal, shattering the weapons into various pieces. Those that did not shatter beneath his strikes bounced and redirected about to stab him from behind. But Joshua fell upon Frea faster than her tendrilled limbs could reach him again. Joshua poised his blade to slash Frea across her neck. This time, Joshua wouldn't pass Frea, he would land atop her head.

Frea's armor loosened, the solid murk that protected her and reformed into a giant fist, leaving her body completely exposed and naked. But this exposure did not allow Joshua to land a serious strike, for the giant fist that proceeded from her clenched Joshua in its gargantuan palm, snatching him like a fly out of the air.

Joshua grunted, trying to free himself, but it was to no avail. The fist proceeded to squeeze him and crush him. Joshua had made a mistake, he believed that Frea was not capable of changing her armor into other forms. The weapon Frea used was nothing compared to the weapon she was.

Joshua watched the odd girl through twitching eyes. The naked girl smiled, she needn't any defense when Joshua was trapped. This was her mistake. Joshua huffed and puffed. In his lack of movement, a deep-seated heat welled inside his throat. Joshua opened his mouth to a pucker, or whistle. Joshua breathed out, blowing a stream of air through his lips which formed a perfect "o." In an intense shot of heat, fire spewed out of his mouth like a flamethrower, enveloping the giant fist around him. The giant fist caught fire and the intense heat caused Frea to buffet, releasing her grip on the sleuth. Joshua fell as Frea's hand shook and extinguished itself. It quickly returned to her, reforming into armor, protecting her as Joshua swiped at her chest. Joshua's blade bounced, unable to leave a scratch before he plunged underneath the water.

Joshua readied himself from the synthetic liquid for Frea to soar in, lance ready to skewer him with a victorious blow. But, instead, she continued to remain still in her reality, watching him from above like a mocking god.

Joshua was unaware at first what lay behind him, that other beings might coexist with her in this estranged and gothic world. But he began to realize this as a dim light, further into the black mire, became to reveal his surroundings. There, seeded into the shifting sands of the sea-bed were the bodies of polished skeletons. Their heads watched Joshua's decent, their arms reaching for his boots. Joshua tried to swim away but the sludge was too thick, the water dragging him down further and further in a slow-motioning riptide. The skeletons tugged at his coat.

Joshua looked down, kicking at the undead. The light that came from below the ground was sourced beneath the sand. Joshua watched as the light slowly grew brighter. It rose to greet him to Frea's demented world. Joshua began to choke on the ooze as the sand shimmied away from the beast, unable to hold his mouth closed. A large kingfisher burst from the ground. Instead of a lantern about its forehead, an arm was evident. Its single, centered eye shone like a headlight, catching Joshua in his heinous gaze.

The beast wiggled forth and grabbed Joshua in its hand. It redirected Joshua's plunge, throwing the American down its throat and gurgling him down in a puff of sand and bubbles.

Joshua slid down the leviathan's gullet like one would slide down a pool tube. The water slushed about him, meeting trapped air in the beast's innards. Joshua tumbled down into the stomach and slapped the fleshy room with a firm thunk.

Joshua picked himself up and retched slightly. There in the beast's belly, the American smelt the organic, rotting, dungeon. Joshua caught his breath, he could bide some time here. He flicked his hands, watching himself steam the moisture from his clothes, drying them off for comfort.

Joshua looked around the stomach of the beast, it reminded him of a dream he had a time long ago, or so it seemed long. The foul air met his lungs but did not beg him to bunt any longer. Joshua was had adjusted to the putrid smell, and nothing was like the Shaper he once faced. Joshua closed his eyes and rested his hands against the pink stomach lining. He would need time to get out, but he was not in immediate danger within the belly of the whale. Joshua snapped his fingers and pushed his thumbs into the walls, watching as his fingers steamed and boiled the intestines before him.

Frea thought Frea was happy, she enjoyed testing Al Hamra, understanding what sort of man he would become. Al Hamra was a deep-seated man, broken but certain of himself. He would make a good leader.

Frea knew Frea was tired, Frea's world exhausted Frea, and Frea had never fought someone for so long. Frea watched the surface of the water. Perhaps Frea had drowned the poor man. For a time, Frea thought Joshua was dead. Perhaps Frea should've disbanded Frea's world to save him.

Frea looked down at the water below her. The water began to bubble. She smiled, Al Hamra was certainly strong. Frea thought.

Joshua twitched his hands and watched as his flaming fingertips simmered the fish's innards in mephitic odor. Joshua focused his thoughts, his wish to escape coupled by his rage. He couldn't go home if he died there in an unknown world surrounded by nothingness.

Joshua let a torrent of energy rush over him, a caffeinated feeling, an invigorating mental vector that pointed upwards. He opened his eyes and watched his surroundings burn in dark red flame, the acids began to bubble, then boil and writhe. Joshua was sure he could prove himself. He wouldn't be a failure any more. He would never let anyone else die. Perhaps being a king was like that, lifting his people to better heights, putting his hands beneath their feet.

The beast began to cough, then it began to heave. As the bowels began to shift and the diaphragm pushed against the floor, Joshua prepared himself for exodus. The great fish barfed, and Joshua flew on an updraft of heat and bile. The beast retched at his spicy treat, and Joshua soon felt the water splash against his face as he reentered the lake. He emerged from beneath the sand, reaching and pushing himself away from the skeletal bodies that littered the firmament.

The beast fell back to the bottom of the trough with a defeated choke, quickly residing itself in the shallow bed once again. It excused itself from the fight and hid, unable to eat Joshua again with such an upset stomach.

Joshua floated within the lake once more, still submerged beneath the surface. He waited for a moment and reached into his pocket. He felt a wisp of fog; the avatar had followed him into this odd world. He produced it and watched it swirl in his hand. Joshua nodded and the Fog began to nestle itself near Joshua's heart. Joshua stirred the heat around him, the water about him steamed, and the Fog collected each vapor, growing again once more into a beautiful beast. Joshua watched it grow into a monstrosity, its mask now a compound of the bones and burnt scales discarded beneath them. The wet murk of the water encouraged the avatar to grow into a tremendous power. It positioned its face beneath Joshua, whom placed his feet on the mask. The avatar pushed forth, rapidly ascending towards the air, letting Joshua surf upon its body.

Joshua exploded from the depths below against the surface with a great burst of water and positioned his trajectory beneath Frea, crashing his blade against the tendrils of the ever-enthused girl.

Frea giggled, she was having fun.

Joshua freed his left hand and a flame erupted from his palm. He faced his hand down and erupted the air beneath it, generating force and hurling him above his foe. Now free of the weighted burden, the avatar rose thunderously and struck Frea from below, jarring her from her mantle upon the river. Frea was sent sprawling into the air a distance. Joshua descended from his launch and stood upon Frea's shoulders.

He slashed at her tangled hair, but the rings about her follicles shifted to block his blade.

Frea's hair wrapped around the steel sword, clamping it. The hair tried to twist the yatagan from Joshua's grasp, but the warrior held fast to it. Joshua was tossed about, trying to free the blade from the girl's intelligent braids.

The avatar rose and slashed at Frea's thick hide in fury, shaking her inside her dark tin. Frea's hair loosened and the avatar shifted away as Frea's armor erected more tendrils to defend itself. The tendrils honed onto the avatar, who swept around the outskirts of the lake, aptly dodging their trajectory.

Joshua leaped off of Frea's stubborn bangs and descended through the air until the avatar caught him atop its mask. Quickly, they twisted about and entered into the fray for a second bout.

Joshua raised his sword to meet Frea's lance. He pirouetted after the first second of contact, dropping his guard and slamming his blazing hand into Frea's breastplate. The armor shattered beneath the force and sent Frea cascading into the pier and bouncing onto the grass. She was getting slow, and she was finally on the ground.

Joshua watched Frea from above the lake, how the tide had turned. Still, he expected Frea to fly into the air again to reclaim her post as queen of the intangible hill.

To Joshua's surprise, she didn't. Frea stood there on the grass, still smiling, still aggravating. Joshua twitched, snarled, she was so impudent, it frustrated him. He leapt from the avatar's face, ready to continue, upset that he always had to come to her.

Still, Joshua admired her unwavering composure, her commanding and daunting presence.

Joshua landed haphazardly upon the docks. The avatar loomed over the lake behind him, ready for its orders. Frea stared at him, her body still, intensely glad. She waited again to resume on Joshua's mark. Joshua dropped his blade momentarily between the wooden panels of the pier to remove his jacket. He stood there in his jeans and t shirt, his body steaming from anger, magic, and exhaustion. He stole forth to meet her.

The girl's armor had readjusted to cover her body again, but this time, it was thinner. Every time Joshua shattered the solidified ooze, she would lose those pieces, and become more vulnerable. If Joshua was correct in his approximation, this was Frea's main weakness: a reliance on a magical ammunition. Joshua prepared himself as Frea raised her great lance and puffed a stray hair from her eyes.

Frea lunged at Joshua's heart but Joshua moved further right, letting the spear glance off his blade. His left hand quickly followed, wrapping over the polearm and towards the woman. Joshua clasped his hand over Frea's lance. Frea laughed and moved her head from his hand reactively, half expecting him to reach the whole distance to scratch her with his claw.

Frea twisted her body into the air and danced about the rod like an acrobat, landing a firm kick to Joshua's cheek. Joshua's face whipped under the weight of the blow and he quickly rebalanced himself as Frea leapt away, ripping her spear from his grasp.

Joshua twisted under the blow and quickly refaced his foe. The cursed boy dropped his sword and placed both hands on the spear before it retreated away from him. Joshua tore the spear from her hands yet again using her adverse momentum. The torsion of both combatants created a gust of wind about them, rippling the grass and shattering the spear in miniature fragments which dropped into the tall grass in hiding.

Frea smiled a distance away from Joshua, his retreat only half successful. Frea flickered her hand, reminding Joshua of his own movements.

Joshua watched as the girl's armor trickled down her elbow. It solidified in her hand, creating yet another spear for her to strike with. Unlike the last spear, this lance remained attached to her armor, combined by a small shaft that ran along her arm. She would not let go of this one.

This reanimation, or recreation, cost Frea's defenses dearly, as both her legs and both her arms were exposed.

Frea wiggled her palm about the grip, a thin scorch mark was left on her skin by Joshua's heated hands. Both of their bodies toiled to remain standing, but neither of them made a noise, afraid of showing weakness.

Both combatants zoomed forth, each landing a blow upon their weapons. Joshua feinted to the ground and swept at Frea's legs, but she jumped lightly into the air just in time. Mid hover, Joshua watched as the tendrils shot forth from her clothes. Joshua fell back unprepared, protecting his chest and head with his arms.

Before the ooze could strike, Joshua's avatar loomed forth in its miasma and struck the tendrils down, glancing the multitude of them with its face, inches beneath the soles of Joshua's feet.

The mist began to dissipate around the avatar, it was losing it strength, seeping back into the world. It was a toil for the avatar to materialize in Frea's mindscape and its time was up. The lake must have become sentient that something was leeching off its power, and it demanded its body back. Joshua watched as the avatar was sucked back into the lake slowly. Once it alleviated itself of the synthetic liquid, it left its usual token, its boon to help and remind Joshua that it still existed. As the mist faded, the thin wisp that was left of the avatar floated back into Joshua's pocket to rest.

Joshua would have no more help from his spiritual friend.

The American rose and shattered Frea's glassy tendrils beneath his foot. Frea leapt back in expectation. She was beginning to become nervous. Her body was no longer drenched in tight silk. She stood there, covered inadequately, her arms, legs and stomach exposed. In all applications, she could be regarded as defenseless.

339

Frea grasped the remaining ooze on her body and ripped it off like fabric. The tattered cloth contorted and formed a large bow in her left hand. It loomed before her, ten feet tall and cemented itself into the ground as a man-powered arbalest. Frea raised her lance and notched it into the drawstring. Joshua paused, waiting for her to draw the massive coil.

Frea waited, and Joshua heard behind him the sound of moaning. The skeletons from the water had dredged upon the shore to meet them. They crawled past Joshua and broke their ribs before the girl, handing her, aloft, their own bones in adamic fashion. As the ritual continued, the dead broke their frames to create a pile of bones around Frea, giving her substance, giving her shelter.

Frea opened her mouth to speak. "Frea wishes an end to this."

Joshua smirked, sensing a twinge of respect and admiration from her voice. Even if Joshua were to lose now, he could be proud of himself. Pride was a hard feeling for him to muster in any circumstance, but in that moment, whether out of honor or chivalry, he agreed to Frea's request. Like he and Cid exchanged blows at the end of their boxing match, so would Frea and Joshua exchange blows. They would take turns until one was left standing. This would declare the victor.

Joshua waited for Frea to ready herself. His hands shook, his heart pounded. The ex-detective, the anarchist leader, engulfed his body in the darkest fire he could muster. If Joshua won, would that mean he was worthy to be king, worthy to recruit her for his cause? If Joshua lost, would she leave and search the world for someone else worthy of her? Joshua still had trouble understanding the girl. But he did discover why no one else stood a chance against her. She would easily be the most powerful tool Joshua could call upon during the war. Frea would be his trump card, his ace in the hole.

Joshua wanted her at his side, lest she might be against him.

Frea took her turn first and re-notched her massive lance. The ribs of unused skeletons wrapped about her chest to cover her, the spines and skulls protecting her knees and privates. She peered at Joshua through a large skull, her eyes perfectly set in their sockets, perfectly set on him. The girl spied Joshua for vulnerability. She would execute him there and leave his body in the meadow behind Whitecroft's estate. If he could not prevail over her, he would not be the one to abscond the throne. Like much of the world, Frea was searching for a champion, a queen for her chessboard. So was Joshua, in both ways a queen to her, and a king unto himself.

The grass the two stood upon began to grow at an exponential rate, wrapping around the fair maiden's flesh and pulling her into the ground. The arrow she would release would project enough force to send her flying back in reaction without these tethers. This was her best play to kill Joshua, and the true test of her foe's resolve.

Frea smiled from a corner of her mouth, her cuspid creasing her lower lip. She began a small croaking laugh, but it stopped a second after it started. It was a tired laugh, a repressed one. Frea had to remind herself she was being serious.

Joshua didn't budge, which deterred the lass from loosing her arrow. Was he truly planning on facing her final attack without moving? Truly, Joshua Hill was brave. He stood before her mere paces, unresponsive. He must've been a man without peer, Frea thought. Or, her champion was deeply suicidal. Frea hoped Joshua would live, she was beginning to like him. He was a dangerous foe, a dark hero, and she was a dark woman, a dangerous oracle.

Without warning, Frea loosed her spear and let it fly towards Joshua, a burst of energy expelling behind her, tearing the ground and the trees from their placement. Joshua steadied himself, waiting for the last possible moment. As the missile rushed forward The American sank low to the ground, watching the arrow warp through the air to meet him. Joshua felt the ground before his toes and tightened his fingers around the avatar's mask. As the arrows tip loomed before his eye, Joshua doubled over, flipping to his back. He pushed forward with the mask, grinding it against the length of the polearm. The arrow splintered against the makeshift shield, burrowing into the mask and breaking through it. The spear's tip pierced Joshua's shoulder, but had not the remaining momentum to sever his arm from his torso. The man continued to rotate along the ground, rotating the stick into the ground behind him in a piledriving move. The lance's length struck the ground in its own momentum and broke in two, leaving a large shard toppling away into the lake. Joshua watched it cascade with a shudder and a bubble.

The arrow was gone. Joshua survived.

Al Hamra head-rolled to his feet and tossed the shattered remains of his targe into the lake behind him. He reached into his coat with his right arm while his left hand removed the spear's shard from his shoulder. His shoulder spurted with blood; but Joshua's right hand, although injured, was still deft and steady. Joshua produced his pistol and fired his magazine in one swift and precise motion. The bullets flew forth and crashed against the bone and grass that cemented Frea to the earth, tearing them from her body. Once the magazine was empty, Frea's placement was exposed by holes in the bone.

Joshua sprinted forth, dropping his firearm and reaching for the yatagan which lay hidden among the flora. He poised it about his shoulders and continued his charge through the thicket.

But something was wrong.

Joshua watched as the ground exploded beneath him. Frea's bow hadn't crumpled, it had hidden itself in the earth just like his sword. It rose from the dirt and stabbed Joshua through the chest, sticking itself in his stomach. Joshua tumbled at the blow of the massive beam.

Joshua gasped, but his legs continued to move against his will. To Frea's amazement, Joshua did not stop his advance.

Joshua sliced at the beam in his chest and severed it, giving him room to maneuver. He stumbled forth on his feet and regained his lost momentum, still charging headlong into his foe.

Frea flinched.

Joshua plunged his blade into a hole in Frea's armor, stabbing her liver. The girl's stomach spewed blood and she fell upon the ground, beneath Joshua. Joshua wished to stop and finish the job, but his mindless legs sent him tumbling some yards further down the way, unable to stay with his weapon or his enemy. Joshua tumbled and lay there on his side in the foliage, paces from Frea, hidden in the grass.

The blades of grass around Joshua tickled his face. He watched the thicket flow back and forth, even in a world without breeze. Joshua couldn't see Frea from where he lay. He hoped she was down in the grass just as he was. Joshua hoped he hadn't lost.

Joshua blinked and found himself in the meadow, inside the white painted circle. Frea stood above him unscathed, and so was he. She reached down her hand and helped Joshua to his feet, seemingly less tense.

The grass was scorched inside the circle, all life was left crisp and dead. Whatever had occurred between both of them happened in a different world, created by a witch that wished to join his ranks. In the distance, Joan shouted at Green for missing his target again. Dutch patrolled the sparring areas, looking to critique others on their form.

Frea tied her dress around her waist, as was her habit. All of the men Frea fought before had no chance against the woman.

Joshua was slightly confused at the girl's power. It was hard to believe one girl could have so much favor. What was it that she did? Was there magic that allowed people to create their own worlds, could Joshua make his own?

The American continued to stare at Frea until he gave up. He couldn't truly understand her. All Joshua knew was that Frea hadn't killed him or left him in her head on her own planet. Joshua assumed this meant Frea conceded to join their merry band and was grateful. If not for the illegitimacy of their mission, Joshua would be ready to storm the castle immediately.

Joshua didn't say anything of Frea's trial as Dutch came to their ring. Dutch stared at Joshua for a moment and then at the dead grass. He asked his boss if everything was okay, to which he nodded and waved his advisor away. It was another nine minutes before Dutch would call the new set of rounds over, and the participants to change their partners.

Joshua was unsure how much promise his group of rebels showed at the end of that day. But among all the allies Joshua had at his disposal, the girl in the black Victorian dress was by far the most powerful. Joshua argued with himself that night, he wondered if Frea let him win, he wondered if she was the strongest being in the world.

Joshua almost laughed, if he were not so scared. It seemed that anything was possible, anything at all. He was just a small fish in a colossal pond.

How poetic. He twitched. *How pathetic.*

Part 7/Rue

Joshua washed himself days after in the stream behind Dutch's tavern while the others stood inside. Many of them ordered beer to cool themselves after another long day of training in the meadow. Frea stood by the window and gazed down the road, pompously watching the clouds roll by. To Joan's disgust, that woman was still present in their lives. Joan didn't like her, she didn't like any woman who restrained themselves to wearing dresses and other frilly things, and that was not the only reason.

Dutch and the others sat around the collected tables. They heard the door open and looked to see whom had walked in. There before them, casting a long shadow, was an ironclad warrior without a helmet. A white plume stuck out of his knotted hair where white bands held it back. His hair was a light brown, almost ginger. He looked stern; he was stern.

"Dutch, I see you've gathered your company here. That's rare." The man remarked.

"Left tenant Jackson!" Dutch exclaimed, the brief expression of worry on his face was soon covered by false excitement. "It's also not every day I see your face around these parts. What brings you here?"

"I assume you've seen this." The man replied bluntly, ignoring the question, but still answering it. He glimpsed at Joan at the end of the table. His face tightened and returned to Dutch. He handed him a sheet of paper, upon it was Joshua Hill, his hair cut and his face well shaven. Dutch studied the paper carefully.

"This is the detective that escaped Whitecroft's dungeon almost a year back, yes?" Dutch put, taking a sip of beer and handing the picture back. "This pamphlet is very old. I'm surprised you still have a warrant for him."

"I keep pamphlets for all people of interest." Jackson snorted. "I've assumed you've also seen this."

Jackson tossed a smaller paper to Dutch. Dutch read it as follows:

Three weeks ago, the esteemed advisor to our lord, Priscilla Whitechapel, passed away during a nightly gathering at his estate. There, the house caught fire and he was trapped in the flames. While his ashes were recovered, eye witnesses place the culprit as a man of fair build and light complexion, standing 5'11 with yellow and black eyes. If anyone reports the location of a man fitting the description above, and that man is found to be guilty of arson and murder against Gene Chase and his property, they will be awarded five years without grain taxation and a treasure of his or her choosing from our Lord's renowned vault. Any person with information regarding this criminal should report their knowledge to the nearest guard or official, lest be hung by the neck until dead.

~Fin.

Dutch scratched his head while Lt. Jackson passed him yet another flyer, it was Joshua Hill again, but his hair had grown, even a small beard hid his disappointed pout. The portrait must have been taken the night of his bar brawl west of Dutch's tavern.

"You don't honestly think Joshua Hill is back in town, do you?" Dutch scoffed. "He'd be crazy to show his face here."

The lieutenant slammed his hand upon the table with a loud crescendo; the beer shook, and so did the chandelier above them.

"What I think is that you've been neglecting your duties, Dutch!" Jackson barked, "You conscript criminals who deserve to be in jail, and you sit with them as equals at the same table! You are a blight to this state! If you don't find this man soon, I'll strip you of your privileges and hang all of your friends using *your* entrails as rope! Got that?"

"I got it," Dutch grumbled slowly rising from his table. "Let's go men, it's time to find ourselves a criminal!"

"You can't save this one, Dutch!" Jackson shouted, leaving the tavern before them. He met with his guards on the road, whom about faced and marched perfectly behind him.

Dutch's officers rose alongside their captain, just in case the left tenant was to look back and see them sitting still. Appearances were everything, after all. The muscled leader scratched his head once he was sure his comrade was gone, twisting away from the opened door towards his friends.

"Joan, go get Joshua from round back, we need to move him somewhere safer." He commanded.

"Where could I go?" Joshua asked, appearing from his hiding place on the stairway. "It's your job to find me, that won't change wherever I am."

"We could blow up a goat and turn in the scraps to Jackson, claim its Joshua." Hannah suggested, she grinded her fist into her palm with excitement.

"That would never work, missy." Green rebutted. "Too easy to tell the difference."

"She just wants to blow something up," Mortimer analyzed.

Hannah frowned.

"We could capture Jackson and hold him until Whitecroft is dead!" Biarre imputed. He crossed his arms and nodded, pleased with himself.

"They would just look for Jackson; that's too suspicious." Joan thought.

"Fools," Lilith grumbled. She sat on a book at the table. A tiny bottle of milk sat before her, barely touched. "We don't need Joshua to build or train the farmers. We don't need him for any of this drivel. He only needs to be present when we're ready to slay the baroness. Until then, he can sit in jail patiently. We will release him from his cell before we enter the estate. He'll be safer in a dungeon than prancing about the country side waiting to be seen. All we need to do is make sure Joshua isn't at the chopping block before we're ready to pounce."

Dutch nodded, truly thinking Lilith was the wisest pre-teen alive. Everyone nodded but Joshua. Joshua hated the idea.

"How do we make sure Joshua doesn't hang before we're ready? Who can hold back Whitecroft's bloody hand?" Biarre asked.

"Dutch," Joshua started, "When we spoke of Whitecroft's upcoming party, you mentioned that she didn't need to owe *another* baron. Which baron does she owe currently?"

Dutch thought about it for a moment. "Baron Cornelia, the baron of New Spain."

"Maybe we can get Baron Cornelia to call in that favor." Mortimer piqued. "One of my brothers is his personal doctor, maybe I can ask him for help. He might lose his job, but there are more important things than occupations at the moment."

Joshua looked at his boots. He thought about it, "I don't think a baron would answer to his doctor."

"His doctor is the only one who knows, besides me of course," Mortimer refuted, "knows that baron Cornelia is dying."

Dutch grimaced, that meant a lot of the region. Baron Cornelia had brought about an age of prosperity to his people through a trade agreement with American Providences, namely Canada. This agreement led to an abundance of jobs and an abundance of revenue. His entire country was covered in gardens, filled with stallions, lively and bizarre like an Egyptian epicenter. His people never went hungry, and they never looked to their leader with distaste. His successor, on the other hand, was too brash and conceited, a young man named Gilbert Gray. He didn't share the same passion for the people as Cornelia did. He hoarded his possessions like a sniveling child.

If Cornelia was dying, it wouldn't be surprising if New Spain faced economic downturn. Even the knowledge, or rumors, of Cornelia's illness would mean widespread paranoia as people prepared for the worst.

"Get it done, Mortimer." Joshua mumbled.

The masked figure stooped and left his allies to their festivities. If Mortimer could pull through for them, Joshua would be in a good position, when the time was right, to attack. The dungeons winded below the estate, utilizing natural caverns. Joshua would rise from beneath his pray like a shark and snatch her out of the waters.

For the time being, Joshua left words with Dutch in their secret room. The night had turned to silence, and Dutch's officers left the tavern to feign a search party. Eventually, they would "find" Joshua out in the open air and he would be captured. Joshua hoped it was for the best. This was to save their operation and continue building their rebellion in obscurity, after all.

Dutch made sure Joshua knew what was going to happen while he was away. In circumvent, their fiery leader would not be attending the Baron's party as per their original plan. The death of Gene Chase unfortunately alerted the baron to Joshua's presence, and the opportunity was lost for them to raise civil unrest by surprising the barons with Joshua's attendance.

However, as the harvest trucks shifted out for winter to sell the farmer's crops, Dutch would plan raiding parties that would cripple the exports. The looted food would be used to supplement the Farmer's diets, gaining their loyalty, strengthening their resolve to retaliate. The other bundles of wheat not needed would be pushed through Saia's black market "pro bono" in exchange for favors and market goods.

Saia, although disgusted with Joshua Hill's face and position to take her throne, agreed to aid the revolution in preforming small missions beginning with Mortimer's brother, whom aimed to blackmail Baron Cornelia.

A few weeks passed, and the aforementioned mission was a success. Mortimer's brother blackmailed Cornelius into calling in his favor. He asked Whitecroft the let Hill rot in the caverns, after all, it was a punishment far worse than death. But, such a request also left their ally's brother in a tight position, often incurring his Baron's wrath, a mistrust well placed. Cornelius had seen Mortimer's brother as a friend until that day and no apology would make his frustration in such betrayed trust any less dire. Mortimer's brother was on a thin thread hanging over hell, waiting for the string to snap or burn.

Mortimer insisted on stealing his brother to safety to the American shoreline where he could become a village doctor before Cornelius decided to take his head. Cornelius could have any other doctor to help him. But when Mortimer sent his last missive to his brother, he never replied. Neither could Saia's agents find him anywhere.

Further on, as operations went underway, and the time for imprisoning Joshua neared, the farmers would begin small acts of protest. During the winter, the Baron's men would move door to door, inspecting every nook and cranny of the house, often breaking furniture in their endeavors. But a small display of arms at every house would dissuade them from entering. The farmers would rally at their houses with their new rifles, swords, and bows, ready to respond in force if the guards were to enter the house. Others would follow the patrols closely, applying pressure into them, circling them like vultures incurring judgement.

The baron would hopefully be furious, having her namesake spat upon and turned on its head. She would begin to double her active guards, pulling them from her own garrison which was located within her estate. This dwindled the guards around her, making it easier for the moment when Joan would slip in and unlock Joshua's cell. Joshua would then sneak through the basement and assassinate the baron while Joan moved to unlock the front gate, allowing others to join in the reverie and bear witness their new king.

Joshua, the day before he was to be turned in, met with farmers at their doorsteps, giving them a face to the name of their leader. Although it was commanded that Joshua's name not be spoken until he was put into jail, the farmers silently chanted his name in their minds that day. Joshua was going to be their new baron, their new king. They had already fallen in love with his deeds and his kindness, but when they met him, they wished they could storm the castle immediately.

The morning came when Joshua would be turned in. Dutch had to be the one to commit such an act, in order to remain in Whitecroft's good graces and paint himself a friend of his ever-immaculate queen. Along the road, in which Joshua was bound and tied, he had time to talk with Dutch and understand him. They talked of many things, for it was a long walk. But Joshua grew in full faith of Dutch's abilities to lead his men while he was absent. Dutch truly deserved to be the new baron, and Joshua was waiting to force it upon him.

There comes a time in every man's life when they begin to think about their actions and the consequences that became them. It was later in this week that this thought came to Joshua's mind. As the Baron's castle loomed in the distance and Dutch dragged the blindfolded man by his feet, he began to think of why he once agreed to being turned in.

The reason Joshua thought this was because the baroness wasn't a logical woman, she didn't need to answer to someone hundreds of miles away (such as Baron Cornelius) and, therefore, was able to reign at any fancy or whim. Whitecroft could snap her fingers and shrug her shoulders at Baron Cornelius, telling him she still owed him a favor. She could let the New Spaniard stew on her misstep and betrayal. She might do such a thing because she knew she had the courage, and the Barons, in summation, were cowards. There was no guarantee Lilith's plan would work.

Joshua felt the dirt road become cobblestone. He kept his head aloft to keep it from bruising. It wasn't the best sackcloth bag for Joshua's head either, as he could see well through it.

It was the late afternoon, the trees surrounding the stone fortress cast a cool shade on the land. The baron's forest was the only place wild game roamed in the region, she made sure to trim it back so that no citizen would think to head north and try to poach there. It was her forest, her meats and her shade. If anyone was caught, they would immediately be hanged and left there.

The outside of the forest regarded that fact. Many farmers and adventurers had been caught trying to sneak through the woods, trying to find food. They had made the fatal mistake of not entering through the beach on the north side, and now swung like ornaments along the tree line. The baron never took them down, their carcasses served as a reminder not to cross her. This is mentioned because it was these swinging farmers that Joshua watched enter his view, one by one like a parade of corpses, as he was brought through the first entrance of Whitecroft's hallowed ground.

Dutch dropped Joshua's feet as they walked into the main entrance. The building was beautiful. Stained glass windows let in supple golden light which brushed the long purple carpet. That carpet led to the courtyard behind the Baron's throne where she sat, splitting into two separate vectors which wrapped around the elevated chair towards the doors in the corners. A large window loomed behind the Baron, but instead of a cross or a dove or the Virgin Mary, Whitechapel stood in as the imagery, luminescent and judgmental. The mural had been constructed back before her lover's death, back when she was beautiful and people took pride in her.

The building was the same as Joshua remembered it when his life first took a turn for the worst. However, this time there would be no party and no Haddock to save him. Elizabeth wasn't paying attention and nor did God seem to care for the following:

"Your elite majesty," Dutch bowed, "I have brought you Joshua Hill, as requested through your esteemed Left Tenant Jackson."

The mustachioed man lifted Joshua to his knees and ripped the cloth from his head. The coarse fabric scratched Joshua's nose and the perpetrator blinked until his eyes adjusted to the new saturation. Joshua stared at his target, his enemy, a look of disgust on her face evident before him.

The American wanted to burn his tied hands and tear her in two that instant, but he suppressed the urge, and brought Lilith's plan back to his mind. It calmed him. He walked through the steps described at their meeting, imagining every plotline. Joshua slowed his breathing, anything to keep his ambitions from ruining the plan. Joshua had to focus on the long term. He couldn't jeopardize his legitimacy. By waiting until Dutch finished his duty in raising a true revolt, Joshua could reduce innocent bloodshed and push the farmer's plea into the spotlight. He needed to make sure the barons were watching, rooting for him. Most of all he had to make sure Solomon knew where he was to be found, and that the media put his face on every screen around the world.

Joshua needed to wait for the barons' blessing, which took time.

"You've done well to bring him to me." Whitecroft stated, her long finger screeching against her stone armrests. She reminded Joshua of a newt; her body swallowed by her throne, her mind swallowed by her narcissism. She was a small bead in a large cup.

"But why did you wait?" Whitecroft continued. "You had him days ago, did you not?"

Dutch gawked, the once stalwart and whimsical personality shuttered by apprehension and fear. Joshua had never seen him so afraid. From the right of the room, he heard the clang of metal. Jackson loomed through the door and came to stand in witness.

"Your majesty," Dutch stuttered, "I meant no disr-"

Dutch could not finish the words on his quivering lip, and Joshua felt a warm spot on his neck. Joshua looked back at Dutch. A small dagger, a kris, struck through his ally's chest. Blood gushed from the wound. Dutch hadn't finished his apology. The unknown words, and his body, hung there by the blade.

Joshua twisted around to find the blade had not a wielder. It merely floated there, flying, pinning his fallen friend aloft like a puppet. Dutch stared at Joshua under dead eyes. Joshua thought to scream, but he didn't. They didn't kill Dutch because they knew about their coupe d'état, they killed Dutch because they knew Dutch's kind heart.

"How long I've waited for an excuse to kill him." The Baron mused, "Soon, even his cohorts will be hunted down. He thought I didn't mind. He thought he could buy me with scraps from his plate, keeping the other criminals away from me. He didn't know I was just waiting for them to collect, to wipe them out in one fell swoop. Now the pieces are in place, and I have you as a bonus."

The baron signaled to Jackson who took his cue to leave.

Joshua looked back to Dutch, the sword slowly slipping out of his chest. He fell with a loud thump to the floor. The sword continued to hover, but slowly, a hand began to form around it. Someone had been there the whole time, invisible. This invisible man was a large lizard, a chameleon that wasn't unlike a human, much like Frea wasn't quite a girl, in Joshua's mind. There was something sinister under its eyes. A dry, lizard-like skin continued its form about the monster. It wore a long coat, with the shoulders moving out from his body

354

into two triangular points. He smiled down at Joshua and licked his jagged teeth. The thing grabbed Joshua by his feet and jerked him back, leaving Joshua on his stomach. He was dragged back down that velvet purple carpet. Watching Dutch become smaller and smaller and smaller.

Joshua was dragged away.

The baron called out to Joshua as the lizard man pulled him through hallways, heading into the dungeons to lock Joshua away for all eternity. "You'll rot this time, Joshua Hill, and no one will save you."

Joshua closed his eyes. Had he failed everyone?

The American realized he would never see Dutch's face again, he could never ask his opinion or advice. Dutch was the first friend Joshua ever had. The man asked nothing of him, never manipulated him or drug him down in guilt. He tried his best to understand Joshua, and defended him when others couldn't understand his rage, his methods of living. Perhaps they were friends because they were complete opposites. Dutch was the happiest and most thoughtful man Joshua had known. Unlike him, Dutch was not selfish. Unlike him, Dutch was good.

In this world, did the good ones always die?

Joan laughed with the group, watching Green, who sat on the end of the table, mock Hannah's freckled face. Mortimer sat on the other end, reading a book to himself, stopping to ponder the phrase, *"To one I have given much, only to lose that which I kept for myself."* He repeated the words again, his voice muffled through his silver mask.

Lilith slept in the corner, her head on Frea's ruffled dress. Sach sat at the bar stool, his long and spotted tongue licking the inside of a shot glass. Biarre challenged the odd creature to a drinking match. Biarre was losing.

Mrs. Hammond brought everyone another round, they all cheered. Joan was worried; Dutch was late. But in her worry, she felt the answer and saw the signs. Before anyone heard it, she heard it, it whispered to her through the ground, tapped on her feet. It was the tongue of death, the pattering of wet tears and the drums of war. A small unit of cavalry men were on their way down the road.

Joan rose and made her way to the end of the house. She looked out the window the see a small cloud of dust looming. She doubted her heart which told her it was the enemy. She waited, but there in her telescope eyes sat Jackson thundering toward the tavern on his spotted horse.

Joan twisted around in a panic.

"We need to go!" She cried.

The trope looked at her in bewilderment. They had just received their next round, Lilith was resting, and Sach had not yet defeated Biarre.

"No," Frea whispered, her voice serene and calm, "It's okay."

Joan turned to see the soldiers loom, they had mere moments before they arrived. Joan watched a thin black speck rise into the air and grow larger. An arrow, from that distance, shot through the window and struck her shoulder with a thump.

The band of officers shouted and rose. Mortimer quickly came over to help her away from the open window. Quickly he picked her up by the armpits and slid her a short distance before she stood. It was just in time, as a volley of arrows thudded against the wall and through the opening, leaving darts firmly embedded into the floor.

Ms. Hammond screamed.

"Prepare yourselves, men!" Mortimer demanded, his voice muffled but firm.

The men didn't need to hear him. They already began their defense. Joan looked upon them as she tore the arrow from her arm, they flipped the tables to their sides and pushed them against the doorways. Hannah walked over to the bar and began to dip rags into beer bottles, creating molotov cocktails for her friends. She placed a lighter on the table. Ms.

356

Hammond reached beneath the bar and pulled out a small sawed-off shotgun. She tossed it to Green who snagged it. Green paced back and forth on the open floor, ordering the furniture against the doors. Biarre opened the stairway door leading to the secret room and collected all documentation of their rebellion, stuffing them into a small backpack.

Joan looked over to the corner where Lilith and Frea sat, but they were gone. In the midst of the chaos Lilith managed to escape to safety. Frea must have taken her away through the backdoor before it was forced shut. The thundering grew louder, and the Baron's men were upon them. They dismantled their rides and formed rows and rows of circles around Dutch's tavern. There were at least seventy of them, all armed to the teeth with muskets, swords, spears, and bows. They were Baron Whitecroft's elite fighting force, the best of her lackeys.

Before the elites, Jackson stood with his sword, clad in his steel shell, swinging his sword in his left hand like a dancer's baton. Beside him, a small man blew a trumpet.

All was silent. Biarre shuffled quietly down the stairs with rifles over his shoulder, he began to pass them out among the crew. He laid the rest of them against the walls, loaded and ready to use.

"You will not be shown mercy today!" Jackson bellowed. His men began to beat their chests with their gauntlets. The sound of metal clacking metal filled the air. Psychological warfare, pumping his men for the fight, preparing his foe for prostration, and then, death.

"The Baron will have your head!" Jackson roared.

"THE BARON WILL HAVE YOUR HEAD!" His men repeated. The first row of elites, pole bearers, knelt to the ground. This allowed the second row to place their rifles on their shoulders, steadying their shot.

"Everyone down!" Joan yelled before leaping over the bar.

A flurry of bullets ripped through the cabin. Mrs. Hammond fell beside the huntress, unable to duck in time. She was dead on impact.

The others took shelter behind their tables, the extra layer shielding them from the brass.

Dutch's officers rose and stuck their rifles through the window and fired back. The bullets grazed their enemy, their armor too thick to penetrate. The steel they wore slanted neatly in an acute angle at the chest piece like the keel of a ship. It prevented the bullets from puncturing their armor, only leaving dents and scrapes.

Hannah lit one of her cocktails and tossed it through the window, pegging a soldier in the face. The bottle shattered and engulfed him in flames before spreading to others. The alcohol creeped between their plates and burned them alive.

Hannah yelled, excited and terrified. "Eat that Crofties!"

Jackson grimaced, "Advance troops, knock down those doors!"

The soldiers began to close in. Joan and her friends looked for holes in their armor. But, as they fired magazine after magazine, only few fell beneath the hail of bullets. Hannah continued to throw cocktails from the windows, slowing their advancement, but there were too many of them to burn, and too few rags.

The fire of the cocktails began to spread, engulfing the surrounding area. As the men began to pound on their doors, so did the fire creep through the floors. Joan looked around for an escape, but they were locked down in the growing inferno. She watched as Dutch's officer struggled to keep the door shut, their backs against the tables as spare bullets fired through the walls.

Nothing had worked, it was hopeless, and they were trapped.

Green stuck his arm through the window, his shotgun poised to go off. He fired both shells into a guard's neck who crumpled to the ground dead and headless.

But Green was too reckless.

Jackson rushed forth and descended his blade upon Green's arm, lopping it off. Green twisted back around, trying to save himself, but it was too late. Jackson reached through the window with his arm and grabbed Green by the neck. Joan rushed forth to help, but just as she grasped his good hand, he was sucked through the window, gone. She could hear him scream from outside as Jackson stabbed him again and again with his blade.

Their friend was dead, and they were next.

Jackson continued to pace in circles about the front of Dutch's tavern, waiting for someone else to try their luck. He had done this so many times before. He was the best of Whitecroft's men, the best at getting things done. He waited for his soldiers to break down the entrance. It was only a matter of time.

Mortimer, Hannah, and Biarre looked to Joan for guidance, but the young huntress had no ideas. The flames rose to lick the swissed walls. They couldn't run, men surrounded them on every side, and the flame was getting ever higher. They couldn't wait inside for help, they could hardly breathe through the smog.

"Let them in!" Joan ordered. "We'll face them out there or suffocate in our own home!"

"It's better than dying like a fox." Biarre agreed, stepping back from the table.

"I'm sure we'll be avenged." Mortimer huffed, "I believe in Joshua... he will make this worth it."

Mortimer and Hannah gripped the table, ready to move it out of the way.

Joan grabbed a small butchers' knife from the table. It was the only weapon they had left besides the stocks on their guns. They steeled themselves.

This was their end.

Mortimer moved the table away and it immediately burst open. Joan charged the first guard and leapt on him, she cleaved her blade deep into the parting in his neck. He quickly expired and fell to the floor. Joan rolled forward off his head, grabbed his sword and quickly tossed it to Biarre. Biarre caught it and twisted around to meet the second soldier, cleaving him through the waist with great speed and force. He blocked at parried at the gauntlet, batting away the men and kicking them out into the burning foreyard. Hannah and Mortimer armed themselves with the weapons of the fallen and rushed forward to aid their friend.

Joan funneled out behind them, finding a bow and quiver on one of the deceased. She scooped them up and began to notch her first arrow. Her first shot landed neatly in another man's neck.

Mortimer moved right and slashed with all his might. He began to feel confident in their plunge. He began to quote from his favorite bards as he moved through the mass of soldiers. This confidence urged him forth in a fervor, but, he never noticed the blades that began to puncture him. The adrenaline coursed through him, he couldn't feel the pain, but to his surprise he fell to his knees amidst the clash, his legs no longer working, his legs no longer there. He looked down at himself in a pool of his own blood and guts. His mask was gone, shattered by gunfire and pommels. He wasn't a handsome man, his face speckled in burns from decoctions and plagues, a side effect of working with diseased bodies in his youth. Mortimer smiled before the blades descended upon him.

"Yes, this was better than a fox in his den." He sighed his last.

Hannah stayed away from the fray. Scavenging for gunpower, she moved from one dead body to the next, stopping only to unload the rest of a magazine. This did not fell many of her enemies, but she posed a considerable distraction, leading people way from Joan and Biarre. She was quick, but soon, there were no new bodies to scavenge.

So, Hannah ran.

The young girl found herself at the river bed. Spare cavalry men ran along the banks with their rifles trained. Her feet splashed through the cold water. Jackson's men fired, the first volley deflecting from the trees. She continued her flight, ducking beneath a stone bridge. She rushed through the short tunnel, looking for the light at the end. The light soon was seen, an illusion of freedom. As it came she was met by an infantry man who had hopped down from the path to meet her. He stood ready, and cut her down, there in the running water. The young girl fell on her face, she was not ready to die. But, if she was not dead yet, the swordsman made sure. His foot pressed against her shoulder blades, forcing her head underwater until she stopped moving.

They left her there in the cold waters, lifeless.

Biarre continued to hack the enemy. He was a force, flowing with his blade. He leapt and crossed around his enemy, attacking from all sides. He was unpredictable, his blade stance different than his enemies were used to. He held the blade from all ends like a staff. He gripped the tip of his blade and swung it about, striking a group of men with the hilt. The force rotated the sword in the air. As the man released it, it spun to meet the back of a soldier's neck, digging deep. Biarre pulled it out, the sword now backhanded, and flurried in a circle, blocking four lunges in one smooth motion. He rotated back in the swivel and the blade grooved its way through their waists, leaving their guts spilled on the dirt.

Biarre looked about to find Jackson advancing on him, ready to strike him down. Biarre grimaced back at him and charged. Jackson deflected the first strike but not with his sword, he deflected with his elbow. Confident in his armor, the blade glanced off, letting Biarre closer. Jackson reached

361

down to grab the duelist, but Biarre had already regained his composure and swat the lieutenant's hand away with his arm.

It was numbing pain, the feeling of flesh against metal. Biarre rubbed his arm in an attempt to encourage blood flow.

Jackson swung his claymore in a wide arc horizontal to the ground. Biarre held his blade against his torso and used it as armor himself. The force of the heavy weapon jarred him, and he heard his sword crack. Biarre slid along the ground. His arms lost feeling. He couldn't raise them to defend himself.

Joan continued to fell her enemies. Quick with a bow, she allowed herself plenty of space as the men rushed forth. Joan spied Biarre who lay vulnerable before Jackson. She rushed forth and reached into her quiver, notching her last arrow as she sprinted to help her comrade.

Joan released the tension in her string and the arrow flew through the empty lane towards Jackson.

Joan chased her own dart. She followed it through the fray and watched as it neatly embedded itself into Jackson's side. Joan leaped forth, upon the scene, and stretched out her foot, kicking the shaft further into the left tenant's waist.

Jackson flinched and stumbled sideways, grunting in pain. Joan watched him regain his posture from the ground. The large man did not die, for the arrow did not sever his spine. Joan rolled to her feet, unsheathing her knife and her pickaxe, ready to help Biarre. She looked to him, but he was motionless. The remaining men, that Dutch's band had not killed, pierced him into the ground. Biarre clawed at the road, trying to free himself.

Joan heard the men laugh, watching him like a snake caught by the tail. Biarre twisted and pulled, but it was no use, every movement opened his wounds further. He looked at Joan, the last of Dutch's officers. He gave her a small smirk, before closing his eyes and breathing his last.

Joan screamed furiously. Her hands twitched, her body ached and pulsed with anticipation and anger.

Where was Dutch? Where was Joshua?

Joshua was gone, imprisoned or dead, and no one would free him from jail, not if Joan died.

Joan turned around as Jackson descended his sword.

Joshua knelt in his cell, a wooden stock around his wrists. He listened to the guards walk through the decrepit halls. In the corner of his prison was a small bowl which lay under a single stalactite. The drops that periodically collected beneath the conic stone would be all he could drink the duration of his stay. Joshua couldn't become dehydrated, but his throat was dry. He thought of his responsibilities, he thought of his punishment, he wondered if he could've saved Dutch if he had only paid attention.

Was Lilith's plan still in effect, or was he waiting hopelessly for no one to retrieve him?

"These caves are special," Symeon called from the bars. His face was illuminated near the door. "They have an uncanny ability to suppress the thoughts of others. Like a vacuum it just sucks them into its mouth and drinks them away from the mind. You can feel it can't you? Your mind feels like someone else is inside, thinking for you. It makes you feel your crazy, hijacked like a computer. You can't wish for anything down here. You can't melt these bars."

Joshua looked at Symeon with an empty gaze. He thought the ghost had abandoned him, he thought the ghost was mocking him. But he wasn't.

Symeon leaned against the bars and peered at Joshua, a small but sad smile on his face. He hadn't finished talking, he wanted to comfort his champion.

"Don't worry, boy. I'll be here to keep your head intact. Maybe someone else will wish for you. Maybe a child will wish that winter will arrive sooner than we think."

Joan lay on the dirt, Jackson's sword embedded in her thigh. Beside her, Jackson sat on a stool of bodies as the flames were doused around them. His handful of men roamed about, stacking bodies. Joan could see Green, Mortimer, Hannah and Biarre in the pile. Blood trickled from Joan's forehead. She never stood a chance against Jackson.

Jackson polished his knife, looking to savor Joan's death. He paused frequently, paranoid that the huntress wouldn't be there, vanished into the earth, sprinting for safety, or bled to death like a lamb.

Joan blinked, witnessing a shadow from the roaring flame, the rotting tavern. It was the outline of a queen. Joan watched as Frea stood behind the group of soldiers, walking quietly with her parasol, taking a gander through the inferno towards her. No one seemed to notice Frea's wayward walk. No one seemed to look in her direction. She took her time inching closer, slowly, with a rotten smile on her face.

Joan began to hear the muffled words of Jackson, he began to hum to himself, something of moonbeams and pedaled grottos. It was a song, something she had heard when she was a child. It explained his height, his character. Jackson was also from the North, from the Scandes, like Joan was.

And the dame had cried, saying no, no, no, not into
France I won't go, go, go.
I have my own house, and I shall not leave, I do not care for
reckless dreams.
I've built my world in the cold, where the weather is safe, I
won't go
I love him to the earth and back, but on his ship, I won't go,
On his ship I won't go.

Joan mouthed the words along. Jackson raised his brow, and his lips puckered slightly, thoughtful.

"So, you remember the words too? I make sure to sing them at night, reminds me of home... I want to go back one day." He sighed, running his finger along the edge. He cut his thumb slightly and ran it over Joan's eyelids.

"For our people, a ritual for the gods, so they know who sent you." Jackson reminded.

Frea looked at the bodies around her. The guards and allies who were slain. She knew that it had to happen this way, she knew it. They were not the ones to stand when Joshua became king. But she looked over at Joan, the one who would be there.

Frea watched her watch her.

Jackson didn't realize his men were all dead. Frea killed the rest of them, on by one easing their bodies to the ground, running her parasol through their armor like warm butter. Without a sound she stood behind Jackson who began to raise his blade over Joan's chest.

Frea grabbed Jackson by his knotted hair and tilted his head back. The giant was surprised. He strained his head, his neck tensing and struggling to free itself. But Frea overpowered him. She was too strong. Her titanic strength, her single hand, pinned him still. She looked into his eyes with a thin smile and raised her parasol into the air. Jackson screamed in panic, but the umbrella silenced him, clasped and plunged deep into Jackson's gaping mouth. The parasol broke his teeth and dislocated his jaw.

Jackson choked and sputtered geysers of blood. Frea let go of the Left Tenant and he fell from his stoop backwards onto his back like a turtle. Jackson gasped for air before drowning in his own blood.

Frea removed the giant's claymore from its perch inside Joan's leg and lifted the huntress on her shoulder like a pillow or a rug. Frea strolled away from the carnage, having saved two people.

Frea saved the correct two.

Part 8/Resist

Joshua stared at the walls of his rank cell. Dazed, he knew not how many days had passed, but his hair ran to his chin and his beard grew full. The American rocked himself on his heels in rhythm, trying to understand the minutes, hours, and days that passed. The furthest he counted was somewhere around ten thousand seconds until he lost his train of thought and had to start over. Symeon stood in the corner of the cell, watching patrols loom by. The guards couldn't see the ghost watching over the young rebel, but they knew to watch Joshua's cell tirelessly under the Baron's orders. Whitecroft would not let him escape.

Joshua listened to the guard's chatter for months on end; he heard them speak of the massacre at Dutch's tavern. It was a shame, they said, to lose such a fine bar before winter. They gave Joshua information on the outside world. He knew that Frea survived the battle, Jackson had died gruesomely, much to his pleasure, and that many farmers had begun to take violent actions against the monarchy. Frea and Lilith were most likely the ones keeping the revolutionary flame lit, helping those farmers stay alive through winter.

Soldiers wouldn't kill a child, would they?

Joshua also heard of a woman who led a small band of hunters. These hunters had a reputation for destroying transports along major routes. The guards grumbled, talking of pay cuts and higher grain taxation. The county was choked off from the outside world. These rumors all coincided with the plans Dutch had mentioned to Joshua before he was turned in. Knowing this, he held fast to the hope that one day he might be free once again.

The last thing Joshua would hear rumors of, was his own name. The people began to rally behind "Al Hamra" or

"Joshua Hill," painting the name in red on the baron's walls, shouting it before firing their first shot. Joshua wished he could change that name, to replace his fame with "Dutch."

Joshua slept in the corner, tried to sleep, but the constant splish-splash of the water, the beat of feet, and his brain breaching the halls of insanity, kept him up at night. It was when he felt the most demented that Symeon began to talk to him. He told him about his days in the park, his days behind a desk. Symeon also taught him some history regarding magical species and what existed out in the world.

Recently, there had been increased sightings of magical specimens outside of The Americas, which rose an alarm to city officials around the world. The Russians had found the Shaper Joshua slayed, their expedition successful. They erected a military-science outpost to study it. The fats on its body refused to decompose, the cold preserving it. They released the data for other countries to look at, in hopes of gaining a better understanding of the ecosystem and the strange phenomena.

"World's changing, boy," Symeon would say, "And you'll be able to see it one day."

It wasn't that Joshua didn't believe he would be free one day, it was a matter of when he would be free that concerned him. If the rumors were true, the farmers were getting restless. Frea might be over-empowering them, leading them down a path of war that would create too much bloodshed.

According to heresy, farmers would attack guards at random, and were now considered armed and dangerous. Farmers hung orange cloths from their roofs and over their corpses. This a symbol of remembrance and rebellion. Civil hostility unified under an orange flag with the word "Dutchmen." It bore a blazing sun in the center. Dutch's kindness in life, his willingness to look the other way, meet people in the middle, and understand the citizen's strife, put him at the forefront of the people's hearts, even if Joshua was on their lips. In life, Dutch was a saint, in death a martyr, and now he was a war cry much like Joshua.

"Al Hamra" was a promise for a future, "Dutch" was a loathing for the past.

But this wasn't what Dutch wanted, was it? He wanted Joshua to wait because he was afraid the people would become hurt. Dutch wanted to wait until all the odds were stacked against the baron so that the citizens would be protected from whatever fallout ensued after her assassination. Now enraged, the populace's death toll skyrocketed.

The Crofts was a warzone. People hung from the neck along the rivers, polluting the fresh water, and making soldiers and rebels alike sick and diseased. Blood turned the snow red and corrupted the soil, giving rise to odd species of plants, barbed and poisonous. Children stayed inside after one had ran through a thicket of these "bloodthorns" and died the day after.

None of it was what Dutch wanted. He didn't want the people to lose their innocence. He didn't want the people to lose their lives.

Had Joshua waited too long? Was he expected to come out of hiding and kill Whitecroft? If that were the case, he missed his opportunity. The isolation of Joshua from the world and the magical presence in the caverns siphoned his energy, his willpower to fight. Joshua was helpless to lead himself out of captivity. So, waiting day after day, each minute passing with the length of an eternity, Joshua waited.

In moments of lucidity, Joshua took command of his dreams, imagining every which way he might kill Solomon. That was his end goal, after all. That is why he was there in the first place. He was a fool to think it would easy. He was a fool to think about making friends, and a fool for not relying on others. Joshua pushed everyone away, he faced it all by himself. His guilt, his burdens, were not meant to be snuffed under the guise of strength.

Joshua needed help, but he had no one to ask. It had been during first week in the darkness of jail that Joshua pleaded to Symeon to free him. Symeon laughed at him, told him he couldn't even if he wanted to. The old man was not a poltergeist or avatar who had a strong hold on the world, it was much for him to simply appear. Symeon could guide Joshua, give him advice, or tell him a story, but that was all he was good for in that cave. It was one of his only strengths; to be there for him like a father.

But was that enough to keep him sane?

Surely, it was not.

Joan watched from the barn the long dirt road which winded towards the border. She counted the seconds as her crew gathered in a circle with their bows, watching the red pulse of a landmine, waiting for the next shipment to come storming down the road.

Before Joan left with Frea the day Joshua was imprisoned, she made sure to pocket the blueprints Biarre hid on him. He had everything they needed, shipment dates, schematics, routes, and itineraries. Because of Biarre's quick thinking, Joan could hit the Baron's franchise hard and fast, quickly disappearing unnoticed thereafter.

Joan heard the trucks, saw the headlights through the cracks in the window. She closed her eyes, waiting to hear the blast.

Now.

Joan opened the barn door just as the cargo truck passed the mine, the mine exploded in a vertical, controlled, explosion, leaving a hole in the engine block. She drew her bow and quickly guided an arrow through the window into the driver's seat, killing he behind the steering wheel.

Dead.

Her crew rose from the ditches beside the road in kind. They sniped the two other drivers and fell upon the car, gutting the rear passengers with their knives.

Dead, dead, dead, dead, dead.

Joan rushed to the truck and helped the men remove plastic boxes from the beds. They quickly hid them inside the drainage pipe beneath the road and continued their mission.

Joan grabbed the first steering wheel and put the truck in neutral. With help, she pushed the car down the hill until it ran into the ditch at the crossroads. Joan placed another landmine in the seat of the broken vehicle. It faced the door, ready to kill whoever opened it next. The villagers had the memo not to go near them, but the guards had not caught on yet to their booby traps. Eventually, one of those unlucky soldiers, on an excursion to find the missing cargo shipment, would meet his doom in that roadside ditch.

Boom, dead.

Life was death for Joan now. She was death.

Joan watched as her elites covered the drainage pipe with orange cloth. A sign for the scavengers to collect the packages so that Joan's squad could go on their way.

There were drainage pipes all over the countryside. These were common places for the rebels drop supplies for scavengers, unless other squads decided to claim the trove.

Joan rallied her people and they began the long ten-mile sprint to the next checkpoint. They had half an hour before the next shipment would pass outside the border. This was Joan's territory; no shipment would leave. She began to pant, her heart bursting with anger harbored for months. Eventually, Frea would be ready to end the war, but for now, Joan had a long night ahead of her.

Lilith drew plots along a map, showing Frea's assassins the locations of key officers. The girl separated the group into small teams of two based on skill and the nature of their targets before sending them on their way. They were the finished products of country bumpkins, the bravest and most agile of men in The Crofts.

Lilith missed Dutch, often thinking she would pass him on the road. But after turning over their bodies, she would realize her mistake and catch up with Frea who played the role of her new mother. It wasn't so much that Lilith didn't believe Dutch was dead, she had been told time and time again he was. The resistance even brought his body to her, which was found strung by the ankles as a warning on Whitecroft's gate. Dutch was buried in the meadow to the north in a circle of burnt grass. A wooden cross and his sword were embedded in the center to mark his place, even if the flowers grew back.

The reason Lilith thought she was seeing Dutch was that she needed another Dutch. She searched for a surrogate, a replacement, someone to look after her, to treat her like a child and take pride in her mind. Lilith needed a father.

In Frea's care Lilith was put to work, constantly studying the enemy's movements and discovering their patterns. She was tasked in understanding the enemy's chain of command. She also sought out Whitecroftian defectors who had fled across the border. Frea was not keen on sparing their lives or letting them forget their crimes. It was a dark war, and Lilith didn't mind ordering others to do gruesome things. It was logical to her to be savage. Savagery beget power.

Frea watched over Lilith, her personal bodyguard. It was Frea's word that meant the most to the people. She was the figurehead of the revolution, Joshua's tongue. She united the county under one promise, that there was a king waiting to lead them, that they were close to the end of suffering. She spoke with an even voice, a tinge of hope garnered with sadness and conviction.

Most of the farmers who rebelled, had seen this "Al Hamra." But the way she spoke of him reminded them of their plight, their purpose. They wanted to meet this man again, whatever the cost. They wanted Al Hamra to bring prosperity to them, return to them their rights, clean their lands. Despite their anticipative excitement for revelations, Frea kept the commoners in order, and they would not assault the Baron's mansion, much less breathe, until she said so.

In these months, Frea had a taste of what it would be like to be queen. Suffice it to say that she liked it. Frea liked ruling, possibly too much.

Lafayette sat on the couch in his house and watched the world from his television. He leaned back watching a special on civil strife, a newscaster with beautiful laugh-lines now gaunt and serious, reporting the deaths of loved ones in the Red Rebellion. It was for this reason the Marquis never left his city, which floated like an idol above the clouds. Mortals only wanted violence and could never find peace without turmoil. Anything else, any delegations or treaties were only a farce, a snide way of stealing and trading.

The Marquis knew war, and he left it behind. But something about this war enthused him, asked him not to change the channel and watch his Sunday cartoons as per usual. Church was over, but The Marquis found himself praying softly when the helicopter panned over the blood-bathed countryside. The camera continued to pan until focusing on Whitecroft's estate, her walls reinforced by wood panels and small watch towers. The news anchor opened her mouth to speak.

The Marquis missed her beautiful smile.

"The rebels claim their leader is Joshua Hill, who, reports say, was a Paris detective before being convicted of murder under Baron Whitecroft's jurisdiction…"

The Marquis rose in his seat suddenly revolted in his lazy demeanor. He told Joshua not to become like him, but never in his dream would he think Joshua would become like *this*. War never led to victory. How could Joshua let this happen?

The Marquis left his living room and moved to his foyer. He placed his hands on his front door, waiting to turn the handle. He paused, hesitated. Even if Joshua was leading these people to their death, they still did so willingly, the Marquis thought. Even if Joshua was leading these people, he was still making the world a better place, wasn't he? Did The Marquis ever leave a legacy, did he ever do anything to help the world? How long had he waited for the world to change?

The Marquis grabbed his coat from the white rack by the door and strode outside.

The Marquis rested his arms on the handrails, his house sat in the middle of his small city lifted above the lives of everyday people. He watched them, sitting on benches by the pond fueled by cloud vapor. They took strolls down the sidewalk, perhaps to visit a neighbor or return to work. Laffy lived in heaven, surrounded by fine people with ample joy and needless money. Everything anyone could ever want was here, built above the earth, built on LeCeleste.

But, everything was too grand, *too* peaceful. When he had left the world to enjoy his immortality and study it, he took his friends with him. His comrades were also tired from the meaningless struggles of the world. They too saw humanity as a blight, something to be removed, but they had not the selfishness nor the cruelty to end another life. But now, that generation had passed away, and the generation after had passed too. The Marquis was the last member of his era in the city, the only one to know strife among the population.

Did these people look down at the earth as he did, worried, angry, sorrowful in their plight; or where they ignorant in their numbered days? Perhaps The Marquis coddled them too close, fed them with their silver spoons until they no longer looked down at all, never once feeling human, never once feeling broken.

The Golden Baron griped the rails harder. He thought about Joshua, the man he had taken under his wing but for a short time. Joshua never knew the full extent of how The Marquis saw him, how The Marquis envied his resolve, his ability to survive in the darkest situations. Joshua conquered his fears and faced the world head-on. The Marquis wished more people were like Joshua, struggling to live, and thus, actually living.

It was those days on the front lines, during the time when Lafayette would meet with Washington and Thomas, that he felt the weight of hunger and the pain of loss. It was when he pushed out of France into Europe with his men and listened to the bullets striking the dirt that he understood the value of life, the uncertainty of tomorrow, the way life was meant to be.

Unlike Laffy, Joshua wasn't a coward, he didn't hide when he heard gunshots in France, he didn't run to safety when the world began gunning for him. Joshua Hill wasn't a coward; The Marquis and his people were cowards. They pretended nothing was happening. They changed their channels away from the news while men and women spilled blood in an attempt to create a better world. The Marquis admired Al Hamra, this Frea who spoke for him.

Joshua had sparked something within him, the want he had as a child came back like a fever or illness. Lafayette wanted to help the world again, help people again. He wanted to be a hero, but could he jeopardize his people for that dream?

The Marquis made this truth in his mind, that he would try to do *something*, for nothing good came from stagnant water.

"Is everything alright?" A mechanical, processed voice interrupted.

Gnat stood below the terrace, in the small garden Lafayette kept. The Marquis walked down to him. His helmeted friend watched the plants, scanning them. The boy scanned everything.

"What are they saying?" The Marquis asked.
Gnat looked up. "They're in pain, a good pain… They're growing pains."

The Marquis nodded and smiled. It was a good thing to hear.

"Let's plot a new course, Friend." The man smiled, "Let's go back to France, let's go to Whitecroftia."

Gnat straightened himself. If anyone were to guess, a look of excitement wore beneath his helmet. The man sprung off down the white roads of LeCeleste, darting between batches of people. In the distance the control center stood waiting. He bounded forth, climbing the long steps by sets of two. He reached with his hand and burst through the double doors.

The control center was a spherical building, the innards of a large globe. The building sat above empty air, held forth from the city by a ring of bone in which the dome neatly sat. It was the front of the ship, the head of LeCeleste. The interior was a turquoise blue, machinations beeped and swooped along the walls, providing holograms of nations and a small red dot, their location on the earth hovering over the Atlantic Ocean. In the center of this building was a hologram of LeCeleste, floating in an empty void surrounded by clouds and virtual birds. It was their stern, and Cid stood there with his hands around the image like a child guiding a paper airplane or model set. Many scientists buzzed about the globe, collecting data, organizing papers. They were Cid's flight crew, tasked with understanding weather conditions and bird migration patterns, careful not to endanger their golden home or the wildlife about it.

"Cid!" Gnat called, "turn the ship around, were going to The Crofts!"

Cid looked down through the glass flooring which held the stern in the center of the building. Gnat stood down by the entrance, his voice carrying around the metal walls. Cid, and the staff surrounding him murmured amongst each other. Cid looked back at his friend.

"Is that old man crazy?!" He shouted through the floor.

"There's a civil conflict occurring there, we can't go!" one scientist said, adjusting the clipboard in his hands.

"Why would The Marquis want that? He's clearly not in his right mind. We should wait until the war is resolved before we move back above Europe." Another agreed.

"Enough, all of you." Gnat demanded, "the Marquis knows what he's doing. Chart the nearest current and put it on the map. We're going to The Crofts. This is an order from the Baron!"

Cid looked at Gnat, first with disdain, then a twinge of admiration and pride. "I want all readings on my vector, storms and Russian satellite radars, you know the drill." He ordered his crew, turning back to his virtual ship.

The scientists resumed their hustle, grumbling to themselves. To them, the Marquis always had something childish in the back of his mind, and this was another one of his antics. Nevertheless, they had their orders, and never dreamt their king was aiming to conquer Whitecroft's estate.

The Marquis stood on his balcony as the citizens collected below, wondering why the city began to turn. He watched all of them gather before addressing them.

"You are all wondering why we are heading the other direction." The Marquis began. The crowd murmured, nodding. A single "yes" from a courageous man was shouted from the back of the masses. The crowd shifted in their fine clothes and whispered amongst themselves, nervous.

"You're wondering if we are going to be safe…" The Marquis continued. "… we will not be safe."

The crowd grew louder in disbelief, hushing ensued from those intent on hearing their baron out. They negotiated socially against rioting.

"I have watched generation and generation go by, watched them sit on their golden chairs eating their delicacies… I have watched them eat, and I have eaten. I've thrown away countless plates of food without a thought for the people below us starving.

Look around you, yes, look around. We ride the heavens on limitless energy, we touch the skies with a simple stretch of our hands and we have never gone wanting."

The crowd nodded and smiled; they were amazing in their own eyes. They were the prime examples of peace and prosperity. They smiled and chuckled until their baron began to cry.

"We are a foolish, ignorant people! We play an uncaring god against men who squalor in the dirt without ceasing, trying to make ends meet! We think we are better than them, but we are the ones who need help! We are dying! We are sinning! We can't continue to live our lives like this!

We are going to Baron Whitecroft's doorstep and reminding ourselves what it means to be human, what it means to carry others! We should be down there helping, leaving our footprints on the sands of time!"

The crowd continued to grumble. Gnat watched the Marquis from below. The two met eyes, and the soldier encouraged his king to continue.

"We need to be there for our fellow man. We need to break out of our prison because we aren't living! We have to wake up our soul-less hearts and care about our fellow human race! I'm tired of playing the perfect king! I'm tired of giving you everything you want when you should be out in the world reaching for your own futures with your own arms! Every one of you has to take hold of your dreams and never let it go! I cannot protect you any longer, I refuse to leave you in your nest, in your tree, forgetting what it means to fly, to be truly free! We have to stop serving ourselves! We need hearts if we want to live! We need to go out, and we need to let people in! We have to save people! God made us to be heroes, not heathens!"

There was a silence over the city, no one cheered or nodded their heads. The people simply stood. Lafayette didn't expect them to erupt in admiration for his words. He didn't want them to. He wiped his eyes; his arms shook. Lafayette's voice quivered, it was the first time his citizens saw him break composure, the first time ever.

"Each and every one of you needs to make the decision for yourself. If you don't wish to join me then feel free to hide inside your homes. Evil cannot reach you there. But if you are strong enough, and if you are as disgusted as I am watching the world shake on the precipice of chaos. Then help me now or once the war is over. Help me end this tyranny and repair what these people have lost."

The Marquis paused before finishing: "We'll be in The Crofts by the end of the week…"

The Marquis swiveled around and left the crowd to think amongst themselves. Opening the doors to his house, he found himself passing by the television again. He had forgotten to turn it off, but that was okay. He uncorked a bottle of wine and watched from the corner three revolutionary leaders, three girls, who stood before the farmers with the world in their hands.

"Life is certainly more than finding happiness... Joshua taught me that." Elizabeth chimed, sitting in an armchair before him.

The dark room was illuminated only by the TV. She looked comfortable, considering she had just broken into a house. The Marquis turned to her, she sat impressively on *his* chair, commanding the room.

"Why are you here?" The Marquis asked solemnly from the corner.
"Because you're right." Elizabeth sighed. "We can't hide from the world any longer."

The Marquis chuckled bitterly, taking a large gulp from his glass. "Connor always had that effect on people. He made you think anything was possible, that nothing was beyond repair. He still doesn't think he's Mr. Shaw, does he?"

"He doesn't need to be, not anymore." Elizabeth replied, she looked at her lap for a moment before saying something that had been on her mind for months.

"He's so much better than Connor ever was. It's one thing for a loving man to save others; it's quite more for a man who hates to do the same."

Part 9/Rope

Joan stared at Frea in frustration. The woman stood there in silence atop Hiker's Folly. The fields below were dented from mortar rounds and grenades, the once fertile soil now fine and lifeless. The fences were torn down, the buildings made holy by bullets. Taverns burned in the distances where Baron's search parties roamed, looking for stragglers behind an ever-changing warfront. They had retaliated well into the night, pushing back the rebels a few miles. This concern for stability kept Frea's hand from pointing to the Baron's estate, poking above the leafless tree line.

"There," She aimed, "set up a checkpoint there."

"Are you sure?" Joan asked through grinding teeth.

"Yes, I can see it, tomorrow there will be a dispatch there." Frea smiled thinly, her posture still akin to royalty.

Joan shrugged, she was never wrong, but that didn't keep her from hating the Victorian woman. Frea seemed timid on the battlefront, always waiting, never striking large targets. She was timid, Joan wanted her to move the front, push to the estate and end the bloodshed. She once asked Frea to send their army into the castle's bowels and recalled her cryptic answer; whenever Joan prodded her to act, to take more drastic steps, she always responded with the same slogan.

You'll know when the time has come, when the second sun crosses the sky, and right hand of the gods counts the time.

Joan always thought she had meant two days, but it had been yet another month. The Baron was becoming smarter, her men faster and more-deadly. Frea had scraped Joan's supply runs for the remainder of the year and prevented the rebels from capturing grains. They began to starve, rationing their days to single meals in a vain attempt to survive.

Frea was killing them.

Joan leapt from the rock and grappled down, she only applied tension the last hundred feet, slowing herself enough to release with a thud and a forward roll. She motioned for her waiting hunters to follow, rising enough to creep along the surface. They began to shuffle through the night, moving from position to position, weary of enemy riflemen. They could be anywhere, hiding in dents or the back of exploded vehicles. The enemy ghillies were perfectly still the fields, you only saw them during the muzzle flash. If you ever saw or heard the rifle fire, you couldn't move. You could only pray that the sniper was far enough away to miss.

Joan crossed over the stream and laid on the other end of the field. She spied something, something small, something quick. It moved through the fields like a tiny fox. Joan motioned her group to a halt and they waited, counting their heartbeats until the moving shadow passed the field.

"Must've been the shadow of a buzzard, they've taken to feeding at night." The man on her right whispered.

Joan nodded, and started across the next field.

It was a long winter, the blood began to stick under the dead stalks, becoming one with the permafrost. Joan lifted her boots, careful not to make a sound on the crunching, slick ground. Crunching the snow was the one mistake she could count on. The Baron's men still wore their plate armor which weighed them into the ground, ensuring the noise beneath their boots, a signature crunch, like the snapping of beaks. It told Joan exactly where they were and gave her an advantage over her adversary.

Forward, Joan looked over a small stack of bodies, the only true barriers left in the flat warzone. People made too many mistakes, she lost too many men who moved to a house instead of behind a corpse. The ghillies would fire and the bullet would rip through the thin wood. If the bullet didn't kill them, the wood shrapnel was sure to shred their skin. They would spend the rest of their months in a bed, waiting for the least of the rations, their leg infected with gangrene.

Forward. The worst part was the mercy killing, watching a man cry for help in the middle of a field, the bullets flying past him, begging for the pain to end. Be it the fool who tripped on a land mine or the fool that crouched too high. Joan would always close her eyes before letting her arrow go. She thought she was doing them a favor.

Forward, and to the left, under the cover of another stream, a path leading to their new destination, they continued. Maybe the worst part was watching the slow deaths. With Dutch gone, the black-market shipments had ceased, there was no food left outside of grains. Those who couldn't help were fed the least. It couldn't be helped, there was not enough food each day. That was the slow death, when farmers watched their friends shrink a little every day until one evening you're on task and hear that they passed on in their sleep, died hungry, wondering why there weren't enough buzzards in the sky.

The buzzards ate their fill and moved on. Even they knew when the dead were too much.

Joan tracked along until she stumbled upon a dim light. It was a camp of guards, a band of twelve men by a fire, stoking the flame. They ate gingerbread and poured canned cheese in their mouths. They laughed quietly.

Joan slowly inched forth, each second scaling an inch closer, an inch closer. It took them minutes to become close enough about the guards. They hid in the shadows of the soldier's bodies which were cast by the fire. This is why you never use light, Joan thought, it pampers the eyes.

Joan prepared to kill again and raised her hand to strike. Her men drew their bows, and she almost descended her blade upon the first victim. Before she could, she hesitated. She stopped. She listened.

"Yeah, he's still down there."

"No piss. The jailers don't feed him enough. I'm surprised he hasn't keeled over. Strong guy, can hear him talking to himself when I'm on jail duty."

"Yeah, Joshua Hill, the one that killed the Baron's wed."

"No Piss."

"No Piss."

"I heard Whitecroft is going to pull him out soon. She's probably going to torture him again, try to break him so that he'll stop clinging to his life. But damn, that man is like a mummy, both inside and out. I never thought such a dark person like him would last so long. It's the unhappy ones that die first, you know?"

"No piss."

"No piss."

There was a grumble, a sound of hunger. One of Joan's hunters reached for their stomach, hunger pains, folding him over. He bit his tongue, struggled not to make another noise, but the guards already heard. They rose from their seats.

"The hell was that?"

Joan closed her hand.

Arrows flew forth from the darkness, each meeting their mark precisely through the eye slot in their helmets. The arrows struck deep into their brains and they fell dead instantly. All of them were dead but for two. The first person was Joan's target, she was still in his shadow. Joan quickly moved forth to place her knife firmly into his lower spine. It severed his nerves.

Dead.

However, the second target loomed behind her and not one hunter had the shot. Joan fell back under the weight of the heavy hunter she had killed and was pinned beneath him.

Joan looked up to see the enemy's sword descending. She flailed, but she couldn't toss the body off her to save herself. In that moment a small shadow loomed from the thin canopy, a vulture, a dog, a cougar that sailed down into the light in a brown blur.

The fur ball opened its mouth and closed its jaw about the plume that sat colorfully on the knight's helmet. The soldier's head lurched to the side under the newfound weight, his weapon brushing Joan's sternum. As the soldier twisted about, he tumbled over the log where he once sat.

Sach stood and ripped the helmet off the guard's face, sinking his teeth into his foe's neck. The blood gurgled and dripped to the ground, the rodent growling and shaking the man until he was still.

Dead.

This was the first time Joan had seen a soldier without his helmet on. She glanced in horror. The men all knelt down to remove the enemy helmets, they were all the same.

None of the fallen knights were human. They stared with their hollow eyes, a flat, ugly humanoid, something between man and lizard. Their skin was soft but dry. Small flakes of skin fell off their exposed necks. They were shedding.

What was this monstrosity, why were they here, and how did Whitecroft get them? This phenomenon explained why Whitecroft's numbers hadn't dwindled over the past few months. She was, at the very least, hiring her troops from another area. But this was a different world altogether, and Joan knew Joshua very well.

In Joshua's battles, magic was always involved.

Joan clutched her chest, the blade left only a gash between her breasts. She held up her hand and immediately a hunter came beside her. He moved her hands and began to pour a small pouch of alcohol into her wound. They couldn't take any chances, especially when their enemy never cleaned their weapons. The medic helped Joan to the floor, sitting her as she winced in pain.

While she was being treated, Sach began to hobble over but was halted by an arrow striking at his feet. It was a warning shot. Joan waved her team off frantically. "He's okay, he's okay!" She hissed.

Sach continued on all fours, lower to the ground this time.

"Where the hell have you been?" Joan coughed, "We couldn't find you after Dutch's cavern was burned down."

"I was running errands for Ms. Hammond. I returned long after everyone was gone. I found Mrs. Hammond's body, burned to a crisp... I couldn't leave her laying there. After I buried her behind the house I wandered around. I didn't know what to do, but I'm here now." Sach frowned, a beady tear dropping from his fur.

He stood there with a salute, his chest puffed. "Reporting for duty, Joan."

Joan nodded, it was good to have him back. Tomorrow morning, they would have to prepare an ambush. She leaned and lay back on a log. Joan nodded once more, and her elite went to work stacking the bodies for barricades.

Joshua listened as another patrol approached. He watched them, expecting them to pass. They didn't, instead they beat the bars of his cell with their steel gloves.

"Away from the door prisoner 53!" One shouted, "Lay on the ground with your legs apart!"

Joshua laughed hysterically. They wouldn't enter until he did, so he obeyed. The main guard slowly turned the key to his gate.

"I wonder what they want with you." Symeon said.

Joshua giggled.

"No talking, prisoner, and stay down!" The guard shouted, opening the door. But Joshua rose to his feet. Joshua rushed forward and slammed his shoulder into the first guard, knocking him against the far wall outside his cell. The guards drew their bludgeons and struck Joshua repeatedly across his back.

Joshua laughed beneath the pain, he felt something, he could still feel something. Oh, how the pain was better than waiting in a cell. The young man twirled about and landed his stock against the second guard who grunted. But the wood cuffs would do no harm to the iron clad man. The guard quickly seized Joshua's hands and struck him on this shoulder.

"Stop laughing!" The guard ordered, continuing to beat Joshua. "Stop laughing, stop laughing, stop laughing!"

They all beat Joshua until he stopped laughing. He lay on the ground, waiting, he tried his best to not to laugh, but it was difficult. They were all going for a walk, which was good for Al Hamra's health. Joshua had cabin fever.

The guards drug Joshua by the leg along the rigid ground, leading him to Whitecroft. It was through a series of tunnels that Symeon followed them, past doors and doors of prisoners, each of them cackling, whispering to themselves.

"Away from the doors!" The jailers shouted, beating at their fingers, beating at their cages.

Symeon couldn't protest his anxiety about Joshua. The first few weeks were painful enough. Every moment and chance he got he would appear to talk to the American. Joshua would smile, say something in response, offer knowledge on the subject where he could, but around the second month he said less and less, reverting to moans, small words or incoherent phrases. He didn't talk back to Symeon, he began to talk through Symeon. Now, four months in, Joshua never talked, never looked his comrade in the eye, never reacted to anything he said. It was as if Symeon didn't exist. Even worse, it was as if Joshua didn't exist.

"Have you lost your mind, boy?" Symeon asked, watching as they began to drag him through the entrance.

The entrance of the cave was carved in ancient letters. The cave led to a large cellar that was emptied. But one piece of furniture still hung on the far wall, alone and haunting. The painting was grotesque, a horizontal image of men and woman walking in a parade of torches and pikes. The painting abused the colors green and red. In the center, whether it was being chased or followed, was a man with three eyes that coddled a centipede between its fingers. The man had the face of a fruit bat, and the furry body of an ape.

The carving sat neatly in the room so that the beast could watch those who would come, and who would leave. Symeon wondered why anybody would enjoy such a painting. It was ungodly, amateur. But as he walked from its left to its right, passing with Joshua to the stairs, the eyes seemed to follow him, the whole head seemed to swivel. Before the painting was a large bucket of unknown contents. Something floated inside of it like a cucumber inside a pitcher of water.

Joshua never responded to Symeon's question. The young man stared at the ceiling, the marvelous ceiling. It was the first time he saw architecture in four months. He forgot how mathematical it was, not that he remembered basic arithmetic at all.

The guards twisted Joshua around and up the staircase. At the top of the nest floor, Joshua would hear the sound of a woman and a hiss. Joshua glanced up once he emerged from the stairwell to find the Baron before him. Whitecroft didn't walk, she was held in the hands of a lizard man. The Lizard carried her shriveled body like Joshua once carried Elizabeth a long time ago. She watched him as she opened her mouth to speak. Her voice was weak.

"All of this was because of you." She snarled and coughed, a twinge of sadness in her tone. "My kingdom is falling all because of you."

Whitecroft was moved to her throne and placed there like a rolled shirt in a moving box. Behind her giant throne, her marvelous incandescence watched down from the mural. The walls about the atrium were spattered in blood. From the stone rafters, farmers and citizens and soldiers hung, their blood dripping to the stone, soaking the purple carpet, wetting Joshua's back.

Joshua could see a dried stain underneath the thin pools, a small blotch of sanguine under a thin film of crimson. There was Dutch's blood, the first of the martyrs. It had dried long before this artistic barbarity began.

When did this hell begin, and did he truly cause this? Joshua thought, hell must have begun once he stepped into his apartment, returning from paradise, running from Elizabeth and the feelings in his heart. Maybe hell began when he chased his director through the streets and locked eyes with the yellow devil himself. When he watched his own leader die, his own, small, king. Maybe hell began when Baron Glass traded him like a business card. Did it really matter now? Was any of it worth it?

The farmers believed they could overcome their obstacles, empowered by the promise of a new king, a new baron. Was he that king? Did he even want to be? Joshua wanted to hand the mantle to Dutch, but Dutch was gone.

Joshua was placed on his knees in the center of the room. The baron rubbed her forearm in anticipation, a toothy smile creasing through her lips. Joshua looked at the wall behind her. She had adorned her throne, redecorated her hall with her own soldiers who failed her. They were scattered in a mound behind her, pinned on their own swords. Those who couldn't be thrown to the top of these mounds were pinned to the walls, hanging like butterflies in a collector's box. Perhaps this is how she created her army of lizards, and why there were so many to be found. She sacrificed her humans for monsters, hoping it would gain her victory over the rebellion.

Was she this desperate to quench her opposition, or did she have this in mind long before Joshua was given over from Baron Glass?

She was mad, he was mad, it made sense to the both of them in that small world to be mad. In those last moments, it was okay to be at least flustered.

Yes, Joshua thought. For Whitecroft, all began when Joshua killed her lover. Joshua had created her. Joshua's first child was born of an emptiness, born of a series of bullets which changed their lives forever. They both spiraled into the heart of despair. Joshua, plagued by nightmares and the children he passed, knowing he ended lives just like theirs. Whitecroft, plagued by cold beds in the night, waking every morning alone in this giant estate.

The Marquis was right, people were evil. People were broken.

Was any of this worth it? Joshua asked himself, again and again.

"When your friends come for me, they'll look first on your rotting body!" Whitecroft cackled. "You'll hang here in the center, right at the top of the archway and the world will know that 'Al Hamra' is dead! You'll be forgotten, Joshua Hill, and I will never take you down from that place, so rot! Rot like your friends will! Rot like Dutch rotted! Rot, rot, rot, rot!"

Whitecroft coughed in her fervor, her small body fidgeting under the weight of her own words. It was hard for Joshua to tell if she had lungs or not, that was all he thought about. He giggled.

Joshua felt the noose hang down and tighten around his neck. Above, a ceremonial sword was pinned neatly into the wall, the rope cascading from it. The guard's lifted him higher and higher and higher until he stood on a tall platform overlooking the carnal vestibule. Joshua waited for the floor to fall, so that his neck might be snapped. Unlike the first time he was there, he wasn't holding on to hope. Neither Joan, nor Frea, nor Elizabeth would be there to rescue him. He couldn't do anything to prevent his death.

Joshua imagined all the ways he could have died, he imagined all the ways he died in his dreams. Out of all the dreams and fantasies he had of death. He thought this one to be the most beautiful. At least Whitecroft, who continued to laugh, could have her closure. Maybe through death, he could save her too.

Joshua almost smiled as the floor gave way. He looked down at the moving gallows, and back to the feeble, broken woman in the stone throne. Either way, he had won. He was finally about to die.

"Fool," Al Hamra whispered.

The rope pulled tight and Whitecroft worshiped the scene she had created.

Frea smiled grimly as LeCeleste broke through the clouds. It shined against the sun, its brassy shell casting large uneven spotlights over the estate. Although a hundred miles away, the sky city could be seen in every detail. It floated there proudly, waiting in anticipation for its virgin battle.

Frea looked at her farmers. They approached her from the tower where she stood, marveling at the sight.

"Be ready!" She cried, the once quiet lady louder than ever before, vibrant. Her cheeks blushed. "Rally the others!"

The farmers nodded and raced off down the spiraling staircase. Lilith stood beside the Elizabethan lady and handed her a red flare gun. She held it above her head and fired.

Joan looked up from the trees to see the red marker streak across the sky before bursting into a lovely radiance. Following the arc, Joan could see something shimmering above. Joan moved out of the river bed to behold a ship, a behemoth, that floated above the land. She watched the reflection of the flare on its belly, reflecting the light back to the earth. She rose from her place with her men. It was the signal. It was time to take the castle.

"It's the second sun!" Joan exclaimed, "The second sun!"

"What the hell are you talking about?" Sach asked, moving towards her.

"It's time! It's time to end the war!" Joan shouted, her men rising from their stupors.

Sach stood into their camp and looted a bowie knife from a nearby corpse. He lifted it forward to Joan like a sword.

"Let's do this!" He snarled, "Let's free Joshua!"

Joan sprinted forth from the stream with her band in tow. They ran fiercely to meet the others at the front line. They ran fiercely to meet their king. For the first time in months, Joan felt alive. The end was near, they would be united again, Joan and Joshua, just like in the beginning. It didn't take long before the squad met resistance. But full of new life they sprinted into the explosions and upturned dirt, drawing their bows and firing. They were relentless in their charge, swiftly dispatching rouge enemy squads as they went, miraculously bypassing sniper rounds.

The Marquis watched the red bullet soar into the sky. A warning sign, he thought, an announcement of their arrival. He clutched a rope in his hands, watching the Baron's men collect *en masse* around the estate.

Whitecroft was ready to repel their attacks, all of them, if need be.

The Last Baron looked back at his friends, half of the citizens of LeCeleste hung beside him about the hull of their city, ready to rappel. They were armed with old flintlocks and bronze swords. They were ready to fall into their foe, clash so they might learn what it meant to err, to learn what it meant to save a life. The Marquis smiled, proud of his family, proud of his home.

Gnat counted the men, their numbers reached eight hundred and still more flocked outdoors. After the Baron's losses, he expected there to be much less. How could she have raised such an army at a moment's notice? Something was wrong about them, their hearts stood on the right sides of their chests, their gait misplaced, their spines crooked and bent inside their tin cans.

"Sir!" Gnat called out over wind, "These are not humans!"

The Marquis nodded in understanding, it did not change the situation.

"Let's hope they still die like mortals then!" He shouted back over the wind.

Gnat rolled his eyes. Unlike his immortal captain, he had a life to lose.

"We can still turn back, boss." Cid called through the intercoms, "the media hasn't picked up on us yet."

The Marquis pondered the words. He looked at his ragtag band of citizens, he watched the explosions outside the compound. Small dots began to collect, bright streaks of bullets stretching across the fields. The people began to move closer, moving slowly, zigzagging to their hovels, making headway to the estate.

Did they know LeCeleste would arrive, and charge at this opportune time? The Marquis thought. *Did they aim to take the estate and his floating fortress? Or did someone inside contact them about their arrival?*

Elizabeth had left weeks before, bound to her duty as a witch. But it wasn't impossible.

"No!" Lafayette bellowed, "We are no longer the heartless!"

Laffy raised his sword above his head, his family followed suit. They let go of their coiled ropes and let the strands fall to the roof of the estate.

The Marquis was the first to descend.

Frea marched with her people to the estate. Altogether, the fighters numbered a few hundred. Bullets flew through the air and all but Frea took cover along the ground, crawling from battlement to battlement, body pile to body pile.

Frea clasped her right hand around a long spear, a scarlet red flag flowed from the pole, waving in the air as she stole forth. The bullets ripped past her, seemingly bending before they could strike. She walked straight into the fray, the empty space between makeshift trenches.

"Left side!" Joan screamed, pointing to a small, displaced band of Whitecroftian lizard guards. They knelt there with no regard for safety, their armor deflecting oncoming fire. Joan leaned about with her bow, killing one with a well-placed shot at the belt. She quickly rotated back into the human barricade as a stream of bullets flew by. It would be a slow advancement, but they were cleverly gaining ground.

Joan's elite spread themselves along the field, slaying the monsters as they approached with their bows trained keenly.

Frea stood paces before her troops and raised the flag to wave in the sky. The long cloth rippled triumphantly, ordering her men to fire upon the emerging army. Their enemy bore large claymores in Jacksonian fashion, steadily approaching their positions. In a flurry of bullets, the troops began to fall. Thankfully, Joan had stolen a few armor piercing bullets from shipments and storehouses. Frea's large army allowed Joan to run about the battlefield, silently whittling their numbers and surrounding their foe on two fronts.

The farmers rose from their positions and began to fire at the oncoming enemy. The noise from their rifles quickly aggravated their oppressors. The enemy shifted their movements left of the battle field. Joan quickly rushed around them, her hunters circling around to puncture the lizards from behind. They swung towards the gate and charged through as the first battalion moved away from the entrance. The bullets flied, and Joan rose her knee into a guard's chest as she entered the courtyard, quickly rolling along the ground and lifting the lizard's rifle. She sprayed the bullets from her waist, spading the troops before her in a fan. Sach leaped from her back and quickly vanished through the crowded armada of legs. As he ran, he brought his knife to the Achilles tendons of his enemies, leaving his foes crawling on the ground, helpless.

Frea watched as Joan slipped through the created opening. They would be dividing the armies in two. From there, the farmers would be responsible for handling all enemies outside the gate while the officers and the elites fought closely with those inside the walls. It was time for Frea to follow suit. The lady unclasped her dress and stole forth. In the blink of an eye she was gone, leaving Lilith in the protection of the farmers. The little girl blew her whistle, the sound of the second phase.

Beneath the ground, hidden under a sheet of rotting wheat, the Dutchmen assassins emerged beneath the battle. The enemy line was broken as men tripped into their traps and were swiftly behead by the assassins. The Farmers continued to fire, slowly defeating the horde of guards who faced in every which direction, panicking while the assassins danced in their midst. The assassins buckled and flew through the long weapons, their adversaries too slow to cleave them. They further divided the army, pushing half of the outside force back towards the wall.

Lilith commanded her regiment well and ordered her men to charge. The farmers fixed their bayonets and fired whilst moving forward. Their bullets sundered the enemy. Amidst the commotion, many farmers, assassins, and soldiers died, furthering the dreams and ambitions of others. They formed the soil and wrote the history which Lilith would walk upon as she grew up. She was born in this land, and this is where she would stay.

Lilith trudged behind her troops, careful not to die. As the tactician, she was the most important unit, the king on the chessboard.

The Marquis saw the combat from the roof of the estate, Whitecroft's stronghold was breached by a band of bow-wielding warriors. But that small group was not enough to hold the enemy back from the entrance. He watched as they struggled and fell against the sheer numbers of fiends.

Gnat fired his gun upon the lizards below, clustering his rounds in the kinks of their armor. He was not the most accurate shooter, unlike Reeves had been, but their enemy wasn't a giant landscaping monster. Gnat wouldn't fall to something so small and insignificant as a lizard. The soldier led his fellow citizens in their volleys, directing their fire where enemies were thickest along the ground. He was certain he could protect his friends. He was certain he would prevail.

The King of the Golden City ran forth from the roof where his men sniped and fell down into the small pocket where the red-haired maiden, whom he had seen on tv, deftly dispatched another guard. The Marquis landed and buckled under the impact. He moaned, slowly rising behind her. It wasn't quite the entrance he was expecting, but it would have to do.

Joan twisted about to punch a hole in the Marquis' face, but his hand clasped around the arrow in hers, stopping its momentum.

"Don't worry," the sky king smiled, "we're here for the Baron too."

The Marquis released his hand about the arrow and Joan placed it back against her string. The Marquis continued to smile, pressing his back to Joan's.

Joan turned her back to The Marquis. She needed to focus on saving Joshua. The Marquis slashed about, unsheathing his weapon, a beautiful gilded handle on a simple blade. It flowed about striking his enemies down. He stayed at Joan's back, making sure no one would overtake her.

At the entrance, Frea bustled through with the confidence of a queen. She was late to the fray. She smirked as foes neared her, she didn't raise her hands. Whitecroft's lackeys struck down their blades upon her head, but instead, were struck down, an invisible force of death reversing the cause and effect. Whomever looked to harm her would be harmed.

The girl paused and stood at the entrance, embedding her flag into the ground. Lilith's Dutchmen rushed through from behind the opening she created. They had vanquished their half of the army and came crashing through the enemy lines, leaping over dead bodies and plunging their blades between the guard's necks.

Frea stood watch, waiting for the end which would soon come.

The conflict continued, and many lives were given. Once Lilith's farmers had succeeded in eliminating the outside forces, she ordered them to return to their homes. They were no longer needed. Lilith followed them as well. She had no need to see what would become of Whitecroft, she should hide away with her pawns, so that she might be safe.

The Marquis sank his sword into the last foe, the lizard hissed and crumpled to the ground among its fellow beasts. The Golden King wiped his face free of blood and proceeded to bless his enemy with a small prayer. Even though he knew not his foe, he wouldn't wish hell upon them.

As he turned back he looked at the huntress who shook in rage and anticipation.

Joan paced in front of the doors.

"We need to prepare!" She shouted. "We don't know how many more there are inside! Stock up on bullets, grab a sword. We storm the palace in five minutes!"

Gnat motioned for the citizens of LeCeleste to climb back to their homes. They had done well and were no longer needed. In the house below them, only those worthy enough should enter. The soldier did not want to crowd the entrance with bodies, only to be slaughtered. They needed the best, and only the best. The Russian climbed down from the roof and watched The Marquis close the eyes of the fallen, praising them for their willingness to die for others. Frea watched the doors, a thin smile on her face. Sach lay by her feet, grumbling.

"This is impossible," He whined, "She could be on the other side with a rocket launcher, or another hundred of these creeps!"

"If you don't want to die, you can leave!" Joan hissed, her arms shaking. "I'm going to go find Joshua and he's going to kill Whitecroft! That's the way it's supposed to be!"

"I am also here for Joshua." The Marquis chimed, looking up from his ritual at Joan.

Joan looked at him, her eyes stern and cold, "It's not that I'm not thankful for your help, but what business do you have with Josh?" She puffed.

"I have come to help, need there be any other reason?" The Marquis defended.

Joan chided The Marquis with her eyes. She felt that he had other intentions, but for now, she shouldn't worry for more than one thing.

"He's in the prison somewhere in the compound." Joan huffed. "We need to find him before we confront Whitecroft."

"Whitecroft is right behind those doors," Gnat added, the faintest heartbeat on his sensors. "At the least, we should occupy her time while someone fetches him."

"There is no need to fetch Joshua," Frea smiled, her face returning to her typical sly gravitas. "He hasn't been in the prison for quite some time."

"Damnit!" Joan spat, moving to Frea and putting an arrow against her neck. "You better not have done anything! You left when you could've saved us. You could have saved Dutch's friends, my friends!"

"Hey! Let's not have a cat fight. I hate cats." Sach piped, but turned hypocritically to the mage as well, "Where's Joshua, you hag!?"

Frea smiled, she didn't answer, but her eyes fixed on the doors to Whitecroft's mansion.

Joan looked at the large doors in front of them. She was scared.

The doors were surrounded with a small arcing window. Inside a thin shadow swung back and forth.

Joan ran to the doors and kicked them. They didn't open. She tried the handle. It was locked.

"God!" She cried, "Open, damn you, open!"

The Marquis watched her fight the inanimate object. He closed his eyes, unable to watch her claw at the wood, her fingers beginning to bleed.

What have you done, Joshua? He thought.

"Open! Open! Open!" Joan screamed, punching the door and turning back to those in the courtyard. "Will any of you help me! Please?!"

Gnat approached Joan but didn't help her. Instead, he grabbed her by the arms and held her still, hugging her like a bear while she kicked and sobbed.

"Open the doors! Open the doors!" She begged, tears streaming down her eyes. "He's alive! Oh God, he has to be alive!"

The Marquis moved to the doors and placed his sword between them. He leveraged his body about the seam, preparing to pry it open. The immortal captain pulled with all his might but in the end, it was his sword that broke, and not the locks.

"Gunpowder, gas?! Anyone!?" He barked, his worries surfacing, his countenance fading. "Anyone!? A bomb, anything!?"

The wake shook their heads. They hadn't the tools to open their bullets and gunpowder never did much by itself.

Joan continued to cry, a muffled sound, rasp and breaking. Sach stared at his feet. The Marquis ran his hands through his hair again and turned to the door. This time, he began to kick it.

"Open up Whitecroft!" He screamed, "Open, damn you!"

This continued, the silence, the sorrow. Until, the door clicked.

The large wooden door began to open, at first it shuddered, then it chimed in its gears like a music box, then, it whined. The Marquis looked forward at his host, the last of the serpentine men.

"Hello, guestsss." The serpent hissed, its body twisting camouflage between green and the purplish red carpet beneath him. This lizard was a chameleon.

As the doors continued to open, more of Whitechapel's morbid collection was ready to be witnessed. The morbid interior design was much to take in.

The Marquis looked at the beast and detached the knife from his belt. As the serpent bowed in welcome, Laffy descended his blade upon the its neck and watched its head roll along the floor, its forked tongue jutting out. The Marquis kicked it into the corner and he marched into the room alone. The others had not yet followed.

The Marquis quickly stopped and fell on his knees. He looked up at the next set of arches which stemmed from the pillars. He stayed there for a moment, unable to move.

Joan broke free of Gnat's constriction and ran into the mansion. The others followed, leaving no one to guard outside. She wiped her eyes, unable to see. But as her vision focused, there she saw Joshua.

Joshua hung from the rafters above them.

The band of friends stood there in silence. Joan fell to her face, she didn't cry anymore, she hadn't the energy. All of their pain and suffering, all of the lives she took led to an empty dream.

"Tragic, isn't it." Whitecroft mockingly pouted from her throne at the end of the room. "All you ever wanted ripped from you in an instant. That's how I felt. Now you feel it too, hmm? Tell me you feel it, little girl. He's gone, I strung him there days ago. I haven't left this chair since. I've just been watching him and watching him, swing, swing, swing. Swing,

swing, swing, I knew he had it coming, he was a killer, didn't you know?"

"Shut up!" Joan screamed. "Shut up, shut up, shut up!"

The Marquis rose from his knees and looked down the hall at Whitecroft. He poised his knife forward like a rapier.

"It's time to end you, Whitecroft. I don't know if you will be the first death I enjoy, but your tyranny is at its end."

"You think you can end me!?" Whitecroft laughed. "You think I'm alone?! Let me tell you a little secret. I built this estate here because of the caverns underneath, as a girl I made a deal with someone I found down there. I gave him bodies, I gave him minds, I adorned my walls for its pleasure with the flesh of my friends and family, and now, in my hour of need it will defend me!"

Whitecroft laughed as the ground began to bellow. The caverns below almost breathed life through the building. The group listened as this breath crescendoed into an animistic howl which reverberated off the walls. The room began to grow dimmer although the sun did not set.

The rays of ambient light behind Whitecroft, her mural of stained glass was quickly covered on the other side. A shadow stretching over the window. No, it was not a shadow, it was a color. The glass had begun to change to a sickly purple hue which prevented the light from filtering in. The image of young Whitecroft began to move, contort. The eyes began to follow them.

The glass was alive.

The Mural unpinned its body painfully and moved forth from the wall leaving the window a plain violet shade. Its arms and torso become thick, more than two dimensional. It hunched over Whitecroft on all fours, an image of herself, webbed together by mastic like tendons and muscles.

Whitecroft sat there grinning, impressed with herself. This was her last champion, gifted to her by the devil himself. She would not let him down, she would continue her rule.

The Glass swiped its hand through the air before Joshua's friends, launching glass missiles from its palms. The Marquis swept forth and raised his arm to protect Joan whom had trouble moving under the weight of her heart. The glass punctured along his side and he grunted. He turned back to look at Joan, at his friends, pulling the stakes from his body.

"Don't just stand there!" He barked, his body re-stitching itself in glowing golden wire, he looked like an angel, like Gabriel or Michael had joined them in their hour of need. "We have to fight!"

Joan nodded and notched her bow, beginning to find the energy she needed to fight. If she couldn't save Joshua, she would avenge him. Joan fired a volley of arrows over the Gold King's shoulder. The arrows loomed into the creature, leaving only small cracks on the glass. Joan grimaced, and sprinted around the vestibule.

"Circle around it!" She called, sliding through the bloodied floors and stopping behind a column.

Frea watched as the rest charged forth. They held their weapons to the sky in a battle cry, bold and reckless. The beast lashed about, toppling columns, upturning tiles. The small band of miscreants were trying to salvage whatever they could of their rebellion. They were fierce heroes, each and every one of them, willing to go where others wouldn't and willing to stay where others left. She watched them strike the beast with their steel, their blades barely chipping the furnaced sand.

Where The Mural stood, no one could reach the Baron, as it hovered over her like a shield. Gnat and Joan had tried many times to sneak an arrow or a bullet in, but they were soon blocked by the shifting sculpture. It was a lean adversary, a surrealist depiction of the younger Whitecroft who once had a reason for kindness.

Frea did not pretend to understand the Baron's intentions, the reason she let them in the building, the reason she sacrificed her men like goats and starved her people.

Regarding herself, Frea's inaptitude to fight was the nature she imposed upon her lifestyle. She could be a champion over the foes and have saved many people, but it would not have been the course the war should have taken. She could see it there like a far-off dream for she was a seer and held the ability to understand the course things can and might take. Frea chose the stream with the highest probability of success and rowed her comrades through the mouth of the beast. Now, all she had to do was wait for the dice to roll.

Frea placed herself exactly in the center of the opened doors. Waiting for the battle to end, waiting for her next role.

The battle continued in the foreground. Frea's pawns evading endlessly the multitude of the enemy's blows. They struggled, pushed back into corners and struck into the floor only to rise up again with the same vigor as when they had begun. They would not allow themselves to fall before the beast. They would fight not only for their survival, as Laffy had originally thought and tutored, but for the survival of others, even at the cost of their lives.

The Marquis slid beside Joan and let the glass spears pierce his body again. The whole ordeal had him playing a human shield. All those present but Gnat and he were used to fighting such mythical creatures. Laffy huffed and removed the glass from his body with a shout of fervor. Joan watched a golden light pour out of his wound and slowly seal it shut. He was immortal, but his energy was waning.

"We need to be more precise!" The Marquis told the huntress. "Tell everyone to aim at one point, take away the mastic, the glass is too thick! We all need to aim at the same place if we're going to do any real harm."

Joan nodded. "I'll focus everyone on the left leg, can you distract him?"

The Marquis replied dryly, "Yeah, I'll give it what it wants."

Joan ran off through the room, leaping over broken pillars to spread the word.

The Marquis dropped his knife and rose his hands. "Hey!" He shouted. "Right here!"

The Beast looked over to him in curiosity. There on its right stood a velvet man with no defenses. It took its opportunity and twisted at the waist, slamming its palm down upon Lafayette. Lafayette was crushed beneath the weight, forced to the ground under the smooth purple hand. He grimaced in pain, gritting his teeth.

"I'm not dead yet, beast!" He implored, wrapping his arms around its finger like a golden wedding band. The monster raised its hand and slammed The Marquis to the ground again. Yet his body didn't break, he didn't pop like a grape. The beast was enraged, it closed its fist, taking the Marquis into its hands and began to strike the floor repeatedly, trying to squeeze the life out of the Golden King.

Joan stood with the others as the beast focused on its luminescent bait. Joan pointed at the ankle, where the smallest pieces of glass met the biggest lines of mastic.

The troupe nodded.

Gnat and Joan took aim in wait while Sach stampeded forth along the ground. With all his furry might he slammed his blade into the beast's leg. Then the duo opened fire. The bullets and arrows stole forth, clapping against the stone glue. It cracked, it chipped, and altogether broke upon Joan's last arrow, drawn back until the string snapped naturally. The Mural shuddered, its foot detached from it body, and fell back on one knee unable to rebalance itself.

The Marquis coughed from his place on the floor, paralyzed and dizzy.

Gnat reloaded and began to strafe behind the Glass giant. He stood behind it's left shoulder blade, aware that if it reached back, the sudden shift it weight would leave it falling over its broken leg.

The Mural waved its hand out to the gunman, but it couldn't reach him and protect the baron at the same time. In response it continued to stream glass from its arms, but the

403

Russian soldier easily weaved between the pattern of bullets, his helmet calculating the trajectories. Gnat continued to fire his rifle at the beast's face while Joan climbed to the second floor for a better angle. Sach foraged for used arrows to fill Joan's discarded quiver while she ascended.

Joan watched carefully and moved across the alcove. She looked down and unsheathed her dagger. The huntress watched the good ankle shift along the ground as the beast tried to remain upright. Joan was confident she could aim a little higher. She backed towards the wall and counted, mustering her strength.

Joan breathed deep, if she missed, she would be sitting right underneath the beast, but, right in front of Whitecroft. If she missed, and she was fast enough, which was unlikely, she could still kill the Baron before The Mural sat upon her.

One, she counted, remembering the days she would wait for a deer to pass below her.

Two, she huffed, thinking about Joshua's still-hanging corpse.

Three.

Frea heard the sound of slow feet behind her. But it was not Lilith nor any vilified man. The footsteps were confident, gallant and sure. She needn't to be a seer to know who'd joined the party. Before her, The Mural struggled to protect its ward between the three remaining warriors. Whitecroft fidgeted in her seat, nervous, staring up at the purple visage in disgust.

It was supposed to be bigger than this she thought, had she not sacrificed enough?

"It's been a long time, Sister." Elizabeth smiled. Frea turned about and returned the same grin. The Witch of Val-Ashoth stood there in her haori with a steel katana strapped about her waist. She stood there, unimpressed underneath her straw hat and she strode forth into the mansion.

Elizabeth's chin jutted forth, pointing at Joshua's body.

"Don't you love a man that takes his time?" She sighed.

Frea ginned, the same sheepish, sly grin that ran in the family. The two girls waited there watching the festivities, waiting for their moment.

Part 10/Reverie

Joshua walked behind the children who led him. There in the haze he watched them skip, Bucky, Lucky, and Ducky. They were full children, no longer skeletons and flesh. The children were fed and happy. They led him without certain destination, almost zigzagging along the invisible road they walked.

Joshua looked at them, so peaceful, so gentle, never knowing pain or suffering. They moved through an irrelevant void, surrounded by stars, blanketed in green light.

"Where are we going?" Joshua asked happily.

"We're going to the park!" Bucky laughed.

"We're going to get a puppy!" Ducky shouted, her feet tacking against the transparent sidewalk.

Joshua watched them intently, waiting to arrive at the intangible park. He loved his children. He loved to spoil them, and he loved to heckle them. Joshua sat on the thin air and watched the children run in circles downwards of the wind. Lucky held a toy in his hand, taunting it before the dog Joshua could not see. Joshua leaned back on his park bench and moved to light a cigarette.

If there were days in this place, it would be a good day.

Joshua listened to the cars behind him. No one honked, no one screamed profanities out the window, no prostitutes stood at street corners under neon signs. The breeze was cool, and the cigarette tasted just right. He closed his eyes. Joshua needn't worry about a thing. He listened to the dog bark and pant, the children giggled and shouted at each other.

"Joshua Hill?" Symeon asked, standing behind the bench, the well-dressed man held a manila folder before Joshua's eyes, waving it in front of him. "The precinct sent this for you."

Joshua waved off Symeon and closed his eyes again.

"I just retired." He insisted. "My wife would kill me if I started another case."

"Elizabeth would kill you if she caught you smoking too." Symeon chuckled. He waved the folder before Joshua again. Joshua sighed and snagged it from the old man's hand.

"I'll take a look." He grumbled.

Symeon took a seat beside Joshua on the bench. The old man watched the children while Joshua read the document. His arm stretched back over the rest. Joshua fiddled with his cigarette between his lips.

"You have beautiful children, Josh." Symeon smiled. "But they're not yours."

Joshua looked up from the folder. "Excuse me?" He asked, his eyebrow tight and raised, offended and bewildered.

"They're not your children, boy, none of this is real." Symeon sighed under his breath. It was something Joshua didn't quite understand.

Joshua grunted and resumed reading. The document mentioned a man in a yellow raincoat, a serial killer, most of his victims were children. Joshua knew the type, it was the reason he got out of the game.

"This is quite the case, sergeant." Joshua grimaced, handing the folder back, "But like I said, I'm retired."

"No one retires," Symeon retorted. "Especially Al Hamra."

"Who?"

"Especially you."

Symeon stood and rebuttoned his jacket. The children had fallen to the ground, the dog licked them tirelessly. They giggled. Joshua smirked.

"Let me know when you're ready to be a hero again, Joshua." Symeon chided. "The people sure need you."

Joshua ignored the man and watched him leave. He passed down to the invisible street corner and waited for the light to change. Joshua looked back at the park.

Joshua blinked.

At first, Joshua didn't see his kids, but then, he didn't want to. They lay there on the ground mangled, the dog was gone and there stood a slender, spider-like creature. The creature had long white arms and an eggshell face. The creature from his nightmares stood over his maimed children in their yellow raincoats. Joshua stood fast and reached for his gun. He rose it to meet his eyes and spied the beast between the iron sights. Joshua squeezed the trigger and blinked.

Joshua sat on the bench, watching his children play. Behind him a beautiful woman with black hair passed her arms around his neck, kissing him on the edge of his ear.

"Hey, handsome." She whispered. "How did the captain take it?"

"Hey…," Joshua replied, "Not too well."

"Well, there will be plenty of cops to replace you." Elizabeth chuckled.

"I sure hope so." Joshua sighed. He rubbed his eyes.

Elizabeth ruffled his hair and gave him a kiss on the cheek. "Come on, hero. Let's go home."

Joshua rose and waved to his children playing with their dog. They all saw their mother and ran to her.

"Mommy, mommy!" They cheered, hugging her at the waist. She smiled and hugged them back. Joshua knelt and attached a leash to his Labrador who licked his face. Joshua wrinkled his nose and smirked,

"Come on Sach, were going home."

The children were put to bed and their dog was left on the living room sofa. The house slowly drifted to sleep while Joshua stared out from the condo's balcony at the invisible city. It had been a long day.

Joshua collected his first stipend and let his old boss chew him out for a few minutes before punching him in the face and leaving, the envelope tucked smoothly in his back pocket. He had enough time in the rest of the day, after surfing the subways and picking up the laundry, to surprise his kids at the elementary school they attended. They were happy to see him, and he finally made good on his promise to buy them a dog.

Today was a good day, and Joshua knew that tomorrow would be a good day too.

Joshua turned around to see his wife laying there on the bed. She blushed and motioned for him to come closer. Joshua didn't, he stared at the only thing she wore, a yellow raincoat.

"Please take that off," Joshua asked, gripping the black coffee in his hands with white knuckles.

"We'll get to that." Elizabeth giggled.

"No… seriously." Joshua frowned.

Elizabeth's face frowned, she could tell Joshua was upset. He was always emotionally distant, and they both hoped quitting his job would help him grow closer to their family. She quickly rose and got dressed, suddenly self-conscious.

"What's wrong, hero?" She asked, moving towards him.

Joshua backpedaled slowly, finding himself sitting on the reading chair in the corner. He ran his hand along his face, worried. "It was just something I saw today."

"Are you still having nightmares?" Elizabeth asked, sitting on the bed cross from him.

"Yeah, I think they're getting worse." Joshua replied as Elizabeth took his hand in hers, she examined it like a piece of paper.

"You know what could help." His wife began. "If you woke up and helped us."

"Excuse me?" Joshua asked. This was the second time he heard something out of place in conversation.

"You need to wake up and help us." Elizabeth repeated, her arm stretched across his body, reaching for the small table by the chair where Joshua had left his dinner sandwich plate. At first Joshua thought she was reaching for her coffee. But as Elizabeth snatched the butter knife, twisted the blade in her hands, and plunged it into his chest Joshua knew he was mistaken.

Joshua sprang from his chair pushing Elizabeth down to the floor. His love rose from the ground, laughing.

"What are you doing?!" Joshua hissed, backing his way to the living room.

Elizabeth walked towards Joshua while he pulled the knife out of his body. She still smiled at him, nothing was wrong to her.

"I'm just trying to get you to wake up, hero." Elizabeth cooed.

"Stop calling me that!" Joshua huffed.

Behind Joshua, the doorbell rang. The American detective twisted around and turned the handle, trying to leave. He swiveled the door on it hinges, but the second it opened, a pair of firm hands grabbed him by his shoulders and tossed him into the hallway.

Joshua looked up dazed from the carpet. Everything was blurry, everything was gone again. The rooms, the architecture, all invisible again, un-crafted, dismantled. He looked up to see Symeon in his officer's uniform. Elizabeth exited the apartment to join them.

Joshua felt Symeon's gloved hands squeeze around his neck. Joshua choked, sputtered. Elizabeth watched him as he reached for her, reached for help. But no help would come, only their words served to aid him.

"You have to wake up, boy!" Symeon grunted, struggling to fight Joshua's writhing.

"Wake up, Joshua." Elizabeth agreed.

"I don't want to wake up!" Joshua gagged, pressing his hands against Symeon's face. Symeon flinched at the hand, trying to keep Joshua's palm from his face.

Elizabeth placed her hand on Symeon's shoulder. Symeon looked at her and she nodded, conveying some unknown understanding between them two. The officer let go

410

of Joshua's neck and retreated behind Elizabeth. The lovely girl sat beside Joshua on the invisible floor. Symeon panted, his eyes baggy and dark.

"I've been trying for months." Symeon complained, "He just keeps reliving this day over and over."

"Relax," Elizabeth commanded, "It's only been a few real days and we still have time."

Joshua's wife placed her hands on his cheeks and sat him up. She pressed her forehead against his and closed her eyes.

"I don't want to wake up." Joshua pleaded, "…Please don't wake me up."

"You have to wake up, Joshua. You need to stop thinking of us as we could be but remember us for how we are." Elizabeth whispered. "This is no time for Paradise."

Joshua stared at her. It was true, none of it was real.

Joshua didn't have children, they weren't married. Lucky, Ducky, and Dutch were dead. Elizabeth was condemned to dance until her feet bled. Joshua was condemned to dream about the children he killed for the rest of his life. He couldn't hide from broken people or fix them. But as Elizabeth kissed him he realized that was okay.

"Can you help us?" Elizabeth asked, staring into Joshua's eyes.

Joshua frowned, he didn't want to leave this world behind, but perhaps remembering it was all he could do. Maybe, if he looked back at this fondly, he might be able to live a little longer, love a little deeper, and run a little further.

Joshua nodded. "Let's go home, Elie. Take me home."

Joshua watched as Joan leapt past The Mural's leg and fell beneath its thighs. The monstrosity looked down at the girl in surprise as she quickly rolled upon impact into a sprint toward Baron Whitecroft. The huntress charged forth, ready to kill the baron at the cost of her life. But the beast threw its arm beneath it in a sweeping, bowling, motion. Joan leapt before the baron, raising an arrow above her head.

Joan wasn't fast enough. The glass guardian's hand swatted her body and launched her along the ground. Joan was sent rocketing along the floor, her helpless body slammed into Frea who stood neatly along her trajectory. They crashed into each other and both were sent zooming across the estate.

In midflight, Frea's clothes began to solidify and morph into a shell of silk, providing her protection in the shape of a hamster ball. Together, they crashed into the outer perimeter wall, safe.

Joan moaned, alive and rescued by Frea. Frea smiled down at her. She had executed her job perfectly. Frea waited by that door for that moment, seeing it from beyond and preventing the death of a great hero. Joan would one day do great things, things Frea couldn't ignore. In Frea's motherly arms, Joan passed out, tired and defeated. Frea sat there and watched the huntress intently. Joan's role was over for the fight, and she did well.

"Finally awake?" Elizabeth chuckled. "Took you awhile, hero."

Joshua looked down from his noose, his brain collecting itself. He glanced at the beast before him, a thin curve to his lips. The boy flicked his fingers and burnt the noose about him, sending him cascading to the ground. Joshua left the tile chipped where he landed.

"Thanks for bringing me back, but next time, you could wait until morning." Joshua bickered flatly.
"It's good to see you too, Joshua." Elizabeth chuckled. She blushed.

Joshua stood there before the enemy, a serious look on his face. The baron looked through the colored glass to see Al Hamra alive. Joshua met her eyes sternly, transfixed on her gaze.

"Impossible!" She screamed. "How are you still here!?"

"You can't really hang someone who doesn't have a spine." Joshua laughed darkly.

Joshua bent forward, his head pointed like a bull, on cue, his body erupted in black flames. Joshua smirked, unlike before, he was altogether different.

Joshua had permission to kill. His fingers flared in anticipation, his eyes shimmered.

Gnat spied the inferno through the corner of his helmet. Quickly he sprayed the last of his bullets and dropped his gun. He did not want to interfere from that point going forward. Gnat swiftly moved across the atrium to lift The Marquis into a fireman's carry. As Gnat sprinted by, toting the Marquis to safety, he stopped momentarily to stare at Joshua in disbelief. Gnat nodded silently, admiring the spectacle of Al Hamra.

Joshua stared at Gnat, his yellow eyes violently fixed. This gaze reminded Gnat of the day Joshua killed the Shaper.

Gnat was scared of Joshua, and quickly bustled off. Joshua wouldn't hold back, and anyone in the immediate vicinity would be hurt.

Al Hamra looked forward at the beast as Elizabeth met him at his side, she unsheathed her blade.

"Are you ready Elie? Hold nothing back." Joshua half asked, half commanded.

"Just follow my lead, hero." Elizabeth smiled.

The witch sprinted right, and Joshua mirrored to the left in tandem. Elizabeth quickly buckled and slid under the beast's swooping arm, placing her sword into the ground next to its thigh. She continued her run, leaving her sword in the ground until she was well outside her foe's range. Waiting where Gnat once stood, Elizabeth focused her incantation.

Joshua leapt atop the Mural's right knee and proceeded to land a quick one-two punch into the monstrosity's stomach, shattering pieces of glass before leaping yet again above it. Joshua leap twirled him above into the rafters. Ha landed firmly on the first crossbeam, his feet touching the stone for mere seconds before he slid his feet off the edge and fell back. The monster reached up to the ceiling to catch him, but quickly found it had caught the American. The beast looked at its palm in curiosity, wondering why it couldn't close its hand and pop his foe.

The black flames around Joshua forced an out-draft of air. This incredible heat pushed out in waves about Joshua, emitting from its origin and forcing The Mural's fingers away. The Mural was unable to grip the man as he stood upon its palm.

The force of the draft quickly subsided, but was replaced with an even greater flame, this flame, burning like a sun, began to melt the beast's groping hand. The glass began to liquify, leaving Joshua standing carelessly on its nub.

The Mural's other palm was pointed at Elizabeth, shooting a volley of glassy icicles in her direction. She watched carefully, her body bending back to avoid the first burst of glass bullets. The witch tilted, compressing a batch of air to form a thick shield. The compressed air formed before her and the glass rockets cleaved in two upon impact. Elizabeth drew odd symbols in the air behind the spectral barrier, odd designs and shape one might find in alien hieroglyphics.

Elizabeth finished her wish and her sword began the glow with a blue aura matching the designs she formed in the air before her. The blade dislodged itself immediately, humming with power. It erupted from the ground and slashed vertically, severing the whole of the Mural's thigh with unprecedented force. The blade rose into the air in an acute parabola. At its crest, the steel blade shattered, leaving not but the handle intact. The steel fragmented into many filaments, almost naked to the eye if not for their reflective properties. The shards whipped about like a snake, pummeling the mastic

414

and whittling it like some would whittle soap. Eventually, these shards wore down into powder, helpless and drifting in the room's gale.

Elizabeth twitched.

Joshua kept one hand in his breast pocket, and another in his pant pocket. He needed to be weary that his pistol didn't misfire, and the fog didn't evaporate. He kept his hands around both of them, providing a pocket of cold where his hands did not catch fire. In the intense heat, the second Joshua released both grips, he would lose a few bullets, and a useful ally.

Joshua jumped from the melting arm and landed on the stone flooring. The stone beneath him began to contort under the intense heat. He strode forth to the beast, placing his torch body between its knees. The beast leaned forward, trying to bat Joshua away with its forearm, but the glass instantly turned to slush the moment it touched the flame. The Mural lost its arm.

The beast leaned forward to headbutt Joshua, who stood there with an odd look in his eyes. The Mural loomed, trying to punch Joshua's face with its own, but quickly retreated once its face began to melt, leaving Whitecroft's once beautiful visage a hauntingly wax doll.

Joshua chuckled quietly, no one could touch him. Joshua winced, his eyes began to bleed, he began to sweat blood and ash. He was using too much energy, but the pain was to wonderful to stop. Did Whitecroft's torture create a sadist of Joshua? Joshua clutched his palpitating heart through his coat, he squeezed it. He was going into cardiac arrest, or something akin to that.

The Mural backed away from Joshua, retreating from the flame like one would a spider or a scorpion. It maintained its guard over Whitecroft, but much closer. The elemental being was on its last legs. Thus, The Mural stopped any semblance of a willingness to attack the burning man.

The glass giant, having lost an arm and a leg in mere seconds knew it was beat. It couldn't approach Joshua in his schizophrenic splendor, nor could it harm the witch behind her barrier.

The Mural had one option. The beast, with its solid body, would protect Whitecroft at the expense of its life. The noble creature bent over backwards to form as shield over the baron.

The Baron screamed, unaware that The Mural's duty to protect the baron surpassed its duty to kill those whom sought her harm.

"What are you doing? Kill them!" Whitecroft demanded.

But the beast didn't listen. It simply lay around Whitecroft like a bridge, forming the best shield it could. It wasn't the beast's fault that, when it was summoned through sacrifice and sanctity, it was ordered to protect Whitecroft above all else. The selfish baron couldn't see past her nose, and so, was stuck with a blessing that payed more attention to her than to that which Whitecroft paid attention to. Perhaps it was because Whitecroft was selfish, and therefore prioritized herself over her goals and dreams.

Nevertheless, The Mural felt chastised. It was trying its best to save Whitecroft. Why couldn't mother understand?

Elizabeth looked over to Joshua where he stood, paces before his foe. He stared at Whitecroft from the other side of the glass windows. He watched her like a gerbil, a lab rat. Elizabeth didn't like the look on Joshua's face, it was worn, empty, and evil.

The young girl walked towards Joshua, she wanted to help him end the fight. But Joshua didn't pay her any attention. She neared as close as she could without dying from heat exhaustion or become the fire herself. Whatever this black flame was, it was not given to Joshua by favor. The flame was not pure nor natural.

The Baron watched Joshua stand there, his arm against his heart and in his pocket like some kind of creep in a city slum. His darkened eye sockets, his red-wrung neck, his bleeding eyes and his beady, dark, sweat all pointed to a man who was a drug addict.

Joshua was not a drug addict.

Joshua stared back into Whitecroft's eyes, his yellow retinas contrasted with his black sclera. He panted from exhaustion. From behind, Elizabeth moved around the inferno and pressed her hands against the fallen Mural. She felt the mastic at the tip of her fingers and ran her hand along it. She determined herself to destroy Whitecroft's only protection, with or without Joshua's help.

Whitecroft looked back to Joshua as Elizabeth began to carve magical etchings into the mastic, preparing it for demolition. It would only be a matter of time before they made their way through to her.

The more Whitecroft watched Joshua, and the witch who stood before him, the more she began to reflect on her life. This reflection saddened the girl as she missed the days when Joshua was defenseless, a simple man without a clue. Whitecroft hid her tears, remembering how she teased him as if they were rivals. No witness could have told, but Whitecroft was still a young woman, still naïve and selfish. Despite her withered body and her gaunt features, she was still looking forward to the rest of her life, no matter how wretched it might have continued to be. But now, as Al Hamra knocked on her door with the reaper before his toes, and somehow it was fitting that the tides of war should shift so suddenly.

Whitecroft began to believe she was ready to die, at the hands of Joshua, it seemed so fitting. First her bride, now herself.

This whole fiasco was a lewd chess game with the detective, or so it seemed, and Whitecroft had lost. Joshua kept all his pieces on the board and used them well. Joshua was the champion, and he was moving on to better things,

417

forming his own future, taking orders from nobody. But would Joshua really kill her?

Joshua closed his wounded eyes, he thought of Solomon who would know his name and chase him once he heard, so was the plan. Joshua wouldn't forsake revenge just yet, and hopefully, he could find a way out of becoming king. Joshua had to trust Symeon's plan, he couldn't abandon the people now, not when he promised to help them. But he wished Dutch was present. He would force the role of king onto him, he would shove Dutch's hand into Whitecroft's neck if he had to. Joshua couldn't think of anyone else to take the throne. He didn't trust anyone else to lead the state either.

So, what did this mean? When Joshua killed Whitecroft, would he be placed in the custody of citizens, forced to lead them to their own salvation? Joshua gritted his teeth, he bit his lip until it, too, bled. Joshua didn't want this, he didn't want this, he didn't want this.

Joshua also wondered why the voices in his head wouldn't hush.

The American could hear them screaming, the voices, the voices, the voices. Something was wrong with him, of them, because they wouldn't shut up. Joshua's head jerked sideways, his fingers twitched. Joshua felt something in his stomach, it scratched and begged him to scream. Something was wrong with Joshua, something was terribly wrong.

Elizabeth finished he wish and watched as the mastic began to dissolve, flowing like water from the crevices and spilling to the floor. The glass fell to pieces in large chunks like ore or beach balls rolling from hills and dunes.

Elizabeth looked back at Joshua, expecting him to thank her, to say anything, but Joshua looked right through her and walked ever slowly to the baron. Elizabeth was scared, much like Gnat was scared. She had never seen the *worst* of Joshua. Perhaps she was about to. Elizabeth wanted to grab Joshua, to hold him. She took a few steps behind him, trying to wish the flames about him to part. She wanted to hug him

418

for just a moment, to remind him that, no matter what Whitecroft had done to him, he was still human.

Was Elizabeth so dense *not to* remember? Joshua was no longer human.

Elizabeth wished, but the wish wasn't granted. She took another step forward, but quickly backpedaled as the hems of her haori singed. She worried, watching her love from behind. He stood before his torturer, his opposite, his aspirations.

Part 11/Red

The tyrant sat there, unapologetic, a look of disgust on her contorted face. She didn't say anything, she wanted to die with her pride, in thinking of her righteousness, however misguided it was. Whitecroft believed she was right. And it wasn't so much the way she did things, that she judged, while looking back on her gluttonous life, but the way she felt while she did those things. The baron remembered a time before her reign. When she was young, and sneaking about the estate her father, the previous baron, sat beside the fireplace one night talking to his advisor.

"How can we know?" Her father asked, "How can I know that I'm *not* the only person this world was made for?"

"How can anyone know," the advisor responded cynically, "You can choose to live only for yourself and believe that no one else really has a soul. There's no way to prove any of it. In this selfish life, really, it's all a gamble. Are we animals or are we more? What do you want to bet on, sire, that you're the only one alive, or just another meaningless face in a populated sea?"

At that age, once she heard the conversation, Whitecroft chose to gamble the former.

Whitecroft didn't see a future king in Joshua, who reached out with his flaring hand, Holding it before her as one would a carrot. He pointed two fingers at her, preparing himself to tap her withered forehead and set her on fire. Whitecroft saw another worthless pawn. She gazed at him through his flame. If Joshua killed her and she closed her eyes for the last time, the world would cease to exist. That was her gamble.

But why did Joshua hesitate?

"You do want to kill Solomon, don't you boy?" Symeon asked.

"I do," Joshua whispered.

I do I do I do I do.

Kill her, I have to kill her.

Shut up.

"Kill her Joshua, she's waiting for you to kill her. Tell Solomon you're here, you're so close." Symeon coaxed.

"But I don't want to be king." Joshua whispered. "Please, there's another way."

"Kill her," Symeon demanded, "You've come this far, don't chicken out now. Think of the villagers, think of everyone that died just so that you could get here. Do you honestly think their lives meant nothing?"

Joshua shook his head. He couldn't tell whether Symeon was there in the atrium with him, or if it was just his own imagination.

The American steeled himself and reached again for Whitecroft. He poked her above the brow and watched as the fire contorted around his finger and enveloped her.

The baron burned like a piece of tinder, a piece of twig. Her pale flesh began to brown like chicken. Whitecroft closed her eyes and admitted defeat. But instead of finding herself in a void of nothingness, she saw something flash before her eyelids.

Whitecroft opened her eyes and found herself standing in the hotel he fiancé died in, she looked out down the hall to his room. Joshua stood before this door, steady and stoic, as he was known to be.

Whitecroft felt an odd sensation as two of Charlie's friends pushed a small group of underage girls through her spectral body. She watched the two brutes shepherd the virgins to Joshua, who stood still at the door, trying not to make eye contact with any of them.

The girls looked scared and beaten. Whitecroft knew what was about to happen.

The baron listened as Charlie cheered his guest's arrival. Next came the sounds of something terrible, something that Whitecroft didn't want to hear.

Whitecroft began to cry, she didn't know Charlie was like this. She had no clue he was a rapist, a monster.

"Kill him!" Whitecroft begged Joshua, who stood unhearing at the door. The man lit his cigarette and took a long puff, letting out the smoke from his nostrils.

"Kill Charlie!" Whitecroft pleaded.

Whitecroft couldn't do anything to stop her fiancé, she made her way to the suite of his room and tried to beat the door down. She didn't weigh enough to move a thing. Whitecroft sobbed, hearing Charlie's crimes. She reached for Joshua but could not touch him. She wanted him to do it.

Joshua extinguished his cigarette and pulled the gun out of his pocket. Whitecroft watched him open the door, watched him kill Charlie and his friends. The girls ran away, out of the room, free and safe. Joshua fired the last of his rounds into Charlie.

"Thank you." Whitecroft cried, "Thank you."

The flame about Joshua subsided and the new king looked through Elizabeth beside him. Joshua had become the next baron.

Elizabeth grabbed Joshua and held him as he fell to his knees. They stayed there on the floor for a time while Joshua rocked on his toes. He whispered odd words to himself, trying to regain a sense of humanity. Elizabeth pressed her hands against Joshua's temples, her fingers wrapped in drooling blood. She tried her best to comfort him, to hold him above the darkness in his heart. It seemed, even in killing Whitecroft, Joshua had lost something.

Elizabeth didn't know what.

Once Joshua regained some semblance of etiquette, Elizabeth cleaned his face of grime and plasma. She helped her shaking love onto his feet and turned him around. He would feel better once they left such a cursed place, Elizabeth thought.

Together, the two found their way slowly down the stairs of the throne and through the room. It took them a few minutes, but the witch managed to carry Joshua outside the doors of the estate as the tapestries and rugs caught fire. Much like Gene's estate, this place would hopefully become but a ruin, a shadow of the evil that lived within the castle.

Once Joshua emerged from the front gate, the night was in full orchestration. At this time, the news had caught word of both the appearance of LeCeleste and the assault on Whitecroft's keep. The news reporters and the farmers grouped together in mass to try and catch a glimpse of Joshua, the so called "Al Hamra." They wanted to know what had happened in the estate, why there were lizard corpses about them, why there was a golden city in the sky. More importantly, they wanted to know whether their futures would be protected under their new leader.

Joshua answered none of these questions and simply stood before the entrance, locked in by the sea of witnesses. He eyed a distant horizon barely noticeable against the dark sky.

The Marquis, having recovered greatly in such little time, moved to where Joan and Frea had landed and ran his hand into the huntress' shoulder, shaking her gently. Joan woke with a sudden jolt, instantly remembering the conflict.

"What happened?" Joan asked.

The Marquis smiled down at Joan. "Joshua happened. He's here, and he's alive."

The young huntress, with joyful tears in her eyes, looked across the masses, but immediately, felt cast aside. In some odd form or fashion, she imagined herself beside Joshua, standing with him to stake their claim over The Crofts. Was she not with him before any of these others? Was it pride that she felt, was it envy, watching as Joshua held on to a strange and exotic woman?

Joan rose to join Joshua but was quickly caught among the masses. Unable to squeeze herself through, she watched silently like another commoner. Joshua didn't see her, he didn't seem to see anyone in that moment. From his place over the exotic woman's shoulder, Joshua began to look down from the cameras, almost at the ground. Something was on his mind. Joan knew this because this was the same shaded face he wore after finding the children in Gene's mansion. Whatever demons he had harbored in his heart had not been released.

Joan's tears of joy quickly became tears of worry. Was this not the closure they wanted? Was this not reason she fought? She wanted Joshua to be happy, she wanted Joshua to become a kind man. Joan wished Joshua would look at her, wished that he would smile and let the world know he was alright. Joan wasn't alright so long as Joshua didn't smile.

Frea awoke thereafter, watching her king stand before Whitecroft's estate. The people cheered his name, the name she gave him, "Al Hamra."

Frea stood up and made her way before the citizens, standing a distance behind Joshua. She had made him, this was what her efforts had born, the fruits of her labor. Frea was excited for what was next, she could almost see it all. Not only did she bring Joshua to this point, she thought, she had also dragged herself along with him. Frea was about to taste the higher things in life, she no longer had to hide from mage hunters and magic-stealing cults. Joshua would protect her in his mighty kingdom. This is what Frea wanted, and this is what Frea would have.

The Marquis tried to hide his face from the cameras, from the commoners. He didn't want people to know who he was. Plenty of historians watched the news, and soon, they would come in search of his city, invading his privacy, asking him to pay flight taxes. The man kept from looking up and motioned to Gnat that they should duck out. So, they did, and made their way back to their ship. The morning after, they would assist in helping those from LeCeleste pick up their fallen comrades. The day after that, their people would begin to burn the dead. It had been a rough day. Many people would cry after seeing their loved one's dead and lying on the deck of LeCeleste. Many of them would scream at the Marquis. The Immortal Baron knew they would hate him the rest of his days, but somewhere higher than they could fly, the spirits of the departed had flown. The righteous dead become greater as they were cut down, worthy of martyrdom, worthy of being called human.

Elizabeth let Joshua stand on his own. He stooped slightly over the edge of the main foundation and looked down at the ground. Joshua fell upon his knees and Elizabeth quickly motioned to help him up, but Joshua pushed her hands away. Joshua wanted to be on the ground.

Joshua raised his head to the sky while the helicopters streamed the event to the world. The barons would watch their new rival from their beds, from their chairs in their castle. They would prod him for weaknesses, ask him for favors, and plot behind his back. But most of all, they would watch as opened his mouth to speak this one time. They would hear his new citizens pledge loyalty by speaking his name.

Joshua was a promise to the villagers, and without Dutch to take the throne, Joshua knew he couldn't break such a word. Joshua had to stay with his new people to honor Dutch. He had made the news, he had shown himself to the world, hoping Solomon would be watching somewhere. But even if his title granted him absolution from his crimes, he was trapped, a slave to aid his citizens for the rest of his days, forever forced to wait on them, instead of waiting for Solomon.

If only Dutch were alive, Joshua thought. *If only I could have walked away.*

Joshua's other promise, the promise he made to himself, tore him in two. He had to kill Solomon, but he couldn't if he was locked inside his country. He wanted to go to Paris and hunt him, play a game of cat and mouse. It would have been better than the torture, it could have been over. Why did he let Solomon goad him so well? Was this truly the only way to reach the yellow-jacketed man?

Joshua closed his eyes as he opened his mouth to speak, everything inside of him, his dreams, his ideals, his anguish in life and months of torture and isolation poured out in one word. Joshua screamed, but it was not a triumphant roar as those before him believed it would be. They expected a word of encouragement, a word of power or a mantra to live the rest of their lives by. Instead, what Joshua let out was enough to create his own avatar, even without his death. Joshua shouted the name of his oppressor, the name of his plague and affliction, the name that brought him to become king.

Joshua screamed Solomon's name at the top of his lungs, calling him out. Beckoning him to come and end this charade.

Joshua was waiting, and he couldn't wait to have his kill.

"Joshua, Joshua, Scratch, Hill, Break, Bleed, Kill... Scratch ... Scratch Scratch, In death, Hold... Scratch. Me... here.
Listen, Scratch. Kill. Scratch.
Oh Joshua Hill
Scratch Joshua, Scratch. Joshua, Scratch. Hill.
Monster"

Joshua thought.

Act 3/Resolve
Part 1/Reign

Joshua watched his workers build his temporal home, it stood there beside the Rhine on a warm spring day which rushed anew, carrying cold water from upward melts. Still, a year later, LeCeleste floated above the fields which had grown with newly sprouted grains and treelings.

Joshua read a small sheet of paper, a report that the providence found and removed a dam further south, providing his people with more clean water.

Joshua looked up from the document to watch Elizabeth bark orders at the constructors. Joshua felt something scratching his head.

Joshua was a busy man. The barons were keeping their eyes on him, often sending messengers to scout out the lands. He spent countless hours in discussion with each of them renegotiating tariffs and rescinding export promises. Despite his hands-off approach towards the farmers, letting them keep their grains and sell them without intervention, they often came to his seat to ask if they were allowed to sell something. Joshua would bark and tell them never to come back unless they had an emergency, but they never listened.

Joshua was a stern baron. His quiet resolve evoked his people to revere him, and he never argued with that. They were so used to a tyrant, however, that he went to bed some nights fearing he would become one. Joshua was a good king, but something scratched at the back of his *head*.

Elizabeth hadn't been in Hill's country long. She often came to see him once every few months before having to return to Val-Ashoth. Joshua missed not being able to carry her home or waking up to her elbow in his face, but they made do. She was everything Joshua wanted in a queen, strong, stubborn, and graceful. But, she was never present.

Joshua felt the small diamond in his pocket which sat inside his black jacket and frowned. He was so busy he hadn't found the time to set it into a ring yet, not that he could ever propose to the witch. The land needed a queen that would stick around in case their king couldn't. Still, Joshua liked the anticipation, the knowledge that at any moment he could pretend to be selfish and take a knee. The only thing keeping him from being so reckless, was something that *scratched* at the back of his *head.*

"It looks like your mighty fortress is almost complete, your majesty." Elizabeth mocked, bowing clumsily. She wore a white sundress, her hair down in waves above her jawline. Her eyes sparkled, her skin glowed. Life was good, on the surface.

Joshua took her by the hand and watched as the small building's final piece was set and hammered.

"What do you think?" Joshua asked, slightly less present in the moment than he wanted to be.

"You could have been more original." Elizabeth sighed, "But it really is home away from home, isn't it?"

"It'll tie me over while the rest of the state grows. I don't want to have a castle when the people haven't any proper towns." Joshua promised.

Elizabeth opened the wooden door and peered inside. Everything was perfectly placed. The mattress lay against the far wall and the wicker chair sat staring at it. It was a good replica of their house in Val-Ashoth. It was everything Joshua wanted.

The workers went their way after Joshua paid them their dues. Tomorrow they would return to work on irrigation and a town market. The whole area was going to be rebuilt along the river, allowing for a natural and eco-friendly living center. Joshua had also mandated safer crop cultivation, demanding the citizens alternate which years they could grow their fields. This allowed the soil to heal and prevent over farming. The farmers would save their money, which was given back to them from Whitecroft's treasury, at Joan's request, for those years. They were able to buy grain from other farmers, and they were not shy to share.

It had taken the best of two months to clean up after the short war. The bodies were burnt or buried, prisoners were retried, and the old prison beneath Whitecroft's estate was demolished, collapsed and filled with gallons upon gallons of cement. Joshua transferred those criminals found guilty to Paris for temporary safekeeping, not that there were many of them. He leveraged his time on the police force and his knowledge of Dominion law to create a small window in which Joshua could house his convicts, buying him time to create his own prison.

This agreement also aided in restoring a strong alliance with the military power as Joshua agreed to provide trained liaisons that would help the capital city prevent crime. He had trained those Liaisons himself and the public nicknamed them "The Red Hand," Joshua's first specialized fighting force.

Even though Joshua managed to roughly patch things together with Baron Glass, all of their communications were professional. Joshua was waiting for him to die, but the man just wasn't old enough. The Red King hoped that the assassin prostitute he never caught was gunning for the mobster. He wanted to read of her success on the news, killing baron Glass before biting her own bullet. Wouldn't that be grand?

Scratch, scratch, scratch.

Among the changes that occurred over the past year was the world's understanding of itself. Watching a carnival of lizard men on live television piqued many interests among in the world community. To educate the people, Joshua and The Marquis held a worldwide conference in which they shared their knowledge of cryptids and the world at large. The world slowly began to realize that magic, although uncommon, existed. But despite the Joshua's willingness to tell the world the truth, there were many things he didn't tell them. Val-Ashoth would forever remain a mystery, like much of the world still was.

"It's almost time for me to go," Elizabeth grumbled, falling to the bed. Joshua lay beside her; the long day was ending. "When you wake up I won't be here."

"I know," Joshua whispered, burying his yellow eyes in her neck. The tired man quickly fell asleep, not that sleep did him much good.

Scratch.

Elizabeth watched as Joshua dozed beside her. She kissed him on the temple and rose from the bed to leave. The witch tiptoed out the door of their house and climbed the first hill, vanishing into the night behind the silver moon.

That morning Joshua reached for Elizabeth, but she was not there. He frowned. It was another warm morning, although a cool breeze drifted through the open windows and the unlocked door.

Elizabeth loved to leave the door open for him.

Joshua rose and walked outside after putting on a pair of pants. He ran his hands along his many scars, most of them inflicted by Whitecroft, who had studied him like an alien. Joshua shuddered. She had done much to him, cutting his ashen body in pieces, watching to see what did and what did not grow back.

Fortunately, everything did. Unfortunately, everything grew back so fast, they were all cut off again a few days later.

Outside Sach stood upon a high-chair at the small porch table. The mongrel handed Joshua a cup of coffee.

"Morning asswipe," The gremlin snickered.

"Morning." Joshua returned half-heartedly, taking a long sip.

Sach has become something a personal pet to Joshua; and Sach no longer had to do chores. Personal, however, the pet was, Sach still had his own job and his own house further down the river. He served as a leader of his own small platoon, part time.

The rodent tilted his cap in apology and looked out to the fields. He shook his healthy fur and reclined in his chair. "So, Elizabeth is gone again, huh?"

"She is." Joshua replied, "But she can quit, right? I mean, it's not like she *can't* quit."

"It's more a matter of whether the land lets her go. It gives her a few days every once in a while, from pity, I guess."

"The hag could at least try." Sach mumbled.

"She likes her job." Joshua defended, "and watch yourself, you're technically royalty now. You can't have the locals hear you bad-mouth your own king."

"It's a nervous twitch, you know that." Sach excused.

The rodent paused for a moment, watching the clouds loll across the sky. They both drank in peace. In the distance, horses galloped across a knoll, all chasing each other, enjoying freedom. Their long orange manes bobbed against their necks, reminding Joshua of a certain friend he once had.

Joshua scratched the back of his head.

"Do you like your job?" Sach asked The Red King, "I could always take over if you wanted to go off and play footsie with your girl."

Joshua chuckled dryly into his mug, "Like hell anyone would let you run a country, much less an ant farm... As much as I would love to leave, I know I'd have to come back just to kick your ass. I don't want any more rebellions in my lifetime."

They both shared a laugh. Sach knew it was true.

"You need a wife, Joshua." Sach began again. "Hell, Joan is actually on her way to talk to you today." The brownie ran his hand along his sides, outlining her curves. But Joshua's face didn't budge.

Sach frowned, "It's just a thought, she's a good gal."

431

There was another silence, it lingered longer still. Every other day had been like this, it left Joshua to his thoughts, waiting for someone who needed him. There were no papers nor meetings to complete today, and he couldn't be a hero when a country wanted him to wait hand and foot. Neither could Joshua be a vigilante when there was no crime. Joshua lived in a newborn country, pure and innocent.

Joshua had waited for days after killing the baron. His face was all over the news, newspapers, magazines, websites. But still, he never found Solomon, the killer never revealed himself. It had also been months since Symeon last visited him, gave him advice, talked to him. He didn't know whether he had failed or if Symeon was a liar somehow.

Night after night he stared at the door to his house. He left it unlocked; he left the windows open, waiting for the man in the yellow raincoat to walk in, ready to kill him. Underneath Joshua's flat expressions, he burned incessantly for a chance to hurt Solomon.

It didn't help that Joshua's heart beat like a machine gun when he passed people on the streets after a meeting in Paris. *Was that Solomon?* Joshua would guess. *Did I miss my chance?* It also never helped on the days when it rained. Paris was a cesspool of fashion, and the color of choice that spring was yellow. Joshua would look down to the streets, yellow umbrellas at every corner, yellow jackets, yellow everywhere. So many times, he was tempted to aim his pistol from the balcony of his hotel, pointing the barrel at those yellow circles like they were carnival balloons and squeeze the trigger. Joshua never knew where Solomon might have been; Joshua never know who Solomon might've been, and it frightened him.

Solomon was probably playing game with him. It could be another year until he arrived, walking up to Joshua when he least expected it, as a friend, as a messenger, as Elizabeth, and gut him while he sat on his temporary throne in his temporary tent, waiting for a castle with defenses to protect him. He could be in the middle of listening to the mediocre plights of his citizens, and suddenly look to find the man in his tent, disguised as a man with a complaint.

Yes, Joshua thought about Solomon more than he did his own country, more than he did Elizabeth.

"Josh!" Joan called, waving her hand from the back of her horse.

How long had she been sitting there, waiting for him to reply?

"Earth to His Majesty!" Sach barked.

Joshua scratched the back of his head. "Joan, good morning."

"Look, we need to talk later, but right now we have a problem!" Joan asserted, her horse pacing and rearing excitedly. "Some idiots are heckling one of Baron Gurdard's messengers by the beach!"

Joshua quickly rose to consciousness and bustled about to the rear of his house to fetch his horse. He sprinted about, all the while snagging a shirt from his clothes line. As he approached his mare, he found his head through the collar of his shirt just in time.

Joshua's horse stood there proud and excited, a black stallion neighing and stomping furiously. The king settled her and quickly tossed a thin leather saddle upon her back and buckled it down. He mounted swiftly and eyed for Sach. The furball looked up from the ground with a sword he fetched from the house in his hands, it was the yatagan Frea had given him in their skirmish, re-gifted upon his birthday.

Sach tossed the weapon into the air. Joshua quickly snagged it just as his horse began to give chase to Joan, who rode fast to the north by the river. It was crucial that they arrive there before the situation grew worse. Baron Gurdard, the King of the Scandes, was one of Joshua's closest and most treasured allies. The Baron, although rash and abrasive, was a warm-hearted man than understood and followed an honorable code of law. It was imperative that Joshua's people maintained good relations with his country, being that they supplied the cold-mountain peoples most of their grains throughout the year and Gurdard supplied them fishing boats and other woodcrafts in turn.

Joshua's subjects were good people, but one of their most prodigious flaws was their immense sense of nationalism. Years of social isolation left them vulnerable to pride and often they would bully travelers who used the now-open roads to cross through northern Europe. It didn't help that the country saw a tremendous economic rise in such a short time and new freedoms were being burdened on their shoulders. It fed their inability to understand other peoples, often leading to small matters which had to be resolved.

However, in this case, the harm of a messenger from another baron was paramount to declaring war.

Joshua's horse leapt from the grass onto the sand. Joshua looked about for Joan. His red-haired friend had ridden too far ahead of him in their rush to aid the foreigner. Joshua looked out to the ocean to spy a ship adrift in the waters, no doubt the messenger's. Somewhere along the shore was his rowboat where he landed.

Joshua closed his eyes. There was a faint shout in the distance, something left of the beach front where he sat. Joshua stirred forth and galloped towards the sound in haste. Hopefully Joan had already resolved whatever heinous intent Joshua's citizens held.

Joan stood between two men and Gurdard's messenger from Scandinavia. She shoved the two citizens back quickly. The men had been tossing sand and spitting on the messenger.

"Stop it!" Joan shouted, "As the right hand of The Red King I'm ordering you two to back off."

Joan huffed and looked to Joshua as he approached. The baron slowed his stallion and climbed down. The two citizens looked at him in fear as he strode before them. They were short men, each suffering a serious case of balding, one from the front of his head, the other from the back. As Joshua stomped between them and the messenger they fell back upon the sand.

Joshua stooped down in front of them. He fiddled with his sword, pulled it from the sheath slightly, moved it back in, pretending to contemplate extreme measures.

"I won't pretend that you two are smart enough to understand how important foreigners are to me." Joshua commented, "so I'll just give you a warning."

The men cringed, shivering under the weight of their king's eyes.

"If you ever mess with someone who's just passing through again or start *any* fight with *anyone*, I will bleed you slowly from your privates. Whether you started the fight or not, I do not care. You will *still* be found guilty." Joshua threatened, "Now run along and pray I never see you two again, or I just might change my mind."

The duo didn't move, Joshua smelt the piss collect on the sand. He sighed and lifted both of them to their feet. He kicked them in their asses like dogs and they began to run back through the woods for their home.

The King placed his sword on his shoulder and scratched the back of his head with his scabbard. Joshua turned about to greet the traveler.

The traveler was a brawny man with blonde hair which was braided back into a pony tail. A long thin scar ran down the man's face from one corner to the other. He was fierce, covered with forehead lines, laugh lines, and crow's feet. These creases, due to long days in the sun, disillusioned his company how old he was. This man could have harmed the two miscreates that scrutinized him, but he honored Joshua by sparing them.

The messenger bowed slightly in reverence.

"Thank you for not harming my citizens." Joshua nodded.

"It would hardly be fitting on my first visit to your territory." The man replied, "I've come with a message from my lord, Baron Gurdard."

"Let's hear it, unless you would rather rest after such a long voyage."

"That is not necessary but thank you." The man bowed again, "The message is this: Baron Gurdard strongly suggests your presence at his son's aging ceremony in five days' time. He wants to sit you and your esteemed huntress to his left while his son preforms his ceremony of adulthood."

"Baron Gurdard wants me to attend a birthday party?" Joshua asked.

"The coming of age ceremony is extremely important when someone in Scandinavia turns thirteen. It's the time when they stop being coddled and are seen independently of the father and mother." Joan piqued.

"What does it mean that am I invited?" Joshua rephrased, still lost.

"When a Father asks you to sit at his table during the ceremony, he is showing the son and example of the company he should keep. Now that he is considered an individual by the tribes he will be judged for his own actions; his punishment will no longer be prescribed by the father but by the law of the tribes. Gurdard's son will no longer be Gurdard's son, he will be a child of the tribe, and Gurdard will give the boy his first name along with his first title." the messenger explained.

Joshua looked at Joan, she stood there and nodded her head, her eyes alight with excitement. Joshua crossed his arms and looked at his bare feet. He would need to delegate power while he was gone, as Gurdard's lands were days away by ship. He would have to be gone a week at least.

"Consider his invitation accepted." Joshua nodded. Al Hamra reached to shake the messenger's hand. The man took him by the elbow and quickly turned his back to them. The man promptly pushed his boat into the ocean and started to row away.

Joan grabbed Joshua by his forearm, jumping with excitement.

"I can't believe I was invited too!" She screamed, her face brimming.

Joshua watched the messenger's boat slowly move towards it's mother vessel.

"We'll need to get our bags ready. And you need to prepare your boat." Joshua replied, mounting his horse.

"What do you mean by my boat?" She asked confused.

Joshua gave a weak smile and rode back into the tree line, a thin but certain laugh resounded off the trunks back to her.

"What do you mean by my boat!?" Joan asked again louder. She saddled her horse and chased him into the woods. "Tell me!"

Frea stood in the tent watching Joshua's advisors delegate. They stood there before the round table shaking their hands in frustration, unable reach a conclusion without Joshua. The Left Hand rolled her eyes and waited for the rabble to stop before speaking in her small voice. "How do you expect to run this land once The Red King leaves?" She barked.

The advisors were all afraid of her. They shifted uncomfortably while the seer began to pace around them. The men and women who stood before her were all hired on a trial basis. Joshua asked for them once learning he was requested in Scandinavia. He wanted to explore the possibility of creating a council to act as his surrogate. Because there was no queen present, and Joshua was frequently absent on business ventures, a surrogate was in dire need. What no one else knew, was that Joshua was hoping the council could replace him entirely.

Frea looked at each of the members with disgust. They were ex-militants, having fought in the rebellion. Now they bickered, fighting over whether to implement a *small* taxation policy that would garner a larger standing army.

Personally, Frea knew of a young girl who could do better than their lot. But Joshua ordered that Lilith be moved to a school in Paris, worried that she would not have a bright future stuck in the undeveloped countryside. This made Frea smile.

Unknowingly, Joshua had become a father.

Frea waved the advisors off, "Leave! You're all fired! The Red King would be disgusted with you."

The advisors left, stammering on words and their own toes.

Frea leaned into the table and stared at the country's borders, the jagged edges, the smooth lines. Sadly, she could not see what lay beyond this moment in time. Something wrong had occurred, and Frea could no longer see the future. The sorceress moved small tokens into the center of the map, the wooden figurines marking the locations of barracks and patrols. She created a large disgusting pile of color from them. What did they need to fear from the barons? What did they need to fear from anyone? Frea thought.

They had to be afraid.

"A franc for your thoughts?" The Marquis asked.

Had he been standing through the tent flap while she thought?

Frea stared at him with her chastising eyes. The Marquis smiled back, unfazed, and moved to the table across from her. He reached down to the table and grabbed a large oval piece the size of his thumb. The words LeCeleste were written in marker across its top. The Marquis slid it back to position above Whitecroft's forest. He then began to grab each other piece and moved them to their prospective encampments by memory.

"Would you stop that!" Frea puffed through grinding teeth.

The Marquis looked up at her slyly, "Not a fan of strategies?" He asked.

"How could I be? How you can *ever* be certain something is going to work?"

The Marquis rolled another piece between his thumb and forefinger. "I get it now," he thought aloud, "you're a control freak."

Frea swiped the pieces off the board and they softly rolled across the green grass beneath their shoes, hiding themselves, especially the green ones. She lifted the map and tore it in half before dropping it to the floor.

"There's no point in doing anything when something random can just happen in return." She retorted stressfully.

Lafayette dropped his piece to the ground. "What ever happened to the Third-person dialogue? Are you no longer certain of yourself? You used to be so confident, you used to be so… knowledgeable."

"Watch your tongue!" Frea retorted, "I can still cut it off! You aren't a baron anymore. I could have you executed for your words!"

The Marquis chuckled, backing away from the table. "Are you sure? You don't *know* whether you can catch me or not. Do you know, Frea? Are you certain?"

Frea reached down and lifted a knife from her boot. She darted quickly in her dress around the table, but the Marquis quickly ran around to the other side. He smiled, taunting her. He wanted her to hate him, he wanted her to break down and cry. Frea growled and ran about the table again. Lafayette was too fast for her and they ended back where they began, staring at each other from the opposite sides of a table. The Marquis chuckled softly, his breathing lightly labored from the sprints. He was out of shape.

"See, you don't know anything anymore, do you?" He mused.

"Why the hell are you still here!?" Frea cursed, "Weren't you supposed to disappear with your crap city months ago?"

The Marquis waited, watching her. He ignored the question and leaned forward over the table. Frea snatched his collar and pulled his body over to her.

"Got you! Now open your mouth, swine!" Frea demanded, unhinged.

Frea raised her knife into the air to rest near The Marquis lips. The Marquis still played cool. She waited for him to open his mouth. But the knife grew weak in her hand, she grew tired of yelling. She was tired and had never been tired before.

The Marquis clasped his free hand over hers and pushed her blade into the table. Frea let go of his shirt and Laffy rubbed his neck.

Frea stormed out of the tent, furious, quiet.

The Marquis chuckled to himself quietly. He walked around and collected the pieces of the strategy set. When he had finished he placed them back on the same table with the torn map. He began to put it all back together.

It had been two days since Joshua left across the North Sea, he could still recall their conversation before he left.

Joshua stood before The Marquis with his arms crossed. They leaned over the railings at the Whitecroft's old estate and watched a small flock of birds droop by. They had many conversations like this after Joshua became baron. Joshua often asked Laffy how to run an empire.

The Marquis always shrugged and waited for the real question, the specific question Joshua wanted to ask him. Joshua stood there juggling a rock in his palm, waiting for it to fall from his hands.

"What if I fail?" Joshua asked, "What if I can't do this? What if I don't want to do this?"

The Marquis shrugged again, he always shrugged, wanting to give his friend doubt with his answers.

"Well, someone will pick up where you left off I imagine. But who would that be?"

Joshua tossed the rock to Laffy, who snagged it and began to juggle it in turn.

"I'm worried about leaving. What if something bad happens while I'm away?" Joshua asked.

"You could have more faith in people." Lafayette suggested, "Or you could play sentry all your life and stay in the country. One day or another you'll have your back turned, and something bad will happen. That's just the way things are. This is not heaven and we're not saints."

The Marquis dropped the rock. He chuckled.

"Frea really hates you, you know." Joshua warned.

The Marquis nodded, "We didn't get off on the best foot after the war."

"I'm glad." Joshua responded. "She needs someone to be angry with. Someone to hold a grudge against. She's never experienced failure before and she will if she wants to stay in my cabinet... I want you to do me a favor while I'm gone. I want you to be hard on her when you can."

"Why is that?" The Marquis asked.

"She needs to understand what is like to fail. So, force her to fail. She should know that feeling before something serious happens. I'm afraid she'll break down under the stress of trying to be perfect. She can't be perfect."

The Marquis smiled, "You're giving me all the fun jobs this week, aren't you?"

Lafayette opened the tent flap and looked to the distance where Frea continued to march off. He rubbed his arms; the night was beginning to grow cold.

The Golden King had asked Joshua if he could stay above his country some time ago. In truth, just like Frea, he was scared of the unknown. If he left The Red King's airspace, what would happen? The Golden King was afraid the defenseless city would be hunted down, tracked, tagged. He didn't want to lose her. He didn't want to lose his people.

It was to his joy when Joshua told him he could stay as long as he wanted. The Marquis didn't think he would ever leave. He looked up at his city in the heavens and watched the lights flicker through the windows. He had stolen the sun centuries ago, and now, in some shape or fashion, he was giving it back. It was in the right hands, parked above the right lot. The Marquis was sure of it.

Laffy began to walk that way, ready to go back to his house and read a book, or, perhaps watch cartoons. But in the middle of a field he stopped and looked back towards Frea, concerned. The girl didn't have much of a chance when surrounded by chance.

Did Joshua really mean to give her a seat on his council after all the innocent blood she spilled during the coup?

Joan stared at the schooner ecstatic. She pulled Joshua onto its deck which floated softly upon the Rhine with soothing rocks. She ran her hand along the rails and felt the helm. She laid down upon the polished flooring and listened to it creak in anticipation for the North Sea. She made Joshua lay down too.

"I love it!" She exclaimed, reaching her hands into air, trying to grasp the wind.

"Dutch showed me the catboat you left on the shore," The Red King started, lying next to her on the floor. "I always thought that your price was going to be a new one, so I was having it made the second we raided Whitecroft's treasury. I was surprise when you asked me to spread the gold among the citizens... I figured you deserved this anyways."

Joan rose to open the door to the captain's cabin; a king-sized bed lay in the center with plain white sheets and a cover.

"I figured we could design it with some things from the Scandes, we can fill your room with whatever you want once we make port." Joshua called, sitting up.

"Thank you, Josh." Joan replied, moving to her knees before Joshua and hugging him there on the floor.

Joshua frowned, but Joan couldn't see his expression, her head buried in his chest.

Joshua toted his bags onboard. Although it was a sea vessel, and not quite as smooth as a skyship, everything was familiar to him, so perfectly familiar. Joan stood at the helm pretending to steer it through the ocean, the soft hum of a shanty was heard from her tongue. Joshua dropped his bags down the hull and made his way below.

Joan watched him descended. She was almost ready to push off. The sun was about to break on the horizon and she didn't want to waste another second. The beautiful huntress stared at the mouth of the river. Before her lay an old and familiar frontier. The vast blue sea and the vast blue sky would soon be their room, perfectly joined like a single color, a single void. Joan always thought she would be afraid to return to the ocean, but in her excitement, all of that fear vanished. Maybe it was her company, maybe the war had changed her.

Either way, she was ready loose the sails at Joshua's command.

Joshua delved the depths of Joan's ship until he reached the very bottom. He didn't want to sleep in the hammocks right below the deck, used to the darkness and size of the lowest portion. He spread out his sleeping bag and prepared his old watch to ring early the next day. It would just be the two of them this time around. The king did not want to burden the tribes with a vessel full of rowdy and heated sailors.

Joshua stretched and stared at the floor for a time before beginning to ascend back into the sun. He was uncertain of his country, afraid his people would forget him. It was ridiculous, he thought, how much he had changed after winter. He knew it was because his people looked to him as guidance, and Joshua had to put on quite a show for them.

So that was it, Joshua discovered. Nothing had changed he was just pretending to be a good king, pretending like an atheist hiding in church.

Joshua poked his head from the grate and looked up at the orange sky. The birds began to wake and chirp and sing lackadaisically as they do. There was no sign of a storm on the horizon and the King amicably wrapped a band about his head to keep his hair above his ears. He had cut it down a few days after the war ended, also shaving his beard. But he didn't have much time to keep it shaven and often showed greying stubble, even at his young age. He untied the rope connecting the boat to the small pier and waved to Joan. Soon the sails were down and catching a well-angled wind. They were on their way.

"What should I name her?!" Joan asked as Joshua met her by the wheel.

"That's not up to me; it's your boat." Joshua denied.

Joan thought for a while as they listened to the gulls. The birds seemed to chase them, their flapping wings waving them off.

Joshua hoped that the Marquis didn't take his request too seriously, and Frea would keep her head above the water. It was after Joshua fought Frea the day they practiced in the meadow that Joshua understood what she was capable of. The girl could take a small space and contort it, altering time, splicing it with her own imagination. The girl could also see the future, or rather, she used to see the future, but no longer.

Frea confided in Joshua and Sach after the battle while telling the baron what had occurred during his absence. Elizabeth had told The Marquis about Frea as well since he had taken interest as to how the young lady knew LeCeleste would arrive above Whitechapel's estate at the opportune time. It was this escape of knowledge that upset Frea, creating a rift between the seer and the immortal captain.

The Victorian girl had never seemed so scared as that following week. After Whitecroft died she bumped into tables, spilt drinks. She was outside herself, a regular klutz. In that moment of vulnerability Joshua knew Frea needed work. She had a whole different side to her she kept locked away. Frea's dishonesty and fear of failure encouraged him to set The Marquis on the warpath against her. She wouldn't be a good advisor if she was afraid to take chances.

"I think I'll call her the Red Empress." Joan decided, looking over to Joshua expectantly.

"Sounds like you." Joshua hummed.

Joan smiled. "Yes, I suppose it does."

Joshua felt the salt air run through his shirt and looked to where the invisible gale might go. Behind him, the inland had become a thin blue line on the edge of the earth, small and obsolete. Joshua stood in Joan's kingdom now, aboard her land. He was thankful his title didn't mean a thing until they were back on solid ground.

The day was long, and Joshua made sure he relaxed until Joan was ready to be relieved from steering, but, even hours later, she did not seem to matter at all. She still stood beside the wheel with a keen smile on her pretty face, her dominant hand resting between the pegs. Yes, Joan was content, absolutely in love with her position and duty to escort Joshua to her homeland.

The waves lapped and beat against the hull while Joshua read, sitting on the railing with his legs dangling over the water. Joshua looked down at the azure ocean imagining what life would have been like if he had decided not to overthrow Whitecroft. He would still be in his apartment reading case files and examining crime scenes, or maybe he would be content for once and stayed with Elizabeth in her cottage, watching her dance, strolling with her through the town as if the world never ached.

Joshua squeezed his fist around the railing. His thoughts begged him to take a minute, so he closed his book.

If only he were less worried about others and more worried about himself; he would have never missed Elizabeth for a second. She was there, and he let her go, afraid of living some fantasy when that was all he ever wanted. It was uncanny, the man-made curse that need not magic nor wishes. The curse was named Discontent, and its effects were that the victim always wanted something they did not have, whether good or bad.

Joshua scratched his neck.

Joshua was egregious in defending his point as he watched the waves sidle by. He passed about the picket fence advocating for either side as if he could go back and see how the other path ended. That idea stirred within him, the idea of never knowing, the same fear Frea began to feel.

What if Joshua could, what if he could return to Val-Ashoth and pretend he didn't feel guilty for the sins of others? What if he could discard his urged to help others and abandon the world? Could he sleep at night? Joshua didn't know any of these answers, and for the first time in a long time he felt weakness. *Good kings aren't weak*, he thought, *they have no weaknesses, no emotions*. Kings were perfect creatures, able to do whatever was necessary to protect others. The King was supposed to lift up his civilization much like Atlas held aloft the earth. Damn the King that waits in his castle and isn't the first to pick up his sword and charge into battle. Damn the barons.

It was that entire day Joshua reflected such things. Al Hamra reflected on his duty, his philosophies, and scared himself into his own submission. Joan had never noticed him carve his sins on his heart, and nobody else but her was there to notice him begin to carve the sins he thought he might commit in the future. He was certain to make mistakes, and he wanted to be the best possible. Joshua laughed quietly, he was a hypocrite for asking The Marquis to break Frea, when he wasn't fully remade himself.

Joshua clutched his heart, he felt something pierce it. He wasn't feeling well, and this feeling occurred too often. The young king ran his fingers beneath his eyelids, checking for blood; he hoped he wouldn't get sick this week. He didn't want anyone to see him weak, retching blood and ash into the ground.

"I think it's your turn, Josh." Joan shouted out against the gale, her ears red from the sun and the wind. Joshua nodded solemnly and made his way up the steps. Joan watched as he slid his rough hands into the pegs. He hadn't said much after they departed. Joshua didn't look at her. Her King stared ahead, waiting for something to show in the water.

"You're doing it again." Joan poked, "you're shutting the world out."

Joshua looked at her, his eyes slightly emptied, but it was hard to tell. The eyes were the windows to the soul, and all Joan saw were the yellow eyes of a demon.

"How did you know?" He sighed, looking back into the distance again. Joan sighed too. It didn't seem that he truly cared to pull himself out of his own brain. She wanted him to. She wanted Joshua to pay more attention to her.

Joan stole one more glance of her king; his crown of cloth was beat by the wind, small strands of hair and sewing ruffled with the breeze.

"Because I know you." Joan smirked softly as she began to retreat into her quarters, "But don't worry," She called, descending the stairs and entering the captain's cabin. "I have a solution!"

Joshua heard her vanish and expected her to return immediately, but it was to his surprise that she didn't. Minutes passed, and he began to worry if she was alright. He began to count all the things that could go wrong.

Had he steered too hard and sent her crashing into a cabinet, rendering her unconscious? Maybe she had fallen asleep or was afraid to return empty handed, not having a plan whatsoever.

Joshua thought too much.
Scratch, scratch, scratch.

Part 2/Resentment

Frea stared at the line of farmers waiting patiently outside her red tent. Citizens, and all of them waited to see her, as she stood in place of The Red King. It was the middle of the week and she did not have the patience to deal with them. She sat there in the center of the crimson tent in a feigned attempt to enjoy the shade it provided her, but her black garb caused her to perspire, almost profusely. Frea tried to hide this.

There was a guard standing in the tent flap, holding it for the next person to enter.

In most situations, a farmer's request was simple, something arbitrary and trifle. The young farmer, a woman this time, stepped into the shade before her temporary queen and bowed in respect. She wore a long shirt which covered her pockets and short jeans which stopped at her calves.

Out of all things, it was the farmers' way of life and culture which disturbed Frea. Their lack of decency both in public and private domains. They had nothing nice for themselves and carried their backs as if they were a burden within their body. They hunched over and slapped each foot to the ground before the other with no elegance, no certainty. They never bought themselves anything new either.

Here, this woman talked without tact, and it troubled Frea.

Frea stared at her while her mouth moved, unable to understand the audible jaw. She stared until her mouth ceased moving and stared some more. She was tired of listening to common rabble day in and day out. Where were the bankers, the lawyers, the businessmen who wore suits and dresses that matched and complimented her elegance? Where were the soirees where men offered to buy her drinks, their lips forming pleasant sounds unlike the cacophony she was enduring? Just months ago, The Red King had given them ample amounts of money for their years of hard work under their previous ruler, and yet they didn't know how to use it, their lives still utterly the same, simple, dumb.

The seer fell into line under the new order Joshua laid before them. She stood by his side while he was given his crown from the other barons, a jewel he quickly tucked into the vault to collect dust.

Joshua also didn't know nice things when he saw them.

Frea knew, and Joshua knew, that she would be by his side to aid him while he redefined his kingdom. It was something Frea had seen in her visions. Yet, she no longer remembered what she was supposed to do as one of his highest officers.

When she laid in bed at night aboard LeCeleste in her small limited apartment, she expected to wake up again with a revelation, another glimpse into the future. That glimpse would allow her to redirect and manipulate the ebb and flow of causality, ultimately writing her own story as she saw fit. That was her strength, the most powerful and rare of all affinities. But now, she was useless and timid without her courage, her ability to see the future. Asked to pick up more duties in his absence, Frea only wished she could remember how each day was supposed to go. She had forgotten everything, and she would hate to make a mistake.

The farmer still stared at her, waiting for a reply. Frea rubbed her forehead in hope of daunting her daunting headache. She cut her eyes to The Marquis, another cohort of her king, who stood just slightly behind her in silent mockery. Frea used to be someone, and now she was no one. The Marquis nodded to her, filling in the blanks as to whether she should or should not let this peasant have what she requested. It was The Marquis who listened to them through her, helping her get through each day, silently reminding her how pathetic she was. Frea was surrogate for Joshua, but also, a marionette for The Marquis.

"Fine," She huffed and rolled her eyes, "As you say it, it shall be done."

The Villager began to thank her, Frea trying to wave her off with her hand. She wouldn't leave, she was still thanking her. *Why? Just leave.* She begged.

The Marquis grabbed the woman who began to cry in joy and guided her outside. The Marquis reminded her not to keep the other citizens waiting. He was polite, chivalrous, looking deep into her eyes with sincerity and grace. Ill known to the temporal queen was what request she had granted this woman. This woman was a mother, and her daughter had become deathly ill. With the help of royalty, with the help of Frea, her daughter would be treated in Paris.

Frea watched as people came and went. She tried her best not to hate them, to loath their simplicity and their lack of understanding. Every little thing about them was a red flag to her, sirens blaring in her brain, begging her to point out their flaws. She knew exactly caused these feelings. The flaw she saw in others was due to her social defenses that prioritized highlighting the chinks of others. This virus, this anomaly, was birth by her newfound insecurities. She wanted to point out everyone else's mistakes so that no one would see her issues, so that no one would look down on her.

It was a discriminating bully complex, something she had adopted when she was young. It was caused by the Meeting of Sorceresses once every few years. She would watch her family threaten each other, watch as each of them exploited the others until they got what they came for. It was just like the council she had discarded a day or two ago. The Meeting of Sorceresses was the grouping of alpha wolves who held a philosophy of kill-or-be-killed. She tried her best to keep those tendencies at bay, or in the least, subtle and less obvious, so that she wouldn't hurt others. It also helped her maintain a low-profile, so that she would not be caught by other mages and picked on. She adapted a smile, her way of laughing and her composure all to hid and denied how much she hated people and how much she doubted herself. This was ironic, stemming from someone with her particular gifts.

It was just like the barons, she thought.

Frea looked to Lafayette again who shook his head.

"Request denied." She muttered, her hand on her chin. The man walked away angry and stomped his feet outside the tent, cursing her and the new order. The guards watched him carefully, hoping he would not do anything brash or unnecessary.

It was Elizabeth who helped Frea learn to bear with humanity. Elizabeth, her non-blood related sister, was the only one to protect her when the mages got together at the Meeting of Sorceresses. It reminded Frea of a school dance like prom, a school anything for that matter. The meetings were riddled with childish accusations and intentions that she couldn't protect herself from. There were niches and groupies and flirtation and reputation. The worst part was that Frea was the freak in those scenarios, the teenager nobody asked to dance with. The one with the freckles and the braces. But that all changed when she met Elizabeth who protected her like a little sister. Elizabeth showed her how to defend herself, how to gain the upper hand.

Frea looked at The Marquis, she had zoned out again, thinking of the past. The Marquis shook his head again, a resounding negative look on his face. Whoever stood before her certainly did not deserve his wish granted so Frea waved him off without words. The skinny man before her looked angry. This, Frea did not notice. She expected him to sulk away in shame.

Instead the farmer strode forth, brandishing something sharp from his shirt. Frea looked at him, his killer intent, his hunger for recompense. She began to stand, she didn't know which way to turn. Her feet began to buckle, her arms shook on the armrest rattling her wooden throne. As she watched him loom closer and closer. The guards sprang from outside the tent, slower than the man who wished to attack. The assassin sprinted forth and raised the shiv above his head. It was a gruesome shiv, metal flakes were barely attached to it, places where the blade had been sharpened abrasively.

The Marquis took half a step, his saber ready for the berserker. In one swift motion he neatly cleaved through the assailant from underneath his armpit through his neck. He fell into two pieces in a shower of blood that stained Frea's coat, dripped on her face.

She knew in that moment, her eyes wide open, how vulnerable she was.

The Captain of the guards screamed at his men, "Who didn't search the civilians?! Maxwell, you were supposed to search every one of them head to toe!"

"Quiet!" The Marquis hushed, "Don't make a commotion. Send the rest of the villagers home, we're done for today."

The Captain grumbled and Frea watched them drag both segments of the man out the back of the tent. They would notify his next of kin. The Marquis opened the front tent, careful to keep them from seeing the bloodstain on the floor. He waved the line of Farmers off. The crowd of swine would run back to their murky water for the day, only to resurface the next with their trivial complaints.

Frea prayed that she wasn't hoping they would die before tomorrow, but she wanted them to.

The Marquis knelt before Frea who hadn't moved and inch. She was glued to her chair, unable to rise. He tried to say something to her, she couldn't answer him. Frea refused to answer, not to him. Laffy removed his coat and gently dabbed her face with it, the white cotton ruined. It was a waste of good cotton, and Lafayette should have known better than to stain it over something trifle like blood.

Frea knew her one victory today would be in this: to leave the tent immediately. She would leave The Marquis in the tent alone, waiting for a "thank you." It would be the one thing she could control.

Frea burst from the chair once the Marquis briefly turned away. She left through the back. Again, she marched away into the field. She unclasped her stained dress and let it waft to the dirt. She could not allow herself to wear stains. She tried her best to stand straight, but she could feel the twist in her spine, the effects of sitting in a chair for too long. She must have been slumping in her throne, how did she not notice?

Frea tried to race away to the old garden, to the burned estate, or to Hiker's Folly. She wanted to hide somewhere where no one could see her. Back in the distance she could hear The Marquis walking slowly after her, following her. He would wait for her to be vulnerable and gawk at her. He would chastise her as he always seemed to.

Frea picked up her pace, she would not be caught in black hose.

Joshua finally saw Joan emerge from her cabin. She bit the blade of a knife and raised two large bottles of rum in her hands. Joshua smirked, that was her solution to his silence. His accomplice was aiming to get him drunk. Joan quickly stole through the flight of stairs and placed the glass of one against his neck like a knife.

Maybe the girl had drunk a few bottles without him, or perhaps she had been crying.

Joan lifted the bottle from her chest and placed it on the stern.

It was a peculiar thing, Elizabeth's magic. Joshua needn't eat nor drink, but if he did, he could still feel the side effects of the chemicals such as caffeine and alcohol as if he was human, or perhaps ifrits could enjoy drink and food too. Elizabeth's magic had a tether to his brain, monitoring his lifestyle so that it might logically react in most ways a human would, under certain circumstances Elizabeth deemed legal for

454

his body to feel. Unfortunately, this made Joshua feel like an android, a robot with settings. Fun Mode, off; Blood Mode, on, and so forth.

Joan whined, "How are you supposed to get happy if you won't loosen up? You need to stop being such a zombie, zombie."

It would almost sound encouraging, Joshua thought, if he weren't operating what he considered "heavy machinery."

"There are more things to life than happiness, Joanne." Joshua replied.

"*Oh…*" Joan replied lazily, "I see, using my full name, trying to distance me, huh? You're trying to be the *cool* king who's *too* good for friends."

Joshua shook his head, his eyes still pasted to the ocean. There was so much empty space, which both comforted and daunted the baron. At any moment the loose water could break, something from beneath, something old, something mythic, could rise out and swallow them without so much a warning or "hello." But, Joshua digressed, one could also look forward to that sight, look for it and remember it, if one didn't die, of course.

It was a dark world, an unknown world, and more so an unknown sea. Some time ago, scientists discovered penicillin, engineers created cars and planes and rockets. Ingenuity soared with technological advancement, but the world rose so fast that it seemed to leave something behind. Humanity was like a child in a dark forest, the child built a lantern to chase the demons away. The boy was successful, he never knew the demons, and never saw the fireflies either.

Joshua chuckled quietly, with power comes philosophy, he guessed. Unused to his mind scouring for wisdom. A year ago, he would drive at the edge of his seat. He was reckless, youthful. Now, it seemed he was growing up too fast.

"See?" Joan chuckled too, "I can make you laugh too!"

Joshua twisted his mouth, was Joan making jokes while he thought? Had his missed something she said?

It sounded like the young lady was comparing herself to someone else.

Joan was jealous of someone else, who occupied Joshua's mind. Little did she know it was not Elizabeth that grabbed Joshua's heart. It was another man, a man in a yellow raincoat.

Frea sat in the garden, she had made it. She believed Lafayette had left her alone. What she didn't know was that her vilified friend was pacing outside the entrance, debating whether to enter or leave her be for the night.

Frea waved her feet to and fro under the bench, she clicked her shoes together and keenly noticed another speck of blood. This red ink blotch found its way through the dress, staining her favorite pair of boots. The fair lady lifted that blemished shoe to her seat and began to scrub the mark with her thumb, but she made a mistake, and scratched the leather with her nail. Staring at it, she shook, the small line where the skin was damaged was unnoticeable to any spying eye. It should have been a minute causality of wear, but Frea judged the damage inadmissible.

The seer untied her laces and tossed the shoe to the ground in frustration. It was unbecoming of her to wear such ruddy trash, and now, it was unbecoming of her to wear only one shoe. She discarded the good boot as well. She would never wear those shoes again; she was too good for them.

Frea looked down to find more red. Splotches of sanguine were now witnessed on her bodice. She was infuriated, how much more would she have to throw away to achieve peace? She began to untie the leather behind her back fuming in discontent with her attire.

The Marquis placed his toe on the first square stone in the garden, it was an ill-placement for the slab which wiggled beneath his foot, knocking against the stone after it. If Frea didn't know he was still here, she definitely knew now.

That loose stone served as a warning sign, an alarm bell.

The noise gave the immortal man the courage to brave her anger yet again. It was his duty as Joshua's friend to look after his staff, even if it meant hurting them. It was hard to imagine the girl could be any more hurt than she was, however. After almost being killed mere hours ago, it would be trying to imagine anyone else having as bad a day as her, unless that person hadn't survived.

That would be a bad day.

Lafayette looked around the corner of the ruins, the old estate that was burned down. Perhaps somewhere inside, Whitecroft's body lay under the rubble. Lafayette hoped it had turned to dust, that her grains left the area on a viscous breeze.

Lafayette careened the corner as he spied Frea. She had removed her outer shell, and now sat in a black cloth undergarment. She was truly old-fashioned. Even her knickers revealed nothing of her curvy body. Lafayette approached the girl quietly and sat across from her on the opposite bench.

"Go away," Frea mumbled into her drawers, her knees tucked to her breasts, "You've done enough for today, don't you agree?"

The Marquis couldn't tell if it was the cold spring night or her emotional condition which made her sniff uncontrollably. If he asked, she would make an excuse for the pollen which floated sweetly in the air, not that she would be conceding enough to admit she had allergies.

The Marquis didn't say anything, he stared at the floor in front of them. He wished there were another table between them, just in case she had another blade hidden somewhere along her thighs.

"It's okay," The Marquis began, choosing his words carefully. "It's okay for me to be here… you know?"

Laffy fumbled a small stone in his hand, just like Joshua and him did in their talks. He thought it peculiar that she would decide to go there instead of anywhere else. This was also where Al Hamra spent his time when he needed to think. Laffy looked back to the girl, she seemed younger than he had originally thought. He didn't have the boldness to ask. He smiled.

What did age matter to a man hundreds of years old?

He didn't wonder that for his own sake, for his own heart. The Marquis had loved a girl once, and he thought it was enough for his lifetime.

Frea spied him through one eye, almost cheating at a game of hide and seek, except, she was the one hiding, and he was the one trying to find her from where she hid behind her legs. Perhaps it was closer to a game of peek-a-boo.

"It's okay." The Marquis repeated, through the silence his words were fresh in his mind. The girl still shivered so he found himself removing one of his layers and tossing it upon her head. He couldn't have a dame get sick on him, especially when she had a country to run.

"Stop saying that." Frea retorted, catching on to his message. It was a call for her to accept her failure. It was call to her to become average, she surmised.

"You know," The Marquis sighed, looking back to the space between them. "I've made mistakes too, a lot of them."

"Good for you, you can afford to make mistakes. None of them are fatal, you outlast them all. Your mistakes don't shape your life."

The Marquis thought about it before answering, "I once had a friend, a comrade actually, who stayed with me when I ran from the world. He was a good friend, not a great friend but a good one.

One day, a few years later, after we had a steady population due to picking up so many vagabonds, we started seeing less of each other. I would have these spells of depression, lock myself away with my books for days. He had

458

his own problems, he was almost a town drunk some would say. I never thought to stop him from his pleasure…"

The Marquis paused, he had dropped the rock from his hand by accident.

"One day I had finally gathered the strength to go outside after a few months of reading. I decided to meet my people again, show my face around. It was going to be a good day, I told myself, a damn good day. I decided sometime in that day I would go look at my skyship, an old rig I had found in India, and, walking along the lowest floor of terrace, I see him just standing there on the other side of the rails. I looked at him and for some reason I smiled. I didn't want him to let go of the rails, I was just so happy to see him again and thought nothing of it. He actually smiled back. It was a small smile, something he gave me right before he disappeared through the clouds."

Frea looked up from her knees, "But that's not your fault, when someone else decides to die."

The Marquis tried to smile, young people were a funny thing.

"Isn't it?" He asked, "All the times I could have checked on him, but I was too concerned with myself. People like Joshua, they have the strength to save people, they save people all the time. Indeed, he is saving lives. But regular people can save a life too. They just need to be there. To kill someone, all you need to do is make them lonely. To save someone, all you need to do is be a good friend. So, I do think it was my fault, for making him lonely, for not being a good friend. Ignorance and negligence are cruel weapons to use, especially against those you love. The worst part is that, sometimes, you don't know you're using them."

"You aren't being clear." Frea spat softly, still guarded.

The Marquis re-centered himself. Perhaps he had been rambling. How could he explain what he meant, why he had told her this originally?

"Erik died after eight minutes of falling. Eight minutes of mistake that happened nearly two centuries years ago. I still feel it, I have to carry it around with me. I made a mistake, Frea. But, I do believe that mistakes make us who we are. I wanted to come here to encourage you to make mistakes, not ones as big as I did, but make mistakes that are small at least. It's better than living your whole life afraid of screwing up. Either way, perfection is a fallacy. Adam and Eve saw to that long ago."

Frea remained silent, her cards close to her chest. After that silence became unnerving, she watched her comrade rise from the bench slowly. She heard him whisper something to himself, something unintelligible.

For once, she had doubts about whether it was directed against her.

"Oh, and lass?" The Marquis called back to her.

The handsome man stood underneath the moon, his hair in the subtle breeze. She felt her heart and it hurt her like punch from within. She waited for him to speak, her eyes rising from her arms. He stood there proud, but she noticed his skin was becoming pale, almost blue without his second layer. His faint perfume still floated down from the discarded jacket she wore about her head. It felt like he was standing right above her, the velvet cloth was still warm. She heard his next words clearer than any bell, and louder than anything he had ever told her before, anything any one had ever told her before.

She waited for certain words, already blushing.

"You sucked today," Lafayette chuckled, "do better next time."

Frea hesitated in her smile, not that he could see her mouth in her cotton disguise. The seer expected something quite different from him, but that was her mistake. The temporal queen was left alone as the moon began to rise above her head. The night was halfway finished, and she should begin her trudge home. She waited until Laffy's shirt had lost its warmth, and she was sure not to see him in the distance, walking back to LeCeleste.

Frea put her boots back on and laced them tight, the smudge of blood and the scratch ever evident without her skirt to cover it. It would do, it was only a short walk. She would discard them once she was back home.

Frea wore The Marquis' jacket around her shoulders while she walked home. Although it did not match well with her attire, Frea was comfortable.

Joshua watched as Joan twirled about the small fire she had ignited on the deck. It flicked there energetically in a wide firepit that illuminated the whole of the ship.

The girl was crazy, but that wasn't such a bad thing, Joshua always admired the energy of others. The Red King admired her attitude as well. Perhaps she was fueled by the promise of seeing her people again. Albeit, she had too much to drink.

"Join me Josh!" She begged, dancing in circles to a song no one heard. Joshua was surprised she still remined upright despite the rocking ship. In the darkness, the boats motions tempted to lull the boy to sleep.

If only Dutch were here, The American thought, the bald man would have loved to dance with her. It never occurred to Joshua how much Dutch might have been a father figure to the two of them. He wasn't an old man, but neither was he young enough to be seen as her brother. It must've hit Joan hard when she found out he was dead. After all, it still stung his soul.

The pair visited Dutch's grave often, which often caused the huntress to cry quietly on the dead grass. It was the only spot in the meadow that hadn't grown, perhaps eternally effected by Frea's residual magic.

Joan still pranced about the wooden column, free of doubt. Joshua looked down to the bottle of rum besides his feet and picked it into his hands. Maybe just a few sips, Joshua thought, or maybe he could down the bottle.

No, he had to pay attention. Scandinavia was a dark sliver now, softly reminding him of his chore. He had to remain sober, for in the morning, they would pass through treacherous waters. The Scandinavians, Gurdard's people, were a seafaring people who enjoyed fishing and docile labor as much as raiding ships on the open seas. Many men grew up in the Scandes who decided to become pirates later in life. Many of them lost their lives and their boats in the North Sea, never straying too far from home. Thus, the area that Joshua and Joan would be passing was full of these rotting vessels, jutting from the ocean waiting to pierce any passerby. To strike one would send their float down to join a graveyard crew.

Joshua would have to tread slowly, only using the foresail to move them along. It would be a long morning of squeezing through tight spots and praying he hadn't missed something lurking below.

Frea sat the next day in the same chair she always had to sit in. Surprisingly, she found herself able to listen to her subjects. She tried her best to be fair, to do what seemed right for the country as a whole, but not being able to see the future dampened her hopes.

Frea wanted to be frugal and send every citizen home, to let them take the risks, let them handle their petty squabbles and monetary troubles. She was less reserved about failure today, but that did not change her hatred for her humanity as a whole. Whatever they asked, although she tried to give them the benefit of doubt, still upset her.

The people should be apt to defend themselves, provide for themselves and yet somehow, they weren't, or so Frea thought.

Frea nodded until the last citizen of the day found her way out the tent. It had been a long night for Frea. The girl couldn't sleep, being away from the premonitions she was used to, her current dreams seemed candid, stale, and eerie. During the last few weeks she would sit in her bed rocking herself, afraid of closing her eyes.

"Miss," The Guard Captain interrupted, "Although the commoners are all taken care of, there is a traveler who wished to see The Red King, may I show him in?"

Frea nodded, whether from dozing or actual compliance it made no difference. She watched as the man bowed low to the ground, lower than any other man that regarded her.

Finally, she thought, someone who knew manners and power when he saw it. He also looked decent in style, wearing the latest creations from Paris.

"Your excellency," He announced, slowly raising his head from the grass beneath their feet. "I have come from Paris to meet with your esteemed ruler, the Magnificent Red King. However, I was rife with disappointment to find he has left on a diplomatic errand overseas. It would be my greatest gratitude if his office was to loan me a few coins so that I might wait for his return at one of the local inns. I promise my presence will be both discreet and rewarded as I am sure the merciful Al Hamra would be overjoyed to see me."

Frea liked the way the man spoke, he utilized a feathered tongue which plodded paper delicately. The strange man considered his words carefully and praised often those he spoke about. He didn't ramble about his opinions nor his feelings on the subject. He spoke his peace and waited for a response silently, still bowing in admiration for his company.

Frea was inclined to agree with the man. Besides, room and board were trifle expenses at the inns. She was sure the man would behave himself and found no reason Joshua wouldn't be interested in seeing the character upon his return.

"Your expenses will be paid for, traveler. A guard will retrieve you when The Red King returns. He will summon you at his convenience or meet you where you are staying. Is there anything else?" Frea replied.

"No, your majesty. A thousand blessings." The man thanked. Swiftly, he retreated from the tent, leaving her and her officials alone under the red-filtered light.

That was how it should be done, Frea thought, quick and painless.

Frea smirked as the man slowly disappeared into the distance. She admired his mind for Paris' seasonal color, a yellow raincoat was both stylish and functional during the monsoon season, after all.

"Do you think that's wise?" The Marquis asked, still looming behind her as all other days. "We don't know this man or his intentions. We didn't even ask."

"The King can handle himself," Frea snapped, "You asked be to take more risks so I'm taking one. Isn't that what you wanted?"

The Marquis sighed, "I suppose I can't complain against that logic. What's next on the agenda?"

Frea looked to her left where a small note was laid on an even smaller coffee table. The whole tent was full of antiques like this, moved about pieces on a stage to accommodate the current task. She lifted the parchment delicately and began to read quietly.

Work with people, talk to people, listen to people, watch people... Frea frowned, why did she have to do so much people work? She missed Joshua, he would do these things without hesitation and Frea would only have to wait to see if he needed help. Plus, he never needed it so greatly she would have to speak at length. She was supposed to be in the Marquis' position, standing there minding her own business, overseer to a single and menial task, Joshua.

The King never needed anything and preferred to keep to himself. In his free time, unless Elizabeth was around, he had taken to reading literatures, trying to soak up knowledge whenever he could. Royalty had changed him, his stern and quiet rage was directed, sedated perhaps. He had more strength than ever before, and his power allowed him to carry his guilt well.

If he were not so taken with Elizabeth, Frea might have thrown a glove into the ring for queen.

"Must we do any of this?" Frea gawked.

"Is something wrong?" The Marquis sighed again. "Don't tell me you're ready to call the day over *again*. We've hardly begun."

"All of these jobs require me to listen to people, its horrific."

"It's horrific that Joshua allows you to stand in. How did that man ever come upon such a child like you and think it okay to place you on his roster?"

Frea scoffed, The Marquis never could be one-sided, his kind tones did nothing to cushion his verbal blows. He was silver-tongued, a sphinx. The girl waved the paper in her hands, and the Marquis retrieved it between his index and middle-finger like a crane. He paced before her, reading the list. The Machiavellian covered his mouth. Outside, the rain began to pick up, pattering softly on the tent.

"Look at this one!" The Marquis pointed out, tapping on the paper. "there's a new transport of stone that needs our approval. You can do the signing while I talk to the drivers."

"Fine." Frea snapped, still not liking the prospects.

The Marquis lifted his umbrella over his head and opened the tent flap. He stared out at the rolling clouds, hopefully the current weather would hold, and not become worse. Wrinkling his nose, he motioned for the darling stand-in to join him. Frea twisted her face at him.

"I have my own, thank you." She huffed.

"You won't mind finding your own way to the shipment, then? I'm getting tired waiting on you, your royal sluggishness." The Marquis joked sheepishly.

Frea jerked her chin and lifted her dress in a wad, she did not want to soil yet another outfit that day. She would

465

have to bear with the mud below her high-heeled boots. She lifted her umbrella and strode out with The Marquis in tow. She was going to beat him there.

The Marquis didn't mind staying behind her brisk pace. He wanted to be there when she tripped over her vanity and watch every second as she struggled to compose herself again.

Lafayette started to think he was a cruel man, if not only for a moment, as he trudged behind the beautiful girl. He held the odd feeling of doing evil for good reasons. He didn't like pressing the girl's buttons, it made him feel foolish, flirtatious, even. But, neither did he want Joshua to return only to discover no progress had been made with his promise.

The Marquis did not want to break a promise, even if it meant hurting someone else's feelings. It was for Frea's own good, anyway.

The Marquis was appreciative of Frea's character. He had to admire anyone that was consistent in any personality. People who tried too many characters, changed between styles and emotions, pretending it was Halloween every day, were people to keep away from.

Frea did remind Laffy of Halloween, however. Frea almost always wore her dresses, the same century with the same "poof" under the skirt. She always wore high-heeled leather boots and a bow about her waist with whatever the color or design. The fine and key elements were always there, but there was always tones of black. If she was an artist, she would have painted the Mona Lisa, a stunning and brilliant piece of art. But, she would have painted the Mona Lisa so many times any given critic would question whether the piece was of any value. A wise man could indulge in monotony, indulge in Frea.

The Marquis was not that wise.

During Laffy's senile ramble, he finally beheld the tragedy. A few miles from where they began, the last baron watched as Frea's heel sank into the shifting mud and snapped.

The woman fell into the mud beneath her.

Lafayette smiled, it was her consequence of trying to bring her city clothes into the countryside. There was a reason the farmers, even the women, wore pants day in and day out. They made sense given the environment.

Splat went the girl, her bum caked in brown soil. Her boots were ruined as the ooze sank beneath the laces and seeped inside to slather her legs with grime. Frea felt the cold earth; it could be compared to something like a dog's tongue.

She didn't need this, she didn't want this. She looked back at Lafayette, mortified to see him watching her with a thin smile stretched across his lips. He looked like a demon ready to strike a deal.

In a brief burst of rage and humiliation, Frea tore at her skirt and removed her boots yet again. She hated this hell. She hated everything. She stood up as the rain soaked her hair, her socks began to turn a sickly brown, the color she detested most. *Brown.*

Where was her castle? Where was her sanctuary? Frea thought. She was supposed to be inside, she was supposed to lay on a chaise lounge while people fed her grapes. She would only answer to Joshua. She could do whatever she wanted within his law.

The Marquis began to chuckle, moving his umbrella over her. He knew how much she hated people to be close, so he held it out from himself and let the rain do its worst to him. The Last Baron didn't have the heart to wait until she broke apart, he really didn't have the heart to make anyone cry.

Frea looked at him, the water poured over his head and drenched it. His long hair matted against his forehead, his eyebrow twitched to block raindrops from his pupils. He wasn't Frea's enemy, she knew this. It was just because Frea felt frustrated. Because she was refusing defeat, The Marquis treated her like a child. He wasn't incorrect in the matter.

The Marquis was sopping, imperfect under the heavy torrent of sloshing rain. That imperfection led him to care for others, led him to keep his eyes of his vanity and focus on others.

Perhaps she was being too selfish. Frea guessed.

In that view of The Marquis something fostered in Frea. The girl wanted to be like Laffy, she didn't want the weather to hurt her pride. She wanted to be humble, and therefore become a titan among her peers, unapproachable, flawlessly flawed. There, smothered in mud, the girl wanted to admit defeat.

Frea finally understood that she couldn't be perfect. Yet, The Marquis didn't know of this mental decision. Neither did Frea know how it would change the course of her future. The changes wouldn't come suddenly in her future, she would have to fight defeat again and again over the following years. But one day it would begin to wane, her self-consciousness, her walls. One day she would be an angel, if she wasn't already.

Frea rose, slapped the umbrella from over her, and pushed it back to Lafayette. Without a word she took off her shoes and turned away from him. She walked barefoot, the slimy mud rising between her toes made her shudder.

The Marquis smiled and unfolded the umbrella, he was already wet, through and through, there was no need to use the umbrella anymore. He was proud of Frea. She wasn't going to give up too easily. But she was, at least, letting go of her baggage.

Frea sighed. Whatever grace she had in her cadence was undone, crippled by her sliding feet. Her leggings were ruined, her straight hair began to fringe and twist. She could be immaculate without her clothes, couldn't she? She wanted to show The Marquis that her fall hadn't destroyed her. She wasn't fragile, she was strong. She would show them all, even if every last strand of her clothes unfurled and her makeup continued to stream and stain her cheeks. She would show them all she didn't need them.

But she knew she did.

Everyone needs friends.

On purpose, The Marquis chose the furthest distance to make Frea walk. He wasn't a seer like his peer, but he knew beyond doubt that Frea would fall, if not now, then later. It was a cruel deed he did, dragging her out into the storm, but it was for Joshua, it was for Frea, it was for the whole country. It was a cruel deed much like it was a cruel world. Laffy prayed he hadn't taken his task too far.

Part 3/Repel

Joshua stood at the bow of The Red Empress and called back ship positions to Joan. He served as a human mine radar. The whole morning had Al Hamra scampering about the deck to ensure their ship didn't join the forsaken graveyard they waded through. He watched the shadows, the edges, and the protrusions carefully, allowing his captain to navigate through the treacherous waters smoothly. There had been only a few hiccups, moments when sloshing water made a rouge attempt to budge them a few inches in a bad direction. Still, they had made it through to the end.

The day broke upon the ocean and the duo watched the coast, now just meters away. They could spy smokestacks from cabins and small villages. Fishing boats sat on the shore while fishermen emptied their nets. The breeze and mist cooled the spring air and made Joan slightly cold. She differed back to her fur clothing, the hide wrapped about her body snuggly, comforting her with a familiar feeling of security. The huntress gleamed from cheek to cheek.

While looking far off at her beautiful homeland, Joan almost split a small fishing boat in two. She apologized as the fishermen cursed. Joshua moved to the stern and promptly removed the mesmerized wheelman from her position. Joan was too distracted by her homeland, even more so than Joshua whom beheld the beautiful landscape for the first time.

It didn't take long for Joan to tie her ship to the docks. The local villagers glared at the marvelous schooner, their own peoples used to flat cogs instead of tall French ships. Together the envoy unloaded their luggage and climbed down to the shore. They still had a few miles to venture inland. The Ceremonial hall in which Gurdard waited for them was placed on a large plateau inland, right at the base of the biggest mountain.

"Don't you just love it!?" Joan exclaimed, "The fresh air, the smell of the mist, the smell of the fire, it's all so amazing!"

Joshua nodded. He did love it. He almost wished he had staged his rebellion here instead.

The American made his way behind Joan through the village. Men and women were busy with work, sawing, cooking, fishing, milking. Everything the locals did was magnificent, worthy of art and inspiration. It was the joy of labor in a rich and resourceful land, to be able to do many different things, each one contributing to society equally. Joshua's people only had grain fields, and a few grape fields, at the moment. But one day he wanted to bring game back to his province, bring markets and mines to diversify his lands.

Joan arrived at the base of the Scandes and ran her hand along the path marker, a thin strip of yellow linen which waved under a pile of rocks. They were about to ascend along the mountain. Joshua hoped he hadn't overpacked, or the weight would burden him needlessly. They began their climb slowly, the slope hardly noticeable. But further along Joshua could see how dangerous the paths were, and why so few people walked it.

Joshua twitched after every yellow marker they passed. The cloth flickered in the wind, mocking him. This estranged Joshua to his thoughts. He imagined yellow coats pinned beneath the rocks, perhaps he could smash Solomon's head with a rock.

Joshua blinked and pressed his hand to his eye. He looked at his fingertips and ran his thumb over the blood splotch. The felt a wrinkle in his nose, he wiped beneath it, expecting mucus from the cold, but it was blood as well.

The back of Joshua's head scratched endlessly.

Scratch, scratch, scratch.

"The winter season usually blocks these paths. Come springtime, the melting ice carves the path away or leaves loose rocks. So be careful Josh." Joan warned. Thankfully, she did not look back at Joshua.

The road did indeed begin to look worse. The duo shuffled up the path, resorting to all four limbs for traction. The gravel beneath them slipped and broke off in small shards, kicking up dust which floated down into the valley. The two were practically scaling the sides of the mountain. Joshua wondered how the natives could brave such an incline. The path was treacherous, a 45-degree angle.

"Hold on," Joan started, "Let me lean back a minute. Could you hold me up, Josh?"

Joshua reached forward and pressed his palm against Joan's back. She let go of the sheet before her and placed her weight on his arm, sitting back on his palm. Joshua found the resourcefulness to cheat his grip. His ifrit talons could be abused, serving as a much need piton. His talons helped his hand stay in place, helped him climb.

Joan looked out to the valley below them. One false move, one rightward slip and they would be tumbling down into the trees below. Nevertheless, the view was gorgeous. Mist had covered much of the peninsula, giving them much needed cold and shade. The mist weaved its way between the trees and covered the mountaintops, providing a sense of mystery for what was yet to be seen. Despite their dangerous position, Joan and Joshua wanted to stay there on that path for a few minutes longer, so that they could paint the rest of that colorful picture and remember it by heart.

"Joan, as much as I enjoy letting you rest, my wrist is starting to get tired." Joshua complained.

"Sorry, Josh." Joan huffed. "Let me grab my climbing axe from my bag real fast. It'll only take a second."

"You could have done that before we started climbing, or two minutes ago." Joshua winced.

"Well I didn't think the slope would continue for this long so stop whining. You're the one with "magical powers," why don't you grow a pair of wings and fly us up there? The end is just over there."

"Were it so easy, I would." Joshua huffed. He waited few more moments. "How's it going?"

"I almost have it, calm down. Say, Joshua, you're not trying to say I'm fat, are you?" Joan teased.

Joshua chuckled, staring at his claw embedded in the rock. If only Elizabeth were here, he thought, she could probably just teleport them to the top.

But there was no adventure in that.

"Got it!" Joan whispered, moving her pack behind her again. She dug the metal blade into the shale and began to climb again. Joshua shook his hand, trying to flow blood into his arm.

Joshua wondered if ifrits had some sort of blood flow which made them tired, especially as exhausted as he was. Perhaps it was just his illusory body that made his arm grow numb.

Joshua wiped his face and continued.

It was that moment when Joshua looked back up from the view that he realized he had been watching Joan climb for guidance up the mountain, unintentionally staring at her rear. Joshua found it hard to stare anywhere else but up, given the fact that he wanted to watch where she climbed. It would be reckless of Joshua to look anywhere else.

Joshua concluded to close the eye closest to her as to not feel perverted, but he could still make out her butt, even with the infraction.

Joshua recalled Sach's words when they were at his house. Here Joshua was, alone with Joan, just the two of them facing the world, scaling a mountain.

They made a good team.

Joshua couldn't help but imagine Joan in a throne beside him, but it made him feel guilty. Joan was a great personality, but she wasn't Elizabeth. The more he thought about it the more he realized he didn't know what he thought on the matter.

Elizabeth was amazing, she was comforting, but she didn't challenge Joshua much.

Joan was adventurous and headstrong. She pushed Joshua out of his comfort zone and helped him enjoy the moments they found themselves in.

Elizabeth would never go hiking with Joshua, she was too posh. But she was also very posh.

Joan was a regular traveler, and Joshua felt he could go anywhere with her.

Joshua wiped his forehead again, stopping to let Joan clamber further away from him. He couldn't allow himself to get that close if he thought about her that way. It was going to be a rough few days if he couldn't be comfortable around her. He hoped he wouldn't become nervous. He hated relationship tropes.

"You better catch up, old man!" Joan teased again, looking down to him.

Joshua also thought about how much harder it would be not to kiss her. The man was enamored, but also, something else. He felt another strain of blood flow down his cheek and quickly wiped it away.

Joan rolled over onto even ground, her arms on fire. They were not done yet, but they had made an impressive start. She looked up from the ground to where the Ceremonial hall should be and traced her hand along its hidden ridge. It was the ridge she couldn't forget, the one she stared at every day as a child. Joan's home was somewhere along that spine, her home before she moved to the shore, before her father left her with her uncle. The small shack would be but a speck in the distance, but like a star it would glow like a lighthouse. Whether in the valley or the sea, Joan could spy her home better than a hawk spots food along the ground.

Joshua heaved himself over the small lip and stood there on the terrain. Joan stared up at her king's rugged face, expecting him to tease her for being so tired. But her looked at her briefly and looked away further along the path as if spotting another person. He seemed hesitant, silent all over again. Joan held her hand up for Joshua to help her and her king lifted her safely to her feet. She noticed he was putting on more muscle, which made her heart beat a little faster. He also smelled of chalk, which suppressed the thought.

"You good?" Joshua huffed, taking the lead in front of the girl. He set a brisk pace, cold shouldering his friend.

Joan pinched her shoulder, getting her mind back into the present. She had to focus.

Joshua was already in the distance, about the edge of another corner, standing there, watching her as she began to move. He was waiting, seemingly impatient to go. At the moment she caught up to him, his back was already turned, heaving itself over the large steps. The following obstacles were small rising stairs meant for giants. The stone stood well over their shoulders, requiring them to pull themselves up. Joshua was already far ahead of her. He didn't stop or take a breath, he looked tired, his chest heaving in exertion. The King seemed to be punishing himself.

"What your deal?!" Joan called from behind him, trying to pick up her pace.

"What do you mean?" Joshua asked under labored breaths.

"You're doing it again."

"Doing what?"

"Being a brick wall; being an asshole." Joan snapped.

"I'm sorry, Joan, I have a lot on my mind." Joshua deflected.

"When do you *not* have enough on your mind?"

Joshua shrugged and stopped. He placed his back against the next step, but it was too high for him to jump, or Joan. The baron thought about propelling himself with fire, but he advised himself against it. He didn't know how much of a lasting toll it would have on his energy, and he was sure it would disturb the mountainside.

Joan levied herself up the second-to-last step and met Joshua. "Do we need to talk?" She asked him.

"What about?" Joshua sidestepped.

"You've been different lately."

"A lot's been different."

"You're so full of crap." Joan sighed. "I know when something's up with you."

"I'm fine, really." Joshua defended, lacing his fingers to make a step. "Ready?"

Joan shook her head and placed her foot in Joshua's palm. The Red King moved his hands and lifted her until she had a firm hold of the edge above them. He watched as Joan disappeared for a moment and reappeared.

"I don't suppose you're going to help me up, are you?" Joshua inferred, watching Joan stand above him, not on her stomach reaching down.

"Not until you tell me what's wrong." She chided.

Joshua ran his hand through his hair and sighed. "I don't know how to behave during the ceremony tomorrow." Joshua lied.

"Bullpiss," Joan chided, "Try again, tough guy."

"How about, I don't feel confident leading a small nation?" Joshua tried.

"I liked the first one better." Joan chimed.

"I don't know what to tell you." Joshua shrugged again, huffing condensation from his mouth. The world was growing colder.

Joan reached down, and Joshua leaped to grab her hand. She helped him to the ledge and he climbed up. Al Hamra dusted his pants off and continued down the path. Joan frowned at him and followed. The area was widening now, which reminded Joshua of the Siberian Tundra. There was a finite amount of grass which found its way through the rocks and a small frozen palette of soil over the path. Clumps of snow pushed into the sides of the stone path, signs of the trail's use. Just in the distance the warm light of their destination village glowed, the faint sound of partying caressed their ears, a welcoming sound after the long climb.

Before Joshua reached the village, Joan swiftly stepped before him and grabbed him by the elbow. She stood closer than he would have liked her to. Her big blue eyes pierced him. They seemed worried for him. Her lower lip either quivered beneath the cold or beneath fear.

"Are you sure you don't want to tell me something." Joan asked a final time. "We might not have time to talk inside the longhouse."

"I'm fine, really." Joshua lied, taking half a step back.

Behind Joan was the longhouse. A series of wooden huts accompanied it, plotted along the steppe. Each building was adorned in colorful cloth and paint, a perfect glimpse into Valhalla. The longhouse was the most decorated of all the buildings. Lined with furs and family shields, it looked like an upturned boat with walls, a round oval made of thick wood, an upside-down bucket with smoke rising from its butt. Even at their distance, the warmth and happiness of partying and bonfires could be felt from inside. It was a wide lighthouse, marking the end of a pilgrimage.

Joan nodded. Joshua could tell her disappointment, he would be disappointed in himself too were he not torn between his mind, his heart, and his vengeance. Joan turned and walked towards the village slowly, her decorated hair waving with each step.

Joshua followed behind the huntress, catching the door before it closed on him. The second Joshua stepped across the threshold he heard Gurdard at the other end of the table. He banged his giant iron pitcher full of booze, rattling the plates.

"Joshua on the Hill, The Red King and his guest, Joanne the Wave Breaker!" He shouted triumphantly. The partygoers echoed the name back and resumed their festivities.

Joanne the Wave Breaker, Joshua thought, quite the suitable name for her. Before Joshua could make out Joan's whereabouts in the crowd, Gurdard jumped over the table, strode across the bonfire in the center of the room, and embraced his fellow baron like a bear. The man had long black hair which intermingled with his ringed and knotted beard. The man wore another ring in his septum, and one around each finger. He was a big man, his muscle covered in fat. His rosy cheeks were the only thing that softened his fierce brown eyes and his board shoulders. He was the image of a good king, a happy and conquering king, standing well over six feet tall.

"How are you, Joshy boy?" He asked with a brimming smile. "I haven't seen you since our meeting in Paris!"

"I'm good, Gurdard." Joshua insisted, grumbling into Gurdard's fur clothes.

Gurdard gave Al Hamra a stern but gleeful glance. "You can't lie to me Red King, especially not tonight, while we are surrounded by all this mead! I'll have you speaking the truth soon! Oh! To see Joanne here again is such a treat as well! I was such a good friend of her father!" He bubbled.

"Was?" Joshua asked.

"She didn't tell you?" Gurdard hushed, suddenly holding back his tongue. "Well… you better find and ask her then. I'm sure you two will be spending plenty of time together tonight, before the ceremony."

"What happens during the ceremony?" Joshua asked, "I haven't been taught much regarding your customs."

Gurdard laughed, and guided Joshua to his table. "You'll see soon enough, my boy! There is nothing to worry about. Us Northerners won't be offended if you don't do things our way! We aren't like those prissy Frenchies in Paris. Let me go get you something warm! Sit down I'll be right back!"

The big man bustled his body away through the crowd, almost hobbling. He reminded Joshua of Santa Claus. A younger, stronger Santa Claus that could hog tie a wildebeest without batting an eye.

Joshua sat there and watched the Scandinavians dance on the main floor. The men puffed their chests and beat their pectorals like apes while the women twirled about. The feminine dance reminded Joshua of Joan when she first saw her new ship, when she first saw the shoreline.

Joshua stifled a yawn as Gurdard placed a pitcher of ale before him. He motioned for his friend to drink. Joshua gave the mug a good few gulps before placing it down again on the carved table. It was good booze, the kind that could keep you going all night. Gurdard nodded his peace and slapped Joshua on the back with a good harrumph before taking his own swig. His "swig" finished his own cup and the baron tossed it into the fire with a loud ring and a quiet belch.

"So, Joshy, what's wrong between you and Joanne?" Gurdard asked.

"That obvious?" Joshua asked.

"She hasn't come to see me yet, and she's not around your arm. You need to grab your girl by the waist, boy! Show her that you care!"

"She's not mine." Joshua retorted.

"But you want her, don't you? Yes! I can see it. What's keeping you from her?"

"My actual girl." Joshua bluntly replied.

"Oh... I see." Gurdard mumbled. "Not the best feeling, being trapped between two mountain lions. You turn your back on one and the other will bite you on the neck before you can pray. Tread carefully and be patient, you'll start to think about one more than the other, and then you'll know who's right for you."

Joshua nodded and raised his jar half-heartedly. "To women."

"To women," Gurdard chuckled.

Joshua knew Gurdard's wife died a few years ago. He saw the news, she had died of complications during birth, even the baby didn't survive. He wondered how the big man could be so happy despite losing someone so close to him. Joshua thought he would go crazy of anything like that were to happen to him. But, Joshua already knew he was crazy.

Scratch, scratch… scratch.

The American saw Joan on the far side of the room, greeting people she once knew, exchanging a few slugs with the guys. She was a tough woman, full of heart.

"I should warn you I'm rooting for Joanne." Gurdard said, before taking in another "sip" of ale. He moved to point at her. "The best women come from here, not because they're beautiful or because they're strong or they're great in bed. They're all those things, Red, but most of all, they're loyal. They'll never leave your side no matter what. And that's all we want from a companion when the gods rain their piss from the heavens, really. We're all looking for someone to have our back."

"Where is your son anyway?" Joshua asked, redirecting the conversation. "I haven't seen him anywhere."

"He's with our ladies." Gurdard cackled, "Not in the racy way, mind you. But when a boy or girl becomes of age, the night before his ceremony, he goes into the wilderness to hunt with our best huntresses. A young child will always listen to a strong woman over a man any day, and it helps them understand how to respect and cherish the hunt. The biggest animal he kills, my table will eat, and everything else will be shared among the other guests. It'll be his duty to feed the tribe, not just himself. He best get it into his head now, how much of a burden that can be. He'll be pullin' his biggest catch all the way up the mountain by himself."

"The smart hunter would chase his game up the mountain before killing it." Joan interrupted, a confident smile on her face. Gurdard rose and she leapt into his arms, both squeezing the other with all their might. Joshua was surprised he couldn't hear her coming, but that was Joan, quiet and stealthy.

"You've risen far, girl! To think just the other day you were a fat-headed baby picking shells off the shore. Now, you're the right hand of a baron! How does the office of Red fare?"

"Thanks, Gurdard!" Joan chuckled as she was let down. "It's not easy, as pig headed as Josh is, but I make due."

One of the baron's laughed, the other asked for another pitcher of ale, quickly downing his first. Joshua tossed the empty cask into the fire and watched it glow much like the others did. Joshua tried not to eavesdrop on Joan's conversation, instead looking about the hall. It was a truly spectacular place. Joshua watched as two men began to tussle. The spectators in their immediate circle began to laugh and toss their ale on them. They were both middle aged men with wide-cut shirts. The only mortified girl there seemed to be the one they were fighting over.

"HEY!" Gurdard shouted, "You two buffoons settle this outside. Indoor fighting is only after the son shows up!"

The men looked at each other, turning docile under the traditional laws. They rose together and carried each other outside, their arms around each other's neck so that the other wouldn't run.

Gurdard laughed and addressed Joshua, "It is our custom to settle matters of the heart with our fists, especially love. It's not to say whoever wins, wins the girl, but it's a good display for her. She can think about who loves her most by who's still standing at the end. She can make a good decision from that, if she wants. We should go watch, come on."

Joshua followed Gurdard out of the main house. There, the general populace shoved the two quarreling men into a pig pen adjacent the short mansion. From within the slush, they would settle the matter.

The American wrinkled his nose, he might have drunk a little too much, for the two men, who were both middle aged, had the same hair and the same face. Gurdard noticed Joshua's look of confusion and nudged him in the ribs.

"Born of the same parents, twins, Oski, the Moon and Tet, the Sun, born ten hours apart in winter. Quite a rare sight to see them fight over anything. Girl must be quite the dame."

Oski and Tet struck with all their might. Oddly enough, both had no inclination to dodge or block attacks. They exchanged blows evenly, both of them refusing to budge an inch. This went on for minutes in what was seemingly a forceful game of tag. Eventually, one fell, presumably Tet, and was quickly meet by a girl with silver hair and grey eyes. She was astoundingly beautiful. The brother who fell was quickly picked up by the other. The silver-haired women kissed the fallen brother on the cheek and the victor ruffled his brother's black hair before leaving him outside the pen.

"A kiss for loser?" Joshua asked.

"It is so." Gurdard explained. "If the defender loses his girl after the fight, the girl gives him one last kiss. He deserves it after getting the piss kicked outta' him at least. A tradition started by Antionette the Fierce who had to choose between her childhood friend and her ship captain, who once saved her life. She was so heart broken by the end of the match that she kissed her savior on the lips. He had been so beaten to a pulp that no one could recognize him. The fellow just wouldn't back down."

"Sounds sad." Joshua sighed, wondering why the crowd hadn't dispersed yet.

Joshua soon received his answer. Through the crowd, another man had jumped into the ring and tore of his shirt. He had a tattoo of a snake on his chest which coiled to his neck and up the back of his head. He was almost bald, if not for the thick mutton chops that ran down to his jaw.

"I, Ogram of the Black Stone, challenge anyone who might defend Joanne the Wave Breaker. Let me fight him to prove my love!" The man shouted.

"Looks like you're up, boy!" Gurdard cackled.

"What do you mean? I'm not her-" Joshua stuttered, but was quickly pushed from behind.

Joshua watched as Joan brushed by him and nimbly hopped the fence to meet her knight. She stood there and crossed her arms, unenthused by Ogram.

"I'll defend myself, Ogram." She spat.

Joshua looked to Gurdard, puzzled.

Gurdard laughed so hard he began to cough. "I've never seen this before. I suppose Joanne, being single, is in a relationship with herself. It seems rational."

Ogram stared at Joan in disbelief. "You can't challenge me, I'm fighting for your arse!" He complained.

"I won't take any man weaker than me, or a wuss who thinks I'm just a piece of arse!" Joan retorted.

Ogram rubbed his empty head, confused. Joan moved forward through the mud and twisted her hip about, smashing the fool's nose in. Ogram fell into the mud. Joan stood there over him, and he began to slide away from her. He was afraid she might hit him again.

Ogram stood in a hurry and ran away through the pen's gate. Everyone laughed at him in his humiliation. Joshua felt nothing if not a little sorry. He certainly picked the wrong girl to "defend."

"Anyone else care to fight me for Joan's heart?" Joan asked, a wry smile on her face. The crowd murmured, the men shook their mangy faces. Joan straightened herself, proud. In proving her point she walked back to Gurdard.

"Hey ho, you've done it now girl! I wouldn't be surprised if they give you another title before you leave again!" Gurdard whooped.

Joan truly was a force to be reckoned with and Joshua, for one, was glad to have her on his side. He wondered what would have happened if he had accepted the challenge.

"Reminds me of a certain bar fight." Joshua mused. Joan grinned slightly, she was still somewhat upset with Joshua. "Once I get a few more pints back, it sure will be." She replied, motioning to flex her arm proudly.

"Yes," Gurdard hissed, "there will be plenty more challengers throughout the night. Maybe even our young baron here will throw his hat in, if not for fun, hmm?"

"That would be a sight… If he's not too busy whining like a wet dog." Joan joked.

Joshua heard a horn in the distance, thin yet clear. He looked out to the peaks, unable to pinpoint its location.

"It seems my son is ready to show his skill as a hunter!" Gurdard hollered.

The people outside rejoiced and began to move back inside the longhouse. There they would judge the boy's skill and slowly roast the animals he killed over the fires. Joshua followed Gurdard back into the house and sat to his left. Joan sat to Joshua's left thereafter. The room fell silent and every occupant watched the front door in anticipation. Perhaps out of respect, they did this, awaiting the boy who, at any minute, would burst through the entrance with his prize in tow.

Joshua tried not to tap his foot, tried not to cough nor stir a muscle. He did not want to offend the baron. Even though Gurdard gave him the okay to be himself, Joshua couldn't help but maintain restraints in all forms and fashions. He worried about the off chance. He worried that state relations would become ruined due to something small he did, something that was significant to the Scandinavians. Joshua looked to Joan for help, a silent explanation. She nodded her approval of his demeanor, and then, pointed at her vibrant eyes to the doors.

Keep watching. She meant.

But then Joshua felt something odd. He felt a small tremble below his boot, the sound of horses, perhaps. He also felt Joan's hand grip his elbow tightly, her shoulder pressed against his bicep. Joshua tried not to become flustered at the touch. Her hands were warm, much warmer than the fire in front of them, flickering behind the table.

The noise began to subside, and then it left altogether. Joshua fidgeted slightly in his chair.

The doors slammed open, all the doors. The doors to the right, the left, and behind them. Joshua almost jumped out of his seat, his hand beginning to spark, but Joan's tight grip kept him firmly planted to his chair. No one else reacted.

All about the hall were female huntresses. They stood tall, almost like giants, Gurdard's height. They wore green shirts tied with feathers, bones, and other oddities. They looked like human dream catchers, Joshua thought, but maybe they more inclined to inflict nightmares than prevent them.

The warriors waited, and Joshua spied a small silhouette skulk through the door in front of them. Joan ran her smooth hand up Joshua's arm, it tickled in the best way. She pressed into his chest and made him rise as she did. Joshua, therefore, found himself standing with the baron and those at their table. It seemed they were supposed to rise. Joshua began to notice the huntresses shift slightly and look at each other. They looked disheartened.

Joshua felt humble to be Joan's puppet for the ceremony. She still gripped him tightly, making sure he didn't budge and inch or shift from the position he was in. She looked straight ahead, watching the young boy trudge through with a rope over his shoulders. Behind him a large animal, a large bird, bigger than the fire it was to be struck upon. The bird squeezed its way through the door. It was carried and pulled upon a small cart, until it stuck between the door's posts, and slid in the momentum onto the floor in a defeated slump. The boy stood there with his arms at his hips, a proud look on his dirt-smudged face. He had brown eyes just like his father and short black hair no more than half an inch thick.

"What have you done, boy?!" Gurdard grimaced, his fist pressing against the tables.

Joan's iron grasp grew ever tighter. Joshua tensed under the volatile air. The boy hadn't brought back any ordinary creature, this Joshua knew. But, given the size, Joshua thought the baron would be proud. It came to tell him how little he knew. The boys next words cut his father deeply.

"Father, it's the biggest game there is, I brought back a griffin!" The boy protested.

"Yes, you brought back a *griffin*!" Gurdard seethed. "You killed a sacred creature, or have you forgotten what griffins did for our ancestors!?"

The boy paced back. Joan threatened to pop Joshua's arm. The house knew the punishment for such a crime, but Joshua didn't.

"Gurdard, we tried…" a huntress to their left began.

Gurdard held his hand up and silenced her, "I know it is not your fault, Hassi. It is no one's fault but my boy's. But he is no longer my boy… Here at this feast he will be named, and then face trial for his actions…"

"Gurdard!" the honoree to his right broke, "This means we have to eat the beast, doesn't it?"

Gurdard placed his chin to his chest in shame, "Indeed it does, the beast will be cooked here overnight, and the ceremony will resume."

"You'll put a curse on all of us!" the man cried.

"We have no choice! We are bound to this tradition, this table must eat the biggest game caught!" Gurdard hissed. He then turned to the commoners, "Everyone here is dismissed until the feast tomorrow! Go to your beds or run back to where you came! Leave my boy here to pluck his sins alone…"

The boy remained silent and fell to his knees. Slowly Gurdard walked around the table and to his child as the partygoers and huntresses disassembled, vanishing through the exits back into the cold.

Joshua didn't know how many would stay around after such a bad omen. Perhaps they would be the only people left on the mountain, left to eat the carcass of a magical beast. The Scandinavian King knelt beside his boy and both of them wept softly. Gurdard rested his big hand on his child's shoulder and cold tears would fall from their eyes.

"The lad always reached too high," the rightmost member sighed.

"Icarus in the sun..." Gurdard sobbed. Not looking at Joshua nor Joan, nor the other two guests beside him.

The Father addressed them. "Begone with you, my honored guests, I will be out shortly."

Joan tugged Joshua out of the long room in silence and the duo found themselves outside the pig pen. They leaned against it, staring at the door. They said nothing, the setting sun birthed frost which powdered their hair with small flakes.

The two other honorees stood there on the other side of the square, closer to the door. The first man, whom sat closer to the Baron, was tall and slender. He wore a long black gambeson with extended neck paddings that rose behind him like a peacock. It complemented his thin gray hair and made him seem effeminate. Even though the man was Scandinavian, he looked more the foreigner than Joshua did. Beside that man was a much shorter man, perhaps standing five feet and an inch or two. He was a bald, baby-faced, a creature with a stupid expression on his visage. He conversed with the tall man extensively, something Joshua couldn't, but would have liked to, hear over the wind.

Gurdard exited the longhouse with a worn look on his face. Joshua rose with Joan to intercept the sorrowful baron, but the other two reached him first. Joshua and Joan waited patiently for their turn. After a few minutes, the men gave a light bow as Gurdard turned away from them.

The giant made his way to Joshua and Joan. He wrapped his meaty arms around the two in embrace before he spoke. He sounded sad, this was unlike any emotion Joshua had ever experienced from the man.

"The Ceremony will begin tomorrow when the sun is highest in the sky. I expect you two to be ready. I do not know what will become of any of this, and I am sorry for bringin' you here."

"Baron Gurdard, our prayers to your son as he begins his rites. And our hopes for a peaceful trial when all of this is done." Joan consoled.

"Thank you, Joanne, your words fill my heart. I would advise you to leave as soon as the ceremony is over."

"We will do no such thing," Joan insisted, "I am still a part of the tribe. I will cast my lot in your boy's favor if my King would allow me to do so."

Joshua nodded solemnly, Gurdard needed all the help he could get. The Red King didn't see why they should leave until all matters were resolved. But he thought it was best to let Joan do the talking.

"Thank you both!" Gurdard choked, wiping his eyes, "You do me honor. Your cabin is the one with the elk on the door. I suggest you two get some rest."

Joshua watched Gurdard kilter and loom off, the other pair of honorees joining him. The two men proceeded to pick up their conversation, seemingly unabashed by the event. They seemed to goad the baron.

"Leon and Brigga," Joan huffed once the trio were out of earshot, "they pay most of the sailors for their haul."

"Businessmen, then." Joshua hummed.

Joshua hated businessmen.

Joan opened the door to their cabin and looked at Joshua to follow. However, Joshua was entranced by the three silhouettes now in the distance. The three stood by the ledge, near the path they had come from that morning. The man named Leon, the tall one, had his hand placed gently on Gurdard's back, patting it, rubbing it. Joshua couldn't tell what was being said. However, the way Leon smiled at Gurdard was nothing less than wanton, begging the baron to fall over the edge. Joshua would keep his eye on the weasel during the ceremony, lest misfortune befall them.

Joshua entered the cabin to find Joan stoking the fire. She stood there with her arm over the mantle, watching the flames rise and the sparks fade in the air. Joshua put his bag down near the door and looked around.

The wooden cabin was well constructed. The thick walls kept the cold outside, not a single crack between each length. They were sanded to a light brown, the color of fine grain. The beams were carved with extravagant knots and animals which paraded about the fixture until vanishing behind hanging blankets and small rugs. Tall jars sat on the floor in the corner filled with wines and frigid water, the liquid cold due to hour spent outside. A small basin was place on the other side of the room along with a bathtub. Both were shadowed by a foldable blinder. The whole room was open, and a single bed sloughed close to the fireplace.

Gurdard was really rooting for Joan.

Joan took off her shoes and sat in front of the fire. The radiance made her hair glow, blending it with the flame.

"Bring the wine jug, will you?" She asked.

Joshua did as he was told and set it beside her along with a mug. Joan dipped her mug in and immediately chugged the wine down. She wiped her lips and sighed. It had been quite the day. Joshua, under the flurry of unexpected events forgot all he wanted to ask. After much deliberation, and a few more glasses of wine, Joshua finally remembered at least one of his questions.

"What will happen to Gurdard's son?"

"I don't know." Joan replied, "It's up to the tribes but it won't be a slap on the wrist. Griffins are sacred here; they're intelligent creatures."

"I didn't think a whole nation would acknowledge a cryptid," Joshua replied.

"It's kept from the world, ever since the Legend of Carmine." Joan sighed, tucking her knees to her chin.

"The Legend of Carmine?"

"Carmine of Iceburgs, a tale our parents told us as children. A fabled shipwright, Carmine was, navigated between the islands, a cartographer. One day she was attacked by pirates and her ship was left sinking in the middle of the ocean. Days had passed, and she waited on the bow to starve to death. But in the sky, she saw a griffin with golden feathers. Mistaking it for a god, she called out to it, but it didn't come to save her. The second day passed and again she saw it, she called to it again, but the bird flew by without giving her notice. She continued to do this for two more days. On the fifth day the bird snatched her from the waters and brought her back to her nest."

"Just like that." Joshua replied.

"Just like that. But they're just stories, who are we to know?" Joan mumbled, chugging yet another glass. "The Griffin saved Carmine, so I guess we feel we owe the damned birds something."

Joshua was surprised the girl hadn't a beer belly, perhaps all the beer sat in the right places for northern women.

"So tomorrow we'll eat the griffin, then what?" Joshua followed.

"We eat the damn bird. We give the boy his first name. The boy gets his title from the father. The boy is celebrated through the night and the party is over when everyone wakes up in the morning wasted. But no one will want to celebrate a griffin-killer," Joan replied wiggling the mug in her hands. "No one will be there but us to celebrate, the honorees required to stay at the father's table."

Joshua rose from the floor and put his mug on a hook in the wall before sliding onto the bed. He stared at the ceiling. It looked so far away, so out of reach. Joshua traced his hand along the arches, forming triangles with his finger. Joshua felt the bed move and looked over to see Joan join him. She lay on her side and watched the baron articulate his finger like someone would watch an artist. Joshua talked to himself, his lips forming letters and words. Joan took in his image in the moments she could afford to watch him, while he thought she was closing her eyes.

Joan couldn't simply fall asleep. She pretended to stir back to life and lay on her back, slightly closer to him than before, their arms close enough to touch, should her king start to trace to outer edges of the rafters. She was so close and so far, not knowing how he felt about her. His silence, his attitude at times, was infuriating. She felt like she was infatuated with a robot, emotionless, dead, careless. But at other times, when he was working, he would somehow become somebody different, someone lively, moving. He had a purpose when he had something to react to, someone to help. Left alone, he was just an empty shell, a paperweight waiting to be used again. Joan wondered if he was simply a mirror, a human that worked to fill a void, reflect the images given to him.

Did Joshua have any dreams left since he became baron? Was he past the point of ambition, now just a tool for others? If he wasn't, what was he waiting for? Joan wanted to know whether a kiss would give him purpose, whether he needed someone to care for him. His face looked gaunt despite his growing muscles. Small dark circles lay below his discolored eyes. Joan even saw white hair in his sideburns and about his stubble. He was getting old, older than he should be getting. Joan was reminded of a dog, one that waits on the world, waits for a soldier coming from home, waiting for the promises he fought for to come true. Was that it, was Joshua waiting on something someone promised him?

Joan began to find herself leaning closer, her lips began to pucker, her body shifted so that it press into his. Her heart pounded, Joshua would soon know how much she wanted to care for him.

"Look," Joshua said.

Joan rolled back, almost embarrassed, but Joshua couldn't tell. Joan looked back at the ceiling, trying to act casual, trying to hide her blushing cheeks.

Joshua had traced the outlines in their eyesight using golden embers which floated above them. It was a holographic painting, made in glowing ink which outlined every contour of the house. The ember was created much like Joshua could create flame. It floated there in the spaces of air, pushing itself into levitation on the heat it created.

Joan never took Joshua for an artist, but he had captured the cabin in his own expression. The golden lines created geometric shapes, tangles of straight lines intersecting like a puzzle which hovered above them. It was both a copy and unique piece of art at the same time. Joshua really was the red king, a king of embers, a lord of fire. Joan could feel the warmth of the art fade as the ash slowly and methodically drifted away like a thousand fireflies. They extinguished, naked to the eye, flying somewhere no one could see. But still, a warmth remained. That warmth was Joshua, his body like a dying sun, cold enough to touch, warm enough to stay.

"Thank you for everything," Joan whispered, turning away from Joshua and onto her side. She began to work on burying her feelings underneath the dirt of her brain. She thought herself away from anything more but her grip on him in the longhouse and closed her eyes. She traded her ambition and admiration for a prayer, that the man she was beginning to fall in love with would be okay.

Joshua wiped his eyes and scratched the back of his head. He felt small dots of red liquid and hid them away, rubbing them between his fingers.

Joshua drew his thoughts away, it was something Elizabeth had taught him to do every night. She would hold his free hand while she watched him draw. It helped Joshua think of her, helped him go to sleep at night. It reminded him what she meant. It reminded him of the promise he made to himself, that he would fill the void Connor had left.

Joshua thought he had promised to be with Elizabeth if Connor Shaw never arrived. And after he talked with Frank Penn, he knew that would never happen. He never told Elizabeth about Connor Shaw burning to death. He didn't know if she could handle that. Perhaps he wanted to pretend he was Connor Shaw, although he didn't say that out loud.

Perhaps he did it so that she could believe he was still alive, and with her, as Joshua.

Maybe, if Joshua hadn't drawn what he did, he and Joan wouldn't have gone to sleep that night. He would have forgotten his promise to Elizabeth, and he would never be able to live with himself.

Because Joshua was nothing if not a mirror, reflecting a lover from days long gone.

Part 4/Rapine

Frea stood before the Marquis, her arms hung in the air like a scarecrow, stiff, uncomfortable.

"They'll do." The Marquis chuckled wryly.

"Like hell they'll do, he hasn't cuffed the sleeve." Frea barked, making the tailor red with embarrassment.

The Marquis waved off the remark, his personal tailor would not be commanded by a child. The tailor bowed, he was a prickly man in a billowy tailcoat. His lips pouted, it was possible he had taken something sour beforehand.

The trio stood in Frea's apartment, cotton lying about the floors. They had picked her, or rather, Lafayette had picked her, something better for her duties on Joshua's council.

Frea's new clothes were capable of withstanding the heat, the rain, and walking long distances. She wore a flat pair of brown boots over a small pair of breeches, ruffles still sewn about a single hip. She clasped a belt about her waist, frustrated. Her torso was a short-sleeved hybrid between a shirt and gambeson with synthetic fibers weaved in lieu of seems to provide ample breathing. A small scarlet cape draped about her left shoulder bearing The Red King's insignia, a series of triangles with a small sword through the middle. It was a simple design. The drape stopped at her elbow, in which the sleeves had been haphazardly rolled. The last, and least important part of her new costume was the large bow that sat on her tailbone, a semblance of the dress she used to wear, something of a creature comfort.

Frea quickly leaped from her pedestal as the tailor vanished from the room. She strapped her old corset about the shirt, wanting to cover herself more. Her cheeks were pale and red.

"I feel like a man." Frea huffed.

"Well, you can move, can't you?" The Marquis goaded.

Frea nodded solemnly. It was painful to admit that she was comfortable.

"And you can jump and sit and bend over without having to keep your clothes from lifting?"

"I'm not fat." Frea snapped, "I could do all those things already."

"If you want to tear another dress again, be my guest, but you'll get used to dressing down. If you give it a chance, you might begin to like it. Besides, you still look regal."

"I suppose... I do look rather cute." Frea sighed, looking in the mirror and rotating about.
"I'll be waiting outside, we have a lot of walking to do today." The Marquis chimed.

Frea looked in the mirror once more and sighed. She looked like someone whom had to lift things off the ground. How miserable she was.

Frea about faced a few more times and admired her figure before conceding to do what Laffy asked of her. She plodded her feet down the stairwell, noticing her hands floating in the air where her dress should be held. Frea felt odd once she put her hands down to descend the gilded steps. She felt like a gorilla.

It was going to be another day of work and she hoped no one stared too long at her.

The Marquis guided her through the golden streets to the small elevator they used to reach the ground. Truly, the contraption was a primal piece of work, a large wooden basket with a rope and pulley, from the days when water would be fished from wells and not pumped to the surface.

"Woah boss." Cid interjected, waiting at the elevator for a ride. "Who's this dame you have here, you haven't been hiding her from me, have you?"

"Cid," The Marquis smirked, "I'm sure you've met Frea before. She has been staying with us while her house it being built."

Cid stopped his greasy smile; the skull kid even began to sag his face. "Oh, Frea, right."

Frea twisted her face at Cid. He twisted it back pointing out his tongue. He had one encounter with the lady after the rebellion ended, and it ended with a heel up his ass. She was a vicious fiend in Cid's mind, a force he loved to reckon with.

The trio boarded the elementary lift and waited to be cranked down to the grass below. The skies were clear that day, the third last day Frea would rule the country.

"What business do you have below?" The Marquis asked his friend.

"I found some good guys to get soused with." Cid snickered.

The Marquis rolled his eyes, "What happened to Gnat? You used to drink with him."

"He never gets drunk, it's no fun. You can't make a joke or do anything imaginative with him. The guy's pretty much his helmet now. You never know what he's thinking, and when he speaks, it's like he's a broken record. No fun at all." Cid gossiped.

The two men continued to converse while Frea looked out to the rolling hills. She stared thus until the basket plodded the ground and the group departed from it. The Marquis said his goodbyes and began to usher his helmsman onward so that Cid might not exchange more verbal bullets with Frea.

Then, he let Frea exit the basket, helping her down.

Today, they were to meet the small towns, every single one, and survey their living conditions. If they hadn't adequate housing, foodstuffs, or clothing, an inquiry would begin as to what created the fault and steps would be taken to remedy the situation. It was Joshua's plan to kickstart the country this way. For the next year he would watch his kingdom and provide for the people until the next winter.

He would teach the baby to walk, so that it could run, so to speak.

However, Frea was afraid they would spoil the child and create a dependent system in which the people looked to their ruler for anything free. Joshua had a big heart and was chalk full of ideas, but he was easy to manipulate, too ready to help instead of chastising his people. Maybe that was Frea's purpose as an advisor, to mitigate the damage dealt upon Joshua's throne by providing a callous viewpoint, a different viewpoint. Or so she thought.

They had not walked far later that evening before one of the final towns came into sight. All Whitecroftian towns were originally erected around the taverns. Each house was a small wooden building that would stand temporarily until more building resources shipped into the country. The country had no mine deposits at the moment, and the farmers hadn't the skill to smelt iron or form rock.

Frea walked among the people, they were unbathed, odorous, and dull under their clothes. Just in passing, Frea could hear their bodies shudder as they scratched and belched without manners. Again, she was revolted. She found herself covering her nose with her red shoulder cape.

The Marquis took to the populace in stride, leaving Frea to watch. He asked each person how they were getting along with the new order. He even prodded deliberately for negative feedback. He seemed to dance about the center between people, somehow remaining discreet enough as not to arouse anger. He was influential in the queried conclave. He smiled at each of them, his nose unfurled, his eyes bright and welcoming.

People eventually began to overhear him and made their way to discuss with the Golden King their opinion on the matter. Some fussed, others encouraged and even defended the throne. But, no matter what they had to say, The Marquis took their opinions gracefully and memorized them. His humility in his mission begged others to speak their piece. Eventually, the

Marquis no longer asked people to approach him, they swarmed to him like a prophet or a male-geisha.

Frea watched him outdo himself again and again, town after town. She blew hot air from the distance at him, her hair shifting above her face under the current. Subsequently, Frea decided to give conversation a whirl. After seeing how easily The Marquis commanded the masses, she doubted it would be so difficult.

Frea spied a man in passing, watched him avoid the crowd and make his way around. Frea could intercept him, she could do her job, she encouraged herself. The miserable girl walked forth to ask the man whether he had a complaint about Joshua's reign. She opened her mouth and lightly uttered the first syllable, yet, was stopped by the man whom quickly adjusted his course and breezed past her.

Frea was rejected and left alone in the small square. It wasn't a feeling of defeat that embedded itself, it was a feeling of disgust for how rude the man had pushed her off, interrupted her. She began to feel contempt for her people, her face red and sour.

The Marquis laughed with the crowd, he was a regular swindler, Frea thought. He spoke with a different tone that calmed people's fears. He knelt down among the citizens, giving himself a distinct advantage in the conversation. He orchestrated them, formed them much like a bottle shapes water. Frea looked away and eyed the tavern. She could use a stiff drink.

The young lady abandoned her post and entered the open door of the tavern. The far corner boasted a small quintet of musicians who played something lively, something whimsically fierce. People drank to whatever reason they could, shouting over each other. Men became bulls and swung their metaphorical penises around. The whole scene was a cockfight, a thoroughfare of masculinity. Frea quickly began to realize that she was the only girl in the tavern, and the only person both fully dressed and well dressed.

Frea sighed again, a favorite pastime for her as of late, and made her way to the bar so that she might find the tender. The bartender danced there, pouring taps and sliding pitchers down the line. He was a well-built man, if not a little skinny, who didn't take to wearing a shirt. He had the tattoo of an eagle on his chest, and his medium blond hair was tied back loosely into a small tuft at his nape. He eyed Frea as she sat down on the barstool before him. She rubbed her head and placed her elbow on the table to prop her chin.

"What will the lady have?" the tender asked.

Frea looked at him, a small tinge of hatred beneath her eyes. She pointed to the rack behind him, the biggest bottle, the highest proof. The bartender raised his eyebrow, it was his only bottle of wine.

"Are you sure you don't just want a beer, it's cheaper." The bartender insisted, not to save him the trouble of breaking the seal, but to protect her from running against the standards set by to rest of the guests in his establishment.

"Does it look like money is an issue?" Frea scoffed, pulling at her red cape and her black-velvet corset.

The bartender shrugged and grabbed the bottle off the rack. He uncorked it for her and placed it on the table.

"You should get out of here, girl, before someone notices you. I doubt any of these men have seen a pretty girl before, and these lot aren't the type to ask women on romantic dates."

Frea stayed, ignoring the man, pouring her wine into a small wooden cup. She didn't need someone else telling her what to do. She didn't mind being approached either, it would give her an excuse to hurt someone.

While the Marquis did his work Frea made her way through a few more glasses. The bartender kept his eyes on her cautiously. She was asking for trouble, and the man didn't want to be a bystander.

"Damn." The bartender whispered, watching another group walk into the door of the tavern. Their presence stopped the music with tightened notes which screeched to a halt. The guests looked at the new arrivals, a look of worry on their faces. The men were large apish creatures with small cudgels about their waists. They were covered in warts, riddled with flies, and pasty. They made their way to the bar and stood into the stools, bumping them to the ground without notice.

"The usual, Dirk." The first man said, his face reminded Frea of a pig, the nose pushed in and up. The man was also missing quite a few teeth.

The Bartender, Dirk, began to fill seven large pitchers to the brim and placed them on the table. As he filled them, the group or apes looked at Frea, perverted glances worn on their faces.

One of the men licked his lips, "Who's this whore?" He asked ambiently, bluntly. His voice punched through the room, the slur evident on his tongue.

"She's from the royal office, Horace" Dirk answered, "so you best drink outside before you get any ideas in your thick skull."

Horace mumbled, picking up his pitcher, the others followed suit.
"And pay upfront. I won't have you guys 'forgettin'' to pay like last time." Dirk insisted.

"We're good for it Dirk," Horace grouched, his eyes still pasted on Frea.

Frea swiveled to stare Horace in the eyes, the bottle clenched in her hand, her eyes sharp as knives. The men smiled their toothless smile, some of them seemed to drool through the gaps in their canines.

Horace placed his money on the table with a loud thump, followed by the rattling of glasses. "Yeah, we'll drink outside, why don't you let the whore join us around back, we can show her a good time, right boys?"

"Get the hell out of here," Dirk hissed, "I won't have you ruining another girl. Not in my tavern."

Horace shrugged and made his way to the door, "We'll just wait until she leaves, then, when she's not *in* your tavern."

Frea watched the brutes make their way to the door and exit. They waved goodbye to the stand-in queen, gesturing obscenities. Dirk snatched the cash from the table and dropped it into a bucket with the other bullion, cursing under his breath.

"You can stay the night here if you want lass. I won't charge you a thing. They'll be bored and gone by the morning..." the bartender said, a look of worry on his face. "I told you to leave, but you women never listen, do you now?"

"This has happened before?" Frea asked and took a long slug of wine.

"Horace and his boys make these threats to every woman who comes along... sometimes they make good on those promises, sometimes they don't." Dirk sighed.

"And the guards haven't put a stop to these rapists?"

"The captain of this area grew up with Horace as a kid. He was a regular bully in his childhood, and now a bully in adulthood. The captain might even be *more* afraid of the man than I am."

Frea took one last sip from her bottle and rose. She placed a bill on the table to pay for the alcohol and turned to leave.

"I can't let you go out there." Dirk contested, "You can't take that risk, trust me, just look at you. You're no gladiator."

"Call the captain of the guard for me, then." Frea mocked wryly, slamming the door behind her before Dirk could approach from behind the bar.

The young girl stood outside and quickly turned right down the street, glancing at Horace before she made good distance. Horace's men rose and began to follow her, they snickered beneath their breaths. The seer walked out of the town to a nearby tree which stood upon a hill but a hundred yards up from the town. Frea turned around and waited at the base, the shade cast over her face, but not hiding the shine of her eyes.

The men slowly scaled the hill to her while she looked down at them. The hill was cliché, to imagine it would be trivial, but it was a beautiful tree, something out of a painting.

"You're really asking for it, whore." Horace spat. Already, he reached for his cudgel. "we like it when they scream, and we won't make it fast for you."

Frea ignored the perverse commentary. "So, you rape women, then? You don't deny your crimes?" She asked.

The men nodded like animals, thirsty hyenas.

Frea frowned.

"Then, by the name of The Red King, and as the highest-ranking officer present, I condemn you seven to death. You will be gutted like the pigs you are and hung by this tree."

The men laughed, Horace blinked and began to loose his pants so they might fall about his knees. Horace smiled. His men smiled. Then, they all stopped smiling.

The Marquis heard a loud feminine scream in the distance. The crowd looked out to the fields hidden behind the wooden buildings. Right past the roofs of the shallow houses, there up on the golden hill, a group of shadows loomed beneath the tree. The Marquis looked about for Frea, but she was not in the square. From the tavern, a shirtless man ran out the door and into the distance where the wail came from. The Golden King looked to the crowd as they began to rise and make their way towards the noise.

"Everyone, stay here!" Laffy commanded, "It would be safer if I see what happened."

Lafayette waded through the people and began to stride out of the village through the knee-high grasses. He looked at the ten shadows on the hill behind the small town. Seven of theses shadows, growing in detail as the immortal approached, were hung upon the tree, their organs oozing out of their bodies, covered in pus. These innards fell to the ground, unfurled and decaying. Some of the men were hung by their necks, others by their legs and their waists, haphazardly poised like ballerinas in mid-flight. It reminded The Marquis of an ambitious puppet master who maintained a few of his thralls while abandoning the others to sulk lifeless. Their skin was sickly green, and pus dripped from their mouths. One of the victims had not a head it was missing somewhere.

The victim's hairs were grey, and their bodies concaved where there was once fat and muscle. They had been up there for ages, but the Marquis didn't recall the scene as they walked into the town. The tree before him was gnarled, dead with age. A perfect circle of dirt was left around the base. It was the presence of something supernatural, the manipulation of time. It was as if the small hill was placed inside a snow globe and shaken until all that was within died. Whatever the explanation was, the reason was warped out of logic and science.

The first of the surviving shadows was the man whom had run to the hill after the shout, he stood there staring at the hanging tree his hands on his head in disbelief, "Thank God," he murmured, to the shadow next the him. The second shadow, with whom he talked with, was an older lady who cried slightly, shocked at discovering the mutilated men. This woman must have been the siren, the one who screamed and alerted the town.

Lafayette was interested in the third of the living. He already knew her, the enigmatic and haughty girl known as Frea. He determined the death of the men was her fault. The signs of the incident more akin to a massacre.

The Marquis shuddered slightly, he knew Frea was capable of great evil such as this. Moreover, it was her form, her smile, that twisted in Lafayette's stomach. The Marquis had found the missing head.

Frea sat there at the base of the tree holding a brand-new skull in her hands. It was cleaned, the skin and muscle torn away like a mask and left sitting beside her. The red skull, still a little moist from its contact with flesh and blood, sat neatly in her hands. The girl stared at it with a sinister smile, enjoying the scarlet color. Black liquid crept up through her clothes, the ink sat thinly upon her skin like a tattoo, a slab of colored-in pictures that moved back and forth. The oil wrapped about her neck and pointed to her eyes in sharp vectors.

Frea hadn't noticed anything around her, to in love with her work.

"What did you do, Frea?" The Marquis asked, calling the girl to attention. Laffy's hand sat across his body, gripping his sword at the hip. Frea looked up and smiled at him actually smiled at *him*, as if she were normal or even better than her usual self. Frea never smiled at him.

"I heard a complaint. I solved the problem." She mused, looking back to the stained bone. The black tattoos on her skin began to settle, hiding beneath her shirt until they vanished from Laffy's sight.

"They raped women, sir," Dirk added, "they were monsters. I suppose this is recompense."

"That's no excuse!" The Marquis barked and pointed at Frea, "What is she now?! She is a monster too, unable to give them fair justice, a trial!"

"I gave them a trial!" Frea snapped back at him, beginning to stand. "They pled guilty, they were going to rape me!"

"Shit!" The Marquis huffed, stomping the ground. "you have a lot to answer for, girl!"

The man strode forth and snagged Frea's wrist. He tugged her aloft and back in the direction of LeCeleste. The ship could still be seen from faraway, a small darkening blotch over the horizon that began change color as night approached. They would finish their conversation somewhere else, somewhere private.

"What's going on here!?" The Captain cried out, appearing from the town. He and his troops had gathered themselves to the hill. "Damnit, those are Horace's men!"

"Horace *and* his men are dead." Dirk informed, "This woman did what you didn't have the balls to do."

The Captain looked at the young lady with the black bangs and sinister eyes. She still held the skull in her free hand. It dripped with collecting blood. The captain unsheathed his sword and his men followed suit.

"As captain over this town, you are arrested, demon!" The man shouted, "I'll see you hang once this is over!"

"She's not going anywhere with you!" The Marquis roared. The Golden King gripped Frea's cape and lifted it towards the guards. "Do you know what this is? It's the symbol of *your* baron, she is his viceroy. She will not be going anywhere but to her home!"

Frea slapped Lafayette's hand from her clothes. The man flinched and let go of her. She began to pace forth.

"You're the sheriff of this town?" She asked.

"I- I am, and you're coming with me!" The Captain answered, his sword in front of him. He was uneasy with her approach, almost quivering. He adjusted his stance, readied himself.

"You let this man rape women. You knew all about it and did nothing. Why?" Frea asked, pushing the tip of the Captain's sword away with her fingers. The Captain dropped the weapon, rather, it flew away from him a keen distance, forced from his loose grip.

The Captain stuttered, backing away, "They w-were whores! T-they had it coming!"

"That whore was my daughter!" The woman on her knees sobbed from the hill, she was too weak to turn about fully and face the captain. "You knew she was a good girl, a pure girl, Sheriff Gerald. No whore slits her wrists after she's been had."

Sheriff Gerald felt a tear in his eye. It was true, he was a coward, still afraid of a man who bullied him in his youth. He was ashamed.

"I'm sorry, Dorothy, I shouldn't have said that." Gerald murmured, before turning to Frea. "Please, you may-"

Frea lunged at the Sheriff with the skull in her hand and tackled him. She pressed the bone to his mouth, pushing in his teeth, causing his mouth to bleed.

"You'll eat your sin, you bastard!" The stand-in queen screamed. Gerald's guards backed away out of fear. Frea slammed the skull against the sheriff's forehead, cursing him while he twisted beneath her. He couldn't escape and if not for Dirk and The Marquis quickly coming to his rescue, he would have choked on his own dislodged teeth. The two men each grabbed an arm and dragged her back from the soldier. Dirk kept Frea restrained, letting the Marquis do something else.

"Sheriff Gerald," The Marquis addressed, "You're no longer the Captain of this regiment. Whoever is next in rank will take over your duties until we assign this town a new protector. You're clearly unfit to lead."

Gerald sat there in his urine, the men around him gone. He watched as the demon child was lifted onto The Marquis' shoulders and carried away from the town. She went limp, trying to free herself like an upside-down chicken.

Once all witnesses had gone, Gerald rose and made his way up the hill. He began to reach for the first body, to cut it down from the tree but he stopped mid-motion. He saw something in Horace's chest, a movement, a pulse, a heartbeat. Headless Horace was still alive, and very much in pain. Gerald looked to the other men, taking a moment to feel their pulses, they were all still alive as well, their hearts racing in agony.

Whatever Frea had done, she had not killed them.

Gerald cut the criminals down and plunged his sword into their hearts. He waited for the pulse to stop. This was the first time he experienced magic, and he learned to hate it. The young girl had tortured these men in their own bodies, condemning them to watch as their flesh rotted away, as their stomachs burst like Juda's Iscariot. She had even scarred the men, writing words on their bodies like *lust* and *gluttony*. Their eyelids were torn from their sockets and their toes lopped.

Frea was something else. She had to be some special kind of devil to make these men undead, strung on a tree while their bodies decomposed. It took Gerald a long time to bury them, and still, he was worried their graves would be too shallow. He hadn't the time in the day to continue, and he had to help Dorothy home.

Before The sheriff made it home himself, he had one last look at that cursed tree and thought one last time about that demon girl. He had never been so scared in his life, and he would never experience anything else that terrifying for the rest of his numbered days.

Part 5/Repast

Joshua walked in a red desert, the same one he had dreamt of before. In his dream, he watched a bear and a tiger attack each other, they rolled in the sand, blood dripping from their eyes and nostrils.

In that same dream there was an iron ship that moved through the ground like it was water, pushing the chestnut sands to either side in its plow along the ground. It was a poorly constructed vessel with holes and graffiti smattered about it. The machination stopped in the distance, hiding the horizon, four shadows stood on the deck, locked in combat with their swords. It was a free-for-all, each of them aiming to kill the other, three were men and one was a woman. The woman had long white hair and pale skin like the one he saw at the pig pen. She slashed about with a rapier, thinly grazing her opponents, making the best out of every situation. She wore a red top and a red skirt with white embroidery about the edges. A large red sheet draped over her the side of her head and covered half of her face like an asymmetric bride. The sheet was tied into knots as it cascaded down the right side of her body. Her clothes flowed on the wind like ribbons, her serenity and barbarism unmatched. She proceeded to slowly kill two of the three men before the third had her by the throat, hanging her over the edge of the ship. He slit her throat and dropped her into the sand below.

The Red King ran to the gypsy and found himself dragging her across the dunes. Hours, or so it seemed, later, he had found no help or civilization. Joshua pressed his sandy hands to the girl's throat, hoping to stall for time, to keep her from bleeding out. The girl

placed her hand on his cheek, she mouthed words, but no sound came out.
What was she trying to say?
The young girl faded in his arms. She died.
The bear, he thought, what had she said about the
bear?

Joshua looked around him, shadows loomed outside of the sandstorm they found themselves in. These shadows were men and women, charging towards Joshua. The Red King watched them flail in the distance, trying to sprint towards him, to eat him. But it took them a long time to near. But even as they fell upon Joshua, Joshua knew he would wake up.

Joshua startled from the bed and gasped for air. Joan, startled in turn by the sudden awakening, rose with him to comfort her baron. But before she could say a thing he had already risen and stormed out of the cabin, coughing and holding his hands to his face.

Joan was left by herself in the dark.

Joshua knelt at the edge of the plateau and watched the ocean in the distance. It was a trial to see the boats which hovered over the water as a thin storm of powder kept him from seeing across the peninsula. Joshua rubbed his wrist in worry, looking at the bloodstains on his palm.

His dreams always meant something.

It was still quite early when Joan dressed and came to meet him outside. She sat there with her legs dangling over the edge, silent.

"What happened?" Joan asked, a calm erasure about her.

"A nightmare… it was nothing." Joshua lied. This time, Joan believed him.

Joshua and Joan sat there and waited for people to leave their cabins. But the silence between them continued under the shrill of the breeze. There was nothing for them to say or do. The minute snow cover made the world seem white, blank and lifeless. Joshua had peered into the white for some time. He expected something to loom through the expanse. Whether it was something sinister, or something simply colossal, the young man couldn't distinguish. If something were to come, he would have to face it as he always did.

Little did Al Hamra know the gravity of his dream, and that he was facing east.

"We are the only ones here." Gurdard, appearing behind his two friends, huffed over the brewing storm. "You two, Leon, Brigga, the boy, and me. The rest of the village went home over night. They rather face the inclement weather and frozen paths than do their duty to name my son."

Joshua stood to face the small party, leaving Joan to question the red and black snow Joshua left where he sat.

The son still waited inside. And it was time to finish the ceremony by eating his catch.

Leon and Brigga nodded their hellos, a stale gravitas about them. Joshua couldn't help but grimace slightly when they did. The American would be watching them carefully. They turned and walked toward the longhouse and the door swept shut behind them by the wind with a loud bang. None of this aided Joshua's uneasy mind.

In the center of the longhouse was the large fire, as known by Joshua when he saw it first. But little did he know how the fire could change. As the boy twisted the bird upon its rotisserie axle, the fire that licked the animals savory skin turned a neon green color. This change in color flickered on the archway above, setting a dual scene. The bright red flame created the warm flooring like earth and the green flame created a sinister sky in the rafters. Joshua was stuck in a painting expressed by a man with bipolar syndrome. Any second either color could dominate the room, and the terrible consequences ensue. Joshua was worried for those who must participate, he knew not what omens would occur if they ate the bird. Joshua imagined eating the Shaper and cringed.

Neither could he eat The Mural or the Lizard men, such things were out of place.

Joshua sat between Joan and Gurdard just as before, this time they watched as the young boy carved the oversized chicken, placing each slab on a wooden plank. He served it to the father first, and then the people on his father's right. Joshua watched the boy as he served him and Joan next, he looked sad, tired from a long night of work. Moreover, he looked terrified of his meal.

No one had ever consumed a griffin.

It was the flames that concerned Joshua, the way they changed colors meant the bird might have some Favor in its veins. Whatever fantastic energies that were within the bird had not left its body while it died, it was locked within the meat. Could it have adverse, or even positive effects once swallowed? Would they grow feathers *and* beaks, or just one?

Joshua grabbed a tender piece of meat and peeled it from the bone. He watched the others. They were also apprehensive. Gurdard closed his eyes and lifted the meat to his mouth; he dug his teeth into the fat and chewed. Joshua followed suit in smaller portions. The meat was gamy, mostly tasting like chicken, much as would be expected.

Perhaps it was okay to eat the beast, Joshua did not feel anything odd within him, but perhaps that was because Joshua did not have a conventional body. The American watched the others for signs, waited for one of them to choke as pillows of feathers spewed from their throats. To his joy, everything was fine, and the posse began to finish their plate.

Now, what had possibly been explained to Joshua before or through the course of implication was that the whole bird was to be eaten that day. However, the nature of this bird, being much larger than any bird or even a bear, intimidated Joshua, who hoped Gurdard would pull most of the weight. Moreover, Joshua had never consumed so much before in an ifrit's body and soon found that he was not getting full when he should have been. His lack of a stomach kept the food from

511

pushing against the stomach lining inside him. He didn't bloat either. Perhaps in truth, there was a furnace in his body, and he was simply dumping his food back into another fire, burning his food into a crisp. Would his flames become green? That would make sense to him.

Joan and Leon stopped their intake. The girl felt her stomach and looked at the others. Joshua caught her eye and she tried to smile. She would be done for a while, waiting for her food to settle. On the bright side, only an hour had passed by. But, the three remaining to devour the feast began to slow their pace.

Although Joshua wasn't full, the taste began to make him feel sick, coupled with his tense emotions that stirred from his dream he decided it was best to pace himself unless discover what ifrits do when they vomit. Perhaps it was magma, or just a pile of dampened soot. Joshua cringed at the thought, thinking of vomiting was the road to vomiting.

Eventually, thirty minutes later, the five had stopped their conquest. Joshua asked the boy for water, wine, beer, whisky, and anything else he could bring to diversify the meal and get his tongue off the monotonous taste. He waited for his request to be fulfilled while the others moaned. Joshua noticed that Leon barely touched his plate. It looked like that in which a child might do with his vegetables in an illusory attempt to leave the table. The meat had been cut into small bits with a knife, but few bites were consumed, and the rest were scattered around the plank to make the portion look smaller than before. Joshua wrinkled his nose, was Leon trying to cheat them? It seemed to him that Gurdard had begun to catch on to the man's "small belly," he chastised him.

"Come now, Leon, I know your mother fed you more when we were children, you had a bigger appetite back then." Gurdard smacked.

"I haven't the room anymore. I'm afraid I'm not the eater I once was." Leon replied. He didn't sound full.

Joshua decided not to mention the tactic, the boy had brought him seven different drinks and small leaves like spinach. Joshua resumed to eat and drink. This helped his food stay down. The assortment of taste kept the king from the fowl's fouling taste, it encouraged him to continue while the others took a break.

"Look at Joshua go!" Gurdard applauded, "Pass him your food, Leon, so that he can show you how it's done."

Leon rolled his eyes and moved the plate to Joshua's side of the table. Joan watched Joshua move from plate to plate with awe, she hadn't known he had such a big appetite. She enjoyed a man with a big stomach. It wasn't such a big mark on her list of characteristics, but seeing her King decimate portion after portion reminded her that Joshua was not a shrimp nor a scrawny boy. Joshua was a man, and in that moment, he even bested the men from Scandinavia at their own hobby, feasting and drinking.

That morning, Joshua had devoured a third of the bird. The rest pulled together to eat the rest. Gurdard helped eat another fourth, and Brigga, although short, licked his thumbs happily after finishing his last strip. Between him and Joan, the rest of the bird was devoured. Leon protested that he had at least gone through a significant portion, but Joshua knew better. The skinny business man had yet to prove his worth.

Gurdard picked his teeth with a griffin digit, having conquered the bird, he had a newfound distaste for the legends of old. His boy had killed a griffin, and nothing bad yet occurred. Still, Gurdard watched the bones of the animal, superstitious, cautious despite his lax demeanor.

"I suppose it's time to give you your name, boy." Gurdard huffed. His son approached the table before them. He stood in front of a space between the fire and the main table. He took a knee. Joan grabbed Joshua by his arm again and lifted him in synchronization with Gurdard and the others. This time, her cheeks seemed scarlet beneath her blue eyes, flush from a new embarrassment. She remembered trying to kiss Joshua the night before.

"Given the circumstances, and the village's absence in the matter, I pray your role models will understand the decision I have come to without their consent. But, before I do this, I want you to take a look at them and know them well. Watch them as you continue to grow and let their actions guide your decisions. You will roam far and wide, or you may just find yourself settling down here in a few years. Wherever your path leads you, let it be with these heroes in mind: Leon the Mane, who has flourished our people through his wise understanding of business. Brigga the Dull, who fought for one of our Chiefs. He bore a proud heart even after falling in battle. Although he lost his wits, he still perseveres and lives a full life. Take Joshua, The Red King, also known as Al Hamra, a man who once prevented crime both day and night, working as a detective in the slums of Paris. Even when he was accused guilty of murder, he rose under his accusers and placed himself above the law, becoming his own judge. I have not met many men like him with such a flame in their hearts. He is now his own baron and leads his people with compassion and honesty. Take Joanne the Wave Breaker, who crossed the sea with nothing but a catboat and her wits. Her courage is ferocious and was passed to those who rose against tyranny in Joshua's name. She was his unyielding hand, loyal and honorable. She fought beside him even when the world turned their back. Even though they were leagues away from each other, she held true to their goals. Will you scald these virtues into your heart, wisdom, perseverance, pride, compassion, honesty, loyalty, courage, and honor, so even when the world breaks, it will not break you? Will you become a man like these men, and this woman, are in your age, so that when the world breaks, you can put it back together?"

"I take these virtues and will watch these heroes so that I might be like them." The boy answered.

"Then the village, and your father, name you Icarus, griffin slayer!" Gurdard shouted.

"Icarus the griffin slayer!" The boy shouted back, his voice piercing the wind howling outside the hall. His name echoed in the empty spaces, where people were supposed to shout his name back to him again, it provided a karaoke, as if the dead were there to whisper his title back, over and over.

"The ceremony has been complete. Live your life well, Icarus, we will be watching." Gurdard said, a slight break in his voice. Icarus bowed his head and rose. Joshua watched him, the power in his name. The boy looked older than seconds before, tougher. He was ready to face whatever the village had in store for him when they returned to the shore. Icarus turned his back to them and marched to the door, he pushed it open and it was caught by the growing wind. He vanished behind the torrent of snow.

Gurdard didn't stop him. The father wouldn't even suggest he stay. His son was a man now and would forge his own future. The five honorees extinguished the fire and left the longhouse to return to their cabins. They would pack their bags and wait until the storm calmed down. They did not know where Icarus went, but he would be there for his trial tomorrow.

While Gurdard and his heroes descended the mountain, Icarus trudged through the snow in his winter coat, the tumult catching in his fur hood and swiping it back down about his neck. The wind had begun to pick up, and there were no signs of shelter. There wouldn't be, where Icarus would rise. Despite this detriment, the young boy waded through the building snow determined to reach the peak of the mountain.

It was at that peak that the boy found the Griffin nest and waited. The boy recalled the ambition that made him fond of the idea. He thought bringing back a griffin for his father would be his biggest achievement. It was his greatest failure.

Icarus' name left an odd feeling in his heart. He was torn between being proud of what he'd done and feeling ashamed. Icarus did not want his father and the people to look down on him as a killer of a sacred beast. On the other hand, he was so proud of his skill in killing the bird as it flew towards its nest, that he didn't feel the full weight of his consequences bearing down on his shoulders.

The snow climbed up to Icarus's chest. With all his might, he brushed the ice from before him, carving a path up the mountain. He was a brave child, determined and courageous, just as his father asked him to be. The boy wanted to make things right with himself, he wanted his people to be as proud of him as he was in himself.

People killed people all the time. Icarus heard about the wars and the pillaging their ancestors embellished in. Surely human beings were more intelligent and sacred than wild birds, and yet, his own species was killed was slaughtered with more confidence and in more numbers every day. What harm came from killing one griffin? There had to be more along the mountain range, they couldn't be endangered.

Icarus felt his foot against something slick, he looked down into the hole he had cleared with his body and saw the liver of the griffin he killed. He had gutted the beast right there near the nest in order to make the bird lighter and easier to move down to the longhouse. The boy was close; he could tell his position on the narrow ravine he walked.

There weren't many options to get lost when the only ways to travel are backwards or down the side of a cliff. His destination was only a few more yards before him. Through the wind he heard a small sound, something distinguishable above the cacophony, something sweet. Icarus smiled, his blue lips dry and cracking. The boy had arrived just in time.

516

Part 6/Remove

Joshua dipped his feet into the sea and watched The Red Empress rock against the ripple of the waves. Once Icarus returned, the trial would begin. Joan remained in her quarters, and Gurdard spoke to the people about what they thought was a fitting punishment for his son. Despite Gurdard's stature as baron, Joshua discovered he was less than a cornerstone of society, and more of an ambassador that maintained relationships with other providences. On his own land, he was simply a well-respected man with a high social value. When it came to ruling his land, the people acted as one unified government. That was the power of tradition in the Scandes. Even though Napoleon came and went, placing his French flag in the soil, the people still maintained a distinct identity. If anything, Napoleon's conquest of Europe only determined cooperation among separate people groups. Once they could not find an heir to follow his reign. If they had ever found Napoleon's heir back then, the Scandinavian peoples would be answering to a different regime instead of living peacefully and symbiotic with their neighbors.

Joshua imagined how loving the first baron of Scandinavia was, to be given authority by the French to rule over a land as far as his eyes could see, and yet, that baron chose instead not to ratify their culture to suit his own dogmas. Joshua wondered if he was infringing on his people's culture by promoting trade between other providences. Joshua wondered if the Scandinavians truly wanted to proceed into an age of technology and policy as he did. The American wanted his home to be akin to Paris, yet a peaceful land without slums and poverty and crime. He wanted to build a better Paris. But what if the world's advance towards the future made criminals possible? The advent of technology gave form to documentation, complication, categorization and then discrimination… That would lead to civil disillusion, a precursor to crime.

Joshua flicked his hand and watched sparks raise into the air. He noticed how unusually dark the flame had become as he lit his second cigarette. Joshua thought he was growing ill. A year ago, he used to much favor and had been paying the price for it, so he guessed. But what if it was something else.

Al Hamra scratched the back of his head. He had begun to hear voices in the caves, long before Whitecroft descended to cut off his limbs and study him. The pain of torture only made the voices worse. Joshua remembered learning about trauma, it could create multiple personalities, a way for the victim to categorize their emotions, or isolate certain memories. He doubted he was suffering from this. Perhaps the voices in his head weren't other people, and he was simply telling himself to kill others, to make fountains of blood and cakes of bone. It was an odd thing to think about, an odd thing to want, not that he wanted it. He could never want that, could he?

The thick storm on the mountainside had begun to settle and exposed the rock to the villagers. There on the path was a small boy. Icarus had returned for his trial. Joshua watched as the villagers began to usher him out to the docks where Joshua began to stand. Joshua would not be allowed to accompany the jury while they determined the boy's fate for he was not Scandinavian.

Joshua quickly climbed The Red Empress and knocked on Joan's cabin. She emerged.

"Is it time?" Joan asked, looking down at the commotion. Joshua nodded, and she quickly descended the side down to them in order to join.

Joan had described the event to Joshua prior to Icarus' return. The villagers would take Icarus out to open waters in a cog. There, they would sit him in the center by the mast as they sat around the edges of the boat. They would discuss what to do with him there, where no one had any distractions, and the world was neutral. Joshua would follow from a distance in The Red Empress, staying a few miles out until the council was over. He was allowed to pick up Joan after the verdict was made so that they could be on their way home and closer to their pre-conceived schedule.

Joshua watched the group of judges board the cog and shove off. The men rowed through the shallow waters until the main sail was dropped. Joshua left the front sail down, and trudged behind slowly, only to keep them in his sights. There was no particular breeze that day, just enough for a slow roll over the vast blue ocean. The oars on the Scandinavian vessel and its smaller size made the difference in their speed.

Joshua wondered what would happen during the conclave, perhaps Joan would tell him after, if the meeting was not as confidential as it seemed.

Joan watched her ship in the distance; it was far enough that she could pretend to hold it in her hand. She waited as the boat began to slow and the anchor was dropped to the sea floor. It was a peaceful and sunny day, not a cloud in sight. The deck began to warm the cold air where they sat, providing an uneven temperature that was more or less adequate for spring. Joan took her position along the railing and sat down with her legs crossed. Each villager would say their opinion on the matter, and only once was each of them required to speak at length so that all opinions were noted.

First, Icarus would start the trial with a statement to defend himself with.

The young lad sat in the center of the boat and watched the people stare at him. They judged him, some snickered. He was too young to give a compelling and adequate answer to his actions; thus, the boy simply spoke his mind.

"I killed a griffin two days ago, but I don't feel guilty for it. Nothing happened, nothing *bad* happened, so we're all okay. I don't hold to traditions, because traditions just hold us back. I understand that I offended people, so I won't do it again. I *think* I'm sorry."

Gurdard shook his head. His son did not say anything to help his case. If anything, he unknowingly ostracized himself through his honesty.

The group murmured to themselves, awestruck by the boy's honesty and bravery. No one was ready to speak their turn yet, but in the group, and after some time, Leon began to chime in. The slender man stood up and walked to the center of the boat giving everybody his full attention.

"It's only been a few days; the boy could be cursed. I spoke with each of you about this individually before we boarded this ship: The gods enjoy making us *think* we're safe, but then they will curse the many for the sake of the one. I have full confidence that we will do the safe thing and exile Icarus, the Griffin Slayer. Kick him off the island, I say! We can't risk harming the villages! Cast him into the sea!"

Joan gritted her teeth, Gurdard rose from his place among the people.

"You bastard!" the baron grunted, "You've cooked up this little scheme from the beginning, didn't you? You're trying to sever the baron lineage so that the people will vote for the next baron. *You* want to be the next baron, don't you!?"

Leon smiled and did not reply, he had spoken once and was not obligated to speak again. Joan thought about it, Leon had always been a slippery fish. She waited for the others to speak, they expressed worry for the consequences, both from casting the boy into the sea and sparing him. To her horror, most of them sided with the businessman.

Joan looked to Icarus who seemingly stared at Leon, but why Leon? Why didn't the boy look to his father?

"Icarus," Joan asked, "Who gave you the idea to hunt a griffin?"

"Leon did." Icarus responded.

The crowd murmured in surprise.

Leon scoffed, "It was a passing suggestion, a fleeting idea! I didn't know he would actually *act* on such a small notion!"

"It's your fault Icarus is cursed!" a villager replied.

"But he's not the cursed one! Icarus is the one on trial, not Leon. We still have to get rid of the boy!" Another replied.

"Yes, it's the boy that killed the griffin, so throw him into the water and let the gods sort him out! Exile him!"

Verbal sparring broke out among those onboard. They shouted over each other and cursed each other's names. They found every reason to blame someone for their verdicts. Joan and Gurdard were the loudest among them. Gurdard targeted Leon with his slander, accusing him of nefarious intentions ever since their birth. Joan called out to the people, begging them to come to their senses.

Joshua watched the boat sitting calmly in the water. It had been near an hour since they took their places. As Joshua watched them through his telescope, things seemed to become pretty heated. Joshua squinted. Through his lens he could see something peculiar, a glint in Leon's clothing, a sharp shape.

"What are you doing Leon?" Joshua asked himself.

Hours later Joshua rose his telescope again, he looked at the people on the boat, they stood still on the boat. Every one of them stood, even Joan. Joshua traced their silhouettes until he spied the skinniest man, spied Leon.

Joshua began to shake.

Leon held the boy by his arm, pushing him towards the edge of the boat. The boy squirmed and tried to fight him.

Were they really going to kill the child?

"Bastard" Joshua muttered. He dropped the telescope, shattering the lens to pieces.

The young man quickly turned around and walked into the hull. Joshua sank into the depths next to his cot. Next to the bedding, he grabbed one of his bags and curtailed, thundering back up the stairs. Joshua moved to the bow and placed his bag on the floor. He opened the satchel methodically, producing a long pipe, a firing pin, and an assortment of gun materials. He began to assemble it, as fast as his hand would allow him.

Not again, oh God, not another kid. Oh God, oh God, oh God.

Joshua, Kill. Joshua, Scratch. Kill, Hill, Kill. Break, Bleed,
    Kill Kill Scratch Scratch Kill Scratch.
In death, Kill. Hold Scratch. Kill Me Here.
Listen!
    Scratch, Kill Kill Scratch Kill Oh Joshua Hill Kill
Scratch, Joshua,   Kill Scratch. Joshua Scratch. Hill, Kill.
Monster

Gurdard stood before Leon who held the boy to the railings of the cog. The thin man looked fierce. He reminded Joan of a jackal.

"You can't do this!" Gurdard demanded, almost begged. "Your verdicts are wrong! Let my son live!"

"Oh Gurdard, my oldest friend." Leon smirked coyly, "There's nothing I can do now. The tribe has made up its mind."

Joan clenched her fist. She didn't know what to do, she hadn't expected the trial to run so awry. If Leon dropped Icarus into the water, he would die in minutes. His body would enter hypothermia in seconds. He would be condemned to death the second his head went under the water. It was hopeless, Leon had his way.

Gurdard shouted and stormed forth, tackling Leon onto the deck and ripping Icarus from his hands. Icarus wobbled into the rail at the collision, tumbling over the side. Joan sprinted to catch him, finding her hands around his thighs. The little boy hung head-over-heels before she could drag him in. His hair was wet, but altogether, he was unharmed.

Gurdard punched Leon across the face, quickly drawing blood. "You will not take my son!" He roared.

Leon smiled and reached into his doublet, he pulled out a small knife from his pocket and unfolded it. Leon proceeded to stab Gurdard in his sides repeatedly. Gurdard bellowed in pain, placing his hand on Leon's hand, letting the knife skewer his palm. The Scandinavian baron gripped Leon's fist, forcing it against the deck.

"Father!" Icarus called, he tried to sprint to Gurdard, but was soon stopped as Joan wrapped her arms around his waist and picked him up.

"Let your father handle this!" Joan chided, "You can't help him now!"

Joan looked about the cog, the other villagers began to awaken from their fear and punch each other. Among them was Brigga, whom, upon seeing Leon harmed, spurred into a half-minded frenzy towards Joan. Brigga shouted lamely, his tongue against his open mouth like a dog. Brigga doubled over himself, crashing into Joan haphazardly. Joan dropped Icarus and crashed into the wall at the blow. The huntress grappled with the old midget, exchanging fists and elbows. The rest of the villagers shouted in the fray, attacking those whom held different opinions than them. They hit each other relentlessly, believing that their aggression would differ the other's judgements. It did not, it only solidified their desires to do what they thought was necessary.

Icarus ran to his father, now free of Joan's protection, but the man held his hand back, pushing his son away.

"Get to safety, boy!" Gurdard ordered as Leon landed a blow to his face. The slender man rolled over Gurdard and wiggled his blade free, raising his hands above his head.

"Die Gurdard!" Leon screamed, slamming his knife into the baron's belly.

Joshua rested his rifle on the ships railing. He took a deep breath and squeezed the trigger. The sound of the bullet

523

alarmed those on the cog long before the white streak met Leon's head. The bullet caught the slender man through the skull and ricocheted inside, severing the spine from the brain perfectly. Leon fell to the side, dead.

Scratch, scratch, scratch. Kill, kill, kill. He thought. The words bouncing off his skull, echoing and careening around his cranium.

Joshua breathed in, his bleeding eyes pasted to his scope. He waited for Leon to stand up, he dared him to. Joshua *wanted* to shoot him again; he *wanted* to watch the bullet tear through his head. He *hated* Leon. In that moment he saw Icarus over the railing he knew the man deserved to *die*. He was *just* like *Solomon*. Joshua began to *mutter* to himself. Who else could he *shoot*? Who else voted to toss Icarus over the boat? He *wanted* to know, he *wanted* to know who the *kill*ers were.

They're all like Solomon, they're all like Solomon, they're all like Solomon. Scratch, scratch, scratch. Yes, yes, yes, Joshua. Kill, kill, kill. It's all you're good for. Save by killing. Kill, scratch. Kill, scratch.

Joshua began to see yellow raincoats. It was like his nights in Paris. He'd shoot them all. But which one was Joan? Was Baron Gurdard alive? Where was Icarus?

Joshua panned left, he saw something short, he saw the baby face, the round body. It was Brigga. Joshua took a deep breath. He was sure. Before, He had seen Brigga talking with Leon, he had to know what was going on. Joshua put his finger on the trigger and squeezed. The second bullet rang through the air like a thunderclap.

Yes Joshua, yes.
Scratch, scratch, scratch.

Joan watched as Brigga fell under the weight of a bullet. The man stumbled back. There was a third shot, a loud roar. This one found its way higher up his torso. A fourth loud noise, the fourth bullet killed Brigga in a rupture of blood.

Joan quickly rose and leaped on the railing of the cog, waving down the manic Joshua. She was horrified, not knowing if he would kill yet another sailor on their boat. She was scared, not knowing if Joshua would even shoot her. Joan was scared of Joshua. Joan waited, her hands above her head, her eyes closed, waiting for the bullet to move through her head. Joan was wrong to think Joshua was okay. The world had asked to much of him. Whitecroft had done too much to him. Joan didn't blame Joshua.

Joan still loved Joshua. He was trying his best.

The bullets had stopped firing.

They were safe for now, safe from their own savior.

After a silence, The Red Empress slowly made its way towards the cog. Joshua was sailing to meet them. Joshua didn't know whether to finish the job and purge the boat of sinners, or to do what he had promised to do, and steal Joan away from the turmoil.

Was Joshua crazy? Half of the council on their boat would have his head before he even stepped foot on the deck.

Joan looked back to see Icarus kneeling by his father. Gurdard bled on the floor. He placed his hand on Icarus' shoulder who stood before his father. His son begged him not to die.

"Run-away Icarus," Gurdard commanded, choking, "even though you were kept from death, the verdict is the same. You can no longer step foot in Scandinavia, ever again. So *please* run, my son, don't let us catch you. Run!"

Gurdard coughed. His citizens, calmed by the sound of gunfire, flocked to their baron. Closing Icarus off from his father, blocking his view of his wounded father. They pressed their clothes into his body. Gurdard was a big man, and he had survived worse. The big man looked at Joan with a nod through the legs of his many citizens.

Joan moved and wrapped her arms around Icarus again and he cried. She held him tight and lifted him up. The griffin killer squirmed and flailed, trying to be free, trying to make it back to his father, to be beside him again. Joan held him back across the chest, fighting the boy's rocking body. The Red Empress loomed close behind her, she turned to grab the ladder.

As Joan grabbed the bar, she looked up to see the Joshua on the railing. Further up, he stood over the ledge, staring down at the cog with judgmental eyes. The crowd below looked at the man who blocked out the sun behind him, casting a long shadow over the boat. The crowd was scared of the killer, his yellow eyes bled profusely. They thought he was death, but certainly, they knew he was worse.

Joshua didn't say a word as he looked down at the cog. But his mind fluttered with rouge voices. His fingers twitched, he could burn it all down. With a flick of his wrist he could burn all evidence of their existence, prevent anyone from knowing what they tried to do Icarus.

He didn't. But he imagined it.

Joan hung on the ladder as The Red Empress sailed away from the cog.

"Father!" Icarus screamed, being separated from the last of his family. He was handed over to strangers, people he didn't really know. Gurdard held his hand up to the sky so that Icarus might see him wave through the crowd. The boy cried, he didn't think being an adult would be so hard. Moreover, he didn't know whether his father would live. He didn't know whether he would ever see his father again. Chances are, he would never see any of them ever again.

Gurdard gave away his only son. But perhaps this saying was truer, the traditions of the Scandes failed his son. He would most likely never see his son again. He would be unable to notice him in the world, unable to hold him or watch him grow up. Indeed, yesterday was his passage into adulthood, and look how far his son had already flown. Icarus would be a great man one day. Gurdard hoped to watch him do just that, even if it meant he had to watch from the heavens.

Before Gurdard closed his eyes, he took one last look at Joshua Hill. He stood on that railing with a hand in his coat pocket, and another against his chest. The man looked ill and in so much pain. Gurdard wasn't scared of Joshua, who hunched like a madman, his eyes twitching as he murmured something to himself. No, Gurdard wasn't scared of Joshua, even though he could tell Joshua wanted to condemn them all for even thinking to hurt a child.

The baron looked at Joshua's judgmental eyes, dead and soulless. The Red King was a savage grim reaper, an empty man with a vendetta. He was a terrible man, he wasn't a hero or a villain. Joshua Hill was King that was born only to kill. Joshua's dreams, his loves, his hopes, the detective had killed those too. It was what he was born to do. He was cursed, in more ways than one.

Gurdard was happy however, even for this. This grim reaper, this bitter saint, saved his son, saved him. He would be eternally grateful to Joshua, despite his methods.

Somewhere within Joshua Hill, there might be a heart, but it would be a miracle if it ever started pumping.

Icarus screamed until the Scandinavian cog disappeared over the horizon. It was the last he would see of his homeland for a long time. The boy exhausted himself as he struggled to become free of Joan's grasp, eventually falling asleep before Joan even climbed aboard the deck.

Joan quickly moved to place the boy in the captain's quarters so that he could rest, ignoring Joshua for the time being. She locked him inside after tucking him in. Joan didn't know what to do with him; she didn't know what to do with either of the men on board.

Joan walked up the stairs as Joshua lit a cigarette and took the helm. She slapped it out of his hands. Joshua watched it tumble to the floor and blow along the breeze through the rails and into the ocean. Joshua's hands shook.

Joshua turned to Joan, expecting to be chewed out. Joan looked at Joshua, the blood caked across his cheeks. How didn't she see it before? The help Joshua needed. Joan only thought, truly she knew, Joshua was the darkest of saints. Joan wrapped her arms around Joshua's shaking frame. She held him tightly, for nothing good ever came from chastising those already hurting.

"I understand now." Joan said. "I understand why you're so quiet all the time."

"I lied to you." Joshua exhaled unevenly, his hand still on his chest. The American's voice was strained, the words on his lips struggling to be spoken. "I am a killer, Joan. I've killed more than I care to count."

"It's okay Joshua, I finally understand," Joan replied, "Joshua... how many kids have you seen die around you?"

Joshua looked the hand in his coat pocket, he fingers for a number, trying to do the math. He didn't really want to answer her, but the voices in his head made him thirsty to know. He wanted to put a number on his pain, an integer to define himself by. Joshua remembered his dreams, but the number in his head didn't match the number in his heart. The Red King folded his fingers in and out, fluttered them inside his pocket, tapping the seams. He tried to understand why he was so confused.

Joshua felt something on his cheek, it was wet. It wasn't blood and it wasn't raining. Joshua's knees buckled beneath him, he hit the deck and sat on his heels. His fingers continued to twitch, they made triggering motions between his counting, motioning the death count.

Kill, kill, kill, kill, he counted.

"There were the children, in the house... and- and" Joshua began, "There were the children in the house, there were the children in the house, the children in the house. T-the children in the church... the children in the mansion... oh, God, why can't I count them all?"

Joshua cried.

Kill, kill, kill.
Kill, kill, kill.

Once Icarus recovered from his stupor, he helped Joan man the sails after the captain forced Joshua to sleep. They didn't know Joshua was eating the pillow, twisting in agony, still trying to count.

On sweeter notes, Icarus was a good helper, apt to listen, quick at work. Gurdard had raised the boy well, and much did the father know he would be using the virtues he gave the child. Icarus had never done much wrong in the Scandes. He was never the one to be called a troublemaker before he killed that griffin. Joan quickly grew fond of him that day, and quickly thought of him as her own child. For all purposes and the course that vessels would take, Joan was Icarus' guardian. The huntress made it her responsibility to keep him safe and make sure he lived a full life. The boy was quiet, but in the coming days he would begin to talk more and more.

On another day, Joshua sat on a barrel near the bow, looking at his foot. Joshua, although avoiding contact with Joan after displaying emotions, found that Icarus would often try to talk with him. The boy asked him about where they were going and what the land looked like. Joshua explained everything he could in as few words as possible. It was the most Joan had ever seen Joshua talk.

Icarus might be good for Joshua's health. He might have been the medicine he was looking for.

When that day had closed itself like the end of a play, Icarus had begun to grip the pegs by the stern and guide the boat across the navy waters. There was nothing for the troupe to worry about for they were upon the open sea, obstructed by nothing. Joan used this time to call Joshua into her captain's quarters. Joshua poked at the small fireplace.

Joshua didn't know whether she would still be mad at him for what he did. He had started to feel better. His eyes had stopped twitching, his anxiety subsided. He almost felt normal if not for the whispers in his ears.

Joshua didn't regret killing Leon or Brigga, but what he did wonder was how Gurdard would calm his people. The Red King didn't know where the relationship between their two states would go, but he hoped they would not go to war. Joshua had traded a good standing with the small country to save a small child, the baron's only child.

It was worth it, he thought.

Joan watched Joshua and thought about their return to regular schedules. Soon, the baron would be too busy for her unless on official business, or sheltered in his house, reading, waiting for Elizabeth to walk through the front door with her overnight bag. Even now, Joshua preferred seclusion to Joan's presence. He hadn't addressed her since she entered the room.

Joan hoped that Joshua would get better once they returned. Perhaps it was best for their king to stay in his house all he could. It would be better to buy him books and other hobbies so that he could stay away from the people all he could. They needed to keep him stable, and maybe Elizabeth wasn't doing her job at helping him live a full and happy life.

Joan could do that.

It wasn't until minutes after that thought, when Joan brought about the courage to tell him how she felts, that he opened his mouth to speak.

"I'm okay, you know." Joshua said, still poking the fire.

Joan shook her head, "That's… not why I called you in here Josh."

Joshua looked over to her, his eyes looked empty, something dark was on his mind. Joan wondered if she was utterly insane, or somehow redeemable. Why did Joan have to love a man who never so much as batted his eyes at her? She had no idea why she was infatuated by him. All she knew was that she wanted to give him everything, the whole world if she could.

"Is there something you need?" Joshua asked. He asked the question like a genie, his words spoken from some written duty, not because he cared. Joan opened her mouth; how could she say this to someone so callous? How could she express something on her heart without giving her heart away? No, Joan had to play the hand she was dealt.

"I want," Joan began, but she faltered for a moment. She recollected herself, she had faced more challenging things before. She could do this.

"I want to be your queen, Joshua."

Joshua continued to stare through her. His cheeks didn't blush, his facial expression didn't change. Joan was disheartened, Joshua was withered. It seemed to her that Joshua had relapsed back to his old self. His persona before he was king. Maybe she should have waited longer. Maybe she should have waited for Joshua to resume his schedule, to collect his heart again. Then he would have been more receptive to her.

"You would make a good queen." Joshua replied, almost looking away from her. "But I don't think you could make *my* queen."

"Because Elizabeth?" Joan spat.

"Yes," Joshua replied, as if it needn't any explanation.

Joan clutched her fingers. She didn't like Elizabeth, not one bit. She seemed like a whore. She refused to stay with Joshua, always leaving him in the middle of the night. Joan would wage war against Val-Ashoth if it meant finding her way to Joshua, if that's what it took to win his love. Elizabeth didn't act to improve her relationship with Joshua. She was complacent, unwilling to make sacrifices. She didn't seem to care. Joan didn't like Elizabeth, yes, Joan hated her.

"Why?" Joan buffered, retaliating against her circumstances, trying to convince her king she was the one he needed, the one he should want. "She's so far away! You never see her! If I remember correctly, she manipulated you and treated you like a slave! What do you owe her, that keeps you from me? What must you pay to be free of that witch?!"

Joan's voice broke, her voice softened.

"It's guilt isn't it? The great king still feels guilty for everything, doesn't he? You think that you would deny her Connor Shaw if you didn't love her back. But you know he's dead."

"That's not true. Not all of it." Joshua replied slowly. Looking back to the fire he spoke through gritted teeth. "I need to protect her... I don't need to protect you. Don't you see, she needs me. She can't have Connor, so all I can give her is second best."

"That's shit Joshua! You're not some king of watchdog that has to stand in front of her house! You're your own person! You don't have to keep serving people like some slave, some... kind of cop! You're a king! You're a damn king! You have to take care of yourself and do something you want to do! You're over your people, not under them!"

Joan paused, huffing, catching her breath. It then occurred to her, something that never occurred to her before. Dutch and Joan always mentioned that Joshua would become king, but, never once, did Joshua agree with them. In the beginning, he had told Joan he wanted to kill Whitecroft.

He never said he wanted to take her place.

"Did you even want to become a baron?!?" Joan asked.

Joshua looked back to Joan, tears welling in his eyes. He shook his head no. "I never wanted this. I was going to make Dutch king. I was going to abandon him with the throne. All I wanted was for Whitecroft to die. And now she is, and I'm stuck."

"Stop!" Joan barked, almost interrupted, "There's more to life than killing people! You're not some kind of avenger! You need to stop this! You're going to run yourself into the ground before you see the world become a better place, you already have! You can't change everything Joshua!

You can't change nature or the whole world! You're just a man and you're at your limit!"

Joshua continued to stare at Joan, his eyes unexpressive. But tears that welled in his eyes and tricked down to his chin almost flowing like a waterfall.

"Don't say that Joanne," Joshua asked, begged, pleaded softly. "It can become better; all of this can get better. One day, people will no longer hurt. I want to give that to them. I want to protect Elizabeth from hurt too, even if it means lying to her..."

Joan scoffed and left the cabin, she wouldn't listen to the suicidal man anymore. Joshua really was insane, and he was long past redemption. The door slammed behind the huntress as she left and rattled the chairs.

Joshua looked to his feet for a moment and decided to stay in that cabin. It wasn't until further in the day, the dead of night, that Icarus came in to sleep.

Icarus lay in the bed, staring at the ceiling. Joshua moved from the fireplace to leave.

"I think I want to be like you." Icarus said before Joshua twisted the door handle and exited. Joshua looked back at the boy who continued to stare at the ceiling.

"What do you mean by that?" Joshua asked.

"I want to be a hero, like you." Icarus restated plainly, "I want to save people like you saved my father."

"Don't say that." Joshua replied, reaching into his pocket for a cigarette. He lit it, this was the last in his pack. Old habits die hard, he thought he had quit, but here he was smoking every day. "Be better than I am, kid. Promise me you'll do better than me when you're older."

Icarus looked up momentarily, his eyes caught the killer's glance. Even in the boy's youth, he could tell what Joshua was, how much pain his ideals brought him. Icarus saw the same look of hatred and emptiness in the eyes of bears and wolves. Icarus also saw the fear in Joshua's eyes like that of a fawn.

Even though Joshua warned Icarus, the boy wasn't worried about happiness, he wasn't concerned with how his life would turn out. The boy had become enamored by the man in the black jacket. He wanted to save people like he did, even if it meant killing others.

"I promise." Icarus half-lied, putting his head back onto the pillow. The boy heard the door open and Al Hamra stepped out into the night air.

"If I can't," Icarus whispered to himself, "then I'll at least be exactly like you."

Joshua stood there by the door to the captain's quarters, afraid to walk further and be spotted by Joan. But Joan already heard him and broke the silence with stern words.

"I'm going to drop you off near shore tomorrow."

"You're not staying, then?" Joshua called back from below, almost expecting this conversation to happen. The good ones always left. "There's nothing I can do to keep you here?"

"No, it would be best that I leave. I'm not going to stay around to watch you kill yourself slowly." Joan replied, almost choking, holding back the tears.

"No, you don't want to watch that." Joshua agreed. "I don't think anybody should watch something like that."

Part 7/Reason

The Marquis stopped by early that morning to check on Frea. He let himself through the door and perused through her house until finding her in bed. She was under house arrest for a few days. She had killed seven men, and the punishment was the lightest he thought he himself could accept. The Marquis was expecting Joshua that day, and the king would sort the stand-in queen out.

Laffy didn't know it so much, but he sure saw it. Frea was unmolded, at the very least changed, more flexible, less conceited. His job was done, as best he could do it at least. The woman didn't raise her disheveled head to greet The Golden King as he placed her breakfast on the nightstand and removed her uneaten dinner from the night before.

Frea hadn't moved from that bed since, perhaps ashamed of breaking countenance three days before, losing her cool. Whatever had snapped in her heart truly did its toll. She no longer combed her hair, changed out of her pajamas, or worried about her health. It was an odd arrangement, in which Frea now spiraled into a rabbit's hole of bad hygiene, but, Lafayette was confident she would resume her normal duties beside The Red King in due time.

"You should eat before you lose weight, not that you could. You'll get sick if you don't eat."

Frea moaned, her face buried in a wadded-silk blanket.

"Suit yourself," The Marquis sighed, "Joshua will be back today, I'm sure he'll want to see you."

Frea didn't respond. Lafayette shrugged and backed out of the room, closing the door gently behind him.

Frea house, or, all houses in LeCeleste, were made of white cedar and embellished with animal bone and gold. That material formed everything tangible in the city and curved organically as one fluid piece like a melted igloo that refroze in a more… slushy… state. Everything was one cohesive and curved piece of art. The bookshelves were carved from the walls which sloped down to the floor and segmented by golden grooves. The stairs were carved from the walls, providing a set of spiraling stepping stones. The entirety of LeCeleste was carved from a single tree. It radiated an incandescent white and yellow like the sun, in which it proudly held the name.

The Marquis was proud of the French achievement, much more elegant than the Russian military juggernauts who built their machines on heavy steel and iron which stumbled through the skies loudly, clanging after each bump. The difference between Russian engineering and ancient French craftmanship was the difference between a foil and a mace.

Lafayette whistled as he descended to the earth in the small elevator basket. It was hardly ever used, as most of his citizens still preferred to stay in their high-horse city. Even after the conflict had settled down a year ago, they held a certain neglect for those bumpkins below. The Marquis spied, as he looked up from the elevator, his skyship, neatly tucked into the side of the leviathan. It was tied down and waiting for him to take her out on another spin. The Marquis wanted to but had not yet an idea of where to go. He thought back of the week when they had Joshua aboard. It was funny how far that detective had gone in such a short time. From detective to renegade to king, the man truly impressed. Perhaps there was destiny about him.

The Marquis laughed, Joshua was like a grenade that popped out of a gumball machine. The barons pulled the pin and now the man was exploding in all of their faces.

As the descending basket scraped the grass, the ancient man carried himself over the hillsides towards the docks on the coast. The workers began to finish the pier in this early hour. The woodworkers had toiled endlessly on building the country a trading port. As the Marquis was heading to the coast anyways to wait for Joshua, he decided it would be splendid to see how this pier was coming along.

It took Laffy some time to reach the beach where Joshua and Joan had parted to attend Gurdard's ceremony. He wondered how they fared and hoped they didn't step on too many toes while they were present. The Marquis began to walk along the sandy shoreline, tracing his eyes on the horizon in vain hope of witnessing the red schooner floating along, early in its schedule. It was a warm day and the smell of salt was thick and rich. If he wasn't careful, Laffy would leave the beach with a headache and a bloody nose.

The pier was well made, simple yet trustworthy. Walkways stretched out from the shore into the ocean some fifty yards to accommodate the biggest of ships. Still, missing planks scattered the landing, leaving nefarious holes where a cartoon cat might find himself falling after several seconds of levitating over the gap.

The Marquis smiled. One day, Joshua hoped that the piers would serve as a marker for people to settle there on the bay. Eventually, as trade routes were reestablished, and contracts were signed with other barons, Joshua would even build his own series of houses along the shore and sell them to traders capable of buying whole shipments on the king's behalf. These merchants would also serve to station a market for the ships, so they wouldn't need come ashore or inland to peddle.

Joshua had big ideas, The Marquis liked that.

"Are you sure you don't want to stay?" Joshua asked, his voice dark and tired.

Joan shook her head, "It's about time I began exploring the world again. There's much that I haven't been able to see."

"Be careful." Joshua exhaled, lifting his bags onto the dingy.

"Goodbye Josh." Joan replied.

537

Joshua moved the dingy over the water with Joan's help. Icarus watched them from the rails as the two adults waved their goodbyes.

Joan would take care of the boy, she needed a good sailor. Neither did the huntress want Joshua influencing the boy, not knowing he already had. She hoped for Joshua's future, but, in her independence, knew she could move past the memory of her time with him. It would be nothing but a chapter in her life. Hopefully, it would be the smallest chapter in her book, perhaps never mentioned when people wrote of her epics.

Joshua began to row away from The Red Empress, and Joan watched him as he grew ever distant.

"We could've let him off closer." Icarus mentioned.

"Let the man work for it." Joan smirked, "I think he would like time to think before hitting land anyways. Come, boy, let's be off."

"Where are we going?" Icarus asked, plodding after her to the wheel. Joan ran her hands along the wood of The Red Empress, thinking to herself.

"Let's shoot the dark and find ourselves an adventure." She smiled, rotating the rudder.

Joan and Icarus were off to the great unknown. Perhaps they would become something of import themselves. Maybe they would create their own crew and make their own names.

The captain of The Red Empress felt the wind in her hair and watched Icarus scamper about the deck to adjust the ropes. Even though Joshua was gone, she still had a brand-new world ahead of her. Joan and Icarus would make the best of it. They would have the adventure of a lifetime; the girl was sure of it.

The day soared by as Lafayette watched the waters chop and foam along the wooden pillars. Eventually, come two o'clock The Marquis could see the painted sails of Joan's schooner loom over the horizon. He gathered himself for their arrival, they had much to discuss, but, Lafayette found himself standing at the end of the pier longer than he expected. It seemed the ship had stopped but a mile away. The Golden King squinted his eyes to see a small rowboat tossed over the rails, and a single identity make its way closer.

It took the better of fifteen minutes for Joshua to arrive in his dingy and mantle onto the wooden pier. His hair was smattered and wet from the ocean spray.

"What's wrong, where is Joan?" The Marquis asked blatantly.

"She decided to go her own way." Joshua replied sadly, wringing out his shirt and saddling his pack over his shoulder. He was already raring to go. He didn't want to wait on anyone, he didn't want to look back or linger on the coast.

The Marquis looked back to the vanishing vessel with a short hum. He didn't wish to ask further. The man had a small bundled newspaper under his arm and walked alongside Joshua back across the dock and into the rolling hills. They passed many farms and taverns as they made their way back to Joshua's small house. The Marquis informed him of the goings-on and the failure of his advisors leading to Frea's brief reign and quicker killing spree.

"Where is she now?" Joshua frowned.

"Moping in her bed under guard." The Marquis replied, "It will take her some time for her to regain her bearings. I suggest you meet with her as soon as you can. I'm sure she would be glad to see you."

Laffy paused before brandishing the paper from underneath his arm. "There's… also this."

Joshua grabbed the newspaper and unfolded it. He began to skim the headlines.

"I had someone deliver it from the providence over. It seems Russia has made quite the show of itself while you were gone." Laffy informed, "hopefully it's all grandstanding and empty notions."

"It's saying here that Russian soldiers were found across the 15th. That's a breach of the treaties... They were found and shot on sight by French soldiers." Joshua said, letting The Marquis know where he was on the page.

"Much like those children you found, they found themselves in the back of a car making their way across, most likely drunk or desperate for French... proclivities."

"Prostitutes, because prostitution is banned in Russia but not France." Joshua restated.

"They're a mean but clean people." The Marquis added. "Everyone has a job, and the government likes to keep the cap on population growth as well as disease. Prostitution ruined that."

Joshua groaned, "What has Russia done in response?"

"Apparently," The Marquis began, his bright face losing tone, "The Russian government is discussing war."

Joshua walked into Frea's bedroom to spy her under the sheets.

"Go away," Frea moaned.

"Oh... but I heard you had something to tell me." Joshua excused.

Frea looked at Joshua through the corner of her eye. She rose with the covers strapped around her like she was sushi, or in a mental ward; it explained all the white. The girl stared at him for a moment, her eyes half closed, her hair standing on end, touched by static. She jerked her chin to a small note on her nightstand. The note lay next to the food Lafayette left her that day. Joshua waltzed forward and read it to himself.

"Some random person that wants to meet with me?" Joshua asked, "Did you get his name?"

Frea shook her head, "No, he's down at the Lamprey inn, waiting for you."

Joshua shrugged and left the note on the stand. He sat on the side of her bed while she lay back down. Joshua stared at the chiseled walls of the bedroom.

"I have a job for you." Joshua began.

Frea didn't want to work with people, but upon hearing Joshua's request, her ears began to perk up. She watched him explain his intentions, and nodded with each pause in his speech, assuring him she was listening. Once Joshua rose again and left to meet the strange man at Lamprey inn. Frea soon found herself eating the lunch The Marquis had left. She was excited to get back to work. She got dressed quickly and stormed out of the building, freed under Joshua's permission. She had a lot to do that day, and for many days after.

Joshua made his way back to the surface with the guards he had dismissed. He ordered them to come with him to the inn. The reason for this being he was unarmed and uncertain what he would find there. Al Hamra worried that he had missed out on something important, that the man would not be there when he arrived, having waited too long for an audience with the baron.

Joshua soon found himself sharing a horse with one of the men, speeding him to their destination miles away like a cabbie. It reminded Joshua, however remotely, of the cab he took to the park in Paris but some time ago. He could almost feel the deja-vu. It was odd how and investigation went so wrong and went so right. Joshua's life was completely changed that day, all because of an encounter with a strange killer in a yellow raincoat. It all started with a ride, a scream, and a radio.

It was midday in which Joshua and his two cohorts arrived at the inn. The trio entered the housing and spoke to the barkeep. She seemed confused at first, not sure what to think of the prospect, unsure whether someone had been staying with them that long. The keeper was also an older lady that reminded Joshua of Ms. Hammond. He was patient while she ran her gnarled finger along her ledger, a furrow in her brow and a thin frown on her face.

"It says here that your highness has been paying for one sir to stay at the inn, but I don't know his name. I don't believe he left one." The lady said, her voice feeble and shaking.

"You didn't ask for one?" Joshua insisted, "Don't remember his face or when he left?"

"No, your highness. I'm sorry. I didn't want to impress on him in fear he was someone important. You shouldn't anger important people, now. And I haven't been too good with faces, not with me turning that age an' all." The keeper excused.

"Well, thank you for your help." Joshua sighed, before making his way out of the tavern.

When Joshua emerged from the wooden building he was met by a blinding flash of lightning. A storm had brewed and was quickly moving towards them. The sudden change in weather from that morning took Joshua by surprise as small drops of rain began to puddle beneath his feet. He didn't quite understand the sudden change, the heavy air. These signs did nothing to peak Joshua's interest. But as The Red King looked up, he understood the sign behind him, he understood the odd poke in his back.

"Call your men off." Solomon demanded, prodding Joshua's spine with his gun.

Joshua could hear the men unsheathe their swords once they heard Solomon's voice. He had appeared before them out of nowhere. If only they were smart and quick enough to not react.

As the men drew their swords, Solomon reacted accordingly and shot them each in the face in one quick movement. They were dead, not knowing exactly what had occurred.

Solomon quickly twisted his pistol back only to place his gun into an erupting flame. Solomon cringed as his right hand was charred and his gun melted in his hands.

Joshua turned his head to look over his shoulders at Solomon. The villain leapt back, looking into the king's bleeding eyes with a smile. Joshua didn't blink, but Solomon had disappeared from existence, hiding in another world.

Joshua looked back to the fields to see Solomon standing in the center. The rain plopped on his pale and scarred face, pattered loudly against his yellow raincoat. The man rubbed his wrist in his hand, letting the pouring water soothe his burnt hand.

"Learned some new tricks, Joshua?" Solomon asked.

Joshua didn't say anything.

Al Hamra took a step towards Solomon, moving into the field, but immediately felt a sharp pain in his chest. Joshua clenched his heart and coughed, wet ash seeped down his bottom lip. The ex-detective looked at Solomon who waited for him in the field. Joshua grit his teeth and shuffled forward, hunched over his stomach, feet dragging in the mud.

Solomon laughed smoothly, he waited for Joshua to come a little closer, close enough to hear him.

"You don't look so well, Josh." Solomon hissed.

Joshua winced; the sanguine flame that had erupted about him now dissolved. Yes, Joshua was sick, but he didn't know with what. His heart felt stabbed by shrapnel, constantly berated by knives and flails.

"Bastard, b-blood. Kill, scratch, kill, monster." Joshua murmured, moving forward slowly, step by step, inch by inch.

Solomon shrugged vanished, teleporting behind Joshua and grabbing the back of his skull. The foe pushed Joshua to the ground, and dug his face into the mud, rubbing his nose in the soot.

"You should talk louder if you want me to hear you." Solomon huffed, grinding his hand down.

"Kill, kill, kill." Joshua muffled, gurgled.

"What was that?" Solomon asked, "Speak louder!"

Solomon watched as a thin wisp of smoke fizzled from beneath the mud. The soil began to evaporate about the two adversaries, the ground began to smoke and the rain hiss before touching the ground about them.

Solomon wat his neck, feeling a speck of boiling water touch his skin. It was getting hot. The man looked down to see Joshua turn, his eyes opened, his face half submerged. The American was smiling, almost laughing, a mouthful of mud in his open mouth. Joshua showed his teeth, a stream of blood collecting in the puddle, changing it from muddy brown to black.

Solomon rose and stepped back, warping into the distance where the rain wasn't boiling. He ran his hand over his exposed skin, wiping away the feeling of burnt skin. He chuckled softly, his eyes wide open, curious.

Joshua rose from the mud and turned to face Solomon. His hand still clutched his heart and his open palm faced upwards. Five crimson flames the size of marbles sat around Joshua's fingertips, flickering in the subtle breeze.

Killkillkillkillkillkillkill... Joshua whispered, his light air caressing Solomon's ears.

Solomon readied himself, he never felt so alive. Joshua leapt forward, suddenly full of energy. He rose his knee, his leg on fire, propelling himself across the field and into Solomon's chest. Solomon couldn't teleport away in time, he felt the kneecap slam into his sternum, cracking bone immediately. Solomon cackled and fell to the ground, Joshua's knee still in his chest. The yellow man gripped Joshua's leg, trying to push against it, for air, to keep the detective from crushing his chest into a crater.

Joshua kept his hands in his pockets, his eyes streaming blood, his mouth wide, smiling just like Solomon.

Solomon laughed and bucked from the ground, tossing Joshua over his head with a body roll. Joshua nimbly redirected his momentum and landed on his feet. Solomon stared back at him a moment before tucking his head and charging forward. The villain took a knife out of his coat and held it forward like a torch. Upon nearing, his direction stopped and his hand slashed horizontally, grazing Joshua whom tilted back in time.

Joshua rotated and dug his fingers into the side of Solomon's face, searing his scalp. Solomon slit Joshua's wrist and retreated back. Joshua followed him in his retreat and tried to punch the monster, but Solomon teleported away a few paces as Joshua descended his fist into thin air.

Solomon cackled and lifted his foot, kicking Joshua in the forehead and sending him flying back into the mud. Joshua rolled, then slid a few feet, before coming to a stop.

"You can do better!" Solomon chided. "Or does the king have a tummy ache? Hmm?"

Joshua huffed, he was well past coherent words, but not from insane rambles. He hissed at himself, his excitement for killing starting to surface ever more.

"Solomon!" Joshua cried.

Solomon raised his brow. Was Joshua ready to get serious. The author of Joshua's life watched the ex-detective stand. There was on odd look on his visage, something akin to this: a mixture of anger, happiness, and pain. Joshua twitched at the corner of his eyes, his cheek lifted to squint. The boy sniffled, his nose bloody.

Joshua bent forward and was encompassed by his own flame, it mixed between black, red, and green, something spectral, something sinister like in a folktale of headless horsemen with jack-o-lanterns and ghastly ghouls. The flame surrounded Joshua, it flickered, and the man kept his hand in his pocket, protecting something important.

Solomon cackled and wiped his mouth from rain and dirt. He began to walk forward, watching Joshua clutch his chest with his other hand. Was he so immersed in his lust for revenge that he was willing to kill himself for it, to work his body into a heart attack, a mental breakdown?

Solomon frowned, if not for a moment.

Joshua leapt forward again, meeting Solomon's knife with his arm briefly. Joshua let the blade catch in his skin and kicked his enemy in the thigh, following with a punch to his ribs. This gave a satisfying crunch. Solomon Grabbed Joshua's leg and tackled him to the ground. He took the knife out of Joshua's arm and stabbed Joshua in the shoulder, once, twice, three times, before being kicked off and backwards.

Solomon was thankful for the rain and his raincoat, they were the only things that kept him from burning to death. However, his face was badly singed, and his eyesight waned from heat damage.

Joshua's back waxed in a quick flame, pushing him up to his feet. The detective hunched there, his hands still hidden. He felt that if he removed his hand from his heart, he would die, his own heart would stop beating. Joshua felt the rush of blood to his brain, the rush of energy to his heart. He cringed beneath the fervor, the favor. This was the price of wishing Solomon dead.

Perhaps Solomon was his sickness, and the reason why Joshua was sick.

"Die Solomon, just… Die already!" Joshua coughed, the blood tricking down his neck and staining his shirt.

Solomon grimaced, trying to keep his eyes opened. He watched Joshua carefully and reached in his coat, producing another small knife. The favor of his coat was that he could pull anything out of his jacket. It was an infinite pocket, he could have anything anytime, as long as it could fit in his pocket. But he didn't want what he wanted to pull out of his coat, not just yet.

"Die Solomon, Die, die, die!" Joshua shrieked, charging forward.

Joshua was so angry.

Solomon drove his blade into Joshua's thigh as the detective's shoulder met his neck. Joshua opened his mouth and bit Solomon on his collar, puncturing his skin and tearing at his muscle. The villain screamed and tumbled back, but before he hit the mud, teleported away from Joshua, appearing twenty yards across the field. Joshua immediately spied the man and twisted about.

Joshua immediately curtailed and charged forth, rocketing through in a maelstrom of heat that boiled the ground behind him. Before Solomon could react, the red king dug his toe beneath Solomon's ribs, shattering his sternum.

Solomon felt the blood pool inside his body. He coughed bile, spit, and blood as he was sent sprawling into the fences across the field. Solomon wheezed, hacked. And before Joshua could close the distance again, he vanished once again.

Solomon appeared another distance away from the ex-detective. He stood still in the field, his free hand feeling beneath his jacket. Where Joshua had kicked, the skin was left seared and lacerated. Solomon raised his pistol and looked down his sights at Joshua. He looked at the hunk of flesh in the detective's teeth. Solomon was scared. He had created a monster. Joshua looked to him like an animal, his mouth open and breathing out steam. The man should have been happy, Solomon thought; he should be happy to be king. Nothing was going according to plan. Solomon was supposed to win. Solomon was supposed to be the villain.

In looking at Joshua, Solomon could tell this was not the case. He looked into the eyes of hatred and death. For a moment, Solomon felt like a hero facing the big, bad, dragon. This was not right. How did everything go wrong? The villain asked himself. Joshua was supposed to be the hero. Joshua had to be the hero. Solomon wanted to play the villain because it meant he could push Joshua like a rival. The man wanted to embody everything Joshua wasn't supposed to be, so that Joshua would want to become someone else, someone happy. Solomon hadn't predicted that Joshua's hate and lust for revenge would drive the hero to be *more* like villain.

They were both villains. Solomon concluded. But he had to be the one to die.

Solomon pulled the trigger, watching the beast before him charge. Joshua watched the bullets tear through his body. As he sprinted forth, the two knives he had been stuck with fell out of his body in the jarring run. Joshua hunched forward like a raptor, the flesh falling out of his mouth. Joshua would take another bite, he would tear Solomon to shreds with his teeth if he had to.

This was all Solomon's fault, this was his fault, Joshua told himself. He told himself this, even though he knew, killing Solomon wouldn't change a thing.

Joshua continued his disquieted sprint as the bullets flew past him, through him. The detective twisted and grabbed Solomon's wrist with his mouth. Joshua twisted about, hurdling Solomon over his back and into the ground. The motion and impact dislocated Solomon's shoulder, almost taring his arm from its place on his torso. Solomon's wrist bled profusely, the blood staining Joshua's white canines.

Joshua looked down at Solomon and kicked his face with his boot, the wrist still in his mouth.

"Die, die, die!" Joshua seethed, his eyes streaming, both tears and blood and ash. He was unhinged, all semblance of happiness or humanity discarded by a will of retribution.

Solomon wondered if he should have left Joshua in Paris. That was his purpose after all. Joshua's purpose was to be a detective. The man in the yellow jacket thought Joshua was going crazy in Paris but did removing him from Paris actually help. Solomon felt he had made everything worse. If only he had stayed with Elizabeth in paradise. Joshua could have been happy, if only he could close his eyes for a second and forget about the world's problems.

Because Joshua saw Solomon as so evil, Joshua wasn't happy.

Solomon smiled, he would be happy soon.

Solomon warped on last time away from Joshua. He held his hand to his wrist, trying to stop the bleeding. He reached into his pocket and produced a small metal bead.

Solomon, put this bead into his mouth and swallowed it like a pill. He watched Joshua carefully. The young king had turned to him, the flames about his body contorting, the look in his eyes so devoid of peace.

The man in the yellow jacket was happy it was raining. Joshua couldn't see him cry.

Solomon thundered forward at Joshua. He screamed at the top of his lungs, his burning legs struggling to gain traction on the slippery mud. Solomon screamed for the future, he screamed for the past. The villain leaped into Joshua, pulling yet another pistol from his jacket and shoving the barrel into Joshua's gut.

Solomon squeezed the trigger, hearing the thump of brass contact.

Joshua fell back to the ground, the flames around his body waning, vanishing. Joshua watched the sky from the ground, he coughed, his eyes hurt.

Al Hamra watched Solomon quickly stand over him. The man in the yellow jacket aimed the barrel at Joshua's face. This was it, Joshua had failed. He heard the voices in his head, the boiling in his heart. It couldn't be over, Solomon had to die, Joshua had to kill. Joshua looked up at Solomon, the man who started all of this, the man who was supposed to die. He was supposed to die. Why didn't he just die?

Die, please die.

Solomon chuckled and pulled the trigger.

The gun clicked. The gun was empty.

Joshua rolled left, toppling Solomon to the floor. The detective buried his hands in the mud and clenched one of Solomon's knives beneath the mirth. Joshua pulled it from the soil and rotated it aloft, descending it into Solomon's yellow coat, straight into his heart.

Solomon retched at the blow, dry heaved. He was pinned under the blade. Joshua punched Solomon in the face, again, again, again.

"Die!" Joshua begged, "Stop breathing and die!"

Joshua raised the knife and began to stab Solomon relentlessly.

Stab, stab, stab, stab. Scratch, scratch, scratch.

Joshua plunged the knife again and again and again. He didn't tire.

Solomon looked up at Joshua once he finished. The man grinned. Joshua hadn't noticed the gun Solomon still held in his hand. It wasn't the unloaded gun, it was a new one entirely.

Solomon rose the gun to Joshua's face and fired. The bullets ripping into Joshua's face. Joshua fell back into the mud, motionless.

Solomon sputtered, his hands to his chest, giving him more time before he bled out. He chuckled wryly and looked at Joshua on the ground. He regretted everything. The man in the yellow raincoat cackled, the blood making its way through his hands. Solomon looked at the sky, felt the rain on his cheeks. This was good. This was going to be a good ending, nevertheless.

Solomon winced as a long shadow covered his view of the grey sky. Above him, a silver fox stood in his black suit, staring down at the killer.

"You know," Symeon sighed, "I still don't agree with all of this."

"This is no time to be coarse, father." Solomon croaked. "Be kind to me in my last hour."

Symeon huffed and ran his hands along his forehead. The fancy elder sat on the mud at Solomon's feet. Solomon looked down at him. They both watched Joshua, as many people watched Joshua, with worry, sadness, a bitter pride.

"All of your life, you tried your best to do good by people. You tried so hard to help others that you ended up destroying yourself." Symeon whispered. "And now look at you, betraying all you believe in, just so somebody can have a chance at a better life."

"Look at him," Solomon coughed, "We placed the world at his fingertips. How is this not better than when he began?"

"He gained the world... you gave him a world." Symeon scoffed, reaching into his pocket and producing a cigarette. He lit the fag and placed it on Solomon's chest. "But you took his soul. You pushed him so hard that you forgot about what he wanted. You thought you were giving him something amazing. But how can he enjoy his life when he paid for it with his heart? You kicked him when he was down, trying to make the boy tougher. You put your ambitions on Joshua, hoping to make a hero out of him, a savior. But all you did was make a monster, because you never thought to help him. You pushed him to the throne, you didn't carry him there."

"But he *is* there." Solomon assured, grabbing the smoke and putting it in his mouth. "He can let go now. I was his closure. I was the end of his pain, he put it all on me."

"No, son. The pain never leaves. He could have Elizabeth or Joan and everything in the world. He'll never forget this. He'll never stop trying to save others. He'll never stop dreaming about you."

Solomon coughed and closed his eyes. "It seems, only time will tell what we've done."

Symeon sighed, "If only you could see it."

Solomon nodded placed his head back into the mud hand. The cigarette dropped from his mouth. He closed his eyes and exhaled the rest of his lungs, the last of his air.

Solomon was dead.

Symeon rested his hand on Connor's back. He smiled at his creation, he was proud of his child. Although estranged in his methods. Joshua had Connor to thank for becoming king. Solomon baited Joshua. Like a horse, he became a legend, a wealthy and powerful man, all because someone held out a carrot before him. Solomon was the worm on the bait, the reason Joshua was championed. The man really would do anything for Joshua. Anything but actually love him.

Symeon knew Connor would miss Elizabeth, wherever he was. But he wanted Joshua to meet his old love. Connor knew, just as he fell in love with her, Joshua would too. Connor was afraid, after being incinerated and left for dead in America, that Elizabeth wouldn't want him. So, Connor gave himself to her in another way. Connor couldn't see her, not like this, not after he found out his childhood was made up, implanted in his mind. He became a little crazy, he did a lot of bad things, trying to make the best of a bad situation.

One might suppose anyone would go crazy, having been born at 25.

Within a few hours, Symeon watched as the Marquis and Frea found Joshua. They had grown worried, wondering why Joshua was gone for so long. They didn't quite know the demented history between Connor and Joshua, and neither did The Marquis notice the dead man in the yellow jacket was his old friend. They paid Connor no mind and huddled about Joshua's body, feeling for a pulse.

Symeon accompanied them while they marched off with Al Hamra. They couldn't see, nor hear, nor feel Symeon's presence as he followed them, watching over his youngest son quietly. They didn't hear him call his name and apologize for disillusioning him.

Symeon wasn't always a good dad, hell, Symeon wasn't even a good dad. Symeon wasn't even called Symeon, in the past.

As Joshua was toted off to be repaired, Symeon sent one last blessing with his child. His job was done, he somehow allowed Connor to "secure" Joshua's future, allowing his oldest son to take his youngest out of the darkness of Paris. Although Joshua wasn't the brightest soul, he prayed Connor was right. Symeon prayed that Joshua would learn to love deeper and feel warmer, now that his revenge was finalized. Symeon wanted his son to have a promising life ahead of him.

Thus, was the end of Connor Shaw, a thread that led to the beginning of Joshua's beginning.

Joshua Hill was four when he ascended the throne. Joshua was five when he unknowingly killed his brother, must to his brother's joy.

And this was only the beginning of The Red King's life.

Epilogue
Story 1/Research

There was a time, a long, long, distance behind, that a man who would one day call himself Symeon walked down the stairs in his office while reading the newspaper. Yesterday, after many trials, experiments, and human guinea pigs, this man, and his company, had made a break through. And, this breakthrough came at an exponential cost: infamy...

This is where it all began...

42 ECore Employees plummet to their deaths from city rooftop. Symeon read. The businessman sighed. How was his company ever going to explain this?

The well-dressed executive quickly stole away from the windows that viewed the Paris skyline and hid in the elevator. He was growing paranoid. No one knew about what Symeon was doing but top brass executives, buyers, and select scientists. Besides the notoriety, Project Kindergarten was going swimmingly.

The elevator rang Symeon's arrival and he stepped out onto the floor, his heeled loafers clacking against the tile floors. He opened the glass door before him and pressed the lighting button. The glass became opaque and soundproof. Symeon approached the single scientist located behind a single monitor and motioned to the switch he had just pressed, reminding him the project was top-secret.

"How's progress on BD1-4?" Symeon asked.

"I think he's ready to go sir." The scientist said, rising to meet him and passing him a clipboard. "Cellular atrophy is minimum; the subject is properly aged and running the latest creation software. I'm positive this one will last longer than the first model before going crazy. He has a reinforced bone structure; cellular regeneration is twice that of our last model. He can take a beating, that's for sure."

Symeon huffed and crossed him arms. He looked at the fluid tubes across the room, vertical and bubbling. Inside the red bioregenerative ooze was a limp, male, body. His was hair long and tangled, floating above him to the roof of his canister. He wore nothing but a breathing apparatus which was tubed to an oxygen tank.

Symeon grunted and twitched. He always hated being in this room, looking at the experiments. He wondered what strand of DNA it was, which infinitesimal helix was chosen from the batches of blood tubes to become the next series. Symeon remembered his pictures as a boy, getting married, playing sports. The subject looked almost like him. It born from his life's work, but never once did Symeon stop to think the young man in the container was his child. The experiment was just a toy, a moving, fleshy doll made of synthetics and proper cultivation.

"He won't grow a conscious and vanish like the last model, will he? He won't suddenly think he's from the Colonial era or anything like that?" Symeon asked.

"BD1-4's neural programming automatically creates, and stores memories based on a preset childhood. These memories will only be available to him for a set period of time, preventing him from second guessing his past. He will never find out he was never a child, he won't doubt his birth or his past. He certainly won't have a glitch like the last model."

"Good," Symeon replied, "That's good, AR3-9 wasn't the best start we could've had. Hopefully this model will be more promising. All that's left is determining his occupation and his name."

"Mr. Vice-President," the scientist interjected, "May I suggest putting him closer to ECore, perhaps as an accountant or clerk?"

"He'll stay close to Paris, I agree. But this specimen won't be no damned desk worker. Our backers need to see their potential. Nobody is going to buy this product to count numbers for them." Symeon chided. "Make him something trying, something that really pushes the model's limits so that they can see how well made these machines are. Make BD1-4 a cop, better yet, make him a detective. Create the file and make him a detective, program him with the virtues that make a cop so – so perfect. A desire to save others, loyalty, unwavering, stoic, strong, quiet. You know, the good stuff people see in movies."

"But sir, isn't that dangerous?" the scientist interjected.

"Why good ever comes from buying desk-jockeys and janitors. Think about it, if Baron Glass catches wind of this and he'll want in. If we can pitch him that he can buy man-made human beings to do his dirty work for him. He'll buy it. Hell, he'll buy a whole army and send them into Russia. It'll be our edge over the Russian government, our own armada, a weapon and a shield."

"Yes, sir." The scientist grumbled, moving to punch numbers in his computer.

Symeon shifted and looked about the room one last time. Open canisters were arrayed against the walls, 42 of them. The only model that survived the last batch of tests was BD1-4, the lucky dick. Symeon traced his eyes along the lose wires and tubes. One day they would have their own factory, their own hero factory. They would sell each model like a car or a cellphone. He smiled at the thought, all that cash running through his fingers. He could sell wives and husbands and prostitutes. He could sell slaves.

Symeon turned and moved to the door, ready to leave.

"Mr. Vice-President-sir." The Scientist called again.

"Yes, Dr. Eisenwhal?" Symeon sighed.

"We still need a name. We need to make BD1-4 a human name." Dr. Eisenwhal reminded.

Symeon smirked, "You did good work on this one. He's more your child than mine so you pick,"

Symeon left the room, letting the doors hiss close behind him.

Eisenwhal looked at his clipboard and ran his finger down the list of names. One caught his eye in particular. The doctor looked up at BD1-4, his hair growing in tangles. Large tufts of twisting hair grew from BD1-4's hair, the strands like strokes from a paint brush.

Yes, it would be a fitting name, just like the tree that survives the desert, BD1-4 would survive too, unlike the last model.

Eisenwhal typed the model's name into the program quickly. He sighed and leaned back into his chair. He swiveled in a circle about his desk, his pencil brushing his teeth.

"Well, Joshua, tomorrow, your life begins."

The Vice President walked down the street and coughed into his handkerchief. He grimaced and looked at its lavender silk. It was ruined, stained black by blood. He needed to see a doctor, and soon. It had been a week of coughing and fits in the night, most likely a symptom of his anxiety, or maybe even a sign of cancer. Symeon would wake up in vivid dreams, watching people roam about his house as if they were ghosts. He wished his wife was still around to console him, to help him focus on his work and help him relax. Symeon thought to himself for a moment and coughed again into his glorified napkin. He was too busy to get it looked at.

Symeon was lonely, so it was no surprise that, in the night, he found himself an escort service and brought the dame to his flat just outside Paris. The man began to undress, he had ordered a new girl this time. He wanted something different.

Symeon waited in his bed for the knock on his door.

"Come in." Symeon called, making himself presentable. He was ready for a good time.

The door slowly creaked open and the girl was stood in the doorway. She was wearing something unprovocative, which made Symeon question whether he had ordered the right girl or not. The call-girl was not wearing a slinky dress nor a playboy costume; she wore a black stealth suit, a pistol in her hands. She pointed a laser dot to Symeon's chest.

The assassin fired repeatedly, the bullets tearing through the naked executive. Symeon died there, sad that he did not see his project completed.

Little did Symeon know that he would be cursed to care for them, a ghost of guidance for the children he didn't care for.

Story 2/Resolution

"Joshua."

"Who is it?"

"Guess."

Joshua Hill opened his eyes from his bed. He looked over to the door to find Elizabeth in a white sundress, her hat nestled like a bird's nest on her head. Joshua smiled and moved his head back to the pillow. He wanted to kiss her hello.

"What are you doing here?" Joshua asked, "I thought you weren't coming for another few months."

"I heard about what happened. I can't believe some random guy attacked you yesterday..." Elizabeth exhaled, "Val understood... when I asked for some time off. Besides, I have a surprise for you."

Joshua moaned and slowly propped himself up. Elizabeth strode forth from the doorstep and helped him sit.

The witch ran her fingers over Joshua's face. He was beat up, a few new scars in place where Solomon had fired. She traced her finger over the scars in Joshua's short beard, they prevented his hair from growing in certain angles, leaving pale lines running up and down his chin. A small scar ran about Joshua's outer eye, it was wide and deep, where the bullet had lodged itself. Frea told Elizabeth that it took all day to patch him up, to sew his face back together.

Elizabeth's sister had to steal spectral strings from the Marquis' body and use them to speed Joshua's healing process. Over the past four days, Joshua was bedridden, constantly guarded by the best sentries his kingdom had to offer, Gnat and Sach.

The witch of Val-Ashoth traced the last scar, a thick collection of tissue running beneath Joshua's eyes and over the bridge of his nose. Her eyes began to water. Joshua brushed her hair back and looked at her calmly.

"Hey, you can fix it if you want. Frea could only do so much." Joshua piped softly, holding her.

"No, I just wish I was there to kick that guy's ass." Elizabeth cried a chuckle.

Joshua held her for a time, waiting on her. Elizabeth wiped her eyes and kissed Joshua's forehead.

"You said you had a gift for me." Joshua asked.

"I do, it's outside." Elizabeth laughed. "You're such a kid sometimes."

Elizabeth helped Joshua rise from the low bed. Joshua reached and grabbed his sword that lay against the corner. It was the sword the Marquis gave him, something he only recently got back.

As Joshua exited the house he noticed a looming cloud over his head, a darkness. Joshua listened but no thunder nor rain marked a coming storm.

Gnat stood before Joshua and quickly took the reins from Elizabeth, helping him from the porch onto the grass. Joshua used his sword as a cane to help himself along as Elizabeth moved ahead of him. A slight wind ruffling through her clothes. Joshua watched her smile and run her hands through the tall grass at the top of the hill. Joshua remembered a dream he had a long time ago, a dream about a girl treading through high grains. It only took tell now for him to realize it was Elizabeth he had dreamed of.

Elizabeth turned back and watched as Joshua and Gnat ascended the knoll. She watched Joshua's dark and hollow eyes start to tear up. Altogether, his glance became full of life, present and peaceful. Joshua was happy. He understood now, he was in heaven.

The cloud above him moved from his behind his head into view. It was a large and smooth slab. It was a hand soaring in the sky. On its palm grew trees and towers. Birds flew about the canopies and people stood on its edge watching the ground below. The rivers stopped at the side of the earthen paw, contained by an imaginary force.

This palm continued to sail across the sky until it neatly sidled beside LeCeleste in the distance, hovering over Whitecroft's estate, hovering over the Baron's forest.

It was the hand of Val, in its palm was the village of Val-ashoth, Elizabeth's home, Elizabeth's people.

Joshua looked at Elizabeth who fit perfectly into the frame of his sight. She stood underneath the distant cities and looked back at him. This was her gift to him. She looked so beautiful against the backdrop, her hair twisted back, untied and flowing in short ripples. She held her hat in both her hands, letting it rest before her knees.

"We're here." Elizabeth called to Joshua, who stood but a pace or two down the hill, "I'm here- I'm here to stay."

Joshua didn't know how to say thank you. He didn't know if he could jump for joy. But everything he wanted was there. In under two years, maybe he could see a life ahead of him, a home and something to live for. Joshua looked about at his friends. He didn't know how to express gratefulness, but he felt it.

Elizabeth looked back on the two cities which hovered above Joshua's nation. The breeze caressed her like an angel. She was serene and graceful. This was her gift to him; this was the best day of his life.

Sach scurried along the ground beside them. Despite the vulgar propensity of the mutt, he stayed silent. Sach winked at Joshua and motioned to his pocket. Joshua reached in and realized what Sach had done while Joshua was gone.

"Gnat." Joshua whispered.

Gnat looked at Joshua, his duct-tape helmet scanning for a complete sentence.

"Help me to a knee."

Gnat moved Joshua forward as the king passed his sword to Sach below. He moved quietly through the waving wildflowers behind Elizabeth. Gnat placed him there on his knee. Joshua pulled the stone out of his pocket and aimed it at her like he would his sights. He waited patiently, and Elizabeth started to turn.

"Elizabeth?" Joshua asked.

"Yes?"

The End

Joshua sat on his backless throne many years later.
It had been a long time.
He looked at the tattered banners. He looked at the broken columns. Through the fallen walls he surveyed the debris. The second sun touched the ground outside, forgotten, lost underneath the red sky and the iron airships. Its golden sheen was tainted, its white blemished, and its purity dirtied.
Joshua fingered his sword in one hand. He balanced it on his toe, reminding him of someone he used to know.
It had been such a long time.
Al Hamra ran his fingers into his shirt and found a thin leather string. He looked at the metal ring on it. The diamond once set firm like his mind was one firm. Like his mind it was gone, lost in the explosions of many battles. Joshua waited there for a long time, but no one came to greet him, to ask anything of him, as people used to. No one asked Joshua stupid questions about grains or taxations. Joshua didn't impart any wisdom.
Al Hamra sat there, waiting for something. Had he done something wrong, and, when did he make such a big mistake?
In the distance there was a faint sound, something Joshua listened to. Down by the Rhine a lonely boy stood on the edge of a bridge by Joshua's castle, what was once his wife's castle. As the boy marched over the boardwalk he blew softly into the fake-golden cask. He screamed something familiar into his trumpet. It

was an ode, an emotion Joshua hadn't felt in a long
time, even in his old age.
Joshua looked at his last blade and remembered the
first time he'd used it. He had killed a monster many
years ago, with the help of someone he once knew.
What was his name, and whatever became of him?
Had he died, like everyone else did? That was the
trend, after all.
Joshua closed his eyes.
What was that emotion?
The Red King scoured through his mind like a
mole in soft dirt. He found the faces of people he once
cherished and he struggled to recall their names. He
struggled to remember their faces.
What was it that Joshua felt?
Joshua listened to the trumpet, its lonely cries
for attention. Somberly and painfully, the boy played
on the Rhine by Joshua's broken home.
That was it.
On the boardwalk parade ever so far away,
that little, humble, musician reminded Joshua that he
was the first of a broad flame and a long shadow.
Joshua was the first of the boardwalk trumpets.
Indeed, Joshua was the first of all the heroes, and he
was certainly not the last of heroes to come.
This, as we all know, was the first of the
boardwalk parades.

Made in the USA
Columbia, SC
15 November 2018